LADY LOCH

As published in **THE TATLER**, November, 1976

This full page portrait of the author by society photographer Rosalind Mann was commissioned when Sylvia was living and working in the Algarve and had just completed the main part of this book. After the death of her late husband, Henry, she married Richard Hawkins an environmental lawyer, also a writer. Their home in the Scottish Borders provides a haven for their beloved Lusitano horses, dogs, cats, geese and sheep as well as an inspiration for her work.

An Algarve Affair

Sylvia Loch

Black Tent Publications

First published in 2010

by

Black Tent Publications
145 Durham Road
STOCKTON-ON-TEES
TS19 0DS

www.black-tent.co.uk

Printed & bound by Lightning Source UK Ltd
Chapter House
Pitfield
Kiln Farm
Milton Keynes, MK11 3LW
UK

ISBN: 978-1-907212-04-8

To my Family

Acknowledgements

This book has taken rather longer to finish than anticipated – that is an understatement. I wrote the main part just after Portugal's 1974 Revolution when events in that dear and beautiful country were clear in my mind and life was a little less hurried. Then it was put to one side.

After we returned to the UK in 1979, my novel remained hidden away as I became immersed in the day to day running of our large East Anglian dressage centre. The sudden death of my late husband, Henry Loch, led to an eventual scaling down of these teaching activities but my writing skills were tested to the hilt as I attempted to write about the wonderful horses we had brought back from Portugal and how to ride them in the time-honoured way. This led to 7 books on the subject and over 10 films.

Despite a crazy schedule of work, I could never quite get *An Algarve Affair* out of my mind. I gave it to a few long-suffering friends to read, but since my life seemed carved out with horses and I was lucky enough to be in demand as a columnist, lecturer and trainer, there wasn't the time even to consider its future. One day, around the time she was off to university, my daughter Allegra discovered its whereabouts. After reading it from cover to cover, she told me 'right – no more horse books. You have to finish and publish this!'

Although some more equestrian titles were smuggled in, I have many people to thank for the final completion of my novel. Richard, my lawyer husband, has always given me excellent support and advice about the disciplines of writing as well as its research. My great friend Lesley Sendall was patient enough to read *An Algarve Affair* through several drafts, including the most tattered and torn. Like my daughter she was warmly enthusiastic and gave me the courage to finish it. There were many kind friends and students who were good enough to 'take a peep' – or rather more – and provide much needed feedback. I would particularly like to thank Mary Davenport and Nell McCarthy in the USA for correcting my colloquial Americanisms and Mariana Lubomirska de Vaux, here in London, for indefatigably sorting out my Portuguese language and spelling.

In Portugal, I wish to thank Francisco and Michou de Bragança for giving up their dining-room table to my laptop as I wrote between teaching duties at their welcoming equestrian centre, *Quinta do Archino*. I also want to thank Joan Yaest. Joan is a generous, lifelong friend whose beautiful cliff-top cottage – perched high above a golden beach – provided me with a base in my early twenties. As an American ex-pat of some 30 years standing, she has helped me with my '*lembranças*' of a time when our peaceful Algarve was only just taking off as a holiday destination.

Finally, I want to thank my editor and publisher Lesley Skipper for all her calm commitment, understanding and belief in this book. A big thank you must go to Melanie Wilkes, also to Angela Hinnigan and Elaine Andrews – for transferring and printing out files and files and files of text, all without losing a single word, for this nervous pc-incompetent. Jane Drake diligently proof read the last edit whilst fellow writer Jonathan Steffen added support in the last nail-biting moments.

As for my lovely daughter, Allegra, I very much doubt this book would have come to fruition without her. It was she who insisted, I cut, cut, cut! She then surprised us by taking over the design of both front cover and back covers. Not only is she artistic, she is a very good photographer and I am constantly amazed by her talents.

I am sure there will be many others too numerous to mention, who had a hand in encouraging this first time novelist and I thank you all from the bottom of my heart.

Part 1

1

Scotland – August, 2004

'**W**ho's that?' came a far away voice. 'Is that you, Archie?'

For a moment Kate Fraser wished it was. Archie was strong and always said what needed to be said – her father respected that.

'No, it's me!' she paused for a moment under the old gas bracket and gazing up, remembered the little girl who had also paused here, long, long ago. Then, with a tilt to her chin, she was marching down the endless hall before she could turn around and flee.

Her father's dogs escorted her to the library. Across the panelled room, past row after row of faded books, Jock McKay turned to face his daughter and frowned. 'I didn't expect to see you here today.'

'I didn't exactly expect to come,' she said, and despite her trepidation, looked round and sniffed in appreciation. She loved the smell of this house. Old Scottish pine, leather bindings and honey-wax polish all merged together by a strong undercurrent of burning peat; it had a peculiar mustiness but it was home. Sunlight from long windows lay in pools over a bleached Persian carpet and through the glass she saw a peacock and a pheasant strolling across the lawn in apparent harmony. If only we could all be as easy together as that, she thought … what a lesson in relationships!

Her father had been sleeping, she decided. His big tapestried chair had been pushed back from the hearth and his slippers lay awry; but never one to be caught in the act – he rarely gave in to his four score years – he was standing very upright by the fender, hand on hip, the other elegantly extended along the marble mantelpiece, an unlit cigarette lightly balanced between his fingers.

'Well!' the glimmer of a smile was hovering now; it took time for him to become civil after being disturbed, her mother always said. 'What brings you here on a Sunday afternoon? I thought you'd be snugly in bed, entwined in the arms of that poor man of yours. You see little enough of him as it is.'

It was so true she was caught off-guard for moment. With a guilty flush she thought of all those late nights on the internet, estate accounts and staff problems, the Red Eye from Inverness every Monday and the poky London flat that awaited her husband night after night, week after week. Even his short weekends must have been disappointing. She'd been so preoccupied of late, she hadn't made time for him. There'd been less warmth, less family time, and she had to face it – less sex. He must wonder sometimes if it was worth flying home at all.

'You're right, Pops,' she said lapsing into the name she had adopted during her art college days; Papa had seemed so upper-class. 'I should be at home, but I went to church this morning and it focussed my mind. You see, there's things to talk about… things that should have been discussed long ago.'

'Church, eh? I thought you'd have had enough of that after… after the funeral and everything.' He cleared his throat, 'Not like you, Kate, is it?'

'Not exactly – but maybe I need help,' she said, remembering the young curate whose kindly eyes and outstretched hand she had managed to avoid as she hurried away at the porch step to escape the curiosity of the locals. 'The point is Pops, I need answers, and since I didn't find them there – I was hoping you could help.'

'This is a bit sudden, isn't it?' he narrowed his eyes and looked at her thoughtfully. 'I did think you were extra strained lately, but it's hardly surprising –' he took a step back, 'given the circumstances. Shouldn't we let the dust settle a bit?'

'No,' she said shortly, 'I can't do that. I *had* to see you …' she stepped nearer and looked into his still imposing but now dimmed tawny eyes, 'I'm not talking about the last few weeks, I've been tormenting myself for months! It's not fair on James and the boys. We need to talk. There are things I need to know … only *you* hold the key!' It all came out in a rush and she stopped, breathless, her voice, higher than normal echoing back at her.

'Well! we *are* in a hurry! This has to do with Catalina.' It was a statement of fact, not a question. As usual, he referred to her mother by her Christian name, rarely as 'mama', the Portuguese term, and never 'mum'. It had always been like that.

'Yes,' she said, drawing back and awkward. Playing for time, she ran her fingers through a vast arrangement of drooping flowers which someone had sent after the funeral, showering the floor with pollen, 'It's something she said, Pops. Something she wanted me to know – just before she died. She hinted at some sort of confession, and wanted me to understand she'd made it. The point is it involves me so I need to know exactly what she meant.'

'Well, spill the beans.' To her, he'd always been a man of few words and age had not changed him. He bent his handsome leonine head to light his cigarette and took a long hard drag. 'Of course, if life was fairer, it should have been me, not her, you know. I was the smoker, the boozer who abused his body; she was the one who looked after herself. Besides, she was far too beautiful to die. '

'It's not just about lungs,' smiled his daughter ruefully. 'You've got the constitution of an ox. If life was fair, you'd have gut and liver rot as well, *and* skin cancer. But look at you! Still tall and upright, still skinny as a rake, with a perma-tan and never a day's illness in your life – at least not as long as I can remember.'

'Life's never fair,' he replied. 'But it's hardly been an easy ride, and – er – I've suffered in other ways.'

'I know,' she said, reaching for his hand.

'And now, you've come to taunt me with questions I probably can't answer.'

'Can't or won't?' she said, suddenly terse. 'Pops, I have to say it – this is no idle visit. I'm at the end of my tether. I need to know. There *are* questions but most of all, I need your help, not …' she searched for the right word …'your antagonism. I've the whole of life in front of me, but I need to get things clear. In my head. I can't go on not knowing.'

She had thought about what she would say all the way up the hill. The drive from their own house on the other side of the valley was only ten minutes away but it always seemed longer because you had to concentrate at every point, and it was tempting to stop and look at the views. She'd lived on the island for almost twenty years now, but even today she'd taken a moment to brake halfway up and gaze through a gap in the landscape at the sprawling mass of sandstone that formed Lochaig House. As she wrestled with her speech, there was the vague hope that the sight of its formidable outline might give her strength.

The main section, inhabited by her father was perched above a series of natural terraces, commanding strategic views to the south of the island over the sea loch which surrounded them. The fifteenth-century keep and a couple of crumbling turrets lay to the north, built into the hillside itself. McKays had lived there as long as anyone could remember and it was one of the last islands still in Scottish hands. 'Mainly because no one else wanted it!' her father always said.

Unfortunately, he was right. Too small at under thirty square miles to be a serious estate, too hilly for cereals or beef, too far from the mainland for most businessmen, it was a challenging place to run. In the old days, when her father boasted of rowing it, the stretch of water could take up to an hour to traverse but this was rare. Nowadays, in a powered dinghy, things were much easier.

Kate adored her island home. For most of her life she had lived near the sea and the thought of not having it close nowadays, seemed incomprehensible. She often wondered if it was the lack of sea that led to her crazy days in London. At art college, she ran wild, pushed boundaries, got anorexic, burnt the candle hard at both ends. There'd been dedicated drinking and days where she couldn't remember where she'd been, but she managed to stay out of serious drugs or real trouble until she returned to the island to help out in the summer of '91. It was at Lochaig she had met James Fraser, who'd come north for the shooting. A group of London highflyers had rented one of her father's cottages, and the best looking one had fallen for her.

Kate was in no doubt her father had engineered that she ferry the all-male party to the mainland on the first evening of their holiday. Archie and his mates were mysteriously unavailable, and the visitors wanted a pub. The slim blonde girl who declined their offer to join them but who deftly manoeuvred them to and from shore, had every eye on the boat on her. Kate was convinced the return to the sea had smoothed out the edges enough for her to respond to James's obvious admiration without an immediate rebuffal. At art college she'd hung out with outrageous or arty types, and a few years before she'd have dismissed him as impossibly conservative and chauvinist.

All Kate's family could sail a boat, even her spoilt, comfort-loving mother – it was in the blood. The difference lay in the handling. Where Catalina treated each vessel as an inanimate machine, Kate's approach was that of a good rider; she loved the feeling of the live animal in her hands as she balanced the rudder to perfection. She was also meticulous about leaving the tackle in order. She vaguely remembered how much her mother exasperated her father during her early childhood in Portugal as she beached their sleek little vessel and swaggered off, leaving someone else to clean up the mess. Which brought her to that other boat in far-off South Africa … she gave an involuntary shudder … that was why she'd come today.

'Sit down,' said her father, pulling out a high-backed Queen Anne chair, before returning to his own and sitting down heavily. She wondered if he'd noticed the shudder; there wasn't much that escaped him, even now. 'You'd better fire away. What did she say that's upset you so?'

Kate raked her shoulder length hair back from her forehead and screwed up her face as she thought back. 'It was the day before she – well, you know …' her eyes slid across to him and he nodded gravely. 'Surprisingly, it was one of Mama's more lucid days. In fact she was looking better and speaking clearer than she had in weeks. Her eyes were bright and she seemed agog to tell me something. Then out it came, she seemed very pleased with herself – in that way of Mama …' her father nodded again, seeing it too.

'I waited a bit, then she calmly announced she'd "made her peace with her Maker". Those were her exact words! Apparently she'd just received absolution from Father O'Grady and although …' she gulped, '… although I'd been "a brave girl" and held my tongue loyally all these years, everything was OK. I wasn't to worry about things any more.

'The question is, Pops – *what* things? What did I keep quiet about for so long? Is it what I think it might be and did Mama actually allow that accident to happen? Worse still, could she have set it up? I've absolutely got to know before I lose my mind – am I the daughter of a murderer – a murder-*ess*?'

Her voice had gone very quiet at the end and she uttered the final sibilant syllable as though it was profane. There was a silence; only a log sparked in the fire. Her father was expressionless. Then he gave a bark of a laugh. 'I've never heard anything any so ridiculous in my life. But if you're so worried, maybe you should go and talk to that evil-smelling old priest yourself. Why bother me?'

'Oh *Papa*,' she found herself formal again as though distancing herself from him, 'does that mean I've guessed right? Is that why we left South Africa in such a rush… and came home – to you?' She felt the blood drain from her cheeks and the tears began to roll silently down her cheeks. There was another long pause.

'Oh, Catkin dear, come *here*,' said her father patting his knee, in the way he used to in the Algarve when she came to him with some small woe. It was always he who comforted her, rarely her beautiful Portuguese mother. But for once she couldn't go to him. The last time she'd sat on his lean and bony thigh was only last summer, when Snap, her Jack Russell, had swum out after the boat and got into difficulties. It was the second time they were to lose someone at sea and it unnerved her terribly. Later, his small cream, black and tan body was swept up with the evening tide and she had wept her heart out into her father's arms. What she never told him was how the nightmares had returned. Only James knew of the cries in the night and the panic in her heart as she struggled for breath.

But today was different. She felt her father was deliberately misreading her, refusing to take in the seriousness of her question. 'Papa – this is no good!' she exclaimed with some anguish. 'Can't you see, I've got to face up to things? I don't want reassurance or comforting, I want to know the truth. I've waited long enough. She must have told you *something*. I need answers – and I need them now!'

'Kate,' her father seemed maddeningly calm as he bent to fondle the spaniel's ears, 'I'd love to tell you, but I honestly don't know. I wasn't there. Try to understand that.'

'But I don't mean the actual accident,' she protested, irritated that he couldn't read her mind. 'I know you weren't there – you were here – I remember *that* much. I mean the whole thing – the whole idea – you know, the Plan!'

'What plan?'

'Oh, don't tell me you didn't guess! All that time we were in hiding, Mama used to refer to the Plan. It always involved you, like…we were only leaving for a few days, the Plan being you would join us. Then – when that didn't happen … you'd been taken ill – or so I was told – another Plan was dreamed up. Then came the Revolution – a change of Plan – you'd gone away! Finally, another Plan altogether – the Cape!'

As she continued her voice took on a new, reproachful tone. 'All through that time, little seeds of information were dropped, to keep me happy I suppose… but always the hint you and she had mapped something out. Didn't it involve some sort of pact, where Mama would tempt that awful man away from his wife, milk him for all he was worth and then having got rid of him at a convenient moment, she – we – could return to you, bringing with us …' she choked slightly, '… all the loot?'

'Kate, my dear girl – I'm not sure what you're trying to say, but it doesn't sound very nice,' Jock swung his long legs out of the chair again and began to pace up and down, 'neither is anything in life that simple.' A log fell out of the grate and he paused to push it back with a brass poker.

One of the Dobermans came and placed a long, wet nose in Kate's hand as she listened and held her breath. 'As far as I was concerned,' he continued, 'Your coming home was a complete surprise. Prior to that, everything was nebulous, constantly changing. I couldn't keep up. Your mother did what she wanted. She'd always been like that.

'Your abduction was the most terrible shock. Oh yes, people said I should have read the signs, but when you don't want to see something, the mind has a wonderful way of concealing the obvious. Then came the Revolution! Your mother could hardly have planned that but it served her well. All my endeavours were dead in the water and by the time the borders re-opened, you could have been anywhere. Spain, France even South America ... there were the postcards ... I got thrown off the trail again and again. Your mother was playing a wonderful game. I seriously think she made up the rules as she went along and didn't quite know herself where it might end. That was probably half the challenge.'

He went back to his chair, and since she didn't speak, continued as though to himself. 'The problem with Catalina was her beauty. Because of it, she'd got away with so much in her life, she thought she could do anything. It gave her a sense of power. What you saw as a *plan* was simply her exercising and enjoying that power. Of course, a serious games player sticks by the rules, a person doing it for fun may change the goalposts at any time.'

'Are you suggesting Mama killed someone as part of a game?' Kate rose up, aghast.

'Shit, Kate! I never said anything about killing,' said her father coldly. 'I believe the whole affair, I refuse to call it a love affair, started as fun. Catalina was flattered by all the attention she was receiving and the whole thing got bigger and bigger until suddenly it was no longer containable. Before her feet had hit the ground, she was swept along with the whole idea. Elopement is terribly romantic, you know.

'As regards the accident, it may have been rather a convenient one as far as you and I were concerned – but I'm not at all sure about her. For my part, I had to have you back at any cost. So I grabbed the opportunity.'

'But you must have known I'd come back when I was older,' said Kate.

'Maybe, but after how long? Besides, I wanted her too, despite everything. But whether leaving her lover was in her overall 'plan' – as you call it – I can't be sure. I gather he was – er – rather good in bed,' he coughed and turned back to the fire.

'But if she hadn't intended killing him, why go off with him in the first place? I can't believe Mama ever loved him; if she ever loved anyone other than herself, it was you.'

'I've told you,' he said quietly. 'She got carried away. There was the sex; she was very passionate and I was getting older. Besides, he was a strong, fit bloke – if you like that kind of brashness; then of course there was the money. That must have been the main attraction. Money means power – at least it did to Catalina. I hoped she'd get fed up, leave the bugger and settle for the equivalent of alimony; a clever lawyer and she might have done it. I confess I did think in those terms, when she first deserted me. '

'But half of that money belonged to his real wife,' said his daughter.

'Precisely,' said her father 'and the courts wouldn't have liked that.'

'So there you are, she *had* to kill him – if she was to get it all.'

'I don't know what you mean by 'there you are'! Surely we're not scoring points here, Kate? Can't you see, she didn't have to kill him at all! He had the money and she was enjoying it.'

'Ah, but even *I* could sense that didn't fit in with her plan,' said Kate. 'All that time in South Africa, she was clearly marking time. Besides, remember how we arrived back here and how she immediately took over! She was quite triumphant; her actions were hardly that of the grieving lover. In no time at all she was revamping this place!' she swept an arm around her. 'You must know Pops, she was terribly proud of Lochaig, its grandeur, its history and all that. In her own way, she loved it as much as any of us.'

Her father gazed into the fire. 'I know that, and that's why I say what's done is done. Her lovely face … I'd missed it so. You know, it's not fair, Catkin, a man would give up anything for a beautiful woman. Your mother broke my heart, repeatedly… but one look into that face and I always forgave her everything. And she knew it.'

'You're not only a man, Pops, you're an artist too,' said Kate sadly and went to sit down at his feet. They both stared into the fire together and immediately Kate was back at number 9, the *Esplanada*. 'Do you remember the castles in the fire – in the Algarve?' she said.

'The *what*?'

'I'll never forget it, we used to look at things, lots of things …the sea, stars, clouds... we'd see funny shapes and forms and talk about them. And once, in the fire, we spotted castles and a knight in armour and a dragon.'

'Did we?'

'Yes. There wasn't much I forgot about those early days. I held onto them when we left; it was those memories that kept me going, and hoping. Children are much stronger than you'd think, but they need a solid base. *You* gave me that when I was little, not Mama. She loved having a child to show off, you loved *me*.'

'Well, I hope I've done something right in my life.'

Silence fell between them again. Then she said, 'It would make things a lot more right if you can promise me something.'

'I don't like ultimatums, Kate, you know that.'

'No, but if I'm ever to rest happy again, I need to know this one. Promise you never *planned* for Mama to leave you and go off with a man with lots of money in order that she might eventually come back to you.'

'Kate, how *could* you?'

'You heard me! Promise, Papa – on your honour?'

'I'll be damned if I promise anything of the sort!' He turned to face her full on and a curious light shone in his eyes; they might have belonged to a man half his age. 'It's a pretty dishonourable thing you're suggesting, and I have my pride, you know.'

'But what if it wasn't an accident? What if Mama did it because she thought you wanted it? That some drastic action on her part might save Lochaig and make you happy again?'

'For God's sake, Kate! Haven't I said enough? Everyone said it was an accident. Your mother, the coastguards, the police, even you.'

'Me!' she screamed at him. 'But I was only a little girl. Everything went blank!'

'And that's how we'll leave it,' he said and sat down heavily. The two big dogs crossed the room to sit on either side at his feet. A moment later, the spaniel got up from her basket and followed. They formed a tight little band and she knew she'd gone too far. His defences were up and she'd get no more out of him. They all remained silent for a while, and just as she thought of one more question, she saw he was asleep. Quiet as a mouse, she placed another log carefully at the back of the fire and tiptoed from the room. Now in repose, his face looked tired, old and very vulnerable.

She got home to find James playing French cricket with the boys on the lawn. Eldest son was bowling, father fielding and the youngest stood, knees bent, back braced at his post to bat. 'They can't get me out, Mum!' he called shrilly and that moment, a cheer went up and Charlie had him smack on the shin.

'L.B.W. you cretin!' he yelled.

'Just as well it was only a tennis ball or that would've hurt!' cried his father.

'You lost concentration!' said his brother, rubbing it in.

'It was my fault, said Kate and joined in. She loved this game and they loved her being in it. James treated her like one of the men, Charlie was gentle with her and Maurice thought it a hoot and kept getting the giggles. Charles was still bowling but sent soft underarm bowls, unlike the hard over-arm spinners he sent his younger brother. In the end, she took twenty runs before sinking down exhausted on the grass. The boys played on and James came and sat beside her.

'I wonder how harvest is going,'he said. 'I feel guilty not joining Archie and the lads. The boys did their bit this morning and Charlie's going back after tea.'

'No one expects it,' she said. 'They know how exhausted you get from all that commuting, and let's face it, farming's not exactly in your blood, so why pretend?'

'For the sake of the family,' he replied.

'Oh fuck the family!' she said, suddenly terse. 'Too much has been done in the name of the family.'

We've been here before, haven't we?' said her husband, gently as he leaned across and threaded a long piece of rye grass through her silver bracelet. He'd brought it back from Mexico last birthday and she never took it off. 'I thought we'd laid most of that to rest when I went to Lisbon. What's up now, is it something to do with why you had to go and see your father?'

'I didn't *have* to go and see him,' she said fiercely, then her face crumpled – 'well yes, you're right – I did,' she could not lie to James, 'but it didn't really help.' Silence fell between them like a stone. She'd related her mother's last words to him at the time, but like her father, he'd placed little importance on it.

'Just a bit of melodrama, if you ask me,' was all he'd said at the time and then events had overtaken them in the way that preparations for funerals do. During it all, there's rarely any time left for grieving or brooding, especially when it comes to big family occasions. That's why so many people need funerals – thought Kate, glumly.

James did not try again, other than to say 'Well, I'm sorry about that, but you know your dad, he's never been a great one for opening up. And nor are you, sometimes …' He was careful not to look at her. 'Never mind, I'm sure with time you'll work things out in your own way, my sweet. Don't forget – I may be away a lot, but I'm always there for you.'

'I know,' was all she could trust herself to say.

2

That evening James made love to her, hoping to stir her from her melancholy and bring back a sparkle to those grey-green eyes he loved so much. It wasn't a huge success. Instead of falling into a deep slumber, the old nightmare had returned and he awoke to feel her shiver damply against his side as she called out in the middle of the night. It was always the same. ' I want to go home, I want to go *home* ...'

She had often described it to him. She was a small child again, out at sea and with the promise of a wonderful adventure ahead. They were on their way to meet her father and she very much hoped that 'Uncle' would leave. At her first bout of sickness, they'd insisted she was a good sailor. Indeed, she had been – but this was different! All those times circling the bay back home with Mama at the helm, trailing her hand in the water, watching the seagulls hover and swoop, there was never a trace of sickness. But a big ship was different; no one had explained how she rolled and swayed like a big, lumbering woman and how down below, flat on your bunk, you couldn't even see the sea.

But it was the memory of her next environment that brought on the real nightmares. The claustrophobia of their life together in a brand new bungalow hung over her dreams like a malodorous mushroom cloud. Weeks on the ocean, sick of the sumptuous food, she had grown pale and listless. By the time they arrived in Cape Town, there was a permanent ache in her tummy. One night in a grand hotel, and they were on the move again. Would it never stop? Her whole life had become one of travelling hither and thither, running and hiding, ducking and diving ... and then, quite suddenly, another place, a new sensation. Mama was full of excitement – already calling it home. How could she? Pristine and pretentious, there was nothing reassuring about this building, and worse by far – there was no sign of her father. With a sinking feeling, it did not take long for the young Kate to understand that she had come this far only to be stuck ... trapped!

She was unsure what she had feared the most. Was it the heat, the blackness of night, those low ceilings or the smell of the parquet floors? Even the pale light of dawn creeping under the door to highlight unfamiliar objects and scary shapes filled her heart with deep dread. She felt far from anything she knew or trusted. She could not even cry or rush into Mama's bed, because *he*'d be there. And the sense of loss – where was *Papa*? With no one there to stroke her hair or comfort, she had held herself so tight she thought she might burst.

Thirty years on and the old insecurities still remained. Hyper-ventilating and clinging now to her husband, Kate tried to exhale, hold ... and count to thirty. 'You must let the carbon dioxide build up in your lungs again, Mrs Fraser,' her doctor had instructed with rather over-stated patience. 'These shallow breaths let in too much oxygen, and it doesn't help your stress … your – er – panic attacks.' She'd never told him that it was the flashbacks that were the cause; that there was nothing new about this, simply remembered responses from the horror of her early childhood. He clearly thought she was some stressed-out mother who had decided she could not cope with her daily round. What was the point of disinforming him? And who would listen? Not even James could understand, let alone an over-worked young doctor from the local health centre.

Calmer but still cold, she cuddled into her husband, spoonlike, for warmth. Her hands folded round his stomach, her fingers finding comfort in the short wiry hair. As she settled her chin into the little hollow behind his shoulder blade she was almost asleep again when with a small sigh, she felt him stir. She should have known better. Now he might want sex again and it was the last thing she needed. But what do you do when your husband works away all week? Send him into the arms of another woman by refusing?

She knew that the pattern of their lovemaking had acquired a worrying inevitability. A few sleepy kisses, and then wordlessly it would start. Sometimes she bit into the pillow, the cotton material dry, yet comforting. If she gritted her teeth, she was less likely to protest. How different from the old days, the little gasps and screams of excitement. Where did they go? Did he miss them too? Did he really care? She tried to convince herself he did. So despite the fact that nothing was ever said and she could not wait for it to end, she always remained compliant. It was very important, she felt, to focus on his needs and to make up in some small way for being such an unsatisfactory wife.

She held her breath; he draped an arm around her and held her tight. Then he was back to sleep and relief flooded over her. As she cuddled into a safer place, she finally let go. As her breathing evened out, she realised her feelings had become a mystery to herself – a betrayal of her womanhood. One moment she craved the closeness of his body, the next, she longed to pull herself from under him, curl up in a ball and cry. What did it mean? This virile, healthy man at her side was not some one-night stand, he was her husband – the man she loved! And of that she was sure. To reject him outright – as she'd so often been tempted, would be the ultimate insult, a denial of their union. And that was the trouble; she really did still treasure that, which was the tragedy of it all.

The next morning, as though to make up, she drove him to the airport. Usually he took his own large Audi which was kept garaged up with Kate's run-about by the ghillie's cottage on the opposite shore, but this time she insisted. 'We hardly had any time together this weekend, and besides – there's something I've got to talk to you about. I know you'll think me crazy,' she said as soon as they'd left Archie and the boat, 'but there's something I've simply got to do.'

He frowned as he arranged his long legs as comfortably as he could in the small car, his briefcase balanced on his knees. He had too much to think about already today, with important meetings pending. What was coming this time?

'The thing is,' her voice was appealing, 'I really want your blessing. I don't want to be like my mother, selfishly springing things on people when they least expect it and refusing to listen to reason. I want you to think about this slowly – at your leisure in a quiet moment during the week ahead. Perhaps you can let me know when you come home, or ring me before – if you've time. Of course, if you don't want me to do it yet, I'll respect that. Only...' there was a pause, and her voice dropped almost to a whisper, vulnerable, childlike, '... I've got to do it *some* time – it's very important for me. In fact, desperately so.'

James Fraser was no fool. He'd guessed all weekend she was brewing up to something. The visit to church and the family home merely confirmed what he felt in his bones. Something was gnawing away at his wife – had been ever since her mother became ill – and he didn't like it. There'd always been a side to her which he felt she held tightly in reserve, yet in most ways, she was the most honest person he knew. Indeed, openness was one of her greatest qualities, so entirely different from past girlfriends with their ploys and games. Long before their marriage she'd unburdened most of her life history to him, so 'there'll be no nasty surprises later' she'd said, and he respected her for it.

Things had run remarkably smoothly during their early marriage. Once, when business had taken him to South Africa, the land where she'd spent the most troubled period of her childhood, she'd asked to come too. They'd toured the Cape and whilst admiring its grandeur and beauty, she was irked by how little she recognised. Finally, they reached an attractive seaside town where, in the lee of the main beach hotel, the remembered bungalow had stood at the top of high cliffs. She'd been glad to learn it had been pulled down as the hotel had expanded outwards, and he felt that was one hurdle over. She just about recognized the beach where she used to play, but that was all. Thus, when they visited the scene where her mother's lover had died back in 1978 she coped remarkably well. Hazily remembering the place, but not the event, made her pitifully grateful and she said it had helped. It seemed to James then that her loss of memory was complete and it was probably a blessing in disguise. Thereafter, she had seemed content to leave the matter of her past alone.

A few years on however, the doubts had returned. It came to a head when Kate learned that James was to fly out to Lisbon to support one of his clients in a take-over bid. She had begged him to find the time to set up a meeting with the American widow of Catalina's dead lover in between work commitments. It would free her conscience, she said, since despite reports to the contrary, she had worried for years that this unknown woman might be living on the breadline.

James was reluctant but despite his father-in-law's advice to leave well alone, he had managed to trace the woman's whereabouts. He soon learned that she was in no hurry to see him, but when finally they did meet, it was as inconclusive as he hoped. Clearly, she too had put the past behind her and wanted for nothing. At least he was able to report back to Kate that she seemed hale and hearty and they had done their best. In fact, the woman had positively refused any help. This had cheered his young wife greatly and indeed relieved his own mind. He now hoped they could let go of the past and return to normality.

With the advent of the two children, those danger areas – South Africa, Portugal and particularly the Algarve – were rarely mentioned. The smile returned to Kate's earnest face, and she became outwardly more confident and bubbly as she juggled family life with social events and business trips to London and Europe whenever James needed her. As the children got older, they were soon living life to the full. There were the small shooting parties that brought in important revenue for the estate, fishing and sailing in the summer, skiing in the winter, hillwalks and picnics. Catalina's lively dinner parties at the Big House provided light relief and despite the hectic pace; their marriage felt strong and solid.

Then the cancer struck. The change in his mother-in-law from being bright, bossy and wildly extravagant in both behaviour and dress was radical. It hit Kate and her father hard. `Not long after Catalina started to go downhill, James sensed a resurrection of the old family worries and difficulties. It soon became apparent his wife was still haunted by something to which even she could put no name. Certainly, *he* couldn't and he sensed it would be wrong at this stage to probe too far.

As the sex got bad, and he felt her shrink from his touch, he wished she would seek counselling but she had firmly rejected this as a cop-out. Patiently he held out. Most of Kate's grieving had been done before her mother's death – they all knew it was coming – what he hadn't expected was so much pain afterwards. Catalina's farewell speech was the last straw; clearly it had wrung the last vestige of confidence out of his wife and he could see she needed to release herself once and for all from those lingering ghosts.

'Well, fire away – what is it you need to ask?' He tried to keep his voice even and calm.

'I'd like to go back,' she said. 'No, not the Cape – we've been there, done that!' she forced a glibness into her voice that she did not feel. 'The thing is – sooner rather than later – I'd like to go back to the Algarve.'

There was a sharp intake of breath. 'But you always said you wouldn't,' he said in wonder. 'You didn't want to 'spoil the good memories' and there was nothing to be learned there. That's not where he died!' The last words sounded brutal, but he had to say them.

Her knuckles turned very white on the steering wheel but she kept her eyes fixed ahead as she said quietly, 'I know – but I think I've been missing the obvious. That's where it all started – it's where we all were. If I go back far enough – perhaps then I'll be able to fill in the blanks that I need to know – about Mama and that man! And Papa also – where he painted, and saw his world fall apart. And maybe that's where the Plan, if there was one – was hatched. I know it sounds crazy, but I just need to go there ... talk to a few people ... find out – how it *really* was.'

'Darling, is this wise?' Now James felt real concern and for the first time in years, a moment of panic. It was not unlike the feeling he'd had when his mother told him his father had been hurt in a road accident, but they did not know how badly. He pushed it aside, squared his shoulders and tried to sound normal. 'What about the boys?'

'I've thought of that – Mima McCrae will have them. I'll only be gone ten days – or at most, a fortnight. And besides, the holidays will soon be over, harvest too and they'll be busy back at school. They enjoy Mima's because she lets them stay up late, use the internet and watch their favourite programmes. She also spoils them *rotten* over food, allows them all the things that I don't.'

'We-ell,' began James. 'I'll think about it, but I really don't see much to be gained. The past is the past, what's done is done, and in my experience delving back into stuff over which one's got no control, is an utter waste of time.'

'Not for me,' she said and he noticed she had tilted up her chin in that way of hers. They travelled the rest of the way to Inverness in comparative silence, but as they drew up to

Departures, she said brightly, 'Of course I don't *have* to go now, but there'll come a time when I do. Sooner rather than later – might be best for *all* our sakes.'

James gathered up his coat, his briefcase and turned to haul his hold-all out of the back seat. Her serious face flashed before him as he climbed out. Thoughtfully, he came round the car and kissed her long and hard through the open window. 'Okay,' he said, 'I'll think about it and let you know. And in the meantime don't do anything silly. I love you.' And with that he was off, his long swinging stride carrying him into the small airport and away from her – a very erect and purposeful figure in a well-cut navy suit.

He settled down in business class and pulled the relevant papers for this morning's meeting out of the neat perspex folder his secretary had prepared. His career was going pretty well, his recent promotion to a partnership not bad at just 37. Accountancy was all to do with staying ahead of the politicians, knowing the tax law backward and second-guessing the next budget. Being the youngest on the board had made him few friends internally and quite a few enemies. There were several older men who had been with the firm much longer and thought they should have got his place. If only they knew!

Apart from the money, he couldn't have cared a stuff about his hard-won status at Goddard & Goddard. Although he enjoyed his work, it was only a means to an end. Yes, he was a good workhorse, yes he was devoted to the ethic, no – he wouldn't let the old firm down, but there was far more to life than number 15, Fortescue Place, SW1 to which so many of his colleagues were steadfastly shackled. Instead, the idyll James wanted most in the world lay far from the metropolis.

James Fraser could be ruthless at times but not for the reason most of his colleagues thought. His partnership was all about making enough contacts and money to retire from Westminster aged 45 and set up as consultant at home. Then he could move permanently to Scotland where his real life's work could begin. Ever since he had first set foot on the island of Lochaig, he had wanted to run the estate. Kate's father had little business sense and there was much to be done if their sons were to inherit a viable business. Farming held little appeal since it brought in a derisory revenue but conservation and field sports were something else.

Returning the landscape, the flora and fauna back to a practical, balanced state fascinated him. It would require specialist care and investment but it would be so worthwhile. Since the political climate in Edinburgh and London had done little to help the growing crisis in the countryside, and his father-in-law had been too busy with his own career, the estate was crying out for someone who understood it. James knew that independent and preferably overseas investment was required to get things back onto a sound footing. Holyrood would never vote any money to the Highland estates, which they considered rich men's playgrounds. Neither would the ramblers with their spiked boots and kagoules provide the islanders with their bread-and-butter. What they needed was work that motivated and paid good wages as well as investment for the future.

He fervently hoped that by the time his two boys left university, the island would be running in a form of partnership with its inhabitants whilst the whole family poured heart and soul into its growth and welfare. Their obvious care and participation in every area of island life had earned James and Kate general respect both at home and across the water but the thought of his wife going to pieces now, just when he needed her most, was a worry gnawing beneath the surface.

James's father, a Scottish engineer but based in the south, had died in a car crash when James was only fifteen. With no elder brothers and only a traumatised mother and sister left in the family, the teenaged son had to grow up very quickly indeed. Instead of the annual return to their roots, the wonderful family holidays to the west Highlands simply stopped. After years of yearning, it was a huge joy when at the age of 26, James could afford to go north again for the field sports once shared with his father. It was on his first return trip that he had met Kate, thanks to a colleague discovering the little known island of Lochaig. Thirty square miles, lying just south of Skye, it was a sporting man's dream. That summer, James joined his friends to take the last cottage for let, and six of them booked themselves in for ten days. It was a genuine stroke of luck.

Things were changing in other directions too. James had been in a relationship with a fellow accountant, Suzie Latimer, one of the brightest young women around Westminster. In fact, he'd begged her to join them on the trip. 'I know you've never been stalking before, but you don't need to know anything. You're very fit from the gym so coming out on the hill won't present a problem and there's always plenty of breaks. Once you get into the swing of things, you'll love it and I don't mind betting it'll be hard to get you back to London.'

She'd laughed in his face, 'You must be joking, darling! What would I want to do clomping about in green wellies and eating hunker-munker sandwiches in a howling gale? Now if it was a yacht off the south of France you were offering – that would be something else!'

He tried again. 'Suzie – you've got it all wrong! First of all you don't wear green wellies for stalking, you'd get blisters in no time. Secondly, the weather can be perfect – the brownest I ever got was on the hill with my father. Third, you can skip if you want it, but you won't be able to resist our Highland suppers – or the malt whisky.'

'Sorry,' she said and he often wondered just how sorry, when he broke the news. He called her up a fortnight later and took her out to lunch in Mayfair. He'd always been straight with her, so he told her the truth. How he'd met Kate, fallen in love, wanted to marry her and that it was the end of their two-year affair. He tried to do it gently and she took it like the professional she was. The next time they met she looked through him with eyes of slate and as though he'd never existed. She was so very different from his soft Kate, he couldn't understand how he'd never noticed the hardness before.

He turned the fifth page of his document, his eyes travelling over every section of the contract about to be tied up for one of his most successful clients in Bermuda. He'd scarcely taken in a thing. 'Damn you, Kate,' he said under his breath, 'I'd better decide now or I might blow this. I'll ring you tonight and agree – you'd better go! But my God – I love you far too much to let you go all strange and ga-ga on me now. I want you back! But I want my old Kate, the warm, wistful girl I fell in love with – not this cold person I've been living with for the last eighteen months.'

A few weeks later and it was Kate's turn to while away time in Departures. She was flying with Portuguese Airlines on the advice of James who declared that the Portuguese were lethal on the roads but brilliant at sea and in the sky. 'Faro airport is out on a limb on the salt flats,' he'd explained, 'and I always reckon they know their own coastline better than anyone and you'll be treated royally. The wine's better too!'

She had declined his offer to upgrade her to first class. This was after all *her* expedition, on her iniative and she wanted no special favours. In fact, she was unexpectedly looking forward to travelling tourist, just like all the other holiday-makers. It would help her feel more normal, she told herself – she might even relax into holiday mode like them. Certainly she had felt far less tense and unhappy since the decision to go had been made.

James had been very good about it all although she knew he was still mystified by her request to return to Portugal. She'd come down from Inverness the night before to spend one night with him at the London flat before taking the train to Heathrow that morning. Rather pointedly they'd kept off the subject of what she would do once she got there. Frankly, she did not know herself, but it might have been nice to discuss things – if only he'd pressed her. Never mind – at least she had her mobile.

It had been decided James wouldn't return home until she did. As usual she had no qualms about Mima looking after the boys. 'Have a good time, Mum,' they'd called cheerfully as they waved goodbye from her old chum's modern timber house high up above Loch Buich where she dropped them off in the second last week of September. 'We're going water-skiing on Sunday, so think of us!'

'I will,' she said 'Brrrr!' Latterly, the weather had turned autumnal and it would be good to find the sunshine which had abandoned the Highlands and islands for the last several days. Her father was left in charge of the dogs whilst Jessie, one of the crofters' wives, would attend to the cats, the geese, and the guinea fowl. It was never a very big deal leaving Lochaig, because there were always people about and the door of their farmhouse was rarely locked. Strangers who came to the island were few and far between and with only one natural harbour, no one could steal in anonymously.

Dragged rudely back to the present by the strident tones of the tannoy, she scurried to her feet. The top fifteen rows of seats had been called ahead of the rest of the plane and she was amongst them. She caught up with the rest of her section and was soon ensconced in her window seat just aft of the wings. After a while, the other passengers filed on and she was pleasantly surprised to find no one seemed to be occupying the single seat next to her. Now she could stretch her long legs and avoid the intrusive chat that is all part and parcel of air travel these days.

She had already stowed away her carry-on luggage, glad to have brought so little. With no business conferences or formal parties to dress up for, jeans and a T-shirt would be the order of the day with a change of top for the evening meal. The small family-run hotel sounded unstuffy and it was unlikely any one would bother with her much. The overall package included a hire-car at the airport and she had clear directions and a map. She had driven abroad enough not to be daunted by the hour's journey from Faro to Santa Felicia. It sounded simple – turn west along the main auto-route, past the Vilamoura and Albufeira exits, and the next junction would be clearly marked and lead her straight into town. After thirty years, the layout might have changed but according to the brochure, the hotel was easy to locate in a side street just off the main *praça*.

A sense of adventure and freedom was already taking over and it was nice to be a free agent. She could settle in, get her bearings, then simply come and go as the mood took her. It was all a question of seeing what the days ahead had to offer. She did not know who was still left from her early childhood, nor indeed what or whom she would recognise. All that was still to be discovered. What was certain was that no one knew she was coming – so with no expectancy on anyone's part – things could take their course. This, to Kate, seemed the very best way of going forward. There was a problem to solve; whatever was meant to happen, would no doubt happen and if nothing ensued – so be it. At least by making it possible, she had taken positive steps to square up to her past. Now it was all in the lap of the gods.

The rest of the plane seemed to have settled down. It looked like being a fully loaded flight, apart from the seat beside her. The raven-haired airhostess came down the rows, smiling and handing out newspapers, 'We weel be leaving shortly,' she announced in the husky accents of a well-bred Lisbonian. 'We're just waiting for two passengers for whom the paperwork was not correct. They'll be weeth us soon.'

At that moment a bucolic, red-faced gentlemen came forcefully down the aisle and Kate's heart sank. He seemed to be aiming straight for the vacancy next to her, but mercifully he strode on and she relaxed. A second later a slightly panting, tousled young man with a rumpled raincoat dived into 'her' empty seat, with a 'Phew! that was damn close! Some idiot at the travel agents got my name wrong on the tickets, serves me right for not having checked!' He wasn't so much addressing her as the whole plane, so she made no answer, only smiled sympathetically and moved her stuff back onto her lap. At this point, he turned, looked straight into her eyes and apologised profusely, 'What a bore I'm being! I'm so sorry to disturb you – I guess you thought you were in luck!'

She murmured something, but he wasn't listening. He got up again, dropping his ticket on the way, took off the raincoat and after some difficulties with his duty-frees, tried to bundle an enormous battered briefcase into the overhead locker. The stewardess watched him pessimistically as he became flustered, but finally he won the battle. Checking everything was properly shut, she raised a well-plucked eyebrow at one of her colleagues. There was still a plastic bag stuffed with books and papers, which needed a home. Obligingly, Kate moved her legs closer to the window and suggested the space in front of her. He shot her a grateful look and still breathless, settled down just as the overhead signs for seatbelts came on.

There was something familiar, but Kate could not quite put her finger on it. He had the look of a third year undergraduate, but the expression in his eyes was just a little too mature and self-deprecating for that, despite the bookish manner and possessions. It was only when the lapel of his jacket fell open and she observed the dog collar underneath, that she knew at once where she'd seen him. Of course! The young vicar from the church at Loch Ullich - it had to be him! How extraordinary! What a very strange twist of fate!

She glanced at him sideways and hoped he had not recognised her, since he'd certainly given no indication so far. She convinced herself that someone in his position must see hundreds of strange faces every week, and no doubt staring down from a pulpit would be as anonymous as looking out from a stage in some school play. Should she leave things as they were? There was really no need to talk at all now the ice had been broken yet for

24 *Sylvia Loch*

a moment she felt quite disappointed. It might have been comforting after all, to chat – especially since, despite the harassed look, he had such a kind face.

The stewardesses took up their positions, straight-backed and sedentary, ready for take-off. As usual Kate shut her eyes tight shut as the powerful Boeing engines revved and the thrust up the runway got underway. She had done this as long as she could remember and it had become involuntary. Although intrepid in so many ways, she never much enjoyed flying and James would always be amused when she clutched his hand or dug her nails into his arm each time they ascended or came into land. It never seemed to matter how many flights they did, it was always the same. Soothingly, he would mutter in her ear, 'It's OK darling, it's going to be OK'. He was nice in that way and she suddenly missed it.

Was it superstition, or real fear that made her remain like this until she felt the plane adjust from its sharp ascent into the horizontal? She often thought it was the fear of being afraid but once clear of the clouds and gliding effortlessly in a silent world of blue where the sun or moon seemed just an arm's span away, she felt safe. Today there was no one to cling onto, but as usual she had prayed the unspoken prayer of so many passengers, 'Dear God, please keep us safe. Don't let us crash. Let me be OK. For the sake of the family, please!' It was roughly the same each time, echoed again on the way down, often with the promise to be a better person if she could just get safely home. She wondered how many other people did the same. Many, she suspected.

When she opened her eyes, she saw her companion looking at her quizzically. 'Were you praying then?' he asked, quite bluntly.

She felt stunned. Nobody asked such questions, not even James. Neither would she want to admit anything; the excuse of ear pressure, a headache – anything but the truth. 'Well, ye-es ... I guess I was,' she blurted out to her own surprise, 'doesn't everyone?'

He smiled at her. He had a nice smile; good, straight, white, even teeth and lips which curled gently up at the corners which despite shaving, already showed the shadow of a moustache just above the white line. His eyes were slanting, green and twinkly and he had the nose of someone who might have boxed or played rugby – she was sure it had been broken – which somehow seemed rather incongruous with the dog-collar. He was broad of shoulder but gangling in posture, bending over all those books, she thought, which gave him an apologetic air. Perhaps all young priests had to be like that these days. It wasn't very cool to be a man of the cloth in the modern world, so little wonder he looked embarrassed about it.

She'd been so busy studying him, she realised he hadn't replied to her question. Perhaps he just took it that no reply was required, so she asked again. 'Well, doesn't *everyone*?'

He noted a hint of defensiveness in her voice. 'I guess so,' he replied. 'The difference is you looked as though you meant it.'

Crikey! he's been watching me, she thought – and felt herself turning pink.

'I'm sorry,' he said, as though he meant it, 'I didn't mean to pry, it's only I remembered you from church in Inverness-shire and you were praying quite a lot on that day too.'

She was taken aback. She was so sure he hadn't recognised her. This was a blow. Now it meant she might have to talk to him on the journey; he was bound to want to know why she'd left Scotland and why she was flying out to Portugal. She couldn't exactly blame him.

The last time he had seen her she was very much the countrywoman, living in a remote rural environment; now she looked like someone off on holiday – perhaps for an illicit affair. Another twist of Fate!

'It's OK,' he said, seeming to read her mind. 'Don't let it worry you, if you don't want to talk I understand. It would have been hard not to remember though. It's not every day you notice beautiful women right under your nose in the front pew, then hey presto! they're sitting next to you, two thousand feet up in the air.'

3

*T*hey were about half an hour out of Heathrow when the drinks trolleys came rattling down the aisle. All this time she had tried to concentrate on the colourful autobiography of a disgraced Blair cabinet minister. 'It's highly readable,' said James thrusting it into her hands as she left that morning, ' and if you think women are bitchy... think again! It'll certainly take your mind off your own troubles!' Unfortunately, her mind really wasn't on the job, so she shut the book with a bang and was in the middle of ordering a Bloody Mary when the young vicar cut in.

'Hey, I'm just about to have a g and t – let me get this.'

Afraid of being rude, she hesitated just long enough for him to get there first. He placed her drink in front of her, together with some nuts. 'Ten euros' said the airhostess, 'or six pounds, fifty.' He found a five pound note and was fumbling for change when Kate got her own back by slapping down the coins. Whilst trying to look grateful, she felt inexplicably resentful – all too conscious of the fact she wanted to talk and it might show in her face. She was also aware that if anyone could help her, it just *could* be this man of the cloth whom Fate had so inexplicably thrust beside her. Coincidences like that were not in the game plan. She had just left home to be alone, to sort things out her own way. And yet ...

Clasping her drink, she turned away to the window. Two idiotic reasons had attracted her. One, he had mildly sworn; two, he was drinking spirits! Since neither went with her experience of clergymen, it was a surprise that some might be half-human after all. She did not regard her mother's priest as even vaguely approachable, which is why she'd never taken her father's advice to talk to him. He had white flaccid hands which one couldn't shake properly, spat when he talked and smelt of mothballs. As for his manner, far from instilling confidence, he was far too deferential and whilst her mother may have found that comforting, she didn't. Kate very much doubted she had ever met a truly devout person before. The school chaplain had been decidedly creepy, the Presbyterian minister up the glen was stern and forbidding, but somehow here in this unlikely scenario, she was convinced she was in the presence of someone quite spiritual – despite the swearing. Not only was he nice looking, modern and normal, but there was a sincerity that was compelling. 'Thanks so much,' she said turning back, 'My name's Kate by the way.'

'I'm Michael – Michael Hargreaves. I'm pleased to meet you – properly – I mean. That's a very stunning part of the world where you live. I wasn't there for long but I did enjoy it. You see I'm one of these travelling clerics at the moment. Young, inexperienced and on the move. Having to fill in for others, I'm only gradually finding out what it's all about.'

'How long have you been qualified? – sorry that's not the right word, is it?'

'Ordained, ' he grinned. 'Well actually, I'm not yet, at least not fully. It's only official when you're given a parish. In fact I shouldn't even wear a dog collar, but I've been told I should for this job – to reassure. They obviously think I look too young without it, which wouldn't go down too well with all these colonials I'm about to meet.'

'Heavens,' said Kate, 'It sounds awfully complicated.'

'It is rather and I wasn't sure about the whole thing for ages. Oh, I wanted to read theology all right, it's an amazing subject. But before I had this crack at being a curate, that's when the doubt set in. Having got my degree and so on, I didn't *have* to go into the priesthood but I guess I'm kind of committed now. Otherwise, I wouldn't be here.'

'What decided you?' she asked, genuinely interested.

'People, I guess. They're so many confused and unhappy people around, and so many bitter about religion – can't blame them really – I began to think maybe I could do a bit of good. That's not meant to sound conceited. It's just I'd been there myself so thought it might help. You see religion's not about recrimination, it's about freedom of choice and that's the message the Church needs to be getting across.'

'I think most people give up on religion because they feel they don't measure up,' said Kate. 'There're all these holy, rather boring people busily going to church on Sundays and it's quite off-putting to anyone normal.'

'Yeah – that's exactly why I've decided to stick at it,' said Michael. 'Jesus wasn't interested in worthy individuals 'measuring up'; he wanted to help ordinary people especially those in a muddle with their lives.'

'OK,' said Kate slowly, ' I sort of know that, but then there's this thing called commitment. Not everyone wants to reform and lead a pure and selfless life, so you could be wasting your time.'

Michael said nothing for a moment, then smiled. 'It doesn't quite work like that. Yes, one does have to make a commitment but then people make commitments every day and don't feel threatened. Being a Christian just means that you don't have to face everything alone and when things go wrong – as they so often do – you've got someone to lean on, share the load.'

He ran his fingers through his tousled hair and looked a bit embarrassed. 'I guess it's a question of letting go, rather than having to fight and struggle. I never think of myself being better as an individual, I simply say ' Dear Lord – I'm not much good at this. Would you take charge?''

'If only!'She stared at him. A moment later she was giving herself a mental kick on the shin for letting down her guard, so added flippantly, 'Are you a mind reader or something?'

'Not at all,' he said, looking puzzled. 'I was just trying to tell you the way I look at things – for what it's worth.'

'It might be worth something to me,' she said. 'You've just said in two sentences what I'd like to believe but what nobody's ever convinced me about. My problem is I've never been able to let go – I've been carrying this huge burden on my shoulders, for I don't how long. I've tried to pray – a couple of times, but nothing seems to work. Clearly I'm just not meant to have things so easy in my life...' her voice trailed off as she worried how naive and exposed she must have sounded.

He stopped looking at her and fiddled with his papers again, 'Perhaps you've just been asking in the wrong way. Perhaps you've been so busy carrying your burden that you haven't given God a chance to shift it for you.'

She turned away and looked out of the window. All around them the sky was stunning, clear blue and burnished gold – you could only describe it as heavenly, endless space. If I wasn't such a cynic she thought, it looked as if the scene has been specially set for this moment – by Him up there. She felt resentful again, it was all too easy – what did this young guy know about life anyway? He could only be 25, much younger than her and totally inexperienced. 'That's actually the reason I'm going out to Portugal,' she said firmly. 'I've got to find out certain things which will help remove all the baggage once and for all. But I've got to do it on my own.'

'Ah,' was all he said.

There was silence again. She longed for him to ask what she'd meant by that, so she could continue to de-stress herself a little more – it was after all rather pleasant to chat in such a low-key sort of way with a drink inside her. The fact that he wasn't involved, made it easier to be honest. She waited, but he stayed quiet. For a moment, she had a wild desire to place her hand on his thigh – it was after all very close to hers.

'Well, aren't you going to ask me why?' she said, unconsciously fluttering her eyelashes.

'No, it's none of my business,' said Michael. 'That is, not unless you choose to share it with me and I suspect this is the wrong moment. One of the reasons I remember you from that Highland church was you were visibly struggling under some powerful emotion and I felt you'd gone there as a last resort. Still, now you're determined to work things out for yourself, it would be wrong to deter you. However, if I were allowed to offer a word of advice...' he paused...

'Go on!'

'...it would be this. I don't know anything about you as a person, or your circumstances, but generally in life when something goes badly wrong, the more we try to *make* things right, the bigger the muddle. It's often better to cut and run. '

'How d'you mean?'

'Well, in the end, a new start might be the thing. The good thing about having a faith is that rather than leaving things in a nasty untidy mess for someone else to stumble over, you simply hand everything over... warts and all. *'Come unto me all ye that are heavy laden...'*

'Yeah – but that's pure God squad, isn't it?' she said, disliking the sarcasm in her own voice. 'Anyway, I thought God was only supposed to help those who help themselves.'

'But I thought you had tried that and drawn a blank?'

Kate began to feel defeated. 'Well – not everyone sees things in the same light and for me, it's not that simple. There are things to be done, people to be seen and I've got to work things out in my head. If I don't find the answers to certain questions, they'll haunt me for ever.'

He shrugged, 'Good luck to you then. But whether you find your answers or not, if you want to talk again, here's my number. I'm taking over the Anglican Church of St Vincent in the Algarve whilst its regular padre enjoys a much earned holiday in England. I gather the church out there is a pretty social affair, but hopefully I'll get some time for myself, so if you feel like a chat over coffee or a g and t – I'd be delighted to see you.'

'Thanks,' she said, taking the piece of paper. 'I hope I won't need to – oh dear, that sounded rude! It's not that I don't want to see you again, but – well, you know!'

He smiled, 'Of course – and maybe it will all work out the way you want.'

'Well I'm determined to try,' she said, glad to be rescued by the appearance of their lunch.

Kate found she did not have much appetite for the delicate slivers of smoked swordfish and watercress salad. It had been an extraordinary coincidence meeting Michael and there was something endearing about him. Of course, he was very young, so how could he possibly guess at the thoughts that were going through her head, particularly the fear that one or both her parents had planned a murder. It was nice of him to offer to help, but what he proposed sounded like a whitewash – as bad as hiring an analyst! She, Kate Fraser, was not going to allow her responsibilities to slip away in a moment of self-indulgence at an altar rail. Look how her mother had behaved!

She dozed off to sleep for the rest of the flight but they saw each other briefly as she passed the luggage carousel. It had been a good landing at Faro; the visibility excellent. She saw the white salt flats that James had talked about and was amazed at the width and depth of the sand dunes encircling the bay of this capital town of the Algarve.

'You're lucky!' he called as she headed towards Customs with her carry-on luggage, 'I've got to wait for two suitcases and a package of literature sent out by the church at Lambeth!'

She smiled ruefully, and was just filling in the documents for the Rent-a-Car when she saw him once more. He'd got all his stuff and now in the main foyer, had been swooped upon by two blue-rinsed ladies in flowery dresses, obvious stalwarts of the church in the Algarve. 'Oh Dr Hargreaves! – welcome!' they were saying indulgently, 'It's such a pleasure! *such* a pleasure!'

'*Dr!*' she thought as she went out to collect her car, 'so he's already a PhD – just to be a priest! He *must* be committed … and bright. Maybe I underestimated him.'

It was coming up to five in the afternoon when she drove into her old home town. All the way from the airport, the adrenalin, the anticipation had mounted within her. She'd been not quite eight when they left this southern tip of the Peninsula, but despite the new road system and a plethora of billboards blotting out the sun, there were odd moments when a cluster of pines, a dip in the rocks, seemed familiar. It was the final turn down to the coast that bothered her most – this seemed strange and unknown. Her mind harked back to a winding road, squat windmills high on the skyline and a green valley that had simply disappeared. Now there was concrete as far as the eye could see. Everywhere was shining, white, pink or beige – the contours of the hills marked only by houses. This was not the Santa Felicia she remembered.

Driving an unfamiliar car, she had taken time to adapt to the right only to be haughtily bypassed. Endless superior vehicles flashed by, sleek BMWs, long Mercedes, a shiny black Golf, even a red Ferrari as well as the inevitable 4 by 4s all contributing their spurt of dioxins. Clearly, the 'locals' lived life in the fast lane – whilst tourists like her cautiously crawled – demoted by default. The centre was disconcerting; the streets were narrow, many had no entry signs. Hoping to end in the main square, she rounded a corner and there was the Fisherman's Beach. Recognition hit her in the stomach like a blow. She parked the car by the low seawall, expectation and excitement raging for supremacy. Feasting her eyes on the sight before her, she gripped the steering wheel, her hands slipping on the vinyl. But it wasn't the heat.

It took some minutes for the sick feeling to pass. Thirty years had just flashed by and she was there again, in a place she knew far better than she'd ever dreamed possible. Transported back in time, each physical feature spread itself before her – the bay, the rocks, the yellow cliffs, the headland – she knew it all – how could she have forgotten? Every day she had sat on this wall, paddled in the tide, climbed over the rocks, scuffed her feet in the sand and it was all still there.

There were superficial changes of course. The rutted boatyard, where her father would smoke his Gauloise and chat with the men as they mended their nets or hung up squid on lines to dry in the sun, was now a smoothly paved plaza. The air, once heavy with diesel, gruff laughter and thick guttural voices, was now fresh and undisturbed. There were no nets, no smell of sardines, and the big heavy boats had given way to surfboards, small slick windsurfers, the odd ski-jet and just a few people left, hanging about in wet suits.

No one looked up as she stared at them through the open window of her car. That in itself was odd – in the old days, everyone was interested in everyone. Tourism had been in its infancy and the town was too small not to notice new faces. Her father had spoken of the relentless gossip in the bars at night and if someone had guests from England or a party, the news would flash round the nightspots like wildfire. Whilst the locals had owned the *tavernas*, main restaurants and bars, it was the ex-pats who ran the disco, a couple of bistros and two pub style watering holes.

The Anchor in the main square attracted almost everyone on arrival. Opposite the gardens where the sun obligingly honed in all day, people could sit outside with a pint of bitter for hours. For those serious night-owls who wanted to continue into the wee small hours, the short stroll downtown to the Fisherman's Beach, provided the more intimate VIP. Kate remembered whitewashed walls and hanging baskets, and how sometimes, for a treat her father took her in for a ploughman's. Eccentric both in character and appearance, standoffish to the point of rudeness, Jock caused a stir wherever they went – and no matter how crowded, a table always appeared. She looked now in vain and sighed; a huge hotel had replaced the snug little bar and along with those shadows of the beautiful people, the VIP had long since passed into oblivion.

It was all coming back now … the old family stories, hobnobbing with stars of sport, screen and entertainment, George Harrison, Dusty Springfield, Frank Ifield, one of the Stones, the tall lanky one, what was his name? Her father would have known. He still spoke of George Best and his laughing eyes, how he and the great Pelé talked together in Portuguese and the generosity of Austrian racing driver Niki Lauda who always bought them a drink. Many, like Cliff Richard had their own villas up the coast near Albufeira, and Cat Stevens had found inspiration here for *Morning has Broken*. It was clearly a golden time.

Her father's nightlife had amused him, thought Kate. It was probably his only means of escape from the financial troubles that had besieged him ever since he inherited Lochaig from his own father. Over the years, he had sold off the furniture, the old master paintings and the best porcelain, but still the Inland Revenue demanded more. Since Jock McKay could never bear to be beholden to anyone, his quick pen and sketchbook with its wicked caricatures provided an original way of repaying his drinking companions. 'You shouldn't give these away,' her mother had scolded after one boozy evening, when he'd produced an excellent likeness of the actor Terence Stamp and his model girlfriend, Jean Shrimpton – or was it Twiggy? 'One day these little portraits will be worth a lot of money.'

Kate had grown up knowing many of these things since she was a toddler. She guessed how her mother would have resigned herself to letting him go. He was a restless man, a loner at heart, but it was well known he worshipped his wife. Whilst she did not approve of his drinking habits, Catalina would never seriously have worried. He rarely looked at another woman and he always came home to her.

Apart from Sundays, when he conceded to stay in, the pattern had always been the same. Unless they'd been invited out, her parents would dine at home at eight, whilst she lay tucked up in bed. Then, at nine thirty precisely, he was off on the short walk to The Anchor but not before he popped in to see his daughter and give her a goodnight kiss. He was very much a man of habit. 'You would never get a Portuguese husband behaving like that...' Mama sometimes sighed. If the company was stimulating, he'd stay there a couple of hours, but he was always in the VIP before the clock in the main square struck midnight. You could set your watch by it, Catalina told their friends who never quite understood why she never joined him.

Her husband did, however. Brought up on rigid Catholic principles, first at home, convent school, then at the university of Lisbon, Catalina had studied under the tightest of budgets and had very little in common with the casually dressed, cafe society that Jock so enjoyed. As for the Algarveans themselves, since tourism was in its infancy and most of the locals came from farming or fishing backgrounds, his city bred wife stood out like a swan amongst a crowd of scrubby ducklings.

Raised in northern Oporto, Catalina's parents, both schoolteachers, had instilled in their bright and intelligent daughter from day one, that she had a natural right to better things. Proud of her wit and looks, but regretful they had been unable to provide more in the way of travel and the arts, they soon convinced her that study was the passport to future happiness. Overjoyed, when in her last year at Lisbon, she won a bursary to finish her education in London, they did not altogether appreciate that their daughter's apparent zest for the world of academia, was simply a means to an end. It was not love of the work itself which drove the young beauty; instead, a strong ambition for material comfort, entertainment and pleasant surroundings.

For this reason, Kate's mother had very soon disdained her own age group as being either irreverent or impecunious, and turned to older men. Her early adventures into sex amused her and she surprised herself with her ability to charm and empower herself with people who were mentally and socially superior. There had been several flirtations, following by two initially exciting but ultimately unsatisfactory, affairs. The first involved a married don which had caused a small scandal; the second was with her own professor at Lisbon, who broke off a long term engagement to become her lapdog. Flattering at first, the guilt he bore about his former lover soon bored her. By the time she arrived in London she was looking for something rather different.

A chance meeting with Jock on a visit to Canterbury had opened her eyes to what she really wanted in life – sophistication, a sharp intellect, originality and someone who could arouse passion. She hated subservience in men, and loved the idea of a challenge. She met Jock at a time when he was flush with money after a successful exhibition in the West End and he was immediately besotted by her beauty. He wanted to paint her portrait and she willingly complied but within a month, it was she who was out of control – he had swept her off her feet!

Tall, elegant and with all the sophistication of the older man, he had wined and dined her, but unlike everyone at university seemed in no rush to take her to bed. From ancient monuments, he introduced her to the opera, ballet and the galleries. On intimate terms with so many in that world, there were numerous private views as well as fine art sales. At Christie's, Sotheby's, Bonham's and Spinks, she gazed on in wonder. On one occasion – it was Jock's family Worcester going under the hammer – the sight of those beautiful plates with their small heraldic coat of arms emblazoned against each gold rim excited her enormously. More and more, she wondered about the island home which had been in the family for more than eight generations. As he spoke of Scotland with such passion and of all he had left behind, the more determined she became to work her way into his heart so that she might one day go there.

When finally, they consummated their relationship, it was romantic in the extreme. Her wish had come true and they flew to Inverness in a friend's private plane. First, violent, passionate lovemaking in a Scottish fourposter, and the next day out on the hill, he took her again amongst the heather. By the end of the weekend and for the first time in her life, Catalina had fallen wildly in love.

It took another year for Jock to propose. Challenged by his reluctance, a result of his inability to take her back to live in the western isles, she had worked hard on him. By this time she had fallen back on her studies and broken too many of the college rules, but there were more important plans afoot. Finally, he succumbed. 'But it's going to be tough,' he insisted. 'It may take another six or seven years before we can live there and by that time I'll be in my mid-fifities. Do you really want to be married to such an old man when you'll be in your prime? Think of it, Catalina, you'll only be in your early thirties!'

But as usual, she got her way and when they made their engagement official, her family, although a little shocked by the difference in their ages, were much comforted by the social elevation their daughter would enjoy. After all, British husbands were known to be much more faithful than Portuguese ones and this was a famous one!

After a modest wedding in Oporto, a whirlwind honeymoon to the West Indies and a period in London, everyone was surprised to hear the couple would return to Portugal. Not to the north and bosom of the family, but to the hedonistic Algarve. Taking out a lease on number 9 the *Esplanada*, Santa Felicia, was not quite what her relations had in mind, but they were reassured when they realised it was only a temporary measure. The ultimate plan meant that their talented daughter would become mistress over a grand house and estate in Scotland. By and large, it seemed worth waiting for.

'Let's face it – you're just a little snob,' Jock used to tease. 'Your parents may have worked hard to educate you, but there's no need to think yourself so above everyone, you know.

You ought to mix more, meet some real people occasionally. Why don't you come down to the VIP with me tonight?'

But Catalina wouldn't be drawn. A serious dresser, she was only interested in those invitations of the stiff white card variety. Smart dinner parties, consular cocktails, embassy garden parties, or the occasional trip to Estoril or Sintra to mingle with the international set, were her preferred choice. Otherwise she chose to stay at home. There was her small speed boat, her society magazines, and just occasionally she might lunch with the ladies, none of whom she could quite bring herself to call a girlfriend. Like her husband she was very independent and a law unto herself.

Kate was aware of most of this, not only from remembered childish observations but humorous snippets passed down by both parents over the years. There were the albums too; her mother at a ball, amazing in red gown with swirling skirt and nipped in waist – big diamond earrings accentuating an elegant profile; as a dinner party guest, leaning forward in animated conversation, Spanish combs pulling back her hair to expose a beautiful neck. Across the table, other guests could be seen. It wasn't just the men who were watching Catalina McKay – it was the women too – which probably accounted for those tiny dimples lurking at the corners of a passionate mouth.

Kate gave herself a shake, jerked on the handbrake, slipped out of her shoes and evacuated the car. Briskly, she walked down to the water's edge. She would need big gulps of fresh air to shake off the memories that were flooding in. First there was the hotel to find, then she'd take a walk around town; a few discreet enquiries at the local tourist office might give her a feel for how or where the older ex-pats resided. How her mother would have hated all those developments! Yet here at the heart of things, the old seaside resort was as charming as she remembered. Perhaps a few of the original residents might still be around?

There were at least three people she hoped to find, but the most important of these was 'Uncle' B's widow. It was some six or seven years ago since she'd given James the run around, but she couldn't be that antagonistic, Kate mused. She had after all agreed to meet him. Kate reckoned she must be at least sixty seven by now and there was a good chance she could still be here – unless she'd returned to America to retire. Who could blame her if she had?

4

It was all so much easier than Kate had thought. Once she had found her small *pensão*, only two blocks away from the Fisherman's Beach, she took a pre-dinner stroll down the street where she used to live. She recognised the old marble-mosaiced *Esplanada* at once. Passing the big hotel she remembered from her childhood – the Maritimo, still dominating the main beach – she was glad to note that whilst so much else seemed foreign, this residential part of town had changed little.

It was no surprise that several of the houses hanging over the seafront had been smartly refurbished – 'tarted up', her father would have said and probably no longer in the hands of local townsfolk. Generally however, the traditional features remained and despite the addition of a restaurant here, a boutique there, it all looked amazingly familiar. She knew that 'Uncle' B's wife had rented a shop shortly after the revolution, but it was unlikely to be here – too expensive now – thought Kate, and besides, all that could wait for now. What she wanted most at this moment in time was to find her cherished number 9, and to that end, she strode resolutely on, crossing her fingers in her jeans pocket.

Unwittingly, she had steeled herself for the worst and knew she might find a mere shell of all that had been before. Papa's studio had probably been pulled down years ago, no doubt replaced with a snazzy roof terrace. Alternatively, the house might now be a pricey *pensão* for those backpackers from Australia or South Africa who could just about afford one night in the coolest place on the coast. Everyone back home would have heard of Santa Felicia and postcards from this, of all destinations, were a must. With these thoughts close to her heart, she forged on. The familiar bend appeared in the road, and much sooner than expected, all speculation ended. She was there!

How short the road seemed; she had remembered it as endless. Indeed it was just a stroll from the Maritimo: she'd been expecting half a mile. She couldn't believe her luck. Yes – number 9 was still here, virtually unchanged and still, it seemed, a private house. This was too good t6 be true. Pausing outside, she longed to knock. The western sun was casting long shadows in the street as it began to retreat behind the rooftops, there was a golden gleam on a church spire in the distance, and again time was standing still. Were her eyes playing tricks on her? She could have sworn the forgotten knocker on this shadowy door was indeed the very same Mama had installed long ago? It was slender, made of brass and wrought in the shape of a woman's hand; 'very Portuguese' declared her father and she'd got the impression he didn't care for it. But if it was – wouldn't that be a marvellous omen? She saw it was well polished, a small but important indication that the house was in caring hands.

In the end, she gritted her teeth and clasped it with trembling fingers. What did she have to lose? She might be told to go away or come another day and that couldn't hurt, surely? Gingerly, she tapped. If they were meant to hear they would; if not, she wouldn't try again. Having paved the way, Kate liked Fate to make the crunch decisions. That was something she'd omitted to tell young Michael Hargreaves because it was hard even to admit to herself – she did let go, allow things to take their course – but only having set the scene first.

A scuffling sound of feet, shrill laughter and then a young woman in very tight white trousers threw open the door, a baby in her arm and two small children, peeping round her narrow hips. 'Yeah?' she said with a drawl that was neither quite Canadian nor American, and she noted European undertones. 'Am I expecting you?'

Kate decided she might be Dutch and had been watching too many Hollywood movies. 'I'm sorry – er ... I hope you don't mind – I was just passing, but I couldn't help ... Look, what I'm trying to say is, ' she pulled herself together, 'I used to live here. I was curious.'

'Oh really?' said the young woman who could have been no more than twenty-five, 'that's neat. Do you wanna come in?'

'Oh, I don't think I should, I mean – you don't know me. But, we-ell, yes *please*! I'd really love to. Are you sure?'

'Sure, I'm sure – it's not every day the ex-owner comes round. You certainly look harmless enough!'

She stepped aside, and Kate went into the small hall. How tiny it looked, and goodness, how dark, despite two little windows cut into the street side of the house. She felt a shiver pass down the length of her spine. It was surprisingly cold after the evening sun and it was all so odd somehow – coming back, being invited in. She felt momentarily as if she was in a dream.

'Hey, my name's Janie,' said her hostess, switching on a lamp. 'This is Baby Amy and these two are twins, Max and Heidi and they're *real* trouble.' There was a giggle, then a squeal and the pair went scampering off. 'They'll be off up to the playroom in the tower at the top of the house – it's a great place to keep them out of mischief and reasonably safe. We had the glass reinforced though. Was that there in your day too? How long is it since you lived here? We've only been here around eighteen months.'

Kate did not know which question to answer first. She started with the last; it seemed easier. 'I lived here from the age of nought practically until I was seven. That was 30 years ago, pre-Revolution, and I haven't been back since.'

'Wow!' Janie's blue eyes opened wide. 'That's a while, that means I wasn't born – not even thought of – when you left!'

'Er– no,' said Kate, feeling suddenly quite old. 'By the way, my name's Kate – Kate Fraser.'

'Scottish, eh? you don't sound Scottish though. Still, I guess if you lived here, you wouldn't, would you? Silly me!'

'Oh, but I've been away for years. In fact,' suddenly she wasn't sure how much to say, 'it's the first time I've been back to Portugal since I was seven. I've only just flown in.'

'Wow!' said Janie again. 'Hey, come into the kitchen and we can have a glass of wine, it's about drinks time. You look as though you could do with one. Then I'll take you round the house if you like. I get so bored at this time of day, my husband is the manager up at the hotel and tonight he won't get back 'til around ten. I could do with some company as well as the kids.'

She led Kate through to a lower level and suddenly they were standing in a kitchen which bore no resemblance to anything she could remember at all. In her parents' day, the kitchen had been very much the domain of Philismena, their elderly housekeeper. With most meals served upstairs, her mother had spent as little time here as possible except to give orders. But it had been Kate's refuge. She found comfort at the old woman's side when her parents rowed and there was always something to do, rolling pastry on marble, shelling peas at a worn table and stirring the *bouillabaisse* soup her father loved so much. At a safe distance, her eyes would pop as clams and mussels opened up in a steaming pan of herbs and olive oil. And the forays into the cold larder; Kate would gaze up in wonder at the home-cured hams, *chouriços*, and the inevitable bunches of herbs, all hanging neatly in a line, a must for every self-respecting Portuguese household. She remembered stuffing olives; taking out the hard little stones while Philismena prepared a filling of red peppers sealed with split almonds. All these things, forgotten, were flooding back. She remarked to her hostess how everything seemed transformed.

'We had a dresser here, and a gas stove there and a tiny window over there, but – er – none of this,' she said in wonder, spreading an arm round the smart work surfaces all illuminated.

'Oh yeah,' said Janie. 'The last family had a lot of fun knocking down walls and enlarging the rooms; I think there used to be a poky little room up those steps and the same happened upstairs in the master bedroom.'

'That was where Mama had her morning room,' said Kate excitedly, suddenly getting her bearings. 'Look , the door's still here, it's just the kitchen's been expanded and eaten it up!'

Janie had lost interest. Instead, she poured two glasses of white wine from a bottle in the fridge holding the baby at a rakish angle. Miraculously, she didn't awake. 'What did you say your name was – I mean your parents' name?'

'I didn't,' said Kate, at last beginning to relax. How different people were when they lived in the sun, she thought… this would never happen in an English seaside town. 'It was McKay – my father's Scots, my mother Portuguese.'

'I see,' Janie was pulling a pack of Marlboroughs from her jeans pocket and happily lighting up, despite the sleeping Amy. 'I must say you don't look at all Portuguese. McKay, eh? Doesn't ring a bell for me, but there's a lot of people around who would no doubt remember. Take old Leah Bloomfield down the road there!'

Kate almost dropped her glass. 'Who?' she said, having heard quite well but unable to take it in. She must have misheard. Nothing could happen quite so soon in her quest – surely?

'Old Leah,' said her companion. 'Getting on for seventy now but you wouldn't think it. She and I talk a lot. She likes to hear about New York – used to live there, and we seem to be the closest tie – it's only two years since my husband was one of the assistant managers at the Plaza but she hasn't been back for years. I don't think she really hankers after it; she just enjoys all the gossip, especially about the antiques trade. Luckily, Hans is able to fill her in there; he's wild about antiques – one of his hobbies actually.'

Kate looked around her with throbbing heart. She hadn't noticed the furniture when she came in and the kitchen was startlingly modern. She was still reeling from the shock of realising that 'Uncle' B's widow was still here and that if she wanted to meet her now, it could happen. No doubt, she only had to make her request known to this friendly girl and everything would click into place. It was somehow too easy, too soon – and too scary. Fate had just dealt her a very strong and open hand.

She sipped her drink and attempted small talk. 'I was wondering how you got your American accent,' she said, 'but you're not from there originally, are you?'

'Shit, no!' her companion had a rich husky laugh, and there was something a little masculine about her, despite the baby in her arms. 'Both Hans and I are from Bavaria, but we've lived out of Germany ever since we met. He went to uni in Atlanta, and I was working out there as an *au pair*. It was great to find someone from home and we hit it off pretty quick. Fact is, I was only nineteen when I fell pregnant with the twins. We got married in Washington DC – very romantic – and not long afterwards, he landed this great job at the Metropole. Later he went to the Plaza. He's kind of bright, I guess and people really like German managers – they seem to think they'll be in efficient hands. They certainly are with Hans, he's a workaholic and since we've been here, I hardly see him.'

Kate could see why she'd been asked in. The girl was plainly lonely, despite the children, and was desperate to talk. She felt rather sorry for her. 'Could we see the rest of the house now?' she ventured, steeling herself against the tempting thought of Leah Bloomfield. That had waited 30 years, a day or so longer shouldn't hurt.

'Sure,' said Janie obligingly and leaving the sleeping child tucked into a baby-buggy, they set off up the stairs. 'We'll hear if she wakes up – she always yells blue murder!'

It was in the room below the tower that Kate knew she'd really come home. The large square studio-type room with its mammoth plate-glass window looking straight out over the bay was just the same. The original fireplace was still there on one side with jutting out chimney-breast and hand-painted tiled mantelpiece. Even the basket-shaped iron grate, in which the present owners had placed a dried flower arrangement, was still in evidence, whilst opposite where Mama's chaise-longue once stretched regally in an alcove, there was an ornate Bavarian console. Dark wood and heavy paintings of game birds, fish, stag and wild boar seemed somehow incongruous in this bright and peaceful room. For a moment Kate closed her eyes and tried to will Papa's vivid canvases back into their place – the wild slashing primitive colours, blue, yellow, orange and scarlet lending life to the stark whiteness of the walls.

'It's a great room, isn't it?' drawled her hostess. 'It's what sold it to us. You get the sun all day in summer and then in winter, we have a big fire burning and it's so cosy. Hans loves it then, it reminds him of Germany and there's more time to spend at home with the kids once the bulk of the tourists leave.'

'I'm glad you've kept the room white,' said Kate, 'It was like that in my day. My father is an artist and he hung all his work here, but he did his actual painting round the corner – in that L-shaped bit upstairs, we called the tower.'

'Let's go and see then!' said Janie, mounting six steep steps to where the noise of children gave evidence of the fact that this room had been put to other uses. They found the twins bouncing on a small trampoline, pink cheeked and breathless, but they stopped the moment their mother walked in. 'I told you *not* to do that, if I'm not here!' she scolded, but she sounded as though she did not really mean it and they wheedled round her, before darting off to some new pursuit in the toy-strewn room.

Kate was surprised by how small it was. Again, she had expected something altogether bigger, but it was more of a boxroom than a studio and she wondered how he had ever fitted in the heavy workbenches she remembered. The north-facing window remained however. It was really a large skylight, but it did the trick. She saw him standing at his easel, his patient brown hand with its familiar liver-spots painstakingly working and reworking the canvas, whilst the all-pervading smell of turpentine and oils filled the nostrils. There would be music playing – Elgar, Grieg or Vaughan Williams just as there was today at Lochaig – but the record player, with its tirelessly revolving turntable on the shelf above his head, had long since died a natural death. For all that, she looked around, half expecting it still to be there and a lump came into her throat as she noted it was now home to a large teddybear and some books. For a moment she was at a loss for words. Then she said, 'It's nice to see the children's pictures up on the wall here – in a funny sort of way they remind me of my father's painting.'

'Oh?' Janie looked puzzled.

'Yes, he was a modernist,'she explained. 'He had a big following in the sixties and seventies when people like Hockney and MacTaggart etc were all the rage. His pictures are still worth something, but whilst others became really great, he somehow went out of fashion, never quite making it to celebrity. Things changed a great deal after Mrs Thatcher came in; people went conservative again and unless one was up there in the 'big time', it was a difficult time for artists. Unfortunately, he was always too busy trying to pay off his overdraft instead of concentrating on PR – you need good promotion as well as talent if you're going to stay ahead,' she added thoughtfully.

They went back down to the kitchen and she finished her wine. 'Have another,' said Janie eagerly, opening the fridge door and causing Amy to wake up and look around her. Her face was puckering up as though she was about to cry.

'No – really, I've taken up too much of your time already,' Kate put down her glass and stood up. 'It's been really nice and I'm so glad I came. It's lovely to see the house in such good hands, thank you.'

'Come again,' said Janie, picking up Amy who had started to wail and jiggling her on her hip, as they walked to the door. 'I mean it.'

'I'd love to, 'said Kate. Casually, she added, 'You did mention Leah Bloomfield. I know my parents knew her, where would be the best place to find her ? I don't suppose she still has her shop?'

'Shop!' said Janie, 'she's got more than one and that's an understatement. There's two in this town and she runs quite a few more in all the other tourist spots, Albufeira, Armação, Portimão, Loulé, Lagos – you name it, she's there.'

'Gosh!' said Kate in genuine wonder, 'how amazing!'

'Why amazing?' Janie was shushing the baby with a kiss and a dummy, 'she's got a brilliant business brain. I gather she caught some sort of cold back in the revolution days, didn't everyone? – but she's certainly made up for it since. She does well.'

'I'm glad,' Kate swallowed hard. 'So, where would I find her?'

'Oh, she's still here in town and the shop a few doors up is the one she's at the most. Not surprising, since she lives above it! It was her first, I gather and she likes to hang around there and see all her friends. People like me,' she grinned, 'who pop in and out and waste the time of day!'

'D'you mean in this actual street?'Kate was trying to keep the incredulity out of her voice.

'Sure! if you'd walked on another hundred metres or so, you'd have come to it. It's called *Caverna* and it really is a cavern, a treasure trove of bric-a-brac, but there are one or two real treasures too, if you like Iberian and Moroccan stuff and all that sort of ethnic thing. Hans thinks it's awful, I think it's fun and the tourists really go for it.'

They said their goodbyes and Kate promised to call back, since Janie insisted she must. 'Maybe before the end of your vacation? – we could go out for a meal?' The girl really was lonely, she thought as she turned into the dusk. She still could not quite believe her good fortune; so many questions answered before she had even starting looking... but it had already placed her in a dilemma.

She stood stockstill, tempted but uncertain whether or not to proceed up the street and away from the centre to look for the successful *Caverna*. Again, decisions, decisions. At that moment her tummy rumbled; she felt suddenly hungry and it was getting late. No, it would be better by far to turn back to her small hotel, have dinner at a reasonable hour and go to bed early. She was tired after her journey which was hardly surprising since she'd started out at six that morning. If she got a good night's sleep she'd be in a much better position emotionally to deal with whatever life had to offer her in the morning.

'Leah Bloomfield!' the name kept resonating in her mind as she retraced her steps up the Esplanada, watching the lamps light up along the bay and out to sea, struggling to make sense of it all. She simply must not screw up now, having come so far. She guessed, if she went early enough the following morning, she'd be bound to find 'Uncle' B's ex-wife *in situ* before the shop opened up for the business of the day. But if she were to do things that way, then inevitably, she would have to announce herself. Did she really want to explain who she was and why she had come? Would this be wise? Easier, perhaps to wander in like any tourist, act innocent – a fly on the wall – and play it by ear.

And what about Leah? She had already, a hundred times over, tried to imagine how she would behave if she were the American woman and in similar circumstances. It was not unreasonable to assume that things might turn out very awkward indeed. Of course, much depended upon Leah's character. She knew little about it, except that Leah had behaved in a surprisingly dignified way when James had engineered that Lisbon meeting, not long after Charlie's birth some eight years ago.

She had tried not to think about it for a very long time because whenever she did, the old guilty feelings crept back. Now it sounded as though she need not have worried so much but she often wondered if the outcome would have been different if she had had the courage to go instead of her husband. After all it was *her* mother...

The sole purpose of that one and only meeting had been to try to make amends over some of the cash which 'Uncle' B had stashed away in a Liechtenstein bank account. It was this small fortune, the Bloomfield savings, which had eventually found its way to Lochaig when Catalina was re-united with her legal husband. On the face of it, Catalina had been perfectly entitled to this money. Her lover's savings had been placed in their joint names and with no one to argue that half of it might have been obtained by deception, the passing of the proceeds at the time of his death was a mere formality.

The fact that no one else had claimed the money was taken as acquiescence. Many years later when questioned by his daughter, Jock had been quite vehement about that. No one had come forward, so nobody cared and that was his firm opinion. He certainly would not hear of sending any of the money to Buster's widow at this late stage. 'I've no idea where she is, ' his eyes were hard, 'she's never written to your mother or me and as far as I'm concerned, she's probably sold her big house for a fortune and is living the life of Reilly. Who wouldn't, after losing that creep?'

As for her mother, Catalina had drawn a firm line over the past and by the time Kate was old enough to probe further, they'd been back with her father for over a decade. It was hardly surprising that by then too much water had passed under the bridge and she refused to discuss the subject with her daughter. Moreover, she made it abundantly clear that the whole episode had caused her great distress and she never wanted 'Uncle' B and his money mentioned – ever again. Jock was even more insistent; if anyone dared upset his wife there would be big trouble. Kate was always a little afraid this meant never being allowed to set foot in Lochaig House again. There was a ruthless side to her parents and after all her childhood trauma, this was a risk she could not take. Besides she had her newborn son to think of.

There was only one occasion later on in their marriage when James, plying his father-in-law with fine malt whisky, was able to ascertain a couple of points. Under the influence, Jock admitted that Leah Bloomfield had finally been in touch through the lawyers, but only to confirm certain formalities about her husband's demise, years after the event. Yes, as far as he knew, she was still living in Portugal and although her address had changed, she might still be in the Algarve. No, there had been no claim on the estate so he felt no compunction to help her. Once she had been put in touch with the South African lawyer who had handled Buster's affairs after his death, there had been no further communication and he'd been greatly relieved. Now several years had passed and his conscience was clear. He felt he owed her nothing

Encouraged by these admissions, James had mildly voiced his wife's concerns. He suggested that Leah must have suffered huge deprivation and it might not be too late to help her now. He was not prepared for the anger in Jock's response. 'Suffered!' he had shouted, '*suffered*! Don't talk to me about suffering! I was the one to be deprived of my family for over four years and for much of that time, I did not even know if my only child was dead or alive. Mrs Bloomfield had no children, she only had herself to worry about – why stir things up now? Fuck the lot of them, I say!'

And that was that. Once he had calmed down, Jock simply could not be persuaded to look at things from any other angle and it always came back to the same statement 'I've suffered enough not to reap some benefit from all this brouhaha,' was his unswerving stance. 'As for your mother, she worked damn hard for every penny she got, living with that bone-headed man. It wasn't her fault he took a death wish at sea and quite frankly, she's gone through enough not to be disturbed now. I'm not going to have recriminations at this late stage of her life!' And nothing they said would change him.

Morally however, even if 'Uncle' B's death had been pure accident, James and Kate both felt it could still be argued in a court of law that some of the American money should be returned. After all, Leah was still his legal widow and whilst Lochaig and its inhabitants prospered, she might well be on the breadline. Mindful of all this and Kate's concerns about the past, James had finally managed to track Leah down without his father-in-law's knowledge. He and Kate had recently moved into Island Farm House which Jock had made over to them to avoid death duties and to give his first grandson the very best start in life possible. 'That should leave you two with enough money to pay school fees and all the rest,' he had beamed. 'This place needs a son and heir and I hope you'll be encouraged to have more!'

They had. Maurice had been born three years afterwards, but in the meantime James had been out to Portugal with the idea that he would offer Leah the equivalent of the valuation on their house. He had discussed it all with Kate, explaining that he had always found it hard to accept Jock's offer when he could well have arranged his own finance. This would be his way of 'putting something back'. Kate had been touched when he added, 'It'll be killing two birds with one stone. Sure, we'll have to make sacrifices, but it will be well worth it. You'll feel less guilty for your mother and I'll feel I've done *my* bit. I never want our sons to think that I married into this family for its assets.'

'Don't be ridiculous,' said Kate, 'you've been propping up the estate accounts at Lochaig ever since we got married, so nobody could ever think that.' However, in general she liked the idea, provided she could be kept out of things. It was all so painful still, the years spent in South Africa, her deep disdain for her mother's lover, and the shock that followed the accident. As far as she was concerned, she never wanted to have anything more to do with South Africa, the Algarve or anywhere else that could possibly remind her of 'that man'. Nevertheless, there was no doubt that she, Kate had benefitted, so if some of that load of guilt could be lifted from her shoulders, she would be a much happier person.

She also knew her husband well enough to recognise the need in him to have his pride restored. It had not been easy for someone of his calibre to accept the house as an outright gift, when by this time, he could have raised his own mortgage. By encouraging James to seek out Leah, he could once again take the moral high ground. They both knew that any contribution of theirs would probably fall well short of all the damage 'Uncle' B had wrought on his wife – all those years ago – but surely their gesture must help?

Running a small shop sounded pretty dire and must be humiliating for an American business woman at the peak of her career. By all accounts, Leah and her husband had come out to the Algarve to retire in style. Like so many others they had pursued a dream only to have it dashed to the ground and shattered in a way too horrible to contemplate. It seemed grossly unfair that left on her own, Mrs Bloomfield had been forced to start all over again. It would be nice to make amends, even so late in the day.

What neither James or Kate could ever have expected was to have their offer turned down.

5

*L*eah Bloomfield woke early. It was another heavenly Algarve day and she stretched luxuriously in front of her sea-front window, barefoot in boys' pyjamas, her short hennaed hair spiking up from a restless sleep. It could only be about six am but already she could feel the heat from the morning sun pouring into her bedroom, giving lie to the fact that it was almost October.

She pulled on her dressing-gown and pottered round the open plan flat, talking to the cats, waiting for the kettle to boil and heading for her desk. She must read that letter again, just to make sure there were no hidden catches. She'd thought about it half the night.

The headed paper from the Amsterdam hotel chain, was designed to inspire confidence. Embossed with the company's logo and of thick texture, the typing was bold and the English excellent. '*Dear Mrs Bloomfield,*' she read aloud for the tenth time – '*Following our meeting of* ... de-dum-te-dum ... *and discussion between your goodselves and our Lisbon agent* ... de-dum-te-dum... *we are pleased now to have come to a decision regarding your chain of shops 'Caverna'.*

'*You will be glad to know that our independent study of Caverna's stock, ledger books, on-line sales history, audited accounts* ... de-dum-te-dum ... *has proved satisfactory. On this basis we are prepared to make an Offer of two million, two hundred and fifty euros for the purchase of the entire business.*

'*We understand you wish to retain the apartment above the Santa Felicia shop* ....de-dum-te-dum... *your exclusive use for a further twelve months. This will be agreeable to us on the understanding that the name, together with its internet site plus the leases on all seven remaining shops are transferred to us on completion of Contract. Perhaps when you and your lawyers have* ... de-dum-te-dum ... *will let us know if you are willing to accept our Offer.*

'*Faithfully yours etc*'

The kettle was whistling, and she drifted back to the work surface, filling a cat bowl with biscuits on the way. Absently, she popped a saccharine into the mug and stirred her black coffee, her head full of turmoil. What should she do? Did she really want to give up work? – after all this time? Apart from those lost two years in cloud-cuckoo land, work was her way of life. She lived for it. It had to be said, it was also great for body, mind, spirit and soul. Working solo and without a man to poke his nose in, making her doubt and delay major decisions, had been an eye opener. She had really thrived on being her own master – and look where she had come! What she had achieved, single-handed? She was almost 68, but she looked and felt 55 or less. Moreover she was happier and more in control of her life than she had ever been, so did she really want to give all that up now?

She wandered back to the bedroom. She would shower, get dressed and go for a long walk along the beach. The fresh sea air would clear her head – it always did. This afternoon she might call Manhattan and see what Wally and Melinda would have to say. They knew something was up and were always so positive about everything she did. They'd probably say – go for it. It was one helluva lot of money and she probably couldn't do better. But – on the other hand – money wasn't everything.. She'd learned that long ago.

She stepped out of the shower, and let the towel slip from her waist as she looked for her clothes, carefully laid out. She caught sight of her own reflection. The truth was her body was ahead of her face, she *was* getting older and it would be crazy, in a way, not to get out while the going was good. Oh shit! Despite her slimness, her boobs sagged, the once neat ass was spreading, and the hint of cellulite around her thighs was sobering. Still, as she'd already discovered, it could all be covered up, but the one thing that really got to her in this warm climate, was the lack of muscle tone under the arms. There was no getting away from it – she had crêpe! And no amount of swimming, working out or over-arm stretches could get rid of it – which was why she'd given up sleeveless tops long ago. Why do some women never realise that necks and underarms are the biggest giveaway?

'Oh well, if you can't fight it – go with it,' she thought, pulling on bikini pants, her wonderful wonderbra and a smart pair of black stretch jeans by Moschino. Her candy pink shirt was Turnbull & Asher and she fixed a pair of platinum Gucci cufflinks into her cuffs, then rolled them up carefully for the trip along the beach. Slipping her feet into trainers, later to be replaced by smart slip-ons, she opened the door of her apartment and went carefully down the wrought-iron steps that the cats liked so much, to the garden below. It was just a step into the street and round the bend to the communal path around the cliff to Santa Felicia bay.

Although it was not yet seven, there was already a scattering of people. A couple of sun worshippers spreading out towels, a family with three young children walking, a solitary jogger with a German Shepherd at his heels and some health fanatic taking an early morning dip. Truly, she thought, Santa Felicia is a haven – the safest beach in the Algarve and probably amongst the cleanest sands in Europe. The dog would have to be off by eight o'clock or the warden would have something to say and she missed those weekends when the local stables used to canter their prancing Lusitano stallions across the sands. Oh well, it was all about European standards nowadays and one had to move with the times.

As she walked, she wondered where she would live if she sold up. She hadn't actually owned a property since the sale of Casa Amarela and that had taken eight years after the Revolution to get shot of. It had kind of put her off owning property of any description ever again. What a nightmare! She very much doubted she would want to live out on a limb again and a big property with big responsibilities was a definite no-no. You certainly learn by experience.

The problem was that buying property in the centre of town was hard. Relatively little was residential nowadays and even commercial buildings that could be converted to homes were hard to come by. Whenever a tobacconist or retailer closed down, they were nearly always snapped up by the *Camera* and turned into yet another government office, if not a euro-bank. To top it all, prices were crazy. Not that that would be a problem, but the right location was something else.

The thing was – she adored where she was. She loved the fact that people popped in and out of the shop all day and when she wasn't there, she was simply repeating the experience further down the coast at one of her other stores. She had gotten to make a great many acquaintances all over the Algarve since she'd first expanded her business. How could one be lonely when so many, clients and colleagues alike, had turned into real and often unexpected friends? She'd learned a lot about life in the process and found her tastes had completely turned around from her days in Manhattan.

Once upon a time, she, Leah had been carefully selective. She and her husband had enjoyed a close set of fellow-minded professionals, mainly from the arts and the world of innovation and design. In general, their tight little circle was filled by bright, highly successful, streetwise people who dined at the same restaurants, went to the same film premières, wore the same labels, imbibed the same wines, thought the same way and generally voted Democrat. Curiously, of all those people she'd left behind, less than a handful had remained as friends – the others had vanished into obscurity.

When, finally, news of Buster's death had leaked out, she very soon knew who actually cared. Wally and Melinda had always stuck with her, there was an old flatmate from college days and that was about it. Then of course there was Howard and Benjie – but that was more from necessity than love in the latter days and altogether another story. Even so, Howard's sudden heart attack still hurt, especially when one considered the stress he'd endured – but no, now was *not* the time. She pushed it all hurriedly to the back of her mind. Even now, some things were too painful to recall.

Things had been different immediately after Buster's defection. In the first place there was real sympathy. Few appreciated that she'd been completely wiped out and were therefore eager to come forward and advise her. Unfortunately, what it always boiled down to was all manner of costly legal consultation coupled with more expensive action in the courts. Although she could not afford the former and the latter was impractical, they blindly urged her on. She must pursue Buster to the *hilt*; he must *not* be allowed to get away with such deceit. Fair play must be seen to prevail! They made it sound like child's play, brushing aside her very valid objections.

Whilst a decent American judge might have leant favourably on the side of the injured party, a European judge might not. The paperwork was not in dispute so one would need to look to the moral question. In a country not famed at the time for its human rights, let alone women's, this could be a long drawn out affair.

But that was beside the point; the over-riding issue was the disappearance of her husband. Clearly the birds had flown so she was in a hopeless situation. As she wearily pointed out time and again, you cannot take someone to court unless they are available! An injunction only works if there is someone upon whom it can be served! And since the 'crime' had taken place in Portugal, it would ultimately have to be a European court that dealt with it. It was extraordinary how people whom she had once rated as above average intelligence found all this so very hard to understand.

It was often those self-same people who told her they'd never much cared for Buster in the first place. Yet these had been their mutual friends and she was not sure she liked what she was hearing. Somehow it made a mockery of so much of the fabric of their former life; she began to wonder just whom she could trust. Sadly, as the truth of her circumstances finally dawned on everyone, their enthusiasm dwindled away. Disbelief turned to disinterest as she explained that any useful evidence had been scattered to the four winds when the Portuguese Revolution broke out in the middle of it all. With the armed forces, police and judiciary system in total disarray, what chance did *she* have?

Leah was shocked by how few North Americans seemed aware of what was happening in Europe. Events in Portugal were all too far removed and no one seemed much interested in becoming better informed. The fact that her adopted country had gone through political meltdown with not just one military coup, but a series of major upheavals resulting in a temporary Communist take-over during the summer of '74 and a failed right-wing counter-coup in October of the same year, seemed not to penetrate. As she patiently spelled out the difficulties of her case and the fact that it was impossible to find anyone to testify on her behalf, it became clear that she had lost the sympathy of her fellow countrymen. Her continued love of Portugal and of the Algarve in particular was seen as a sign of weakness. Few back home could begin to understand why she stayed on. The fact was – she had no choice. She might only own part of it, an arguable third – but at least here she still had a *roof* over her head.

During the muddled years of the coalition that followed the first general election in '76, with a dozen parties jockeying for power, Leah had accepted her lot. Any hope of an improvement in her situation was moonshine. She had never been a person to waste energy when the chips were down, so accepting defeat in one area merely strengthened her resolve in another. She determined to start all over again, and the first obstacle to tackle was her own state of mind. Looking back, she realised it could so easily have gone the other way.

The worst time had been the return to Portugal after her nervous breakdown. She had already accepted that she was broke, but the loneliest moment had been entering the empty suite in their big house. She knew in her heart that all attempts to find the missing couple had failed but the visual evidence of their betrayal poured salt on an open wound. Gradually, the pain subsided. As the months and then the years had rolled on, and a misleading set of pointers and false trails all led to a dead end, Leah resigned herself to her fate. She might have lost her assets, but she still had her energy, her quick brain, and her talent. No one could take that away from her, least of all that 'rat'. She was also well aware that she had far more chance of starting all over again in the relaxed sunny atmosphere of Santa Felicia than the hurly-burly of New York. At least there were no heating bills or massive wages, rates and insurance to pay, and if you ate like the natives and went with the seasons, it was perfectly possible to subsist on surprisingly little.

Inevitably, at the beginning, there had been the odd rumour. Various 'sightings' of the runaway couple had taken place, and painfully, hopes had been raised. As with the English Lord Lucan affair – which a decade earlier had given the newspapers a field day – South America seemed the most likely hideaway. One of her old colleagues was adamant he'd spotted Buster in a beach bar at Copacabana. A few weeks later, someone else had seen him on the island of Bahia, but when a third perceived him in a market place in Tuscany with a blonde on his arm, Leah banished all further conjecture from her mind.

She was not alone, however. It was the season for missing people. Straws were being clutched at all over the place. The Lisbon newspapers, swinging from one political persuasion to another as heads rolled, were full of stories as to the latest sacrificial lamb to flee the mother country. People-spotting became a national past-time in Rio and São Paolo: you did not have to be a politician to awaken interest; any *capitalista* was fair game. Fortunately, money still counted in South America and the Brazilians had been swift to close ranks and protect their own. A large percentage had blood-ties in Portugal, and loyalties ran deep. Arms were held out and whole families were literally swallowed up and disappeared quietly for a time.

Leah had never quite convinced herself that this was where Buster and Catalina had gone although with Catalina's Portuguese passport and connections, it seemed an obvious option. It was an enormous country and with the avalanche of displaced people flooding in from the now abandoned Portuguese colonies – Mozambique, Angola, Cape Verde and Guinea – confusion reigned. With rumours of spies, secret police and plotters from the old regime peppering Brazilian society, who would care a dime about an ex-pat from New York and his sloe-eyed mistress? All the missing couple had to do was lie low for a while and let the whole thing blow over. It could take years.

Ultimately, it had been a massive relief when finally she received the news. South Africa, eh? Who would have thought it?

Her reactions to his death shocked her initially, mainly because she had never even considered the possibility before. It turned out he had changed his name by deedpoll which explained why none of them had picked up on the story before. Had it not been for an American reporter writing a story about the movements of whales round the rocky coast of a small seaside resort, she might never have known. It turned out peaceful Hermanus was not only famous for its whales; a tragic drowning had taken place close to those same jagged rocks a few years back. Records showed that the man concerned, one Bertram Roache who hailed from New York, was something of a mystery man. He could not be found in any US military records, neither did he appear as a taxpayer, so no one from the state department back home showed much interest. It was assumed he was a drop-out.

It was a couple of years before more facts emerged. A sharp-eyed American student working at a notary's office in Pretoria faxed the newspaper to fill them in on the fact that their so-called tragic Mr Roache in the whaling story had once been a Mr Bloomfield and it might be in their interests to contact his family in the US. This they duly did, but after a lot of time-wasting investigation, they could only locate one elderly cousin, who had nothing further to add, so the story died a natural death.

It took a further five months for Buster's cousin to track down Leah's address in Portugal. By the time she finally received a copy of her husband's death certificate, she had been tied into the joint ownership of a house she could gladly have done without for over six years. The anger over Buster's betrayal was now replaced by the anguish this time lapse had brought not only to her, but to her old business partner Howard, who was also involved. But it was no good looking back. Soon the house should be off her hands, and she renewed her energies in her growing business as finally *Caverna* began to take off.

It wasn't often she looked back on those days now. If truth be known, the thought that her faithless husband was no longer humping the person she'd trusted as both friend and soulmate, had been liberating. She hadn't much enjoyed imagining the two of them in violent passion night after night, his rasping breath so vivid, she often had to switch on the light to make sure he wasn't actually there. Too often she'd pictured him, virile and rampant – standing over a bed on which *she* lay – her voluptuous and acquiescent rival. How could she have trusted her? It was still a wonder to her, but what was the point? Now, she was being offered closure. Knowing they could do no more to hurt her, she was being given the chance to let these embarrassing imaginings go. The man was dead! Gone for ever! She need never care or wonder where or how he was again.

In the interim, she had worked like stink, built up her one tiny shop leased for a peppercorn rent at a time when no one was prepared to take a risk, and then opened another. Within two years, Leah had worked off the loan she'd brought back from America and things were looking bright. One of the first to see in what direction to go, she saw the tourist economy change before her eyes. Prior to the Revolution, the Algarve had been favoured by the discerning traveller, people who valued privacy and peace, good food and good service. For such visitors, the idea of shopping was a romantic journey into the hills for one or two well chosen pieces of hand painted pottery, or a dalliance in the market place for a handwoven basket, olive oil and fig cake.

Pre-Revolution, there was little outlet or demand for cheap clothes, gifts and trinkets. There was even less accommodation for cheap development. Ironically, it was those factors which had attracted Leah and Buster, and many like them, to the area in the first place. To challenge and test the strictures of the local planning office by designing their dream home and the triumph of getting it passed, was made all the sweeter by knowing how tough it could be for the next person. They themselves had learned the hard way, sacking one architect after another until they understood the rules of the game. Those tasteful villas landscaped so prettily into the hinterland were not there by accident but the result of wheels within wheels. That was – until the Revolution.

It was frightening how suddenly the President had been swept away, and his ministers too. For those who remained and tried to brazen it out, the knock at the door could come at any time. Detained without trial, seized land, frozen bank accounts, no one quite knew what would happen next. The ex-pats watched in horror as each day brought news of another burning *quinta*, sequestered estate or another company director or banker in jail. Their only saving grace – the victims were all Portuguese. But what about *them*?

Worryingly, as the left wing element took hold, there was strong anti-American sentiment. It was not so bad for the Brits – the Portuguese regarded them as their oldest allies – but in such a climate, anything could happen. The upheavals were mainly in Lisbon and the Alentejo – a hotbed of anti-capitalist activity. Crude, painted slogans warning of the exploitation of the workers made for uncomfortable reading and were travelling south by the hour. People like Leah kept their head down as they went about their daily business, only too well aware of their vulnerability. It did not help that Leah's was one of the few really big villas still occupied by its owners. Those grand holiday mansions belonging to wealthy Portuguese now stood shuttered and empty – the word *fascista* painted across their walls. She wondered for how long.

If most Americans seemed to be giving Portugal a miss in the mid '70s, it was comforting to note that the middle-roaders remained. The Brits felt close enough to home not be put off; it was the same with the Dutch, Germans, and Scandinavians. Leah might be American, but unlike so many, had taken time to learn the language. She was friendly and respectful of the locals and this had been noted. So she gritted her teeth and worked her way through the Revolution. She began to feel like one of the people; she needed to survive, and like them – she would do so – without a fuss.

All around her, a modest way of life was being embraced; in her new found poverty, she slotted in well. Now it was time for the country folk to flex their muscles whilst the townspeople held their breath and bit their tongues. The price of bread, of pumpkin, olive oil, figs and melons shot sky high. The Algarve had always been the garden of Europe, so there was no shortage, but the cloth-capped men in their mule carts and the black-hatted women with their donkeys were commanding more respect and higher prices. So were the fishermen. No one dared to argue or haggle too much over a kilo of sardines as in the old days – you too might be accused of being a *fascista*.

Overnight, standards were overturned. In the bank, tellers rolled up their sleeves and blue jeans were the new uniform. No one wore ties in restaurants. Even the newly built casino at Penina threw away its membership cards and opened its doors to all who cared to spend their money. In this climate, Leah was renting two more shops, her profits soaring as the Algarve opened up to the new dawn of the package tour, apartment blocks and the self-catering village on every available green site. She rubbed her hands in satisfaction; she, Leah Bloomfield, was definitely back in business!

She dragged herself back to the present as she had reached that point of the beach where you could go no further except by sea. Time to turn around and get back. Her reminiscing had brought her no nearer to making a decision than when she'd started out. 'Oh well,' she told herself. 'There's no real hurry; I guess I've got two or three days to think about it. Better really to keep them waiting; if they think I'm too keen, they'll regret making such a generous offer.'

She took a different route home, involving a lot of steps and a tunnel through the cliffs. Now in the main square, she popped into the Maritimo to collect a copy of the *New York Times* and some fresh newly baked rolls from the *padeiro*. They were still warm from the oven and she clutched the bag against her chest as she rejoined the *Esplanada* from its opposite side.

Back at the flat, she kicked off her trainers, made up a breakfast tray with more coffee, olive oil spread and fresh honeycomb for the rolls and plonked herself back on her bed. If she looked up, she could see seagulls, a vase of late bougainvillea spilled over the open fireplace; spread open before her – the newspaper. This was her favourite time of day. Generally, the phone would be silent for at least another hour. With only the cats to disturb her – she felt blissfully at ease.

It hadn't always been like this, which was why she enjoyed this quiet time so much. All those old worries about Buster, the business, the Boys, Casa Amarela, it was behind her now – but what a saga! And how it had gone on and on and *on*! She'd been well and truly dragged through the mill and it had not been pleasant. She often wondered what had become of all the rest of the people involved. Was that old fox, Jock McKay, still alive? He had done absolutely nothing for her, but his daughter – if one could judge by the son-in-law – had obviously turned out a decent enough person. She would never forget the satisfaction she felt when she turned down that anxious young man with a firm 'no thank you' when he'd offered to make good.

Perhaps, on reflection, she'd been a bit hard on him. He might be upwardly mobile, and ambitious, but it was clear he had heart. She'd have given her eye teeth for some of that dough two decades before when he and Jock's daughter were still in short socks, but he'd come along much too late. She'd made it on her own, well almost – but no thanks to any of *that* family. She was damned if she was going to be beholden to them now. What was done was done. More fool her for marrying Buster in the first place – and as for that Power of Attorney… how careless could one be?

The Algarve dream! The moment she'd set foot on this blessed soil, she'd allowed a softer, more feminine side of her character to take over and had simply got carried away. She'd never regretted the move to Portugal, but she deeply rued the way in which she'd handled her business affairs. She'd been far too trusting all round. She'd also popped too many pills. It was as simple as that. Well, she'd learned her lesson – the hard way. She now knew to trust no-one. It was much better like this, because no-one could hurt her any more.

On the social side, things had been equally bad. Having built their house, they should have lain low. Old money, titles, keeping things under wraps and the way you behaved was what counted in post-Salazar Portugal. Instead, they had tried to please and impress, which in ex-pat society merely exposed one to amusement, generally coupled with contempt. The Brits were the worst – those who had lived in the Peninsula for years could be patronising in the extreme; others, nosey, prone to gossip. She could see now how others had viewed them: flashy and *nouveaux*, obvious and spoilt. Displaying their wealth and tasteful things might work in Manhattan circles, but it cut no ice in Europe. She could see now they had tried far too hard – and paid for it.

Now, ironically, she did not try at all and had to keep people at arm's length – they all wanted to know her! People admired her for what she was – a worker, a cool head and a woman who was not afraid to say what she thought. Thankfully, there was nothing now to distract people from the real Leah. If only she'd had the courage to bring her out in public before!

Her mind moved on to the last decade. She'd been pleased to collect the odd lover here and there and was gratified to note some self-esteem creeping back. For years after the elopement she'd stayed faithful to Buster; not by choice, but because she'd been too busy. Apart from that she'd felt too wounded to face the thought of a man's rough body close to hers – there'd been enough of that. When she did allow herself the luxury of an affair, it was only because the Portugese lawyer she met on the plane to Lisbon was the absolute antithesis of everything she'd ever seen in Buster. He was finely built, soft-spoken and slightly effeminate, but for all that he'd made a delicious lover. She made it clear to him she neither wanted nor felt inclined to fall in love again, but her sense of self worth had soared!

There'd been her toy boy too! A young Liverpudlian, Adam, with an earring – not her type at all – working for one of the tour companies, had followed her around one summer like a devoted puppy. He started writing poems for her and resistance became increasingly difficult as he insinuated himself into her life by helping in the shop and throwing out long languid looks when they shared a coffee. In the end she succumbed to the regular and persistent erections she couldn't help but notice in his tight jeans and they had a few good romps in the bedroom. The problem was he fell heavily in love; she felt flattered and was physically aroused but nothing more. She'd had to handle him gently to get rid of him, but luckily his contract and his money ran out so she was able to wave him off at the end of the season.

In a way it was sad that she craved no great passion now. She still felt young enough – but, no. Reluctantly, she'd come to terms with the fact that Buster, for all his horrible faults, had been the one great crush of her life. He had also very nearly crushed her in the process. That, together with the pills.

As she gently removed the cats, folded up the paper and slipped her legs over the side of the bed, she realised she hadn't read a word. It was morbid thinking back like this … there were important decisions to make … but sometimes it was hard not to hark back. Perhaps the time really had come to free herself of this place. If only someone could give her a nudge.

6

*A*lthough her latest recruit to *Caverna*, the attractive Maria José, a language graduate from Coimbra university, would arrive in the shop well before nine to get everything ready for another day's trading, Leah decided to go down early. It was only half past eight, but she wanted a chat with elderly Fernanda who came in every day to dust the surfaces and shine up the floor. Leah had had her eye on a particular property for some time, but she now saw a need to seize the moment.

The big question was – had the tobacco shop belonging to her maid's family on the outskirts of town been snapped up by the municipal authority or not? They'd been sniffing round it for some time with Fernanda's sister and brother-in-law on tenterhooks. They obviously wanted the best price possible and since Portugal had joined the European Community, local government paid very well.

It was a nice little building with a roof terrace and tiny orchard, tucked into a high hillside as one exited the old part of town eastwards towards Albufeira. Leah thought it definitely had possibilities but felt irritated with herself for not having shown more interest earlier. Unlike her beloved apartment, there was no sea view, but over red roofs and pepper-pot chimneys you could see for miles across olive and lemon groves. The problem was – would there be more development in this small corner? One could never quite be certain.

She sighed; decisions, decisions. Could she really bear to give up the old routine? Should she try to cling on and let fate take its course? If she turned down the Dutch offer, she might never get another chance. The thought of being lumbered with the business when she was really old and grey was less appealing. Come on! she thought – you're grey already! Few would guess – or did they? Perhaps she had kidded herself you're only as old as you feel. But there again – it was the adrenalin associated with the job that kept her fired up and energetic, so would it all die if she gave up?

She was almost relieved when her maid told her that the shop had been sold to the *Camera*. They got a good price, and so did the couple next door who'd been persuaded to sell their adjoining property along with it. Now the family could go to Madeira and retire. Fernanda too would go one day. It had been a family dream for many a long year.

Dreams – thought Leah, so other people have dreams too but look where my last dream landed me! She shuddered – she hoped theirs would be less complicated. Oh well, that was another possibility out of the way; it was a relief really to have the decision made for her. She could postpone worrying about where to live now until some inspiration came along. After all, they'd promised her twelve months. She could still sell the business and cling on up above for a while, but it would be very hard to see a stranger in this shop.

She had her back turned to the door when it opened. Maria José generally came in with soft step and unlike old Fernanda, addressed her in English. 'Hi, you're early, honey!' she called as she rummaged through a basket of soft, woven scarves. She'd had them sent in from Marrakesh and with their vegetable dyes and mixture of silk and goat hair were proving popular with the young – pashminas with a difference. 'These are going like hot cakes – how many did you say you sold yesterday, dear? I'd better order some more – I wish our source was more reliable – remember the trouble we had with those braided belts?'

There was silence, then an embarrassed cough behind her. 'I'm sorry – er – are you still closed? I saw the door ajar and – er ... are you Mrs Bloomfield?'

The last words came out in a rush; Leah straightened up and turned slowly to see a tall, slim girl with shoulder-length, blonde hair. She was casually dressed in tee-shirt, jeans and trainers, but something about her manner was disturbing. It was the way she regarded her through nervous, downcast grey eyes as though she was expecting something nasty to happen. For a moment, the older woman was at a loss for words. Something about the young woman made her heart stand still. Did they know each other? Had she made a mistake and failed to recognise someone important – someone who appeared to know her better than she knew them? Was she one of those bright young things from the tour companies who brought her all their clients week after week and expected now – at the end of the season – some token of appreciation such as lunch out, or a gift from the shop?

Maybe not. This wasn't a rep, not even a tour operator – she was different. For once Leah was at a loss; she felt her jaw gape, but no words came. Then, with a sudden shiver to her shoulders, she heard herself say in foolish tone, 'Hey! – hang on a minute, I guess I'm being crass, but – do I know you?'

To her amazement, the girl blushed deeply. 'Yes, you do! The amazing thing is – I knew it was you! Of course I can't really remember, at least ...' she broke off and suddenly the blood was draining from her cheeks; Leah thought she was going to swoon. These kids, so often they didn't eat breakfast, what was going on? She hurried to her, and supported her arm. The girl seemed to stumble, then pulled herself together, 'I'm sorry – can I sit down?'

'Sure,' Leah was eager to salvage the moment. What was going on? Who the heck was this? She fetched a wooden chair, and sent Fernanda scuttling into the back kitchen for a glass of water. 'Look, I'm sorry – you say I know you. I think you're mistaken because I sure as hell can't remember you! Could you jog my memory?'

The colour was returning to the girl's cheeks. She swallowed the water gratefully, then said 'Look, I realise there'll be customers soon, is there anywhere we could talk – have a coffee maybe? Or shall I come back another time? I'm really sorry to walk in like this. My name's Kate – Kate Fraser – but it used to be Mckay. I was seven last time you saw me.'

Leah felt her heart drop away from under her – and all at the same time, the door opened again and in waltzed Maria José looking sleek and coquettish in a strappy top and pink denims. 'Hi!' she called out, then her voice grew concerned 'Are you OK, Leah? You look as though you've seen a ghost!'

She rushed to her boss, and the situation was almost comical as another chair was brought and the stalwart Fernanda stood between her mistress and the stranger, looking from one to another and gabbling rapidly in Portuguese. What was happening? Everyone was fainting! It was too early in the morning for such things! Why had this girl come and why had she upset her *senhora*? Why had her *senhora* upset her? Maria José must please take charge! It was all beyond Fernanda, she couldn't cope. She was an old woman and it was only nine o'clock in the morning!

But, as usual it was Leah who took charge. She recovered almost as soon as she'd sat down, vexed with herself for reacting at all. 'Thank you Fernanda, that will do,' her voice sounded softer in Portuguese. 'Look – Maria José,' she reverted to English and tried to sound businesslike, 'this is an old family friend. I wasn't expecting her, so it's a great surprise. And now she's here, we're going to go up to the apartment for coffee and a chat and I may be away for some time. We have some catching up to do.'

'Of course,' said Maria José, game but curious. Life at *Caverna* was usually pretty predictable, but there was uncertainty and a definite buzz in the air this morning. 'Family friend' – Leah had never mentioned family in all the time she'd known her. Tempted to discover more, good manners prevailed; besides, she had a job to do. No doubt she would learn in good time. 'Do you want me to start the autumn stocktaking, or shall I get on with the new window display we talked about?'

'Forget the stocktaking, forget the display – just run the shop!' said Leah, distracted but peremptory. 'We'll deal with all that this afternoon. I guess I may be off for most of the morning.'

They went out and the two Portuguese women heard them mount the iron staircase. Nothing was said, but they looked at each other with expressive eyes. Maria José guessed it wouldn't just be the morning; more likely the whole day. She'd been privy to a look on her boss's face which was hard to describe. It really was as if Leah had seen a ghost, and there'd been something else. Was it hurt? Resignation? Betrayal? Definitely more than a family friend should warrant; instead, a very big question mark loomed like a mushroom cloud. She only hoped for Leah's sake that the pretty English woman was not a harbinger of trouble. Maria José was really getting into this job and Leah had promised it would lead to better things such as buying and management. As a post-graduate she had wasted months since leaving Coimbra with no work, and it was such a relief when Leah took her on. It was not what she had envisaged for herself but now she was settling into things, she hoped nothing would threaten her position.

'And so,' Kate was saying, 'I couldn't bear the sense of mystery any longer. Mama used to drop these snippets of information, here and there, like scattered seeds – but there was never enough for me to piece them all together. All my life I heard things, gleaned a little here, picked up a little there, even overheard when I shouldn't, but rather than help the overall picture, I was simply left fazed and confused. I got to a stage in my teens where I began to convince myself I was in their way – I had absolutely no self esteem. After the first homecoming when he couldn't do more for me, Papa became gradually more distant. All the love that I had remembered and yearned for – after that terrible time away – seemed to dry up. There were times he seemed so remote I wondered if he even noticed me. I seriously thought of running away at this time.

'As for Mama, well she'd never been very maternal except when it suited her. She'd always had her own agenda, which rarely seemed to concern me though I tagged along.

Once settled in Scotland, she was far too busy turning Lochaig into a showpiece, giving drinks and dinner parties, being seen at the right functions and generally lording it around the Highlands. People had never seen anything like her; she was a far cry from the nice relaxed tweedy ladies from neighbouring estates who rode, gardened, trained gun dogs or simply mucked in. She was terribly aloof, exotic and rather put the women off, but as usual the men were drawn to her because she was so different! Of course, she loved that.'

'She would,' said Leah regretfully, 'Catalina always had to be the centre of attention. The awful thing is we all indulged her, and despite being female, I was the worst offender. In those days, it was not so much Buster – believe it or not – it was me and the Boys. They thought her thoroughly delicious and I, for my sins, could see no wrong. I guess we kind of basked in her reflected glory – she was like a gorgeous butterfly and we were delighted she'd landed on our patch!'

There was a pause, whilst they both thought back. Kate had been in Leah's sunny apartment for over two hours now and much coffee had been consumed. She had recovered her colour and after a tense start was beginning to relax. God – what a decent woman this was! She'd been so scared when she entered that shop, so uncertain of what to say. Right up until the last moment she was going to be just another tourist, feeling the vibes as it were, sizing up her options. Only after that first visit had she intended to come clean about her identity – but that would be for another day.

But it didn't turn out that way. Kate was not a person to deceive. One look at Leah bending over her wares, the careworn, honest face as she straightened up, and the surprise in her eyes had changed all that. This woman had suffered enough not to be the victim of yet more deception, and throwing caution to the wind, she swept reservations aside and said what came naturally – the truth. What she hadn't reckoned upon was turning to jelly at the knees and almost collapsing in a heap. She was surprised and disappointed at herself for giving way to such weakness, but it had been such an emotional moment. What would her father have said? What would he say now, seeing the two women with their heads together and hearing their conversation?

In two short hours she had learned more about her mother than in her lifetime. The extraordinary thing, that despite her appalling behaviour, Leah bore no grudge. According to this exceptional American, the scars had healed leaving mind and soul intact. It had taken many years she said, but if anything, it had made her a better person; tougher anyway. Since this was the closest Kate had come to thinking that good really might – after all – prevail over evil, it was a revelation. She had longed to believe such things, but no amount of talking to others, or going to church, had convinced her. For years, she felt contaminated and besmirched by what had happened in her background and had seen no way out. Yet here in front of her was a woman who had survived all manner of misfortune, mainly at the hands of Kate's mother and possibly her father too, yet she remained untainted.

Neither was there a hint of bitterness, anger or revenge as they talked. Regret, naturally, but what struck Kate straight between the eyeballs was the fact that Leah had never allowed what had happened to sully her own *persona*. She had held herself separate, removed herself from the misdeeds of others and struck off on her own. That required huge strength of character. And if she could do it and make a success of things – then there was just the tiniest hope that Kate could do it too.

'Look, honey, before we talk further – I think you ought to meet Benjie. You see, there's no point in me mentioning names, unless you get a bit of a feel for who these people are. A lot of them have left the Algarve and gone their separate ways, several have died, like our once glamorous Johanna – you'd have seen that in the press – but those few who are still around might be worth taking a look at. Places too! There's no point me starting at the beginning without you having a sense of where it's at, or rather where it *was* – if you see what I mean.'

Kate nodded. As Leah had been at pains to explain, it was impossible to make judgements about what had happened between her parents without understanding the social strictures and structures of the time. The ex-pats formed such a tight community, there was an energy about that might have led people to do things they would never, normally, have considered. 'We were all living in a bubble,' said Leah – 'it was such a rarified atmosphere. During that time – remember, we had just moved out of the Sixties – the decade ahead stretched full of promise and there were people about who thought anything was possible.'

'So unlike today,' said Kate. She'd been sitting on the floor with her legs stretched out, and now as she brought her knees up to her chin, pushed her hair behind her ears and squinted up at Leah curled into a basket chair, she thought for the umpteenth time. 'What an amazing lady!' Finally, she said aloud, 'Are you sure you've got the time?'

'I'm sure,' smiled Leah. 'To be honest, I could do with a diversion. I've got a business decision to make in a few days, and it will help clear my mind to focus on something completely different. We'll call this Project Kate – a splendid change from Project *Caverna*! Besides, it'll blow away a few more cobwebs to take you around and show you where things happened. Santa Felicia's changed a lot since your mother and father lived here, but I'll enjoy explaining how it used to be, where we did this and that and point out the hotspots where the beautiful people hung out. We may even meet a few more faces in our travels, so much the better, then the jigsaw puzzle will really start to take shape.'

'You are *so* kind,' said Kate. 'After all that's happened, it's hard to believe this.'

'I'm not *that* kind. It's not all altruism. Apart from my business conundrum, it could be quite therapeutic as well. I made up my mind long ago not to let anyone get under my skin or hurt me any more, but there are still a few bad moments when I lie in my bed. This might be a way of saying goodbye to the last of them, you never know. I'm going down to the shop now for an hour or so, but I'll tell my staff they're on their own from lunchtime onwards. You kill time with whatever you have to do, and I'll meet you for a drink and snack in The Anchor at one. Some of the old crowd still hang out there, and it's likely we'll discover Benjie and Roger at the bar. Of course, I won't say who you are – that'll be our little secret – but at least you'll have a few faces to back up the saga as it unwinds. I've always believed you learn more by being a kind of fly on the wall, if you're willing?'

'I thought it was Benjie and *Howard*,' said Kate.

'Oh it *was*, honey,'said Leah, 'didn't I tell you? Poor Howard died some fifteen years ago and Benjie finally teamed up with his old friend Roger Grafton. They're quite an item!

The Anchor Bar lay just off the main square. It could have been an English pub from Shakespeare country with its blackened timbers and daub walls. Missing was the thatched roof, but the iron sign that hung lifeless in the still air looked genuine with a faded Jack Tar, propped up against his vessel. Overall, it seemed designed to attract those far from home, with an inclination for manly talk and a pint of strong bitter. How different was the reality!

Inside, the place was thronged – but with customers of all types and arguably more women than men. Kate edged her way through the mêlée as instructed by Leah, aware that any hope of securing a high stool at the brass rail was futile. What did it matter though? She was quite happy to stand in a corner, melt into the crowd and to observe. Feeling much better now, it was hard to believe she was the same person who had gone down to breakfast with huge butterflies in her tummy. No wonder she had been unable to do justice to the generous spread of ham, smoked cheese, and fruit facing her across a crisp tablecloth.

After her time with Leah, she had walked along the beach and tried to reach James on her mobile. They had spoken the night before. 'Please be careful,' he had warned. 'This woman may be highly resentful and she may have some really upsetting things to say about your parents. If she becomes unpleasant, just walk away. Whatever you do, don't get into a slanging match – you don't deserve that.'

She had tried to convince him that anything was better than the uncertainty that had festered within her over so many years. Not knowing is far worse than knowing, she'd pointed out, but he still seemed dubious. If you've never been there yourself, you never really understand when another person is in mental turmoil. It was a pity she hadn't got through to reassure him, second time around. Today the reception on her trusty Nokia was non existent; perhaps it was the sea breeze or was it the cliff? James would find it hard to believe that the dreaded meeting had not only taken place, but exploded into something that might have taken place in a film.

When they had first entered her apartment, the element of contempt on Leah's part was tangible. Kate felt it was less to do with who she was, more to do with her motives. Clearly, Leah could not imagine why any sensible person should want to stir up the past except out of idle curiosity and perhaps even a chance to gloat. 'Look, honey,' she'd said, hands on hips, her nasal twang more pronounced than in the shop. 'I can't blame you for what your mother did, but I want you to know I've put the whole thing behind me, rebuilt my life, done my own thing. If this is just a jaunt to see the Algarve and revisit your past, you've come to the wrong person. In fact you're wasting your time. I'm simply not interested, d'you hear? Not interested at all.'

A few more words in this vein and Kate had lost her tongue, very nearly her senses too. She'd stuttered, put her hand to her head and started to shake. It was all so unfair. So completely the opposite! She'd agonised about such a meeting for so long, but the reality of it taking place so suddenly, so quickly, was altogether too much to bear. In less than 24 hours she'd seen her old home, felt the strangely familiar *calçada* under her feet, smelt the seaweed, sat in the lee of the bay and come face to face with the woman whom her mother had betrayed. The enormity of it had struck her speechless.

Worse than that, this woman, this tough wiry American, imagined that she, Kate, was like everyone else in this crazy charade. She knew, could sense she was being regarded as a superficial materialist without scruples or conscience. To Leah she obviously represented someone who could just order up a ticket, hop on a plane and come all this way to satisfy some idle whim – dropping in as a *voyeur* on someone's else tragedy. Unfair as it was, she couldn't blame her! Leah must have thought she was her mother's stooge and somehow she could not bear that. It was all so totally untrue, so terribly, terribly unjust. 'You've got it wrong!' she burst out, 'for a start, my mother's dead!'

At this point, everything changed. She didn't exactly collapse again, but the hot tears started to sting her eyes and with a murmured excuse, she had sat down heavily on Leah's big studio sofa, her head in her hands. Then she started to rock, gently at first, then more vehemently to and fro. She knew it was absurd, but as in the old days when all was stacked against her and she felt out of control, she had to do something! Without this physical outlet, she knew she might break down completely and that was the very last thing she wanted, under the circumstances. All at once, something jerked back in Leah's consciousness and she remembered the young Kate. A small fair-haired girl with worried eyes – little Katy McKay! Her mother was always complaining how the child rocked herself into a state of oblivion when she felt insecure – and wasn't it silly? Problems at school were blamed, but once or twice Leah had seen this so-called behavioural problem for herself and the cause was obvious. It happened when Jock and Catalina had one of their blazing rows. Jock would drink, Catalina would nag – dramatic and aggressive – she admitted it herself, and the child would be caught in the middle.

'Poor kid,' said Leah, just as she had all of thirty years ago and suddenly she was crouching down beside her, a strong warm arm round the grown-up Kate's shoulders. 'Poor kid,' she repeated. 'I can see now why you've come. You're all screwed up, aren't you? You see, I've been there myself – so I know.'

It was a relief to tell someone. It was then that Kate Fraser cried as she'd not cried for a very long time indeed. She cried for herself, she cried for her dead mother, she cried for her father. She also cried for the future. 'I've spent my whole life wanting to know the truth about my past,' she said between the tears. 'There's been so much I couldn't understand, wasn't allowed to understand and the worst part of all it's left me with a feeling of such guilt, it's been impossible to throw off. Part of me, the inner part which I can't quite reach, seems to think I could have stopped it all happening in the first place. For years, I felt I'd let my father down when we went away and I'd like to know why.

'Then there was the accident. I was there, you know, but I can't remember what happened. Again, I wonder if I could have somehow stopped it happening. Did I play some part in it? Why did my mother never discuss it with me? She used to give me a knowing look as if somehow we were in it all together. Now I shall never know and I'm so scared all this is going to affect my children. James just doesn't see it,' she blurted out, 'but if ever my sons found out the truth – whatever the truth is – it could hurt them terribly. It could blight their lives – there's so much that I don't know, the doubts grow within me like a cancer and I can never see a light at the end of the tunnel. And the thing I worry about most is ... how can I say it ...?'

'... whether his death was an accident or not?' finished Leah. 'No, there's no need to flinch like that. And don't think I haven't thought about that many a time myself. I guess it's one of the great unsolved mysteries and it's probably better left that way.'

'But don't *you* want to know?' Kate's eyes were huge in her pale face, her voice incredulous.

'Not really,' said Leah. 'To be truthful, it was one helluva relief when I knew he wouldn't be coming back. I had dreaded that more than you'll ever know. Besides,' she smiled wanly, 'at least it gave us all a chance to get on with our lives and sell the house. His name was on the deeds as well as ours and as long as he lived – we'd no idea where – we were impotent, stuck in a house we could no longer afford. It was so hard on all of us, not just the expense of it all but the memories too. The Boys in particular were desperate. I still think all that worry brought Howard to an earlier death than he deserved.'

'I hadn't realised,' murmured Kate. 'I always thought you'd be devastated and so bitter. I also thought, despite everything, you might want him back.'

It was the only time since they'd met that Leah showed real emotion. Her laugh came as a shock – a high pitched bray, verging on the hysterical. Then silence and a very long pause. 'After what he did? Oh no, honey,' said Leah, her voice resumed normality, 'you mistake me. You can be a sucker once, but not twice. I'd never have had him back – even if he'd come on bended knee the day after he left and said he'd made a big mistake. His death just made it easier to cope with the aftermath. I just wish it had happened a whole lot sooner. It would have been nice to have had some fun, in between! Instead, I was always waiting for that rap on the door.'

Again, Kate found her jaw dropping, and this latest revelation almost brought a smile to her lips. The more she talked to Leah, the more she felt the stress lifting from her shoulders. There was still so much to share, to lay bare and explain, but she felt all the urgency had gone out of her mission. As for the guilt – inadequately, she tried to explain and as Leah saw her struggling to articulate, she changed her tune. 'Forget what I said about not wanting to rake up the past. I only said that because there seemed no point, more harm than good – but not in your case. You need to get your mind sorted and if the only way is by going over the past, then I'll do my best. There's so much I don't know myself, but after your mother and he took off, I did a lot of talking to people. You see, I still hoped to find them – despite the Revolution – so although I never traced them, I unscrambled a good deal of what had gone on behind our backs and under our noses – we had been so blind!'

'I think *anything* you feel you could share would help,' said Kate. 'It's my father I worry about. I want to know how much he was involved – it's possible to accept one of your parents is thoroughly bad, but when it comes to both ...'

'Oh, even Catalina wasn't *all* bad,' said Leah. 'Don't judge her too harshly – I think things just escalated out of control and circumstances egged her on. My husband exuded a kind of power I only recognised after he'd left. He was very physical and it takes two to tango after all. Just please remember one thing – we're not talking about the Leah of today. I was much too intense in those days and on all kinds of pills, which gave me an unrealistic perspective of life. Look, the way I see it is this. There was this naïve woman, Mrs Bloomfield, newly arrived from New York – a real innocent abroad. And through sheer blindness, dependency and a nutty ideal of following a dream, she allowed herself to get embroiled in a mess.

'And so!' she took a deep breath, 'whatever I have to say now about that poor woman will be as I see it today, not as I felt it then. We'll keep feelings out of it if you don't mind, because even with all this – ' she swept a vague arm around to indicate the apartment and the shop, 'I need to keep my distance from that whole crazy scenario. It's OK from the outside looking in, but I must never do things the other way around. I learned that under therapy.'

'Leah, if this is going to be damaging for you –' began Kate.

The American brushed her aside. 'No, on the contrary – as I said, I'm regarding it as a project and since *I'm* in control this time, that's fine! After lunch, we'll drive out to where you can see the whole of this peninsula spread out before you. We'll sit in the sun and I'll start on this story about four people who came to Portugal with stars in their eyes and an incredible dream.'

'I'd really appreciate that,' said Kate. 'If ... if you're absolutely sure?'

Leah nodded. 'Remember, we're talking about the time of the beautiful crazy people when the world seemed squeaky clean and shiny and new. And if this detached and sometimes sardonic glimpse of a time capsule long gone helps you make up your mind about your family and banishes those ghosts forever, I'll feel I've done a good job. If not – ' she looked suddenly vulnerable and shrugged her shoulders – 'well who knows, probably only the sea, the birds and the wild wild wind – it comes across from Africa and we call it the *Levante.*'

'I understand,' said Kate getting up to give her a hug. 'This has been the best thing that's happened in years. I can't thank you enough.'

'I've done nothing yet,' smiled her new friend.

But she would soon, thought Kate, wiggling her toes against the cramp creeping up one leg from her propped position near the bar. It was getting hot and uncomfortable and still there was no sign of Leah, but it was early yet. Some German tourists were getting up from the back of the room, so she seized her opportunity, squeezed through the throng and launched herself into a chair by a small table, crowded with beer glasses. She had just made room for her bag when a shrill Mayfair voice hissed in her ear, 'I say – *we* rather had our eyes on this table, could you *possibly* give it up I wonder? After all there's only – em – *one* of you and as you can see – em – *four* of us.'

Kate jerked her head up to see a wafer-thin blonde in what had to be a Versace pantsuit – a look of injured self-righteousness on her finely chiselled face. There was another woman, a brunette, equally thin, plus a man who could have been a male model. The three of them were flanked by a much older man with a puffy face and a fat cigar cocked between the fourth finger and thumb of a white, fleshy hand. 'Now don't go bullying people, Maysie,' he said in smooth languid tones, wagging his finger and scattering ash all over the floor, 'the lady may not be for turning?' He gave Kate a mock bow while they all waited expectantly.

She looked at their collective faces, and was slightly amused. Who were these people? She judged the women to be somewhere in their fifties and who obviously thought themselves quite special. It was tempting not to give them the wretched table, but she'd already decided Leah might not see her from there. 'Oh, don't worry,' she said as magnanimously as she could muster, 'I don't want it anyway.'

'Thank you *so* much,' said the male model, 'You are *too* kind,' and they surged forward as one, with the blonde giving her a cold, sideways look.

By the time, she had filtered her way back to the bar, she was relieved to see Leah who had been hailed by a tall good-looking man perched on one of the bar stools. The man's younger companion seemed more engrossed with his cocktail – a florid affair with sticks, a mass of greenery and little paper umbrellas. For a moment, Leah seemed not to notice her and Kate hovered awkwardly as she heard her say, 'It's a darned shame for you, Benjie, but knowing you – it'll all come right in the end. It generally does.'

'But I told her what a *scumbag* he was,' he was saying, 'I said 'Anna-Maria my girl, it's not *tony,* and it will all end in tears. You leave me to work for him and you'll be out on your butt before the year is out!' He swivelled an elegant neck round to indicate a direction far over his shoulder and came face to face with Kate.

'Why hull-*o!*' A pair of very bright hazel eyes, with dozens of little crows' feet set in a tanned face, met hers, whereupon, Leah jumped into action.

'Benjie honey, this is my guest, I asked her to come and join me for lunch – do you know Kate? – er – Kate Fraser?'

'Oh! Delighted, I'm sure!'he said, slipping off his stool and pumping her hand, 'Fraser, hmm… isn't that the name of a distinguished Scottish clan? Any relation of dear Lady Antonia?'

'Er – no' smiled Kate, politely 'There's rather too many of us all to be related.'

'But you actually live in Scotland?' he pronounced it Scatland, as though it was one of the remotest places on earth, 'How simply *wonderful!*'

Leah broke in to rescue her, 'Yeah, Kate's out here for a week's break from kids and family. It's her first trip to the Algarve and we got talking in the shop today. I haven't much on, now the season's tailing off, so I said I'd show her around.'

'That's good to hear,' her companion raised an eyebrow, 'Distractions are good. They tell me sweetheart, you might be selling *Caverna* – is there any truth in that?'

'I can't think where you heard that,' said Leah, 'but aren't we forgetting our manners here? Kate, can I introduce Roger Grafton – he too is from the UK.'

A freckled face turned sleepily round, and grinned. No attempt was made to offer his stool, but the green eyes were friendly enough. 'Hi!' the voice was unmistakably Oxford, 'you'll have to forgive me. We were partying rather hard last night, and this is my way of chasing it all away,' he twirled the little parasols with a shaky hand.

'Well, *you* seem OK, Benjie,' smiled Leah. 'Whose party, by the way?'

'Oh, you wouldn't know them – don't *ask,'* said Benjie, darkly. 'Anyway, I'm on tomato juice – I don't need chasers!' and for Kate's benefit added, ' I learned my lesson years ago – one needs to here in the Algarve.'

'Well, we're off to have some lunch,'said Leah. 'I can see we'll never get anything here, it's all much too busy and the barman hasn't looked my way once. Let's go, Kate!'

'I'd have gotten you a drink if you'd waited' said Benjie. 'Nice to meet you Kate, be sure to drop by my offices if you're passing that way. Leah will show you where I am.'

They went out into the square together. 'So that was Benjie, a rather important part of the story,' said Leah. 'He'd simply die if he knew you were Catalina's daughter; it's lucky your colouring is rather different, although the shape of your nose and the chin is identical.'

'Is it?' said Kate genuinely interested – no one had ever told her that before. 'By the way, what does Benjie do? – his offices sound impressive.'

'Oh, they are. He's done well for himself. After all the upset, he – like all of us – had to start more or less from scratch again. He revolted against interior design after what happened up at the house – the 'desecration' was how he described it – so he went into real estate. There was a killing to be made in land after all the turmoil of the Revolution and he's become one of our leading property people here on the coast. Now! Let's go and eat and then I promise to start at the very beginning.'

7

New York – February 1973

$\mathcal{N}$ew York was cold that morning; almost as cold as the international situation relayed via the breakfast news. Rwanda was heading for civil war, the Israelis had just shot down a Libyan plane over Sinai and Brezhnev's man in Washington was yet again in telephone debate with the President's number one. The exchange had been frosty. As though to emphasis matters, February's climatologists' report in *Science Digest* was warning everyone 'to prepare for the next ice age.' Whatever the temperature, it was business as usual for Leah Bloomfield, seated at her enormous mahogany desk on the 16th floor of Astra House, just off Times Square. Her only concern was that none of these catastrophes would get in the way of her latest consignment of salon furniture due to leave Madrid later that day. She was on the phone to her favourite agent when Buster burst into her office. 'I'm told it's Portugal – *tomorrow*!' He was holding a bulging travel wallet which he waved in horror at his wife.

'Hang on! Bill? You say you've located the consignment? Yeah, yeah! five crates, each carrying an L62 document, but we're still waiting on the valuation from Christies for one of the Prado pieces. Mind you – it shouldn't make much difference – we've already entered a figure well over the EVA. Can you hold a moment?' She cradled the instrument against the crook of her arm, nodding furiously at her husband, 'What's the problem? why *not*? We'd more or less agreed – it was just a question of which darned day ... Are you still there, Bill?'

'But it's crazy!' her husband stormed, 'We've only talked! I know nothing about the deal – not in any depth. You've done everything – as usual. You know the site, set up, officials, lawyer... the lingo, that *helps*!' his voice was heavy with sarcasm. As always, you know all about it – down to the last nitty gritty little detail – I don't!'

'Buster, hon – you'd think you'd never been out there! You always said – if it came to the crunch ... Bill, I'm sorry - can I call you back? I've gotten myself a small problem here.' She put down the red handpiece, rolling her eyes in exasperation As if on cue, the mustard phone – a mile across the desk – set up a low persistent ring. She reached for it with a 'Hold, will you?' placing the other off the hook and smothering its complaining whine in a cushion.

'Look, honey! I can't see what the problem is. It's only the paperwork to complete. It couldn't be more simple. Only – look at me! I'm snowed under. You know I can't get away!'

'*Can't?*' he retorted, 'I thought you didn't recognise that word – or won't? Why can't I hold the shop here, for Chrissakes?'

'But that's just it Buster, you can't…' she bit her tongue, 'er – you're not in a position to, honey. Too much can go wrong at this stage, Snape & Addington are dying to step in and take this deal off of us – whereas, all that's needed in Portugal are signatures. Plain and simple. There's nothing to lose – trust me! You've gotta go! One of us has to – our future depends on it.'

He flung himself, tightlipped, into a high button-back leather chair, throwing his feet onto a coffee table and showering the room with trade journals. 'Precisely,' he retorted, 'That's my point!'

'Look, Buster,' her eyes were imploring, 'I'd give anything to go swanning off to the sunny Algarve right now, but if I did, I could lose this contract. It's been months in the making and I've got to see it through. Don't forget, it's the last real money-maker. Mark up? five hundred per cent – to *us*! If we leave for Europe without this under our belts, I'll never forgive myself – or you for that matter. I need you right now and I need you in Portugal!'

'Convince me!' She knew that voice; despite the play of petulance, he was weakening.

'Don't you see, Portugal's a done deal. A kid's game – everything's been arranged. All they want is a signature on five different documents – they're called *escrituras* – you know, registry of title and all that. We did the land, we did the permissions, but now it's built, there's a process for the villa itself. Howard's already been over and completed his share. Now it's down to us before the legal boys get everything stamped and notarised at the *camera*. I've arranged a power of attorney for myself with Goldsteins this afternoon; it has to be translated into Portuguese but the consulate will hurry it through. All you have to do is take it out, hand it to the lawyers in Faro, then you can sign for both of us. It'll be over in a day, and afterward you can enjoy yourself. Think of us shivering here in the ice!'

She leaned over, a neat figure in a wool trouser suit, and replaced the red receiver. Her personal line on the mustard phone was emitting a high pitched wail, 'Don't bust my eardrums,' she said and put it back on its cradle. Immediately it was ringing again and she gave her husband a long meaningful look. It was a dismissal.

'Leah Franklyn and Partner!' She still used her maiden name… 'Why, hullo there! *Suzanne*! It's been an age. No, we haven't moved…not yet – but we've finished the construction stage – and we're getting there! Buster's off tomorrow to do all the signing. Look, I can't talk right now – but say, what about lunch – in a week's time? Then I can fill you in.'

She was back on the red, dialling out. With a shrug of his broad shoulders and a look of weary resignation, Buster Bloomfield heaved his long athletic frame out of the chair and ambled towards the door.

'OK,' his voice was low, 'I guess I'll have to go. But if I sign the wrong god-darned documents or something goes badly wrong, you'll know who to blame.' He cocked a finger at her like an imitation pistol and backed out of the door.

She blew him a kiss, cupping her hand over the mouthpiece. 'You're a peach! I knew I could count on you. I'll see you at two thirty to fix that power of attorney.'

A moment later she was back on the red, clipped and decisive as she grilled one of their retail managers, 'How come Michigan were down on budget by a working 7. 5 per cent?

Yeah – I know it was a poor Christmas generally – but you can't blame the politicians for everything. I'm relying on you to kick a bit of ass up there in the frozen north and tell them to get their act together. Oh, and remember, Lou, there's no such word as 'can't'!'

Another successful completion under her belt, Leah let herself into the apartment. It was convenient for the office at 79th, just off Park but despite the fatigue she was walking on air. Three days had passed since she'd last seen her husband but there'd been no time to miss him. In the meantime the delayed Spanish consignment had left Europe – a hefty bribe had done wonders – and the big Beverley Hills deal was finally through.

'Six months of playing games and we made it!' she sang, flinging her bag onto the sofa as she moved automatically to the bar for a vodka and tonic. 'Thank God I was here to modify the contract! Despite those concessions and massaging all that professional ego, we've still come out winners! Only now they think they've got one over us and that's just fine with me!'

Deals! She knew she was good at them, and as she sank into a white moiré sofa and put her feet up, she wondered how much she would miss this buzz. It would have been more appropriate to open a bottle of Moët, but champagne wasn't much fun to drink alone. She laughed at herself for having talked out loud. She did it too often when he was away and it was developing into a habit. Forget the buzz – she thought – it was definitely time to retire.

Funny how the apartment always seemed so huge without Buster. He and his sprawling ways took up a lot of space! Well, he'd be back by the end of the week, hopefully in the best of spirits – pleased with himself, the villa and life in general. The sun always did him good. In the end, he hadn't needed that much persuasion; he simply liked to dig his toes in and make her feel bad for giving the orders. It had been that way all of their married life but he'd hung in there and enjoyed the benefits – he was hardly going to throw in the towel now, just as things were moving up a whole gear. Together they'd worked hard for this. Once they made the break, they would wonder why they hadn't done it long ago.

It seemed incredible it was all now so close. In two months they'd be handing the keys of this place over to the new tenants – along with the business and everything else. They were about to embark on the biggest venture of their lives and literally to start again. It would be a new beginning…'a new life'. She was saying the last three words aloud again, the enormity of it all hitting her forcibly in the pit of her stomach. Until now she had never allowed herself the indulgence of dreaming on in this vein. Besides, things had a habit of changing at the last moment and Leah was superstitious enough never knowingly to tempt fate. But now, short of Buster ringing to say there was some legal hitch over the title – which he'd have done by now, surely? – their combined fate was moving inexorably towards total, irrevocable change. Life would never be the same again. It was as though someone had opened an unwritten book; it was now up to them to fill the empty pages.

Suddenly she had an urge to laugh hysterically. Instead, she gulped her vodka down, retrieved her handbag, fished out a couple of valium from her enamelled Cartier pillbox and popped them into her mouth. She hadn't really meant to take them, but it had been one helluva week and she needed a good night's sleep tonight. Tranquies … she thought ruefully, shame on you Leah! and she shook her head in disapproval. This time next year, she promised herself, you'll be truly independent of these – you'll be calm, settled and fulfilled.

Kicking off the high heels which had punished her all day, she curled deeper into the sofa and thought about the last time she and Buster had been to Portugal together. It had been less than six months, yet it seemed like six years. The final, time-consuming stages of building the villa were undoubtedly the worst, since the smaller things had to be checked constantly and the local builders had a habit of interpreting the minutae on the plans in their own way which was often not *her* way.

The early stages of erecting the main structure had moved forward splendidly. They had no complaints there and besides, their architect, Aurelio de Moura from Lisbon, was in constant attendance and the foreman respected the brightest young partner of a firm which had won two government-backed contracts for the Algarve's latest golf hotels. But lately, things had changed. Aurelio had bigger fish to fry and now that Casa Amarela was almost complete with most of the money already paid, the builders had become lax at responding to her urgent telegrams. On top of that, the complications of selling, then transferring their business whilst still maintaining a high profile with last minute contracts, had taken its toll. No one knew better than Leah that despite the highs, she was exhausted. Living on her nerves was not only debilitating in the short term, but could store up health troubles for the future. Indeed, Wally, her psychologist, had warned that if she kept up her present schedule, subsisting on less than five, even four hours sleep a night, she'd be finishing the winter in a body bag rather than a body warmer.

Clearly therefore, the time was ripe to leave New York. She had no regrets about going. She'd used this great city, but it had also used her and she did not need her shrink to tell her that. She'd made the decision to get out, long ago. The fact that everything had escalated at the last minute was unfortunate, but nonetheless normal amongst highflyers. There was no need to put either business or apartment on the market. They simply allowed it to be known within the trade and amongst a carefully chosen circle of media friends that things were up for grabs. After the expected lull and inactivity while everyone held their breath – everything happened at once. It was their closest competitors in New Jersey who made the final successful bid, but because Buster actively disliked one of the partners, stress had piled on stress during the frenzied negotiations. Fortunately, the firm itself was as established as they and the capital was swiftly raised. The offer was too good to turn down and Buster assuaged his pride with wise-cracks about 'the devil you know…'

Her eyes swept around the room without affection. Things had reached the stage where she longed to leave it all behind. There was a hand-carved plaque which Buster had hung at a rakish angle over the top row of bottles in the cocktail bar. Someone had given it to them at an office party and it was so kitsch they had kept it, unlike the less offensive staff presents that went to the charity shop. It read 'Home, Sweet Home' and as Leah looked round, she reckoned this had never been her idea of home. Home was somewhere out there, somewhere way beyond the horizon of her east-facing penthouse window – on the other side of the Atlantic. Aware of her roots, supposedly Flemish, she felt her heart had been in Europe for a long time. Each overseas buying trip confirmed the feeling. As the invisible strings that bound her to that historic and diverse continent had drawn tighter over the years, it had become a spiritual thing. Now the long-awaited dream of returning for good was about to become reality.

She shut her eyes and began to picture it all. It seemed only yesterday that she and Buster were standing on the dun-coloured apron of smooth concrete that separated them from the brand new building and its uncluttered view to the ocean far below. The villa spanned out in a gentle curve with a central block etched against a cloudless sky topped by a gently sloping pan-tiled roof. On each side a long arm stretched to east and west, landscaped into the rolling hinterland to house the public rooms at the lower level. The winter sun glinted on tall French windows as though someone had turned on all the lights. The original design had involved three large squares in a complicated cubist effect – 'pure Manhattan' Buster had called it – but having failed to satisfy the town hall, Aurelio admitted defeat and returned to the drawing board. The result he came up with was, in Leah's opinion, much the prettier of the two options. A submerged basement housed the gym, sauna and wine cellar, whilst the ground and upper storeys provided the living quarters. With a cupola effect over the hall, classical lines and arches to the front, Buster was concerned the villa had lost its unique designer look along the way.

'But it's so much more practical, honey,' she'd placated, 'and at least the whole thing spans twice the width of anything I've seen along the coast. It's really imposing! Compare it to our apartment and there's a danger we'll get lost.'

'I doubt it with four of us,' he'd growled, 'I liked the separation of the other design.' But since nothing could be done the subject was dropped and the plans approved. Now, even he had to concede that Casa Amarela enjoyed a sense of glamour which he personally found exciting. It was almost as though the house threw out a challenge.

With an abundance of gesticulations and frequent flashes of strong white teeth, Manuel the builder indicated the finishing touches. Here, on a tiled parapet from whence the natural terracing of the land fell away like the ha-ha of an English country manor, three pairs of heavy cast iron urns would be rivetted into place. A flourish of spatulate fingers and he had conjured up for Leah an image of trailing greenery and clouds of pink geranium, spilling over walls, cascading down a paved stairway to the rockery below. To the side, shaded by a bamboo pergola, would go the seventeenth-century Italian stone conservatory table, presently lying in a bonded warehouse at Lisbon docks. Here they would eat their patio meals – Manuel patted his stomach to show he was well ahead of the brief, locating a copy of the shipping document, together with Leah's photographs and scribbled notes on his clip-board.

Onto another level, and a retaining wall would soon be adorned with hand-painted tiles of birds and fish. Smoothing motions showed exactly where each piece was to be cemented into place. Finally, an enthusiastic sweep of a thick hairy arm, and the site of the swimming pool was indicated. They all knew this by heart, but had decided to defer its excavation until after the move. Now with the landscaping and the villa itself as near completion as anyone dared hope, it seemed as logical a place as ever. Leah was especially pleased to note the pre-arranged ledge of shade Aurelio had promised her once the roof was complete. With her auburn hair and fair skin, she wondered at what precise time of the day the mathematical brain had calculated that the sun would be blotted out by the overhanging eaves in her own private corner of her garden. She was less of a sun worshipper than the others but she trusted him on this – the Portuguese liked the shade too.

Well satisfied with all they had seen, she and Buster were preparing to leave. The only fly in the ointment had been a glimpse of some figures in Manuel's notebook. Their last minute alterations and embellishments had bumped up the balance yet again. They might be over budget but as Leah pointed out, compared to home, the margins were risible. Suddenly she found, she couldn't care less. Especially with their latest deal. Besides, she had no stomach for depriving Manuel of the inevitable little baubles he had in his mind for his pretty young wife. It went with the culture!

As though reading her mind, Manuel was finishing the tour with an expansive shrug of his shoulders. 'With this guy around, who needs to learn the lingo?' said Buster, 'He knows he's in the home strait now and it's all he can do not to rub his hands in glee. And aren't we the suckers?'

'Stop worrying, hon, let's just *enjoy*,' Leah reached out and drew him to the end of the terrace. Now they were about to leave, all she ever wanted to do was gaze and gaze at the sea until it burned into her subconscious. She had bought the land for the view! How could she explain that the sight of the Atlantic, navy-blue and endless, surging away towards the heel of Europe as it crashed against the rocks of Cape St Vincent could turn her city-born knees to jelly. And the reassurance right here – where the ocean came gently, nuzzling its way round this modest little bay with its softly sloping almond-clad land, as if questioning its welcome like a nervous cat – did he not feel it too?

Here there was no roar, no crash of surf upon the beach. Salt did not hang in the air, or wind pierce the worn crevices of the yellow cliffs. She had never sought grandeur in Nature. It was too emotional, too threatening. That was why she had fallen in love with this soft Algarvean hillside. Undulating land, tranquillity, a view – who could want more? The peace of the spectacle eased her soul, beauty lay all around in an unhurried, wanton way like a lazy woman waiting to be despoiled. She hoped that Buster could embrace it too.

'You realise,' he was saying, 'despite the machinations of our friend here, we've been pretty smart on the real estate side. An English guy in the bar last night was telling me about his brother in Marbella, Spain. Apparently a plot with a coastal view like ours is double the price of anything in the Algarve, building costs too. He reckoned he's already spent a million bucks, with the house only half started!'

'Yes hon, I *know*,' she replied, sighing at his habit of measuring everything aesthetic and romantic with dollar signs. 'But that's *not* why I chose here; I simply fell in love – it could have been Marbella, it could have been anywhere, it just happened to be this spot.' The sea today was the colour of spring hyacinths and the glitter from the sun as it sparkled and leaped across the little bay made her eyes water. Beauty and brightness! They had the same dazzling effect on the senses.

'Well I'm glad it *was* here and not Marbella,' Buster was saying. 'But isn't that my clever little business lady, all over? You see - you've done it again for Leah Franklyn and Partner. But as for the "partner", I guess old Buster B can't take too much credit this time. That old bastard hasn't had much to do with this little exercise, now has he?' he swung her round and looked into her pale eyes with his piercing hazel ones and for a moment, he looked very virile, strong and stern.

She broke off from her daydreaming, 'Oh, honey,' she felt suddenly anxious, 'but you do love it too?'

For an answer he held her still, then spun her round and sent her away – playfully slapping her quite hard across the seat of her pants. Recovering her balance, she felt herself flush up as she saw a look of real surprise on the builder's face; he was clearly unused to such demonstrative and intimate behaviour. Buster mistook the look for something else. 'You see you can't go wrong around here! Even the locals think you're neat with your red hair and trim ass – don't forget half their women are build like heifers, destined to breed and not much else. The guy simply couldn't take his eyes off your fanny then.'

'Oh Buster, I don't think so,' said Leah ruefully, 'and please don't talk like this!' She lowered her voice to a whisper. 'He may not speak English, but he's no fool.'

'No fool indeed!' laughed her husband, 'but as for liking it all – how could you doubt me? I'm mad about it, it's a great place. And more important for the economics – Howard likes it too.'

'I know,' said Leah allowing Manuel to help her over an unfinished ledge, whilst wishing for the thousandth time that Buster was a sensitive as their old friend in New York. 'Despite the fact he's coming in halves, I still worry about Howard from time to time. He's real solid in so many ways, a rock in business, but socially, he can be quite unpredictable.'

'It's the Irish in him,' Buster always had an answer to everything and in the meantime was stuffing a thousand *escudo* note into Manuel's breast pocket. '*Irlandés* Manuel! There's one for you to mull over!' He slapped the man on the shoulder in jovial fashion. '*Irlandés – Senhor* Howard! ... *pouco* crazy ... er ... *pouco louco*, huh?'

Leah sensed, rather than saw, a certain look cross the builder's eyes. As she worried it was one of distaste, even contempt, the moment passed and he was beaming at them again. '*Sim, sim,*' he smiled dutifully and inclined his jowly head. It was the second massive tip he'd been given in two days; if one had to play the dumb idiot to get it, who was he to worry? It would mean another pair of designer shoes for his little wife – she couldn't get enough these days! As well as understanding her, he also understood his clients. It was politic not to speak their language.

Leah was still mulling over the thought of them all sharing, as she murmured absently, 'Honey, you shouldn't overdo things – with the money I mean. You said yourself, the bills are mounting – there's no need to over-ice the cake.' A moment later, she was picking up their things and preparing to go, when she added 'You know, I still can't help worrying about Howard because of his moods. One moment he's over the moon with this whole project, then other times, he seems real gloomy and one wonders if he's regretting it all.'

'Well, he's too late to do anything about it, if that's the case,' said her husband cheerfully. 'You worry too much. It's much too late for any of us to regret anything.'

In an unpretentious Portuguese restaurant in down town Greenwich Village, two men were studying a menu with anticipation, when one called the waiter back.

'To think I've come all this way to read this in English!' complained the elder, a large walrus of a man, his curly grey hair beginning to thin on top as he peered at the starters through thick, pebble lenses. '*Inglês!*'

'Yes sir,' the waiter beamed, then bowed.

'But I wanted it in *Portuguese*.'

'I'm sorry sir, we only have eet een Eenglish.'

'Then I'm walking out!'

The waiter's jaw dropped as the large man pushed his chair noisily back and made to heave out his bulk. There was no getting it right with people these days, he thought; most of their clients congratulated them on their efforts. He visibly relaxed as he saw the man's younger companion put out a restraining hand.

'Howard, come *on* ... don't let's make a scene. What does it *matter*?' Benjie Liebermann hoped he was not in for one of those evenings where everything went wrong from the start. There'd been too many of these lately and Howard was getting more and more twitchy by the moment as the date for their long-planned exodus from New York loomed ever nearer.

'Simply, Benjie – in case it had escaped your notice,' the growly voice was heavy with sarcasm, 'I have, over the past six months, succeeded in paying out hundreds of dollars in Portuguese lessons and tutorials. I've read a Portuguese newspaper on my way to work every day, I've slept with Portuguese cassettes playing by my bed and I've even dreamed in Portuguese. Now, I take the trouble to seek out some down-town Portuguese restaurant that no one I know's even heard of, and which looks –' he cast a withering eye over the room – 'about as fashionable as somewhere frequented by Frank Sinatra's mother's cleaning lady. And now I'm told I can't even choose my *food* in Portuguese – and there was I comforting myself that I could display my little bit of hard earned knowledge for real! So you could say, dear Benjie, that this whole exercise has been a complete waste of effort, energy and ... what's more ...' he struggled for the word ... 'emotion!' The last syllable came out in a hiss; he took a deep gulp of white wine and fell silent.

'Oh, cut out the bitch-witch, Howard!' said the younger man, knowing that to sympathise would be fatal. 'Nothing's been wasted!' he added sharply. 'You'll be able to practise to your heart's content in no time at all.'

'And what if there, in the middle of the Algarve, I get handed a menu in English, too?' said Howard, now mournful.

Benjie had to laugh, remembering how this had happened on their last visit to Europe. 'Then I'd say you were ill-fated, Howard old son!'

'Precisely,' said Howard McDermott, ignoring the starters, and to Benjie's disappointment, jabbed his finger gloomily at the fillet of sole and ordered for them both.

8

'*W*ho the hell are these people moving into that yellow monstrosity on the other side of town? You know, that huge villa – up on the hill? Jock McKay heard himself shouting above the din. It was almost midnight on a Friday night, but the atmosphere was oppressive, stale smoke mingled with equally stale coconut oil.

'I can't hear you, old boy – it's too damned noisy! Let's get out and find some fresh air.'

The two men extricated themselves from The Anchor Bar to savour the peace of Santa Felicia's cobbled square. The taxi rank was empty, all the motorbikes had gone and apart from the usual couple of *Guardas* low in conversation and an amiable trio of dogs, snuffling beneath empty market stalls, the busy night was transformed. 'That's better,' said McKay, taking a deep gulp of sea air tinged with a trace of acacia. 'I never quite understand what attracts people to that place. It's like honey to a swarm of bees, but not half as sweet.'

Someone had once written in a travel journal that The Anchor was not so much a bar, more a last bastion of the British Empire. The point was debatable, since no corner of Portuguese soil had ever lain in British hands. Even Gibraltar – 'the Rock' – separated politically and spiritually from Spanish Cadiz, was at least a day away. Nevertheless, the laid-back Portuguese seemed to welcome the influx of *estrangeiros* who had claimed the Algarve for their own. It might be a colonial backwater but what did it matter? – it brought in good money. With English now dominating the resorts, visitors were encouraged to throw away their *dicionarios* and treat it like home.

'You're surely not complaining – you're a regular here, yourself!' McKay's companion remarked, swotting a moth.

'That's different. I'm drawn here from necessity, not pleasure. '

'Oh come, *come*, old boy!'

' There's no "come, come" about it, ' retorted the Scotsman, drawing himself up to his full six foot one. 'It happens to be true. Look, Patterson, I may live here, but beyond a certain point in the evening, my wife won't allow me to booze at home – so I need *somewhere* to go.'

'The lovely Catalina – I don't believe it!'

'Believe what you wish,' an impatient hand swept back thinning strands of pepper and salt hair that gleamed silver in the moonlight. 'Up to the first glass of brandy she'll put up with me. After that, I'm politely – sometimes – impolitely – told to drink elsewhere. And like the perfect gentleman, I go. I know when I'm not wanted!'

'You were asking about that rather vulgar house that's just been finished,' his companion prompted; McKay was well known for running on for hours about the questionable merits of his young Portuguese wife. They'd been married some years now, there was a kid too, but he still seemed to regard her as a princess. Only time would tell, thought Patterson, and who really cared? Marriages came and went in the Algarve and with so many relationships ending up as seven-day wonders, it was hard not to be cynical. 'As a matter of fact, I met a couple of the owners only this morning. We were all queuing at the bank.'

'You say that as though there were several?' McKay raised an eyebrow.

'Oh yes, it's common knowledge at least four are involved. Business people from New York. It was McDermott, Irish-American, that I met. Fifty-something, seemed a decent sort, solid – *you* know. He was with a woman, forties maybe? One of those highflying sorts, auburn hair scraped back, earnest and fast-talking – said I *must* meet her husband. Eager to be friends, recognise the type? Couldn't wait to explain why they were here and all that…' He drew on his beer, taking time to wipe his moustache.

'They sound as dull as ditchwater, but go on!'

'McDermott's business partner was mentioned. Youngest of the foursome, but not actually present – I'll remember his name in a moment, Ben! No, Benjie… something… Jewish name.'

'Hang on a moment, you're losing me. What you're trying to say is *four* people are sharing this house, not the proverbial family, but a couple and – two men. Partners! – is that it?'McKay's other eyebrow was threatening to join its companion in upward flight.

'Well obviously I didn't ask. They're all from the world of interior design.'

'Well, aren't you just the detective! What else did you glean, Patterson?'

'Not much – just that things got too big, too stressful and they decided to pool their resources and pull out.'

'Having made a pile of money along the way?'

'They didn't say, but I suspect you're right, old boy.'

'Of course I'm right,' snorted McKay, 'they wouldn't be here if they hadn't. Who'd be crazy enough to build a house like that if there wasn't plenty of lolly around. I heard that builder, Manuel Pereira, had swapped his old van for a Merc recently – he's the main contractor. It may be the Algarve but I reckon the locals will be doing nicely out of this and there'll be more in the pipeline when the maintenance bills start flooding in.'

There was silence, finally broken by Patterson. 'I have to admit, it does seem rather an extravagant set-up. They've picked a great site, but – if it was *me* – I'd have gone for building two smaller villas with a gap in between – not as if there's not enough land. I can't imagine my Molly wanting to share a vast home with business friends – doesn't seem natural, somehow.'

McKay roared with laughter. 'You've no imagination, Patterson, no wonder they slung you out of advertising before retirement age! Either it's some form of *ménage à quatre* – or perhaps these people have ideas of grandeur. You know what these self-made types are. Decided to pitch in together and produce something along the scale of Beverley Hills which they probably can't afford back home. It's just a pity they've produced such a gin palace! Never mind, it's a good wake-up call for the neighbours. Look, I'm off for another of these, shall I get you one while I'm at it?'

He drifted back into the crowded bar, a bizarre figure, tall and angular in skin-tight faded yellow cords. But for the silvery hair curling over his collar, most would have supposed him a much younger man. The curiously arrogant swagger seemed more appropriate for a pop star, not a former war-hero fast approaching his sixth decade. The heat of The Anchor came rushing out to meet him as he paused to allow a party of Swedes to pass. Undeterred, he fought his way through and the crowd of young people lining the rail, made way. Jock McKay had that kind of effect on people; a lean and hungry look made him stand out like a golden-eyed tiger amongst a herd of buffalo.

The buffalo came in assorted colours. From the raw-red of newcomers who had overcooked, the honey-tan of those who knew better, the deep mahogany of the veteran sun worshipper to the tired ochre of those who had forsaken the sun for the solace of indoor retreats and cheap liquor, they all came together at night. Above a steady hum, the plaintive words of Nilsson ... *'Oh I can't believe this evening, or your face as you were leaving...'* penetrated the haze of cigarette smoke, and lingered in the drapes of fish-nets, hanging from blackened beams. For some reason it made McKay sigh.

'Why – hello there, Jock!' a pretty, bronzed brunette rushed up and made him jump. She kissed him warmly on both cheeks, 'How *are* you?' and not waiting for a reply, 'And how's Catalina?'

'She's well, thank you and so am I,' he recovered himself. 'It's good to see you, Jacqueline. Is Karl here?'

'Over there, come and join us!'

'Well, only for one,' said the Scotsman, 'I'll be on my way to the VIP shortly.' McKay allowed himself to be pulled into the throng of residents, intent on drinking until the bars closed at two when most would move on to the disco which stayed open until four. Somewhere between those hours, he would leave the noise and the laughter behind him and wend his way slowly home along the sea-wall.

'He may be as tough as old boots, but I can't help liking Jock McKay an awful lot,' Jacqueline van der Stel said, as she undressed in front of the full-length mirror in their bedroom.

'That's because he's a toff,' replied Karl mildly, emerging from the bathroom. 'Why you ever married a simple Dutch man like me is a constant wonder.'

'Because you're all male,' grinned Jacqueline, 'I can't stand chinless wonders, but Jock's generation is different. He may be an aristocrat but he's a real man ...'

'You mean the hard-bitten war hero?   OK, so he may have bayoneted a few terrified Italians at Anzio, but that doesn't mean he's trustworthy. Although I find him a great drinking companion and could listen to his stories for hours – there's something about the guy I'm not too sure about.'

'But he is magnetic,' pouted Jacqueline, 'and he can pull the birds. Which brings me to Catalina McKay – now there's someone I wouldn't depend on. She's very tricky – oh my God!' she broke off and made a face, 'I swear I'm putting on weight. Just look at that roll of fat!' She pinched her side and pirouetted round to see if he was watching her.

'Oh? I thought Catalina was one of your best friends,' said Karl, amused.

'She's fun,' said his wife, 'but if we were still in London, things might be different. It's probably because there's no one else in this damned place!'

'Does that apply to all your so-called friends – Johanna, for example?'

'No-o, Joey's different, one of *us* you could say, ' she frowned, 'but Catalina's a wild card.'

'And stunning with it,' mused her husband. 'You may dismiss her, but from a man's point of view, she'd stand out anywhere – Amsterdam, LA, Paris – even your beloved London.' He loosened the towel from his waist and stretched out on the bed, observing her. 'In fact if I didn't have you, I might fancy her myself!'

His wife tossed her long dark hair over her shoulders scornfully and stood before him, hands on hips. 'But that's just it, darling, she wouldn't have you! You're not a toff – as you so quaintly put it. Put on the radio darling, I want music!'

The late night station pumped out the latest soul hit in Lisbon and she turned to face the mirror again. Karl lit a cigarette and lay back watching as she danced with her own image. 'You're too fast,' he said. 'It would be more erotic if you moved your hips slowly, more deliberately – as if you had all the time in the world.' He found himself thinking of Catalina.

'But that's just the point, I'm not *trying* to be erotic,' he felt she had read his mind. 'People who try to be sexy, seldom are – deep underneath. They simply prey on the gullible – like Catalina with poor old Jock – and obviously, you too!' And a smile came to her lips, as she moved rhythmically, thrusting her stomach in and out.

'Miaow, miaow... don't be so sure,' Karl let the smoke curl over his lower lip, then upward in a long spiral. 'Sometimes I think Jock's the clever one. I mean, he's no young buck, is he? He's lucky to have held her so long.'

'*Lucky!*' Jacqueline stopped dancing and stared at him in disbelief. 'Now I really fear for your judgement. You don't think she stays with him for love, do you?'

'I don't care what it is – maybe he's great in bed. The fact remains they've been together almost a decade – quite an achievement in this climate.'

'What balls you talk!' snapped Jacqueline. 'Age doesn't enter into it. It's a status thing – anyone can see that. Although he's always pleading poverty, Jock's generous beyond belief. She shops relentlessly and life is just so easy – why? – she doesn't even cook! Just as long as Jock churns out the funny sort of art he does, so she can swan along in her latest designer dress to join the in-crowd at all his exhibitions – then he's got nothing to worry about.'

Karl held out his hand to her. 'You've got very hard and bitchy all of a sudden. It doesn't suit you. Come here, I want you.'

Suddenly supine and gentle, she climbed onto the bed and he pulled her to him. It had been a long day and a long night, but there was something hugely seductive about this climate. Soft warm air, soft warm smells, soft warm skin ... the desire rose in him and he sighed with contentment. London indeed! He simply couldn't imagine rising to the occasion nearly so often if they lived in the cold. When would his wife realise? – it was a great place for couples.

Johanna Vincent had just put the finishing touches to her display when Catalina McKay arrived in the boutique. The former actress was on her own, prepared for a quiet day. She had worked solidly on the big bay window since well before breakfast.

'Hello *darling*!' she greeted Catalina warmly, then stepped back to admire her handiwork. 'I was just finishing, how does it look from outside?'

'Marvellous!' said the younger woman, beaming at her from under a pretty straw hat. 'But then eet always ees so, when *you* do it, Joey.'

'Flattery!' smiled Johanna, moving to her leather-topped desk on a raised dais in the centre of the shop. 'Ye gods, it's hot today,' she fitted a gold-tipped cigarette into her holder and lit up, 'I can put up with heat like this after lunch – then I can take a siesta – but before half past ten in the morning, it's positively immoral!'

'I too feel the same,' said Catalina, looking cool as a cucumber. 'But at least you have the air-conditioning at home. Jock refuses you know. He says ees bad for the child, or some such nonsense. I blame those Scottish nannies ... you have no idea, Joey, what I have to put up with.' She pronounced it *'ave* and giggled at the amused smile on Johanna's face. She knew her accent was considered charming. She was suddenly diverted by a full-length gown hanging on its own between two potted palms and a gilt mirror. '*Olha!* That ees nice, Joey – is it *Marroc?*'

'Yes darling, part of my Marrakesh collection. Try it on if you want, you always look delicious in turquoise. Those tiny mirrors woven in will make your eyes sparkle – even more.'

'Thank you!' The young Portuguese woman disappeared into a changing room, a proprietary hand already grasping the fine lawn. Johanna smiled, despite her conscience pricking her. How easy it was to tempt Catalina! Poor old Jock. He once told her he winced every time he saw his wife in a new outfit, but as Johanna pointed out, as long as he allowed her to buy on credit, she would spend the money anyway, so it might as well be with her.

Lately, she had noticed Jock growing more morose. Rumour had it that far from paying off his debts in Scotland by living the life of a tax exile, the couple's lifestyle in the Algarve was costing more than he was earning. Clearly, it would take a miracle to turn his finances around. Oh well, it was not for her, Johanna, to worry about; setting aside the fact that Catalina was her best customer, she was fond of the girl. She might be the spoilt wife of an older man, but she possessed an endearing mixture of gaiety and fun which was hard to resist. Compared to London and theatre land, there was a dearth of talented, vivacious people which was why Catalina and her husband were an important part of her inner circle.

Johanna Vincent was a highly social animal. Something of a people-collector, the subject of character fascinated her. Her razor-sharp antennae missed nothing – accents, manners, the way people spoke, dressed and deported themselves were seriously scrutinised. Many called her a snob, but this was not strictly true – her main requirement was that people were themselves, outgoing, colourful and above all different. Born the only daughter of an impecunious peer, Johanna had virtually run away from home in Devon at the age of fifteen to go on stage. After years of drudge, mishap and failure, interspersed with two disastrous marriages, she finally pulled herself together and, forgoing the quest for glamour, plunged herself into serious rep. From jobs backstage to walk-on roles, 'bit' parts, bigger parts and on and ever upwards, sheer guts and strength of character allowed her eventually to make the West End. For over a decade she saw her name up in lights and enjoyed every moment of her hard-won fame.

Neither did her talent diminish with age. The turn to the screen was inevitable. As a mature, character actress she was signed up by some of the biggest names in the industry:

Warner Brothers, Columbia, 20th Century Fox, Paramount – she'd worked for them all. She travelled relentlessly from continent to continent, whilst her only child, a daughter from her second marriage, boarded at school in Switzerland.

Occasionally, Johanna had endured pangs of conscience, believing it was time she found husband-number-three, so Maysie might enjoy a more stable background. There was no shortage of contenders, but she could never quite bring herself to make all those promises she had broken so glibly before. Gradually the thought of a comfortable existence as the wife of a successful stockbroker or lawyer with a house in London and another in the Shires appealed less and less. She found herself yearning for something a little more adventurous, challenging and unpredictable.

When finally she decided to quit her career at its peak, her love for the sun and dislike of the rat-race took her to Portugal. She bought an old villa with three hectares of orchard in the small fishing town of Santa Felicia. As one of the first British residents to set up permanently, and with a face to which everyone could relate, she was welcomed with open arms. A brilliant mimic and communicator, it was not long before she spoke the language and was accepted by the locals, almost as one of them. From the fisherman who brought fresh mullet and crab to her gate, to the town hall officials who organised her *residencia* papers, everyone knew and respected *Dona* Johanna.

It took two years to convert the house to her liking. A healthy yield from investments over the years enabled her to indulge every artistic whim she possessed. A flock of local artisans worked solidly, her patronage endearing her to the local populace more than ever. She adored her rambling Casa Mariposa, which, despite ruthless modernization in the plumbing department, retained a delightful air of restrained decadence within wisteria-clad walls. By the time it was all finished, tourism had come to stay in Santa Felicia. Some of her land was sold off for new villas, and when she had tired of real estate, it was only natural that Johanna, who loathed being idle, should open the first fashionable boutique in Southern Portugal.

The Lisbonians discovered it first and were enchanted; the Andalusians followed and finally the tourists. Everyone agreed it was a resounding success and at the shop's first birthday party, the British Ambassador himself flew down from Lisbon. The local papers saluted her and the Anglo-Portuguese News carried a three page feature which set a smile on the face of the Mayor and the town hall. From then on, Johanna could do no wrong, which was why so many English residents turned to her in times of trouble or when strings needed to be pulled.

As for *Estrela*, her boutique, meaning 'star', it quickly became one of the social meeting places in the Peninsula. Here Johanna felt almost as much on stage as in London's West End. It was noted that whoever entered her dazzling radius, client, friend, sychophant or rival – in the Algarve there were plenty of each – it was impossible to resist becoming enmeshed in whatever play was being enacted in her living theatre. That was part of ex-pat life in Santa Felicia. Only Johanna herself stood apart – a true professional amongst a bunch of amateurs, she seemed content to remain in a small role, able to slip into the wings whenever she wished. From that vantage point, she could stand back and observe the action. It was not hard therefore to discover just what the main cast were all about.

'Oh, there you are, darling,' she trilled, as Catalina emerged from her cubicle in brilliant turquoise, ruched with silver thread. 'That looks divine! Only someone with your raven black hair could wear that colour. Jock will adore you in it!'

'It ees rather fun,' Catalina twirled in front of the mirror to make sure the dress did not over-emphasise her generous hips; she was aware of her weak points. 'Oh dear! Am I too awful? Jock said no more dresses this month, but I can't reseest… maybe a small deescount? So special and there won't be another, will there?'

The Americans moved into the big house on the last Monday in April. After months of debate, they had registered the name with the local authority as Casa Amarela. The builders were already calling it by this name, simply 'yellow house'. The dun colour was completely natural, achieved by rendering the outside of the building with the residue of an unusual sandstone, transported at great cost from further down the coast. 'The colour of sunbeams,' Leah had raved to their architect, 'I want there to be warmth in my house, morning, noon and night!'

It was unfortunate that on this auspicious day, the heavens chose not to smile sunnily on the new villa, instead rending themselves asunder, to produce the heaviest rainfall for years. Within minutes, the drenched walls had turned a murky beige. The sky growled all around like an angry dog whilst bulging black clouds descended so low, the breathtaking ocean view was blanked off. Not unnaturally, such hostility from the elements cast an aura of gloom. Not one of the four newcomers was prepared to admit it, but it put a real dampener on what should have been a joyful event.

Prior to the move, it had been an exhausting month. Weeks overdue, the builders were still in residence when they all flew in together from New York, having endured long delays between flights. A temporary base was set up at the Maritimo on the front, but since daily commuting had never been in the game-plan, there was bound to be friction. The three-mile route involved a narrow hill road. Passing was a nightmare as tractors, donkeys and mule carts, all heading for market, assumed priority.

Dipping and rising, their journey meandered over a rugged headland littered with windmills before plunging down to sea level again to circumvent a series of small bays before heading upward and inland. From the shadows of stunted trees and scrub, hairpin bends gave way to sunlight, a gentle coast road opening up to the glorious apron of the Algarve. A mile or so on, a line of giant eucalyptus and a couple of white cottages guarding a discreet entrance, and there was their own private road, finishing on a high promontary. As Leah pointed out, it should have been a time to enjoy, so why were they biting each other's heads off?

Several months previously their lawyer had found them a small Fiat, a simple runabout for their occasional visits from New York. Ideal for isolated sojourns, when the couples had taken it in turn to visit, it was evident that the car had outlived its usefulness for shared transport. Leah felt vexed with herself for not having foreseen these difficulties. Unfortunately, the damage was done. Their very first day got off to a bad start when Howard, more at home in a limo, became neatly wedged between the front and back seat with the gear knob adding insult to injury. Despite being swiftly rescued, the large man was unable to see the funny side of things. For Leah, who had known Howard for two decades, this came as a shock. If this could happen away from business – away from New York – away from all the stress of their past lives, she wondered, not for the first time, what the future might hold.

She was on the telephone to the showroom in Faro for an Opel saloon the next day. It was a shock to discover all the red tape involved when you are neither tourist nor resident – but something in between. Instead of taking delivery there and then, she was warned it might take up to ten days just for the paperwork. By the third day, and still no car, she found to her chagrin she was popping pills as easily and frequently as she had back home. From thenceforth, she persuaded a grudging Buster to let Benjie and Howard use the Fiat, whilst they themselves took a taxi. By the time it came to moving day, the Opel had arrived but the atmosphere was at an all time low.

The furniture had preceded them from America, travelling by cargo ship. The sea voyage was uneventful enough but the container's safe release from one of Lisbon's bonded warehouses at Alcantara docks was not. The export-import dockets were in order, but each packing case, each separate piece of furniture or equipment now required a landing document, hitherto unmentioned. Even Buster had been unaware of this and it taught them all a lesson concerning the national character and the true meaning of the word *paciência*. The lack of urgency which dominated the system and the mindless bureaucracy blew one away. For every piece of paper extracted from one department, it seemed another was required to ensure its viability and then everything had to be stamped. For four people who prided themselves on getting a job done, it was all strangely foreign.

Thus, the final arrival of their goods and chattels was tense. They stood at the door, peering through the mist as three sleek but old-fashioned removal vans loomed out of the driving rain, bumping and groaning up the last steep lag. One vehicle ('That'll be the one carrying the porcelain…' said Howard) had a syncopation all of its own. Leah seemed transfixed in silent prayer, her two hands pressed together so her knuckles showed white. As one wheel swung over the edge on the last corner, there was a sharp intake of breath. Miraculously the van righted itself and they all came to rest in the forecourt.

'They're probably all drunk!' said Buster going forward to meet the drivers. 'We'll be lucky if anything comes out of there in one piece!'

'This is supposed to be the good part!' said Leah, desperate to lighten the atmosphere.

Unloading was slow. Doubt hung in the air like a lead balloon. The smaller unmarked packages were being carried into the basement but before a stick of furniture had come out, the men were back in the cab for a tea break, a bottle of brandy in evidence on the dashboard. 'Holy smoke,' groaned Buster, 'no wonder those trucks had a life of their own!'

Long before it left New York, each item or crate had been clearly marked with a number; this represented the room singled out for its final destination. Despite Howard's carefully drawn map, the men seemed to have difficulty in understanding. As the only Portuguese speaker, he explained again, '*Entrada – 1; cozinha – 2; sala de jantar – 3!* It's all in order. All in Portuguese, surely you don't need to be a cartographer to understand?' He had addressed the crew at large, blinking and bewildered. Since no one understood him, no offence was taken – except on his part. Despite a photocopy for every man, no one paid any attention. '*Paciência*,' grinned the foreman, peeling the skin off a large black sausage with his penknife.

Benjie busied himself about the kitchen; 'If you can't beat them, we might as well join them,' he said filling the cafetiere. Huddled round the table, steaming mugs warming their hands, the unspoken thoughts were almost tangible … have we come all the way across the world for this? This inertia, this rain, this gloom, this getting on each other's nerves, this worry about out precious possessions? Have we all made the biggest mistake of our lives, and is this weather the outward and visible sign of dark days to come?

Already furnished, the kitchen was the only sane and habitable room. Leah had chosen local pieces – predominantly pine – table, ladder-back chairs, dresser, stools and cupboards; the surfaces of pink marble, the floor tiled in traditional *ladrilhos*, it now provided a haven. Off the kitchen and into the hall, the ceiling rose up like a cathedral. Next door, a great reception room loomed cold and forbidding. Of rectangular proportion, its cedar floors and long French windows gave way to ocean views through arches that spanned the entire length of the central block, but all they could see was a grey mist. What to call it had been the subject of many a discussion back in New York when all had seemed romantic and rosy. 'I don't like the name drawing-room,' said Benjie, 'it's *much* too English, 'but lounge sounds too American – this is Europe after all.'

'What's wrong with living room?' Buster had asked.

'Provincial!' pronounced Howard, whose lessons in Portuguese were reaching a high. 'We'll call it *sala*, as the Lisbonians say – and that's an end of the matter!' Meekly for once, they had all agreed.

There was a library off the *sala* and both rooms enjoyed open fireplaces. With wood plentiful and cheap to acquire, there was nothing so good as the smell of burning pine even if it sparked a bit. The fireplace in the *sala* was of the hall type with colonnaded supports and a carved scroll effect above. As high as a tall man's chest, it dominated the room and for the fifth time that morning, Leah bemoaned the fact the fuel had not yet been ordered. A bright fire might have put a whole new slant on things. Funny – it was always the small things that made the difference – who would have thought it could rain like this in April?

The men were humping bigger pieces now. Despite the map, the foreman couldn't be everywhere at once, so firm guidance would be needed. No one spoke English and since even Howard's stalwart attempts at the language were in vain, it was easier to touch someone on the arm and point. 'We'll have to watch them like hawks,' said Buster. 'We don't want everything ending up in the wrong place and having to start all over again. Come on boys, to work!' He got up, pulled on a jacket and strode out into the driving rain. Howard and Benjie followed in their Burberries, looking oddly out of place. Leah tidied up the kitchen table feeling Fate had let her down. No one had warned them about the weather … a few showers maybe, but where was that famous Algarve sun?

But it went further than that. She had, after all, given birth to the original idea. She'd found the site, the land agent, the architect, the builder, the engineer and the lawyer. Even their bank transactions had been down to her; she'd flown to London, dealt with a small firm who understood the mysterious workings of the Bank of Portugal, and the whole business of importing and changing their dollars had been accomplished smoothly and without the usual exorbitant transaction fees. Others in the know had marvelled at her efficiency; currency dilemmas and tales of being ripped off within the ex-pat community being rife.

Then there was the water diviner! Here too, she'd made an inspired choice. With her usual sense of purpose, she had found the ancient man they spoke of as the best in the land and charmed him into coming. Long ago retired from his goverment post, he always refused all pleas to venture out, but for her he agreed. Within an hour of arrival and with just two plain birch twigs, he'd located an underground spring at only sixty metres down. This was far less costly than anticipated and even Aurelio, who knew the coast well, had exclaimed at their luck.

With firm answers to all the problems that might present themselves, Leah had drawn up everything as a package. It was easier than she ever dreamed to sell the idea of the villa as a *fait accompli* first to her husband, later to their most trusted business colleagues. In fact, both Howard and Benjie seemed to leap at the opportunity. Strange how so many who came into her orbit felt about their lives as she did – caught in a trap, eager to escape. But few it seemed were sufficiently endowed to say goodbye to stress and invest in their own personal dream – and besides, talk was one thing, action quite another. Who would have thought that she, Leah, not only had the vision but also the courage and the energy to go out there, pull it all together and make it happen?

And happen it did. So now, didn't that little lady deserve just a small slice of credit? Yet what had happened today of all days? She'd woken up to black clouds, dark looks from all and sundry and worse by far, not a word of thanks, smile of gratitude or a clap on the back from any of them. Life simply wasn't fair.

She glanced from the window at this strange, hostile landscape and shivered. Right now she felt as though someone was walking across her grave. She gave herself an impatient shake and got out of her chair. Why was she thinking like this? It was crazy – having come this far, fruition was almost in sight – she'd probably popped too many pills. They were all tired but once they were sleeping in their own beds again – things could only get better – surely?

Outside, Buster and the others were up in the trucks, looking even more incongruous as they issued commands and gesticulated at the men struggling under their heavy loads. An assembly line was starting in the porch and resolutely Leah marched to its head, taking charge in the way she did best – and immediately feeling better. The first big sofa was appearing and she nodded *sala* to two small men. Just in case they had failed to understand her, she herded them gently and felt the smile return to her lips.

9

By mid-afternoon the beds were in *situ* and those for immediate use had been put up. 'I'd forgotten just how many screws some beds need,' said Benjie, chuckling as he realised what he'd said. Howard frowned. Despite a long search, there was no sign of the bed linen, so another night at the hotel seemed inevitable. The manager had promised to hold their rooms but with everyone putting in a real effort as evening drew on, the idea of returning seemed all wrong. 'I'm for staying put,' said Buster, 'we've come so far today, it would be a crying shame not to sleep here.'

'I agree,' said Leah, 'It'll be like camping. I'm going to snuggle down in my clothes and be damned!'

'Good idea – I'm all for camping it up!' said Benjie.

Howard remained unamused but was finally persuaded. He had acquired a queen-sized Edwardian brass bed just before they left New York but of all the furniture, it had given the greatest grief. Much time had been wasted with the removal gang downing tools to scratch their heads over a structure that now lay in bits before them. Inertia set in and had it not been for Buster weighing in with army tactics, they might have been there all night.

With the bed finally assembled, instead of being grateful for everyone's attention, Howard could do nothing but moan that it might collapse in the night. His pessimism was getting them down. Finally, his partner snapped, 'I told you to leave the darned thing behind, it doesn't look right in this room – you should have stuck to your old divan with the Louis Quinze headboard – at least it's continental!'

'I was sick of it,' growled Howard, 'too many memories – and besides, it was lumpy. I told you I wanted a fresh start.'

'I'm not sure what that's supposed to mean but if you'd been set on brass, I could have told you – they have fantastic brass and wrought iron pieces in Lisbon.'

'I like its proportions,' said Howard petulantly, 'and since it's got little to do with you, I wish you'd leave the subject alone.'

Leah detected ice and shivered. None of this was good for them. She must take charge and brighten things up. 'Don't you love those taps, Howard,' she said, breezing through his bedroom to the bathroom. 'Such a gorgeous outlook too, look at the fig tree sheltering from the storm just below your window ledge – and haven't those tiles worked well?'

'They seem OK,' said Howard grudgingly, 'the plumbing needs a good testing, but at least the generator seems up to its load, we've had every light in the house on today – not that I know much about these things. As for the tiles, well – I'm *trying* to let them grow on me – a pity you failed to get the ones from the Manuellian period. '

'I didn't exactly *fail*,' said Leah carefully, 'I tried everywhere. These were your second choice. We think they're real neat. Besides, those others were rather too stuffy for a house like this.'

She ran her hands over the pretty, hand-painted pastoral scenes, good kiln-fired copies of a nineteenth-century set, popular in the *quintas* of the Tagus valley. Why did her voice sound so defensive? Someone had to take responsibility for all the orders but it was hurtful just how picky the Boys were concerning matters outwith her control. Portugal was not exactly the US. She disliked the element of blame which seemed to hang like blue smoke over her head.

It was the same in the kitchen, preparing for supper. It should have been a triumphant occasion. Instead of thanking her for all the supplies she had brought in, Benjie moaned about a lack of electrical outlets over the worktops. Did she imagine the unspoken accusation that *she* had messed up – again? She must get out of the habit of questioning everything like this; there was nothing to be gained. After all, this was their *shared* home. Each area of planning had been discussed jointly, every request relayed with meticulous precision. The old leather diary and its scribblings in her bag bore testimony: ... *Benjie – louvre doors in walk-in wardrobe a must!* (underlined) ... *Howard – raised dais for grand piano – 4/5 ins.? ... Buster – not enough light in study – glass pane in door? Master bathroom – swap position of bidet? ...* and so on – the list of amendments for Manuel and his team had been endless.

Thank the Lord, Buster was OK, hard to read sometimes but rarely a moody man – no snide asides, no bitchy innuendos. A loner at heart, happy to do his own thing, he plodded along, rain or shine. If things got him down, he was like a dog – simply removing himself and slinking off. The Boys were altogether more complicated. Fussy old women! She could see now how temperamental they could be. Strange, how in over 15 years of business negotiations, they always seemed so relaxed, all-accommodating and as though nothing could ruffle their smooth, sleek feathers. Clearly however, when discord or self-doubt set in – particularly one with the other – the easy charm and willingness to please could evaporate with the wind. Was it a character flaw? Or were they all just tired?

Buster came to her rescue, 'Who's fussing about outlets when the roof and lintels have just had the biggest test of their short lives,' he said, peering out as dusk dropped like a curtain. 'I'm amazed that driving rain hasn't penetrated. Even the floor in front of the French windows is dry so I reckon that Manuel guy, for all his little extras here and there, deserves his dollars. Even the patio shows no surface water.'

'That will be the *cisterna* pipes doing their job,' Leah thought to buoy them up with local information. 'Did you know, half the population live off collected water from roofs and surfaces? With every rainfall, each drop runs into an underground chamber, all ready for use. Ours is for the garden, you know, but most rural people rely on them totally; they can't afford bore-holes and there's no city water outside the towns. I rather like the idea – no chemicals, you see.'

'Remind me therefore not to accept drinking water at any country retreat,' muttered Howard. 'The thought of water sitting there and stagnating sounds most unhealthy.'

'Oh no, it's OK!' said Leah, 'they've a way round that. It's real neat! The town hall supply the locals with small fish to place in their tanks, which eat all the algae and bugs and keep the water fresh. Apparently, it really works.'

'I'll know where to go when I want fish-soup then,' said Howard and it was at that point that they decided to call it a day and go to bed. Leah tried to convince herself things would be better in the morning and she was much too tired to worry any more. As usual, she had simply tried her best.

The following day, the skies cleared and the sun was peeping out. Everyone seemed in better humour as Buster and Benjie threw themselves into the tedious work of erecting the more delicate armoires and tallboys, which after the bed debacle, Howard had insisted were quite beyond the capacity of the removal men. This was a task in which Benjie took little joy, but if he did it without complaint, there was a good chance he could move on to pleasanter things such as sorting out their suite – soft furnishings, pictures, ornaments and priceless *objets d'art* – being much more up his street.

Long ago, they'd decided to combine resources in the public rooms. The *sala*, the music room, library and dining-room were being jointly shared so it made sense to meld and arrange their preferred pieces until it was pleasing to all. The upper storey was reached by an elegant double-sided staircase, two arms curving to meet a long landing, ballustraded like a minstrel's gallery. To either side fanned out their apartments with balconies to the front, linked by guestrooms across the central facade. The Bloomfields' master suite lay to the east, the Boys' double one ran westward. Since each would be furnished individually, Casa Amarela provided plenty of scope for personal taste.

At present, all Howard could think about was the library and music room. Neither Leah nor Buster were particularly selective about music or literature and were glad to give him a free rein. Howard had been bookish all his life, and amongst his collection of classics, Scott and James Joyce most satisfied his Celtic soul. While he would never admit it to a living soul, there was a sense of guilt that he did not miss his homeland more. He had assuaged much of this by investing time, energy and money into some very fine first editions, which satisfied an even deeper need, an unquenchable desire to prosper. Bound in leather, with many engraved plates, these volumes had been restored and catalogued. An old copy of *Debretts* had given him an idea for a bookplate. The fact that a certain Baron McDermot of Kinlachan in County Down was absolutely no relation, and even spelled his name differently, did not deter Howard from displaying an all too similar coat of arms. This prized collection together with a vast library of records and tapes should, Benjie reckoned, keep his partner sufficiently preoccupied to allow him some precious hours alone upstairs.

The entrance hall with its lofty walls and high ceiling had swelled in importance with the fixture of an 18th Century chandelier from the court of St Petersburg. Leah had been hoarding this for years after the Texan oil baron client for whom it was first acquired had suddenly changed his mind. 'Take it away,' she'd been told with a sweep of the arm; and so she did. One day she knew it would come in useful.

'It's the first thing you see,' said Buster swinging back on his heels, and gazing up appreciatively, 'and it's sure impressive. That'll set the tone and no doubt some tongues wagging! So will that curlicue mirror on the landing.'

No one said a word. Buster always said too much and Leah disliked this emphasis on impressing people. There was no ulterior motivation in her taste – at least she hoped not. She just loved beautiful things. The silence was broken by Benjie hammering his thumb-nail for the tenth time that day. 'Shit!' he said sharply, 'There must be an easier way of resurrecting these pieces without decimating my hand the whole time.'

'I thought that was what screws were for,' said Buster maliciously.

'Not when you need a fine nail for a minute piece of wood that shouldn't have fallen off in the first place,' retorted Benjie.

'You ought to make a list of all damages however small, so we can claim back on the insurers,' Howard emerged slowly and without much sympathy from yet another packing case.

'I don't *think* so,' said Benjie, 'The contract will be full of caveats and you can bet your bottom dollar these removal men don't feature on any internationally approved list.'

'Excuse *me*!'said Leah, tossing her pony-tail as she felt the need to defend herself yet again. 'They're supposed to be the top firm in Lisbon! It was our *road* that was the problem! Say, honey...' she broke off as Buster brushed by with an armful of dustsheets, 'remind me sometime to get some dungarees; these clothes are all wrong – they're sticking to me!'

'No wonder,' he grinned, brushing sawdust off her bottom, 'You're addicted to air-conditioning and you've never worked up a sweat before. But she's right about the furniture, Boys – we're lucky those vans made it here at all.'

Howard did not reply. Insurance and the mundane were all set aside with the heart-lifting discovery of a case of golden oldies. 'Hey Benjie! Look! ... those Perry Comos I thought I'd lost, and the Frank Bennett LPs, oh and here's Pat Boone. This *is* a find!'

Benjie looked up to share his joy, as expected. Despite a throbbing thumb, he was relieved. He could now slip away and arrange their suite. The linen had turned up and he'd already hung out their bedroom rugs and cushions to breathe on the verandah and wave goodbye to the chemical smell of the ship's container. Before anyone could find yet another cabinet for him to resurrect, he was mounting the stairs, three at a time. Once in his room, he felt his shoulders relax. He hadn't realised just how tense he'd been, down there amongst them all. Throwing open the casement-windows, he inhaled deeply and squared himself up. Ah! That was better, he felt a man again and didn't the air smell sweet! After yesterday, it was a different world. The sea shimmered in the distance and there was a haze over the hillside as steam rose up from yesterday's puddles to meet the sunbeams. It was good to be alive and – after all – it was good to be here. He hadn't really doubted it, but God – Howard could be so difficult at times, not helped by Buster and his aggravating remarks. He could be such a jerk. As for Leah – did she have to take things quite so personally? Could they really all live together?

As he pondered, he felt all the ideas he'd dreamed of, brimming up inside him. How he loved that feeling of total power when he entered a suite of rooms for the first time and there was nothing there. Bareness, blankness, whiteness! The actual hue mattered little – it was the emptiness of it all which excited him – like virgin snow, pure, untouched – all ready for him to imprint as he wished. He had suffered from an inferiority complex all his life; always felt there was something dull and colourless about his personality. The realisation that he could project his *persona* into design and that by enhancing and enlivening an empty room changed his perception of himself, was mind-boggling. There'd been times when he wanted to shriek for joy, sometimes to cry – from real relief and gratitude. At first it was his clients who gave him the confidence he'd never known; later it was the critics. He was inventive, fresh and they wrote of a spontaneity that eluded some of the biggest names in the industry. Eventually, even he began to acknowledge what he read in print. If others could believe in him, so could he.

It was just two decades since Benjie had joined Howard's business, but in the latter years he had run the creative side almost single-handed. Howard had started *Maison Parfaite* in the early fifties and it had always been a one-man enterprise. At the end, nothing had changed – with Howard's name still the only one to feature. But anyone who was anyone, knew who was the real mover and shaker behind the business, the person whose perceptive eye could sweep over the dullest office, studio, patio, or stage set and render it vibrant and memorable. Competitors dubbed him Howard's 'secret weapon'.

For years, Benjie dreamed of his name leaping out of the richly embossed paper, on the dark green trade vans with a shamrock for a logo. But despite several blazing rows, when he'd threatened to walk out, Howard was adamant. Every year, a few more shares were added to his growing portfolio, but alack – no partnership. Benjie could rant hysterically for all he wanted, but the one name remained. He could accept or go. For months, the arguments lingered on, the deep rankling within spoiling the previous steadiness and trust. Then one day things changed. Benjie bit the bullet and was able to accept. He recognised that he owed Howard everything. When the older man had taken him into the business, he had been nothing. Had it not been for Howard and that one great break, he might even now be in the gutter or worse. He had allowed his recent success to push that knowledge to one side. It took just one lost contract to show him just how fickle Fate could be.

One of his more adoring clients, a screen star for whom he'd done a complete makeover at her Manhattan apartment, coupled with a commission for her beach house at Five Keys, was mad about horses. She had bought a large ranch. There were endless discussions, poring for hours over plans and photographs, two visits by private jet to Arizona, but nothing as yet on paper. Despite Howard's caution, Benjie hadn't worried. She loved him, adored him, he was the greatest designer in the world, the only one who understood *her*– until one day he woke up. He'd spent an exhausting weekend of negotiation on the phone with her secretary and much messing about with colour schemes; then, out of the blue, she dropped him, like a hot cake. Nothing had been said. He only knew because he read in the gossip columns two days later, that she'd just contracted with their biggest competitor. She never bothered to call him.

He remembered the flattering words over pink champagne at lunch, the intimate Hollywood chit-chat over dinner, and the thoughtful little presents from Tiffany, all hand wrapped and waiting in his room – 'with love' from the dogs... the chinchillas... the horses... He saw the emptiness of the words. They had meant so much to him; nothing to her. No doubt her secretary had chosen and wrapped the presents. No one who tied ribbons so lovingly could have dropped him the way she had. It had shaken him to the roots. After that, there'd been no more talk with Howard about a partnership; he simply dug in and got on with his life.

A year had passed; by now he was travelling coast to coast, designing homes in LA, the Beverley Hills and the Malibu set, then back via Chicago, Philadelphia and Boston, fêted wherever he went. He loved the spoiling; the getting away meant a lot – Manhattan could be so claustrophobic. People were prepared to fly him by helicopter if necessary to the most isolated homesteads, Aspen, Santa Fé, Cape Cod. Howard said nothing about his stakes or lack of them in *Maison Parfaite*, but neither did he. He had learned to become philosophical and accept each day as it came.

Then came the surprise. He and Howard had dined out early at a French bistro on East 76th, just around the corner. It had been a heavy week and he was about to retire to bed, when Howard called him back. 'I've got something to show you,' he said. Always a little unsteady after a glass of port, the big man went carefully to the wall safe behind a picture in the dining-room and handed him a document bound with pink tape. 'You'd better have a read of that,' he said, his moon face inscrutable.

Benjie saw it was a legal document and what he read made his heart leap. He tried to stay cool and show no emotion, Howard disliked a fuss, but inside he sang with exultation. It was a Will. At last, at last! Recognition and security! The latter was something he'd longed for all his life. It was quite straightforward. Provided they were still together and in the event of his death, Howard would leave *Maison Parfaite*, or its raised capital, to Benjie. All personal possessions, including the lease and contents of their brownstone, his stocks, shares and pension scheme too. There were a few bequests to be met out of a savings account for some long lost relations in Ireland, but the main bulk was to go to '*his dear friend and loyal employee, Benjamin Liebermann*'.

Despite the legal speak, it was all pretty basic and easy to understand. As with most things in which Howard involved himself, the terms of the Will were concise and what you saw was what you got. After that, things could only get better. Benjie went about his work with a new spring in his step, a light feeling in his heart. Life with Howard had never been easy; he was a man of moods, easily offended, rare to please. Despite all this however, there was an underlying solidity. It was this above all else which had attracted Benjie to the job and later to him. Brought up in the poorest side of the Jewish quarter of New York's Lower East Side, he had led a singularly dreary life, losing his mother to bronchitis at the age of thirteen and his father a few years later. The thought of being part of an establishment like *Maison Parfaite*, however humble the role, made him feel safe. In fact, very safe indeed.

Howard's success in the world of interior design before Benjie had come on the scene was largely due to an unerring eye for quality. What he lacked in imagination, he made up for in high standards of workmanship and attention to detail. Clean and meticulous in his personal life – you did not throw your feet up at the end of the couch with Howard around – it was the same in business. Nothing cobbled together or out of place; everything must be pristine and perfect.

Benjie had finished Howard's room – well, almost. He had allowed himself to drift far away to the past, but was surprised by how much had been achieved. How sumptuous the Edwardian bed now looked against the scarlet wallpaper! Howard had been right to go for it, after all. As for the cream drapes billowing graciously over open bay windows, they suited the room better than anticipated, particularly with that crimson and gold tie-back echoing the old brass bedstead.

It had taken forever to hang all Howard's suits, first the summer clothes, then the winter-wear, overcoats, dinner and smoking jackets; would he ever don them again? They all brought back memories of some sort. With all the wrestling onto heavy hangers, Benjie's self imposed valet's role had been severely tested as yet another thin plastic sheath slithered down and crumpled at his feet – like a Beverly Hills facelift gone wrong. He'd seen a few of those in his time! The thought made him smile, not that he needed cheering. Life was going his way remarkably well.

He would never forget the day Leah first mentioned heading off to the Algarve. Benjie had mentally leaped at the idea – it was the answer to every prayer – but he'd been careful not to show it. As his success had grown, he'd worried more and more about Howard. With all the limelight falling around his shoulders and not accruing to his partner, he could see the founder of *Maison Parfaite* growing more introvert and moody by the moment. The signs were clear – if Benjie's personal star went on rising, professional jealousy might grow into resentment and the relationship terminated. A new live-in partner might prove more attractive; Manhattan was awash with hungry contenders – especially when financial security and a smart Brooklyn Heights address was on offer. There was plenty of opportunity at the designer parties.

As for the Will, even the most carefully drafted bequests could be altered, especially if there was a hint of dishonesty in the air. Howard had never pressed him about his past, but it was this that had worried him, haunted him at night. In his teens, he'd gotten in with a rough gang and there'd been a few shady deals down on Lower East Side. One in particular involved an armed robbery. Although he'd been given no idea of what was to take place, he was given the job of look-out. Who would believe he knew nothing of the plans? Why had he been too chicken to go to the police after the event? Deep inside he knew, if ever news of these misdemeanours reached Howard's ears, that would be that. Howard might sympathise, even try to understand but his high moral standards would get in the way. First he would want to know why Benjie had never been open with him. Second, and worse by far, he'd never trust Benjie again. Over the past 18 years, Benjie had been lucky, but for how long could one rely on good luck? One day, one job, someone might recognise him and the whole can of worms would be open. The reality didn't bear thinking about.

No, to ensure real peace of mind, putting distance between him and New York was much too tempting to turn down. That was why the Bloomfields' idea of pooling resources and moving to Portugal seemed heaven sent. Nevertheless, he held these thoughts tight against his chest and was careful to mask the catch in his breath when Leah had first pitched the idea of all four of them retiring to the sun. There was much to be gained by feigning reluctance. It must appear as though it was a real sacrifice, especially in front of Howard and he could run that one for a very long time indeed if he played things carefully.

Now, as he gathered up cushions of all shades, pink, orange, vermilion and scarlet, to plump against the brass headboard, he shivered with a delight. He'd done it! He was here! The crossing to Europe was behind them, the separation complete. He need never think of the grimy streets of Lower East Side and the ghastly gang he used to hang out with, ever again. What had become of them all? He must try not to care any more. They were far, far away – and so, almost, was his guilt.

As he stepped back, to survey his handiwork, the bed beckoned. The brocade cover, the colour of clotted cream splayed out invitingly. Suddenly he had an urge to lie down and savour it all. He had just sprayed the room to get rid of the last vestiges of paint, and the subtle lavender and grapefruit smell assailed his nostrils and gave comfort to a throbbing head as he closed his eyes, a smile on his lips. He, Benjie Liebermann, was looking forward – to his future!

10

$\mathcal{N}$eat piles of vinyl at his side, Howard was down on his hands and knees in the music room. Benjie's banging with the hammer had got on his nerves, and he guessed that in the months to come he would often find solace in this beautifully appointed room with its sweet-scented panels of cork oak.

A little tut of annoyance escaped. He grimaced; this was getting to be a habit and yet again the electric outlets were not in the specified place. There'd been some technical reason – something to do with water pipes, but nevertheless. He would now have to lengthen all his leads – a tedious prospect – when all he wanted was to get on and install his precious sound systems. He might have guessed someone would screw up.

He wondered what Benjie was getting up to in their suite. For reasons which he couldn't quite understand, he found the increasing empathy between him and Leah a tad disconcerting. After breakfast, he'd heard them crowing with delight over some unusual feature they'd just discovered in the kitchen. Giggling like schoolgirls, they were unpacking a forgotten chest of earthenware – 'I never liked it anyway,' drawled Benjie , 'Let's give it to the maid! We can use the real peasant stuff and she can use these expensive Mexican look-alikes! Kinda ironic, isn't it?'

It was all very well for them, thought Howard. Unlike himself, neither had encountered any major obstacles in those areas which personally affected them, and even if they had, they would not treat it very seriously. It was a pity that after nineteen years of Howard's careful tuition, Benjie still failed to grasp the principle that basic lay-out came *before* all else. He might be brilliant with colour, a master of imagination for atmosphere and image, but he had this annoying trait of letting things take shape as they went along. Only Howard had the discipline from drawing-board to finish, so that nothing – simply nothing – was ever left to chance. It was this meticulous planning down to the last finest detail which had given *Maison Parfaite* its cachet from day one.

Sighing, he heaved his bulk onto his feet again and mopped his brow with the effort. Jesus, it was hot, despite the rain yesterday. Somehow he would have to coax himself into dieting again if he was to live comfortably in this country. Being fat made him look older too – Benjie had hinted. Of course it was all right for his partner at only thirty-eight and still in his prime. One day Benjie would be fifty-something, going grey, with a gut on him, and then what?

It was curious how he still thought of Benjie as a boy. He'd come to Howard at the age of eighteen, not only immature in appearance but in almost every aspect. He was gangly, awkward, under-nourished and obviously under-loved. He certainly had no self-esteem.

When he looked at you, although the focus seemed correct, you felt he was looking far beyond, into some dim and distant past which still hurt.

Ever so often he seemed to wince. Howard was sure he had something to hide, but the Irish priest who had sent him was persuasive, 'Mr. McDermott, if you take this lad on, it'll be the kindest act you ever did. The boy's got a good heart, I'm quite convinced of it, but he's had a bad beginning in life. Born a Jew – like all of that unfortunate race – destined to suffer, he's been helping out at my weekly surgery. I've known him now for over a year but I don't think his present environment is the right one. We get the real down and outs, the no hopers and this boy deserves more in life. He's bright, quick to pick up things, and surprisingly practical. I helped him get his driving licence, and he does all the collecting up and fetching for me in between times. I know you've got a job going for a van-driver, and I say to you –' he rolled his blue eyes heavenward, his voice becoming softer as the Irish lilt increased with emotion, 'if you take on this dear lad, you'll get your reward in heaven.'

Howard was more worried about his reward in this life than the hereafter but he'd been sent employees by the priest before and the job of van-driver had to be filled immediately. The thought of advertising and interviewing scores of young hopefuls did not appeal. 'OK, Father O'Connor, you can send him along for me to see. But I'm not promising anything, now.'

'Holy Mother of God, you're a good man, that you are, McDermott. I'll send the boy tomorrow. I've a feeling about this one… you won't regret it.'

And so Benjie had come. The human resources department had seemed satisfied and Howard had taken pity on the skinny youth, who was all arms and legs. He would start on trial the following day. Twenty-eight days later, he'd been signed onto the pay-roll of *Maison Parfaite* as a full-time employee. Benjie's pale face had turned crimson when Howard sent for him and broke the good news himself. 'You'll never be sorry for this, Mr McDermott. It's my first full-time job and I'll make you glad you gave me this chance.' Howard noticed with a smile that for the first time since he'd been in his employ, he squared his shoulders and held his head up as he walked out of the office.

And his words came true. He had made Howard glad. Within a few months, they were all pleased to note that the wincing stopped. From the very beginning, without slacking on the mundane tasks, the pick-ups, the deliveries, the dispatches from the warehouse, Benjie had put in extra time around the showroom. Whatever contract Howard happened to be working on at the time, Benjie would appear after hours and make himself useful. From humping heavy carpets and underlay, to wrapping scrolls of fabric, finding uses for remnants, vacuuming debris, cleaning picture glass and mirrors, as well as dusting here and there, even when a hand was needed for the end of the measuring tape, Benjie Liebermann was there. Occasionally, when no one else was around, he would come and stand at Howard's side. 'Yes, Benjie?' Howard would eventually look up.

'Please – don't think I'm presuming, Mr McDermott sir, and I know it's not my place, but how about some interaction with those two pieces over there? There's a kind of void about that side of the room. Maybe if you placed the blue settee diagonally, opposite the covered footstool, it would take the eye into that corner – beside the tapestry with the blue flowers. Somehow you don't notice it, otherwise – it gets kinda overshadowed by those drapes.'

Howard would frown and say nothing. Then, after a while, when the boy was out of sight, he'd try – and by God, he was always right. It was uncanny how something quite small could change the whole feel of the place and give it more depth. Benjie seemed to have a neat feeling for balance. 'Have you thought about trying those two pieces the other way round? If you had the rose damask over there by the window, it would catch the sun and then pick up the plum in the girl's dress in the portrait to the right maybe, and make it come real alive. I guess Mrs Gable might notice that and … er – like it?' And since invariably, his words came true, Howard began to welcome his intervention without ever admitting it to anyone, even himself.

If they worked late, it was not long before Howard was inviting Benjie back to his apartment for a drink and a snack. It was always Benjie who ended up fixing the food since, as at work, he would not allow Howard to lift a finger. Soon he was acting like a solicitous gentleman's gentleman – refilling his glass, clearing away his ashtray, laying his supper tray and organising everything in the kitchen. It became quite a comfortable arrangement and Benjie's cooking was improving daily.

In the beginning it was just pasta, burgers or something frozen, but one day the boy appeared with a vividly-illustrated cook book, bought with his own money. From that day forth, things on the culinary front leaped up as did Howard's sense of self worth. It was wonderful to be spoiled! He'd never known this sensation before, and whilst his adopted family in Massachusetts had been good to him, real nurturing was hard won. Suddenly, here he was, being lovingly pampered. Moreover, eating at home saved money, and important clients would appreciate being entertained away from the public glare in such a tasteful apartment with its own attentive manservant.

One morning after just such a business dinner, Benjie produced an official looking peaked hat with gold braid, and asked if he might drive Howard to work in the firm's Mercedes. From then on, Benjie always drove Howard's car, whilst he himself sat in the back. It added to his growing feeling of importance. Not once, from the start, did Benjie overstep the mark – a fact which Howard had noted. If there had been any hint of familiarity, their comfortable working relationship would have been doomed.

Once a week, at the same time every Sunday, Howard religiously booked a call to his mother, Martha McDermott, in County Tipperary. He had kept in touch ever since he left Ireland in the summer of '35, but she was now a septuagenarian with time on her hands, so their calls meant more to him and to her than ever before. Howard had been just fifteen when he left home and went to live with his wealthy uncle, Patrick Fitzpatrick, in Massachusetts. Uncle Patrick was his mother's first cousin, a second generation American whom they'd never met but who had made good from the moment he arrived in the US after the troubles. The proud owner of a small chain of haberdashers throughout the state, Uncle Patrick was a widower with no children of his own. Howard's mother had written to him in a fit of desperation from the home country. She had offered her eldest son, a hardworking, intelligent boy, to work in the family business at whatever level her wealthy cousin thought fit. Although he came with nothing, she promised her cousin he would be rewarded with loyalty, honesty and a conscientious disposition. The idea had found favour and a third-class ticket was sent for Howard to cross the Atlantic.

The eldest of seven children, Howard was a plump, serious young man, old before his time due to the weight he bore upon his shoulders over his father's drinking habit. Whilst the younger children hid in their shared beds and blocked their ears with their fists, Howard would wait up, nervous but resolute, to shield Martha from the nightmare of the nightly arrival home from the pub. It was always the same; the dreaded lurching step outside the front door, the thud as one of McDermott's shoulders hit the wood and the struggle to find his keys. Cursing loudly, the big man tried to right himself, an exercise which could take several moments and finally, the clinking and scratching, when – having found his key, he tried to do the impossible – fit it to the lock. If Martha or Howard tried to go to the door and open it before he was ready, there would be a roar and all hell would break loose. By some cussed quirk of his personality, he was determined to go through the whole long painful process himself – as if to prove something. If all went well – which was seldom – he would come in a happy man. If, after several bungled attempts, he failed – then he would lose his temper and bang on the stout door with his fists. Glances would be exchanged between mother and son, and then Martha would hurry to release the snib and let in her man.

Howard was not allowed to answer the door. The only time he had tried, he had been laid cold with an upper cut to the side of his head which had necessitated Father Murdoch taking the lad to hospital to see if any permanent harm had been done. For weeks, Howard had suffered from excruciating headaches and there was the worry that he had bled so much in the eustachian tube, his hearing was damaged for life. After some months, the pain and singing in Howard's left ear departed but, not long after, he developed a severe form of nettle-rash on his hands and wrists. Antihistamine was prescribed and nothing more was said. It was such a relief to hear properly again but the itching resumed whenever things got difficult at home, and he was forced to pull his sleeves down in case he got beaten for that too.

It was a miserable existence for the whole family, but the younger children managed to laugh and play in between the bad times. Sadly, Howard found very little to smile about, and the only good feelings he remembered was when his father went away to Belfast for a few days which he did periodically in his work as a potato merchant. It was during such a venture that Martha received news of her husband's death from alcoholic poisoning and hypothermia early one January morning. Picked up by the *guarda* from a frozen pavement down by the docks, the report said he'd lain there all night and the temperature had sunk to minus five. After the identification, the funeral and the first few weeks of unreality, Martha soon realised that the whiskey had taken its toll of the family business and she was left a poor widow. The idea to send Howard to America was born of pure necessity. Her cousins Fitzpatrick might take pity on their plight and from the money Howard earned, together with whatever she could scrape together herself, she might just be able to keep the house and the children together under one roof.

Howard was not sorry to leave school although he knew he would miss maths and his technical drawing class. Miss Robertson, who had taught him throughout the upper school, had hoped he might qualify for a scholarship to the architectural faculty at Dublin for he was by far the brightest in her class. His work was always handed in ahead of time and with a pristine sense of proportion and presentation. When he came to say goodbye and solemnly shook hands, she said 'Good luck, Howard. Work hard in your new life, but don't forget what you've learned here. Go on with your work, your plans are excellent. Take your portfolio to America, and one day – when you know him better, show your uncle what you've done. You never know, he may be able to send you to a college out there. I hope so.'

As he turned to leave the classroom, she saw the glimmer of tears in his eye. Ever the fat boy of the class, he'd never made any real friends and she guessed she was one of the few with whom he'd shared anything in common. She noticed too that he was rubbing those poor red hands of his. Strange how those same hands could produce such meticulous and painstaking work … she shook her head sadly. It was a hard world.

After four years of working for his mother's cousin, Howard surprised himself by enjoying America and the long hours much more than he thought possible. When war broke out in Europe, overseas mail became a haphazard business, but through thick and thin, Howard remained in contact with Ireland. He delighted in telling Martha how he worked in accounts, 'had gotten on real well' – he was quickly slipping into the American vernacular – and they were moving him on. He had started evening classes in design and technology – and once he had his degree, there was an opening with an interior design firm which bought its fabrics from the Fitzpatrick warehouse. With his uncle now remarried and a new baby on the way, this would give Howard the independence he craved. He was anxious to make his own way in the world, just as he'd promised his mother.

All did not work to plan however. When Pearl Harbour finally forced Roosevelt's hand and America plunged into war with Japan and then Germany, Howard's technical college closed down as all its students were drafted into the services. Having applied for the air force, Howard was refused on medical grounds. Sadly, he wrote to his mother, '*You remember that allergy I used to get on my hands when Pa was drinking? Well, it comes and it goes, but never really clears up. The week before my interview, it got real bad and on the day itself, it was up in bumps and all angry. I never got as far as heart and lungs, they failed me on the spot. It looks like the most I can expect is some kind of clerical post, in a government office …*'

Looking back now, Howard knew he had been lucky. Some of his class never made it home, whilst he had finished his training and got a good diploma. By the time his fellow students were trickling back to make up three precious years of study – he, Howard was all set and ready to go into business. The family Fitzpatrick had been more than generous. In '47, they bought Howard a junior partnership into a new organisation run by two Swiss designers. The specialised business of producing custom-made soft furnishings for the home was flourishing after the war, and with him would go one of their own trained seamstresses. Not only was Howard to be involved in lay-out, he soon showed a natural bent for organising interiors, his knowledge of materials, wallpapers and textural effects earning him serious recognition. By '54, Howard had learned enough about the trade to go it alone. With the confidence of the Swiss bank who'd backed his previous associates, he opened his own small enterprise a week after Thanksgiving and called it *Maison Parfaite*. The French name seemed apt – a small way of acknowledging his continental backers.

Only once after leaving Ireland did he return to see his mother. Some three years after the war, without telling anyone, he took a trans-Atlantic flight on impulse, hired a car at

Dublin airport and arrived in the little town of Kensale on a wet Sunday afternoon. How small everything looked! He could not believe those drab streets, terraced houses, dull shops, had all made up his background. His courage was ebbing fast when finally he found the street of his birth and nosed the car slowly down the cobbled wynd. Curtains twitched on every side and he felt like turning around and heading straight back for the airport, when there it was in front of him – the last but one in the row. And it was too late to run! With its small picket fence and minute strip of grass separating the front parlour from the gutter, little had changed but there was fresh paint on the window ledge and an optimistic plume of smoke rising up from a newly slated roof.

One of his brothers had answered the door. It half-opened, and a face which he recognised only from photos looked out suspiciously whilst a voice with a guttural accent said 'Aye, what is it ye'll be wanting?' Instead of pushing the door wide open and throwing his arms round Edward, his younger brother, as he had so often pictured, Howard just stood there, suddenly aware of his big belly and expensive clothes. In a voice that seemed alien, he heard himself say – 'Er – is Mrs McDermott at home?'

The head was withdrawn, whispering in the hall and when finally Martha herself appeared, he was shaking. His mother too was much smaller than he remembered, a mere wisp of a woman, or had her hard life made her shrink? Whatever it was, the meeting rendered him dumb, but luckily she at least was herself and the moment was saved. With a cry of delight, she ran to him as he hovered at the doorstep, smothering him with kisses and cries of 'I knew you'd come one day!' Ignoring the curious looks of the children in the street, she wept hard into his mohair jacket.

After all the emotion, there'd been a reunion of sorts. The other brothers and sisters were called and they all grouped round self-consciously, but somehow there was little to say to each other. The money he'd sent regularly all through his time in the States had benefitted each member of the family. At first, it had been a meagre allowance, but gradually it had increased and now, because of him, Kathleen, the youngest, was all set for teacher training college in Cambridge – an opportunity unheard of for someone from their town.

Howard did not expect gratitude exactly, but he had hoped for something a little more uplifting than the uneasy looks they all shot him, between snatches of polite conversation in the parlour. Only when the others had withdrawn and he was alone with his mother, a cup of the familiar dark Indian tea in his hand – he hadn't the heart to tell her he only drank China – did a sense of the old companionship creep back. She sat close beside him and he held her hand and they fell into silence 'Howard, laddie – there's something I need to say. You've given us so much; there's no need any more… I mean it,' she looked up at him with her clear blue Irish eyes, and blushed. His heart lurched for a moment but she was serious. Gently she explained how all the older children were now earning, that she had given up working and how grateful she was for all he'd done but that – they'd be all right from now on – they really would.

Back in New York, Howard had poured his energies into his work and for years seemed to need no emotional outlet. He had many contacts, but there'd been no one he called a close friend until Benjie came into his life some years after he opened *Maison Parfaite*. The first year, Benjie was little more than a servant, but as time went by Howard found himself relying upon the youth for companionship. Increasingly, over the months, the boy had been stopping overnight. There was always a reason, new plans on the drawing board, sorting through colour schemes, breakfast meetings with colleagues, or entertaining clients. One day, Howard recognised that even when there were no jobs to be done, he was finding excuses. The large apartment had taken on an oppressive feel when he was there on his own and he didn't like it. Eventually, he took an irrevocable step.

One day, he found himself taking Benjie's arm, 'Look,' he muttered gruffly, not quite daring to meet the other's eyes, 'it's crazy you paying half your earnings away to your landlandy for those squalid rooms you rent down in Sugar Hill when – well, you know – more often than not, you sleep over here. I was wondering – wouldn't it make sense for you to move in with me – er – permanently?'

Benjie thought it would and not long after this, their relationship was changing yet again – this time, more intimate. Now, of course, it all seemed such a very long time ago.

When Leah had first laid her cards on the table and the prospect of retirement in Portugal had gone beyond the dream stage, Howard was in a quandary. *Maison Parfaite* might be reaping the financial benefits of Benjie's fashionabililty and his own good name and business acumen, but the design world was fickle and it didn't take a genius to know that things were changing.

The age of the computer was upon them, and it scared him. No matter how many courses he attended, he knew in his heart the leap from his painstaking technical drawing and draughtsmanship would be too great to encompass. Even Benjie was moaning about the changing technology. A number of designers, particularly those handling the lucrative office and hotel contracts, were doing more and more by computer and the bigger contracts might soon pass them by. The prospect of sending Benjie away for training was not one Howard welcomed. The humble caterpiller he'd picked up and rescued all those years ago had turned into one of the brightest butterflies in New York. Apart from the very obvious risk of headhunters – who was to say he might not be attracted in other directions?

Besides all that ... there was Howard's health.

Recently, his skin allergy had resurfaced. He was prescribed a daily cocktail of new steroids but in his own mind Howard put it down to stress. The word 'heart' had also been mentioned. So had 'diets' and 'lifestyle'. He'd plodded on, but the small words niggled away at the back of his mind. He was therefore amazed and grateful when one day, instead of the reluctance he had come to expect, Benjie let slip that although fanciful, he *could* now see there might be advantages to Leah's plan. 'I thought it was all too pie in the sky,' Howard remembered the light tone of his partner's voice so well, 'Leah's so naïve when it comes to her personal life. I guess you'd have to be – married to Buster! – but it's not such a bad idea, you know. Of course ... I'm thinking of *you*, old friend.'

They were in the office. Howard had just slammed the phone down on the chief of a firm of architects they'd used as long as he could remember and was sitting there, silent and clammy, as he waited for his palpitations to subside. After a while, he muttered, 'You mean you'd consider Europe? Giving up your career to sit in the sun?'

Benjie had nodded. 'I guess we wouldn't exactly be idle. A new villa sounds quite a challenge. And no doubt, if we ran out of money, I could find contracts over there. But

I'm not thinking of *me* right now. There comes a stage, Howard, when after all you've achieved, you just don't deserve this hassle. It might be best to pack it all in. Things are not as they used to be and I think you should seriously consider Portugal. We all know Leah's the eternal optimist, but this just might be worth looking into. Your health comes first, goddammit! '

Howard had mopped a purple brow and nodded. He tried not to look too grateful. 'Get me some Earl Grey,' he said and felt his shoulders sag as Benjie went skipping off. Recently, the eighteen year age gap yawned between them like a chasm and he felt increasingly isolated on the other side. His ability to stand back from a problem was not what it was, and he seemed to lose control of his emotions. Look at him! A pulse was raging in his forehead and he loosened his tie. What about retirement? He was almost fifty-four with enough pension schemes to see him through to eternity, so money wasn't the issue. But how to *let go*?

There weren't really many alternatives. The thought of losing control with Benjie still in the picture was not an option. Once computerised, what would the future hold? Howard would be swept aside, regarded as a has-been and their relationship would lose all respect. It would be much better simply to get out. Cleanly and at a profit! But would Benjie really be prepared to make that sacrifice? Despite his off-the-cuff remarks, Howard was not at all sure. There were many beautiful people clamouring for his skills; clearly the boy was on a roll and who, at his age, would want to climb off? His star could only go up.

That night they had a serious talk. To his amazement, Benjie seemed to have meant what he said. He was showing a maturity and selflessness of which he'd never seemed capable. But it was true! His partner would forego his career for the sake of Howard's equilibrium and health. Willingly, he would tear himself away from all he loved and thrived on – in order to make the ultimate sacrifice. Relief swept over Howard like a warm cloak. So much so, he never stopped to consider the reservations he'd always felt about Buster. Leah, he knew and trusted. The villa was big enough for all of them by the sound of it. What was so different from having an apartment in a block of flats, than having an apartment in a brand new modern beach house? A big one! There was no reason, surely, why it shouldn't work? And if there was a reason, surely they could deal with it? He was being handed a life line.

Now there'd be scope for reading, travelling, his collections, his music. As a couple, they'd never had much time for any of that; here, finally, was their chance! Lisbon, Seville, Cadiz and Cordoba beckoned – grand and ancient places – all within a day's journey of a new home. Hope, gratitude, renewed strength in their relationship and confidence in the future hung over Howard during those last few months in New York, like a tantalizing dream. The only fly in the ointment was the language. Portuguese was darned difficult and when he tried to speak it, no one seemed to understand him.

And now, as Howard dragged his thoughts back from Ireland and far off New York to the present and Portugal, he realised with a small shock that he and Benjie had been together for almost two decades. They had never celebrated the fact but perhaps it would be nice to combine the anniversary of their coming together with a small tasteful party when they'd gotten the house in order. He looked around; they'd only been here less than 36 hours, but already things were starting to take shape. It was amazing what could be achieved with four pairs of hands instead of two. Not for the first time, he wondered why more couples weren't doing what they were doing. It really wasn't such a hare-brained scheme after all and he would be the first to challenge anyone who said it was. Why! Even Buster could probably be brought under control, given a little time. And he made a mental resolution to make a better job of concealing his feelings.

11

*H*e was not sure how long he'd been asleep but when he awoke, Benjie felt clear-headed and ready to take on the world. The last remaining trunks had been emptied; Howard should be pleased with what he'd achieved. It was now up to him to dispose of the things he would never wear again but knowing Howard, Benjie smiled, he would hang on to everything. There were too many memories locked up in these garments and despite his outer show of gruffness, he was a sentimental old thing at heart. It wasn't his fault things had slowed down.

Physically tired, but mentally floating on air, Benjie wandered down to the kitchen. It was time to get some grub. He found Leah surrounded by boxes marked Very Fragile Indeed and clearly debating where to start. 'Care for a bowl of soup and a sarnie?' he asked, delving into the fridge for some bean and beef broth he'd made up the night before. 'Then I'll give you a hand with these, if you like.'

'Oh yeah!' she said gratefully. 'When I'm into things, I kinda forget to eat. I've already had too much black coffee today.'

'Seriously bad for you,' he said, drawing back a chair for her. 'A change of lifestyle should mean what it says. I used to be hooked on caffeine, but now I only allow myself one at breakfast and one after lunch – it's made so much difference.'

'You're right,' she said absently, wishing her husband pulled out chairs and showed the same concern. 'I promised myself a real makeover when I got here, and look at me now – as taut as an alleycat!'

'Don't tell me, I know the feeling only too well,' Benjie grinned, 'but it's early days. Seriously though, when you first told us about the Algarve, that for me was the big attraction! To get rid of all that stress and negativity and start to make time for oneself – and for Howard, of course.'

'I'll try to do the same,' said Leah, 'but old habits died hard. Be a friend and remind me from time to time – I'm good at helping others, but not so good at helping myself.'

'I've noticed,' said Benjie and gave her hand a squeeze, 'and you could start by getting Buster to shape up and do a bit more for you.'

'Oh, that'll be the day,' retorted Leah and they both laughed.

Howard was putting the final touches to his music-for-lovers section, when Buster came strolling in on his thoughts, whistling a tuneless ditty. 'Say, you'd better go and sort out those two giggling kids in the kitchen, Howard, before they make real mischief. As if there wasn't enough to think of, they're already talking about the first party they want to give – some time before the summer is out.'

Howard looked at him in disbelief. Had Buster read his thoughts? No, hardly – he was too insensitive. Odd however, the others were thinking along the same lines. At first irritated, he started to smile. It was the records which had started off his own train of thought – twenty years of partnership! He picked up a well-thumbed Sinatra album, examined the cover thoughtfully, then with due reverence placed it back in the rack, number 139 of a long line; it was already catalogued. Smooch music always had him thinking of anniversaries, parties and dancing. He marched into the kitchen, his smile fading as he saw Benjie and Leah with their heads together over a box full of crystal and glass. They were carefully unwrapping champagne goblets, looking positively conspiratorial.

'Oh Howard,' cried Leah, 'just the person we need! This is all taking much longer than I thought, but if you'd like to tackle the flatware, it would be a huge help. It's over there … '

Howard didn't, but threaded his way through the mess of wood shavings and tissue paper amassed on the floor, feeling demoted. If he stayed, he could at least find out what plan they were hatching. The sight of Benjie so close to someone else always triggered off his allergy – ridiculous as it was. Hell! Already the familiar nettlerash was spreading over his hands and up his wrists. He plucked nervously at his shirt cuffs. 'What's all this I hear about a party?'

Benjie's green eyes sparkled mischievously. He could not resist teasing. 'Oh, Leah and I were just working out the guest list. We reckon we'll get this place shipshape over the next two months and then we can think about launching Casa Amarela amongst the smart set!'

'Smart set!' Howard snorted. 'Apart from Aurelio … oh … maybe you mean to include the new gardener and the guy who brings the gas –' he paused to reposition his spectacles, '… I was under the impression we hadn't quite made it into Santa Felicia society as yet. Besides I always thought in Europe, you kind of waited to be asked before you did any asking back. Nothing worse than looking too eager – could be taken for brashness.'

'Oh, I don't think so!' said Benjie smoothly. 'I'm told the custom is quite the contrary when one's built a villa of this size! Apparently, it's considered standoffish if one doesn't immediately throw open one's doors to the discerning public and we don't want people thinking American hospitality isn't every bit as warm as the other ex pats.'

'Now, don't wind him up, Benjie,' said Leah observing a warning glint behind the small goldrims, 'we haven't decided on anything, Howard. It was the champagne flutes that set us off. I guess the house is getting to us. You have to admit, the ambience is incredible.'

'Hmm … I'd have thought six months might be more appropriate.'

'And have everyone say these Yankees up in that yellow villa are real stuck-up! Oh please – no-oh…' said Benjie. 'If we don't break the ice before fall, everyone'll get the wrong impression and no one will want to know us.'

'He's right, I guess,' said Leah earnestly. 'A little American largesse can go a long way. After all the bureaucracy, it might help smooth our path for the future if we can get into the hearts and minds of the people … you know, in case there are problems along the way.'

'You two are making a big thing of this. I always thought the biggest problem was getting ourselves here! Now we've accomplished that most stressful of moves, it would be nice to lie low for a bit. What sort of "problems" were you anticipating exactly?'

'Nothing ominous,' said Leah, 'but remember all the red tape I had to deal with in getting this house built? It strikes me whatever we need in future, especially planning permission for improvements – take our road for example – it might be useful to enlist the support of those who can pull a few strings.'

Howard was silent. He could see the sense of her words but it annoyed him that his party idea had been sabotaged before it had the chance to flourish in his own mind. What a pity he had not broached the subject first! That would have given him the upper hand, particularly as regards Benjie. There was some balancing up to do, and this would have been a good start. Now Benjie would let his imagination run away with him and he could be reckless and expensive. He hoped this sudden closeness with Leah was not going to encourage Benjie to step over the boundaries.

Leah was warming to her theme and anxious to include him, 'We thought a good move might be to confide in the man who runs The Anchor Bar in town. He must know everyone that's worth knowing. How about some time you and Benjie popping by and have a chat with the guy? No rush of course, but it would be a start.'

The start of what? thought Howard. Things were moving far too fast for his liking and this was not at all why he had come to Santa Felicia. They had left New York to get away from the social whirl, the interminable bandwagon of who you knew, what you did, what you needed to know, how to get on. Having left all that behind, it seemed these two were intent on climbing aboard again – whether in Santa Felicia or New York really made no difference – it was still a bandwagon and he, Howard McDermott was not so sure he wanted to be part of it.

A month had flown by and the villa was definitely taking shape. Every crate, box and trunk had been opened, its contents explored and a home provided. Buster complained they had more stuff between them than Bloomingdales but once they'd knuckled down to shifting the less important items into the basement – their fate to be determined later – and pooled what they 'couldn't live without', things were coming together. With the important public rooms, there had been surprisingly few squabbles. 'I guess we've all worked too closely together in the past to diverge on crucial matters,' said Leah prosaically, 'it's great and somewhat humbling how our tastes seem to merge and dovetail.'

Buster didn't think it humbling at all but for once did not spoil her moment. Even he had to admit the results were breathtaking. The *sala* was everything they'd ever dreamed of and the Baroque yellow walls cried out for pictures. There were plenty to choose from. Between them, over many years Howard and the Bloomfields had amasssed a rich collection of oils and pastels which looked better here by far than in a Manhattan apartment block. Leah's own particular favourite, a small Vermeer of a woman in russet-red, brushing long hair at a dressing table, sat well to the right of the fireplace over a delicate French card-table. The very demureness of this painting made Buster's Rubens-esque hunting scene of the scantily clad goddess Diana chased by a group of satyrs hugely exciting. It rose up and dominated the far end of the room. Lit from below by a subtle Venetian table-lamp, Howard's ruffled portrait of a gentleman from Verona lent an element of sober dignity to the opposite wall. Perhaps it was fortunate that Benjie's rather shocking Heironymous Bosch look-a-like, was small enough by comparison not to overcharge the complex turmoil of emotions it inevitably produced.

Their joint collections of prints and water colours had been tastefully arranged on the stairs, landings and bedrooms. Leah had filled their own suite with a set of German prints from an early nineteenth-century botanical book. The subtle blues and mauves of the wild harebells, iris and hyachinth depicted had prompted her choice of dove-grey emulsion on the walls. 'A bit dull, isn't it?' Buster had complained at first, but now the pictures were up, even he admitted it was an inspired choice.

That night, it had rained heavily again – now it was still. Buster awoke with a start. He lay there in the darkness listening to Leah's regular breathing beside him. For a moment he wondered where he was. Then it all came back to him in a rush. There was no moon and the room seemed very dark. He wondered what had woken him and reached for the torch by the bedside table. Shit! he had knocked over a bottle of Leah's pills and they fell to the floor with a clatter. She moaned in her sleep and rolled on to her other side. Her back felt bony against him, the muscular hardness of her small buttocks digging into his stomach.

He waited until she was settled again, then lay back and shone his torch up at the darkened ceiling. He'd thought as much! It must have been preying on his mind as he slept. The bevelled corners of the cornice on either side of the gabled window did not match. On one side it was rounded; on the other squared – it didn't make sense. Those builders! – one couldn't trust them to do anything without checking first – how could he have missed this? Of course that fancy architect should have spotted it, but once he'd had his cheque, they'd hardly seen him again. Funny how you could go off people. He lay back. It had started raining again. A light pitter-patter on the tiled roof – a pleasant enough sound. It would have been the silence that woke him. He liked noise; even bomb raids didn't disturb him – provided they weren't too close – there was comfort in noise – lack of it was eerie. There'd be some psychological reason, he felt sure; shades of Korea perhaps. Old Wally would know, Leah's headshrinker in Manhattan; he always had an explanation for everything, including – no doubt – why she spent so much money with him.

She'd gone to Wally as long as he could remember. One of the big attractions of moving to Europe – as far as Buster was concerned – was to get her out of that culture of reliance. Thousands had been spent! It was strange that someone so intelligent and capable as his wife, should throw away her hard-earned cash in this way. Sure, she was hyper-energetic and sensitive, but that was no excuse to go and lie on a couch twice a month and pour out one's inner self to a stranger. Not that he was a stranger, worse luck, but he was harmless enough. Whenever Buster remonstrated, it was always the same response – 'Don't you see? Wally *listens* to me!'

'Well so would I if you asked me!'

'Oh Buster! You wouldn't; neither would you *begin* to understand!' was all she ever said.

He wondered if the Boys were asleep. What was the time? He had no idea, and he couldn't see without moving his arm from beneath Leah's head. She was making small gurgly, whistling noises into the pillow ... not the most attractive, Buster decided. She must have her mouth open, to produce that kind of irritating sound. Carefully, he slid the thumb of his free hand under her chin and closed her jaw. That was better ... no sooner had he lain back however, and she was at it again ... a continuous stream of little snores and the odd soft sigh. To hell with it! He waited for sleep.

His mind wandered back to the Boys. It was bizarre how they all came to be here, gathered under one roof, when one seriously thought about. Until it actually happened, he had hardly believed it would. What could have possessed them? The whole thing had started as a kind of joke, a few years back.

It was the winter of '69, and he and Leah had been dining at Howard's fancy apartment in Brooklyn Heights. After a splendid meal, served as usual by Benjie, Howard had produced a very good bottle of vintage port. 'Come on – it's almost Christmas,' he'd persuaded. The time to leave was fast approaching, when suddenly, all pink and girlish, Leah had tinkled her cheese knife against her glass – like a speech before a wedding. What was coming? Had she had too many?

'Attention, if you please, gentlemen!' she said crisply. Leah was either very creative or capable of making a complete ass of herself when she'd had too much. 'I feel the time is ripe to make a pact!'

'Jeepers!' he thought, feeling suddenly sober.

'Now I know you'll agree, we're four very good friends. We enjoy each other's company. We all share similar tastes, good food, good wine, beautiful things, a high standard of living. Yet – here we are – working our guts out in Manhattan and never having any real quality time to enjoy these things – why, I even missed Thanksgiving this year! Neither are we getting any younger. So, do we make enough time for ourselves? I'd say "no"! Tonight's a case in point. Home from work, tired and stressed out, we don our glad rags and struggle out. And it's been fun, make no mistake – great fun – but sure as hell, tomorrow back at the office, we'll all feel like death warmed up – and we'll swear not to do it again, for a very long time.'

'Speak for yourself,' said Buster. What *was* she up to?

She ignored him and went on. 'So, I propose we make a pact and set ourselves a target. We decide to ourselves – no need to tell each other – just how much we still need to earn, before we leave all this behind and get out. Get out while the going's good and not too late to look forward to some sort of life ahead. The good life! That's right! The one out there that's passing us by! Isn't it time we snatched it, before it's taken from us and it's all too late?'

She sat down, solemn now. And waited. No one said anything, so she resumed, but in a calmer, more calculated voice. 'Well, that's what *I* plan to do anyway. I'm going to see my accountant, fix my target, thousands, millions... that's my affair... then, the moment we hit that target, I intend to stop. Stop right there and retire! I'll find a place in the sun, a little slice of paradise somewhere. I don't know where yet, maybe the Pacific, the bay of Naples, Indian Ocean – who knows? But if one wants something enough, it will materialise. The right place will turn up – I firmly believe that.'

They stared at her mesmerised, wondering if she'd finished. She hadn't. 'I propose that if such a place does present itself – and we all agree it's paradise – then we pool our resources and build a beautiful house there. In the sun! Away from here, ' she nodded at the frosted window, 'the cold, the noise, traffic, pollution … the stress. We simply chuck it all away and start again. Then, as the story goes, we live happily ever after. What could be simpler?'

It was a cute dream and when they found their tongues, they laughed. Leah did too. But oddly enough, it seized the imagination of each one of them and although no one spoke of it again, their work took on a new urgency. It was less than four years later when Leah broke the news that she had found the spot.

Leah and Buster had been only children from middle-income families who first met at high school on the eastern seaboard. Leah Franklyn had been raised in their small seaside town near Cape Cod whereas Buster – born in Pennsylvania – had moved there with his engineer father's job, at the age of ten. While Leah's parents were liberal minded agnostics who worked long hours as lecturers at the state university, Buster Bloomfield's parents had become strict Baptists, intent on converting the world. Since they never planned to have a child at all, they found the early days bad enough, but it was even harder trying to cope with an energetic, sports-loving teenager who loved the sea. His mother in particular resented the awkward boy who messed up her tidy porch with his beach stuff and slammed the doors during bible study with the neighbours.

It was probably unsurprising that neither background bound Leah or the man she was to marry with any great ties of loyalty to home. Making their own futures independently, New York was close enough to return if they wanted but far enough to hold them away. Both chose the latter.

In her early twenties Leah had been running her own small antique shop downtown, when Buster re-entered her life. After high school, he had kept in touch sporadically through the draft but when at nineteen he was sent to Korea, the letters became more serious. Not only had he seen more than his share of active service, there was one raid where his sergeant and best friend were blown up within inches of where he stood. '… I found myself covered with blood and body parts,' he wrote, 'I wasn't frightened but I can't help thinking about it.' She only hoped her words of reassurance, support and admiration were enough. It had always been a mystery to her why the proverbial boy next door should have singled out her.

Back in civvy street, he kept in touch. He'd been taken on as a junior manager in an import-export firm near the Brooklyn naval yard and now lived close enough to start a courtship. Could they meet? After the horrors of war, many ex-servicemen like himself, were in relationships. Three of his best buddies were already married. Within months of their meeting up again, they found themselves doing the same. Some years later, her shrink had asked Leah if she had fallen madly in love with Buster and was taken aback when she answered firmly in the negative. 'I didn't need to fall in love, Wally! I just never looked at another man.'

Their friends reckoned it was a marriage of convenience since after only two years at his own job, Buster had joined Leah at the shop. The excuse was they could now expand the business together – and so it proved to be. Soon they were moving to bigger premises and with someone strong and trustworthy to run things at home, Leah was able to travel abroad to find the type of graceful furniture, ornaments and art in which she wished to specialise. It was the lucrative Continental and Middle Eastern market that drew her, and here, Buster's knowledge of freight companies and shipping agents proved invaluable. As old palaces and chateaux were re-opened or pulled down all over war-scarred Europe, much of what had escaped the Nazis was finding its way to America. Leah was developing a sixth sense for fine porcelain, silver, paintings, tapestries and Persian rugs and where to find them.

After a year of proving himself an asset as well as a husband, Buster became a partner. By the early sixties, Leah Franklyn & Partner was one of the leading, privately owned antique dealers in New York. Leah herself had taken a year's sabbatical to work at Christie's in the west end of London. There was talk of a branch in America, but this had yet to happen; instead she found herself first in the Italian section in Duke Street, later in the French and Flemish. Before too long she had a good working knowledge of the Post Renaissance and neo-Classical periods, and by the time she flew home, she was viewed by many as an expert in her field.

It was Buster's contacts that allowed them to steal a march over their competitors. He had developed a real network of people, which included some dubious characters. He would pick up the phone, then via 'a contact' miraculously conduct a consignment of rare lacquer from Goa, ivory from Delhi, or carpets from Persia, halfway across the world to Manhattan. Where others came up against red tape, officialdom or the law, the Franklyn consignment would slip quietly through. Buster always dealt in cash and could be very manipulative. He gave handsome commissions to those people he trusted and Leah learned not to ask questions when she counter-signed a cash cheque 'just for freight'.

From private customers and sale-room success, the Bloomfields were soon approached by the interior design houses. When *Maison Parfaite* began to use them on a regular basis, their future seemed secure. It was Leah who got the McDermott contract. She went all out to get it in the face of much competition but it was personal chemistry that won her the day and tied them into a relationship which started in business and developed into friendship. Howard, slow to trust and generally suspicious, liked her open, fresh and enthusiastic approach to life; she radiated energy, yet carried a cool head on her slight shoulders. He also found her refreshingly honest.

At first he would not deal with Buster. Fastidious to a fault, he found Buster's slapdash approach gauche and unprofessional. The man was always on the phone, kept no paperwork and when dealing with his 'contacts' seemed much too laid-back about the large sums involved. Moreover, Howard did not altogether trust him. Unable to pinpoint exactly what it was, there was something inscrutable, verging on the devious in Buster's gleaming hazel eyes. This, Howard found disconcerting. Yet to be fair, Buster always 'came up with the goods' and never missed a deadline – more than could be said for other dealers. It took some years for Howard to drop his defences but had it not been for Leah, Buster would never have set foot in his inner circle.

Buster himself was blissfully unaware of Howard's reservations. As the two businesses expanded side by side, he took their relationship for granted. They had all worked damn hard, he thought, waiting now for sleep. It did no harm to muse over years of industry, innovation and the steady accumulation of their wealth. He and Leah had gotten themselves a first class financial adviser, so there were no nightmares there to keep him awake – only the prospect of peace and security for life. Neither were there any regrets that he and Leah had been too busy laying up for the future to think about having a family. Early on in their marriage, Leah had said 'I don't think I could ever be a mother; I just don't have the maternal instinct, and besides – I've enough to do picking up after you!' He wasn't too amused by that, but let it go. It was a relief to him that she had no hankering after kids. Kids got in the way – he remembered his mother's daily affirmation of that point – and besides, they had a habit of costing a lot of money. Frankly, he couldn't really see the point.

With no family with which to pride himself, much of Buster's energy was spent on himself. He really prized his manliness. Competitive and successful at baseball, swimming and athletics both at school and in the marines, he kept up a fitness regime throughout their married life. Regular visits to the gym, and running at a local stadium kept everything toned and honed, and although clothes and cosmetic appearance meant little, he was proud of his innate toughness and virility and was determined to maintain it. Despite all that, his introduction to sex had been complicated. Extra-marital affairs were very much frowned upon where he grew up and he was afraid of rejection. He never made a move on the girls in his social circle, but there'd been the odd prostitute on a visit to the city. Then came the Korean war and everything changed. With the anonymity of the one night stand, nineteen year old Bertram (Buster) Bloomfield found himself stationed in Seoul where you could pick up a dozen women as quick as whistle. Spoiled for choice and in every other way by the sloe-eyed Korean girls, he and the boys went mad for a time and confidence grew.

Until then, it had never occurred that his athletic frame, keen eyes, straight, sandy hair and tanned complexion might be attractive to all women. Only when, at a mess dance, he plucked up the courage to take to bed a petite American who worked at the embassy and was feeling home-sick, did he discover one important truth. To his intense surprise, he found it as easy to have sex with a nice, normal girl as it was with a whore! He smiled now, as he remembered the relief.

By the time he met up again with Leah, he had had more women than he cared to remember. It was refreshing to discover that at 22, she was still a virgin. There was enough of his upbringing locked away in the corners of his mind, to know that he would not want to marry a girl who had been tampered with. In his circle, there were few of those around, and even if he wasn't head over heels, he knew at once she would make a good wife and they could live compatibly together. Besides, there was a nice little business.

Affection grew and Buster supposed it had developed into a quiet kind of love. Love had always been a bit of a mystery to him. The sort the poets and song-writers eulogised about was for the romantics of this world, he supposed. Not being a romantic himself, however, he guessed he wasn't missing anything when the heavens did not fall down or the earth move. Physical love was a functional fact of life, healthy, necessary, stimulating and exciting while it lasted. He did sometimes wonder if she enjoyed it, for she never screamed, bit or kicked with delight like some of those girls in the war, but then nice girls were different. And Leah was very much a cut above the others; there was no doubt she was what his dad termed 'quite a little lady.' And ladies, he guessed, behaved like ladies, even in the bedroom.

Somewhere in the dark night, a cock crowed and the first streaks of silver dawn were beginning to creep across the eastern sky. He tried to lie still and concentrate on sleep but these thoughts of the past had stirred him up. And it was hot! After the rain, the heat seemed to be seeping into their room, even as he lay there. Damnit! – he could feel it was going to be another scorcher of a day and with work on the garden now in progress, he needed all the rest he could get. The Boys were fine at ideas and assembling, but it needed a man to shift rocks and boulders and get things into place. The sweat trickled off him as he thought about it. Holy Cow! he was getting randy – well, there was one way for sure he could stop that irritating snoring.

He pressed himself further into his wife as she lay there oblivious with her back to him. He must tell her she was getting too skinny – it wasn't good for either of them. Fumbling, he drew up her long cotton nightie and prized his hands between her closed thighs. She was still fast asleep – he often wondered about those sleeping pills. He'd never fucked a comatose woman before but it might be novel. He half regretted the sound of her muffled voice under the sheet, as she tensed her butt and drew up her knees. Greedily, he folded his arms round her tiny waist and began to ease his way forward. It was a familiar routine, and she'd relax soon enough.

'Buster, what's gotten into you?' She was properly awake now. Pity, he thought, now she'd want to talk.

'Shhhh!' he commanded, breathing fast.

'Well make it quick, I was right out of it then,' she was submitting more out of habit than passion.

'Sure, honey,' his voice sounded faraway even to himself as he moved towards his goal. Now she was awake, he wished she might at least pretend. The passion had long gone out of their relationship, but couldn't it be rekindled? After all, things were different now. Meanwhile, the heat was getting to him … oh well, there was no point in dragging things out – she wouldn't thank him for it. Might as well be quick – and selfish. A few swift thrusts of his strong hips and he'd soon be there. Seize the moment!

It was the aftermath which was the best part of sex – thought Buster. He'd heard himself call out – he couldn't help it – as that tingly feeling of piercing sweetness hit the pit of his stomach. But what came next was almost better. A long blissful ache in his loins, moments to be savoured, drawn out – there was nothing quite like it – only, he wished the woman in his arms could feel it too. Neither could she possibly share the delightful sensation of his own sweat gently chilling on his bare back. In this hot climate, all these things seemed more urgent, more vivid but the languishing afterwards should be longer, much longer.

This climate was made for sex and they should make time for it. The sooner he got Leah off those pills the better for all of them.

He grunted with contentment, squeezed his wife's arm by way of acknowledgement and rolled away. Down in the valley, the rooster crowed again but not before Buster Bloomfield was fast asleep and snoring.

12

*L*eah was up bright and early the next morning. As she showered, she wondered at Buster's show of affection a few hours earlier and rather hoped it wasn't going to be a regular habit. There'd been so little time for sex in New York, she wasn't sure she could handle another dawn raid with so much equanimity.

Feeling cleansed and restored, she wrapped a yellow towelling robe around herself and slipped from the room. Barefoot, she padded down the wide flight of marble stairs, pausing to exult in the peacefulness of the moment. The sunlight came flooding in to bathe the white walls in brilliance, whilst a tall grey horse on a canvas by Wilton gazed snootily down at her, held in place by a turbaned groom against a huge Newmarket sky.

The *ladrilho* floor felt cool under her feet, so different from the soft silkiness of the Persian rug that dominated the *sala* as she passed through to stand silently by the French windows. Slowly, she drew back the long linen curtains and undid the catch. A moment later the warmth of the day rose up at her like a low oven left on all night. Soft air streamed into her nostrils and she felt herself willingly assailed by steamy shades of wet oregano, ocean thrift and wild garlic all vying for dominance from the land below. 'Wow!' she said aloud as she crossed the patio and made her way to the edge of the natural platform where the beige rock fell sharply away. For a moment she felt as though she, the house and land were all suspended in space. With the sky washed clear of all clouds by the storms of the past few days, it was breathtaking. Blazing, glorious shades of blue upon blue captivated, then confused the eye so one could not be quite sure where sea ended and sky began. In ancient days, they called this 'the Vasts', mused Leah. I never quite understood that expression before, now I know what they meant.

If I could paint and put all this on canvas, no one would believe me. Even in art we kid ourselves. When it comes to the surreal – Nature wins hands down – every time! She threw back her arms, laughing at herself as her robe fell open to reveal small up-turned breasts, and she took a great gulp of salty air. She held it there, like someone savouring a good cigar and took her time. She could feel it seeping into the farthest recesses of her lungs, down into the pit of her stomach, purifying, expunging; then she let it go slowly with a long contented sigh. All the doubts of the previous days had fled.

The night's legacy of puddles had almost evaporated in ruts of red soil where once bulldozers and digger ran riot. Weeds everywhere, but not the sort to pull up; they were beautiful in their confusion, tiny petals unfurling to the heat of the waking day. New blades of bright grass struggled between volcanic rocks like emerald spears. Everywhere

Nature was pushing its way through, regardless of obstacles. Trailing over age-old stratas of sandstone, roughly landscaped by the builders, peeping up from every crevice, where bricks, concrete and sand had lain for so long, the wiry Atlantic flora was shooting out signs of brave rebirth.

Buster and the boys had made a good start on clearing, but if they didn't get a move on, the land itself would take over. She was not in the least perturbed. They would have their beautiful designer garden with its pergolas and gazebo, its barbecue patio and tiled bench, a fountain or two, and eventually the swimming pool – but maybe – yes, definitely – they could keep some of this wilderness wild. It had such a life of its own. That would be her piece of land, she thought – under her protection. Let the guys do the formal stuff and I'll potter about on the untamed plot down the hill. It'll be mine to do what I like with. I'll call it the 'wild bit'.

Perched on her warm rock dreaming out to sea, she wondered how it was she had become so reliant on therapy. The last ten months had been the worst; selling the business had exerted more pressure than she cared to admit and only Wally knew how close she had come to the brink. It was hard to imagine now – away from all the trauma, the clients, office, the orders and accounts, the never ending budgets and controls, keeping a grip on everyone and everything, including herself. Wally had been sceptical about their move to the sun; he warned that early retirement might create problems of a different kind. 'You were on the verge of breakdown, you know… but old Wally's tranquies saved the day, didn't they? Just like they did before when you overdid it. They kept you on the level, but that doesn't mean it couldn't happen all over again. And who'd be there to pick up the pieces? – not that husband of yours, that's for sure.'

'Buster doesn't see these things,' she had replied quietly, 'He's never had to. But don't worry, I'll be just fine.'

'But having too little to do can be as bad as having too much. What you need is balance in your life, Leah, you really must be careful.'

'Oh I will, honey,' she was quick to reassure 'Don't forget I may be retiring from business, but not from the world! You see, I mean to be busy all over again – only in a different way. All the things I could never do here in Manhattan…learning to cook a gourmet meal, gardening, keeping a few animals perhaps…oh, and maybe becoming one of the most talked about hostesses in the Iberian Peninsula! You name it – Leah Bloomfield will give it a shot!'

Wally had remained unconvinced and Leah smiled at the memory. She determined to make him eat his words. Her mind went back to the time she'd been stuck at Lisbon airport with several hours to kill after missing her connection. Had it not been for her curiosity and energy, it was unlikely she would even now be sitting on a yellow rock gazing out over an Algarvean sea.

She had been on a routine business trip to Europe, choosing pieces for a Texan oil baron who had a particular penchant for eighteenth-century dressers and chests. Her travels had taken her to the north of Portugal but her connection from Oporto was delayed. She'd arrived back in Lisbon from whence she'd started, just in time to see her flight taking off over the city's seven hills and out to sea without her. It was only eight am and with tears of frustration in her eyes, she marched up to the British Airways desk only to learn of a fourteen-hour wait before the next possible availability.

The thought of a whole day in that airport lounge brought her out in a cold sweat. Neither could she force herself to take a taxi back to the sweltering city, already explored at length; she had enough of crowds every day in New York. On the point of despair, a tannoy announcement caught her attention. 'Will all passengers in transit for Faro, please go immediately to Gate 2b. Boarding will proceed shortly … Flight TP 44 for Faro, please go to Gate 2b.'

It took less than a minute to check if there was a return journey back to Lisbon the same day. A couple more to check in. With seats available on both outward and return flights, jumping stand-by to Faro would give her the best part of a day on the Algarve coast and she'd *still* make her connection. What a stroke of luck! She had never allowed herself either the time or the luxury of seeing southern Portugal before – it was not an antique-y sort of place, but she'd heard it was very beautiful – now was her chance!

Her second stroke of luck came in the form of a taxi driver at Faro Airport. Not only did this important little person speak English, he was prepared to drive her all day. There were smiles all round on this score, his accompanied by a show of raised thumbs and of wide, gappy teeth. He was quick to assure the *senhora norte-americana* that he, José da Silva, knew the Algarve coast better than anyone and that his driving was second to none – or in so many words.

With a reckless disregard for dust or speed limits, they had swept out of the airport in a westerly direction. Leah became aware of a seemingly endless procession of mule carts, vans and small cars, the VW beetle a clear favourite, all of which the redoubtable José made mincemeat. Only when a sleek Maserati or Ferrari approached, at which to Leah's huge amusement the word '*fascista*' was muttered, did the taxi give way. Generally however, they hogged the crown of the road and Leah was loving it.

Delightful detours were taken en route. Without warning, they would dart off the *estrada* and struggle onto minor roads, often no more than a strip of concrete between sandy banks to arrive at some fishing village, tiny cove or burgeoning resort. Compared to the fleshpots of the Italian and French Riviera, served by a coastal road system, Leah began to think the Portuguese planners had shown good sense. By keeping the main traffic inland, the coast enjoyed its privacy and peace, aided by a lack of road signs. She marvelled at the buzz and charm of a fishing town named Albufeira, only rivalled by Carvoeiro, futher on with its colourful gem of a main square. Here the old seemed quite happy to co-exist alongside the new and despite some ostentatious villas on the surrounding hillsides and a bikini-infested beach, she was glad to note a village atmosphere and traditional buildings at their heart.

It was virtually the same at every seaside town. A world of black-hatted women and cloth-capped men on donkeys, laden carts and muleteers spoke of an ancient world which still worked, alongside the new. 'Too narrow for ze charabancs!' grinned José toothily as he nosed his cab past a squatting gaggle of women with baskets of peaches and melon at the verge, 'but not for thees taxi and thees *senhora* and José!'

But Leah wasn't listening. She was lost in wonder at the clearness of the air, the whiteness of the sand. At a glance, she could count at least twenty working boats, with more out at sea, bobbing over the white horses and not an oil tanker in sight. Reason told her such a land could not stay like that for long, but did it matter? The reality was here and it was genuine and tangible. She had never dreamed such faded charm and picture postcard scenes still existed.

At length, Sagres was reached. 'One of ze highlights of ze treep!' José was opening her door with a flourish. Leah stepped out at Cape St. Vincent and made her way carefully to stand at the edge of the most westerly point of southern Europe. Here the hitherto friendly ocean transforms itself into a devilish cauldron of foam; inky whirlpools suck warm air into their depths only to spew up cold spray and a fine damp clinging mist. On the hottest day of the year visitors shiver and huddle their shoulders together. As they gaze out to the wild, open Atlantic, and imagine themselves five centuries back alongside Henry the Navigator, dreaming of a New World, they inadvertently draw back. There is a savagery about this place that only nature can explain.

There was only a handful of tourists, and that day Leah, intrepid as ever, remained the longest. She bought a hand-crocheted shawl from a wind-battered stall and wrapped it round. She could hear the sea rumbling and grumbling, tearing deep underneath and right into the spur of rock on which she stood. There must be caves, certainly potholes; with so much gasping and boiling from the ocean, she half-expected a huge water-spout suddenly to erupt from beneath her feet and eject them all into oblivion.

José watched her from a safe distance. 'Me no like so much,' he explained when she returned. 'Thees not Algarve, thees land of *navegadores* – explorers, yes? Thees already not Portugal, this begeening of New World.' He swept his arm westward and inclined his head. It was time to move on. Surprisingly touched by it all, Leah climbed back in the car and they retraced their route to Lagos and its crusader fort, through Portimão and round the harbour. '*Pescadores*,' said José, nodding at the fishermen and other folk eating grilled fish on the quayside, '*Sardinhas*! Very good...tourists love!'

'You bet,' said Leah, suddenly hungry and keen to join the merry throng. But before, she could stop him, José had dived off the main road again and they were following a dried-up river bed, heading north at a spanking pace and leaving the coast far behind as they wound up into the hills to a greener world. Their route now shaded by tall eucalpytus and fluffy mimosa, the air had lost its tangy savour, instead it hung honeyed and heavy. Dog rose, thought Leah, recognising the clumpy bushes that littered the hillside. I hope you know where you're going, José – I need some food.

As though reading her thoughts, José paused at a fountain to point out the view. From a spectacular height, a spa town, red-roofed and neatly terraced, lay spread out under orange trees and vines. The countryside simmered in a heat haze, the tranquility tangible. Her driver broke it with a loud pat of his belly, 'José already know *senhora* hungry. Just ten minoots, I take you best restaurant in Algarve!'

Leah hoped so. Everything had been 'the best' to date. Now as the road grew more treacherous, the forest thicker, she was surprised to notice at odd intervals a number of stunning villas landscaped into the mountain, clearly commanding magnificent views. As tall, stringy-barked gum trees gave way to even taller pine, with larch and Douglas fir competing to stretch heavenward, the undergrowth grew deeper, richer, giving off the musky scent of heather, broom and gorse. 'Soon we arrive Monchique,' said José, 'many Engleesh and Dutch houses.'

'So I've noticed,' Leah observed thoughtfully, 'They have a real colonial look – I'd have thought they'd prefer the coast.'

'Not for some,' replied José authoritatively, 'They mees the… the – how you say – fog? Thees comes early morning – make them feel good.'

Leah had to laugh. 'No doubt you mean mist, José. M-I-S-T… They miss the mist? I thought they came to the Algarve to get away from all that!'

'Some people like,' José scratched his head and shrugged, 'maybe remind them of home. In the afternoon, sun – he come out. Then they sweem, private pools. Nice villas … people happy then.'

'Sounds like they've got the best of both worlds,' said Leah wistfully.

By three o'clock they were lunching at a rustic *taverna* nestling into a natural plateau high above a valley. A waterfall came trickling out of glinting granite, within a hand's reach of their table, while small rounded orange trees marched straight as soldiers on the emerald terrace. The proprietor of this homely establishment, a balding man with the shortest legs and longest apron Leah had ever seen, came bustling out. He embraced José like a long-lost son, and soon they were joined by the rest of the family. Everyone shook hands with the *senhora norte-americana* and within moments the charcoal under the outside grill had been stirred into life. Several pieces of plump chicken were carefully arranged, all glistening with a rich red oil. '*Piri-piri*…' explained José conspiratorially, and with much smacking of his lips.

A jug of red wine was set down, green olives stuffed with almonds and a plate of sheep's cheese, carefully cut into squares and sprinkled with oregano. Unleavened bread and a plate of smoked *presunto* completed the appetizer and on an empty tummy, Leah felt herself grow heady and flushed as she downed the wine and attacked the ham. It was quite unlike anything she'd ever eaten before, much rougher and darker than the *proscuitto* they ate at home, but delicious. José was full of winks and smiles and the daughters of the house, in their starched white aprons, blushed and giggled. By the time the succulent, blackened chicken arrived with a bowl of salad glistening with olive oil, Leah found herself laughing and gesticulating with the rest of them. It was quite extraordinary, she later told Buster. She hadn't understood a word, yet felt completely at home.

By five o'clock they were ready for the road. José had settled the bill, frowning as Leah produced her handbag for tips and shaking his head. Sweetmeats of marzipan and figs were thrust upon her by the women and a whole rigmarole of handshaking and exclamations of pleasure took up more precious minutes. Leah longed to look at her watch but instead found herself struggling to thank them all in Portuguese. A gabble of dialect from the patron's wife interrupted her attempts and José translated, 'Maria Amalia says eet was a pleasure to serve such a beautiful *senhora*. The *senhora* come again one day and bring all her friends.'

Leah nodded and gave the homely woman a hug. 'Tell her José, yes,' she said. 'I will come back one day. I really will.'

Then they were off. Speeding back down the winding road with little regard for sheer drops and hairpin bends, José drove with one hand on the wheel, the other on the klaxon, scattering children, chickens and the occasional sheep or goat. Leah, still flushed from her wine, felt she was in the lap of the gods. It was a feeling she was not used to, but she found it exhilarating. Back on the *estrada*, she made a mental effort to come back to reality where time governed the actions of ordinary people. She instructed her driver to head straight to Faro. 'I have three hours left before my plane to Lisbon, and I'd like to see Faro before I go. I'll need a hotel where I can wash and change before checking in at the airport.'

José said nothing; in the mirror, a muleish expression had crossed his face. They were about halfway there, when the taxi turned off the tarmac and they were bumping down one of those inevitable sideroads which led to the sea. 'Hey! what *are* you doing, José? I said we must go straight to the city. No more sightseeing, there isn't time!'

José sighed. It seemed he had lost his English as well as his direction. 'Sim, Senhora, sim, Senhora,' he muttered … 'esta bem, 'sta bem …' but still he drove south.

Leah was cross. The wine had given her a slight headache and the thought of leaving this land of gentle people and their gentle way of life was hard to bear. She did not need José to make the parting harder. 'I think you'd better turn around now, José,' she said firmly.

"'sta bem … okay. But the road … ees too narrow here, not safe to turn …' Suddenly, he was bi-lingual again and despite herself, Leah could not help a little grin; for the first time all day her driver was concerned for the rules of the highway! Now he was adding confidently, 'Look, only one corner, you look the view; then I make ze turn.'

There was no point arguing; the man's enthusiasm for the beauty of his homeland was touching. She waited for them to round the corner and the usual view of the sea to rise up. What she did not expect was the tumultous welcome of a fairytale picture of dolls' houses, spilling out over a rugged hillside in all directions to form a cubist Picasso landscape of shade and shape. The late afternoon sunshine bounced off a crenellated wall, onto whitewashed cottages that hung off terraces of vine and bamboo, glanced off the copper spire of a miniature chapel perched high above orange rooftops, then settled and spread, like a cloak of gold, on a distant sea.

Leah caught her breath and forgot to demur as slowly now, the taxi proceeded – slow enough for her to take in the loveliness of the little town before them. 'You see,' José turned round, with a careless disregard for the road, 'Thees ees Santa Felicia! It ees paradise! I saved ze best for last!'

And so you did, thought Leah. Blow Faro! Blow the hotel! I have to hand it to you José – full marks for timing!

One more twist in the sun-baked road, one more descent down a long hill and as red dust gave way to grey cobbles, suddenly they were in the main *praça*. The taxi stopped under a group of blue acacia trees and Leah stepped out into the softest air and an ambience of pure magic.

It was that hour when everything is closing in Portugal. With dusk around the corner, there's a last minute bustle to pull down blinds, close creaking shutters and roll up awnings which have protected doorways all day from the sun. A huddle of donkeys stand tethered around a fountain in the gardens in the square, waiting for their owners to finish work. A very domestic scene and not a tourist in sight; that hour when they too disappear indoors to shower or take a reviving drink – that time of day when the villages become totally Portuguese again – if only for an hour or so.

The minutes were ticking by as Leah stepped out of the cab to explore. Her nose took her first down a long winding street, and as the smell of salt and fish grew stronger, she found herself in a large cobbled open yard ending in a harbour. A small fishing fleet was paddling its way swiftly out to sea, across the turquoise bay tinged with gold – further and further into the blue until each small boat became a mere shadow, a bobbing dot upon the water. Leah watched until her screwed-up eyes could follow no more, then turned regretfully and wandered back to the yard. Lights were coming on in little houses rising up from the cliffs around her. She had never seen dwelling places so cunningly cut into the sheer face of the rock. Might those hanging gardens of Babylon been fashioned in such a way?

She took a new direction, climbing a narrow alleyway heading upwards from the seawall. It would be easy to get lost in the maze of little corridors and patios which opened up to her right. Plucking up courage and passing beneath a whitewashed archway, just wide enough for a donkey cart, she knew not where she was bound. Clearly, she was entering the hub of the fishing community – but what might happen next was anyone's guess. Descending, then rising again, she found herself in the wake of a large bay mule. Together with its portly owner, it proceeded carefully along the cobbled way, just able to avoid brushing its flanks on the dwellings to either side. She followed. Up and up, round innumerable corners, the unshod feet made no more sound than the soft pad-pad of carpet slippers. Quite suddenly, mule and man were swallowed up into the gathering dusk to disappear from view. Leah found herself peering through an ivy-covered doorway set in a high wall. She could just make out a tiled courtyard beyond. Cheerful, guttural voices rang out and by the light of a lamp slung from the eaves, she spotted the good man's wife, come forward to greet him, then leading the mule away into a cavernous depth. It reminded her of a biblical scene, unexpected and strangely poignant.

As promised, her taxi was waiting in the square. The moment had come to depart from this haven and return to reality. José said nothing as Leah climbed into the back seat. Neither did she. Her head was swimming with unbelievable thoughts. Try as she might, she could not forget José's first words to her as they had driven round that fateful corner. Santa Felicia had risen up before them like a subtle temptress, her simple charm adding to her power, breaking down resistance. What had he said? *It is Paradise…?* That was it, Paradise! How ridiculous! Yet, if the truth be known, he was only putting into words what she herself had felt … dammit!

As they drove slowly out of the old part of town, everything was coming to life. Bars were opening, Chinese lanterns in the gardens, warm hues of tangerine, yellow and ruby streaming over patterned pavements, reflected back in darts of light from the little fountain. The beautiful people were beginning to emerge from their hotels, walking hand in hand in the middle of the streets, their thin gauzy evening garments proclaiming they were off to have a good time, in a restaurant, bar or discotheque. The smell of fresh sea-bass, squid and garlic doused in olive oil on outside grills hung in the air, and voices, happy and carefree, rose above the clatter of crockery, as waiters scurried from table to table outside low doorways. Here and there a dog barked, a sports car revved or the low whine of a guitar escaped from a restaurant bar. One thing was certain; the air was very much alive as Santa Felicia slowly and luxuriously prepared herself for the night.

Leah stared straight ahead, resolute this time. 'The airport, José!' she said firmly, wondering why her neck ached so much as she kept her eyes front. There was no time to make a tour of the capital; no time to freshen up at a hotel, but she didn't care. She arrived at the terminal out on the lonely salt-flats with minutes to spare. 'Your number!' she said as she settled his bill and scrabbled for a piece of paper in the depths of her bag. As usual, he was ahead of her.

'Ees here, *Senhora*,' he handed her a battered card he'd been clutching all the while. There was no address, only his name and a rank number, well underlined. He pointed proudly, 'Here you find José, just say ees *senhora norte-americana*, and they call me.'

'I'm not promising anything, José,' said Leah more for her own benefit than his. 'I may come back, but there again, I may not. It's only – if I do – I'd like you to drive for me again. You seem to know your Algarve very well – it could be useful. But it's unlikely it will happen ...'

'You come back, *Senhora*,' he was grinning, 'everyone come back to Santa Felicia.'

'I hope not *everyone*,' she repeated later as she strode out onto the tarmac to catch her flight, 'otherwise it won't do for what I have in mind.'

And as she boarded the plane for Lisbon as one in a dream, she wondered.

And so it had come to pass. She had kept her promise to Maria Amalia, the tavern owner's wife, but who could have guessed that one missed flight could have led to this? Perhaps it had been the wine, perhaps the sun, but now – as she stretched her legs and made herself more comfortable on her yellow rock outside their finished home – Leah liked to think it had all been planned by Destiny.

She remembered the strength of her desire – growing apace within her – as her plane had taken off over a glorious sunset. She was wise enough to know that somewhere so enchanting, so little spoilt, would not – could not – remain like that for long. But while it did, the temptation to return for good to such a place would fill her waking hours and haunt her dreams. *Carpe diem!* From that day forward, she had quietly cherished her dream – admitted to no one – until it became clear that if she turned her back on this opportunity, presented so gratuitously by Fate, it might never happen again.

And now in this moment, remembering – she was grateful for that sense of purpose, that energy which had driven her to this point. Hers was a steely determination; it had brought success and wealth and something else besides. It had given her the will to follow her star, to make others believe, and to push the boundaries – against all the odds. Who would have imagined that four people could change their lives so radically and achieve so much in so little time?

She hugged her robe round her, tested the hot patio with a bare toe, and as she climbed off her rock and meandered back to her beautiful house, Leah wondered – now that they were all here – just where *would* the future lead them? Surely, all she had to do was be herself?

13

Jerry Weaver tweaked the cuffs of his navy blazer, the shine on his brass buttons as immaculate as the glasses he'd been polishing for the last half-hour. Appearances were all important; for none more so than the owner of Santa Felicia's Anchor Bar. No visit was complete in these parts – so the guidebooks said – without a drink at this watering hole and since that reputation had been hard won, Weaver and his wife were determined to keep things that way.

Generally it was Pat who hired or fired the staff. She also ran the books and could spot a dodgy barman a mile off. The first item on the agenda at any staff interview was the subject of honesty – Pat could guess the 'take' on any given day, down to the last escudo – the second was standards. At the slightest sniff of shoddiness, they were out on their ear. Fortunately, the team this summer seemed up to par and his local chap João, who doubled up behind the bar, was shaping up nicely. To celebrate the thought, Weaver poured himself a beer – it was, after all, almost midday.

'Cheers!' he said jovially to no one in particular as he watched the froth settle and noted its depth. He took pride in creating a pristine head, no more than a half inch, his being the only haunt in town to serve beer straight from the barrel. Only the Brits really appreciated the malty taste of barrelled beer. And there were plenty of those. The bar was already filling up with holiday-makers of the home county variety who would in turn bring in the locals. Today, there was a particularly pleasant air about the assembled company. Approvingly he noted an absence of the hippier types with their shredded jeans and dreadlocks – too early in the day, but unavoidable at night. Nevertheless it was a relief to see some proper haircuts. Weaver felt quite avuncular as everyone smiled politely; it was pleasant to feel included in his clients' conversation.

'Industrial unrest again in the North of Spain,' announced a man with the air of a bank manager, 'Rather worrying…my wife and I were thinking of retiring to the Algarve next year, but not if that sort of thing spreads over the border.'

'No chance,' said Jerry, an authoritative ring to his voice. 'The Portuguese government won't stand for disorder, neither civil nor political. We never have strikes – totally illegal, you know – besides, it doesn't go with the national temperament. Your average worker's much too laid back, fortunately for us all.'

'I don't know what you're worrying about Spain for,' complained a small man in a pale blue safari suit, 'England's the place I worry about. Talk of a frigging election in the autumn, too. It's the last thing the country needs. It's leadership what's required – common sense too. I go home tomorrow, and I tell you – with a small retail company struggling to make ends meet – I'm not looking forward to it.'

'The last time I flew back,' said a red-haired girl who appeared to have been poured into a black leotard that did little to hide her generous curves, 'there were no baggage handlers at Heathrow. I said to Steve here, just what's the country coming to?'

'And I says to her,' her companion winked at the assembled company, 'with that outfit, it's just as well, or they might handle something more than baggage.'

The bank manager gave a strained smile and cleared his throat. 'It's – er – hardly surprising so many are getting out of England and starting again in places like this,' he waved a vague arm round the bar. 'There's little incentive at home, even savers are knocked down at every turn.'

'I've given up worrying,' said Weaver cheerfully, wiping a little imagined froth from his handlebar moustache with a folded spotted handkerchief. 'I haven't been back for five years, don't you know – and I'm not likely to these days. What with bombs and picket lines in London, students and foreigners – red banners thrust up one's nose in Hyde Park ... the country's going mad I tell you ... quite, quite mad!' And looking amazingly unperturbed, he pulled another perfect half pint.

'I blame the papers,' pronounced a gentle North Country voice. 'They love to stir things up and make out things are bad, I'm sure it's all exaggeration. My husband and I are only here for a short holiday, but we're already missing home and apart from the cost of living, can't understand what all the fuss is about. Things in the dear old country aren't really half as dire as everyone makes out.'

'With all due respect to you, dear madam – bollocks!'

Everyone turned round startled as a tall, hard-eyed man strode into their midst. It was as though the waves parted as Jock McKay marched straight up to the bar, folded his arms across it and looking Weaver straight in the eye demanded, 'I'll have a campari and soda thank you, Captain!'

From anyone else, Weaver would have basked in the glory of being addressed thus; an officer figure was exactly the image he tried to cultivate. A studied air of condescension coupled with a bluff heartiness and poker-stiff back made up the picture. Unfortunately, he knew McKay was not deceived by outward appearances. It was a permanent thorn in his side that one day, the man would expose him as a mere catering corporal to the officers' mess. As usual, however, he put up a brave front, counting on the support of his customers to ignore or reject this rude intrusion. Surely everyone would be affronted by McKay's language and attitude; it was quite beyond the pale.

'I say. old chap!' He took an ostentatious step backwards. 'Coming on a bit strong today, aren't we?' His eyes rolled conspiratorially at the North Country husband as he reached for the campari bottle.

'Strong?' McKay was both sarcastic and incredulous. 'We can do better than that – particularly about the present government!' he bowed to the couple who were growing quite pink at all the attention. 'But let's be fair, if I've offended anyone, I'll gladly make it up,' he swung round and surveyed the group with a tilt of his left eyebrow.

There was a titter from the red haired girl and McKay pounced on her. 'You, my dear madam – has my terminology upset you?'

The girl giggled, she'd never been called 'madam' before and ignoring her partner, gazed straight back into two very sharp green eyes, finding the leonine head and proud bearing thrilling enough to giggle again. 'Not in the slightest,' she twinkled up at him. 'If you need to use strong language, you've obviously got a very good reason!'

'Precisely,' replied Mckay, beaming back at her. 'What a wise young lady in our midst, Captain! Unlike those who've permanently turned their back on the mother country, she's hit the nail on the head!'

'And why's that exactly?' A tubby man in a white teashirt which did not quite meet up with the belt of his ballooning shorts, wanted to know, ignoring a prod from his wife.

'Since we're obviously amongst intelligent people, let me tell you,' McKay drew himself tall, sweeping away a wisp of peppery hair with an impatient gesture, 'but first things first! A drink for this lady and her – er – friend here, thank you Captain,' he made way for Leotard and her partner at the bar, '– and for both of you, my man?' he smiled at Tubby and his wife who looked flattered. Suddenly confronted by a formidable front at the bar, the beleaguered Weaver fell silent as he poured their drinks.

They were onto their second round, when McKay got dug in. Leotard and Steve were 'into Scotch' a fact that under normal circumstances might have put off a casual host. But there was nothing normal about McKay. Not content with annoying Weaver in the first place, he became more extravagant by the moment. 'Try this malt,' he persuaded Steve, enjoying the red patch on the back of Weaver's neck as he was forced to stretch for McKay's private bottle at the back of the gleaming rows of spirits. 'I'll join you in a glass, I keep it for special occasions.'

Two shots were served, whilst Weaver consoled himself over his high charges for corkage. It was hard not to get annoyed though. Why could McKay never bring himself to say 'please' and why did he always create such a stir around him? More people were gathering round to eavesdrop; it was maddening. 'This one's from home, just south of Inverness, on the mainland,' said McKay, ' Little known except by the connoisseur, I dread the day it hits the market big time, when no doubt they'll expand the distillery, bring in mains water and that lovely peaty taste from the local spring will be lost.'

Steve sniffed his glass with a show of appreciation, before taking a hearty swallow. 'See what you mean,' he said, running his tongue over the roof of his mouth. 'Narse, isn't it? '

'I didn't realise you came from *Scotland*,' said Tubby's wife, worried they were taking advantage. 'You've no accent! Is that because you've lived abroad?'

'No, it's to do with education and where you're brought up. The best Queen's English is spoken in Inverness.'

There was an awkward silence, broken by Steve muttering, 'You learn somefink every day.'

The bank manager was hovering near. 'Tell us about it…your – er – home, I mean. You mentioned the mainland, does that mean you live in the Western Isles? Audrey and I took a trip there last year, stunning part of the world.' Weaver sighed. This was just the cue McKay had been waiting for and in anticipation of a long morning, he called João to replace him at the bar. He couldn't bear to hear the story all over again.

'As I was saying,' McKay's voice had taken on a distant tone, 'you have to hold on to the special things in life; small distilleries, ancient hill farms, traditional fishing and stalking, all of which depend upon each other for survival in a modern world. Once you let go of these, allow the mass market to enter, you lose quality. The old practices, and the knowledge which make a malt like this, go down the pan. It's the same for the tweed industry further north, or the Borders cashmere mills just south of Edinburgh. Too much expansion and you destroy the very quality that makes them special. You also lose the communities.'

'Sounds like you care a lot,' said Leotard, her slightly bulbous eyes full of sympathy.

'My dear madam, I have a lot to lose.' Before anyone could ask the inevitable question, he went on. 'For my sins, I was fortunate – or unfortunate, depending on how you look at it – to inherit a small estate up there on the west coast. Lochaig comprises an island and a loch, sea-loch you know, all of which supports a few families who've existed there as long as anyone can remember. My name's McKay, and whilst one half of the family can trace themselves back to some respectable knight who fought for Robert the Bruce, the others – my half, probably – were the traditional sheep rustlers. Anyway, somewhere along the line they became respectable and built a keep – we call it the Big House. It's been my lot to inherit it.'

He took another slug of whisky, his green eyes piercing the mirror at the back of the bar, as if he did not trust himself to look at them directly. There was another awkward silence and you could have heard a pin drop. 'So, if you don't mind my saying,' said Steve bluntly, 'Why aren't you there today?'

'You mean why do I come and drink in dumps like this?' There was a bitter laugh, 'That's a very good question. Do you really want to hear?'

They all nodded as Weaver tightened his lips and disappeared. 'Because of our bloody politicians! Because of death duties! Let me explain. Look, don't get me wrong, it was never a very grand place, but over the generations it grew. Labour was cheap, stone could be quarried from the hillside and over the generations, new bits, wings and so on got added. My father did what he could with the little cash the estate afforded, but moving into the twentieth century was hard. Plumbing and wiring a modern house is bad enough; imagine dealing with sixteen-foot thick walls! It was already rambling out of control, so we only did one section whilst the rest crumbled. Big or small, it was still home.

'Then came the war. Too old to fight second time around, my father remained to farm the island as best he could with all the young men gone away. I enlisted at eighteen and found myself in the cavalry, armoured car division. We were soon shipped off to Cairo and then it was North Africa, the desert. I remember lying in my bunker waiting for Rommel and dreaming of Lochaig. As the sand blew in my eyes and I closed them, I imagined a newly restored Lochaig, turreted and proud. I'm sure it was this that kept me going. Instead of sand, I thought of smooth lawns reaching down to the water, newly painted windows, roof-tops repaired, slates gleaming in the sunshine… I smelt the heather. When the battle came, and there were dead men all around me, it was this that kept me going.

'We took a direct hit. I ended up in the field hospital. I lost half my spleen and a lot of blood and the padre told me I was "down for dying". He read me a passage from the Bible, and it was Psalm 121. He couldn't have known it at the time, but I believe it saved my life…'*I will lift up my eyes to the hills, from whence cometh my help*…' Thinking about those green hills of home gave me the strength to fight. Each time I felt death's chill settle over my body, dragging me down, I pushed up to those hills. The deer, the sheep, the forests, the salmon leaping upstream, and something else too. It was the people – returning to their cottages after the war and looking for peace. A vision of loveliness, something worth preserving – a better life. I began to recover.'

He drained his glass. 'Put my bottle of malt on the counter,' he said to João in Portuguese, but even Steve was too rivetted to take advantage.

'So what went wrong?…sir,' he added with a note of respect.

'Everything. Armistice came, I was flown home to recuperate. I was still fragile as I boarded the train at King's Cross and headed for Inverness, but felt supremely grateful. Here I was returning with two arms, two legs and a heart that had proved the medics wrong. I arrived on the island, but instead of being greeted by that fine figure of a father I'd left behind, I found this shrunken old man, clinging onto life, just to see his only son again. He'd been fighting Parkinsons for three years and I never knew. The doctors said a lesser man would have gone long before. Within a week of my return, he was dead.'

He stubbed out his cigarette and immediately lit another one. Weaver bustled back into the bar but everyone ignored him; they wanted to hear the end of the story. 'It had always been my dream to follow in my father's footsteps. Not just to restore the house but to give the islanders every possible chance. Father had financed the fishing; he'd laid down scallop beds, restored the river banks, our sea trout and salmon were amongst the best. He gave families certain rights over the loch, dug out a proper harbour to serve the timber yard and sawmills which provided work. He encouraged the women too; our cottage industry had begun to flourish but did he get any help from the Ministry? No! Not a thing! The Atlee government that followed did nothing for the rural community. After the war they only wanted one thing.'

'What was that?' the North Country wife said in hushed tones.

'Money of course! I was the sole heir of an estate I could not afford to live on. Something called taxes and death duties got in the way.'

'What did you do?'

'I knew what I wanted to do,' said McKay and they all craned their necks to hear, 'Line up every member of the post-war cabinet and put my army pistol to their heads. How dare they do this to me and others like me! We had fought for our country, our homes, our people – and now we were threatened with losing everything we held dear, just to pay off government debts!

'Of course I sought advice – civil servants, bankers, the brightest and best in Glasgow and London. Some clever clogs suggested I sell all the homes on the island to private investors, but there was no such thing as real estate in those dates. No one was interested in holiday cottages, not after the chaos of war. People wanted to get on with their lives. I tried the tenants – they weren't interested – even if they'd had the money. Why break with three hundred years of tradition and peppercorn rents? With that slow Highland smile, I was thanked for the privilege offered and a "no sir – we're quite happy with things just the way they are."'

'I'm sure you all know the rest of the story!' a beautifully modulated voice broke in, and made them all jump. The morning was full of surprises – who was this elegant woman?

Johanna Vincent swept into the bar and planted herself coquettishly, hand on hip, right under McKay's nose. Her grey eyes danced as he jerked his head back, shot to his feet and surveyed her. For once, he was rendered speechless. 'Why hello, darling!' she kissed him lightly on the cheek, her eyes dancing as she surveyed the throng, 'now, aren't you going to introduce me to all these nice people?'

Leotard nudged her partner – was the woman being patronising? What did it matter? All this drama had sure livened up the morning ... islands, castles, wounded in the desert ... what next? But *who* was she? There was a familiar ring to the voice and something about that face. She looked to Steve for help but all he could do was blink.

Jock had found his tongue, 'What the hell, Johanna, are you doing here?'

'I've come to finish the end of your story,' she perched herself on the edge of the stool he'd just vacated. 'No doubt you all know who this man is?' she ignored his furious scowl. 'No-o? He only happens to be Jock McKay, one of the academy's most successful post-war modern artists.' There was a ripple of surprise, but undeterred, she continued. 'Yes, this man with all his problems – and boy! does he have them – had the courage and vision to keep his island and promise the tax-man he'd repay every penny. But on one condition – they must first give him a chance! So out he went into civvy street, enrolled at art college, got his degree and started to paint! '

'Johanna – please!'

'And as you can see, he's still here, because being a bloody-minded Scot, he's not prepared to return until all that tax is paid off. But word has it, the return to Loch-thingamejig ... whatever it's called ... can't be that far off. You see, Jock McKay is a very talented, successful man and soon he'll have paid off every penny he owes. Isn't that the gist of it, darling?' she beamed.

McKay was scowling. First and foremost, he regretted shooting his mouth off. Second, he should know better than to buy expensive drinks for all and sundry just because he was feeling sorry for himself. Third, how dare Johanna finish his story so glibly! The way she told it, he might have been some privileged young bastard who'd sailed through art school and fallen on his feet. No one would ever know the self-doubt, the humiliation of being unable to live in his own home and the constant burden of debt which had lasted so many years.

All through art college he had felt utterly alone. It had taken years before his first tiny taste of success and that had only been by a strange quirk of fate when someone had spotted his sketch-pad where he'd experimented with colour in large swirling doodles and begged him to frame it up for them. Then, when his real work was rejected time and time again from the exhibitions, he tried the same trick. And it worked! Frighteningly, it was the non-art that sold his work. The world had changed and the modern day preoccupation with abstract served him well. As his fame grew, he felt in his heart, he had bastardised everything he had ever learned or admired, in pursuit of fashion. And although it made him money so he could begin to pay his taxes, deep down in his heart he still felt ashamed. Apologies to Rembrandt, he sometimes said under his breath at the end of a day in the studio. Then he would top us his drink a little more in order to live with himself.

'Are you very cross with me, darling?' Leotard and her friends had melted away and he and Johanna were left alone at a corner of the bar.

'Very.'

'But darling –' Johanna opened her eyes wide to protest but was cut short.

'You know how I hate to tempt fate. And eavesdropping like that! What were you thinking of?'

'I was thinking it was good you could get things off your chest. And *you* weren't the one tempting fate. It was me suggesting an imminent return to Scotland – not you.'

'That's my point,' said McKay through gritted teeth. 'So many things could still go wrong. For a start – and this was what got me going like a bloody fool on the subject in the first place – if there's an election this autumn and we get an even crazier set of plonkers in power, that alone could mean the end of all my dreams. I'm still way short of my target and time's running out so for the first time I've gambled on the stock market to hurry things up. But knowing my luck…' He didn't finish the sentence and looked so downcast, Johanna wanted to give him a hug but did not dare.

'Oh darling, I'm *so* sorry. I didn't realise. It's just all the columnists have been predicting your return, why only the other day I read in William Hickey –'

'Fuck William Hickey! what does he or she know? Just like those hapless people over there,' he nodded over his shoulder at Tubby and his cohorts, 'no one has a bloody clue.'

'Well, at least we gave them a happy ending,' said Johanna, determined to lighten the gloom. 'After all they're on holiday and they've gone off charmed now. They'll tell all their chums in Essex how they met this famous man and how the toffs no longer have it all their own way these days. How they have to graft just like everyone else! Who knows – you may have changed the face of grass-roots politics!'

Scowling had made his cheeks ache, so McKay gave up his angry stance and sat down beside her. 'You are ridiculous,' said McKay but his eyes had softened. 'OK, OK, Johanna. – I'll only blame you if it goes pear-shaped. In the meantime, I'll buy you one for the road and then I must be off.'

'Thank you but no!' she was up as suddenly as she'd sat down. 'I only popped in for a quickie. I've had a stinker of a morning at the boutique. Masses of people trying on clothes, and no one buying. Amazing aggro and no reward!'

'I know the feeling,' he said as he rose to his feet, allowed himself to be pecked on the cheek again and watched her go out. It was a relief to be left to drink on his own again.

'Queer fellow,' Weaver nodded in McKay's direction as he handed Steve and his partner the menu for a bar lunch. 'Hope you took all that with a big pinch of salt. Verging on the blotto, most of the time.'

'I thought he was nice,' said Leotard, adjusting a bra-strap. 'I like people who have a story to tell.'

Weaver sniffed, '*Story's* the word!' He threw another deprecating look in McKay's direction and was unfortunate enough to catch the other's eye. McKay managed a sardonic nod. What a buffoon Weaver was, always trying to score points with his clientele. Well, he had enough to worry about without caring one jot about a pub-keeper. There was his coming exhibition for instance. Was there enough freshness, diversity, about his collection for this season?

Thank God it would be in London! All the arrangements were so much easier on home ground especially when the house they always took at Richmond was rent-free. Where would one be without old friends? There was a good nursery school down the road, so Katy would be off her mother's hands. Catalina adored London. She'd go mad over her wardrobe of course; she always did, but at least it kept her out of mischief. McKay had never quite admitted to himself that if Catalina had been a normal wife, they might have been back at Lochaig by now.

He was spared the sadness of further analysis by the sudden diversion of two strangers. Approaching the bar, they stood out from the normal tourists with an air of urbanity, the cut of their expensive casual clothes, deportment and height. Something told him they were American, and sure enough, the New York twang was obvious the moment they opened their mouths. Whilst the younger looked confident, fit and muscular with thick dark hair and trim waist, his older companion – a veritable whale of a man – bore an anxious look as he surveyed the room through fine-rimmed gold spectacles. McKay noticed thinning grey hair, carefully arranged strand by strand, as well as suprisingly small hands. Everyone looked up in interest as they heard Weaver's guffaw of laughter in reply to something the older man was saying.

'Ho! ho! ho! That's a rich one! No, I'm not Portuguese – no need to try the lingo out on me, sir. I'm as English as they come – obvious, I'd have thought? But – if you insist – the word you were looking for is *cer-ve-ja* – emphasis on the '*ve*' you know – not the other way round. Get the emphasis wrong, and they'll *never* understand you.'

McKay noticed the big man crumple as though he'd been pricked. It was such a rarity to hear visitors take the trouble to speak the language, his heart warmed towards this deflated stranger. Clearly, Weaver must be taught a lesson. As the two Americans ordered a glass of lager, he noted Weaver taking their money in a condescending way, then quite pointedly – turning his back to fulfill some unnecessary task at the rear of the bar. Marvelling at the fellow's lack of business acumen, not to mention courtesy, McKay seized the moment to make up. Quite suddenly he left his corner, and in two strides had moved in to force the issue.

'Ah, Captain!' there was a peremptory ring to his tone, 'Be so good as to introduce me to our two friends here. It seems some hospitality is required, and I always like to meet new faces in this God-forsaken town.'

Weaver was taking his time; he fitted an optic to a bottle of vodka then turned slowly. 'Just a minute, old boy,' he said, trying to wipe the look of loathing from across his face. His assumption that the two Americans were just passing trade had been ill-judged. One could almost see the dollar signs flit before his eyes as it dawned on him these two might be new residents and in the off-season could prove valuable customers. He could have kicked himself! Once again he'd allowed himself to be upstaged by McKay who, having got what he wanted, was not going to let him get a word in edgeways. For the second time that morning, the wretched Scotsman had taken control in *his* bar.

'So you've just settled in! You must be the happy owners of the yellow house on the hill. We've had a speculative time watching it being built from afar, I can tell you. There's no point in my asking if you're enjoying Santa Felicia because your feet can scarcely have touched the ground. Is everything going to plan?'

'As far as the house is concerned, yes – thank you,' said McDermott. 'But we've scarcely touched the garden, whilst the pool, tennis court etc. are distant dreams. There's a lot to be done. Also, our road – we were lucky to get the removal vans up it. After the recent rains, it's been reduced to little more than a mule track!'

'Like all the roads around here,' said McKay cheerfully. 'Look, don't worry. The local builders are all the same. Full of enthusiasm to start with, then once they've given you a roof over your head, they lose interest and no matter how much they need the business – it's one helluva job trying to get things finished. But don't let it get you down – you'll get there.'

Benjie smiled, 'I've already been telling him that, but he wants everything done yesterday.'

'A grave mistake,' said McKay. 'But it's no good my telling you; you'll learn.'

'I guess so,' said Howard. 'It's just … it's Ireland all over again,' the remark was addressed more to himself than them, but McKay pounced on it.

'That's it!' he said. I knew there was something other than New York there. You're from the South aren't you, County Limerick or Donegal, perhaps?

'Tipperary,' said McDermott shortly. 'Yes, I was born Irish, but unlike most Americans don't make a habit of boasting about it. I consider myself a New Yorker through and through. America's been good to me, Ireland wasn't.'

'Well, I'm a bit of an exile myself, but I don't blame the old country exactly – just the politicians. But I've said enough about that for one day. Were you in business in the States?'

'Interior design,' said Benjie. 'Howard started *Maison Parfaite* back in the fifties. Perhaps you've heard of it?'

'Indeed! I had a very good order from your people for some pictures a couple of years ago.'

Howard had adjusted his spectacles to the end of his nose and was peering at McKay, an expression of comprehension slowly spreading across his face. 'You said your name was Jock McKay… you're not *the* Jock McKay, the artist?'

'I'm afraid so.'

'Well, I'm sure pleased to meet you, Mister,' McDermott pumped his hand enthusiastically. 'You're something of a celebrity with my firm because we had to design a whole villa down in Saratoga around your work. We weren't allowed to use any fabric or wall covering that might clash, and I don't mind telling you it wasn't easy!'

'No, my God! Who on earth was it – some crack-pot? No, let me guess. Was it a certain rather well-known film-star?'

McDermott nodded, 'I can't complain though, she was pleased with the end result and paid handsomely and on time!'

'Bravo!' said McKay. 'Sounds like a tall order, nevertheless. Usually it's rather a case of my work clashing with everything else! Most people who like all that colour, don't care a damn where they put it. To design a house round it – I wouldn't know where to begin!'

'In the end we did it all in pale beige, wild silk, walls, furnishings the lot. Being a movie star, there were the statutory lapdogs, two Pekinese, champagne in colour – so it had to go with them too! We did rather wonder how the sofas would stand up to the constant patter of little doggy feet but she seemed amazingly unconcerned.'

'She's probably into some other artist by now,' said Mckay, feeling quite lighthearted as he warmed to his new companions. 'Look, you've finished your drinks, why not come on back to my house and meet my wife? We generally have lunch on the terrace – a bit al fresco at this time of year – and you can see my small studio, if you want.

'We'd love that,' said Howard, delighted to have found such an interesting person on their first trip out of the villa.

They were about to leave when Benjie remembered something. 'Hey, we mustn't forget what we came for. Leah will be so disappointed if we don't arrive home with that party list. I'm sure it won't take Mr Weaver, long to do. Could you give us two minutes of your time, sir?'

'Party list?' said McKay, as the ear-wigging Weaver literally bounded forward.

'Yeah,' said Howard apologetically, 'it sounds crazy but we were dispatched this morning to seek advice in compiling a list of suitable guests for our – er – house-warming. Leah – er – Mrs Bloomfield – our villa's a joint venture, you know – had this idea to throw a party. It seems kind of premature to me, but she's set on the idea – to get to know the residents, et cetera…' he smiled weakly. ' We guessed the Anchor Bar might help us.'

It was a long speech for him but before Weaver could recover his dropped jaw, McKay interpolated, 'That's settled then – you must definitely come back for lunch! Catalina's the social bee around here. Being Portuguese she knows both sides of the great divide, pat and ex-pat, and besides –' he was already shepherding them out of the bar ' – the Captain's clearly much too busy to help you on *that* score. After all, we must ensure you get the *right* names on your list!' And with a swagger, he had swept the Americans out of the door.

The McKay house was set in a dark street in the old part of town, approached from the *Esplanada*. From the outside it was much the same as the rest of the row, double-storeyed, narrow and clearly built in the last century. Here and there the facades were tiled, others white or pink-washed in Portuguese colonial style, a few balustraded with fading ironwork. All effectively blotted out the sunlight one from the other, whilst a not unpleasant smell of semi-decadence hung in the air. There was certainly no sign of development, and further up the street a group of mules stood tethered to a doorway. Inwardly, the two Americans wondered just what had attracted their new-found friend to this particular area when there were so many more open and attractive streets.

They soon knew however. As McKay flung open the door they were looking straight out over the bay which had been completely hidden from the street above. It was an ideal setting for a painter. The constant activity, and the ever-changing interplay of light and shade upon water, must bring a never-ending stream of colour and inspiration. Led upstairs, they found themselves in an enormous studio-type room where the seaward wall had been taken out and replaced by plate glass. Sunlight flooded this part, laid out as a sitting area with an open fireplace, wing chairs and Chesterfield sofa with occasional tables. Everywhere, huge, exotic potted plants thrust upwards to lend a jungle effect to corners and contoured walls.

The street side of the room faced north and stretched into an L-shape, with a higher level just visible behind a bulkhead and a short flight of stairs. This must be where McKay's work was carried out, where he could savour some privacy. The two friends stood rooted to the spot, struck by the unexpectedness of it all. The range of colour and light amongst the wealth of paintings which hung, lay or stood propped against every available surface burned with an intensity and energy that rendered them speechless. There were pictures everywhere; framed, unframed, half-painted, just begun. Some were recognisable, others not. Some disturbed. In every medium, every size – each creation jostled for impact. It was the quality of colour that united them – startling, explosive, powerful – it snatched the breath away, left one reeling, bereft of emotion.

Wow!' thought Benjie. Howard just gazed and gazed.

'They're unusual, aren't they?' A soft voice, followed by a trilling, tinkling laugh like the sound of falling glass, made them look around sharply.

14

$\mathcal{N}$either of them had noticed the elegant *chaise-longue* tucked away in a shady alcove. They whirled round, coming face to face with its occupant, a picture in herself. Silently, they took in a creamy complexion, long dark hair framing a wide-eyed, flawless face before falling loosely onto firm square shoulders, bare except for a shimmer of blue gauze around the neckline. It was too tempting to trail the eyes downward to find the same blue reflected in a pendant studded with tiny sapphires nestling at the top of her cleavage. Perched high upon an array of cushions, Catalina McKay had the air of a sleek, well-cared for cat, expectant of the attention already coming her way.

So strong was this impression of a knowing feline, Benjie found himself taking two steps backward as at length she came towards them on high-heeled sandals, hands outstretched; he had almost expected her to offer a soft paw. In all his life he could not remember a time when he had seen such an inviting apparition of womanhood. The liquidity of her movement, the way she dropped her chin and angled her neck to smile sideways, the lowered lashes casting a perfect shadow over a retrousse nose – everything about this woman was tempting. Benjie braced his shoulders and gave himself a little shake.

'This, gentleman, is my wife, Catalina,' McKay said, placing a proprietary hand around her waist. 'Darling, let me introduce Howard McDermott and Benjamin Liebermann, our new neighbours.'

'So!' Catalina McKay clasped her hands to her chin to consider her two guests, then, apparently satisfied, lifted a smooth cheek to be kissed. Whilst Howard was taken aback, Benjie obeyed the cue with alacrity. 'How nice to meet new faces,' she beamed, 'and how clever of you, darling,' she simpered up at her husband 'to bring me people to play with. 'You see,' she confided, 'I simply adore visitors and more even than that, I love entertaining.'

'Catalina, these two chaps have just moved into the yellow house up on the hill – the three of us met in town this morning, they'd been sent to spy out the land, as it were. I thought the least I could do was invite them back here for lunch.'

'Well that's wonderful,' cried Catalina, 'and may I say …' there was a tiny pause, 'it's a happy change to welcome people who aren't British! Jock will have told you *I* am Portuguese, and I cannot tell you how many dreary souls I have to put up with, what with being married to such an important man. Yes, darling, I *know* you prefer I don't say such things … but it's true. And I am sure *Senhor* McDermott and *Senhor* Liebermann – also not English – will understand.'

They nodded, surprised but charmed by her candour, and insisted on first names. Regally, she inclined her head, 'Now – having dispensed with all ceremony, I must leave you and tell Philismena to prepare lunch for two more! I can't wait to hear all about your new house and the other people living there.'

McKay laughed shortly as he moved to the drinks tray and uncorked a bottle from the cooler. 'She rather bowls one over on first impact, doesn't she? Don't let her put you off though. She'll walk all over you otherwise! Here, try a glass of this *vinho verde*, and we'll go out on the patio. You'll never see a better view!'

He drew back on the plate glass which now revealed itself as an enormous sliding door, and beckoned them out. All at once, they were amidst the rooftops, sheltered from one side by the chimney-breast, to the other by the high sloping corner of the house next door. There was just enough space on the flat verandah for a few potted plants, a swinging sun-lounger and a wrought-iron table and chairs over which a giant yellow parasol cast its shadow. Benjie was quick to take in Spode china, fine glass and heavy antique silver, on a table neatly laid for two. McKay might cut a dashing Bohemian figure in his jeans and denim shirt, but it was obvious in his own home he enjoyed real style.

Catalina came back apologising that it would only be a simple meal, since the errant Philismena seemed to have run out of everything and how typically tiresome when she had such special guests to entertain. Howard was quick to reassure and apologise in turn for butting in so unexpectantly. 'I feel we're really inconveniencing you, Mrs McKay,' he said, taking off his misted glasses.

'Nobody ever inconveniences me, you may be sure!' was her twinkling retort. A moment later she was distracted by the appearance of a little girl on the terrace, whose bright fair hair was in surprising contrast to her own, although they both shared the same determined chin and flawless complexion.

'Papa! You're back!' the little girl darted past her mother and flew to her father, hugging him round the waist. For the first time that day, McKay's face really lit up. He tossed his daughter into the air, caught her and they kissed each other with resounding smacks and much laughter.

'Come here at once, Katy!' Catalina's voice was surprisingly sharp as McKay set his daughter down again. 'Where are your manners?'

To the Americans' astonishment, the child ran forward, stood on tiptoe and replicating her mother, lifted her face to be kissed. This was new! Unsure what to do, whether to bend down or simply smile, there was an awkward moment. 'It's OK,' laughed McKay, 'here in Portugal you may kiss children – in fact it's expected – in polite society!'

Anxious not to be caught out, they brushed cheeks. 'I don't do that in Scotland,' Kate sidled up to Howard. 'Papa's always reminding Mama. Strange people don't kiss strange people – they shake hands! My name's Katy, what's yours?' Enchanted, he told her. 'Oh, how do you *do!*' She had an old-fashioned ring to her voice. 'Oh dear, I must go now – Philismena's calling. I eat in the kitchen,' she pulled a face and hurried off without a backward glance. An elderly Portuguese servant in grey uniform stood at the doorway, tucked her hand firmly in her own, and they disappeared together.

'What a charming child!' exclaimed Howard, blinking in surprise and undisguised admiration. 'Quite the cutest thing! I'll be honest though, I don't generally take to kids.'

'She's a monkey,' said her father sternly, 'and what's more she gets away with murder. I spoil her, my wife spoils her and that Philismena woman ruins her. Why we don't get rid of the old bird I can't imagine.'

'You know very well this household would fall apart without her,' Catalina produced another of her radiant smiles. '*Diga-me*... how did you all come to meet this morning? Wait – I can guess. You found each other in that dreadful Anchor Bar!'

'As usual, spot on, darling!'

'So, tell me,' Catalina turned back to her visitors, 'what did you think of that Senhor Weaver – the one with the wheeskers?'

'Well, he seemed all right, but we scarcely got talking –'

'He is common,' Catalina was quick to interrupt. 'For me there is nothing worse than a common Englishman. I am not a snob but it is different here in Portugal. You have the worker, you have the cleric, there is the professional and then the upper class. Each of them has his own place, his own dignity but none of them is common.'

The two Americans looked at each other, wondering into which category she might have placed them. McKay came to their rescue. 'Don't believe a word my wife says,' he laughed. 'Firstly, she *is* a snob, secondly she loves to disconcert – throwing a cat amongst the pigeons being a favourite tactic – thirdly, she's spoiling for you to argue back. Why? because this gives her a chance to dazzle! I hope you're not going to let her get away with a remark like that?'

Catalina hadn't finished. Turning to her husband, she remarked about the last time she had seen Weaver at the British consul's cocktail party. 'You may not have noticed, darling, but he tried to kiss me. His boring wife was there so he made it look like a peck on the cheek, but in actual fact he was tickling my breasts with that monster of a moustache. I very nearly slapped him!'

'Why didn't you?' asked McKay mildly.

'Well, you know,' she pouted. 'One did not want to make a scene.'

'But you love scenes, my angel.'

'Aha!' she cried, 'You are right, but only with a worthy audience – and do you know?' she turned back to Howard and Benjie, big eyes opening very wide, 'they were such a dull lot, so *English* – you understand – I couldn't be bothered.'

'Catalina –' McKay shot her a look, 'I've promised our two friends you will help out with something.'

'How intriguing! I will if I can!'

'Well, it's like this,' Howard removed his spectacles for yet another inspection, 'We – that is – Benjie and I, Leah and Buster, rather hoped...'

'Did you say *Buster*?' Catalina swooped on the name, 'now *who* would have a name like that?'

Benjie, having just observed the sharp pinch McKay bestowed upon his wife's arm, giggled aloud. Then, recovering, explained –'Buster and Leah are the friends with whom we share the house. They're a married couple – his real name is Bertram, but he never uses it, it's always Buster – a nickname from the marines – Buster Bloomfield.'

'Oh!' there was a deliberate pause. 'And this Leah, she is his wife? Is this too a nickname?'

'Oh, I don't think so. She's just a very nice and capable lady.'

'A lady?' Catalina raised her eyebrows.

McKay had had enough. 'Yes, Catalina, of *course!*'

'So *you've* met them too? Now I do feel left out of it all! It's always nice – and indeed rare – to meet a lady round these parts. Perhaps I should break my rule and start going to the Anchor Bar too! Then I might meet all these exciting people.'

'Oh there's nothing very exciting about us, ma'am,' reassured Benjie, 'We're just four ordinary business folk who fell in love with your beautiful country and decided it would be kind of neat to throw in our lot together and build a house near the beach in which to spend our … er… retirement.'

'But you are *young*!'She saw a glance flit from Howard to Benjie, and hurried on, 'Never mind – let us start again! You were just about to tell me what is I am to help you with?'

'This is sounding far more complicated than it is.' Howard could feel the perspiration trickling down his back. Too large to benefit from the sunshade, he longed to retreat into the cool of the room they had left behind. 'First, your husband has not yet met the Bloomfields although we hope to put that right shortly. Second, we're looking to give a party, a kind of house-warming. Your husband thought you might be willing to help us with some names.'

'You see we haven't had time to get to know anyone yet and we guessed this would be the easist way to meet our new neighbours,' added Benjie.

'What fun!' Catalina clapped her hands just as Philismena came on to the patio balancing an enormous lunch tray. Salad, cold meats and the usual delicious Portuguese cheeses were set down, and as she arranged her guests, placing the moist Howard beneath an eave, Catalina could talk of nothing else but the impending party. 'Over coffee, we will retire indoors and I shall create a list for you! Really, I can think of nothing more amusing!'

Later, with Catalina re-established on the *chaise-longue*, frantically scribbling whilst the Americans looked on, awestruck, McKay stood in the doorway. He dragged deep on his Gauloise, one ear cocked into the conversation, 'I've already got eighteen names,' he heard her say, 'How many exactly do you want?'

Howard scratched his head, 'It rather depends, doesn't it, Benjie? I mean if one's going to make an effort, one might as well entertain more rather than less. We don't want to miss out on people who could prove important at a later stage; neither do we want to offend those who feel they should have been invited.'

'I disagree,' said Catalina. 'If you ask everyone, no one will think it special. If you ask a select number, those who don't get asked first time round will try harder for the future.'

'I see what you mean,' Howard sounded a little dubious.

Catalina warmed to her theme, 'Twenty to twenty-five should be maximum. That keeps things exclusive without being dull. Also, it's much better you meet less people and recognise them again, rather than fifty and never know who came. Don't you agree?'

'Yes ma'am,' said Benjie reverently.

'And that's a habit you must get out of,' said Catalina. 'Call me by my name! Nobody calls people Mrs or *Senhora* or Ma'am around here unless they are working for you! Besides, "ma'am" – it's so – ' McKay thought she was going to say 'common' and cleared his throat loudly, 'contrived!' she finished triumphantly. What a minx his wife was – yet looking so innocent, aware of her beauty – and almost sanctified by it.

She's a peach, he thought. Sweet, ripe, sun-kissed, tempting. And like the fruit in full bloom, makes no secret of the lushness within. But for how long? Those same beams flirting across her satin skin, could all too soon wither and dry... 'Time's jealous fingers...' a forgotten half quotation formed in his mind. At 34, Catalina was reaching her prime, but the passing years would take their toll when younger peaches, more tempting than she, would jostle into the light. Not that it would make any difference to him; he was committed for life. Nevertheless, he must remind himself to paint her again – soon – so at least on canvas, she would always look like this. He took another hard drag and stubbed out his cigarette as he moved back to the terrace alone with his meditations.

His gaze fell on the busy bay below, but for once no part of him escaped to that vibrant scene. He did not hear the cheerful chatter of the *pescadores* clambering about their boats, the laughter of children swarming over rocks or the call of seagulls swooping and diving. Brilliant light flashed from the church spire, bounced off tall masts with steel fastenings, and met its own reflection in the sparkling water. But for once it did not mesmerise and hold his eye; neither did the clean harsh smell of drying seaweed assail his nostrils. Instead, all his senses were concentrated on one thing – his young wife.

He thought of the night before and the two of them in their enormous bed next door. As he momentarily relived their lovemaking, a bitter-sweet smile drifted over his lips. He had known and loved many women, and some of them had been exceptionally lovely. Yet somehow, all of them – even Sally, his adored first wife whom he had lost, together with their baby boy, in childbirth – had failed to transfix him like Catalina.

He'd waited a long time for her. To quench the pain of losing Sally, he had drunk a lot and run wild all through his thirties. It puzzled but later amused him, why the most stunning women should gravitate towards such a reckless, selfish person. Until he met Catalina he could not remember a single moment where he ever had to make a real effort again. He might forget to phone, feign indifference and neglect the niceties of courtship, but women tended to throw themselves at his feet. The free-for-all of the sixties was still some way off, but after the usual show of reluctance, even the most proper young ladies seemed happy to give away their love. Were they sorry for him? – perhaps, but who was he to argue? A natural romantic, he had expected to woo them with flowers and champagne, but before he even thought of a strategy, they would be his for the taking.

By his mid-forties, Jock McKay was very used to getting what he wanted. The only problem was, he got easily bored and having failed to find a kindred spirit with whom he could truly connect, he became something of a loner. Taking his pleasure as and when he wanted was not always satisfactory. Beauty fascinated him, but he soon discovered that to stay faithful, there had to be more than physical perfection and charm. Above all he valued a quick mind and strong, lively spirit. Perverse in personality himself, he also welcomed unpredictability.

It was not until he met Catalina that he discovered that special ingredient required to keep him faithful. It should have been obvious since he had always liked a challenge, but it had never occurred to him before that a difficult woman might be the answer. Not only was

Catalina passionate, but he loved her inventive mind – she was full of tricks and innuendo. Her passion blew each way – both hot and cold – and he enjoyed the uncertainty of it all. You never knew where you were. She could be ice-cold yet fuck with a vengeance, she could be fiery, then soft as butter. It was this perverseness that excited and drove him into her young arms when they first met in London and by this time, everyone else had given him up for lost.

With Catalina, McKay discovered the mental anguish of desperately wanting and not being sure if that need was returned. She was not a virgin, but she was young and unspoilt in the ways of the world and for this reason, he took his time about seducing her. When it did happen, he wanted it to be cathartic. Instead, he found himself being denied what he had always taken for granted. Where was that giving of the spirit as well as the body? Where was the assurance that makes a man feel the woman is his – totally and absolutely? Loving Catalina was an unnerving experience. The more he gave, the less he felt he possessed her.

When at last they married, he was deeply in love but took pains not to show just how much she meant to him. The truth was he did not trust her. It was ridiculous for a man of forty-five to feel like this, he told himself, but he had to protect himself. With time she will open out like a flower and when that last delicate petal of resistance unfurls, she will be mine, all mine – then, perhaps I can let go. But it never happened, so he held himself taut.

He was already fifty when their daughter was born. As he witnessed her screams and shared the birth pangs, he prayed the time had come. With this much wanted child, his wife's defences must drop and everything will change, he told himself. But there was no such moment of truth. Instead, she made such a feast with her eyes of the handsome consultant as he placed young Katy in her arms, he felt quite excluded. The subtle barrier Catalina had placed around herself had merely strengthened. Was it unreasonable to long to possess her soul as well as her body? Perhaps if she gave way, he would cease to care so much. Like most artists, he knew he could be selfish, he could also be jealous – was it this that kept everything so alive? Now, as his eyes strayed back to her perfect profile as she sat straight-backed, engrossed by their guests, he muttered to himself, 'Be thankful with what you've got, you ungrateful old bastard!'

Leah and Buster were hanging the last picture in the downstairs cloakroom when Howard and Benjie arrived back with a triumphal scrunch of tyres. 'About time too,' thought Leah, struggling with the black and decker while Buster held her ankles as she swayed at the top of the stepladder.

'The Boys are back,' he cried, peering out, 'I thought we'd lost them to the delights of the town!'

'Never mind the Boys,' Leah sounded caustic as she spat out wallplugs, 'Kindly keep a grip on my legs, if you don't mind.'

A moment later Howard strode into the room. 'Hi folks!' he was looking remarkably good-humoured. 'Hope you two didn't wait lunch on us.'

'We ain't had time for lunch,' retorted Leah from her dizzy height. 'Give me half a sec' and then we might fix some – I'm starving!'

'Count us out,' said Benjie with a hint of triumph, 'we've already been well entertained.'

'Judging by the look on their faces, I'll hazard a guess they've been boozing,' Buster let go of her ankles again.

'Aw c'mon now,' there was a plaintive cry from above, 'There's only one more to go! Just hold your horses a minute longer!'

There was a roar from the screwdriver as Leah stretched on tiptoe and threw herself into the job with titanic strength. 'I thought that gadget was supposed to make the whole thing easier,' said Buster as she finally returned to the ground, 'you've been dancing around up there like a cat on a hot tin roof.'

'Thanks a lot, ' said Leah, 'Is anyone going to make me a sarnie? I reckon I deserve it.'

'You sure do,' said Howard wandering around the small room to inspect the fruits of her labours. 'Why, you've got it all done! I'm sorry we've been away so long, I meant to lend a hand.'

'It's only a rest room,' said Leah, pleased to get a compliment.

'And it's the last room,' said Howard. 'Benjie, fix Leah a sandwich and let's have a decent jug of coffee out of decent cups…' he remembered the Spode on the McKays' table. 'And let's all sit down together for once in the *sala* and celebrate.'

It seemed odd sitting there, the four of them without tools or colour swatches in their hands. The room was huge and despite the sunshine pouring in at the open French windows, Leah shivered – she hadn't eaten and felt suddenly tired. As usual Buster was oblivious; it should have been him fixing the sandwich, surely? She must try to re-train him, now that he no longer had a job to do. He was such a restless soul, it shouldn't be too hard! As if reading her thoughts, he was already on his feet. 'You know we oughta be celebrating with something stronger than this,' he swirled the newly brewed coffee round in his mouth, 'What is this, anyway? Tastes kind of nauseous to me.'

'How can you say that?' cried Benjie, ruffling up, 'Howard and I bought it this morning in that cute little grocer's store in the plaza.'

'*Praça*,' corrected Howard quietly.

'As I was saying, it's Brazilian and the most expensive they sell. And I can vouch for it too,' he added darkly, 'I *know* my coffees.'

'Well I'm off to open a bottle of brandy,' said Buster, returning a moment later from the cellar. 'In future, count me out with all that imported stuff, I'm going to stick with Maxwell House.'

'But that's imported too dear,' Leah patted him on the knee. 'The trouble with you, hon, you've become over-civilised. You like everything instant, processed, out of a can! Left to your own devices, you'd be on junk foods and beverages for the rest of your life. We all of us need to go back to nature again. After all, wasn't that why we all came here?'

'Nope,' said Buster, sploshing out brandy into four cut glass balloons. 'And as for cans, this brandy certainly didn't come from one! You can bet your bottom dollar it won't leave scum on your mug either!' He threw a malignant look at Benjie's carefully chosen Royal Doulton coffee cups.

Howard could see a pink flush creep under Benjie's tan. As usual, he was taking Buster's complaints as a personal insult. His culinary efforts were a particularly sensitive subject. They had been down this road before, but Buster never learned. Was he really as thick-skinned as he made out, or was it a deliberate wind-up? Already, the familiar itch had started around Howard's wrists, working up the back of his hands at any hint of an atmosphere.

He eased himself forward in his Queen Anne chair. Leaning across to Buster, his voice dropped confidentially, 'Don't you want to hear how we got on in town this morning?'

'Sure! You mean you actually achieved something other than buying that stuff Benjie calls coffee?'

'Oh, now honey,' Leah put out a reproving hand, 'You know we've been dying to hear. Did you make any progress with the party list?'

'That's just what I was coming to,' Howard smiled with effort, 'we were extremely fortunate.' He proceeded to relate how they had met up with the celebrated Jock McKay, and been invited back to the artist's house.

'You'll just love Catalina!' said Benjie turning his back on Buster to talk to Leah. 'Not only is she very beautiful, but she's chic, vivacious and *so* amusing.'

'Very Latin,' put in Howard, 'really the complete antithesis to her rather dry Scottish husband – but you can see he's mad about her.'

'Sounds fascinating,' said Leah, 'your first expedition into the heart of the town and you end up lunching with a famous artist and his exotic wife! We'll have to invite them back as soon as possible. Did you suggest it?'

'No. They're not the sort of people you want to push too far for the first meeting,' said Howard. 'He's a real upper class type and I think he only took to us because he was trying to prove something to the guy who runs The Anchor. However,' he blinked and thought for a moment, 'I got the impression his wife was pretty curious about the house, so perhaps if you were to drop by – '

As expected, Leah picked up the cue. 'That's great, I'll go tomorrow then,' she said, enthusiastically, 'and what about the party? Did you run that idea past them?'

'Yes! That was quite a charade,' said Benjie, still ignoring Buster. 'We were just about to corner Captain Weaver, owner of the bar, when we got all these powerful vibes coming off McKay. He made it plain *he* would take care of everything and that Weaver would be quite the wrong person to consult … so much so, we might get lumbered with all the wrong people and be socially doomed forever.'

'My!' said Leah, impressed. 'What an escape!'

'Suffice to say, we've got a great list!' Benjie felt in his hip pocket and tossed some folded sheets of paper onto the coffee table. Three pages of thick parchment, covered in purple script from a bold and deliberate hand, opened under her careful fingers. Smoothing them out, she gave a low whistle of anticipation.

'That's right,' said Benjie proudly, 'she's done a real thorough job for us. Not only names and addresses, but all sorts of asides, explaining who's who. She said she felt it was important for us to have a little background on all concerned.'

'I'll say!' said Leah, skimming all six sides. 'Look, honey!' she tried to engage Buster who seemed loathe to make peace, 'this is a literary masterpiece… it reads like the social page from Vanity Fair. Here goes! …. *"number one – the Honourable Johanna Vincent, may have retired from screen and stage, but still stars in S. Felicia. Runs the ultra fashionable Estrela boutique. Without her, your party will be a social flop. Lavish her with compliments and champagne and you'll be success of the year!"* Wow!'

'That's what we said,' smiled Benjie, 'as she was reading out these snippets, her hubbie got fed up and left the room. I had the feeling he disapproved – she was a bit candid. After all, she doesn't know us from Adam!'

'She's seen the house though,' mused Howard, 'at least from the road.'

'Here's another interesting one,' Leah was intrigued, 'number five on the list, I wonder if it's in any order or just as it came into her head? "... *Wing Commander Eustace Stacey – once in jail for manslaughter after a duel, but got off.*" Golly! "*... flies own plane – comes and goes with the wind. Dabbles in politics, environmental issues, business interests in Morocco – nothing he doesn't know – a real character.*" I'll say!' She tried, but failed, to catch Buster's eye. What did it matter? – *she* was enjoying herself.

' *"Number nine... Mr and Mrs Grafton, very British, very dull, but you* need *them"* – underlined three times! '*You'll recognise her by her height, auburn hair and high pitched neigh...*" spelt NAY...' she grinned. "'*Mrs Grafton's brother is second in command at British Embassy in Lisbon, Sir John Warburton (ask him too but he won't come) but important he's asked and will ensure success with Graftons*"... my goodness, this seems to be getting quite political. Who's next? "*number ten ... Mr and Mrs Karl van der Stel – he's Dutch, early thirties, she's from London and very social ... so ask them and you'll be well in. They're good friends with J. V. and often team up together.*" '

Buster suddenly got up and paced around the back of Leah's chair. 'Are you sure we want to get involved with these people?' he sounded unamused. 'Not one of them sounds my sort, and if you ask me most of them could be thoroughly troublesome. You've already gotten us a murderer, an ageing, spoilt filmstar demanding instant champagne, some snooty Brits, what next I wonder?'

'Oh, stop being a spoilsport, honey, this is the greatest fun! Here we go again, "*Lucie and Sebastian*" – no surnames? "*They run S.F.'s biggest disco and will only come for the first half of the evening but they're very decorative! She drives a white MG, he's got a BMW motorbike so look out for them in the square. A bit spaced out, but they think they own the scene.*"'

'Well, that's it!' said Buster firmly. 'One gets the gist immediately. They'll be hip, spoilt and snorting, and I know about the drugs laws here ... invite these kids to our house and we'll be risking a police raid. I've been warned just how tough the PIDE can be!'

'The *who*?' said Benjie.

'*Polícia Internacional...* can't remember what the D and the E stand for – some department or another. They're not your usual police, they're the other lot, Gestapo style. They're there to keep the country clean and I'm all for that.'

Leah ignored him – 'Now this guy sounds fun,' she cried, '... number fourteen, "*Manolo Vaz Valqueiro, half Spanish, half Portuguese; half playboy, half architect*"... hmmmm, what a mixture ... and oh my! hear what Mrs McKay has to say about him ..."*seems very successful in both roles and in other departments! Gucci clothes, chiselled face, dark hair flecked with grey. Not very tall, but the girls go crazy for him!*" '

'Probably makes up for his size in other ways – I've heard of these gigolo types,' growled Buster, getting involved despite himself.

Howard threw him a cold look, 'Do you always have to be so negative?'

'I'd say positive,' said Buster. 'I never knew it was a fault to be over-endowed.'

Leah went quickly on, ' *"Number twenty-one, Gloria Baxter; bottle blonde, over-tanned, over-weight Texan, 29 and desperate for a husband...."* Do you think that's supposed to be bitchy?'

'What do *you* think?' said Buster.

'I doubt it,' said Benjie. 'Don't forget you haven't met her. Catalina's far too pretty to need to put other people down – she just tells it like it is.'

' *"Number twenty-three, Terence O'Connor – big, angular Irishman'*...there you are Howard,' Leah sounded excited, 'a fellow countryman ... *"runs the Maritimo Hotel when not attending shooting parties in the Al-en-te-jo ..."* have I prounounced that correctly? Maybe that explains why we never met him when we stayed there ... *"his pale blue eyes either repel or attract. Leave plenty of whiskey around and he'll be your friend for life!"* '

'And you say this woman's not being bitchy!' Buster made a show of rolling around with mirth.

'Please let me finish, hon,' said Leah reproachfully, 'There are several more names on this list but not all merit a comment. Uh-uh... here's one more... *"Senhor Miguel Mendoza, minister of tourism for the Algarve. It's protocol to invite him. Takes himself very seriously, no sense of humour etc but wife charming and speaks good English"* ... well that's a relief, people like him may well help us in the years to come, so we must be certain to include them. I think Mrs McKay's done a remarkable job and since we've ended on a charitable note, you can relax, Buster dear.'

'I'm perfectly relaxed,' he replied irritably. 'I still think this party's a crazy idea and I'm disappointed Howard's no longer of the same opinion. You've obviously allowed it to go to your heads being invited to this artist's house. The wife sounds a real stirrer and her choice of guests explosive.'

'You're making a mountain out of a molehill,' said Howard, worrying at his hands. 'I agree I thought the scheme hare-brained to start with, but since everyone's so interested in our house, the sooner we show them we're just ordinary folks, the better. With all this speculation around, we sure don't want people getting the wrong impression.'

'What exactly do you mean the "wrong impression"?' Buster was moving restlessly round the room, re-adjusting newly hung pictures. 'All I care is they acknowledge Casa Amarela has had more dollars poured into it than anything else on this god-darned coast. Sure, if they want to see it all for themselves – then I'm happy to welcome them. What I don't want is a whole lot of snobs making us feel we're lucky to have them in our house, just because they've got some title or other, or dodgy ties with some ambassador.'

'Honey, I'm sure there's no danger of that,' Leah was looking through her diary and had pinpointed a date. 'Now you guys, how about sending out our invitations for Saturday in a month's time? That way people will have enough warning and more important – it will give us a chance to let the house settle down. The garden is screaming for attention and by the time we've addressed that, we'll be crying out for a bit of fun. In fact –' she snapped the book shut and looked in a very penetrating way at her husband, 'I'm sure we're in for a real ball!'

There was an awkward silence. Finally Buster sat down again. 'OK, OK,' he conceded. 'Three against one, you'd better have it your way. At least we can show these European

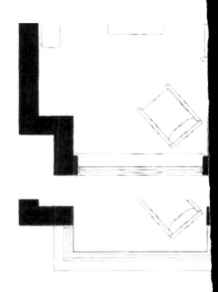

Backed by
HM Government

Help to Buy calculator

Floor Plan

stiff-necks just what American hospitality's all about … only – don't blame me if there are repercussions. With a mixture of guests like that – anything could happen.

15

*T*hat evening, Karl van der Stel opened the apartment door quietly to see his wife standing in the middle of the kitchen, a vacant expression on her face as she stirred a steaming pan. 'Gotcha!' he cried springing up behind her and bestowing a loud kiss on the back of her neck.

She dropped her spoon with a clatter, 'Bastard! You made me jump, I was miles away – dreaming of London!'

'Just for a change,' he smiled, extricating himself from her arms to pour two beers from the fridge. Exhausted, he leant against a unit and pulled her towards him, 'That'll cool you down, my babe.'

I'm not sure I want to be cooled down, thank you,' she said. 'What sort of day have you had?'

'So, so,' he replied, 'but I'm getting bogged down at the *Camera*. They've had our plans now for over ten weeks, but when I went to see the president, he said they were still on his deputy's desk. Nothing on God's green earth will persuade him to see them firsthand.'

'But you gave him a case of Bols liqueur only a week ago! Wasn't that supposed to hurry things up?'

'Oh yeah, it will when he gets his hands on them – we had a wink and a nod about that – but the problem is the in-between stages. I should have given the deputy and his lads the same treatment!'

'It makes you sick,' said his wife. 'Everything's so venal and backward here. It's a wonder any development gets off the ground.'

'Oh, but it does,' said Karl, 'you just have to know how far to oil the wheels. How do you think places like Club Varra got started or Golf-a-Go-Go? August will be the worst month as all the civil servants shut up their offices and go to the beach – but at least I've got everything in well in advance.'

'Hmph!' snorted Jacqueline, 'and when finally you've sweated blood, sweat and tears to get your precious development on the map, who do you think will get all the reward? Not the poor fool who's taken all the flak, but the Chairman sitting on his backside in Rotterdam plus a select few on the Board.'

'That's the way it goes. But you seem to have forgotten the shareholders darling, of which you're one!'

'I know,' she plopped onto his knee as he sank onto the sofa. 'It's just I'm hot and fed up – particularly with this climate, this apartment and Santa Felicia.

'You don't know how lucky we are,' he sighed, 'most people would give their eye teeth to work in the sun.'

'Hmmm,' was all she said and went back to her stirring.

Half an hour later she was in the best of humours. Placing the casserole in the oven, she talked of dropping in on Johanna Vincent whom she'd met in the market that morning. For once she had enough tact not to remind him that in Johanna, she found a little of what she most missed about London – sophistication, wit and West End gossip.

He sighed. Brain-dead from driving up and down the coast, a frustrating meeting at the town hall and juggling figures with his secretary, he longed for nothing better than a relaxed evening in his own home. Yet despite himself, Karl found himself agreeing. Jacqueline would be hell for the rest of the evening if they did not go out first. 'Give me ten minutes to shower and change, babe, and I'll be with you,' he said wearily, stripping off his shirt.

The friendship between the ex-actress and the van der Stels had sprung up since the young couple had first moved to Santa Felicia. Karl's company rented their flat in a modern condiminium five minutes down the tree-lined avenue that led to Johanna's house. This had resulted in a regular dropping-in for the two women who seemed to find such social interaction vital to their wellbeing. But the men too found Johanna hard to resist. Not only was she funny, she was well-read and well-travelled. As she etched out chunks of her life from high society England to the inner workings of Hollywood, interspersed by tales of India, the Argentine and colonial Kenya, people were hooked. Quite simply, Johanna appeared to have known everywhere and everyone at some time in her incredible life.

For her part, there was a compulsive need to be surrounded by young, attractive people. It boosted her own ego, enabling her to forget that her sixtieth birthday was just around the corner, as she blossomed in the warm admiration of her young satellites. A form of mutual flattery existed, accentuated by their somewhat artificial circumstances. There were times however when Johanna preferred solitude. Recently, she had taken to writing poetry. Being who she was, she had no doubt that when the time came, a publisher would appear and embrace her work with open arms. Such were the rewards of stardom. Money was not an issue; it was the satisfaction of being creative that drove her. It was also an ideal excuse for people with whom she had no inclination to spend time '… I'm *so* sorry darlings; I'd love to come to dinner, drinks, your coffee morning – but there's no way! You see I'm *writing* at the moment.' And if a member of the Women's Institute, the Anglo-Portuguese Society, or the English church in the Algarve dared to call without an appointment, it would be… 'I'd dearly love to discuss your fete and invite you in, but I simply can't – you see, the *Muse* is upon me!'

But the 'Muse' was rarely upon her when certain colourful people such as Lucie and Sebastian who ran the disco or close neighbours Karl and Jacqueline van der Stel called. If indeed it threatened to hover, she could easily sweep it aside for an enjoyable hour or two. On this particular evening, there seemed no evidence of the Muse at all and Johanna was clearly in sociable mood. She had spotted the top of Karl's tall frame over the bouganvillea-clad wall and waved gaily from the herbaceous border as they trudged up the steep road below her villa. 'Come through the garden gate, darlings! No point going all the way round!'

As they edged through a narrow iron gate set in a stone archway, she had reached the top of the terrace, looking as fragile and lovely as the bunch of roses and peonies she'd just gathered. Karl went to kiss her, with a smile 'I'm not sure which smells sweeter, you or the flowers. Are you in competition?'

She gurgled up at him with delight; this was the kind of compliment she enjoyed. She greeted Jacqueline with equal warmth before floating ahead of them into the drawing-room, a willowy figure in a flowing cream garment of *crèpe-de-chine*, a trail of perfume and hint of powder trailing in her wake. Karl winked at his wife as he was despatched to do the drinks. There were a couple of bottles of Bollinger in the fridge, and they were on the point of opening the second when they heard a tap on the door. Without waiting for an answer, in strolled Catalina McKay. 'Anyone at home?' she cooed, seeing full well there was. Before anyone could speak, she exclaimed, 'You mustn't send me away, because I'm simply bursting with news!'

'You are, darling?' Johanna, unperturbed by the intrusion, lifted a cool cheek to be kissed. 'Then no doubt we will hear all about it in a moment. But first, Karl will give you a drink and then we can all sit back comfortably and no doubt you'll begin!'

Catalina had stopped halfway across the room to fondle the bunch of roses which lay momentarily forgotten on top of the Bechstein. 'Don't you want to do anything with these?' she said, her eyes round with concern as though she had just stumbled across some orphan children.

'Oh, bless you darling,' Johanna shot Jacqueline a meaningful glance, ' Yes of course… pop them in water, will you?'

Catalina took her time with the flowers waiting for them to get impatient. She loved to be the instigator of fresh gossip, particularly amongst these three. The Algarve was still a small place and news travelled quickly up and down the coast. At last, she conceded to join them on a sofa. Smoothing her skirt she began, 'Jock and I had two most interesting visitors in our house today; Americans – New York it seems – a *Senhor* McDermott and Liebermann. You know them?'

She paused just long enough for Jacqueline to open her mouth, but before any words came out, Catalina continued. 'A most charming pair! They've just moved into the neighbourhood and it would appear we were the first people they chose to call upon. What could we do other than invite them to join us for lunch?' Catalina's English could sound quite stilted which added a degree of theatre to this small speech. She swung her raven hair over her shoulder and looked at them narrowly to see how her revelation might be received. 'Of course – I may be quite wrong – perhaps you've already had the pleasure?'

'No-o,' said Karl, 'Who are they?'

'What sort of age, darling?'

'Where do they live? You don't mean the *yellow* house on the hill?' Jacqueline could scarcely keep the indignation from her voice now she was allowed to speak.

'One at a time, please!' Catalina gestured restraint. 'Yes, they are indeed from the yellow house and they're well-known international designers. They know Jock's work of course! So apparently do the others, the Bloomfields, whom we are to meet shortly – collectors of antiques and all things rare. We were left in *no* doubt of that. As for their age – they have an air of having made it in their world – but I'd hate to guess. I theenk…' she gave herself a little shake – as though preening her feathers, thought Karl – ' I'd rather say no more and let you judge the "whole outfeet" – as Jock calls it – for yourselves.'

'Outfit? Christ!' said Jacqueline, wondering why she felt so irritated.

Ignoring her, Catalina couldn't resist, 'They do seem an unusual pair – for *here* I mean – but they're knowledgeable They talked art all through lunch which would normally bore me rigid but I haven't seen Jock so animated for ages and I have to say I rather liked them too.'

'What do you mean "unusual"?' Johanna pounced on the word and looked at her sternly. 'I have a feeling, Catalina darling, you're holding something back. Now out with it!'

Very few people could outstare Johanna's sharp grey eyes for long. With the habit of turning quickly to ice, they had no effect whatsoever on Catalina. She simply responded by opening her own very wide indeed and adding sweetly, 'There's really nothing more to say – you must judge for yourselves. Besides, you will soon have the opportunity. I've given them your names for their party leest!'

'Their *what?*' Jacqueline exploded. She had listened intently and now felt exasperated by Catalina's air of mystery and importance.

'But of course!' Catalina returned. 'One has to have a leest if one is to throw a party. They're having a house-warming, don't you see?'

Catalina was able to see one of the Bloomfields much sooner than anticipated. She was just putting the finishing touches to her face the following morning when the doorbell rang. Leaving the hard-working Philismena to answer as usual, she popped her head out of an upstairs window to see if it was anyone interesting. Outside stood a brand new red Opel, not a speck of sand on its shining chrome. Its owner was looking up anxiously at the door. It was a woman she'd never set eyes on before. Catalina just had time to take in a neat auburn head, the hair scraped back into a pony-tail, large dark glasses perched on top, and from her perspective, a pair of slim shoulders in what looked like a safari dress, pale khaki and neatly belted at the waist. The image was one of understated efficiency. A moment later, Philismena had admitted their visitor to the hall.

Never one to hurry in the mornings, Catalina returned to study her reflection in Jock's shaving glass and fancied she saw a small stray hair in her eyebrow line. Once eradicated, she pouted once or twice to ensure her lipstick was matte, and satisfied at last, was about to set off downstairs when she heard the doorbell again. This time she saw the postman, but instead of departing, he was hovering expectantly beside his bicycle. There must be something to sign for – perhaps it was exciting!

With a final glance in the mirror, she clicked her way down to the hall on high-heeled scarlet sandals, noticing to her satisfaction that their visitor had been shown into the morning room. '*Bom dia,*' she said as she opened the door, bestowing such a radiant smile on the young man that a slow blush spread up from under his collar. A trace of Chanel wafted over him and he noticed the *senhora* was in tight denims and a tank-top which usually indicated she would be out in the boat later in the day. Everyone knew *Dona* Catalina's little motor vessel, the *Andorinha,* and with so many fishing folk amongst the community, word soon got round when she was out in the bay. For her part, Catalina found it useful to be friendly with the tradespeople. She tipped them well at New Year and always seemed interested in their news, particularly as to who was in town and what might be going on.

Philismena bustled to her side to deal with the man plus his *aviso* slip which her mistress was now signing with a flourish. She noted it was for *Senhor* Jock and reproached herself for not having got there first since she strongly disapproved of this younger generation of public servants. Too often they looked one in the eye with a boldness that was unbecoming and as with this one, tended to linger when their business was done. With the door firmly shut, Catalina had lost interest and as they crossed the hall, was informed of a *Senhora* Bloomfield, '...*uma senhora norte-american... penso...*' awaiting her attention.

With a small sigh of satisfaction, Catalina uptilted her chin and sailed into the morning-room. Shoulders firm and square, she outstretched her hands in welcome. 'Mrs Bloomfield, this is indeed a pleasant surprise! How very nice of you to call!'

Leah whirled round from the casement window where she'd been admiring the harbour below. For once she was speechless. Benjie and Howard had enthused so much about Mrs McKay's beauty, she had built up a completely different image. She had been expecting a tall, aristocratic beauty with aquiline features, similar to the top Italian models from *Signors* Pucci or Schiaparelli, for whom she had provided some of her best Florentine pieces for photo-shoots. Instead, here was a curvaceous kitten of a woman, not exactly short, but certainly not tall, despite the high heels. If one was looking for the perfect figure, one might have lopped a few inches off the bust and most definitely the hips. Nevertheless, she had a tiny waist and the wrists and ankles were slim and delicate. Undeniably, the slightly square face was very lovely and a firm jaw line showed determination and character. But it was the combination of porcelain skin, luxuriant hair and amazing eyes that gave the allure of real beauty. She could well understand why the two Boys had been captivated by this fascinating creature. Great limpid pools of dark, peaty brown, the eyes set wide apart over a pert, retrousse nose, gave the whole visage a sensuous look.

Interest was already leaping in those eyes which Leah could equally imagine flashing with passion once their owner was aroused. It was extraordinary how catlike they became, opening wide as they were now, but no doubt having the capability also to narrow and harden. As for the curving mouth, hinting at a smile, the full underlip spoke of temptation and promise and Leah was reminded of a big cat, licking its lips and lying in waiting. Was it ridiculous to imagine that the woman before her could devour whatever prey she fancied in one delicate snap of that pretty but highly efficient jaw?

Realising that she had stared rather too long to be polite, Leah hurried forward to grip the outstretched hands. The younger woman kissed her coolly on both cheeks, then turned to survey her in a rather calculated way. 'So you are the famous Mrs Bloomfield?' she smiled, fluttering thick, sooty lashes. 'Howard and Benjie had so much to tell me about you. I learned you were one of the most successful business women in New York – so frankly, I admit, I was terrified to meet you!'

Looking anything but terrified she beckoned Leah to a window seat and they sat in opposite corners of a curving bay, facing each other at half angles. 'You'll have morning coffee of course?' Catalina said formally.

'Love some,' replied Leah, feeling oddly nervous.

There was an awkward little silence filled by Catalina getting up and calling instructions in Portuguese through the open door. By the time she returned, so had Leah's confidence and she was eager to talk. 'I can't tell you how pleased I am to be here…we've only been in Santa Felicia a few weeks, but what with the move and so on, it's been non-stop. Incarcerated with only three men for company has its drawbacks. Indeed, it's been stifling and I never thought I'd miss female company so much! I never had much time for girlfriends but funnily enough, it's the small talk I've missed – my secretary's outpourings about her boyfriend, our accounts lady discussing her hair. Always the one to provide a listening ear and dish out advice, it never occurred to me I might actually miss that.'

'I understand,' said Catalina slowly. 'Well – never mind – we shall just have to make up for it here! Maybe I can come to you with all of *my* problems!' She laughed a little too glibly, and there was a steely edge to her voice.

'Mrs McKay, I'm sure you are the very last person to have problems. No, it might well be the other way round. Don't forget I'm painfully new to life in Europe. If you'll permit – I'll probably come running to you for all sorts of advice.'

Coffee arrived on a spotless tray cloth of fine lace, and Catalina noticed her guest popping a small blue pill into her mouth. Never able to restrain her curiosity, she said in a concerned voice, 'Oh dear, I hope you do not have the headache. I see you must take a peell.'

'Thankfully no,' said Leah, 'You see, I never get simple heachaches, but I do suffer from migraines. Heavens no, that was just a "tranquie"…to counteract the black coffee, you know. I ought really to drink decaff, the other stuff winds me up so much … but I always forget and anyway, this tastes so much nicer.'

'A "tranquie"?' Catalina looked perplexed.

'Sure! You know – a calmer – that sort of thing. Some people take valium, I have my own prescription mix. They're fairly mild on the whole but they do help to keep me tranquil – hence the name. Yeah – don't say it,' she put out a pleading hand, 'it's shocking to need anything, I know, but I'm weaning myself off them. In New York I was sometimes on six a day but you should have seen our lifestyle! That's one of the reasons we came here, to leave all that kind of pressure behind.'

'I see,' said Catalina, thoughtfully.

Leah felt both guilt and embarassment for being caught in the act by someone she'd only just met – and for going to such lengths to explain. It did not occur to her that most people would have resisted asking such a personal question. She changed the subject swiftly. 'I must congratulate you, Mrs McKay, on that party list you sent back with the Boys. It's a masterpiece! If you don't mind my saying so, you've missed your vocation in life! I'm sure you'd make a first rate society columnist – your observations are so telling.'

As Catalina said nothing but simply raised her immaculate eyebrows, she found herself gushing on. 'You'll be glad to hear we've already designed the invitation. Benjie and I sat up most of last night until we'd got it just perfect. The hotel will help us over the printing – I nipped in there before coming here. It's kind of exciting planning a party. You don't know how fortuitous we all felt it was, Mrs McKay, the two Boys meeting up with your husband like that.'

'Please call me Catalina. Algarve society is very informal, you know.'

It was almost a put-down and again Leah felt a sense of not being fully in control. This was very alien to someone used to taking the lead. 'How kind,' she muttered and before she had even weighed up the matter, the words were out, 'Look! I know we scarcely know each other, but if you've nothing else to do, you might like to come back with me now and see the house. I can drive you up, show you around – if you can bear the fact it's still kind of shambolic – at least in the garden, builders' stuff everywhere; but it will give you an idea. I'd love you to meet my husband Buster and by the time you've been over the villa and we've had a drink together, it'll be lunchtime. You might manage a snack? Then, it'll just be a case of running you home after coffee. How does that suit?'

Catalina thought rapidly. She had planned to take the boat out, but it was already very hot and that could easily be put off. Jock was bound to be out most of the morning and she did not even have a magazine to read. Yes! she thought. Seize the moment! Nothing she could think of right now would amuse her half as much and how it would annoy Jacqueline van der Stel and that stuck up Lucie Prescott-Adams at the discothèque. Even Johanna would be impressed that she, Catalina McKay, had been invited – ahead of everyone else – to the house that had been the talk of the town since Christmas.

'All right,' she said at length. 'Provided there's nothing in my diary.' She moved to her desk while Leah watched, wishing she hadn't sounded so keen. Finally, the book was snapped shut. 'There's nothing here that can't wait a day or so,' she smiled. 'Philismena will "hold the fort" as they say, and I'll leave a note for Jock. But otherwise…' she turned and beamed so sunnily that Leah immediately felt herself relax, 'there's nothing I'd like more!'

Tearing some paper from a pad, she scribbled a hurried note to her husband, pulled a form from her hip pocket and folded it in. 'Let me warn you about these,' she said as Leah looked on, 'they're called *avisos*, and if there's anything at all to collect at the post office, you have to go there and sign yourself. They simply will not deliver. It's the most tiresome thing, because it can be anything from a small parcel to a registered envelope containing a bill. In this case, it looks like a telegram… for my husband,' she added.

'A telegram?' said Leah, 'Oh dear! I hope it's not urgent.'

'Very unlikely,' said Catalina. 'Jock gets them all the time. He can pick it up when he collects Katy from school. They're normally from his agent about the next exhibition and only sent because international phone calls are so difficult from here. Santa Felicia has precious few lines per head of population as you've no doubt noticed. I sometimes think nothing short of a revolution will make this government move into the new age of tourism and telecommunications.'

And with that, she deposited her note on the hall table and without a backward glance, followed her new friend out to the waiting car.

Provided he wasn't hung over, McKay always considered the early part of the morning the best part of his day. It was cool enough to walk, which made him hanker after those long tramps at Lochaig, through fern and heather, mist or rain. But for all his longings homeward, he enjoyed what Santa Felicia had to offer. The fresh Atlantic air, long golden sands and the hustle and bustle of a small market town as she wakens to a new day, was clean and wholesome – balm to the soul. He also enjoyed having his small daughter to himself. The *Escola Primaria* was on the other side of town and they would stop to look at all manner of things along the way. He tried to answer her many questions with enough imagination to make an impact – just as his father had done for him. It was those childhood memories that had most sustained him during the war; one never knew in life how much one relied upon the past.

They could leave their home by a number of routes and today they zig-zagged down the steps below their street, along the bay when the tide was out and thence to the harbour. Whilst the men busied themselves with their vessels, the older women sat by the quay, mending nets. When Jock and his daughter passed by, they would look up and shake their heads wistfully; one silvery head, one of pure gold – and the father past his prime. It showed the old genes could still carry their mark, they remarked sagely to each other.

'Why do they all wear black, Papa? Mama never wears black, does she?'

'No, you're right Catkin, she doesn't. But then Mama likes gay colours and bright, pretty things … just like her,' he suggested.

'Don't these people like pretty things?'

'I'm sure they do, but everyone lives their lives differently. When one of their relations dies for instance, they wear black as a sign of respect.'

'Why?' said the child. 'Would the dead person want them in black – *all* the time?'

He wasn't sure himself and said so. 'Now! Let's see if we can spot our favourite red boat from here! As usual he was first out of the harbour today, so maybe you can spot him on the horizon.'

'He's not there, Papa,' she screwed up her eyes and wrinkled a small freckled nose against the glare. 'Maybe he's gone past the horizon. What happens after the horizon, Papa?'

'Sometimes I wonder,' said her father, marvelling how often she caught him out.

'Don't you know, Papa?' she looked at him curiously. Oh … look! there *is* the red boat!' she was tugging at his sleeve. 'Just below that cloud shaped like a caterpillar.'

He thought he saw it, but his eyes were not as sharp as hers. Instead he heard in his mind the lyrics of a song which had haunted him when he was courting her mother. '… I've looked at clouds from both sides now … I really don't know clouds … a-at all … ' and the disappointment when she caught him singing it. 'It's not clouds, Jock,' she laughed gaily up at him, 'You are funny sometimes. It's love! *'I really don't know love … a-at all!''*

'Same thing!' he had said defensively. 'What does it matter anyway? It sounded like clouds – we all have different perceptions of the same thing.' All this reminded him now of a moment by the fireside last winter; he in his deep chair dozing, Katy on his knee wide-awake. She had clutched hold of him and cried, 'Papa, look quickly! There's a dragon in the fire and he's fighting a bull. There's a castle behind with people looking out! Oh do look Papa, before they all go!' He had followed her pointing finger into the glowing embers, but although there were many shapes and patterns, he could discern no dragon, no bull, not even a paltry castle.

Nearby in the *praça*, the church bell was chiming nine. 'Come on, Catkin, we're late again!' and together they hurried up the hill, hand in hand. Out of breath – he from his cigarettes, she from her short little legs pumping over the cobbles – they reached the school gate; he was pleased to see some colour flooding into her normally pale cheeks.

'Bye, bye Papa, see you at tea-time,' she raced ahead to join her friends at the top of the steps, then turned and waved. A moment later she was swept away in a gaggle of neat white tunics, dark heads and fair, all merging and rushing to the sound of the bell.

For once on his way home, he did not stop at The Anchor. Seeing only Weaver and a crony, he resisted the temptation of a cold lager. Two doors along at the *papelaria*, his eyes skimmed the headlines. The English dailies were always late, the American ones even more so; both were expensive, so he preferred to get his news at six o'clock from the BBC World Service. He was just translating the headlines of *Le Monde* as the English broadsheets were carried out. You couldn't miss the heavy print ... *Chancellor Hits Landowners – Rates Destined To Rise'*. Bastards! ... he'd been warned about this. Grudgingly, he dug out a few coins from his jeans pocket and picked up the paper as though it smelt unpleasant. There was an empty table at the cafe on the main square, so he settled himself into an iron chair with an *espresso*, wondering grimly what new treat the Chancellor had laid in store for people like him.

At the other end, the market had got into full swing. The last tractor had been unloaded long ago and with wooden stalls groaning under their load of fresh produce, the traders argued amongst themselves over the fixing of the day's prices. The farmers had already been paid off and their empty carts were now rumbling their dusty way out of town and back to their scattered hamlets. Many travelled as much as 40 kilometres a day from Loulé, Messines, Quarteira and Boliqueime and back again. For them life began around three in the morning and for centuries, the same families had lovingly tended what was known as the 'Garden of Portugal' but the profits were small.

It was a different story for the stall-keepers. Tourism had endowed them with endless opportunity and a cunning that many resented. Not wishing to lose the goodwill of the townsfolk, most kept their prices at a reasonable level until the locals had finished their shopping. The canniest of the ex-pats knew about this, and sent their maids. Philismena had already been down before breakfast. After that, the chalked prices on each vendor's slate would be carefully rubbed out and re-written at a vastly inflated price for the rest of the day. The usual mark up was fifty per cent; sometimes in the afternoon, it might have reached a hundred.

Altering the fixed price was illegal, but the authorities turned a blind eye. It was not unusual to see the chief of police dipping a hand into a basket of cherries or apricots as he passed along the line of stalls. A box of fresh goose eggs, or some fig and almond sweetmeats would appear at the guard-room door. McKay had once observed an open fight between a vendor and a young farmer over this very matter. The lad had hung around the market place and seen his melons priced up not once, not twice but three times in as many hours. Seething over the injustice, he had seen red and set in with his fists. As the vendor bewailed his innocence, the black-booted *Guarda* had hauled the young man off to the cells in a very heavy-handed way. There was nothing McKay could do about it, but his sympathy was all for the farmer and he felt a burning resentment against the authorities and a system which permitted such corruption.

Today, McKay's thoughts were too riveted on the plight of British farmers to consider their counterparts in the sun. Too stubborn to wear glasses, he held his newspaper stiffly in front of him and scrutinised the business pages. The overall picture looked bleak and he felt a great cloud of gloom settle over his shoulders. He tried to shrug off the feeling by turning to the gossip column and read an amusing snippet about his cousin's youngest and prettiest daughter canoodling at a West End club with one of the country's more foul-mouthed football stars of the moment.

Unfortunately, the tabloid – already two days old – did not run a stock market report, but not to worry. The last time a Financial Times had come their way, he'd noticed his recently acquired shares in the National Family Insurance & Assurance Company had climbed nicely – just as predicted by that bright young spark he'd been fortunate enough to meet on the plane last summer. In fact, if shares continued at this rate, their return to Lochaig might soon be within reach. What a remarkable achievement that would be – especially when he had sworn not to go until everything was paid off.

Two Gauloises later, he folded up the paper with a withering grunt. Homeward bound, his thoughts continued to hover around finance and tax; he really ought to bring himself to have a serious talk with Catalina, however distasteful the 'money subject'. He might catch her before she went out on the boat. She'd been spending far too freely of late and he should seize the opportunity. After all, she was the one who insisted Lochaig was their rightful home and how she looked forward to bringing up Katy in more suitable surroundings. 'We can give house-parties and breeng her out into society,' she had day-dreamed. 'I can learn to shoot and wear tweeds. I shall go to the very best tailor in London and have proper breeches made up. I always theenk those natural dyes – heather and bracken and so on – go well with my skeen. Can't you just see me darling, posing by the loch on my shooting steeck?'

He had to smile. Real life in the Highlands wasn't quite like that, but he had no wish to kill off her dreams. Instead, he determined to enlist the help of Philismena so that even if the clothes budget did not come up to scratch, savings could be made elsewhere. Prawns instead of caviar, mackerel rather than salmon, and those expensive fillet steaks might just be 'out of stock'. He should have done this long ago.

He quickened his step, anxious to get it all over, now that he'd made the decision. Arriving at the house in record time, he found Philismena polishing the brass door knocker. It was in the shape of a woman's hand and livened up the plain front door. With a nod of his head, he hurried past her. The elderly woman followed him in, slow and bulging in her grey dress, a large white apron around what once had been a waist. McKay noticed the gnarled old hands, clutching the duster and there was a tired look in her eyes. He had no right ever to complain, he thought suddenly guilty; she was loyal and decent and never stopped working. 'The *senhora* went out, sir' she said in Portuguese, 'she left you a message.'

'Hell and damnation!' thought McKay, 'just when I've worked up the guts to do what I should have done years ago.' He saw the note, tucked under the feet of a clawed cache-pot on the hall table and took it to the window. Normally, Catalina's rounded childish hand made him chuckle. Today it did not even bring a twinkle to his eyes.

'Darling,' it read, '*Such an extraordinary person has called to take me to lunch. Mrs. Bloomfield from Casa Amarela! It's too hot for the beach so I'm off to see the famous house on the hill! I have instructed P. to make you a sandwich. Have a nice day! C.*' There were two X's after her initial and then a postcript . *'There's a telegram to be collected from the post office – as usual it's addressed to you!'*

'Thanks very *much*!' exclaimed McKay so loudly that Philismena, struggling to pick up the *aviso* which had fallen to the floor, clutched at her heart. She had a bad feeling about this one, and avoiding his eye, scuttled away to the basement. A second later, the front door banged and she heard the elderly Mercedes starting up.

'Of all the selfish, self-centred, thoughtless women I've ever known, Catalina really takes the biscuit,' said McKay, hitting the accelerator savagely and careering back down the street. 'A more unnatural wife would be hard to find! She could have met me with the car, so we could get the cable together. Someone may have died for all she cares.'

By the time he arrived in a cloud of dust outside the post office, he had worked out most of his anger on the car. As he climbed out of the open coupé, he caught a glimpse of himself in the driving mirror. Tense and ebullient, his hair stood up in spikes, sand clung to his eyebrows and around the cracks of his mouth and he wiped it all off with a handkerchief and took a deep breath. 'It's probably nothing, nothing at all.'

He read the crude message then and there; a reply might be needed. But none was necessary. The message from his accountant was sufficient unto itself. *' … Regret inform you N.F.I & A.Co. crashed on the market yesterday. F.T. writes of seven day wonder. Many casualties and public outcry. Enquiry promised. Suspected fraud. See little hope of salvage but will keep you informed. Very sorry. Jeremy.'*

16

'And what did you do after that?' said Buster, getting up to refill her glass.

'After? It's a long story,' tinkled Catalina, her eyes brimfull of merriment, 'but basically, that was when Jock asked me to be his wife – arriving just at the right moment, like a guardian angel sent from heaven. Indeed, I don't know what I would have done if he hadn't. After all I was in a strange country, with my parents threatening to cut off my money. And yet I was determined not to go home. London was much too much fun to give up. Also, I doubted my parents would have wanted me back!'

'Why ever not?' Leah sounded shocked.

'After being sent down? Oh no, in those days it didn't do to get locked out more than three times in a row and I wasn't one of those boyish English girls who could climb up drainpipes.'

'That's obvious!' said Buster approvingly.

'So you might say I disgraced the family,' Catalina said, without a trace of regret. 'But it was their own fault for making such a thing of it. My parents never stopped telling all their colleagues and friends in Oporto what a brilliant scholar they had for a daughter and how she was the first in the neighbourhood to get accepted for a master's at an English university, but it all – how you say? – rebounded on them. You should never boast – certainly not about brains. It's like saying our genes are superior to yours and people don't like that.'

'So Jock saved the day!' said Benjie. 'What were you studying?'

'Why English, of course,' smiled Catalina. 'And with Jock it was real! I enjoyed more theatre and discussion – real dialogue, I mean – politicians, poets, artists and so on – than any university could offer.'

'I'll bet, ' remarked Buster and after a pregnant pause added, 'In the army they called it the university of life – if you know what I mean.'

Catalina giggled and raised huge sparkly eyes to him, 'You have such a funny way with words!'

'But how exactly did you *meet*, honey,' said Leah swiftly.

'It was rather romantic,' said Catalina, 'In fact it all began in a cathedral in Kent.'

'Wow!' said Leah.

'That's different,' said Benjie.

'Kent! Where the hell's that – not of the cigarettes, I take it?' said Buster.

'Heavens no!' Catalina giggled again and Buster looked gratified. It made a change to see someone actually enjoy his little asides; most of the time he was treated like a buffoon.

What they didn't see was his desperation to lighten the atmosphere – they could all be so deadly serious.

'As I was saying,' Catalina gave herself a little shake, 'I was down in Kent, writing a thesis on Chaucer. I went to spend a day at Canterbury, and there – of all the unlikely places – I met Jock. He was painting in the cathedral.'

'How amazing,' said Leah, 'Was it a whirlwind courtship?'

'You could say,' said Catalina carefully, 'and it was ultimately Jock's fault I got sent down. Yes, I'd been in trouble before – quite a lot…' again the tinkly laugh, 'and since I'd been gated and warned, I told him so. But he would insist I stayed out, so I guess – when the crunch came,' they all held their breath, 'he felt duty bound to marry me!'

'He'd have been mad not to,' said Buster.

Catalina accepted the compliment and folded her hands demurely in her lap. In silent agreement – thought Howard – this lady sure is sure of herself. He'd noticed it before on the terrace of their town house, but was surprised how quickly she'd sucked in the Bloomfields too. If she could do that with strangers… what chance for a single man like McKay? All that seduction and wanton beauty, artists are generally vulnerable. No doubt he was still suffering from the effect!

'But weren't your family a little concerned about the age gap?' Leah was trying to be tactful. Hang on… thought Howard, aren't we going in a little too deep?

'Concerned!' trilled Catalina, not in the least ruffled, 'they were horrified! But they came round in the end. We finally took my parents to see Lochaig and that clinched it, as you Americans say. I think they relished the idea of their daughter in a castle.'

'How sad that you've never lived there,' said Leah sympathetically, 'It sounds a wonderful place.'

'Oh it is,' said Catalina, 'and whilst I think I may die from the cold, in a funny way I want to be there almost as much as Jock. It's been a dream for years. The only time I've seen Jock really happy is at Lochaig. The years drop off him as he strides through the heather – there's a real spring in his step. We don't go much, at least not Katy and me. Jock goes alone and does manly things – the estate and so on – we stay in London and shop. I think it's all too painful for him to go as a family, knowing it's only temporary, and not for real. At least… not yet.'

She broke off, looking pensive; they all regarded her with wonder. Clearly the trilling laughter and the coyness was skin deep; underneath there was something much stronger, at which they could only guess.

'I can just see you as the mistress of a Scottish mansion,' Buster muttered, serious for once. 'It would suit you, standing at the top of a great stone staircase, receiving your humble guests.'

'You make it sound daunting, hon,' said Leah disapprovingly.

Catalina laughed a dry little laugh. 'Oh never fear – there is very leetle that daunts me. And certainly not that kind of thing. In fact that is the part I should enjoy the most. Mistress of all I survey! Rather exciting, don't you think?'

Again there was silence as they thought about it. Each one of them had a clear image of Catalina, the châtelaine, dark, ravishing and beautifully in control. Only the backdrop to this picture of material bliss differed sharply. For Leah, it was dramatically Gothic –

solid grey walls, escutcheon-clad, overhung by gargoyles. For Benjie, it was Beverley Hills, all pink sandstone and turrets by the dozen, spindly and slender. For Howard, it was something between a French chateau and an English country house, whilst all Buster could see was a misty edifice rising up out of water. The only clear part was Catalina herself, her head thrown back in triumph as guest after guest came forth to bow over and kiss an outstretched white hand.

Suddenly Leah burst out, 'You know, it's a cruel thing to say, but I hope you don't get your dream-come-true too soon! We've only just gotten to know you and I had hoped we might get to know you both a whole lot better. Please say you're not planning on going back this year, just when we've all arrived.'

'Heavens no!' said Catalina, tossing her mane of hair over one shoulder. 'I cannot see any possibility for at least eighteen months. Much depends on Jock's annual exhibition. It's scheduled for Christmas but he'll need more under his belt, as they say, before any possible move to Scotland. So you see,' she smiled, 'you may indeed have to endure the pleasure of our company for some time.'

'That's good,' said Howard mildly, keen to diffuse Leah's over-show of enthusiasm, 'but seriously, none of us would deny you the chance to achieve your dream. It must be very hard for your husband to have waited so long.'

Catalina shrugged. 'Jock's a brilliant artist,' she said, 'but if he'd been more of a business man we might have been esconced there long ago. Dreams are all very well, but they can be very wearing for everyone.'

'Now it's funny you should say that,' said Leah placing a confiding hand on Catalina's knee, 'but that's exactly what I felt. OK, OK, the circumstances are all different, but we four had a dream too. And by golly, we had to work our butts off to realise it. But if it's perseverance you're after, you need look no further than these four faces!'

Buster was on his feet, desperate to stop his wife before she adopted the moral tone that was bound to follow this revelation. He always blamed her lecturing parents for a habit of patronising every person that came their way. 'I'll tell you a story about perseverance,' he said jauntily, 'it's what we call a shaggy dog story but it ain't half funny.'

'If it's the one I'm thinking of,' said Leah, 'I very much doubt Catalina would want to hear it.'

'Oh come, come,' said Buster, a glint in his hazel eyes, 'Mrs McKay's a liberated lady, unless I'm much mistaken.'

'But that's not a story for a lady,' said his wife. 'It's a man's joke.'

'And not very funny for men,' muttered Howard.

'Don't worry,' Catalina gave her hostess's arm a squeeze, 'Let him tell it if he wants to.'

Leah sighed. Howard left the room and Benjie began stacking the coffee things onto a tray. Buster ambled over to the fireplace where he struck a commanding position in front of the grate. Clearing his throat very deliberately, he began his story. 'There was this guy, a real Yankee type, fit, lean, basketball-playing – a healthy-living kinda guy.'

Oh no, thought Leah, it *is* the one about being cut short in somebody's garden. Why, oh why, Buster, do you have to do this? I thought we'd left all that kind of thing behind us in America.

'Thing about this guy,' Buster continued, 'is his sense of routine – regular as clockwork. Get up, shit, shower and shave, go to work – day in, day out. A real routine freak ... got the picture?'

'I think so,' said Catalina.

'Thought you would. The pattern for this fella never changes – until – one day he screws up. Nothing happens when it should. What can he do?' He paused to light a cigarette, making a mental note that Benjie was wearing what he and Leah called his 'fish face' in contrast to their visitor who seemed silently enraptured.

'He's got a train to catch and trains don't wait. So here's nothing for it but to pull up his pants and get going. He's heading for the station when – suddenly – it comes upon him and it won't wait. But where to go? In a flash he's over a wall, crouches down and does what a man's gotta do.'

Leah was fumbling in her bag for a pill as the joke rumbled on; Catalina hugged her knees. 'Only problem,' said Buster, 'when he looks behind him – there's nothing there!'

'Oh, Buster!' Leah's voice was a weary sigh. Catalina squeezed her arm.

'Our hero's in a panic! Then he hears the whistle! He sprints out of that garden and catches his train by the skin of his teeth.'

Leah tried to block out the rest of the tale – only certain words permeated her skull – 'haunted all day ... can't work ... journey home ... determined to find ... enters the garden ... in the dark ... thorough search ... unsuccessful. He's a broken man.' For goodness' sake, Buster, just finish the story, she prayed silently.

'Next morning, everything's back to normal. Amazing what a good night's sleep can do! He wakes up, regular time, regular routine – shit, shower and shave – all as before. He'll forget yesterday, lay it to one side. Lightens his step. He's almost at the station when old Matt, their neighbour, leans over the wall. "Hey Buddy!" he looks agitated. "You seen any vandals? You won't believe what's happened here!"

' "Oh?" says our hero, looking at his watch, as usual he's got just two minutes to spare – "What's up then, Oldtimer?"

' "Why – of all the sadistic things!" says the old man. "Someone came into my garden last night, rootled around, trampled down my flowers ... but that's not the half of it, Buddy. The nasty thing was – they shat all over the family tortoise!" '

Buster was heaving with mirth as he delivered his punchline, whilst Leah was painfully aware that no one else was showing any sign of emotion at all. Would Catalina ever want to talk to them again?

Even Buster now seemed deflated as he flipped the butt end of his cigarette into the empty hearth, and pulled in his belt. Rather lamely, he said 'Well maybe that's not your kind of thing, Mrs McKay, but I thought it mighty funny when I heard it in New York. I'm not much good at remembering jokes, but that one kind of stuck with me – if you'll pardon the expression.'

'It's in very poor taste,' said Leah with a long face.

'It doesn't pretend to be anything else – but our guest seemed to have such a sense of fun, I thought she'd appreciate some North American humour.' He looked so crestfallen, that once again Catalina was putting out a hand.

'It did amuse me, really. It's just – I'm not so used to this. Jock can be sarcastic, but he never tells jokes. He's so old-fashioned, sometimes I don't know whether to laugh or cry.'

There was silence. 'Well,' Buster blew his nose loudly, 'having killed conversation stone dead, I'd better go out and do some work. Come on, Benjie, you can take that maiden aunt look off of your face and lend me a hand. We'll leave the gals in peace.'

He bowed to Catalina. 'It's been nice to meet you, Mrs McKay. I'll call you Catalina if I may – the next time we meet. You're the only one around here who looks as though they're glad to be alive – and you'll always be welcome in this house – as far as I'm concerned.' And with that, he half backed himself to the door, before turning on his heel and marching out to the garden.

The two women looked at each other across the coffee table. Leah was so embarasssed, she felt on the verge of collapse but the day was saved by Catalina giggling like a schoolgirl. For the first time in years, Leah felt she had a real ally. 'I'm sorry,' she said, wiping away genuine tears, 'Buster's absolutely hopeless. It's not that he means to offend – he just puts his foot in it, big-time!'

'Don't they all?' said Catalina, 'men, I mean. At least you Americans say what you think, which is more than one can say for the ex-pat crowd. For me, your Buster makes a refreshing change.'

'Tell that to Howard and Benjie,' said Leah, 'The three of them can't be left alone in a room together at the moment.'

'You worry too much,' said Catalina. 'I'm sure it will work out, but that's up to them – not you.'

'I guess,' she said dubiously, 'but it's not how I envisaged things. We were supposed to be a happy band of people, living the dream, but it's not that simple. Hey!' she brightened, 'You haven't seen the upstairs level yet, why don't we make more coffee and take it up to our room. I could do with some advice on landscaping the garden and that's the best vantage point to see everything.'

Together they mounted the stairs. Catalina's sharp eyes swept over the paintings, the alcoves with their displays of old porcelain and the great mirror that took centre stage at the top of the stairs. All at once she noticed the chandelier and there was a sharp intake of breath. For a moment neither woman said anything, then – suddenly selfconscious and uncomfortable with the lull in conversation – Leah ventured, 'Like it?'

'Like it!' repeated Catalina, '*Like it!?*'

Oh lord, thought Leah, she thinks it over the top! Many of these Europeans prefer things to be left where they belong, in old palaces, country houses and so on – not modern villas like theirs. She was about to explain its history as though to excuse their folly, when her guest clutched her arm excitedly and declared, 'It's stupendous!'

Relieved and in control again, Leah ushered the other woman along the landing. 'These are the Boys' quarters, I'll let them show you around there sometime themselves, they're *gorgeous*. We're just coming to the master suite now, we drew straws and I guess Buster and I got the best view, facing south and east – right across what *will* be the garden – to a clear view of the ocean and that wonderful morning sun.'

They were standing in a large light room colonnaded to either side of the window bay, the muted walls showing off the vibrant tones of the curtains, furnishings and headboard. Again, Catalina's eyes were busy; they flew from wall to wall, noting the furniture, the pictures, the rugs, the flowers carefully arranged in what looked like Sèvres vases, cushions and covers. Again, that silence. Leah found herself gently perspiring, wondering what had happened to the hard-nosed businesswoman from New York. A social visit was supposed to be pleasurable, yet showing this discerning *Latina* her precious things was more daunting than taking a top dealer from Saks or Macy's round their showroom.

Expectantly, she waited for some comment but since none was forthcoming, she felt compelled to fill the gap. 'Of course, there's still much to be done,' she said brightly, 'I'm not sure whether that Italian dressing-table works with the Chinese bedcover, but I'm trying it, to see! We've a lot of stuff still stashed away in the basement, but bit by bit we'll get it right. I've always been the first to tell my clients, don't be afraid to experiment – but it's harder when one's doing it for oneself!'

'Or don't have the things to do it with.'

'Oh honey, yes of course – I hadn't thought,' said Leah, flushing. 'But you and Jock have some marvellous pieces, I couldn't help but notice.'

'Yes,' said Catalina, 'but not to my taste. I'd give anything to have a bedroom like this,' and she ran her hand lovingly over a small chest of drawers with a bowed front and elegant, curving legs. 'This for example, is it Italian too?'

'No, French,' smiled Leah, feeling easier than she had all day – this was familiar territory – 'cabinet maker M. Jean de Rouen from the Rue de Faubourg St Honoré circa 1785.'

'It's beau-tiful,' Catalina emphasised the first syllable with such sincerity, that Leah found herself warming to the young woman more than ever. 'You are so fortunate.'

'Well, I guess,' said Leah, never having considered such a point before.

'And that commode, is that French too?'

'No, English, but earlier than the dressing-table. You can mix and match periods as well as styles and countries, but the important thing is to get a balance and above all something that pleases you.'

'It pleases *me* a lot,' said Catalina, finding it hard to keep the envy out of her voice. 'Our furniture, what's left in Scotland, is mainly Victorian, pretty dull. Jock had to sell all the good Georgian and imported pieces long ago to pay off the tax man.'

'It must have been hard,' said Leah, placing their coffee tray on a footstool and settling onto a tapestried ottoman to indicate a place beside her. 'But maybe one day, I can help you establish a collection again.'

'That would be nice,' said Catalina, rewarding her with a dazzling smile. 'I weel hold you to that, if you don't mind?'

'Of course,' said Leah, her spirits lifting by the minute. What a surprising but charming girl this was! 'After all, that's what friends are for!'

'And you are 'appy to be my friend?'

'But of course! I wouldn't have asked you here so soon if I wasn't! My dear, I may come across as a gauche American – but in business, one learns to be the soul of discretion and there are few people I take into my confidence. I have a feeling however you are going to be one of those rare exceptions.'

'That's good to know,' Catalina was moving towards the unlatched window and looking far away to where sea met sky. 'And if this is so – and I have no reason to doubt you – you will be the first in Santa Felicia for *me* to trust. Here, everyone wants to be one's friend and there's a very obvious camaraderie. But I tell you,' she lowered her voice dramatically, 'no one trusts anyone. It's all very shallow and for show, little else. Most ex-pats have too little to do and thrive on intrigue, innuendo and even others' misfortunes.'

'That's unpleasant,' said Leah with a little shiver. 'Fortunately, there wasn't enough time for anything like that, where I came from. I guess I know what you mean though. Small communities can breed envy and contempt.'

'Of course, Jock and I have many friends here,' Catalina was still looking far away, 'but there is not one in whom I confide. If I was in trouble and had to act with impunity, it would be hard to know where to go.' She swung round to face her hostess, her mouth and eyes glistening with emotion. 'Isn't that terrible?'

'It's terrible,' agreed Leah feeling quite maternal, 'but I guess it's life.'

'And this is what I cannot accept!' Catalina went on, her voice raised and her hands held out dramatically. 'I so much want someone, need someone to talk to at times. Someone I can trust. Someone who isn't just in there for themselves, but for me too!'

'Maybe you're looking at her,' Leah tried, but failed to catch her eye. Who could resist such a gorgeous, impassioned figure with this hint of tragedy about her?

Catalina moved towards her, dark eyes focussed on a spot somewhere on the wall above Leah's head. 'I have an idea,' she was saying, 'The only way to resolve this is to create a bond. A pact! Not necessarily sealed with blood, but our own private thing. No men, no interfering English … just you and me. Leah and Catalina.'

Leah was about to say something, but was cut short. Clearly, Catalina had to get this off her ample chest, her hands clenched together as she continued. 'If ever one of us is lonely, sad, we'll be there for each other. If there's ever a worry, however small or trivial, we'll share it … listen. Our confidences will go no further – no one will know about our secret pact, not even our husbands. But *we* will, and that will be our strength. What do you say?'

'I say fine,' said Leah rising up to give the younger woman a warm hug. 'just fine, sister!'

Her cries rang out so loudly that he went to shut the window in case they awoke the whole street. He stood there, watching her bathed in the soft glow of the bedside lamp as she squirmed between the sheets, tearing at her hair which was everywhere. In a ludicrous kind of way, she reminded him of a small furry animal disturbed from its lair and in a panic as to which way to go. 'Here, shut up and cover yourself,' he said shortly, picking up the sheet which had fallen to the floor. He felt totally unmoved by the glimpse of her creamy breasts hanging loose and free, the rounded curve of her stomach, and the firmness of her thighs. She had spoilt all that.

There had been a blazing row. There had been many such in the past, but this had left a bitter after-taste. Moreover, he had slapped her – just once, but hard – on the bottom, like a naughty schoolgirl. She had been outraged but he felt no shame. Indeed, at this moment in time, his love had almost turned to hate. He had stayed up all evening to let his anger dissipate, take stock and have time to think. He hoped now to find her asleep because all he wanted was to climb under the covers, put the earlier hurt and humiliation to one side and sink into oblivion.

Yet here she was wide-awake and aroused, making a drama. The furious tears of earlier had dried; but fresh ones were gathering as she wailed and sobbed. Then came the chanting, which was a new ploy but highly unnerving. 'I'm a bitch, I'm a witch, the witchiest bitch…' The shrill incantation was piercing his ears, driving him back into himself.

'I said *silence!*'

The harshness of his voice surprised him. She must have felt it too as the hysteria vanished as quickly as it had come. Despite the earlier anger, something in his heart melted. She looked so vulnerable. He started to undress. First his old crocodile belt, then the jeans; why did he wear them skin-tight when at times like these they clung to his body? Unpeeling each reluctant garment, he felt her eyes upon him, round like saucers; sensed the quiver of her lips. Maybe for once, she wasn't play-acting and was actually sorry?

The sudden silence was almost worse than the earlier shrieking. He longed for the normal sounds, her breathing, the soft rise and fall of bedclothes which he took such care not to disturb when he came home late. He turned off the light, oddly embarassed to be caught naked. She so rarely watched him. He felt his long limbs stiff and wooden and wondered if they creaked a little as he climbed into the high bed. Now it was he who felt vulnerable, as though he might lose the upper hand, so important to keep this marriage going. He was painfully aware that every hair on his chest was grey. Despite their row and the hurt that followed, he found himself longing to hold her, to brush his lips over her shiny black hair and to lose himself in that all-engulfing warmth. Instead, he lay down and turned his back.

Suddenly her strong young arms were round his and she was burying her face between his shoulder blades. He could feel the wet from her tears cold on his skin, and the thick hair between her legs brushing his buttocks. He sighed, knowing that despite everything, he could not resist her. Already, the blood was coursing through his veins, and he marvelled how he could respond so quickly at such a time, at such a touch. Carefully, he turned so she wouldn't know and held her at arm's length. 'So you're a little witch, are you? Yep… I think I'd go along with that.'

'It's the way I'm made! I can't help it, Jock, you know that. I don't know what gets into me…' her voice was already rising to a dangerous crescendo and he shushed her lips with one hand, as the other stroked the nape of her neck where her hair had parted and swung forward over her breasts.

'You bring it on yourself, my darling,' he muttered and to distract her slid himself down in the bed, until he could bend his knees and prop her up to straddle him.

'Oh my god, Jock" she breathed, taken by surprise. 'You do want me – after all?'

It was a needless question, but he was determined not to let her drop down on him, without some degree of atonement. 'Tell me you love me, Catalina,' he was ashamed to find himself saying – he had wanted an apology – 'just tell me you love me.'

'I love you, I love you,' she said, but he felt cheated, because she'd already sucked him in. Marvelling at her energy, he gave in and went with the flow.

His last thought before falling asleep that night – was the wish she'd said 'I love you' at the end of their lovemaking, too.

He'd been up for hours when she eventually emerged for breakfast. Philismena had taken Katy to school and he had dabbled around with a still-life he hadn't much heart for, today of all days. Now, he was drinking black coffee by himself on the verandah. It was already midday, but for once not too hot. 'Want some?' he pushed the pot towards her on a table still laid for two.

'No, I'll just have orange juice, ' she said, going to the cooler. As she sipped slowly she waited for him to speak, but nothing was forthcoming. She noticed dark shadows under his eyes, but at least he had shaved – a good sign at times like these. 'I thought I might take the boat out today,' she was keeping her tone light and even. 'Might you like to come too?'

'No thanks. I've things to do.'

'To do with what's happened.'

He nodded.

'Does that mean things are really as bad as you said last night?'

''Fraid so,' he said, lighting up a Gauloise and screwing up his eyes to look out at the harbour.

'I'd hoped you were exaggerating because you were so angry with me over the telegram.'

'Nope.'

'But,' she drained the glass delicately and studied the tablecloth, 'there's still the pictures and your exhibition,' her voice sounded unconvinced.

'Yes.'

'Oh Jock! Talk to me,' she implored. 'I'm trying my best to cheer you up … you know, act normal, be positive.'

'There's nothing to feel normal and positive about. The truth is, we're skint – and nothing you can say or do will alter that.

'Well, you've always said where there's a will there's a way. Maybe I should take a job! Be a responsible wife, like you always wanted!'

'It's a bit late for that, Catalina. You are what you are and I am what I am. But being what I am, the eternal optimist and not very businesslike, I seem to have made a right bloody mess.'

'But Jock – things can't just *happen* like that.'

'They do, and they have.'

'I don't believe it's as bad as you think. There has to be a way out. I am sure Jeremy is looking on the black side – you said yourself he's a typical accountant."

'That's why everything he says is black and white,' replied her husband. 'And this time it's all black. Look, my darling one,' he got up and came round to her side of the table to pat her on the head, his voice surprisingly gentle, 'we've already been into this. I explained the whole damn affair to you yesterday evening. I left out nothing. What's done is done, as they say.'

'But last night… in bed… you were a stag! It hasn't been like that in ages!'

'I needed you, Catalina. Hadn't you considered that? When people are low, that's often when they need each other the most.'

'But, I thought … maybe …'

'You thought wrong,' his voice was bitter. 'Fucking has nothing to do with failure… it may have for some people but not for me. I guess it was the one thing I felt I'd got left at that moment in time. Right now, however, I'm not so sure.

'So my darling!' he forced a lighter tone into his voice and looked down at her in a very odd way, 'Why don't you go and sail your boat!' And without waiting for an answer he left her side and disappeared indoors.

17

Santa Felicia had never seen a party like it. It was the party to beat all parties, and as someone later remarked, the new Americans certainly did things in a big, big way. There was enough food and wine to host a battalion.

Guests in cars winding up the steep bumpy road were impressed with their first close-up view. The yellow house had been long in the making, but overnight it had become an empress ship. Ablaze with lights in every window, high above the ocean and against an inky sky – she reared large, proud and extravagant. Down to the last piece of rigging, or more appropriately, the last chimney stack, it was a commanding sight.

The atmosphere within the villa was as electric as the lull before the storm. For days, Leah and Benjie had slaved in the kitchen, baking, stewing, steaming, roasting. Quite apart from the tempting array of meat, fish and fowl, they had dreamt up, mixed up, and whipped up a veritable feast of starters and puddings An air of secrecy had hung over the proceedings. Like partners in crime, each was as determined as the other, that they should surprise their fellow inmates with their audacity and daring.

'No, Buster – you can't go poking your nose in there,' Leah had yelled every time, her husband opened a fridge door. 'Howard, I'll thank you to leave Benjie and me in peace, haven't you enough to do elsewhere?'

Indeed he had. On better terms now with Buster than they'd ever been, the two big men had worked tirelessly, committed to bring the lighting and sound systems to a state of perfection. With the rugs rolled back, bare boards polished, the library made the perfect nightclub. A spare generator stood behind Howard's high-range stereo, his much prized mahogany speakers feeding smaller ones draped in the carob trees outside. 'Great for a smoochy number on the terrace,' grinned Buster.

The sheer volume of vinyl was daunting. His precious 33s from Bing Crosby, the early golden oldies, to the big band sound of the forties, the romance of Cole Porter, Weil, Lernher, Sinatra, Piaf and Aznavour lay in juxtoposition to the neat 45s. Fifties pop gave way to a massive sixties collection, Swingin' London, Merseyside, Motown and California … Benjie was a Beach Boys fan, Howard preferred soul. As for the latest offerings of Bassey, Springfield, King, Franklin, Redding, Sledge, Simon and Garfunkel and a new kid on the block from England, a certain Elton John with a different, wistful sound in his first hit *Your Song*, Howard was confident he'd missed little over four decades.

Then there were his 'classics'. Immaculate opera albums and musicals plus a whole range of ballet suites were now carefully stashed away under lock and key. 'You're paranoid about those operatics,' Buster had remarked the day before, watching him thread the key onto a fine silver chain round his neck, 'anyone would think they were something seriously precious.'

'They are,' Howard gave a final polish to each gleaming disc. Undeterred, Buster went round the room again, checking for spent bulbs and fuses. Apart from the Russian chandelier in the hall, there were no overhanging lights; instead discreet wall sconces, picture lights and gorgeous table lamps clad each sumptuous room in a soft glow. Even outside the villa, a more romantic ambience for an evening event would be hard to equal. It was a place for lovers, thought Buster, mounting the steep path for a final inspection. On such a night, guided by string after string of fairy lights, maybe someone would get lucky.

At 8.55, four hosts, self-conscious and stiff, found themselves in the long *sala*. Everything was ready, down to the finest detail. At the far end, a Spanish refectory table groaned under the weight of so much glass. Bottles of Moët nestled in ice-buckets, whilst jugs of freshly squeezed lemon, orange and iced water jostled for position amid rows of crystal goblets dominated by Benjie's centre-piece of roses, carnations, and hibiscus. Armfuls of pink and white oleander scented corners and draped the picture rail. The clock in the hall was chiming. As if on cue, Buster braced his tuxedoed back and flexed his quads. Benjie looked in vain for another piece of fluff to remove from his velvet jacket. Howard, magnificent in his favourite plum smoking suit, forced himself not to touch the back of his hands. Instead he fussed with the white carnation Benjie had thoughtfully pinned to his lapel.

'Are you sure this dress is all right, guys?' Leah looked nervous and unhappy as she twirled in front of them, 'I'm so afraid to be over-dressed.'

'Better to be over than under,' said Howard, 'Besides, how many times do we have to say it – you're looking great!'

'I don't know – I feel uneasy,' she said, going to the mirror above the fireplace and studying her reflection long and hard. 'I'm not sure how all these people get themselves up for parties round here. I asked Catalina, but she wasn't much help. I get the impression anything – but nothing – goes and you have to be European to know the difference!' Her face stared back at her, a dubious expression round the eyes and mouth. The light was different here, she thought. Making up at her dressing table, she'd looked sallow; now, she regretted that dash of rouge. She felt she clashed with the fuchsia pink of her strapless evening dress, and wished she'd worn the black instead. Too late now!   She tightened a drop earring which had worked its way loose. The diamond caught the flicker of the low fire in the grate and she spotted a bead of perspiration on her upper lip. She must powder her nose again before they all arrived.

Buster had gone to the front door and was peering out onto the drive. 'There's a car coming up the hill. 'Someone's punctual!'

'Oh help!' cried Leah, flying upstairs to fix her face.

'I wonder who'll be first,' said Howard, memorising the list.

'I hope I can put the right names to the right faces,' said Benjie.

They took up position – Howard and Benjie in the *sala*, Buster in the hall. Leah was clacking her way down the long flight of marble stairs to be at her husband's side, when the first guests were admitted. She had just sneaked another tranquie and full of Dutch courage waved 'Hi there!' over the bannisters. Three heads looked up to take in a deathly pale face beaming down at them – Leah had been liberal with her powder puff. There was an embarrassed silence, then Buster was ushering them through. 'Good evening! You must be Mr and Mrs Grafton – very British, huh? – bang on time! Buster Bloomfield is the name, that's my wife Leah – er – up there on the stairs and your other two hosts await you!'

Leah descended, they shook hands and Mrs Grafton introduced her son, 'I hope you don't mind – my brother Sir John at the embassy was unable to come – so we brought Roger along instead. He only got back from Oxford two days ago.' An effeminate youth with his mother's red hair and freckles came forward reticently to shake hands. Leah felt comforted that he stuttered – so someone else was nervous too.

'Oxford, eh?'said Buster, patting him noisily oh the back and thinking they had a cheek. 'Grand place Oxford, so I hear! Like it there, son?'

'Yes, sir.'

'Good, good,' said Buster slightly mollified – at least the kid was OK. He led the way into the *sala* where Howard was supervising a couple of manservants at the drinks table. 'There we are! Howard and Benjie will look after you. Now if you'll excuse me, folks, duty calls!' He returned to the hall. 'What's happened to you?' he said to his wife, 'You look as if you've seen a ghost.'

'Thanks a lot,' said Leah, peering over his shoulder. The Graftons had moved away from the Boys and were gazing around the *sala* as though in a museum. Why was she feeling so fluttery and ill at ease? She had sailed through her New York trade parties with gusto. Since no other guests were in sight, she left her post and hurried up to the newcomers. 'So kind of you to come this evening!' the smile on her face felt ingratiating and false. 'Good of you to make the effort.'

'Not at all,' said Gerald Grafton, a tall man with a prominent, beak-shaped nose.

Kind of haughty looking, thought Leah to herself, and how patronising! Before she could stop herself, she blurted out, 'We didn't know a soul here when we arrived…'

'So it seems.'

'…then Benjie and I had this idea to throw a party.'

'Sensible way to get to know a few faces, what?' Mr Grafton's tone was cool. 'It must be hard without connections – diplomatic corps and all that.'

'I'm sure,' Leah knew she was only getting as good as she deserved; everything she said was coming out wrong. 'Of course we recognised you and your wife immediately!'

'Have we met before, embassy party or something?' he was wrinkling up his brow.

'Er no – I don't think so. But – er – one or two people had mentioned you,' she felt the hot flush creep up her neck. Thank God for the powder.

'Did they, by Jove! How very odd. Did you hear that Christabel? People have been talking about us!'

'What's that?'said his wife, breaking away from a picture of a racehorse.

'Excuse me!' muttered Leah and hurried back to the hall to greet a young couple, the van der Stels. This was going to be much easier, she thought.

Jacqueline, a charming girl with wide apart eyes and a big smile, kissed her warmly on both cheeks, 'Happy House Warming! We've brought you a present, but we thought it better to leave it outside. It's rather big!'

'How very kind, may I ask what it is?'

For an answer, Karl led her out to the front door. 'Oh!' cried Leah, clasping her hands in delight, 'a baby palm tree! What an original present!'

By the time she had shaken a score of hands and several gifts had gathered in the hall, Leah was feeling better. She wished Catalina would hurry; with an ally in the camp she might even enjoy herself. This was supposed to be a celebration! Buster was still greeting arrivals. Thank God he wasn't jittery like her or one of those husbands who couldn't hold his drink. In fact she felt positively proud of the urbane, easy way he remembered and repeated each name, every inch the host, every inch the New Yorker – in his gleaming white tuxedo.

Howard was doing marvels with the champagne. It had been his idea to order vintage and impatient at the slowness of the waiters, he was determined to ensure everyone had full glasses and knew exactly what they were drinking. As for Benjie, he seemed everywhere at once, passing round canapés, hobnobbing here and there, as ubiquitous as a butterfly. Poised halfway between the hall and *sala* so she could usher people through, Leah's mind was still on Catalina. She had only seen her new friend twice in the past few weeks, due to unforeseen circumstances. There'd been some major financial disaster back in England and the McKays had lost thousands of pounds. Shares that had seemed dead safe at the time had been wiped out. The husband had taken a risk, it had not paid off – 'it never does with Jock, somehow,' Catalina had confided in her – and she felt sorry for them.

A woman's South Carolina drawl floated across the hall. 'Good to meet a southern belle in this neck of the woods,' Buster was saying, bestowing a kiss on both cheeks which was reciprocated rather too readily by fellow countrywoman, Janine Baxter.

Close on Janine's heels came a very important little person. With a marvellous sun tan and immaculate hair, going attractively grey at the temples, he could not have been more than five foot seven, but with everything so perfectly in proportion, boasted a dashing and elegant figure. This must be Manolo Vaz Valqueira. Quite unintentionally, Leah moved forward and strained her neck to get a better view. This was precisely what most women did, the first time they set eyes on Manolo. Confidence oozing from every pore, he strode into the hall, tossed his theatre cape to the maid and after a quick appraisal, made straight for Leah, having nicely circumvented Buster in the foreground. '*Encantado!*' he breathed, bending low over her hand, lips just brushing her skin. As he straightened up, she took in a pair of very wicked, nut brown eyes.

'Oh!' she exclaimed, thrilled. 'It must be *Senhor* –'

'Manolo Vaz Valqueira at your service,' he beamed. 'I am *delighted* to be here. I was *delighted* to receive your invitation. Now, I won't keep you – there are many people queuing to receive your attention – but I look forward, to – er – renewing our acquaintance as the night progresses.' And with a meaningful look which made her feel fifteen years younger, he peeled away to present himself to Buster.

'*Senhor*,' again a bow, but not half as low. Before Buster had a chance to say a word, he puffed out his chest and said in perfect English, 'Please! Forgive me! I know you mean to help, but do not worry about introducing me to anyone at all. I know everyone in Santa Felicia – with the exception of your good selves.' With another small bow and before anyone had time to recover, he had swept past them all into the *sala*, a glass arriving in his hand as though by magic.

'Well, the night's full of surprises…' thought Leah and was rewarded by the flash of a backward smile from the gentleman concerned as she followed, as one in a dream. By nine-fifty, all but three of their guests had arrived. Catalina and her husband were amongst them, but an expressive roll of her friend's eyes indicated it had taken a supreme effort to come at all. Pressing a cellophane box into Leah's hands, she hoped this small token of her friendship would make up for not being there to support earlier. As she glided off in the wake of her taciturn husband, Leah found herself gazing down at a delicate green and white orchid resting in a bed of fern and was touched.

Now, as she awaited the last arrival, she thought again of her luck in finding such an unexpected and charming person for a friend, so soon after settling into a strange country. Over an hour late, the entrance of the Honourable Johanna Vincent, was nothing less than spectacular. Never, thought Leah, had she seen a woman with such a magnificent figure at the age of fifty-something. The face she recognised from the screen, but meeting the actress in the flesh came somehow as a shock. She had been unprepared for the sheer vitality and magnetism of the woman.

Energy streamed out of her, and even Buster took a backward step. Undeterred, Miss Vincent advanced smoothly towards him like a long-striding thoroughbred. A moment later, he bent to kiss the extended hand, causing his wife almost to faint with surprise – it was totally out of character. Feeling hideously over-dressed in her fuchsia silk, she moved forward in greeting, wondering why her full length fitted skirt made her legs feel leaden. It was all so different from the liberated lady she felt inside. Suddenly, she longed to tear off her heavy choker of pearls with its impressive diamond clasp. Other women would give their eye teeth, but all she felt at this moment was frustration that someone could make her feel so restricted.

Their gaze locked. Two very penetrating grey eyes looked into Leah's blue ones. Leah held her ground – as quite pointedly – she felt herself under scrutiny. But it was an unfair match. Where she was over-stated, Miss Vincent in black velvet was the picture of austerity. This immediately gave an edge to the contest, if contest it was. A slimline jacket enhanced a neat waist and boyish hips, whilst beautifully cut matching trousers hugged a pair of legs that went on forever, before flaring out over neat ankles. Black braid piping ran round the lapels and cuffs of her coat whilst underneath a white silk shirt ended in a soft ruffle at the throat. Her feet were encased in elegant calf boots, the only jewellery – a plain gold stock pin and a heavy bracelet, made up of what appeared to be Victorian sovereigns. It did not take long to see they were genuine – just like their owner, thought Leah wryly.

At any rate, she'd be the first to speak, the woman couldn't take that away from her. 'Er – Miss Vincent?' Leah forced the words out, 'Welcome to our home!'

'How do you do, darling! What a very nice way to introduce yourselves to Santa Felicia!' Her eyes slid downward – there was a pause – why oh why had she put on such very high heels? Then, smilingly , 'Might I say welcome, too? We're all delighted to see a new villa on our small horizon, and instead of one couple – the usual thing, you know, darling – we feel we're getting two for the price of one! Just a joke of course…' she broke off to glance round the room, '… am I really the last to arrive?'

'Oh I'm sure you're not,' lied Leah.

'Oh I'm sure I *am*,' laughed the other. 'But that's the way it is. So boring to be first, darling.'

Graciously, she allowed Leah to usher her into the *sala* which was now full of people and noise. 'Can I get you a drink, Miss Vincent?'Leah was raising her voice to be heard above the din; but she need not have bothered. Her guest was already surrounded, young admirers rushing forth to embrace her as if they had not met for years. Now they were all thick in conversation. What a fuss! – you'd think it was *her* party, thought Leah, piqued. She spied Catalina amongst them, 'I'm trying to get Miss Vincent some champagne,' she said. ' I presume it *is* still champagne she drinks?'

'It's champagne all right – but Leah, she's already got a glass! Manolo brought her one.'

'Oh!' Leah practically stamped her foot under her tight dress and turned away.

Benjie came up then, a piece of paper in his hand, a sly grin on his face. 'Hi! It's going like a ball – and would you believe it, they're all here – in fact we've got three extra!'

'I wonder who?' said Leah, 'And for God's sake be careful with that list!'

'What's it worth?' he teased, slipping off once more into the mêlée. Leah watched him go and sighed. She felt a total outsider.

An elegant man with Indian features and sympathetic eyes came up. 'May I introduce myself to our glamorous hostess,' he said. 'Augusto Neves at your service,' and for a moment she thought he would click his heels. 'I have a confession,' he said, 'My wife, Corrine and I,' he nodded in the direction of a svelte looking girl with short hair, 'have gate-crashed your party. Will you ever forgive us?'

'I'm not sure what to say to that,' Leah pondered the question, 'Maybe you'll be good enough to tell me how?'

'We flew in from my parents' home in Goa yesterday,' said the stranger. 'We live in Lisbon, I'm a banker, but we come down here for weekends. Our good friend, Manolo, showed us your invitation. He said it sounded like a wonderful party, but not having your telephone number, there was no way I could contact you to ask permission. I guess it was a little presumptous?'

He looked so genuinely concerned, Leah warmed to him immediately. 'Of course not! We're still waiting for the telephone – I gather it takes forever – if you're friends of Manolo's, it's a pleasure.'

'That is very hospitable,' said Augusto, looking as though he meant it. 'Now I feel safe to introduce my wife – she was afraid you might bite her head off! Corrine!' Soon Leah was chatting with ease to this pleasant couple, who were tennis fanatics and already inviting her and Buster to play mixed doubles. It was funny that two gatecrashers should made her feel more welcome than all the other guests put together.

The Neves had just departed from her side, when she felt a close presence behind her and whirled round to come face to face with Catalina. She could not help notice the high pinpoints of colour in the normally pale cheeks and the dark eyes opened very wide. There was a frisson of electricity about her tonight which contrasted with her normally languid air; Leah wondered if she had drunk rather more champagne than she should.

'I see you're beginning to relax at last,' Catalina whispered. 'You looked in agony when everyone was coming through the door. There's really no need! It's a marvellous party and everyone's loving it, so you must too. Come and talk to Jock!' And before Leah could protest, she was being marched to where McKay was finding solace with a whisky at the foot of a Zoffany. Ignoring the danger signals and quite unashamed of the interruption, Catalina deposited their hostess upon her husband, 'You two have hardly had a chance to get to know each other. I'm sure you can make up for it now!'

Without waiting for a reply, she spun away merrily to talk to Terence O'Connor who had been lurking nearby. Leah stared after her departing back. How lovely the girl looked, she thought, the fullness of the scarlet dress showing off her feminine figure, her thick burnished hair flowing out behind her. The masterpiece forgotten, her husband was watching her retreat too. 'You must be proud of her,' said Leah.

'What's that?' growled McKay, his eyes fixed on his wife. They could just hear her infectious, tinkling laugh as she shared some amusement with the big, raw-boned Irishman, who had not strayed far from the bar since his arrival.

Leah was about to repeat herself when he interrupted, 'No, Mrs Bloomfield! I'm not at *all* proud of her. Give me one good reason why I should be.'

Leah was taken aback. This was much harder that she'd expected. She cast a quick glance round the room to see if Buster might help her out, but he was in a tight little circle with the van der Stels and the hippy couple from the discotheque. Both in caftans, the latter looked more like brother and sister than lovers despite their long brown arms entwined about each other's waists. At that moment McKay turned on her with such a bellow of laughter, it quite unnerved her. 'What I said just now," his voice hissed in her ear, 'was perfectly true. I'm not the slightest bit proud of my wife, but I'll tell you who *should* be commended!' the timbre of his voice had altered.

'Who?' she said, baffled.

'I'm proud of *myself*! Yes, proud of me, Jock McKay – for holding on to her! I'll bet you didn't expect that, did you?' he gestured extravagantly with his glass. 'Now – if you'll kindly excuse me, I'll go and help myself to another of these.'

Leah stared after him; what a very odd man! She went to find Howard. It was time to get people eating, otherwise they'd all be drunk, and what a waste of an evening that would be. It was not difficult to encourage people towards the buffet. Several had been eyeing the mountain of delicacies in the room beyond with undisguised anticipation, and soon everyone was surging forward to sample Santa Felicia's first real taste of American hospitality.

The variety was enormous. Smoked salmon from the north, pâté with truffles and wild mushrooms – a Benjie speciality; a basket of steamed crayfish, a vast tureen of ice-cold gazpacho with all the trimmings and an avocado mousse made up the starters. The main course table creaked under the weight of a great fore-rib of beef, roasted dark on the outside and delicately pink where a sharp knife had penetrated; a whole glazed ham, beaded with cloves, and what was surely one of the most enormous turkeys ever reared. Various salads made a blaze of colour against the starched white table cloth; there were sweet potatoes, wild rice, juicy beetroot and pickled cabbage. And more was to come. From Leah's pecan pie to Benjie's baked Alaska, éclairs to cheese-cake, the puddings culminated in a mountain of strawberries which rose in the form of a snowy peak frosted with spun sugar.

Men were taking women into dinner and Buster found himself looking round the room. His eyes rested on Leah's friend, Catalina McKay. Gee! those breasts nestling within her low-cut dress were a feast in themselves – who needed food with a pair like that? Pity she was thick in conversation with that Irish fellow. He turned to look the other way and found himself face to face with the American girl.

'Hi there again!' she clutched his arm, 'I have to say – this is quite a party!'

'I hope so' he grinned, 'The place was crying out for a good show! Look at them all – diving in like gannets! At least now they'll have an idea how we do things in the States. Should shake these Britishers up a bit, huh?'

'You ought to be congratulated,' she beamed. 'I've certainly never seen food like it in the Algarve. Can I go in with you? I'm hungry!'

'Sure,' he said, 'be my guest!'

Howard found himself caught up with Christabel Grafton. She had already taken up his time by demanding champagne cocktails and with each new glass, her face was taking on the hue of her purple evening dress. He looked round for Benjie and saw him already at the serving table with Roger. 'Shall I call your son over?' he volunteered.

'Whatever for? she replied crisply. 'He's quite capable of looking after himself. You were telling me about your decorating business – so interesting – I've done quite a bit of that, myself, you know.'

'Oh really?' said Howard, frowning at the word 'decorating' and wondering how to extricate himself.

'Yes, Gerald's family home near Gloucester. Between us we spend three months of the year there – mainly for the hunting! In other words we're tax exiles. The old abbey was almost *derelict*,' her voice hushed dramatically, 'until *I* got cracking on it. The previous incumbent, Gerald's uncle – Sir William Grafton, quite quite senile – had let it fall into a ghastly state. Yes, I know…' she mistook Howard's raised eyebrows for surprise '… two sirs in one family, one a baronet, one a knight, but *he's* in an institution – William I mean – all of which means – we've got somewhere to go when the season's in full flood.'

'Oh…I mean, yes,' said Howard, uncomprehending and trying hard to control his twitching fingers. He'd lost sight of Benjie and the boy. He must try to relax and not worry so much. After all, it *was* a party.

Manolo Vaz Valqueira was dancing attendance on Johanna Vincent. They were old friends. 'Steady, darling,' she said as he piled her plate high with fat pink prawns, 'Don't forget, I eat like a bird. Half of that will do for me.'

'You ought to keep your strength up, Johanna,' he twinkled. 'You never know when you might need it. Just like me – I always keep a little something in reserve.' Laughingly, she mimicked him.

'Just a *leetle sometheeng*, darling! I take it you haven't set eyes on anything worthwhile this evening, otherwise you wouldn't be wasting your time with me?'

'Oh, *Johanna*,' he looked reproachful.

'Oh, come now, Manolo! I know you far too well!'

'*É verdade*,' he said, glancing round, 'I must confess to being a shade disappointed. I had hoped for – how shall I put it – a little new blood? But it's all the same old faces. The Algarve can be so *limited*.'

'What about mine hostess, Manolo? I never yet knew you to be put off by a wedding ring.'

'Ah, *minha mãe …* ' he sighed, 'That one! She has a pretty face, yes … and the legs and figure, they are good, a trifle thin – but that's only personal taste, you understand. But somehow,' he paused as though struggling for the words in English, 'there's something not right … I can't explain.'

'That's not like you, Manolo – all the fun of the chase!'

'It's difficult to … how you say? … peenpoint. You would think with all the glamour, so much good taste, the lady of the house would be the belle of the ball as you say. But it's too perfect … too earnest!' he pounced on the word. 'That's it! … I feel that nice, *earnest* little lady may get trodden underfoot – and I'm not talking about dancing.'

'Manolo! I've never known you protective! What are you saying?'

'As I said, I can't explain … I just hope these people know what they're doing. They all seem gullible somehow. The men, perhaps, can take care of themselves. But I like our little hostess – I seriously hope she doesn't get hurt by our way of life.'

'Oh, I doubt it,' said Johanna. 'I'll keep an eye on her if it makes you any happier. You make Santa Felicia sound like Babylon. Come on, my little *cavaleiro*! We're holding up the queue. I'm depending on you to find me somewhere to sit.'

'Do you not think you should be going off to get thome food for your huthband?' said Terence O'Connor in his soft lilt that women found so attractive. 'Go and do the perfect wife bit and all that?'

'But I'm not the perfect wife,' replied Catalina, running the tip of her tongue over her lips to shine them up.

'Och, I know you're not, you silly thing, but I don't imagine he'd like it if I took you in to dinner.'

'But that's where you're completely wrong,' said Catalina, 'he expects me to misbehave a little.'

'Doth he say so?' the Irishman opened his blue eyes very wide.

'Not exactly, but he's always bemoaning the fact that he's so much older – as though he wouldn't blame me if I did.'

'So that accounts for your bad behaviour,' he looked her up and down. 'Look, woman, will you thtop doing that and pull yourself together!'

'I'm doing nothing,' she said, moistening her lips again.

'You know very well, damn you. Fluttering your eyes and thrusting your breasts at me like that. I know full well there's some boned contraption under there, so there's no need to overdo it … I'm not blind!'

'You're a very rude man,' she said a pink flush spreading across her face.

'That's better, now your eyes are sparkling! Besides, I'm not rude – just plain thpoken!'

'You are rude – by my standards anyway,' she sniffed. 'I've heard you in your big hotel – the way you talk to your staff – and worse, how you talk to your wife!'

'Look here! I'll thank you to keep my wife out of this conversation. She's back in Ireland at the moment and doesn't come into this.'

'Why not? You were talking about my husband,' she snapped.

'All right,' he said, all smiles again. 'We'll leave them both out – shall we? When are you coming to bed with me, Catalina McKay?'

'What a stupid question!' she said, sticking her chin up scornfully.

'That's debatable,' he replied, 'it's pretty clear to me you want to as much as I do.'

'You must be mad,' she said. 'What makes you think that you're so special? If you must know, every man in this room wants to take me to bed!'

'I don't deny it. But let's put it this way. You don't get turned on the way you are now for every man in the room, do you now?'

She could feel her heart thumping against the tightness of her bodice. Her feet ached in their high-heeled shoes. The room seemed to be closing in on her and she longed to escape, to run barefoot into the enveloping velvet of the summer night. As his slow laugh echoed again in her head, she felt an urgent pulse between her legs, that refused to go away. Wildly, she looked round for Jock. She had felt his eyes on her until a few moments ago, but now he had disappeared into the crowd of people going through to eat. She forced herself to remain still, took a deep breath and heard herself say quite calmly, 'Please, Terence, my feet are killing me, will you go and get me some food? I'm very hungry.'

He looked down at her averted head and knew, instinctively he had overplayed his hand. She was that kind of woman, chauvinistic – despite her extraordinary feminity. In her own eyes, she liked to be the hunter, not the hunted.

'OK, Catalina,' he said. And, half-relieved because he had enough problems in his personal life without adding Catalina McKay to them, he pushed his way through to where a maid was handing out plates.

Jacqueline van der Stel sat at the foot of the stairs flanked by Jock McKay with Lucie and Sebastian from the discotheque on the other side. They all balanced plates on their knees which was somewhat of a miracle since McKay was on his fifth whisky and the young couple looked well out of it. 'I must say,' she confided in Jock, 'I didn't expect them to put on half as good a show as this, did you?'

'I'm not sure what I expected,' he replied. 'Catalina's already at home with them all, but I still find it an extraordinary set-up. All this show and for what?'

'One certainly wonders…do tell me, Jock, I've been longing to ask, are the two "Boys", as they call them, queer?'

'Sweetie,' he replied, 'your guess is as good as mine. Quite frankly, I couldn't care a damn. They seem nice enough and know more about the arts than most people – which for me, is a good start – in this cultural wilderness.' There was a bitter ring to his voice.

Instinctively, she reached out her hand and squeezed his arm. 'I heard you had some rotten bad luck the other day,' she said, 'I'm so sorry.'

He nodded, then recovered sufficiently to say, 'That's kind of you, Jacqueline. I suppose it's all round Santa Felicia so there's no point in denying anything. I did a silly thing. Instead of letting my hard earned savings gather dust in some safe account, I put all my eggs in one basket. Ever heard of a company called the National Family Insurance & Assurance?'

'Of course, it's had a lot of hype – almost a household name!' she moved closer to avoid Sebastian's joint.

'Precisely,' said McKay, ' we all thought that – which is why – now the damn thing's happened, the shareholders find it so hard to believe they could go bust overnight. There'll be an inquiry of course, but it'll probably come too late for me.'

'I'm so sorry,' she said again, 'How's Catalina taking it?'

'Oh Catalina takes everything in her stride, didn't you know?' said McKay wryly,

Buster was in great form. He had drunk well, eaten well and one look around the room assured him that all his guests were equally satisfied. Someone had turned up the music and people were straying out onto the terrace. Others preferred the intimacy of the darkened library where they could shuffle round to the persuasive voice of *My Way*. He could see Leah charging around like a March hare, making sure that everyone had gorged themselves, bossing the servants about and getting in everyone's way. Now she had buttonholed that crazy English guy in the sandals and flowing white gown – the get-up was Moroccan or something. Add a beard and a staff and he'd be straight out of the New Testament! What was the fellow's name? Stacey or something?

Janine Baxter clung to his side. She was becoming kind of heavy-going – not really his type of broad at all and her accent was irritating. She was working here as a sales rep, fixing people up with new villas and apartments. And guess who was the architect? Old bright eyes, Manolo Vaz Valqueira! It didn't take brains to see she was sweet on the guy, thought Buster, remembering the tight fit of the guy's pants when he stood up after kissing his wife's hand.

That Grafton woman was a joke. The champagne cocktails had clearly gone to her head because she'd taken a real fancy to Howard. Poor old guy! thought Buster. Every time he managed to slip away, she was after him with a whoop that would have done her justice in the hunting field. Her husband was fast asleep in one of the Louis XIV chairs in the hall, and the freckly boy had disappeared with Benjie. Just as well Howard had his hands full – an awkward scene could develop and Leah would never forgive them.

'Say, what are you thinking about?' Janine was dragging on a cigarette, the smoke getting caught up in her long yellow hair and reminding him how much he disliked the smell of women who smoked. 'You're mighty pensive sitting there.'

'Oh, I'm just looking around,' said Buster, trying to edge away.

'There's sure plenty to look at,' she said wistfully, eyeing a younger group outside the French windows which included the little architect and his friends from Goa. 'Buster, you're a friend, aren't you?'

'I guess so,' he replied slowly, wondering what was coming.

'I'm kind of hooked on someone here, but I need to know where I stand. So far they've avoided me all night.'

'And you're in a relationship?'

'That's just it…he likes me enough to sleep with, when there's no one else around,' she confided miserably, 'nothing more.'

'Oh, I don't know that's so bad,' said Buster. 'It's a beginning. Let feelings grow!'

'But he hasn't looked my way once!' she wailed.

'The creep!' said Buster, privately not blaming him. 'Well, you know what to do?'

'What's that?'

'Go and make him jealous,' said Buster, anxious now to get rid of her. 'Pick on someone else – not me mind! Make a great big fuss of them in front of this Don Juan of yours, and see if that don't produce the goods. They're mighty jealous, these Latinos.'

'Is that so?' there was a trill of laughter as Catalina approached.

Buster sprang to his feet and in doing so, almost tripped over.

'*Ola!* steady!' she put out a restraining arm, 'There's no need to get so excited!'

'I don't think *you're* the cause of that, Catalina,' put in Janine, resentfully.

'Would you like this seat?' Buster stood aside.

'How kind!' she beamed, 'Oh dear, have I broken something up! Shall I go?'

'Whatever for?' said Buster.

'I'm not quite sure,' giggled Catalina, ' I feel a sudden chill in the air.'

'Not at all,' said Buster, 'Let me get you a drink?'

'Another glass of claret would be splendid – if it's not too much trouble?'

'For you, nothing is too much trouble,' said Buster and wandered off to the bar.

Janine Baxter got up too. 'Do you know what you are, Catalina McKay?'

'I'm longing to hear,' said Catalina, studying herself in the mirror of her powder compact.

'You're a stuck up cow. D'you hear me? A first class, prize cow!' said the other and swayed off in the opposite direction to try out Buster's advice.

Catalina applied more lipstick, and a dab of powder to her upturned nose and sat back. It was really turning out to be quite an amusing evening.

18

Leah came back into the *sala* having completed four duty dances. She could not help feeling she deserved a clap on the back for being the perfect hostess. First, there'd been that funny Wing Commander Stacey, an odd fish if ever there was one, but rather likeable. He was going to revolutionise the world with a programme of self-sufficiency, he told her, and once the UK saw the light, the rest of Europe would follow – except perhaps the French, always a little tricky. He hoped then to launch a powerful campaign in the United States. Some were already on the right track, but people like themselves could spread the word and swell the movement. 'From small acorns...' he said darkly but Leah never caught the rest of the sentence, she was trying so hard not to trip over his trailing *jellabia*.

His idea that immigration would cease as people learned to cultivate their own land and provide for themselves seemed rather optimistic. The West must lead by example, he insisted – how else could Asia and Africa be encouraged to feed their poor? If one owned a plot of land, from two foot square to two acres, it *must* produce. Concrete, patios and paving stones were immoral – the commander's eyes bore into hers – even a window-box on the 147th storey of a Manhattan apartment could yield up some form of vegetation. This would take pressure off the rain forests; why should Brazil be made to fork up for everyone else's water? By now Leah felt quite guilty and said so, but her partner was adamant. It was *criminal* not to use Mother Earth and Mother Nature to their full extent! The time would come when those who stood in the way of the globe's great natural processes, would find themselves up against the firing squad. She hoped it wasn't *his*, remembering his past!

She had managed to escape before the next dance, but not before promising to accept his housewarming gift of a pair of breeding geese to arrive the next day. 'Fine layer, the female – a great start to your self-sufficiency programme provided you let her hatch and keep the first clutch – then you'll be away!' He scoffed when she protested she had nowhere to rear them. 'Easy as wink!' he'd retorted. 'Get that muscle-bound husband of yours to build them a night pen. In the daytime, of course they'll wander free. Save on the grass cutting, they're the world's greatest re-cyclers too!' Leah had her doubts, but he wouldn't take no for an answer. If geese hadn't exactly topped her list of priorities, perhaps it was a step in the right direction.

Apart from the destabilising effect of flowing robes, her next two partners were no less easy. She'd danced with the elderly Portuguese consul who clutched her to his ample stomach in a heavy-handed embrace, complimenting her on her beauty in a monotone of perfect English. Vaguely flattered but uncomfortable, she attempted to raise her head from where he'd positioned it on his starched front, whereupon he switched to Portuguese and merely tightened his grasp. Then it was the turn of Gerald Grafton who had been sound asleep until she stumbled over his feet. He hadn't taken to this too kindly, but after some liquid revival, had escorted her into the library and entered into the spirit of things. They'd managed something between a foxtrot and a quickstep and when he daringly twirled her around in a rock and roll number, she decided he wasn't nearly as haughty as she'd first thought. After all, he couldn't help his accent, and in the slow number that followed, they chatted about gardening and she was promised a cutting from his morning glory.

Feeling quite the country-woman and not altogether disliking the idea she had scarcely left Gerald Grafton's arms when a voice whispered in her ear, 'Eef I don't dance with my hostess soon, I think I will die of frustration!' She spun round to find herself face to face with Manolo Vaz Valqueira and before she had time to reply, he had deftly swept her onto the floor.

'Hey there!' giggled Leah, caught unawares and teetering on her high heels, 'Where did you spring from so suddenly?'

'Spreeng?' he said, eyes gleaming, very close to hers, 'What spreeng?'

'You know – spring from! Out of the blue, like that!'

'A blue spreeng!' his lips were brushing her ear.

'Oh forget it!' said Leah, allowing herself to be guided round the room in a very masterful way. Although she was the taller, she was left in no doubt as to who was in charge. 'I hope you're enjoying the party *Senhor*,' she said a little breathlessly as his hips moulded into hers with magnificent ease.

'*Estupendo!*' he exclaimed. 'Never has there been such a party in the whole Algarve! And,' he lowered his voice confidentially, 'never has there been such a hostess, believe me!'

'Well now,' cried Leah with a coy little movement of her head, 'If that isn't prettily put! Thank you *Senhor* – er – Val de ….'

'Oh – please – I beg of you. Manolo is my name and I insist on calling you something other than Mrs Bloomfield – a cumbersome name, if you'll forgive me – for such a gentle lady.'

'Do you think?' Leah had never thought about it before. 'Names have never meant much to me. I'm not sure Leah is much better.'

'Leah … for us it is very preetty, it sounds like *lua* – you know the moon. Or a sign from the zodiac, I myself am Leo – all fire! Ask any woman who knows me and they will testify.'

It was heady stuff and Leah began to wonder if it were time the dance should end. It was one of those smoochy numbers that seemed to drive her companion's hips ever closer and more angled against her and she was a little afraid she could feel an erection. As though reading her thoughts, Manolo removed himself swiftly. 'Time for a nice cool drink,' he smiled, 'My hostess dances well but she must be looked after.'

He was soon back. 'Here, drink this – the *sangri-a*, I've diluted it for you, nearly all ice and lemonade. You don't deserve a hangover from your own party.'

She was touched, since few would have bothered. His next remark moved her more. Looking deep into her eyes, he gently clinked glasses, 'To you, Leah! And to many happy years in Portugal! You are welcome here, such a change from the usual settlers. Someone who has worked hard all her life and who cares. I know what that is about … I am the youngest son of a big family – if you understand what that implies. Nothing comes easy, you have to strive to rise up. And you have! But don't let anyone knock you down. Welcome to my country, dear Lady! *Bem-vindo!'*

Later, as she stood in the *sala* and surveyed the scene before her, she felt happier than she had for days. All her efforts had paid off, this was her house, her home, her future! It felt good that the natives of this country had appreciated that. First Augusto, now Manolo – even the consul! They'd all made her feel welcome in their midst, suddenly it all seemed worthwhile.

Finally she felt herself relax. All around there was laughter, chatter, music and dancing – some people had even started to eat again! Dinner had long ago finished, but she spied Buster handing Catalina a bowl full of strawberries, Howard was opening a bottle of Lanson – who was he trying to impress? Everyone seemed too engrossed to notice as she slipped off her high heels and crossed the room to exit the open French windows. Ah… that was better! She stood on the terrace and took a great gulp of sea air. It was a magical night. The moon – *lua* – she would never forget that – was on the wane, her pale reflection making little impression on a crystalline sea. But a thousand million stars were out and it was light enough to pick one's way. She skirted the patio with its fairy lights and swaying dancers, and found the little rocky path which ran to the west of the house, before twisting north and up the hillside to the rough land that lay at the back. This part was still in its natural state, the volcanic rock untouched by bulldozer or landscape gardener.

She had explored the path several times, but climbing the cliff at night in bare feet was a different matter. A few weeks before she had come upon a rough stone bench near the top of the ridge. She had remarked on this to their maid and was informed of a local legend. A century or so ago a fisherman had inhabited this land and it was he who had fashioned the bench out of the living rock. As time took its toll and he became too infirm to take the long path to the beach below, he had put together a long length of line so he could still fish off the point, high above the ocean. True or not – it was a pretty tale. Besides, all Leah wanted now was a quiet place to rest as the party progressed without her. Breathlessly, she pulled herself round the familiar spur of rock. Here she would find peace. Surely no one else would venture this far; it looked as if the jutting stone formed the end of the path.

She sat down thankfully and leaned her head against the cool limestone, smooth and rounded, polished by the winds and rains of time. The ledge must have been here for centuries, long before the fisherman… perhaps in the struggles for the kingdom a fugitive Moor or Christian had found refuge here. The resonant tones of Shirley Bassey's *Big Spender* drifted up through the warm air and dragged her back to the present. She tried to shut it out and concentrate instead on the faraway swish of the ocean lapping against the shingle. Like this, she thought, she might lose herself for a few precious minutes in nature, time and space.

Her first reaction when she heard voices on the hillside was to move further up the path. Then she realised they were unlikely to find her, so she stayed quiet and still. Around her corner, she soon found herself an eavesdropper on a conversation she would rather not have heard. Unfortunately, there was no alternative. 'It's kind of you to say you'd like to help…' said one, as she froze to her bench and wondered which of her male guests had such an upperclass accent. The tone was too light for the mad Commander or Gerald Grafton … 'but I really don't see what you can do.'

'You might be surprised what I can do,' drawled the other with a half chuckle which Leah could have sworn belonged to Benjie.

'You must think me a bloody idiot for blurting everything out like that, but I just had to tell *someone*. It's all so bloody stupid … I can't think why I did …' the voice faded into what might have been a deep sigh. 'Why on earth should you be interested, anyway?'

Of course! Thought Leah, the uninvited Grafton boy! That Oxford accent, you couldn't mistake it. What the hell was Benjie doing here, *tête-à-têting* with a callow youth when he ought to be giving Howard a hand?

'Why not?' Benjie was saying. 'I was once in a spot of trouble myself – I wasn't much younger than you – so I'd be a heartless bum if I couldn't so much as listen!'

'Well, it's very decent of you – like a cig? No?' Leah heard three matches strike before he evidently got his light going; it sounded so close, for a panic-stricken moment she thought they'd rounded the corner.

'Calm down,' Benjie was chiding, 'Your hands are shaking.'

'I know,' gulped the boy, 'You must think me a real wet.'

'Never mind what I think,' said Benjie, 'Now the point is you owe this guy around seven hundred pounds, right?'

'Yes.'

'Hmm – that's a lot –getting on towards twelve hundred bucks – Christ! And the guy's only given you to the end of your vacation to pay him back, right?'

'Yup … and –er – term starts again in two weeks.'

'So,' said Benjie, ' we've got a fortnight to find you close on fifteen hundred dollars – Geez!'

'Yes, but Benjie – ' the voice was almost a whisper and Leah found herself straining her ears to keep up with this strange dialogue.

'Hang in there kiddo, I'm thinking. You don't half leave things 'til the last minute – and you categorically refuse to ask your parents for help?'

'I told you – ' the voice rose petulantly, 'That would ruin everything. Provided I get decent passes on last term's exams – which I will, I've turned in some good essays – I'm due a thousand quid on my twentieth birthday. That's in January, it was to have paid for a second-hand car and the insurance. The thing is, they'll never know if I don't buy one.'

'And there's no way you'll get the money if you own up and tell them the whole story?'

'What?' gasped the boy. 'If you knew Ma and Pa, you wouldn't ask that! And it gets worse; I'm due more money – books and clothes allowance from the family trust next term – but that'll stop too if they get wind of this. You've no *idea* what my family's like!'

'OK, OK,' said Benjie soothingly, 'take it easy, kiddo. You're as jittery as an alley-cat.'

'So would you be if you had parents like mine,' Leah heard the bitterness in the swift retort.

'No chance of that,' said Benjie cheerfully. 'Well, we'll just have to think up something. It's a pity there's so little time. I've got shares, but no ready cash without alerting Howard. Besides, I can't afford to mess things up for the future. But there must be other means and I think I can see a way. Now, come on kiddo! We'd better get our asses back to the action or they'll be sending out a search-party. Howard gets stewed up awful quick if he thinks I'm not dancing attendance!'

As she listened to their receding footsteps, Leah wondered if it was her imagination or another of Benjie's chuckles that seemed to prolong itself and mock back at her from the hillside behind. She remained quite composed on her cold bench, wondering at the paleness of her bare arms in the moonlight.

Having given Benjie and the boy ample time to rejoin the party, she was about to get up when she realised with a shock she had not been the only eavesdropper. A man and woman were creeping hand in hand down the bluff towards her. A sense of guilt in the woman's smothered giggle made it imperative that she did not betray her presence. She shrank against the stone, her face turned away from the moon, praying they would not spot her. The voices got louder, 'Gee darlin', that was close! It would have been disastrous if those two had come around the corner?'

'What! That bleeding pansy and his pretty boyfriend? Pity they didn't, we might have been able to show them how it's properly done!' came a slurred Irish voice. 'I promised we'd find a private shpot!'

'We sure did,' giggled the girl. 'You're not only the greatest stud, honey,' she added, 'you're real funny into the bargain!' And completely oblivious of their hostess within touching distance, they meandered off unsteadily in the direction of the house.

Disbelieving, Leah stared after them. She had a sudden ridiculous impression of two life-size puppets swaying in time to the party music, pulled by an unseen hand from the darkened heavens above. With a little sigh, she rose to her feet. It was time to go before anything else happened.

Catalina looked thoughtfully at the plump strawberry delicately balanced between her thumb and middle finger. Turning her head to present a perfect profile to the man at her side, she bit a tiny piece off its crimson head. Slow and deliberate in her devouring of the fruit, she mopped her lips with a napkin, then sucked what was left from the stalk. A red stain had spread over the white cloth, and she folded it carefully before turning her eyes to her companion. 'Hmmm...' she said ecstatically, ' that was so-o-o good.'

'Have another,' said Buster, pointing to the bowl that lay between them.

She shook her head. 'No. I've been rather greedy already – I get carried away. They're such voluptuous fruit, don't you think?'

Buster felt himself reddening, like the napkin, he thought. He did not give a damn about the fruit, but she was voluptuous all right. And those lips ... if only they'd encircled him – instead of the strawberry ... he shuddered deliciously. Then, shocked that she might guess what was in his mind, he changed the subject abruptly. 'Do you like music, Catalina?'

Her eyes danced at the banal question, sooty lashes fluttering as she took time to reply. Horrified, he thought she might have guessed at his thoughts. 'That's a funny question,' she smiled, 'especially to a Portuguese woman! Of course I do! Doesn't everyone?'

'I guess so,' said Buster, chiding himself for his clumsiness. 'But I don't know much about it. Howard's the expert around here...' He brightened, 'I like dancing though.'

'And do you know more about that?'

'Yeah – we had quite a bit of practice in the military.' He shuffled awkwardly to his feet. 'Would you– er – care to…?'

'That would be delightful.'

So eager was he to keep moving, he was halfway across the room before he realised he was on his own. He turned. She was exactly where he had left her, waiting to be helped up. Jeepers! Bashfully he returned to take her arm, this sure was some lady.

'How tall you are!' she remarked as he led her into the barely lit library.

'Six foot three, it says on my passport,' he said.

'Are you really? Of course my husband's tall too, but you're so broad – it somehow makes one feel awfully fragile.'

He looked down at her. Fragile was not a word he would have used; she was actually quite robust, but she was mighty feminine. Funny – he was already feeling quite protective; his wife had never had that effect on him … but then Leah was always so capable. The dance floor was crowded. They edged past other couples and he tried to hold her at arm's length. He'd heard European society ways were more formal than those back home – though, looking around, he wasn't so sure. For all his gauche conversation, Buster was an accomplished dancer. When in uniform, he was often first on the floor at functions and mess parties. You could really pull the gals if your fishtail, shimmy and reverse were in order! Now, after a neat series of turns with Leah's new best friend in his arms, he recognised he had met his match. The music had moved up a beat and he quickened his step to manoeuvre her deftly between and around the other dancers who seemed comatose by comparison.

'Oh stop! Please!' she was gurgling up at him as the number changed, 'I need to come up for air!'

He held her still for a moment, in case he'd overstepped the mark. Instead, she was all smiles. 'You're fantastic!' she beamed, 'Quite fantastic.'

'I'm not sure I understand – '

'You can *dance* – you marvellous man! Don't you see? As soon as I've got my breath back, we can *really* show them!'

Before he could stop her, she broke away and was rummaging through Howard's precious collection. *Favourite Dance Numbers for Lovers* was whisked off the turntable, and replaced with a Spanish album, all within a few breathless seconds. Oblivious to howls of protest, she turned the volume full-blast and announced triumphantly, 'Now it's Tango Time!'

Still reeling from being called a marvellous man and as one in a dream, Buster moved towards her and once again held Catalina McKay in his arms.

'You'll have to hold me tightly this time!' she breathed as he steered her into the centre of the floor which had miraculously emptied. A moment later, they were off, throwing themselves into the compulsive flamenco, exhorted by harsh gypsy voices and the snapping of castanets. Even Howard's sedate speakers seemed to have conspired to enter the spirit of the dance. Buster held her tight. It was vital – her arching back could snap in one sudden fall as she yielded her pelvis to his in total abandon. Heady from wine, mesmerised by music, Buster felt himself bewitched. The fandangos, pirouettes and more fandangos became automatic, synchronised. No need to anticipate the next move, the next step; no time for preparation or recovery of balance, he and Catalina moved together, unfaltering, co-joined. Every time, the chords of the guitar brought them suddenly upright again, her dusky hair hurtled back around her elated face, and in that moment, transformed her into the gypsy-girl about whom the song was written. Then, they were off again, bending backwards into twisting arcs of movement as the whine of the guitar grew to an excruciating crescendo.

Just as it had twenty-five years ago, the old enchantment of the steps enveloped Buster. The other dancers had long since drifted to the side of the floor to watch the unexpected spectacle unfold. He was unaware of this. All he felt was the magic of the movement, the pure physical joy of creating something called a tango through an outpouring of energy. Away, flew the clumsy façade he'd presented earlier. A smooth, streamlined figure had emerged from the chrysalis, and as he and the woman in his embrace covered the floor in graceful sweeping bows and perfect whirling turns, he exulted in his mastery.

Finally, the guitar jealously gave up its last vibrant chord. Catalina, her head thrown back, to reveal a white throat, sank to the floor in a dramatic gesture of submission. Buster gazed down at her, his heart swelling in a rush of emotion. A ripple of approval murmured round the room and someone started to clap. A moment later there was a roar of appreciative applause. Flushed and trembling, Catalina allowed Buster to lead her off the floor. 'That was wonderful!' she cried, 'But I'm so thirsty!'

Happy to be of further service, Buster turned and came face to face with McKay. The eyes that met his were ice-hard. The feeling of elation which had clad him so warmly, fell away instantly. Hell…the man's jealous because I danced with his wife. Better take the bull by the horns. 'Hi there!' he heard his own voice, rather too jaunty. 'Quite a party, huh? Just fetching a drink for your wife; can I do the same for you?'

'No thank you,' said the Scotsman in a quiet voice, standing aside to let him pass.

For some reason Buster stayed where he was; as though the occasion demanded an explanation. 'Er…some dance…some – er – dancer, your wife –' he mumbled.

McKay interrupted. 'She dances exquisitely. Not surprisingly, the tango best of all. It's in her blood.'

So he *had* seen them. Buster had rather hoped not. Oh well! he felt suddenly angry with himself. He'd done nothing wrong. So what the hell was he doing here making excuses? With a grin and a nod, he made to move on but was arrested by a firm hand on his arm. Now what was coming?

'You and Catalina ought to get together more often,' McKay was saying. 'She adores her dancing, but my talents I'm afraid, lie in other directions,' he gave the ghost of a smile. 'It's the first time I've seen anyone match her at the tango. You both did it pretty well. I take my hat off to you, Bloomfield!'

Before Buster had time to reply, the older man had swung on his heel and left the room.

Johanna Vincent answered the door in a gold thread kimono tied loosely around her slim waist. The maid had been sent out early to do the shopping and she had just finished a light brunch of coffee, grapes and pancakes on the verandah. It was a heavenly day, cloudless, yet surprisingly cool for midday, and she noted to her satisfaction a smell of autumn in the air. She was surprised to find Jacqueline van der Stel on the doorstep.

'Come in, darling! You're looking surprisingly bright-eyed and bushy-tailed after last night's little do! Have you been up long?'

'Since eight,' said Jacqueline, with the customary peck on both cheeks. 'I had to drive Karl to Faro to catch the Lisbon flight, then on to Amsterdam.'

'Couldn't he have driven himself? Bad luck he has to work over a weekend, but why should *you* get up at such a beastly hour..'

' I needed the car, and besides – I always get up for him. I hate it when he goes.'

'What time did you get to bed?'

'Too late! Karl got very merry, and I wasn't exactly sober. We were one of the last to go, it must have been after four when we weaved our way down the hill. Luckily no *Guarda* were about.'

'I heard a crate of scotch was delivered at the police station,' said Johanna, 'Bloomfield seems quick enough to have cottoned on to how things work around here.'

'It makes me sick,' said Jacqueline, 'why do we all play their game? Karl's just as bad – on behalf of his company. I hate all this bribery and pandering to the authorities.'

'Until we get democracy, that's the way it will always work,' said Johanna. 'Mark you, a change will come one day, perhaps sooner than we think.'

'And then look out for the drink and drive, we'll all be in trouble!'

'Not for now at least!' rejoined her friend. 'And if you'd like some 'hair of the dog' – there's half a bottle of champagne in the fridge, there should be some bubbles left!'

'Oh, no thanks,' said Jacqueline with a shudder. 'But I'd love some coffee – very black and very strong if it's not too much trouble?'

They settled on the verandah and sipped their coffee in silence. The gardener was working on the lawn in front of them, setting up the sprinkler and picking out weeds from the *calcada* path which led down the slope to the lily-pond. The air was full of the song of birds in the shrubbery.

'That's the nightingale,' said Johanna authoritatively, a finger held up as she strained her ears. Jacqueline could just make out a distinctive fluting sound, quite different from the cacaphony of warbles and chirps. 'I think he only comes to my garden because there's so much water – the fountain, the pond…usually they live in the country round rivers and streams.'

'Or in Berkeley Square,' put in Jacqueline.

'I'm not so sure about that,' laughed Johanna, 'Not when *I* lived in Mayfair! Now,' she ran a languid hand through her silvery hair, 'apart from hitting the bottle, tell me – what did you two think of last night?'

'What a question!' Jacqueline lit a cigarette and looked speculative, 'Where do I begin?'

'The beginning's always a good idea, darling.'

'Well,' puffed Jacqueline, 'Karl and I were among the first to arrive. There was a good deal of awkwardness at the start, but I felt we helped break the ice.'

'Awkwardness?'

'Yes, a slight atmosphere – you know. We had hardly set foot in the front door and were still trying to take in the chandelier, not to mention the Louis Quatorze and so on, when Buster Bloomfield bounds forward in a very hearty way and pumps our hands as though we'd all come through the desert together!'

'Go on!'

'Then we get ushered into that huge reception room where there's a sepulchral hush as everyone tries to make the Graftons feel at home… can you *imagine*! Christabel is wearing that really po-faced look of hers, and Gerald isn't even trying to conceal his contempt. As for Roger, the little drip's got the stutters and it's all too painful for words.'

Johanna nodded sympathetically and fitted one of her gold-tipped cigarettes into a long ivory holder. 'What did you do, darling?'

'I had to do *something*,' said Jacqueline. 'My heart went out to our hostess who was white as a sheet which didn't go too well with all that finery. She was obviously sick with nerves, and embarassed by her husband – I just couldn't let Christabel ruin the evening for her before it had even started. So I gave Karl a kick, and luckily we were able to save the moment with the palm-tree. She was tickled to death, and by that time, thankfully, more people were arriving.'

'I obviously missed a spot of drama, then?'

'Yes, because as usual you were the last!'

'Darling, I may be old enough to be your mother, but there's no reason why I shouldn't still be allowed to make an entrance,' Johanna let out her smoke in a slow, unfurling ribbon.

'Oh and you *did*, Joey,' said Jacqueline warmly, patting her hand. 'You looked simply divine – as usual!'

'Thank you darling … now don't digress… what other little dramas did you observe?'

'You won't believe it, Johanna, but I could swear the dreaded Janine Baxter and Terence O'Connor had it away together somewhere outside. I was on the terrace talking to Eustace – that man gets more extraordinary every time I see him – when who should come wobbling past us, but Janine with sand all down the back of her dress and eye make-up looking like nothing on earth. She clutched Terence's arm as though he was the last man on earth, and he, my dear, looked like the cat who'd stolen the cream. However, once in the house, he dumped her rather quickly and made a dive for the bar. She was crying her eyes out when I went to the loo. Silly bird!'

'I can guess what started that little saga off,' said Johanna speculatively.

'What?'

'Firstly Manolo ignored her all evening, and secondly naughty Catalina didn't help.'

'I might have guessed. What did she do?'

'I can't think how I happened to notice,' Johanna waved a vague arm, 'but there was I with little Manolo, when I spotted Catalina upsetting a cosy conversation between Bloomfield and Janine. Janine charged off like a woman scorned. Let's just say she'd had enough to drink to make her somewhat reckless about the manner in which she needed to prove her desirability.'

'Ah, that explains it,' said Jacqueline, 'and typically Irish, Terence just happens to be in the right place at the right time, and clearly in the right mood! Tell me Joey,' she changed the subject, 'what do you make of the two queers?'

'Darling!' Joanna sounded mildly shocked, 'You mustn't call them that. We don't kno-ow, after all. I believe they're known as the – er – Boys.'

'Same thing, isn't it?' grinned Jacqueline.

'Not at all,' Johanna sounded stern, 'and I must admit, I found them most attentive. The large one – Howard, I think – is so knowledgeable about music, the arts, all sorts of things. He saw me in the West End when I played Veronica in *The Other Side of Wisdom*. Also, when we brought that wonderful Hugh Williams play *The Grass is Greener* to Broadway, he attended twice!'

'Aha,' said Jacqueline, guessing Howard had said all the right things and might soon be part of Johanna's inner circle.

'I was thinking, I must ask them round for drinks. It seems a long time since I had a cocktail party.'

'Won't you ask the Bloomfields too, Joey?'

'I suppose I'll have to,' she said wearily, ''though a less inspiring couple would be hard to find. She's rather too worthy for me and he strikes me as a boor.'

'Oh I don't know,' said Jacqueline, egging her on. 'Buster seems to have made quite a hit in some quarters, so he can't be that bad.'

'Perhaps not. His looks are all right – apart from those appalling horn-rimmed glasses,' conceded Johanna, 'but he has little conversation, and there's something ungainly in his manner.'

'You surprise me – on the dance floor he moves like a professional!'

'Really? I don't think I saw – '

'You missed their *tango*?' said Jacqueline incredulously. 'I thought everyone saw their *tango*!'

For once Johanna was at a loss for words. Silence fell between them as Jacqueline remembered and Johanna waited for an explanation. Since none seemed forthcoming, she asked, 'Who exactly is "they"? …you said "their tango" d'you mean our two hosts?'

'No way!' said Jacqueline. 'Why! Buster and Catalina of course!'

'Ye gods!' said Johanna, 'who would have thought she'd dance with that creep! She usually goes for the aristocratic or autocratic type!'

'Not this time,' said the younger woman, ' She and Buster danced the tango so well, it created quite a stir. I was with Jock but he suddenly excused himself and went off towards the door, muttering. Only he didn't go out. He just stood there on his own watching them, the usual glass in hand. Catalina was showing off, you know how she does. Everyone cleared the floor to see better and Jock looked more and more strained. When the music stopped we all clapped. But not Jock. Then Buster went over and talked to him and for a moment I thought there might be a fight. Then it all seemed to be all right, only – there was a lot of tension in the air.'

'Yes, he's an emotional man, is our Jock,' mused Johanna. 'But he's so deep one never really knows what's going on in that brain of his. Sometimes I wonder if he doesn't get a kick out of Catalina's goings-on. And I'm not so sure Catalina doesn't know it too. Probably encourages her in fact.'

'What? All her flirting and flaunting herself in front of other men – you mean?'

'Hmmm.'

'But Jock's so jealous. He may not say much but you can see it a mile off. I can't believe he would encourage her.'

'I think we know Jock MacKay far less than we imagine we do,' was all Johanna would say further on the subject.

19

$\mathcal{E}$xtra maids were cheerfully at work when Leah ventured downstairs at eleven. Parties like this were a new event in their hamlet and much to be encouraged because of the extra money. 'Bom dia Minha Senhora!' Four bright faces lifted in greeting from the hall and the open sala beyond. There was no response. Out of character and in silence, Leah surveyed their efforts, then turned and made her way haltingly into the kitchen. The women looked at each other, shrugged, then proceeded on their hands and knees to polish the floor.

At that moment, Leah had only two things on her mind. Tranquillisers and black coffee. A mismatch she knew, but a cocktail that experience had shown her would settle such moments of nervous exhaustion. She found the first in a drawer, the second was turning out more difficult. Everything had been moved for the party and the coffee beans she craved had vanished. This was too bad, she thought, as she rummaged about. The night had taken its toll with a few stragglers staying on for breakfast whilst she, determined to play the perfect hostess to the end, had overdone the hospitality – whipping up omelettes and frying bacon for a thankless crowd of youngsters. The night staff had gone home and there was no sight nor sound of Buster or the Boys at the very time she needed them most.

No one had warned her just how drunk these Europeans could get and how precious little thanks she would receive for her efforts. In the end, most of her carefully prepared meal lay uneaten and by the time the last car disappeared over the brow of the hill and into the dawn, her nerves were torn to shreds. So where was the damn stuff? Exasperated she tore things from shelves but to no avail. 'Oh hell!' she cried aloud, as Howard's large bulk appeared in the room.

'What's up?' he said irritably, his normally florid face grey with fatigue and stubble. There was the bitter taste of acid indigestion in his mouth.

'Where's the coffee, Howard?' she whined. 'I've been searching forever.'

'How should I know?' he got out a tin of Earl Grey and put on the kettle.

'Well, I give up!' said Leah, shutting the cupboard door with a bang. 'The only way I can compensate now is to take those pep-up pills I promised Wally I'd given up for good.'

'So why did you keep them then?' said Howard as she made her way to the door.

'Wally said pyschologically, I must always retain freedom of choice, it's a control thing. Also, to keep a few laid by for emergencies – and this,' she added meaningfully, 'is an emergency.'

'What? A hangover?' Howard's tone was not sympathetic.

'No, sheer exhaustion – I was left to deal with everyone on my own at the end last night.'

'I'm sorry – Benjie and I were out with flashlights till four, making sure nobody drove over the cliff. We were cursing you for keeping them up so late. As for that husband of yours, it's hardly our fault he "died" on us when he did – must have been all that dancing.'

'I guess…' she hung her head and sidled up, wondering at the hostility in his voice – as though Buster were a stranger. 'Look, do me a favour would you, pour me a cup of that stuff – it must be better than nothing. '

He made two mugs and they sipped in silence. Finally, to introduce a sense of normality, she asked if Benjie was up.

'He's awake, but staying in his room.'

'Oh. Buster's still sound asleep. He's real knocked out.'

'Hardly surprising.'

She withdrew to look out of the window feeling fidgety and offended at Howard's unsociable behaviour. She was longing to discuss the party, but instead he'd settled down with a diet magazine as he carefully spread his toast.

A knock came at the kitchen door. 'One of the helpers, I bet,' said Leah moving forward, 'they ought to know by now to go round the other way.'

It was as though a whirlwind had entered. A burly man in flapping cream shorts and matching stockings brushed past her, a huge wicker hamper clasped to his chest. 'Well here we are finally,' the voice sounded flustered. 'Five minutes late – sorry about that – but there's a lot of packing to do! We're scheduled to fly out early this afternoon – what? Be damn glad to leave this climate behind. Looking forward to a good day's shooting and a decent Yorkshire mist, what? Then it's back to work, work, work. Did I tell you I'm bringing out a book about it all?' He paused for breath and set the basket down on the kitchen table in front of Howard. 'Sorry to disturb you – there we are, my pretties!'

Leah was still gripping the doorhandle as she searched her mind desperately for a name, a face, some clue that would tell her what on earth this Englishman was doing depositing a hamper on the breakfast table and referring to Howard and herself as 'my pretties'. It was fortunate Benjie was not in the room. Not until the man straightened up and looked her full in the face did it all come back in a rush. Of course! The eccentric wing commander! Only today he wore shorts instead of robes…no wonder she'd barely recognised him. Recovering herself, she hurried forward. 'I'm so sorry, Commander Stacey, you took me by surprise for a moment. I'd er – forgotten you were calling today.'

'Had you indeed? I hadn't – that's why I'm here, ha, ha! Smashing party by the way! One for the annals, I reckon. Now where was I?'

'Leah,' said Howard ashen-faced, 'What *is* going on?' He pushed his plate away as though it had been contaminated. 'Will you kindly introduce this gentleman and put me in the picture.'

'Forgive me, old boy, but we already met,' beamed their visitor. 'Last night to be exact! Different garb, but the same Eustace Stacey at your service!' He clicked his heels and gave a small formal bow. 'Now to business, what?' he glanced at his watch, '…must be quick, airports are strict, even in the Algarve! Now where was I? Ah yes, the pair of them – in there – safe as houses – that is, until you undo the lid, ha ha!…' he made little kissing sounds through the wicker. 'You're going to get an awful lot out of them, I can see. As for names, Cleopatra's the female – and yes, you've guessed it – Anthony. They actually seem to respond…though Anthony can be a bit fierce, he's only doing what comes naturally… to ganders, I mean!'

Leah gripped the back of her chair and tried to steady her legs before she spoke, but she never got that far.

'Oh and one more thing … before literally, I fly! Food! As you'll know they thrive on grass, and the usual grains, handful of maize, etc, etc. You'll arrange a tank of clean water for their daily dip of course – they're keen on their ablutions – it keeps feathers trim and eyes healthy – most important at laying time too! But I tell you what, I'll get my secretary to post you some instructions from England – all right? Bye-bye my pretties,' he rattled his fingers over the basket and there was a faint hiss from within. 'Be good!'

He turned again to face Leah, 'Thanks again most awfully for a topping evening! So sorry I've got to rush off like this, but I've a plane to fly back to England. Good luck with Cleo and Ant! I'll see you at Christmas – if not before. Bye for now!'

One moment he was there; the next he'd disappeared. He shot out of the door as quickly as he had come in. Leah went to the window just in time to glimpse a pair of muscly legs in cream gartered wool vanishing into an old grey Lancia. Then, legs and car took off in a cloud of dust. Long after the dirt had subsided, Leah was still gazing outwards, a look of total disbelief on her face. Then she turned back into the kitchen and, refusing to meet Howard's accusing eyes, scooped up basket and contents in her arms and disappeared in the direction of the wild bit.

Buster awoke with cramp in his left leg. Little wonder, he mused as he strained to touch the bottom of the bed with his heel. Ouch! The movement made it worse, not better. What idiot had told him that was a cure? He could feel the strands of muscle balling up into a fiery knob of pain which threatened to be agony. He slipped both feet out of the bed and tried to stand. The coldness of the tiled floor was a shock to the system; he wobbled and clutched the bedhead. Thankfully his muscles stretched to take the weight and he fell back amongst the covers with a sense of relief. Only now his head was spinning. He opened one eye, and had a vision of a treadmill or was it people trampling grapes…up and down, round and round…the noise inside his head grew more deafening by the moment. Squelch, squelch, boom, boom! How could they be so selfish? At this hour of day! He must demand they stop! But no words came; it might be safest of all to go back to sleep…like his leg. Ah well… if he slept he might dream again of the lovely Cata – Cata – Catalin…

Buster's mouth slacked open as he let unconsciousness wash over him.

Benjie had his back turned to the door, the sheet pulled up around his neck so anyone entering would assume he was asleep. Howard had already been in and Benjie was uncertain if he'd fooled him or not. The way he was facing now, he could just about read sideways. The sun streamed through the slats of the shutters, the zebra stripes of light just enough to illuminate the book resting on his pillow. It was one of Benjie's small luxuries to read in bed. For some illogical reason, Howard disapproved of it, but then Howard was only really interested in books as collectors' items, the thought of a paperback for light amusement inexplicable.

They had had their first row since arriving in Portugal, as the silver streaks of dawn sliced across the sky and the last guests had drifted away. Howard had waited, calculatingly, until Benjie was undressed and about to slip naked into bed. Clothes were for dialogue, birthday suits for sleep, thought Benjie as he clutched a towel to cover himself. Howard tore it out of his hands in one firm swoop, leaving him vulnerable and exposed as he initiated a bitter battle of words. With exhaustion etched in both their faces, the insinuations and accusations were flung like wet cement against a bare wall. And boy – how they stuck! The wounds Howard inflicted never raised welts or weals, reflected Benjie; no one could accuse him of being a violent man. But there was no denying his armoury of weapons, all verbal but nonetheless deadly.

Far from reading, he was turning pages automatically as one of Howard's taunts came back to him now. They tended to echo each other in almost every row they'd ever had. For starters, sharp reminders of Benjie's background, his faith or lack of it, and his early dependency on other's people charity. Words like *low down*, *low joint* and *low class*, liberally peppered each insight into Benjie's former existence. The entrée was mainly about Howard, his incredible philanthropy, generosity and patience in taking Benjie in and then encouraging his dormant talents. Dessert came in a concluding form; a concoction of deductions, all leading to the fact that if Howard had not rescued him from the mire, Benjie might still be wallowing in it – unlikely ever to rise above the scum of his miserable existence. It was all so poignant yet somehow believeable, Benjie could have wept.

Of course his meeting with Roger Grafton had sparked the whole thing off. Benjie could have kicked himself for handling it all so badly. The sense of occasion was partly to blame, the champagne did not help – and for someone who rarely drank, dropping his guard had made him reckless, careless with his timing. Howard disliked the fact that Benjie was a party animal and he was not. Over the years, Benjie had learned to cope with that. He knew for example there was an absolute limit to the stretch of time he could afford to take away from his partner's side, most particularly at functions like these. Anything over, made Howard insecure and nervous. Once this state was allowed to flourish, it generally meant they were heading for trouble; trouble with a capital 'T'.

Really, thought Benjie, rolling over and forgetting to keep his back to the door, the whole situation was getting ridiculous. Years of solid companionship and support should have led to a relaxation of a few rules. They were both older and hopefully wiser, so what should it matter if he made a few friends here and there? He was still with Howard, tended to his every need and that should have been ample proof of loyalty at their stage in life. It happened he had found in Roger a certain freshness and naive sincerity which remarkably few young people possessed these days. It had been interesting talking to someone from such a different culture and background. Hearing about the youth's studies in classics, life at a famous university and difficulties with his snobbish parents provided such a contrast to anything Benjie had ever known, it gave him a vicarious thrill. Besides, what harm was there in simply enjoying the company of someone else? There was nothing more to it than that.

The fact the kid had financial problems was really neither here nor there, although it would be nice to help. In fact, Howard's blast-off last night made the idea more attractive than ever. Here was someone in trouble. For once, Benjie was being given the opportunity to show just how responsible and thoroughly supportive he could be. A benefactor! He rather liked the image. At least Roger Grafton with his fancy accent would see him in a good light! It would never occur to Roger that Benjie was either *low down* or *low joint*.

He shut his book. It was crazy to stay in bed pretending to everyone that he was asleep, pretending to himself that he was reading, and in reality brooding. He got up abruptly and pulled on some clothes. He took longer than usual brushing his teeth as he stared at his lean tanned torso in the mirror. The working-outs were still working … the six pack which had taken so long in the building, still in evidence. As for the face, did he look his age? … maybe, maybe not, but he much preferred himself now to ten years ago – there was a maturity there that he really quite liked. Men were luckier than women that way. He pulled in his stomach, straightened his back and humming a little tune to prove that he, Benjamin Liebermann, was on top of the world, he sauntered along the passage, down the stairs, past the maids on their hands and knees, and into the kitchen. He was just in time to see Leah's departing back, visibly staggering under the weight of some enormous encumbrance. Howard was hunched over the table, a murderous glower on his moon-shaped face.

'Hi, Leah!' called Benjie with a cheeriness he did not feel. As he felt his bravado slipping away, he had already made up his mind that three for company was better than two. 'Where are you going in such a hurry?'

She half-turned her head with difficulty. 'Care to give me a hand?'

'Sure!' he bounded forward with alacrity. 'What in heavens' name have you got there?'

Howard's hands had been twitching all morning. Now he could no longer refrain from worrying the ugly red bumps. 'I was hoping someone was going to ask that question,' he said quietly, getting up.

Leah who had been halfway out of the back door, struggled back in. With Benjie's help she placed the hamper on the floor. 'Look! Is this an inquisition or what?'

'No,' said Howard grandly, 'but since we share this house, I suggest we might be party to this knowledge.'

'I agree!' said Benjie, forcing a smile from one to the other.

'Well, it's geese!' said Leah, ungrammatically. 'Common or garden geese! To live in our garden, as a matter of fact. Other than that, I can tell you no more.'

'*Geese*!' said Howard and Benjie simultaneously.

'Yeah – why not? They're a house warming present from that charming Wing Commander Stacey.

'Fancy!' said Benjie.

'Er– may I ask – are they for the pot?' asked Howard.

'Certainly not. They're a pair!'

'I take it you mean male and female,' said Howard.

'I do,' said Leah, looking him straight in the eye. 'And what's more, I'm going to breed from them. Commander Stacey said it was my duty, you know, environmentally speaking. I'll have you know he's a very clever man.'

'You can say that again – the last part, anyway,' said Howard with a short laugh. 'He goes to a party, dines and wines himself nicely, and at the end of it all saddles his hosts with a couple of old geese he wants rid of. Yes sir – very clever indeed!'

'He didn't want rid of them. He was doing us a kindness.'

'Ah, so he'd been hoping to take them skyward on that plane of his, had he? They've got feathers of their own, but he reckoned they'd enjoy a little trip – on other wings.'

'It wasn't like that,' spluttered Leah, 'We were talking about self-sufficiency and public duty and all that…'.

'Oh, gee…I beg your pardon! I see it all now, you were on the same level, heart to heart and he saw in you another goose fancier. I'm so sorry. I misjudged the guy.'

Benjie giggled loudly but stopped as he caught Leah's eye. He might need her as an ally sooner than later.

'Look!' said Leah, bending down to pick up the hamper again. 'These will be my geese and my responsibility. I'll thank you two to keep out of this whole affair, and I'll see to it that they don't worry you. Now if you'll excuse me…' and she made a brave attempt at sweeping out into the garden.

She left them gawping after her. Then Benjie caught the glimmer of a twinkle in his companion's eye. He heaved a sigh of relief. Thank God for Leah – she had broken the ice. With a grin, he turned to Howard and said 'What's gotten into her?'

'God only knows,' said Howard, spreading himself another piece of toast with a sliver of butter. Benjie knew that tone of voice. It was short, but the venom had gone out of it. He joined Howard at the breakfast table, being careful not to scrape his chair over the tiles. All Howard needed was a little peace and quiet.

McKay put down the half-empty glass and picked up his brush. It was his second shot of brandy and the twenty ninth time he had lifted his brush to canvas since lunch. Only, as yet – nothing had happened.

'Perform, damn you!' he addressed it angrily.

How was it some days it flew through the work in hand, punctuating the canvas with lightening touches here and there, cutting a trail of blazing colour over the desert wastes of white? He had heard of writers' block, what did the wisecracks call this? When a normally lively tool lies comatose between the fingers, when its sheer weight makes everything seem ponderous – when every ounce of life has been sucked from its tow-coloured bristles – does this too have a name?

'Idiot!' McKay flung it down, not sure if he was addressing the brush or himself.

Catalina came into the studio with light step and a pair of scissors. 'Won't you ever learn?' she said, stretching up to expose a bare midriff as she began to snip at the overblown blossoms of the creeping rose which ran around the open casement window.

'I hate your doing that,' said McKay, ignoring the question, 'It seems so final. Why not let them wither away quietly on their own, undisturbed? They do you no harm.'

'They're ugly,' she said, her scissors never faltering.

'So will you be when you're withered up and dry, but I hope at least you'll be allowed to fade away in peace.'

She did not reply; just looked at him in a way that seemed to say that mortality was for others, him for instance, but bore little relation to her.

He swilled what was left of the drink gently around the glass and wished she'd finish. Snip, snip, snip… fullblown heads and brownish petals falling limply. The sight and sound depressed him. To be borne away on a light breeze was one thing, to fall to the floor another. Here would be no peace – no final resting place. Philismena's broom would bang along the skirting boards, and ruthlessly search them out. And then what? Into a pan with dust and cobwebs – to be borne thence to some far-off stinking dump – why must a thing of beauty end with all things ugly? It rather summed up life, he thought.

'You've got your morbid look on,' Catalina was saying. 'Have you drunk a lot?'

'Sufficient to keep my blues and my hangover at bay…'

'Then why bother even to *try*,' she sighed.

He pretended to misunderstand. 'One must always go on trying,' he muttered, 'If I didn't try I'd either go hang myself or be shockingly rude to you right now. But neither would achieve very much, I suspect.'

'To *paint*, I meant. It never works when you've been "at it"… the bottle, of course!'

'Well, it has for others – Goya, Van Gogh, Toulouse… The list is endless. Wasn't some of Picasso's best work achieved under the influence? It can be liberating, you know.'

'You're impossible,' said Catalina. 'Do you want to collect Katy or shall I? She's gone to play with those Jones children from school. Only I want her home for tea here, I won't have her eating chips and all those stodgy puddings the mother serves up. Why do the English give their children all that rubbish?'

'Energy giving,' said McKay, 'that sort of fare never did me any harm.'

'Maybe if you live at the North Pole,' sniffed Catalina, ' or in Scotland, but not in southern Portugal. Anyway,' she added, tightening her mouth, 'since it seems Scotland's out for the future, she might as well stick to Portuguese ways for now.'

'You're really enjoying pushing your point today, aren't you?' said her husband. 'Having a go about everything.'

'I'm waiting to hear if you wish to collect Katy. I said we'd pick her up around four.'

'I'll go,' he said, moving towards the stairs, 'I could do with some fresh air.'

'Well, make sure she doesn't smell your breath. People may say her father drinks like a fish, but as long as she doesn't work it out for herself …'

'Now wait a minute,' he said, turning back. 'Just have a little care with your tongue, will you? I seem to remember you didn't do so badly yourself last night. I might even go so far as to say you were quite abandoned – '

'Jock!' her voice cut in, icy sharp. 'We've been into all this. Don't you remember our little talk when we finally got you home? We had quite a lot to say to each other – or were you so out of it, you don't remember? You'd better speak now if you want to be reminded. Because I think it's quite important. In fact, *very*!'

'I remember exactly what was said. And what wasn't – for that matter. I think we both understood each other perfectly well. But for the immediate future – I'd rather not mention it all again.' His face was suddenly haggard as he added, 'And don't worry – I won't let her know her Daddy's a complete failure – even if her mother thinks he is.'

Leah called round at the McKays' in the late afternoon. Buster was still in bed when she left home. He seemed to think he'd gotten the 'flu, so she had taken up a tray of piping hot turkey broth, toast and butter. There were a hundred and one things still to be done in the house but she'd already done her fair share and it would not hurt anyone if she slipped away. The geese were settled; their odd job boy Carlos had fixed up a temporary pen and they were already grazing alongside a neighbour's goat at the top of the hill.

She hadn't been able to bring herself to discuss the party much with the Boys after their attitude that morning. Besides, it was far more tempting to hear what her friend Catalina thought of it all. She needed some light relief after the stress of last night.

Catalina spotted the red Opel coming and opened the door before Leah knocked. She greeted her warmly, then put a finger to her lips and said 'Shh… Jock's upstairs in a mood, we won't intrude on him. Come into the morning room and we can have tea and talk!'

'Great!' said Leah. She'd been hoping to avoid Catalina's difficult husband. She caught sight of Katy, hiding behind her mother's skirt. 'Hi there poppet!' she cried, wishing this child would be more friendly. 'Come and say hello to your Auntie Leah!'

'Go on darling,' said Catalina, giving her a push.

'But she's not my auntie, Mama.'

Catalina's mouth tightened a fraction. 'Do as you're told darling and then run along and tell Philismena Mama wants tea in the morning room. You can help her decorate the cake she's just made.'

'A chocolate one?'

'Certainly not, it's a light sponge! Now off you go!'

The child danced off to the kitchen, 'She's so cute,' said Leah, adding untruthfully, 'how lucky you are!'

'Oh I don't know,' Catalina led the way into the cool room. 'A child needs an awful lot of attention. She and Jock are both highly demanding.'

They shut themselves in like two conspirators and Leah settled comfortably into a large Moroccan pouffe, enjoying the feeling of having Catalina to herself, 'I'm all ears,' she grinned, 'to hear *exactly* what you thought of last night.'

Catalina was arranging herself, graceful as a cat, on the window-seat. She tucked her well-shaped legs under her, placed a cushion behind her back and looked at Leah with narrowed eyes, 'You don't need *me* to tell you, I'm sure! It was quite the best party ever given in the Algarve. Everyone was saying so! Out of this world!'

'You're not just trying to please me?' Leah's face lit up. With a high pony-tail and no make-up, she looked absurdly youthful.

'My dear Leah! This place is a cultural wilderness! Yes, it's a beautiful land, endless beaches, almond blossom, quaint architecture, fishing boats and so on… but socially!' she raised her eyes, heavenward. 'Most of those people had never seen anything like it… not here. It will be the talk of Santa Felicia for months to come!'

'Oh but surely,' objected Leah, 'your list included a pretty sophisticated bunch – Miss Vincent, the Consul, the Graftons, Commander Stacey…'

'Has beens,' pronounced Catalina, 'they're all retired, or semi… out of touch with the modern world. It will have been decades since they've attended a party like that – and certainly not on their own doorstep!'

Leah still felt doubtful; you could hardly call Manolo a has-been, or his smart friends from Goa, and she hadn't realised Lucie from the discotheque was the daughter of an earl – Gerald Grafton had said – but she let the remark pass.

'Then what about you, Catalina? Did you really enjoy yourself – after all the support and advice as well as keeping a watchful eye out for me?'

'I enjoyed it best of all,' she gave her infectious tinkly laugh.

'Then I'm delighted,' said Leah, 'your opinion means a lot to me.'

Catalina said nothing for a moment, as though lost in thought. Then, with an unexpected edge to her voice, the Portuguese accent more pronounced than usual, said 'I do weesh you would not concern yourself about me so much, Leah. I'm very independent, you know and can take care of myself. Sometimes, you ought to theenk more about yourself before worrying about others. There's a quotation Jock's very fond of using – Shakespeare probably ... "the world is full of trickery..." ' and she threw back her head and laughed.

Leah smiled politely, her mind racing ahead as usual. She had so many questions stored up. How was the food? Had people remarked? The vintage champagne? – was it noticed? And the house itself?...their furniture? Surely someone had said something? It wasn't as though every villa in Santa Felicia could boast a pair of William and Mary consoles or a Louis XIV wing chair – but had they found favour? And even more important – had people liked *them*?

The more Catalina reassured, the safer she felt. Later, Leah wondered at herself – why? Was she hankering after Wally's couch, missing those days in New York where she poured out everything to her therapist? Surely not! She had no business worries now. She was free of all that. No, this was quite different and the thing she loved most about this new girlfriend, was the laughter. There'd not been much time to laugh in Manhattan, and now she was laughing until the tears ran down her face.

'The leest' was discussed all over again – Catalina's observations were witty and dry. Having disposed of Terence O'Connor, Janine Baxter, Manolo Vaz Valqueira and Johanna, they were now onto the subject of the wing commander and his *jellabia*, as well as a colourful scene between Howard and Christabel Grafton. 'She just wouldn't take "no" for an answer,' said Catalina, 'she really had the hots for him!'

'If only she *knew*!' giggled Leah, wiping her eyes.

'Oh, I doubt that woman would twig anything, even if you spelt it out for her. She's so mannish herself, it wouldn't occur to her. No wonder the son is confused about his sexuality.'

Leah nodded; she had decided not to mention what she'd overheard on the cliff the night before. 'I can't help worrying about the Boys,' she said. 'I'm beginning to see a crack in their relationship which I hadn't appreciated before. Maybe it's just the age difference, but Howard is incredibly rigid in his attitudes, it must be hard for his partner – especially when he gets all proper and disapproving. Underneath, Benjie's a lovely free spirit, but lately he's become very over-sensitive and reacts to the slightest little thing. It concerns me too how Buster seems to rub them up the wrong way. So often I have to be peacemaker when the four of us are together. But if I'm on my own, like this morning...the other two gang up on me.' She sighed and bit her lip, 'It seems one just can't win.'

'I expect Buster's sheer manliness makes them resentful,' said Catalina. 'No doubt in time, they'll learn to live with it.'

'I hope so,' said Leah. 'I've even begun to wonder if we did the right thing building the villa together. I sometimes think Howard feels the same.'

'Now, don't be so negative!' said Catalina, patting her shoulder. 'As I said before it's early days and in any relationship, there'll be teething troubles. Things will work out! Look at me! Our whole world's fallen in with Jock's shares going down the drain, but I'm looking on the bright side. In fact, I've already got a scheme half worked out in my head.'

'Have you? That's wonderful news!' said Leah, immediately forgetting her own troubles. 'Do tell me!'

'Oh I couldn't do that! Not that I don't trust your discretion,' she added, 'but we Portuguese believe it very bad luck to talk about something which hasn't yet happened. It tempts the evil eye!'

'Catalina, I'd no idea you were superstitious!'

'Hardly superstition, it is fact. Long before the Moors, we lived under the influence of the Greeks. Like them, we still paint 'the eye' on our boats, looking out to sea, not turning against the men in the boat.'

Leah could not help asking if Jock had managed to enjoy the party at all. 'As hostess, I tried to coax him to get involved,' she said, 'but I made a poor job of it.'

'There's no need for you to take the blame,' smiled Catalina. 'Nothing you could have done would have worked for Jock at such a time.'

'No-o, but it doesn't stop him having eyes for you, Catalina,' Leah clasped her arms round her knees and supported her chin thoughtfully on the back of her knuckles. 'You know his eyes never left your face the entire evening.'

She wanted to say more, but there was a knock on the door and Katy bounced in ahead of Philismena bearing a heavily laden tray.

'My! That was quick!' said Leah, perceiving a large round sponge on a silver stand.

'I did the cake, Mama!' cried Katy, ignoring their visitor, 'but we've made pancakes too! I did the eggs and I spread some with jam for Papa!'

'Was that really necessary?' said Catalina, avoiding her daughter's sticky fingers as Philismena set the tray down on an occasional table

'Can I sit here beside you Mama?'

'No darling, you're all sticky. Go and wash and then you may join us by the fireside.'

'That lady's sitting on my pouffie, Mama.'

'It's called a pouffe, darling and I said to go and *wash*,' said Catalina, her eyes beginning to glint.

'Yes Mama,' Katy hurried to the door. As she went out she said reproachfully more to herself than anyone else, 'Papa calls it pouffie.'

Tea was an awkward interlude. Gone was the cosy informality of their *tête-à-tête*, instead her valiant attempts to win over the child merely made her feel foolish. It must be her father in her, thought Leah. She pecked at the pancakes. 'They really look delicious,' she said, trying again. 'Aren't you clever, Katy, to do all that.'

'I only put the eggs in,' said the child coldly, 'Philismena made them. Mama, can I go now?

'I think the sooner you run along the better,' said Catalina, exasperated. 'Then go to your room and play with your toys 'til bathtime. You're not to disturb Mama any more.'

She turned back to her guest, 'Now!...what were we talking about? Oh yes, I know – husbands? I can see Buster is very dear to you...do tell me more about him?'

With the child gone, Leah began to unwind again. It was so pleasant to have a confidante. With Catalina and a couple of tranquies, one could discuss the most intimate details of one's marriage.

Buster woke up at the last chime of six on the grandfather clock along the landing. He felt ravenously hungry so he called for Leah. It was hours since she'd brought him the soup. What about his tea? There was no response. He tried again – even louder. After all, he was supposed to be ill. One never knew what might strike in a foreign country – there must be all sorts of strange bugs floating about – they could be deadly. Suppose he was on the point of death and no one came? They'd never stop blaming themselves when they eventually stumbled over his dead body. He sank back against the pillows, pleased with the picture of tragedy that stirred within his brain. He could see the scene perfectly now. His own muscular body lying inert, lifeless – struck down in its prime – the last rasping breath being torn from his manly throat. Then the final blow – Death itself! And a vacuum ... nothing ...

But wait! A black veil – and he was moving onto another plane and looking down from somewhere far above. He could see mourners moving into view, gathering around where he lay, shocked and disbelieving at the sight of him. His neglectful wife was clearly defined, pale and wretched, mouth working, hands wringing, clutching at her skirts. Howard was deathly pale too – almost yellow in fact. Too shocked even to worry at his hands, he resembled a huge beached whale, immobile and thoroughly useless. As for Benjie – he was everywhere – darting about, tempestuous, futile – like a moth. Buster decided the three of them would not be brilliant in an emergency

As he closed his eyes, he could just discern another figure emerging. She was clad head to foot in long sombre clothes, her dark eyes misted with sorrow, as she took control of the situation. The other mourners parted to allow her through, the veil parting over a white bosom as she issued commands, in a firm unwavering voice. Only as they lowered his dead body into the yawning grave, did she give way to grief. He could see her red lips parted, moist and shining and she was whispering so no one could hear her...'My love, my love... if only there'd been time... time for *us*... if only...' To his great surprise, he saw the figure was none other than Catalina McKay.

As his coffin hit the ground with a thud, he woke up with a start. Almost immediately, he realised he had a hard-on. The throbbing headache he'd experienced earlier seemed to have disappeared and he knew he was not ill after all. In fact he felt altogether very alive! Ten minutes later he was up, showered and dressed and on his way downstairs to raid the refrigerator.

20

*T*he next time Benjie saw Roger Grafton was at Johanna Vincent's. She had invited a few people to drinks and it was one of those still, stifling evenings that precede the cooler nights eagerly awaited in the Peninsula as September unfolds. Everyone was out in the garden, bare limbs coated in citronella to keep mosquitos at bay. Above this, arose the heavy, cloying scent of the last flowers of summer; rich roses coupled with oleander and peony, screened by bland pampas grass and scented herbs drying behind old walls. An unfamiliar aroma assailed the nostrils from the drinks trolley. Johanna had invented a new champagne cocktail using a local liqueur and liquidised passion fruit which everyone pronounced to be 'divine'. Certainly, it was going down quickly.

Roger had been dispatched indoors to fetch more glasses. Benjie, ever watchful, and noticing Howard deep in conversation with their hostess over a bed of tiger-lilies, seized his opportunity. A second later, he was following Roger into the house, unobserved. 'Hi kiddo! How are things?'

Squatting to reach into a low cupboard, Roger jumped. With his back to him, he almost let go the precious glass stems. Leaping to his feet he became aware of how thin and gangling he must look. He brushed a flopping lock of red hair out of the way and straightened up. 'Oh hello! It's you! I'm sorry...' he stammered, his green eyes averted, 'I – er... didn't hear you come up behind me.'

'Steady there, why are you apologising? What's wrong?' Benjie laid a concerned hand on the bare arm. 'Jeez, you're a bundle of nerves! How come?'

'Oh Christ... everything! Yes, you're right, I'm all uptight.' Still the youth would not meet his gaze. 'It's just that – things haven't exactly improved since I last saw you... in fact I'm in one *helluva* mess and don't know what's to be done. I got an *aviso* – it was for a cable – which I picked up later from the post office. Thank God I answered the door, not my parents – I'm so bad at lying. It was from this chap – the pusher... you know... just to "remind me" – as if I needed reminding! It seems I've got until October otherwise he'll go to my college and tell them everything. Oh Crikey! I've not slept a wink for nights on end. I go back in three days and I'm still no nearer finding a solution.'

'Well I *am*,' said Benjie, surprising himself at the firmness in his voice. 'I've had a brainwave. Now look! I can't talk now, obviously – but if you can get yourself halfway up our hill to the S bend, by the prickly pears, tomorrow early – say eight thirty – I'll tell you all about it. And look,' he added warningly, 'don't go getting yourself caught! Come on foot and stay tight into the headland. I don't want you being seen from the house. Hide behind the cactus until I come down the track and call your name. We don't want folks getting the wrong idea!'

For the first time the youth looked him straight in the eye. Benjie found his chest tightening inexplicably and he swallowed with difficulty.

'I'll be there,' said Roger, 'Eight thirty on the dot … and don't worry – I won't get caught,' he laughed wryly, 'I may be a fool but not a *complete* bloody idiot.'

There was no time to reply. Footsteps were coming and beyond them Johanna's voice drifted down the patio. 'Roger! Roger darling! Haven't you found those glasses yet?'

Benjie slipped past him just in time. He shut himself into a lavatory at the end of the passage and started counting slowly to a hundred. When, he came out, the sound of water flushing behind him, he found Howard.

'Oh there you are!' There was a hint of irritability with which he was getting all too familiar, 'I was beginning to wonder –'

'Yeah,' Benjie smiled weakly, 'So was I …' he patted his navel and grimaced … 'must have been those prawns I ate last night.'

'Hmph … glad I didn't touch them,' said Howard, unsmiling as together they went back to the garden.

If Benjie's manner had been strange at Miss Vincent's house, Howard could find no fault with it the next day. To begin with, there was breakfast in bed. This was a treat for high days or holidays, Thanksgiving or special anniversaries. There had been a time when Benjie had served breakfast in bed every day before Howard went to work, but this practice had long ago stopped as Benjie's responsibilities to *Maison Parfaite* grew more important than his domestic duties.

Nevertheless, it was a pleasant surprise to wake up to such a beautifully laden tray. Only a will of iron could have resisted the smell of fried bacon and mushrooms, or the steamy invitation of lightly scrambled eggs. A crisp white cloth, silver cutlery and the red carnation in its little glass all contributed to a sense of nostalgia. Howard remembered their cosy meals in their far-off brownstone and found himself grow quite husky, 'Why Benjie, how very thoughtful! I'm not sure what I've done to deserve such a feast, but it's a good way to celebrate our first five months in Casa Amarela!'

'Precisely,' Benjie silently thanked the powers-that-be; it had been his only worry – an excuse for the treat. It was hard to believe that almost half a year had sped by, despite Leah's efforts to record every stage of the work in their 'family' album. Propped on the tray was a copy of *Harpers*, borrowed from Johanna to keep his old friend amused. Howard saw the date, and was impressed, 'Aren't you the clever one!' he beamed. Benjie accepted the compliment and casually announced his intention of walking down the hill to fetch up the post.

'But there's no need,' said Howard, 'It's a long way down to the mailbox and Carlos can bring it up as usual when he arrives at nine!'

'Let me do it, ' said Benjie, 'I'll be honest with you, the walk will do me good. It was only as I was cooking the bacon, I realised I needed … er, some fresh air … my stomach hasn't quite recovered from yesterday.'

'Of course,' said Howard swiftly, always grateful for Benjie's stoic approach to preparing food which was not kosher. It was important to seem sensitive over matters of custom or religion.

Benjie smiled and hurried off. He passed Leah who was letting out the geese in her fluffy bedroom slippers. What a row those birds were making! He zipped the parcel he was bearing under his windcheater tighter into his chest – it would not do for her to spot it. 'Just off for the mail!' he cried, cheerily. She was too engrossed to give him more than the barest of nods. It was a good fifteen-minute stroll down the rugged hillside to their mailbox on the public road; Benjie reckoned it would be just like Howard to look out for him. The track downhill was mainly obscured from above by an overhanging bluff, but there were a couple of spots where the snaking bends smoothed out, and might be seen from above. Benjie must take care to follow the whole route even though his purpose lay only at the halfway point.

The sea air was fresh in his nostrils and he felt curiously lightheaded as he jogged all the way to the pre-arranged spot. He arrived slightly out of breath. The countryside glowed bronze and golden all around him in the morning sunshine. It was difficult to believe that this hard, baked earth would again grow lush and green with the rains of winter. He remembered the first time he'd set eyes on it, not long into the early spring of '72. This valley had been swathed in almond blossom, great clouds of pink and white flowers swelling the spindly trees to magnificent proportion and abundance. The change of season marked a rebirth, a miracle of Nature; as though this tiny corner of the peninsula had been singled out as a blessed land, like Canaan in the bible, the land of milk and honey as promised to the children of Israel.

Occasionally, when he was feeling receptive – sometimes in solitude – a rare state for Benjie, he found himself yearning towards something more spiritual. He wished he could recall the forgotten stories from his early childhood when his father had been alive. They seemed locked away in some dusty cupboard of his mind, but he was convinced if somehow they could be located they would enrich his life again. Perhaps one day a visit to a hypnotherapist might help; then he could travel back in time and learn of his Jewish roots and the wise words of those sober but dignified men who had presided somewhere in the background of his family.

But, there again, would that really help? Probably not; there were painful memories too, and he had closed the cupboard door so firmly it was not surprising he could not prise it open now. Better probably to live for the present and enjoy what was on offer in the here and now. The harmonious clang-clang of a goat-bell on the hillside brought everything around him into sharp focus. The whitewashed cottages of neighbours, the brilliance of the sky, bees and sunbeams dancing in unison out of corn-coloured hedgerows, the smells of burnt sage, wild garlic and sunflower all around. It was glorious! Who was he to complain?

A woman on a small donkey was coming up their communal track. She was on her way home from market judging by the full panniers that creaked against the beast's side, slowing its progress. She wore a battered black trilby, green with age at the crown, and with crooked arm, held a black umbrella stiffly in front of her, effectively blotting out any daring ray of sunshine. One of us has to be wrong, thought Benjie, sleeveless and bareheaded, nevertheless admiring her proud posture and sense of purpose. 'Bom dia, Senhora,' he returned, dropping from a jog to a walk so he could step aside to let her pass.

'*Bom dia, Senhor,*' she replied and inclined her gnarled old head in regal fashion, '*Obrigada.*'

They've got real class, these people, thought Benjie. They may be poor, half of them can't read or write, but there's real breeding and manners there. I guess they know what matters in life, and to hell with the rest.

He broke back to a trot and arrived at the sprawling clump of cacti on the double bend. Prickly pears, dozens of them, contorted, twisting, feet above his head, competed, branch to branch, for the sun. Strange, they seemed the only green thing in this tranquil sea of gold and tan. Such an uninviting green too – like the dirty pea-soup colour he remembered as a kid in his school paint-box. He'd never cared much for cacti although he'd used them enough in interior design, some people being inexplicably wild about them. For Benjie, they'd always held something sinister and he knew better than to pick up a mature pear, shed onto the ground to ripen in the heat. As they changed to a bright lime colour, the orange-red heads could attract the unwary but once those barbs, soft and innocuous, fed their way into the skin, painful sores would erupt. Infection could follow and real damage could be done if not cut out. Benjie shuddered at the thought; it had once happened to him – never again.

'Pssst!'

Benjie stood stock still and cocked his head to one side. He had thought he was alone.

'Pssst!' There was no doubt about it this time. Benjie breathed a sigh of relief that the youth was not late.

'Roger! OK, kid! you can come out now. It's safe.'

There was a scuffle. Roger disengaged himself, scrambling out from behind the scrub, and dusted himself down. His face was pale and there were large dark shadows under his eyes.

'How did you get here?' Benjie said sharply, looking him over.

'I jogged from the centre of town. It took less than an hour.'

'And no one knew you were coming here, no one you know passed by on the road?'

'No – to both questions. Besides, I'm not daft. I wore a hat.' He produced a crumpled navy sun hat tucked into his jeans.

'Good – you and that distinctive carrot hair,' Benjie looked relieved.

'Tell me about it,' said Roger, 'Such a give away – has been all my life.'

'There's no time for chit-chat … here!' Benjie produced his parcel. He held it out carefully, letting out a deep breath. 'This should save your skin. Now take it gently, very gently.'

Roger stretched his hands towards him, the palms upward. 'I'm sorry, I don't understand.'

'No, but you will. Have you got it? Sure?'

Roger nodded. He closed his fingers around a brown paper package protected by a thick corrugated sleeve and tied up with string. 'Whatever it is, it's not very heavy…'

'… And it's not for throwing around,' Benjie finished the sentence for him. 'Now listen to me carefully.'

The boy nodded, wonder in his eyes as he held the package tight against his ribcage.

'I already explained to you I couldn't raise any cash, not at such short notice. Apart from buggering up my interest, Howard would find out – we share the same accountant. It's the last thing I need. So I came up with another idea. It's damn risky, but if you don't let me down – it ought to work. I'm probably crazy even to contemplate it, but that's – my problem.'

Roger opened his mouth to speak, but Benjie shut him up. 'In that parcel, you'll find a Dresden figurine. Handle it carefully – it's fragile and very valuable. It's the hand-painted figure of a girl carrying a bunch of holly and it's early nineteenth-century – the factory's coat of arms and issue number is on the base. As far as we know, there's only one other in the world and that's in the Dresden museum. We always bring it out at Christmas-time for the dining table, but for the rest of the year it remains in cotton-wool. Literally! That's why it won't be missed for a couple of months.'

'But Benjie…'

'Shush! as I said, it's worth a lot. Take it to a good pawnbroker. Make sure he's reputable, not some sleazy joint. You shouldn't have much difficulty in Oxford, especially when they see the valuation. Yes, it's in there too – from Spinks, the porcelain people. It's presently valued at seven grand…yes, pounds! Ask them what they'll advance you. Don't settle for less than two thousand. They should be laughing at such a modest request. Make sure you get a proper receipt and arrange to go back and recover it the day after your birthday. I take it – ' he fixed Roger with a long, keen look, 'the promised money really will come through for you on your birthday?'

'No question,' said the youth, who had gone even paler and more hollow-eyed.

'Well, I sure hope so for your sake, otherwise I'll skin you alive,' said Benjie. 'Now, serious again. Keep the piece in the bank once you've repaid your debt – well wrapped and protected, mind. The moment term ends, get your ass plus the holly girl back to the Algarve before Christmas. We'll be decorating the house around the 18th December. Do you think you'll make it in time?'

'We break up on the 12th,' stuttered Roger, 'I'm usually home the day after.'

'Good! Then that ought to see you through then.'

'I don't know how to th–'

'Don't! Just get your ass back here, and don't let me down!' said Benjie sharply. There'll be all hell to pay if Howard discovers the holly girl's gone. He loves that piece of china, like it's his… his own daughter… the one he never had!'

Roger gulped. There was a pause as they both realised the enormity of what they were doing. Finally Benjie added, 'One more thing – don't you ever get yourself involved with drugs again. There's enough misery on this planet for sensitive souls like you and me – without multiplying it all for everyone else. Get your kicks from some place else, but not on grass or coke. It involves too many people and it can't half screw up your life.'

Roger nodded, his face wretched. 'I discovered that some time ago…it was just the money…I couldn't shake this chap off. The more I owed him, the more dope he pushed on me. I was supposed to sell it. In fact, I threw the last lot down the loo.'

'I'm glad to hear it.' Benjie's tone was abrupt. 'Look! I've got to get the mail now. I've been too long as it is. Can you get yourself back to town without being seen from up top?'

'I think so,' stammered Roger. 'I can cut across by the coves and then onto the road behind that point over there,'

'OK – you do that. And if you drop that parcel in the sea – that'll be the end of us both.'

Roger grinned, then fell serious again as he felt Benjie's glance boring into him. This time he looked back, no longer afraid to read whatever messages lay behind that hard glint. Impulsively, he took the older man's hand and squeezed it hard. The contact was like an electric shock and every nerve quivered in his body. Within his grasp, it seemed as though he held the heart of a captive bird, but he was not certain whether it was his or Benjie's. 'Don't worry,' he mumbled, 'I won't let you down – I promise.'

'Better not.' Was there a trace of regret in the voice? Their hands remained locked together for a moment, eyes steady.

Roger tightened his other arm more protectively around the parcel, then slowly, carefully drew back. His eyes never left Benjie as he disengaged his fingers, then his whole hand. Once again, he found himself trying to mouth the same feeble words, 'I don't know how I'll ever be able to…'

Benjie's voice cut in harshly. 'Don't try kiddo. You don't even need to try.'

Roger was trembling all over now. 'Please let me say it!' he pleaded.

The other gave a half-smile. He was unused to this. 'Well… I guess… if it makes you feel better – '

'Oh it does, it does. Thank you Benjie. Oh my God! *Thank* you! I'll never forget this.'

But whether the other heard him, he was unsure. Already the American was striding swiftly away – down the hillside to collect the post.

Part 2

21

Thirty Years on: Portugal, 2004

'So you could say that darned house warming was the start of the rot,' said Leah in a matter of fact way, mopping her lips with a starched napkin. 'Not just for Buster and me, but between the Boys.'

It was their second meeting. Up to this point, she had only told Kate the bare bones of the story. She had begun with that supper all together in New York and the defining moment when she had voiced her ambitions to their business partners, soon to become the other inmates of their dream villa. As she'd built up the tale, the choosing of the plot of land, struggles with the planners, the design and final erection of Casa Amarela, she had been careful not to let personal doubts and concerns detract from the main story. Driven by an overriding desire for a new life in the sun, a utopian existence for all four of them, she had carefully outlined the pressures and constraints of business and city life as though these and these alone had been the only spurs for change.

Now, as she watched this shrewd Scottish girl, she wondered, as she skirted round her real motivation – denied even to herself at that time, but vital in retrospect – if she would read between the lines. Did it really matter? The girl was too polite to say, but she couldn't help but wonder.

Leah's forebears had been European, but three generations spent in America had blurred the blood-ties of which she felt so profoundly proud. Through her work with antiques and old art, she had gallantly strived to re-connect; but it hadn't been enough. How, at this late stage, could one put into words the recollected need to belong? The primaeval desire to retrace ancient steps and root oneself to a continent of which one could feel a part, and where she felt she rightfully belonged, had urged her rashly on – but how could anyone who had not been there themselves begin to comprehend?

Since this inner yearning had been to the detriment of her own canniness, natural suspicion and judgement, it was better not touched upon now. Besides it would be quite irrelevant to Kate's own quest – to learn more about her parents. These people took heritage for granted, but might find it hard to appreciate the feeling of being lost in a continent for which one felt no deep ties, no ancestral link, no real grounding. America had been good to her, it had harboured her family for two generations yet somehow it had never felt like home.

As for their party, which should have been a moment of triumph, this was lightly skimmed over. The remembered snobbery and lack of gratitude had merely accentuated the differences between the four hosts and the other ex-pats but she had long ago put it to one side. To voice those recollections of vulnerability and disappointment would be a mere indulgence. Let the girl read between the lines if she wanted, but of one thing Leah was certain; the misplaced achievement of certain social events in which they had participated, even instigated, had simply widened the cultural gap. By trying too hard to become a European, Leah had allowed negativity and doubt to flourish.

Instead of celebrating the fact she was an American and all that that great country had done for her, she had begun to resent Buster and the Boys for staying just as they were. In so doing she had denied her own *persona* and it was little wonder she had become more and more reliant on a habit she had sworn to kick. This should have been a time for personal growth. Instead, clutching at straws, she had latched too easily onto people who – in her right mind – she would never have trusted.

Coffee came and after a lot more talk, they both fell silent as Leah remembered and Kate wondered. There followed an awkward little moment when Kate had tried to pay the bill, but Leah – true to form – had got there first.

'I don't know what to say,' said her young companion, pushing her hair out of her eyes, and straightening up from a cramped position. They had been at the table for almost three hours. 'You've been so good and so informative, I am not sure I can wait for our next meeting.'

Leah smiled. She had already been on her cell phone to the current owners of Casa Amarela and they were to meet there the following day for morning coffee. Then, so much of what she had told Kate today would, she promised, come to life. 'It's been no trouble,' she said. 'I think in a funny sort of way, I've been waiting for this. I always felt there was unfinished business or something out of kilter or at least unanswered, and as I said before, it's kind of therapeutic – even for me – going through it all again.'

Kate found herself shivering involuntarily. Would the moment ever come when she could say the same for herself? There was one more question, she really wanted to ask – but was it wise? Before she knew it, she had blurted it out. Why had Leah turned down James's offer of recompense? 'You were rightfully entitled it to it, after all,' she stammered, It preyed on my mind for so long, we were sure you would be glad to have it back.'

There was a pause, whilst Leah studied her coffee cup. 'Glad is not the word, I'd have used. You see you don't know me very well, but there's a stubborn streak there and despite appearances, I'm very proud.'

'I can see that,' said Kate seriously, 'but surely – after all you had to go through…' she wasn't sure how to finish the sentence.

'And that's rather the point,' said Leah. 'I had gone through so much and come out the other side, I couldn't bear to tarnish it all with Buster's money – or rather the money Buster stole from me. I just knew if I did, it would spoil everything.'

Kate looked at her. Leah's tired blue eyes had a faraway look in them and she knew it would be wrong to offer another word. She waited, her hands clenching and unclenching under the table, hoping against hope she hadn't caused more anguish than she should.

'You see, I've worked so hard all my life, said Leah. 'Nothing has come easy, everything has been a struggle, success hard-earned. When Buster swept the carpet from under my feet, I would have given anything to get that money back – initially. But then somehow, miraculously, without it – my life took off. I got myself off those bloody pills, I started to sleep properly – God I was tired at the end of each day, I needed to – my energy returned, so did my self respect. All at once I was making new contacts, things were changing all around and best of all, exciting, tempting business opportunities were presenting themselves which would have been nuts to turn down. Within a few years, I was making it on my own and that was precious beyond belief. I guess by the time, your innocent, well-meaning husband came along, I had mustered enough confidence in myself to know I could do without it. You may find this hard to understand, but I believe taking it would have given me nothing but grief.'

'Gosh, I hadn't thought of anything like that,' said Kate.

'Why should you? You weren't me!'

'But even so – ' Kate was finding this difficult, 'but it shows enormous strength of character. Also, what about your family – aren't there people in America you could have given it to, even if you hadn't wanted it for yourself?'

'Nope!' said Leah, 'You could say I'm *toute seule* in the world. Of course, I have friends and employees who'll one day benefit from my Will, but my businesses will provide for them. It would simply be over-egging the cake to give them more.'

There was a silence. Yet again, Kate felt a whole load was shifting off her shoulders and she suddenly felt she must tell her husband. It was all pretty momentous stuff and she needed to share it with someone. Yet again – it was all such an amazing relief.

Pulling herself together, she stood up and gave Leah a huge hug. 'Thank you so much for explaining,' she said, 'I'll never forget this, Leah. You've made me feel a whole load better already, although I know I've a long way to go.'

'One step at a time,' smiled Leah, waving her off, 'for both of us, Kate!'

Her brain racing with the events of the last few hours, Kate drove out to the Fisherman's Beach. As before, she parked by the sea wall and looked out to the bay. She felt the afternoon stretching before her, as far away and uncharted as the sea itself. She climbed out, surveyed the view and perching on the sea wall, found herself dialling out on the familiar 0044 207 number for London. It was a direct line to her husband's office in Westminster but it was rare that James himself would respond. This time the reception was clear and she heard his secretary's voice in its usual cool, brisk, efficient tones as though she was in the next room.

'Oh, it's Mrs Fraser! Oh I *am* sorry, but no – I'm not protecting him! He really isn't here, he's at a meeting with the senior partner at Simmons & Simmons. He'll be vexed to have missed you.

'What's that? Yes, that's right, but why not try later this evening on his mobile? I know they've got a long afternoon ahead, it's to do with the DEFRA decision…you'll know what I mean I'm sure…but he should be free by after seven. Is the weather good? Are you enjoying your little holiday?'

Kate tightened her lip, irritated by the glib words, and rang off. The girl meant well, she supposed, and was always quick to appease when she knew it was the boss's wife on the phone, but even so – there was a lack of real warmth there, when sometimes she could have done with it. She was just about to drive back to her hotel, when something made her stop. As she returned her mobile to her bag, she saw a dog-eared scrap of paper with its hastily scribbled number poking out of a side pouch. '... I'm sure I'll have a bit of time to myself, so if you feel like calling...' The parting words were surprisingly clear still in her brain. She tapped in another number, this time with a Portuguese prefix – just in case.

For some inexplicable reason her heart missed a beat as the writer of the message answered himself. She hadn't really expected it. As though it wouldn't be meant.

'Hi,' she found herself slightly stammering in response, 'I hope I'm not disturbing you? It's Kate... Kate Fraser – the girl from the plane – the other day,' she found herself feeling like a sixteen year old ringing her first date. 'You said to pop by for a cup of tea, if I was at a loose end.'

'Kate!' the warm, welcoming tone embraced her name like a comfort blanket and she immediately felt better, less uncertain, less splintered from reality. It had, after all been a highly emotional lunch. Neither she nor Leah had let on to each other how affected the other felt. 'How great to hear from you – why don't you come on over? You've timed it nicely, I'm between duties and could do with some company. Do you know where we are, out here?'

Directions worked out, she was back in her car with a sudden feeling of elation enveloping her. Her face had flushed up, her eyes looked back from the car mirror less intense, less strained and it was suddenly rather exciting to be driving down the highway in the direction of Lagos to meet the young curate again.

'God, Kate,' she said to herself, 'don't be so silly! You'd think you'd never met a single man before.'

Michael Hargreaves had been lent a pleasant cottage in the grounds of the old *quinta* which dominated the white-washed village of Alveia, a small hamlet that lay a few kilometres off the highway that connected the harbour town of Portimão to the fortitfied port of Lagos. He was standing at the front door of this humble but comfortable abode when she alighted in a whirl of sand at the top of the track, and parked for shade under a fig tree. She felt ridiculously relieved to see him as though he was the one tenuous link with reality after a few days of living a dream.

'Welcome!' he said with a mock bow, exposing a few soft hairs at his throat which straggled upward from an open-necked blue shirt that looked far too big for his slight frame. The fact he looked so different from his dog-collared appearance by which she had originally recognised him on the plane, momentarily alarmed her. As though reading her thoughts, he added 'And do forgive the garb. It's so hot, I just had to break free for a couple of hours, but I'll be all buttoned up again before six, when I have a private service to conduct at someone's villa up the road.'

'Gosh!' said Kate, thinking he looked younger than ever and wondering if it had been a mistake to come. 'They believe in working you hard then, don't you ever get a day off?'

'We've reached a compromise,' he said leading her into a surprisingly cool room with three long windows all shuttered to keep the sun at bay. 'Instead of one whole day, I've traded for two afternoons, but I'm still expected to do evenings if the occasion demands.

And in this case, it does. Someone's elderly aunt has recently died and they're having a very modest memorial for friends and family only.'

'Oh,' she said, wondering why she had suddenly become monosyllabic. She still felt puzzled that Fate had served up this opportunity. Then, searching for more words, 'Does that worry you?'

'Not in the slightest,' he was putting on the kettle in a small tiled kitchen as she looked around. 'The funeral's been and gone so this is the easy part. I'm pleased to be of service, no pun intended ... I don't know the people, but their secretary's been a brick and conveyed all their wishes, personal requests, etc, so I should be able to deliver, I hope!'

She felt herself tongue-tied again, and busied herself with mugs and carrying the tray he'd laid into the darkened sitting room. 'Do you mind if I open one of the shutters?' she said.

'Please do, I don't like the custom myself, but the maid does it every morning as though it's *de rigeur*! It does make sense I guess, keeping everything cool in between whiles which is important out here in the sticks without air conditioning. Also the flies have a habit of flooding in if one's not careful. So tell me – how have you been? I can see you have something to report ... you're all charged up and obviously electric with news!'

Kate found herself flushing. 'I'd no idea I was so transparent,' she said.

'That's not a word I would use for you,' he said gently, 'but you do have an air, as it were. And it's very different from the last time I saw you.'

They settled down with the tea and he offered her some Kit-Kat. 'No thanks,' she said, 'I've just had a massive lunch with one of the people I came to find,' and before she knew it, she was telling him all the things she had been saving for James, only in much more intimate detail. It was funny how talking to a relative stranger made it easier to speak of her hopes and fears, how vulnerable she was feeling right now and what a relief it was to share it.

'The awful thing is, Michael,' she finally paused for breath, 'I think underneath her calm façade, Leah may be almost as upset as I am. And– ' she was stammering again – 'I feel guilty for dragging all this – er, stuff – that was buried in the past – up to the surface again, just in order to satisfy my – er – own selfish whim. After all, she has suffered so much already, is it fair to expect so much from her? She said it might take a few days ... and seems prepared for that, but is it really going to help me with my biggest doubts?'

'Only you and she can answer that,' he said, inclining his head back against a saggy hessian-covered armchair and puffing on a small cheroot which she'd been amazed to see him take from his jeans pocket. 'But from what you say, it sounds like she meant it when she said it would be therapeutic and from your point of view, it's exactly what you came for, surely?'

She slipped her sandals off and tucked her feet comfortably up and under her on the sofa, covered in the same faded hessian. It was surprising how relaxed she was beginning to feel, talking to him as though she'd known him for ever. 'I know you're probably right,' she said, 'but it does feel quite – you know – *selfish*.'

'There's very little we do in life, when it comes to personal ambition, quests, answers, call it what you want, that's *not* going to be a bit selfish in some respects,' he said. 'Even students at college, desiring extra information over and above the normal curriculum, can be greedy especially if it impinges on someone's else time and energy. The point is however, many people love to give out. There's something about offering advice, knowledge that makes them feel valid, important, wanted. Maybe your coming into Leah's life so late in the day helps her to make up for all the bitterness and sadness that must have consumed her, day in day out, when things were hard for her. I think you've just got to play it by ear and go with the flow.'

'But it's difficult with her,' said Kate. 'She talks endlessly, describes so many situations, places, people – but in between all the details, the minutae, I feel she holds back. When she told me about the first time she met my mother, her face changed. She went into a lot of detail, Mama's clothes, her hair, how beautiful her skin was – things like that, but I could feel a slight mask dropping over her face and the voice took on a higher note. There was emotion there, but you wouldn't have thought so from the words themselves.'

She took a gulp of cold tea and watched Michael, thinking he might be getting fed up, but he remained where he was – a trained and good listener, she thought. 'Today we got onto the subject of this party they put on, it was to be their great launch into ex-pat society. At this point, I could feel her shrink back again – more guarded with her words as she described my mother dancing with *her* husband – the dreaded 'Uncle' B. I think I was waiting for some expostulation, but all she said was how good they looked together, my mother's dress, how everyone stopped dancing to watch them… suddenly, it was as though she were talking of strangers, there was no hint of how she actually felt.'

'But that's just it,' said Michael, watching his smoke as it plumed and fanned out into the low rafters, dispersing amongst the faded bamboos which formed a solid mat against draughts and searing heat between each strut of solid eucalyptus. 'She's trying to tell it how it was, but without the personal angle. Don't you see, Kate – she's doing you a huge favour, she's letting you make the judgements. She sounds a saint, this woman.'

'She is, that's the trouble,' Kate's brow crinkled upwards in two very straight vertical lines above the bridge of her nose as she shuffled her feet under her bottom and tried to get comfortable again. 'After all our family have done to her, after all she's gone through, I keep wondering if I should be here! It must be so hard for her. Why! She even insisted on paying the bill at lunch. I feel so in her debt, I'm not sure I like it!'

'Kate!' Michael had stubbed out his cheroot and got up to face her. He looked bigger like this, more mature and determined, with a very steadfast look in his eyes. His hands thrusting deep into the lowset pockets of his jeans squared out his shoulders which she'd remembered as bowed and rounded under the weight of all that luggage in the plane. A rebellious feather of dark mousy hair straying over his forehead emphasised the paleness of his skin which had obviously seen little sun, and there was a shadow of stubble on his chin, which added to his sudden air of authority. Gone was the student figure, she realised with a jolt; this was a man.

'Kate!' he said again, this time with an imperious ring to his voice, 'You've got to stop this dithering and doubting things. You made a decision and you're here now. What you've been offered by this American woman is a miracle! She might have been dead by now, moved to Australia, refused to see you. I have to say I was dubious about your going there in the first place – the little you told me – but now it seems you've been offered a chance to find out all the answers you'd hoped to find. Be grateful!'

'I guess…' she dropped her chin and swallowed hard. He saw tears had gathered in her eyes and wondered if indeed he shouldn't tell her to pack her bags and go home. 'The problem is I'm not sure if this will help. I'm getting answers, but if Leah is not prepared to condemn or forgive my parents' behaviour, it's going to be harder to make my own judgement.'

Michael found it difficult to keep the note of exasperation out of his voice. 'But that's the whole point, Kate. It *is* for you to make your own judgement as it applies to *you*! No one else cares a shit. Even Leah – the most damaged in all this – seems to have put everything behind her and moved on. But you – someone who has benefitted and enjoyed a privileged lifestyle from whatever did or did not happen – are crawling around in a swathe of self-pity and not prepared to take a little responsibility of your own.'

He was caught off balance as she leapt to her feet and turned to him white-faced and tight. 'I knew I shouldn't have come here,' she spat, her eyes suddenly black with anger. 'There I am struggling with myself and you're telling me how pathetic I am! Can't you see – I know that! And you call yourself a man of God!' Before he could recover she had wheeled away from him with rigid shoulders, bent to grab her bag from under the coffee-table and turned towards the cottage door.

As she fumbled with the catch, he caught up with her, seized her wrist and said, 'Kate, don't be an idiot…you can't go now! Not like this, you're upset and I should have been more patient. I'm sorry. Wait!'

She tried to pull away, praying the tears wouldn't spill and desperate to remain in control, but she was surprised by the tenacity of his grasp. With eyes fixed on the door, she was determined not to look at him until her face was under control; she studied the grain of wood and gradually relaxed her body. She was no longer pulling in the opposite direction, but he still held on. For a moment time stood still. There were little creases in the natural pine where years of old polish had got trapped and lay there like globules of honey, smoothed with age but catching the light of the one opened window nevertheless. The old wood gave the whole door a golden look, warm and familiar, comforting in its solidity.

She wanted to let go of the handle and come back into the room, but she was very much afraid she would begin to cry, so she stood there unsure of her next move. What she did not expect was his free arm to come round her neck and his lips momentarily to rest on the back of her neck. He could feel his breath gently fanning her hair. 'It's all right, Kate,' he was whispering into the nape of her neck as the blonde strands fell away and parted over each shoulder. 'Oh, my poor, beautiful Kate,' his other arm had disengaged itself from her wrist and was gently turning her. 'It's all right.'

She smelt him then and the proximity alarmed her. A curious mixture of soap and cheroot and a slight whiff of lemon, which might have been his after-shave, jostled for supremacy and she realised their faces were together, millimetres apart. She could still feel the tears but they were no longer pricking against her eyelids; one had settled on the tip of her nose, the other was already drying on her cheek. She looked up and into his eyes; they were only an inch or so above her own, not like James who stood head and shoulders above her, but just close enough to see right into the flecked irises of aquamarine, and to detect a fleeting, but unmistakeable flash of desire.

Then he pulled away.

She too moved in the opposite direction and wordlessly, they returned to their respective seats, she on the comfortable sofa, he on the armchair. He'd hardly sat down than he was up again. 'I'll make us some more tea,' he said in an even voice and vanished back into the kitchen. She took a compact out of her bag and regarded her face in the mirror. She looked flushed and alive. The nervous look had gone from her eyes, she saw for a moment a beautiful, aroused woman. She shut it with a snap, returned it to her bag and wondered.

Later, when he saw her to the car, there was another unwelcome silence. He had showered and changed while she had finished her tea and she knew the reappearance of the dog collar was to put distance between them and what had happened or not happened at the door. Suddenly, he was back to the old Michael, a little bowed, somewhat gangling and awkward in his movements. He opened the car door for her, being careful not to brush against her as he did so.

Instead of climbing in, she hesitated. Something needed to be said, not about her past life, but about here and now. She had hoped he would start, but in the end she couldn't wait any longer. Desperate to retain the person she had got to know with the jeans and cheroot, she was blurting out words in any order, just to keep the ecclesiastical side of him at bay a little longer. 'Look – I – don't know what happened earlier,' she began, 'I mean this is all so stupid… First of all – I'm sorry I reacted so badly. You were right in what you said, and infinitely patient… I must have bored you rigid with my long story and I didn't mean to lose my cool, like that…Oh dear, I really don't know what more to say.'

'Hush, Kate,' he said, letting go of the car door and turning to her once more. Gently he took both her hands in his, but in a calm paternal way, his face a study in control. Not quite meeting her eyes, he began, 'First of all, you don't have to say anything. Secondly, none of this bored or bores me. You came to me for help and I want to give it to you. I had no right whatsoever to say what I did, to be so judgmental. It's only – oh Kate – my human side sometimes jerks into play a bit more quickly than my professional side…I'm still a bit young, a bit clumsy at being a so-called 'man of God'. I felt at that moment in time you needed a good kick up the backside – if you'll pardon the phrase – but that was very much the wrong moment and achieved nothing. It's me who should be apologising. I handled you all wrong – in every way – ' he dropped his eyes and looked somewhere far away, over her right shoulder, 'I'm very sorry.'

'I'm sorry too,' she said, interlacing her fingers and keeping them there just a little longer than she meant. As they disengaged, she said, 'Please let me come again. I've a feeling the next stage with Leah may be more difficult still. As I told you, we go to the house tomorrow – and she said something about a farm or a shack – after that. It's all a bit scary and unknown, but I would feel so much braver if I felt I could come and talk to you again …just once more.'

'I'm not sure,' he said rather too quickly, a slight pursing of his mouth appearing above the newly shaven upper lip and the hint of worry in his eyes.

'My aim was to help you, Kate. I would hate to do the opposite, God forgive me.'

She wanted to say... *But you have, you have. And let's keep God out of this. You've made me feel alive again and desirable, and not washed up and cold as ice... and... all the other shit things that were happening to me after Mama got ill. And the best thing of all was you listened. I could talk to you and it's been an awfully long time since I could do that with anyone. You made it possible for me. That, and maybe more, who knows...* The thought of being deprived of such intimate conversation was suddenly alarming. Instead, she said, 'Please, Michael, I'd like to come back. Purely for help.'

She emphasised the 'purely' hoping she'd made the meaning clear – to give him an out. He looked at her and thought of Eve and the serpent, wondering as he did so, if this was exactly what the devil was good at. Making you feel you've taken the right decision, when you haven't. But the words were already out. 'Okay,' he heard himself agree, 'But see how it goes. You may well find, you don't need me. And then,' he smiled and this time looked confidently into her eyes, 'I shall be really happy.'

As she drove away, she wasn't sure she quite believed him.

22

Portugal – 1973

October came and went, taking with it the sleepy halcyon days of the mild Iberian autumn. There was a constant buzz of activity at the yellow house on the hill, a cold front arriving in early November, which brought an ever greater spurt of industry.

'Fall was great,' declared Leah, 'but I'm glad winter's coming. Now we can really get on with the garden. In the cold, I can work forever!'

'Don't tell me you're hankering for New York,' teased Benjie, looking up from his knot garden.

'You must be kidding,' Leah's arms were full of stakes as she waltzed up the hill.

They had already done wonders. As with the house, they had split the property into sections, each taking over an allotted share, with its own responsibilites. Doing things this way imbued each of them with the competitive spirit so necessary to drive a task forward. Buster's efforts were the first to bear fruit, or at least visible results. He had taken over the front garden, which spanned the south-facing terrace. Screened by Bermuda grass, the pool would eventually take pride of place at a lower level, amidst velvet lawn and flowering shrubs.

Leah held court on the gentle incline of land to the north west of the house before it ran steeply up the rocky hillside to the 'wild bit' just below the fisherman's bench. The lower reach was to serve as a produce garden and home to the geese. To her great pleasure, Cleo and Ant had already proved their worth by demolishing all the weeds brought on by the damper weather. Closer to the house lay a huge stack of boulders, which would one day form a rockery. They would scour the countryside, stopping the car with a whoop of delight when something rare or unusual was discovered. The best finds were those of irregular shape; Buster had a knack for nosing these out and the mound of rocks grew daily more interesting. To one side lay the rose garden, Howard's domain, to the other, Benjie's herbs enclosed by a geometric arrangement of miniature hedges in the Italian style.

None of the four inmates had any real practical gardening experience, but they had advised and dealt with landscape gardeners in a designing capacity. Howard had always revelled in roses both in his showroom at *Maison Parfaite* and in makeovers. For Benjie, it was a natural progression from the culinary use of herbs to growing them himself. In Portugal, he found a wealth of variety he had never dreamed possible and Maria their maid was forever bringing different strains of oregano, basil, mint and coriander for him to transplant. 'I want this garden to have a slight feel of decadence,' he confided to Leah, 'over indulgent, with many scents jockeying for supremacy, consuming the senses. I'd love to hurry the whole thing up, but I guess we must just leave the bees to do their work.'

Snubnosed Carlos, left behind by the builders as the clearing-up boy, was now a full-time employee. Nephew to Maria, he was hardworking for a southerner, possessing as he did a natural affinity with the earth and her fruitfulness, as well as an intriguing knowledge of inherited folklore. Never sow at full moon, wait till the second quarter before cutting back any shrub, take your hat off before picking lemons, rub your hands in mint before turning over new soil, he confided. He became protective of Leah. With so much digging in preparation for the vegetable garden, the two worked together, but it seemed all wrong to Carlos that the *Senhora* of such a grand house should have to dirty her hands. When he tried to take her spade as she leant on it, breathless, Leah simply laughed and told him in her steadily improving Portuguese to ignore her and get on with his own work.

Carlos lived with his parents and three unmarried sisters on the *monte* just opposite to theirs, which could only be reached by a narrow mule-path running along the top of the cliffs. One evening with the moon already up, Benjie was preparing spaghetti for dinner, when a knock came on the kitchen door. He undid the latch and saw the boy's familiar, grinning face before him. Never able to understand a word he said, he called Leah. She appeared in her bathrobe, her hair in multi-colored rollers, but the youth seemed undaunted and beckoned for her to follow. Benjie watched open-mouthed as the two of them disappeared into the night together.

'Jeez!' he muttered as he grated cheese, 'I wonder what all the mystery's about?'

Buster sauntered into the kitchen and dipped his fingers into the cheese bowl, 'That supposed to be Parmesan?' he said licking them ostentatiously and making a face.

'Do you *mind*!' said Benjie, moving bowl, board and grater out of his reach.

'Not a bit,' said Buster affably, advancing again with outstretched fingers, 'but if you ask me that stuff tastes like stale Edam. In fact,' he snatched another pinch, 'I'd go so far as to bet my bottom dollar that it ain't Parmesan!'

'Look!' Benjie flounced, flinging down the grater, which clattered to the floor, 'I never said it was, did I? Who says it's gotta be Parmesan? It's time you learned to mind your own business and I'll thank you not to come barging into my kitchen – thrusting your great germ-ridden fingers into my cooking and…'

'Temper, temper!' admonished Buster, wagging one of the offending fingers in his face. 'No need to get so excited, is there? And what's all this talk about *my* kitchen, anyway?'

Howard, hearing voices raised, arrived on the scene protective and pink after a hot bath. His sparse hair was still wet and he smelt like a newly washed baby. He had not yet had time to apply his various colognes and body lotions.

'Ah-ha!' said Buster, 'Enter the cavalry, the famous McDermott himself!' and he began to hum a catchy little tune, 'tum-titty, tum-titty… galloping, galloping galloping… and to the rescue came… titty-tum.'

Howard looked bewildered, trying to assess the situation. Something was wrong, but just what, he couldn't be sure. Benjie's eyes were flashing like neon lights and his body so tensed, he looked ready to spring. Buster, on the other hand, appeared utterly relaxed as he leant against the kitchen table, idly flicking through Benjie's favorite recipe book. Flakes of cheese dusted the work surface and scattered the floor like snow, whilst the grater lay on its back waiting to be trodden on. Howard scratched his head.

'You may well look amazed Howard, my old son,' said Buster. 'I'm afraid yours truly has just upset a happy domestic scene. Perhaps you could pour some oil on these troubled waters whilst I slip quietly away and – er – out of *Benjie's* kitchen.'

Leah chose at that moment to return. She threw open the kitchen door and stood quite still, a dramatic figure in her long sweeping robe, back-clothed by the dark hill and starry sky beyond. Her eyes were rivetted to something that lay in her arms. 'Just look!' she cried, her voice quivering with emotion. 'Just take a look at *this*!'

They all took a step forward. There, cowering against the fold of her gown, was a thin black scrap of a dog. Its limbs hung down stiffly. Its coat was dull; it seemed scarcely able to support its head. The only thing that looked very much alive was a pair of wary brown eyes.

'Isn't he cute?' said Leah. 'Carlos and his father found him for me. Poor little pup, he'd been thrown from a car on the main road, and was lying there stunned in the verge when they stumbled upon him. Nothing seems broken though. When they asked in the village, no one knew anything about him. It seems he's been abandoned.'

'With good reason perhaps,' said Buster, 'What are you going to do with him?'

'Why, keep him of course,' said Leah, opening her blue eyes very wide. 'Carlos reckoned we needed a dog, and it's funny, he seems to trust me already.'

'Who – Carlos or the dog?'

'The dog, you dope. But he's right, you know! A big house like this needs a guard dog.'

'Hardly your actual Rottweiler, is it?' said Buster, 'Go on then, put him down. We'd better take a look at him.'

Leah knelt on the floor and immediately let out a shriek of pain as she came in contact with the cheese grater. 'Ouch! What in heaven's name is this? The dog cowered even lower to the floor and tried to climb back into her arms. 'Whoever left this piece of scrap-iron here for all and sundry to splice themselves? Someone get me a band aid – quick! Can't you see I've got my arms full?'

Still bemused, Howard lumbered in the direction of the utility room for the first aid kit, muttering that the house was full of madmen. Meanwhile the dog, back on the floor again, suddenly found an appetite for grated cheese. He devoured it as though he had not been fed for a hundred years. Leah sat on a kitchen stool nursing her knee, which was spurting blood. For the first time Buster noticed her hair was in rollers, 'You look a fright,'' he remarked, 'do you make a habit of wearing these things out in the garden?'

'Oh shut up!' said Leah crossly, 'You're so unhelpful in an emergency... and what's wrong with you, Benjie?'

Benjie's face was ghastly green. He couldn't take his eyes off the blood that had dripped into the mess on the floor. It looked like the dog was going to have that too.

'I think I'm going to throw up,' he said in a dreamy voice, swaying ever so gently beside the cooker.

'Not there you're not,' said Buster giving him a shove towards the sink which he made just in time as Howard returned with lint, antiseptic and a roll of pink tape.

'Oh give me that!' said Leah impatiently; 'someone needs your help over there much more than I do. This is only a scratch ... why don't *you* give me a hand, Buster!'

They forgot the dog temporarily until Buster stepped backwards to admire his handiwork on Leah's knee. A yelp made them all jump before it crept away into a corner holding up its paw with a reproachful backward glance. 'Poor thing!' said Leah.

'I'm sorry,' said Buster to the dog.

Leah got up briskly, 'Well, after that chapter of accidents, I think someone needs to take charge around here. What's this supposed to be cooking?'

'Er ... spaghetti bolo ...' Benjie's voice faded as he rushed for the sink again.

'Then I suggest I take over,' said Leah, wielding a wooden spoon. 'Howard, throw some of that antiseptic down the sink and get Benjie out of here. Buster, you're getting in my way – go and fix yourself a drink and don't come back. It's obvious a woman is required at this moment in time! Mungo and I will manage fine on our own.'

'Mungo?' they chorused.

'Sure! That's what I've christened him ... the dog, you know. My first girls' school was Saint Mungo's! I always thought it was a crazy name for a saint, better by far for a mongrel dog ... and since that's what this guy is – Mungo it is.'

No one said a word. As usual, Leah had presented them with a *fait accompli* and they all felt powerless to do much about it. The timing was perfect; they had missed the moment to object ... unless. Howard opened his mouth to say something. At that moment Benjie began to sway again, this time dangerously and he saw his opportunity slip away. Grumbling to himself, he bore his partner out of the kitchen.

Buster turned to go too. 'I hope you realise just what you're taking on there,' he said weakly. 'Your blessed saint's just lifted his leg against the kitchen table. Lucky Howard didn't see!'

Leah threw a dishcloth at his departing head. After a very long haul, she was feeling in control again – in fact, she was beginning to have fun!

Catalina McKay had been a regular visitor at Casa Amarela ever since the party. A couple of times she'd called to take Leah out in her speed-boat, but with the November winds well up, there'd been no opportunity. Nowadays she just dropped by and with very little persuasion hung around whilst they worked in the garden. It surprised Leah how little Catalina seemed to have to do with her own life. In the end she attributed this to the Latin temperament and was grateful for it. The fact the girl needed company was obvious, but with such a difficult man for a husband and the circumstances in which they now found themselves, it was flattering she chose to share her confidences with her, a mere newcomer.

For someone who prized personal space, it was odd too how she, herself, never resented these frequent invasions. On the contrary, the girl added vibrancy to their lives and Leah found herself scanning the horizon for that first pleasurable sight of the Mercedes as it wound up the hillside. It amused her to see what Catalina was wearing; never the same thing twice, even the makeup, scent and hairstyle changing from day to day as was the news she brought. Tittle-tattle could be addictive particularly since Catalina loved to talk. She always made it clear that her fresh snippets of information were for Leah's ears only. In

New York, neighbours comprised little more than the odd face in the elevator; now Leah was beginning to feel part of a proper community. Looking at herself in the mirror she wondered if she was in danger of turning into the proverbial ex-pat herself!

It was flattering how Catalina never seemed to mind that Leah was always grimy and engrossed when she arrived. In an ancient skirt and shapeless sweater, trowel or hoe in hand, her protestations were swept aside. By contrast, her immaculate friend would perch herself happily on a nearby rock, a cashmere shawl spread carefully under her, with never a thought to help, as she chattered away. When it was time to take a break, she would meekly follow everyone indoors for a coffee and again, not a finger lifted. All of this suited Leah fine. In Catalina she saw a decorative addition to their ménage, an *ingenue* who brought light and laughter on the dullest of days. It was inclusive and fun. Even more important, Leah had not taken a single pill since the end of October.

Today was a case in point. It was the morning after Mungo had arrived and Leah was behind with her work. As she dug in a new line of cabbages, she pondered over the latest gossip, which concerned Lucie and Sebastian. Apparently, the 'beautiful couple' was at war with the club across the street which was enjoying a revival. 'This attractive girl from London's just rolled in,' said Catalina, 'Apparently she's got a real business head on her *and* she speaks the Queen's English! Lucie can't seem to handle that, and has been seen tearing their posters down all around town. I suspect she and Sebastian have been on rather too many little "treeps" lately and feel they're losing the upper hand.'

Leah was always a little shocked at the sheer cattiness of these and other revelations, then reminded herself that Catalina owed these people no loyalty. She admitted as much herself. 'Don't look so shocked,' she would laugh, 'I know they talk about me behind my back … so why should not I do the same?' Nevertheless, Leah could not help wondering if she should share quite so many confidences as she had of late.

Recently, they had touched on the thorny subject of sex. Catalina had been surprisingly vague; Leah downright and honest – even to the point of admitting she did not enjoy it much these days. As soon as the words were out, she'd regretted it. But it was too late. Fortunately, the topic was quickly dropped but to her surprise Catalina brought it up again a few days later and seemed anxious to offer advice. With Jock being older, she confessed she sometimes played a little game which made life in the bedroom more amusing and stimulating for them both. Leah immediately wanted to know all about that. It was simple, Catalina said. One just played very hard to get which had the effect of winding up both partners and creating deeper desire on either side. For instance, wasn't it about time Leah thought of saying 'no' to Buster? Frankly, Catalina felt it would work wonders for their marriage.

Leah was surprised. Wasn't that kind of unfair, not to say immoral to deny a man his marital rights? Buster was a fullblooded male and he might not take kindly to such treatment. Catalina had raised her eyebrows and then the laughter pealed out of her. 'I suspected as much, and that's why it's so good for them,' she had said. 'They actually thrive on a bit of denial. It excites them. Don't forget the forbidden fruit has always tasted sweeter. What they can't have all the time, they want. Try saying 'no' a couple of times, and Buster will be all over you with tempting little goodies and trying a lot harder to win your favours.'

Leah was not so sure about the 'goodies' but she resolved to carry out Catalina's advice. If it tempted Buster to be more appreciative of her, she herself might begin to enjoy the whole experience again. Buster had always been such a mechanical kind of lover. She longed to bring a little romance and mystery into their partnership, and this might be the solution. She would coyly reject him, and wait for him to start wooing her. Had he ever wooed her? She wondered. Well, it wasn't too late. Possibly, it had been her own fault all the way along. She had been too available, and like any man he had obviously taken her for granted.

With this discussion fresh in mind, Leah hoped that today Catalina might give them a miss. She had meant to start her planting early that morning, before the sun got high, so she could water amply without burning the tender leaves, but things had gone wrong from the start. First, there'd been a row with Howard who said it was dangerous to have a dog in the house without first seeing the vet – what if it was rabid? She then wasted an hour trying to ring the only English vet from the pay phone at the local store. Having failed miserably, she decided to take the shopkeeper's advice and set off by car to find a certain *Doutor* Geronimo who attended every morning at the local slaughterhouse.

She got badly lost on an inland road but eventually Leah tracked her elusive quarry down just as he was leaving. With bloodied overall, bushy black sideburns and massive hairy arms which looked more suited to handling carcasses than small, frightened animals, he wiped his hands on his trousers before shaking hands. After a cursory look over the dog and the pronouncement that he was 'clean' as far as he could see, he suggested coming to the house to take a blood sample which would be followed up by inoculations the following day. Leah couldn't help remarking how the good *Senhor Doutor*'s eyes lit up and his whole demeanour improved when she explained where they lived.

There had been another incident at lunch. Someone – she suspected Buster – had left the larder door open. Consequently Mungo was made to take the blame for a certain missing steak pie. With her protegé punished and suitably chastened, Leah found herself smoothing ruffled feathers all round and promising Benjie – who had cooked the wretched pie – that she would make another tonight. Thankful now to work in the peace of her vegetable patch, Leah stood back to appraise her latest efforts, when a scrunch of tyres on the gravel below disturbed her reverie. She heard herself utter a rare profanity as Catalina drew up, waving cheerfully. Damn it…just as she was making headway! Fortunately, Buster was already there, helping their guest out. Let *him* keep her occupied for a while, she prayed, then with luck she might get all her cabbages in on the same day, after all.

Catalina allowed herself to be half lifted out of the bucket seat. In so doing, her short skirt rode up to reveal a frill of black pantie. 'Eet's always the same,' she dimpled up at Buster, 'one tries to be oh so elegant and get out – just so – and then, thees happens, and the whole effect is ruined.' She pouted as she tugged at her hem. 'It looks as though I'll never win the prize for sheer sophistication. I guess I'm just a country girl at heart. Too bad!'

Since nothing could be further from the truth, Buster might be forgiven for laughing. Instead he looked very serious as he declared, 'I'd give you the first, second and third prize, any day!'

'And the booby?' her bubbling laughter was surfacing under the words.

'Never! And you know it – come on, Mrs. McKay!' His eyes and voice were suddenly alive, 'Come and take a look at my garden round the front. Leah's too entrenched with them cabbages and I've a lot to show you.' On the way they passed his wife's concentrated, bent figure high up on the ridge.

'She *does* work hard!' said Catalina, admiringly.

'Too darned hard for my liking,' said Buster, his lips tightening for a moment. 'Don't give her time for nothing else.'

'Oh? That's an ambiguous remark.'

'She's the ambiguous one; not me. I'm a straightforward kinda guy. But,' he smiled, 'you didn't come here to talk about me. Come and see what we've done to the place. I'm hoping you won't recognise it.'

They had reached his embryo lawn with its neatly cut-out flowerbeds and border, all piled up with trim stacks of compost – ready for planting. Standing back proudly, he waited for her to take it all in. She would have remembered how it had been in the beginning and must guess how hard he had sweated and toiled, wrestling with the stubborn ground. The Portuguese were famous for their taming of the land, their clever conservation of natural resources and their terracing; she of all people would appreciate the transformation.

He waited for her to say something and enjoyed studying her in the silence as she cast her eyes this way and that. With her slim legs, teetering slightly on high heels, she made an exquisite figure in soft peach angora, warm and inviting against the blackness of the mulched earth, the coldness of the carefully laid irrigation channels. Still she said nothing and he became transfixed by the rise and fall of her breast. It reminded him of his dream, only now there was glowing colour in her cheeks and he could see her breath hover in the damp air. He knew he only had to reach out to touch her under the fluffy cardigan with its tiny pearl buttons that scarcely met over her bosom to feel the reality. It was all so suddenly tangible and inviting.

She seemed self-conscious, 'It's – er – what can I say? Wonderful – I suppose – what a difference!'

'What is?' his voice sounded sharp.

She turned her great doelike eyes upon him. 'Why, the garden! You asked me what I thought…'

'Of course – I forgot myself.'

'What's wrong, Buster?' she put a hand on his arm, very lightly but he could feel her touch go all the way through him.

'I – er – dreamed about you,' he mumbled. 'Some time ago – the day after the party. But I haven't been able to get it out of my mind. Every time I see you, it all comes flooding back.'

'I hope it was a nice dream?'

Buster shuffled his weight from one foot to the other. 'The bit with you was.'

'That's all right then,' she said demurely.

Silence fell like a stone. Buster thought how clean and fresh she looked. The November breeze suddenly whisked her hair forward so that two wings of ebony black formed a perfect triangle around her face, making her eyes and lips enormous. She pushed them back with an impatient hand and he caught a lingering whiff of her scent. Suddenly aware of his sweat and half the garden on his clothes, he wiped his hands on his stained jeans and wondered if the contrast between them might have offended her Portuguese sense of propriety. He struggled to return to neutral ground.

'Er – how's your husband?' he made his voice casual, 'we haven't seen much of him here lately.'

'Actually that's partly why I came today,' said Catalina quickly.

'Oh yeah?'

'Yes. Jock's had to go to London rather suddenly. You know we had that stroke of bad luck in September?'

'Sure.'

'There have been further complications – something to do with the Inland Revenue, trustees and things. I never really understand these matters, he doesn't share much of it with me. It looks however as though he'll have to speed up the next exhibition. It was to have been in the spring, now it may be just before Christmas – a better buying time, his agent thinks. They've found a new gallery that's prepared to house it.'

'I see.'

'He expects to be gone about ten days, to finalise details of the work he'll take, marketing strategy and so on. I saw him off this morning on the first flight out. What I'm trying to say is – oh dear, how do I say? I'm not much good at these things, but I'm *dreading* being in the house on my own. Weeth Katy at school all day, I find the house so oppressive – only Philismena for company. I get so bored. I can't even take the boat out, Jock made me promise. So what do I do all day? I wondered … if you, Leah – and er – the Boys don't mind – might I spend the daytimes here? It's always so lively and friendly, and … the time flies by …' She didn't finish the sentence; it was a long speech for her.

He squeezed her arm. 'I know what you're saying.'

'It probably sounds silly to you – always so busy – but it would only be ten days and I promise not to get in the way …'

'In the way?' Buster was staring at her. 'Are you crazy?' And then quite suddenly, he had taken her in his arms. 'You, Mrs McKay …' He kissed her firmly on the mouth … 'can come here as often as you want, when you want, at any time you please!'

It was only after he'd kissed her in what was meant to be a spontaneous, friendly, fraternal, call-it-what-you-will kiss, that he realised what he'd done. As he watched her move away to find Leah, refusing to catch his eye, he knew as surely as he'd ever known anything in his forty-seven years, that he wanted her.

He picked up a fork, thrust its prongs into the ground and leant hard on it. She was halfway up the path now and he needed something to steady himself. He was not the same man as the one who had walked her down that path just a few minutes ago. Instead, that single intimate contact had changed everything. It was summoning up every burning desire he'd ever possessed. Not just idle excitement or a passing fancy, but intense frightening feelings which had lain dormant since Korea were now rushing to the surface. The brothel, the anticipation, money passing hands, one special, very beautiful girl in a darkened room…the passion. It was if someone had just stirred up a witch's brew. And into the brew they'd also thrown a handful of magic.

For the first time in his life, Buster Bloomfield knew he was head over heels in love.

Leah got up at Catalina's approach. 'Ever known what it's like to have a broken back?' she grinned, passing the back of her hand under her dripping nose, 'Goodness me – I wanted cold, but this is raw – nobody warned me!'

'It's almost winter,' observed Catalina, 'and Portugal, contrary to popular belief is not Africa, you know!'

'Pity!' said Leah. 'I must be getting old, I can't straighten up.'

'Turn around,' said Catalina and briskly rubbed her in the small of the back, loosening up the tight muscles round the ribcage and gently pummeling her under the shoulder blades. Gradually the spasm eased and all the warmth came flooding back as her busy fingers increased the circulation.

'My, you're a dab hand at that! We should get you up here more often.'

'I spend half my life giving Jock massage,' said Catalina. 'But seriously, Leah, I might just do that. In fact, I was asking Buster only a moment ago if it would be all right. You see, Jock had to go to London today. I'm just back from the airport.'

'Why, honey!' Leah's face showed her concern. 'This was unexpected, wasn't it?'

'Not really. With things the way they are, he was expecting a summons from his trustees at some time. It just came sooner rather than later.'

'So you're home alone?'

'*Mais ou menos.* If I could just escape up here at lunchtime – I'll bring my own contributions of course. It would be so much nicer than brooding at home with that boring old maid fussing round me.'

'Come on, Catalina, you know us better than that! Why not come and stay?'

'Oh no! So kind, but I must be home morning and night for Katy. I actually enjoy the evenings – with the child in bed, a warm fireside, a glass of red wine and a good film on TV – I'm happy as a bee. No, it's the day that drags. Santa Felicia's dead when all the tourists have gone. And I'm not lucky enough to have a whole new garden and imposing house to work on!'

'Like to swap?' chuckled Leah. 'You can take on Buster and the Boys too. Oh! And Cleo and Ant – not to mention – wait for it! I didn't tell you, we have a newcomer – Mungo!'

'*Mungo!*'

'I thought you'd say it like that – everyone does! He's our new addition to the family…' and indulgently she described the misadventures of her charge.

'Oh Leah, what a softie you are!' said Catalina. 'Where is this unfortunate?'

'In disgrace. Chained up in his kennel, I'm afraid. Mind you, he seems quite happy, I gave him a bone.'

'But are you really going to keep him? He sounds the most troublesome creature.'

'I can't throw him out! Someone's already tried that, it wouldn't be fair.'

'I can't believe Howard and Benjie approve?'

' They don't – but they can't stop me.'

'And Buster?'

'Buster goes along with anything, given time,' said Leah.

'I wish you luck!' smiled Catalina. 'I should have thought, however, you had enough on your hands without adding a stray dog to it all.' And lapsing into thoughtful silence, she settled herself down on her favourite stone as her friend got back to work.

The ten days sped by quickly. Catalina would arrive at midday, usually with some edible offering, and soon lunchtime had turned from a hurried snack into something of an occasion. The normal half-hour miraculously stretched and although progress outside was held up, no one really minded. As Catalina pointed out, they were no longer in the States so why not take advantage of the Latin way of life?

The only one who groused was Howard. He was putting on even more weight and blamed the lunches. 'You could try eating less, dear,' suggested Leah, but the remark went down badly. It was sad, she reflected, Howard had been noticeably less *simpatico* since the arrival of the geese, the advent of Mungo only widening the rift between them. On the Sunday before Jock's return, Catalina brought Katy with her. On the same day, Carlos, very excited, announced that Cleo was building a nest. Leah was cockahoop and it became a day of general celebration. Buster – eager to find an excuse – opened a bottle of champagne.

'I've been wanting to pour you a glass of this for a long time,' he said, winking at Catalina and popping the cork before anyone could stop him

Leah gasped as she saw it was Krug '59. 'Buster, whatever are you thinking of,' she said, 'wasn't that being saved for Christmas Day?'

'I wanted to taste it – we've got more,' her objection was waved aside. Catalina took a sip and he watched her closely, the echo of satisfaction hovering on his lips as she gave a small moue of pleasure. 'Anyways, whoever heard of a goose building a goddarned nest this side of New Year?'

'Anything's possible in Portugal!' said Benjie and they all laughed.

The sun came out and it was so warm, they decided to lunch on the patio. Katy ran backwards and forwards carrying knives and forks. She could talk of nothing else but the geese. 'Their nest will be beautiful,' she confided in Howard, 'All downy and soft. Carlos says the lady goose uses her own feathers to line it. He saw her plucking them from her chest with her beak, like this…' she proceeded to give a fair imitation. 'Have you been to look?'

'Er – not yet,' said Howard. Nothing on God's earth would allow him to stick his nose into the smelly hut they called the *casa dos gansos*. He disapproved bitterly of poultry around a house. He had seen too much of that in his Irish childhood.

'You must!' cried the child, jumping up and down. 'Give me a piggy-back, Uncle Howard!'

'OK.' Like many people unused to children he was nonetheless flattered to be singled out by such an attractive creature. She had a winning smile when she wanted. With her blonde hair, bleached white at the temples to emphasise enormous grey eyes, he thought it a pity all kids did not look like this. The ones from his past had runny noses and whiny voices. Those he'd encountered with clients were fat and spoilt. Katy was definitely different – come to think of it – so was her mother.

Lunch was paella. A new recipe, Benjie confided, which he'd been dying to try out on a native of Iberia. Catalina felt she was hardly qualified to judge since the marvellous Krug had seduced her palate and *everything* seemed divine. There was more laughter and Katy wanted to know what was so funny. Leah tried to explain that funny or not, Katy's mummy always said the right thing which was slightly spoilt by Catalina saying how tiresome the child was, forever asking questions.

'Don't grown-ups ever ask questions?' Katy wanted to know.

'There you go again!' said her mother, exasperated.

'Wait!' said Buster and they all turned to look at him. 'It's a damn good question. It deserves an answer.' He looked hard at Catalina and succeeded in catching and holding her eye. There was a pause. 'Well – aren't you going to answer her?'

'There's nothing to say.' Benjie noticed Catalina had gone a little pink and he glanced across the table to see what Leah thought about this little exchange, but she was too busy slipping scraps to Mungo under the table.

'Oh, but there is,' said Buster driving home a point. He turned to Katy, 'Grown-ups *do* ask questions – sometimes important ones – but other grown-ups don't always want to give an answer. Usually because they're scared to. Now why don't you come along with me and we'll find some more champagne for all those scared grown-ups?'

'What was all that about?' said Howard more to himself than anyone else.

A moment later, Buster was back, brandishing another bottle and refilling glasses. 'Hey, steady on, honey – ' said Leah, 'we've already celebrated Cleo's nest once, we can't go on like this all day – '

'Fuck Cleo's nest!' said Buster. 'Now!' he cleared his throat, 'I propose a toast…to absent friends! Namely one missing husband! Please raise your glasses, one and all – to Jock McKay!'

'He means Papa!' cried Katy excitedly, oblivious of the puzzled faces.

'This is very kind,' said Catalina, turning to Buster with raised eyebrows.

'He deserves it – poor bastard,' said Buster. 'Leaving you here with us like this. He must feel very deprived; the least we can do is drink to him!'

'While Jock's away, the mice will play,' said Benjie, ignoring a kick under the table from Howard.

'You're right there!' laughed Leah. 'Just look at us all! Half smashed if you please, at three thirty in the afternoon and half a day's work left undone!'

'That's not exactly what I meant,' said Benjie softly.

Buster had not taken his eyes from Catalina's face since the beginning of lunch. Unlike the others, she'd only sipped at her champagne, but she knew her face was flushed. Slowly she felt control slipping away as more and more she was drawn towards that magnetic pull, beamed across the table. So physical was his gaze she felt as though she could reach out and touch it; she marvelled that no one else sensed it too. Katy had now left the table and was playing with Mungo while Leah looked on indulgently. Benjie was stacking dishes and replacing them with new ones, Howard was cutting cheese. And still, she felt those burning eyes.

As finally, she yielded and lifted her face, there was a sudden defining moment of locking on. In that split second of engagement, everything stood still. It seemed to Catalina that her heart stopped beating. She saw her own hand, clasping a glass – in mid-flight to her mouth – struck immobile. It belonged to a stranger, as did her tongue – stuck to the roof of her mouth. She tried to smile, but her lips stretched tight and froze over her teeth. Her throat was dry and she knew – even if she'd wanted – it would be impossible to speak. The only thing that moved in her entire body, was a muscle which started to twitch, low down in her cheek.

At this point, Katy, in the midst of helping Mungo secure a crumb, got up and ran round to her side of the table. The distraction saved her. As she felt the colour flood her face again, she knew that moment of sheer helplessness was over. With a supreme effort she blinked, finally able to tear her eyes away from Buster's. With huge relief, her jaw relaxed. She swallowed and slowly her breathing returned to normal. It was all over in a second, but she had just lived an eternity.

'Has anyone got a cigarette?' she broke the silence, trying to conceal her trembling fingers.

'I didn't know you smoked,' said Leah, looking up in surprise. 'Are you all right, honey?'

'Fine,' she smiled as Buster fumbled in his pockets, but Benjie beat him to it. As he bent his handsome dark head to offer her a light and carefully held the flame for her, she knew by his expression that he had noticed something. How much had he guessed? How much could he feel the energy between her and Buster? The man was not stupid and she did not dare meet his eye. What would he find there? The reflection of her own naked desire for a start, and what else beside? For a moment Catalina felt ashamed at her own arousal and more so at those undenied, scheming thoughts.

'You must come again for lunch,' Leah was saying to the child, who sensing her mother's withdrawal into a world that did not involve her, had moved to the opposite end of the table. Katy said nothing, just stared at the American woman with the slim face and earnest eyes. It seemed unfair, she thought, she was pretty, but not as much as Mama. 'Perhaps if you come again Cleo will have finished her nest and laid an egg.'

The child's face lit up, 'So soon?'

'I feel sure.'

'Might it …' the little girl paused, breath bated with excitement; '… might it be a *golden* egg?'

'Well dear, I'm not – er – sure about that …'

'She's just read the story of the goose that laid the golden eggs at school,' supplied Catalina, now fully recovered and stubbing out the unsmoked cigarette.

'Oh I see,' Leah sounded relieved, 'Well, poppet – I guess you never know. Why don't you come and see for yourself!'

'I'd like Papa to come.'

'Why not? He's always welcome.'

'He told me he could do with a goose that laid golden eggs,' said Katy confidentially. She was beginning to rather like this woman after all; there was something safe and kind about her, unlike some of Mama's friends, 'just before he went to London.'

'Maybe he's already got one, darling but he just doesn't know it!' Catalina gave a brittle laugh and got up with an excuse to admire the garden.

Johanna Vincent heaved a sigh as she threaded her yellow beach-buggy through the afternoon traffic, all heading in the direction of Faro. Really, the coast road got more impossible to drive along every time she ventured onto it – one day it would have as bad a reputation as the *marginal* that ran between Lisbon and Estoril. But for now it was a journey of contrasts. As if proving the point, someone in a souped-up Mini Cooper shot past, and she was forced behind a mule-cart...oh well! She arrived at the airport only five minutes late, but it did not matter as the plane she was due to meet from London had been delayed.

She made her way to the ladies' room. Silly how much she cared about the way she looked with Maysie, more than anybody else – even her gorgeous man in Lisbon! Her own daughter! It was too ridiculous for words, she thought as she ran a comb through the blonded grey waves which softened a well-bred and slightly angular face – they were hardly in competition. She ran a deep pink shiny lipstick over her mouth and wondered if Maysie would think she had aged. Last time she had told her she had. The way her bottom lip had thinned and the tiny lines between her upper lip and her nose upset her most; there were laughter lines round her eyes but she minded these less. Oh well, there was not much she could do unless she succumbed to a face lift and that was not in the game plan – at least not for now. Nevertheless, children could be cruel – especially adult ones.

Head held high, she strode into the arrivals hall and ordered a coffee. The English papers were late as usual. Perhaps Maysie would have the forethought to bring *The Telegraph*; it would be nice to be up to date for once. The place was heaving with groups of Japanese business men. Clutching identical imitation buffalo briefcases and blue macs, they were being herded up by anxious travel reps and directed outside towards coaches which gleamed in the sunshine. Probably in the Algarve for a business congress in one of the new five star hotels, she thought. They could be anything really – from dentists to dredging engineers – what did it matter? To Johanna, lover of originality and variety, there was something infinitely depressing about groups like these.

An hour later, a guttural voice on the tannoy announced the arrival of Flight TAP 249 from Heathrow. She got up, suddenly jittery. It was always the same when Maysie arrived. Was it a mixture of conscience and guilt that sprang out of the sheer vacuum of maternal feelings she harboured? Even when Maysie was a baby, Johanna had failed to feel any real connection; as a teenager the girl had become a stranger. Now, Maysie was in her mid twenties but the last thing Johanna really wanted was to throw open her house and her life to this cold, judgmental yet demanding daughter. Not only did she cramp her style, it was as though her own hard-earned self confidence could be sucked out of her all too easily.

Quickly, she walked towards the arrivals gate. They were just emerging from Customs. She could not see Maysie but she could see the tall, supercilious figure that belonged to

Jock McKay. Surprised, she looked round for Catalina and spotted her by the bookstand, a brooding, inscrutable look on the normally vivacious face. Funny, she hadn't noticed her before; funny too, the expression – there's someone else clearly not overjoyed at being reunited, she mused. She wondered why.

Jock McKay was tired, very tired. He had had a singularly trying time in London and he could not wait to get back to the slower pace of Santa Felicia. Not that his troubles would leave him here, but at least he could lose himself in the last few weeks of work before the hastily arranged winter exhibition. Damn the change of date! Normally, he would have risen happily to the challenge because he worked better under pressure. But this time it was different – the preparation, the programme, packing and unpacking, the hanging, the final adjustments, the opening night party, the praise and adulation – all part and parcel of a successful artist's celebration of his work – but would it work this time? Having suffered such a major financial blow – could his luck really change?

And the quiet satisfaction of actually seeing all that work hung, admired … it was still a great stimulant … surely? Memories of former exhibitions would flash through his brain in the stillness of the night, remarks that made him grin in the dark – would they still be his? Trite remarks '… are you really the artist? I've been collecting you for years!' from awe-inspired voices. Critics telling you more about your work than you knew yourself. Young journalists keen to make an impression with their fulsome, over-flowery words. Even the old biddies who would sidle up at the end of the evening, apology written all over their faces for not being young, pretty or important, but keen to say their bit '… I *do* like that red composition, so *daring* Mr McKay – but then you always *are*!'… or some such nonsense.

The best part about it and he made no pretence in admitting it, was the money. Sometimes, he felt like shouting out loud – shocking them all – right in the middle of the preview. 'Roll up! Roll up! Your money or your life! You mean-faced old buggers! Forget the chit-chat, forget the compliments! Get out your cheque books and don't waste my time! The colour of your money's what I'm interested in, all I do it for. M-O-N-E-Y! Got it? No sir, of course that's not a ship! Neither is it a tower! No madam, I'm afraid it's not even supposed to portray strength – though, that's a thought. No, it's not supposed to be anything at all. Just a whole lot of meaningless blobs and dabs of paint. All out of my head, like spilt brains! And all I want in return for that rubbish you call "Art" is your *money*!'

It was easy to get hard about it all. He was uncertain if the hardness was a cover-up for something that perhaps did have a soul, and which in some strange way, tried to express the infinite pleasure he got from looking at God's earth. It was a long time since he'd painted a proper landscape, a proper flower – and there certainly wouldn't be time now, that was for sure. Perhaps it was better not to, at least for the moment. He couldn't afford to get sentimental, vulnerable. There was too much else that already hurt.

As he picked up his one large suitcase and headed for customs, he noticed Maysie Vincent's blonde head amongst a bevy of dark ones. She seemed to have a host of designer cases scattered around and was waiting for even more to come off the conveyor belt. The extra kilos must have cost her a package! A pretty girl, he conceded, but not an intelligent thought in her head; he was glad he had avoided her on the plane. Now, he debated –

should he give her a hand? No! thank the Lord – some young man had beaten him to it, half sprinting to her side. That let him out. Phew!

Now, would Catalina be in arrivals? And what sort of welcome might he get? He pushed his trolley through customs hoping he wouldn't get stopped. Luckily, the unsmiling uniformed men were much more interested in a couple of moustachioed hippies and the contents of someone's guitar than him. He spotted her immediately. Why did he have such a sinking feeling in his chest? He was not such a fool as to think things between them would be quite the same again. Fate had already taken a hold of their future and he was not sure he liked the way in which it was moving. Nevertheless, he was determined to put a brave face on it.

'Hello, my darling,' he called and forcing a smile went forward to greet her.

23

'Hello, Mummy! How are you?'

Maysie Vincent planted a perfunctory peck on her mother's cheek and almost in the same breath dispensed with the young man, his gallantry and her cases.

'Oh, just pop them down there, will you? Anywhere'll do – the porter will take them now – thanks most awfully.'

Oblivious of the youth hanging around for a moment longer – the optimistic hope of a telephone number swiftly fading – she chattered on. 'God! Mummy, I'm fagged out! This must be the fifteenth flight I've endured in a month and you know how I hate airports! Hotel after hotel – the worst was in New Delhi – yes I got the dreaded tummy…but it's the air conditioning that really gets to me. My skin's a wreck…Porter! Oh hell, Mummy …he's gone after someone else. How selfish! There must be another porter in this dump of an airport.'

'I'm sure there is, darling,' said Johanna calmly, 'there's no huge rush, is there? If you just have the patience – *Porteiro!* – There, I told you! It does help to speak the language, you know. *Obrigada!*'

The man was already loading Maysie's seven pieces of Louis Vuitton into the back of the beach-buggy. Everyone knew the *senhora* and her unusual car and she always tipped handsomely. A moment later, they were nosing out of the airport.

'Anyway,' Johanna was dreading the answer, 'Why *quite* so many large bags? You'd think you'd come for an eternity.'

'Oh Mummy, it's not a lot, really – not for a top model these days. Anyway, you know me – I never have time to pack or unpack, so it's easier to bring the lot. Besides,' she added, 'there's quite a bit of stuff for you.'

'Really, darling! How very thoughtful! Might I know what?'

'Well,' Maysie paused to think, 'there's some of that cheese you like. I put it down on your account at Fortnums, 'cause I don't mind telling you, I'm stony broke at present.'

'Despite being a top model?' Johanna couldn't help but remark.

'Yah, well – all the expenses, you know how it is. Oh! And I went to Harrods and tried to get that foundation you wanted, but they were out of stock.'

'Ah.'

'Yah, but don't worry, I wasn't idle. I then rushed off to Jackson's and got that Darjeeling you like so much, so you needn't worry about that for a few months.'

'Was that on account too?'

'Yah – but Mummy, I did *try* for you. It takes a lot of time going round these shops – oh and I would have gone to Bond Street to get those dark choccies you like from Charbonnel & Walker, the thought was definitely there … but I simply never made it.'

'Just as well darling, I don't keep an account there.'

The remark sailed right over Maysie's head. A moment later she was waving frantically as a shiny blue Jensen overtook them. 'That was one of the Motta boys! You know the biggest bank in Lisbon … Wow!' she cried. 'Is there anyone exciting in Santa Felicia at the moment?'

'Just the usuals – Roger was home, but he's back at Oxford now. Oh – I suppose you haven't yet met the newcomers, have you? You know, the Americans, who were building that big yellow villa above the coast road?'

'That monstrosity, you mean? I do remember your writing something about a party there. Quite a luxury sort of do – wasn't it? Are they jet set?'

'Hardly, darling. But wealthy, and generous with it, I'd say.'

'Any spare men?'

'Not in the sense you mean, I'm afraid. Didn't I explain to you about the Boys?'

'D'you know, I am *awful*, Mumsie. I never get time to study your letters properly. I do seem to remember something. You're not trying to say they're queer, are you?'

'I'm not trying to say anything. You can find out for yourself!' Johanna tried hard to keep the note of asperity out of her voice. She couldn't bear the thought of a quarrel already.

'It all sounds frightfully suspicious, Mummy – but I got the feeling – you're quite intrigued by these people!'

'Nonsense, darling, but I can tell you who can't keep away.'

'Who?'

'Catalina McKay!'

Maysie let out a long low whistle. 'Really! Then there must be something more to them than you think. Catalina doesn't get embroiled with other people for nothing. If they're not jet set, then what's she after?'

'I'm not sure, darling. People are already saying she's after the husband, but I can't quite see it myself. He's not her type – you know what a snob Catalina is. Well, it just doesn't *fit* – her going for a man like that. He's good looking, but in a healthy, outdoor type of way – Catalina usually prefers the smoothies, lounge lizard type. I don't feel he's sophisticated enough – despite the rather obvious money.'

'Knowing Catalina, it's probably a spot of prick teasing,' said Maysie in her world-weary voice. 'She was the same last summer with Manolo … in front of Jock too. I don't think he minded a bit. Personally, I reckon that sort of thing gives him a thrill.'

Philismena heard them coming and threw open the door. Katy stood beside her in her best dress. At the sight of her father she was suddenly overcome with emotion.

'So you won't come and give Papa a welcome home kiss,' said Jock, looking pathetic. Then he grinned and opened wide his arms and the child flew into them, whooping for joy.

Philismena looked pleased and took the suitcase into the hall as Catalina watched the three of them in silence. She suddenly felt as if she were the outsider; as if the warm, domestic picture before her was too homely to include her. She turned her back on them and crossed the old wood floor, slowly drawing off her long kid gloves. She placed them carefully side by side on the oak table and turned round, as if in a play waiting for her cue to rejoin the others. Jock was speaking in Portuguese to Philismena and Katy was dancing about asking for presents. Catalina's cue did not come and something snapped inside her.

'Katy!' she said sharply, taking out her displeasure on the child. 'Will you keep still for two minutes! Can't you see your father's tired?'

Jock looked up in surprise. It was the first reference she'd made to his wellbeing since he'd stepped off the plane. 'I think you must be tired too, my angel,' he said, not unkindly. 'Let's all go upstairs and Philismena can bring us some tea. I've brought one or two things back to show you both.'

'It *is* presents,' said Katy.

'Now I wonder what gave you that idea, Princess?' said her father, letting her climb on his back. He winked at Catalina to show her she was included and they went upstairs to find a log fire and the smell of pine cones burning in the grate. It felt comforting and familiar, the wood smoke mingling with the faint aroma from above of turpentine and oils. Jock heaved a sigh of relief and put his daughter down. Despite everything, it was good to be back.

It was Leah's idea to have a foursome out somewhere, now that Jock McKay was back in their midst. She and Buster had never dined out without the Boys since leaving New York, so when Catalina announced the return of her husband – apparently a changed man – Leah felt this would give her the opportunity to ring some changes.

Lately, the atmosphere at Casa Amarela had become claustrophobic. It was not as she had foreseen when they had planned the move to Portugal together; the idea had been to share a house, not every waking moment of their lives. It made sound economic sense to lunch together when they were all working so hard on the garden, but evenings were a different matter. Surprisingly, it was Buster who seemed so keen to dine altogether; almost as though he didn't want to be alone with her. Yes, it was high time to break the pattern.

Jock's return was the perfect excuse. Typical of her generosity, Leah had reserved a table at *Cozinha Velha*, Santa Felicia's most fashionable restaurant. Darling of the Michelin Guide, recognised by Egon Ronay and toast of the cogniscenti, its owner-chef Fernando had spent fifteen long years working his way up through the kitchens of the Madrid Ritz, before returning home to open his own business first in Albufeira, now in Santa Felicia. It had been hard graft, but the locals had recognised his endeavour and were quick to support him in those important early days. Now, famed throughout Europe, he still put those old customers first. Friends were friends and if Fernando counted you amongst them, it was special.

Knowing all this, Leah could not help shiver with a pleasant feeling of anticipation as she stepped out of the bath and towelled herself dry. She felt this was an important testing time for Buster and Jock to get together, man to man. Since the blossoming of her friendship with Catalina, it seemed a pity that the two husbands were so diametrically opposed to each other – both in character and culture. She hoped this evening would change all that. Happily, it seemed the artist's London visit had fired him up, there'd been a lot of press interest and he liked the new Chelsea gallery. 'Jock's working so hard, he's even given up drinking spirits,' confided Catalina, 'and I can't tell you the difference. No black moods, he can even laugh at himself these days!'

Leah was glad for her friend and hugged the bath sheet to her, as she contemplated a vision of what the future might hold for the four of them. Eating out at the best places, playing bridge, a visit to Lisbon for a concert or the opera – the list was endless. She was in the middle of this pleasant reverie, when Buster entered the room still in his work clothes, his thick socks leaving sweat marks all over the glossy tiles. Without thinking, she pulled the terry up to her chin protectively.

'Hey, hey! Why so modest all of a sudden! Let's take a look at you! You're always covered up these days, I've forgotten what you look like!' Before she could reply, he had jerked the towel roughly away from her in one swift motion of his hand. She noticed that his fingernails were black and that the veins stood out on the back of his fist.

'Why, Buster,' she cried, 'What's up with you?'

'You mean what *isn't* up,' he growled.

She was amazed. Then she caught it. Mixed with the scent of sweat, a strong whiff – the unmistakeable smell of bourbon. What had gotten into him? He must have had one or two to reek like this. 'Honey,' she decided to ignore the remark, 'I don't want to rush you but – er – shouldn't we be getting a move on?' She went to detach her bathrobe from the hook behind the door.

'You haven't answered my question,' he said belligerently. 'No, *don't* put on that robe – stay as you are! Uncovered! Starkers! I want you to admit the truth!'

He really must be quite drunk, thought Leah. She had better humour him to keep the peace. 'What are you on about, honey?'

'I asked you a question, didn't I? You heard me! I said – don't you like it any more?' He was bellowing at her. '*It*! You know! Sex! S-E-X! Does spelling it make it easier for your complicated mind to understand?'

'There's no need to be offensive, honey,' her voice sounded much calmer than the turmoil she felt inside. 'Of course I still like it.' Did she? 'What funny ideas you get into your head.'

'Don't give me that,' he said, 'Give me one good reason why I should believe you!' His hazel eyes had taken on that glint she remembered him using on wayward employees back in New York, often before a firing. When things were late or someone had slipped up, he was the first to leap into action and give them what he called the 'third degree.' Well, two could play at that, she decided but he overrode her. 'You certainly don't *act* like you like it. When's the last time you put on something real pretty at night, something black or lacy or feminine – you know, instead of those buttoned up nighties of yours? You can't call them seductive now can you, and what about waving your fanny about more? Giggle and flirt a bit, like other girls – *some*thing at least! I mean … hey! Why don't you make up to me right now! Go on – work me up a bit and we can go straight off and *do* it?'

She was alarmed now. This was so unlike him, he couldn't be thinking straight. 'Buster, you're being ridiculous! I've just got out of the tub and we're supposed to be dining out with the McKays. This couldn't be worse timing, it's an important date! You don't want us late, do you?'

'Why not!' said Buster, 'They'd understand. At least it would put a glow on our faces. What's a bet Catalina and that husband of hers ain't doing it right now, this very moment?'

'You don't know what you're talking about,' said Leah, defiantly, snatching up her robe.

'Oh don't I? You don't think that girl blossoms and sparkles the way she does living on art appreciation, do you?'

'Sometimes you're absurd … and ignorant. Jock's not a young man, and I happen to know Catalina doesn't rush to go to bed the whole time. It's quite clear they have other pleasures in life which makes them the people they are. We've discussed it.'

'You have? You mean the guy's not up to it? Did she *tell* you that?'

'Not at all,' she pursed her lips and looked him full in the face, 'I mean some men can hold a woman for other reasons … empathy, sophistication, a sense of the aesthetic. For all his faults, Jock's a very cultured man.'

'You talk crap!' he said, pulling off his clothes slowly and deliberately and dropping them on the floor. 'And what's more, you've let yourself get skinny. If you're not careful you'll lose what ass and tits you've got, and look even more like the virgin schoolmarm you ape already!'

'Thanks a *lot*!' Leah was struggling to rein in her annoyance. 'I might just remind you, Buster Bloomfield, we've got precisely twenty minutes in which to get changed and out of this house.' She brushed past him and slammed the door.

More upset than she cared to admit, Leah went to the full-length mirror in their bedroom, let the robe fall open and took a long hard look at herself. Her cheeks were flaming from the bath and sheer indignation and an angry pulse thudded in her throat. She wasn't so vexed as to overlook the fact that most women would give their eye-teeth for her figure – flat tummy, absence of cellulite, pert bottom and well toned limbs swathed in a honey-gold tan, her level of fitness belying her forty two years by almost a decade.

Neither could she begin to imagine what had gotten into Buster. Firstly, to be drinking heavily at this early hour and secondly, to have spoken to her the way he had. In all their married life together, he had never picked such a quarrel. Argued? Objected? Nagged? From time to time – maybe, but he'd be more likely to tease her into submission, than to lay down the law or challenge her like that. He had certainly, never before, attacked her character. This sudden change had shaken her.

Of course, everything he'd said was unjust. It was true, since the move, there hadn't been much sex – but after all the physical work, it was hardly surprising. Until the other day, she had never refused him, so when she tried out Catalina's advice and coyly said 'no', he seemed quite unfazed. In fact, she'd almost gotten the feeling he was relieved as he'd just sank back in the pillows, asleep within minutes.

As for comparing their relationship with that of the McKays, why that was laughable! She hoped the figure remark wasn't a comparison to Catalina. The girl might be her best friend, but by the time she reached her fourth decade, the ample bosom would have descended and she wasn't so sure about the thighs. Leah had always been proud of her own streamlined appearance. A real city slicker, her friends called her 'tony' – neat in any outfit – pinstripe trouser suit or two piece Chanel! Add fifteen years to Catalina and you wouldn't know where one bulge ended or the other began …

Having reassured herself, she felt happier, applying herself to her make-up with gusto. By the time Buster was back in the bedroom, she was fully changed and coiffed. Just to show him, she'd put on her tightest black pants with a clingy silver top that gave the slightest bump an alluring curve, and six inch stilettos. She'd worked hard on her eyes too, a new silver-blue eye-shadow complemented the lurex, and more mascara than usual. Pleased with the effect, she waited for him to say something. She knew better than to expect an apology, but a mere 'Wow-eee!' his usual exclamation, would have sufficed. She waited in vain.

He dressed in silence and seemed totally oblivious of her presence. She watched him through the triple-sided glass on her dressing table, not a movement escaping her. The minutes ticked by and she was tempted to take a tranquiliser but resisted. Nevertheless, she would slip the tiny emergency pillbox into her bag before they left – just in case. Better to break the rules than spend the evening with shaky hands and fluttery heart; she had looked forward to this dinner all week. Why allow this man to spoil it just because he had broken his own rule and gotten boozed before sundown?

He was ready in no time, looking casually good in charcoal grey slacks, a classy belt with solid gold buckle and his favourite Ted Lapidus button-down shirt. Labouring in the garden had muscled him up even more than all those work-outs in his Manhattan gymn. His deeply tanned face added to the look of youthfulness but the expression was sour as he studied his watch. 'Ten minutes to spare,' he said. 'You see I was right all along – there *would* have been time.'

'If one likes it that way,' she said, looking after him helplessly as he went to start the car.

They had arranged to meet the McKays in The Anchor for cocktails at eight. They arrived on the stroke, to find the only other *estrangeiro* was Jerry Weaver himself. Without checking, Buster ordered her a vodka and a bourbon for himself. 'You see, they're not here. I guessed they wouldn't. Who's to say they're not doing what I said right now?'

'Oh give it a break,' she snapped. At eight fifteen she turned to Weaver, 'Has there been any word from Mr and Mrs McKay this evening? We had a date together for eight.'

Weaver examined his watch following it up with a loud guffaw. 'Might I draw your attention, madam, to the fact that this is not New York – sad as it may seem – only Santa Felicia! It's almost protocol to come late – at least among the natives! When in Rome, you know...' He winked indulgently and twizzled the ends of his moustache. He'd never much cared for wealthy Americans and found the inhabitants of the house on the hill an odd bunch – not really his type of client at all.

Leah's throat had gone a delicate shade of pink which heightened when Buster turned on her and growled, 'There's no need to go and make a fool of yourself, is there? That guy is pompous enough in a British kind of way without handing it to him on a plate!'

Leah suddenly felt as if the whole world was against her. She slipped her hand into her handbag and it tightened round the pillbox. If only Catalina would hurry up! She'd tell her everything, starting with the smell of bourbon on Buster's breath. If anyone would be sympathetic, it would be her. She'd suffered enough with Jock.

At last they arrived. It was twenty-five past and the air was electric as Catalina rushed in – breathless but stunning in a clinging black jersey dress with tiny buttons all the way down to her waist. Leah was so relieved she scarcely noticed there were enough left undone to reveal a considerable amount of cleavage. Both she and Jock were flushed and he, especially, seemed charged with excitement. 'What did I tell you?' said Buster in her ear.

Leah hurried forward to embrace her friend and just had time to mutter that Buster was half-smashed already. 'Great!' beamed Catalina, 'that makes three of us then! Sorry we're a leetle late, but we've just come from Johanna's where we've been drinking champagne cocktails to celebrate her daughter's latest modelling success. Apparently, she's to be the new face on the front cover of Harper's next month! We'll never hear the end of it now!' Laughing, she went forward to give Buster an effusive hug, 'You're looking as though you've just been proved right over something! You're not cross we kept you waiting, are you?'

'Of course he's not!' said McKay, clapping Buster on the shoulder. 'Good to see you again, my dear chap! And good to be back in Santa Felicia too! Now come on, Captain,' he moved imperiously towards the bar, 'what have you got for us there in the icebox? It had better be champagne, the real stuff, not that Spanish lookalike, we can't have Mrs McKay mixing her drinks – can we my dear?'

Shocked to see Jock in such a good humour, it took Leah more than a moment to twig he had turned to her. Already, there was a sense that things were getting out of hand – this was her invitation – so what was McKay doing ordering champagne for them all? She glanced at her husband, but his face had taken on a different hue and he was too busy talking to Catalina to take any notice of her. Her vision of a quiet, intimate dinner, without the distraction of the Boys, was evaporating by the second.

It amazed her that McKay, in his supposedly impecunious state, could afford the expensive bottle that arrived in the icebucket before them – or was it destined for her bill? Only time would tell. Even Catalina was behaving strangely. She was dangling on Buster's arm, whispering something in his ear and the whole atmosphere was threatening to descend into a free for all. Leah almost regretted Howard wasn't around to put a dampner on things.

'Cheer up!' McKay was looking at her through narrowed eyes and raised his glass. 'I know what you're thinking! Why do I do it? Well I'll tell you! When a man's really down and has everything to lose, that's the time to show the world he's on a high! If you don't – they'll kick you as you fall – it's the way of the world. So, instead, we play up beat and show it – especially to that cretin behind the bar! Just think how many people *he's* going to tell.'

Leah looked dubious and was about to reply when Buster butted in with one of his famous, or rather infamous, jokes. Something about a fancy dress party and a guy going as a petrol-pump because of the length of his...oh dear! Buster how *could* you? He was ruining her evening by the moment and as for mixing bourbon and champagne...she clutched at her pillbox again.

Catalina seemed to be enjoying the whole thing. Little trills of laughter scattered the conversation – if you could call it that – like falling leaves. Every so often, Buster would shoot her long gratified looks. Weaver was trying to top up her champagne glass, but she refused, tight-lipped. Nobody noticed. Now Buster was delivering his punchline. Two young Portuguese boys who'd been standing behind them were doubled over with laughter. How humiliating, thought Leah. And how come everyone round here understood English? It was all getting too much to bear.

She begged a cigarette off Jock, as he lit one up for himself. Like Catalina, she hardly ever smoked, but anything not to pop those tempting blue pills into her mouth. He surprised her by putting his own between her lips, it seemed a surprisingly intimate gesture; she wondered if it was his way of trying to make amends. She drew back the smoke and it rasped against the back of her throat – these were seriously strong. Her head spun for a moment, then the old familiar pain of stress thudded against her temples. She stubbed out the cigarette angrily. It had been a mistake to have one. A mistake to come here at all.

Catalina was busy with a story of her own. She had discovered an audience and was evidently enjoying every moment of her limelight. Ever so often she paused to sip a little more champagne while everyone waited patiently for her to continue. The two Portuguese, a trio of tourists, were all in on this one too. Leah wanted to scream at them. Even Jerry Weaver was eavesdropping, his moustaches glistening. Leah caught something about a little girl leading a cow through a meadow.

'Father Santos came up to Maria,' Catalina was saying, 'Where are you taking that fine heifer, Maria? To the milking parlour?'

'No, to the bull, Father,' said Maria.

'Tut, tut,' said the old priest, 'I should have thought your father could have done that.'

'Oh no, father,' said Maria. 'It *has* to be the bull.'

Catalina made a demure face as they all went into paroxyms of laughter. Weaver's face wore a look of amused concentration. One could tell at a glance he was storing up the story to be repeated to clients at a later date. Even McKay was grinning.

Leah cleared her throat. 'Excuse me everybody,' she said shrilly, 'I think we must get moving. We'll lose our table.'

'You wanna know something?' Buster took off his horn-rimmed spectacles and batted them at her. 'You sure are something of a drag tonight.'

'Oh, Buster!' Catalina sounded shocked, 'That's unkind. After all, Leah did arrange this.'

'Just a moment,' Buster sounded aggrieved. 'You don't know the half of it. She's so busy *arranging* things – as you so aptly put it – she's forgotten how to enjoy herself. All that time in New York, it was work, work, work. Now we're here, you'd think some of us could bring themselves to take a little time out. But no! not my wife. And what's more…' he burped into his glass and excused himself, 'she don't want anyone else to enjoy themselves, either.' And he put down his empty glass with a bang.

Catalina whispered something to her husband and took Leah's arm. 'Come on with me to the ladies, Leah. We'll leave the men to sort out the bill.'

Leah followed her out and promptly burst into tears. Catalina let her cry and patted her shoulder comfortingly until she'd finished. 'I don't know what's gotten into him this evening,' said Leah, dabbing her eyes with a paper tissue. 'He's never before been like this…absolutely *never*. Not in sixteen years of marriage!'

'I know, I know,' said Catalina soothingly. 'He was beastly, but I expect it was mixing drinks like that. It was wrong of Jock to order champagne.'

'It wasn't just that,' said Leah. 'He's had his knife into me all evening...' she sniffed loudly.

Catalina deftly removed the ball of wet tissue and gave Leah her own pretty lace one... 'something lacy or feminine'... like Buster's words. 'There! Have a good blow!' She might have been talking to Katy, but Leah obeyed. 'Now let's do something about your face. Have you got some powder?'

Leah had – somewhere. She fished around in the bottom of her handbag, feeling again the pillbox and clenching her jaw against temptation. Between them, they repaired Leah's face. What a good friend this girl was!

'Well done! You look much better. Now stop worrying and relax. The evening's only just beginning and we're going to have a great meal and a fun time. Walk out there with your head held high, and let go!'

'It's mighty hard with Buster the way he is right now.'

'Nonsense!' said Catalina briskly, leading the way. 'Leave Buster to me. I won't stand for his antics.'

Although it was off-season, the Cozinha Velha was doing its usual roaring trade. The bar was jammed with locals and foreign residents alike, but McKay expertly manoeuvred them all into an inner sanctum. The restaurant owed its existence and its name 'old kitchen' to the once rather grand house above, now divided into smart apartments. The lower floor and cellar had indeed been the old kitchen; it still boasted a gigantic fireplace with bread oven and hand-revolved spit. Rows of black sausage and hams hung from the vaulted ceiling; the cluttered feel merely added to the restaurant's undeniable charm and ambience.

Fernando, the owner, had spotted them. 'I swear that man's got eyes in the back of his head,' said Jock as a bull-headed, sumo wrestler of a man bore down on them, a grin splitting his swarthy face from ear to ear. Huge hands were wiped on a white apron that enveloped an ample belly and he embraced McKay like a brother. *'Boa noite, boa noite Senhor Jock! Ha muito tempo não tenho vista!'*

Jock made some self-deprecating motion with his hands and they both threw back their heads and laughed. Leah pushed herself to the fore. 'Our table?' she said, feeling it vital to assert her position – this was after all *her* dinner-party. The two men exchanged a look but finally they were seated and menus brought.

The food at least was delicious. As she sipped piping-hot fish soup, Leah felt her despondency gradually thaw. She turned to McKay and made some headway with talk of his pictures. He told her about a mural he'd been commissioned to paint for a new mosque in London, as soon as the exhibition was over. He was anxious about that, he confided, so little time to prepare; besides, Harold Wilson's government had left such a mess of the economy, it was hardly a buyer's market at present. She felt flattered he trusted her enough for such confidences.

The McKays insisted they ate stuffed squid as a main course. Leah had wanted chicken but allowed herself to be persuaded. It was to be served with a special piquant sauce of crushed chillies and *favas*, a kind of bean. Catalina had pounced on the description in the menu and explained it all in detail; now she was laying odds they'd all adore it. Buster said he never gambled for money, what other stake would she care to offer if proved wrong? For the second time that night, Leah found herself being irritated by the inevitable response, that she never gambled for money either…but?…with a question mark left hanging in the air.

Both Buster and Catalina wanted puddings. She said with a smile that she could never resist sweet things and Buster immediately made the usual crack about her being sweet enough. Oh *puh-lease*! thought Leah. He then ordered for himself. He still had a hole in his belly, he said and only cheese-cake would fill it. The waiter patiently explained they had no such thing. Leah reminded him they had left the US behind and immediately wished she hadn't – such was the hostility in his eyes. After a long embarassing debate, he finally settled for chocolate cake. Catalina had crème brulee.

Leah wondered if she might have decaffinated coffee and was surprised when the waiter seemed confused. McKay went to considerable trouble to explain in Portuguese – it was good of him, thought Leah but unnecessary. It was hardly *his* fault these people were behind the times. The others were now onto liqueurs and Leah's coffee still had not arrived. 'Oh forget it!' said Buster. His voice was thick, 'you've got a bunch of pills in your handbag – shove a couple down your throat and have some proper coffee like normal people. It'll all balance out in the end!'

McKay raised an eyebrow, Leah was quietly furious. 'You know I haven't taken a single tranquie for weeks. I don't know how you could be so cruel.'

'Cruel or cool?' said Buster, 'I used to say,' he addressed the room at large, 'if you give my wife a shake, she'll start rattling!'

No one laughed. There was an awkward silence saved by the arrival of a throng of young people. Leah cheered up momentarily when she spotted Karl and Jacqueline van der Stel amongst them. The latter bounded forward to introduce her to a very made-up blonde girl with hips the size of a wasp. So this was Johanna's daughter – Maysie Vincent, the super-model. Catalina and Maysie greeted each other like long-lost friends, which was ridiculous since they'd all been drinking together only a few hours before, thought Leah. She had not appreciated that Catalina was so close to this cold-looking English girl. She noticed they both called each other 'darling' but put it down to Maysie's theatrical background.

Buster looked on with undisguised interest as the two girls made small talk. 'Why not come and sit down?' he said and sent the waiter off for more chairs.

'We really should be going,' said Maysie brusquely. 'We're off to *Le Club* in Almancil.'

'Oh come on, darleeng, there's no rush, is there?' said Catalina persuasively. 'The discos don't get going for hours yet. Why don't you join us for a drink, first?'

'Oh, all right,' said Maysie grudgingly as she whisked a long forelock of ash-blonde hair behind an ear. 'I'll have a horse's neck in that case.'

'Buster! Will you order the drinks, honey?' said Leah in a pointed way. How casual these people were and it was naughty of Catalina to invite them to their table as though it were her party.

Six more chairs were brought and the party overflowed onto two tables. Maysie sat herself down between Catalina and Jock and did not say a word to either Bloomfield, although Leah caught her staring a couple of times.

'Such a bore!' Maysie was saying to Jock. 'I came here for a working holiday, but Mummy says all the photographers have gone. Am not sure I can afford to stay very long if that's the case.'

'Count yourself lucky,' said Jock, clearly disinterested.

'How long are you in Santa Felicia?' Leah said pointedly, determined to be acknowledged.

'Oh – it depends. I may fly back to London tomorrow,' Maysie scarcely glanced up, 'this place is perfectly *dead* in the off-season.'

'Come off it, Maysie!' Jacqueline gave her a little push. 'Don't pay any attention to her, Leah. It's only because she's landed Vogue, she thinks she has to be so bloody blasé.'

To Leah's surprise Maysie laughed outright! What a difference it made! Her rather sulky face lit up and for the first time there was a striking resemblance to her famous mother. Catalina noticed Leah's astonishment. 'Yes, she's lovely, our Maysie, when she wants to be,' she whispered in Leah's ear. 'Fortunately for the rest of us, she seldom steals the limelight. It's a pity really for she has the perfect face and figure, but she's simply no idea how to use either. No doubt she'd hate it if she knew she provides the perfect foil for my dark and devious ways,' she winked conspiratorially. 'Fortunately, she lacks the brain to see it!'

Leah looked round to see if anyone else had overheard. This was a different Catalina from the one she thought she knew so well. The more she drank, the more physically appealing she seemed, but there was a harder, reckless side to her manner and this worried her. Not for the first time, she thought what a menace alcohol could be. As Maysie and her party drifted off, Leah wondered and worried at that small speech of Catalina's. What could it all mean?

24

It was the day after Cleo laid her first out of season egg that the children brought the kitten to the yellow house on the hill. Fortunately, the Boys were out for the afternoon and Buster had taken Mungo for his daily run along the beach. Leah was alone in the villa with the maid. She knew the children by sight. They came from one of the tumbledown cottages beside the store at the bottom of the hill, and she'd often waved to them as they sat on their doorstep and watched the cars go by.

They stood before her now, shy yet excited, unsure what to say. The eldest one, a thin ferret-faced girl with a runny nose, pushed the middle one forward while the youngest buried his head in his sister's ragged skirt. The middle one was sturdier than the other two with a plump, cheerful face. He regarded Leah thoughtfully for a moment as if weighing up the wisdom of his assignment.

'*Sim?*' Leah smiled encouragingly.

'*Por favor, Senhora...*' he paused, looked to the eldest again, and she nodded. '*Temos qualquer coisa – para si...*'

Maria came hurrying along when she heard their voices. 'What is it?' she said in rapid dialect. 'The *Senhora's* busy. What is it you want?'

A stubborn look passed over the open face of the sturdy child and he shut up like a clam but stood his ground. The eldest took a step backwards. Amused, Leah sent the maid away, 'It's all right, Maria, I can deal with this.' The plump child watched until she was out of earshot. He seemed reluctant to speak again.

'You said you have something for me?' Somehow Leah found the words in Portuguese and knelt down so that she was the same height as this small, silent boy. He nodded vigorously, his dark curls bobbing around a grubby face.

'*Sim, sim!*'

'*Muito bem,*' began Leah again, '*Que....?*'

Slowly, carefully, the child brought out what looked like a pile of dirty newspaper from behind his back. This he held out gingerly to Leah. '*Gato,*' he explained. '*Um gato pequeno...*' Suddenly the rumpled paper moved and a second later a tiny face with huge yellow eyes had emerged, hissing furiously.

'*Cuidado!*' cried all three children together.

She nodded, heeding their warning to be careful, and held the parcel more firmly. Slowly, she peeled off layer after layer of old paper. As the last layer came away, the kitten, its tiny paws flaying with fear and spitting like a tiger, tried to leap from her arms. The children lunged forward to the rescue. But they needn't have worried. Leah held on firm to the seething ball of tabby fur and everyone breathed a sigh of relief.

The kitten's near escape broke the ice. All three children started talking at once and most of what they said was indiscernible. It did not take long however for Leah to grasp the gist of their story. They had found the kitten in the stubble field behind their house. It had been there for a couple of days mewing, loud at first, then more weakly as it began to starve. There was no sign of the mother. She was probably dead, or abandoned...the road was a dangerous place for cats.

They had tried to take food; fish heads, some milk from the goat – most had been disdained. Besides, their father's wrath had descended so heavily for this small act of charity, it was not worth the risk to continue. They knew too that the *senhora norde-americana* liked animals. They heard the geese cackling every day and had learned in the shop how she'd taken in a dog. Surely, with so many mouths to feed, the tiniest of kittens would make no difference? Especially to such a fortunate but kindly lady? Leah had smiled at this; the child already knew how to flatter.

But the thing was – it would make a difference. Not to her very much, perhaps not to Buster either. But, oh dear! – her heart sank as she thought what Howard would have to say on the matter. Alienation would be complete. Nevertheless... How could she refuse the kids? She could not bear to see the hope die in their eyes. It would require a heart of iron to throw this tiny animal to the harsh winds of fortune. Left abandoned for two or three days already, it was unlikely to survive any more.

The children were growing anxious now. The *senhora* had not responded. The sturdy one touched her arm and pointed to the kitten, which had given up struggling and lay quiet against her chest. '*Guarda? A Senhora guarda?*'

Will Madam keep it? Such a simple request! She regarded them for a moment, then without allowing herself further time, she was answering in the affirmative. What else could she do?

They grinned and as one turned away. Ran waving, carefree, skipping down the stony drive. She watched until they were out of sight, round the corner towards the prickly pears, beyond the bluff and out of sight. Crafty imps – not daring to look back, not sparing her the chance to change her mind. Who could blame them?

'OK baby,' she looked at her new charge which had stopped fighting, and looked worryingly frail. 'I guess you'd better stay. But don't blame me if they give us both a hard time.'

A moment later, she was pouring milk into a saucer, but despite wetting its chin, its paws and its chest, the little creature seemed unable to drink. 'Uh uh...' muttered Leah, gathering it up in her arms again, 'I guess I'd better start you off another way.' Soon, she was coaxing the first nourishment in days down the creature's tiny throat. As she held it in her lap and squeezed the rubber bulb of the eye-dropper, she realised she had probably found her niche in life. Looking after animals! Contentment rose within her and she made a mental note that this was better than tranquillisers any day.

Buster had taken Mungo to the big empty beach known amongst the locals as *Praia Branca*. Like its name, it stretched white and long between two generous points which divided the agricultural land around Casa Amarela from the town. Separated from the road by acres of sand dunes, this grand sweep of unadulterated beach was generally avoided by all but the most adventurous of visitors. Too blustery to swim, too exposed to sunbathe, the seaboard floor shelved sharply, just below the tide line to cause a dangerous undertow, whilst white horses huffed and puffed around the edge.

The best thing about *Praia Branca* in Buster's opinion was its uninterrupted hard footing for keep-fit fanatics like himself. Today, he'd seen no other contenders, which worried him not a jot. It was glorious to have this wide open space solely to himself and one black dog and he exulted in the freedom of it. For him the picturesque quality of Santa Felica's main bay with its gently sloping beaches held little interest. Neither did the safe little cove beneath their house. But approaching *Praia Branca*, everything changed. Here the west wind had torn into the sandstone, creating rough fjord like projections which reached far into the sea. The easiest way to approach these hidden inlets was by boat, but after some strenuous walking, it was possible to pick one's way over the narrowest of mule-paths, in between and around the rocks to follow the coast. This warren-like route dated back to the times of the Moors and was still used by a few hardy fishermen out for a day's sport.

Buster had taken pride in learning the local secrets. Exercise was his god, and by constant trial and error, he had explored and run and climbed. Over the weeks, he and the dog at his heels had gone where few dared to tread. He told no one of his new passion, let alone Leah or the Boys. With each discovery, he was learning more and more about himself. Unaware at first, he now saw this physical escape as the only way in which he could make sense of their new existence in the shared villa. When they had first discussed early retirement, it had not occurred to him just how much the enforced idleness would upset his equanimity. Worse by far, was the lack of time and space for himself.

Unknowingly, Buster had thrived on challenges all his life. Unloved in his childhood, he had lived by his wits, disciplined by the sea; then came the draft which gave him the work ethic, and finally the war. Despite life's shocks, all were physically stimulating. Even in business, his role thrived on effort and independence. For Buster, life was all about having the space and freedom to act. And boy – could he get things done!

Today, he was feeling particularly elated. Not only had he run four kilometres, forward and back on lonely *Praia Branca*, but he was celebrating his means of getting there! They used to call him Smart-Eyes Bloomfield in South Korea since he was good at looking out for an opportunity – for himself and the team. Last week Old Smart-Eyes had found a rocky passage that took him from the headland, straight down to a cove and directly onto the beach. He'd now used this a few times, and today he'd beaten his own record. He laughed when he thought of the previous half-hour hike, ploughing over the sand dunes. Today he'd made it in five minutes!

He had parked his car as usual on the minor road that ran between Santa Felicia and a few outlying villages and which was just visible from the beach. There was an argument for running all the way down the hill from their villa before joining the road, but the tides were fickle and he liked to time it 'just perfect' to make the most of his time on the waterfront. The tunnel he used could fill up to above head level with the tide if he didn't get it right, and then one was back to climbing up the dunes again which could take for ever. There was the added risk of pulling a precious hamstring or Achilles tendon in the deep sand.

It always amused him how many vehicles would stop, people get out to gawp, see the problem, then give up and drive on. He'd only once met another runner, a young

Portuguese guy, but even he – it seemed – had not learned the secret of the tunnel. It gave Buster some satisfaction to watch him struggling up the endless dunes after he left the water's edge. He returned a couple more times, then no more. Buster felt smug to be left alone with his secret.

Today was one of those stunningly clear November days, when the sun is bright but the temperature cold. The washed beach felt firmer than ever as it scudded away noisily under his running-shoes, not a granule flying out of place – only perfect shallow imprints from his rubber-soles – as they lapped up the metres. The biting saltiness of the air which seeped into his hungry lungs was delicious – good enough to eat, he thought as he gulped it up. Two minutes spent in the company of the elements on Praia Branca were sufficient to make one feel clean and wholesome again.

It was two days since the dinner party at *Cozinha Velha* and he knew he needed this to cleanse away the excesses of the evening. Too much alcohol, too much tobacco – he'd heard all about it from his wife the next day. But who could blame him when he was forced to sit next to a woman who gave him a cockstand every time she touched him or met his eyes? Did you tell your wife *that*, or did you find some other way to distract the senses?

The dog was a lucky excuse – as if he needed one. Certainly, an incentive. He was also surprisingly good company – who'd have thought it? Funny looking animal, with an even funnier name, but as usual in these matters, Leah was right – Mungo did suit him.

'Come on then Mungo, old guy!' Buster called, 'Here's a stick for you! Come on you son-of-a-bitch! Show some interest!' The dog bounded up to him. He was all legs and wiry black hair which tufted out in an endearing way around his collar. Since he'd come to them over a month ago, he had lost that cowed look and Buster felt gratified and pleased he'd contributed. He'd never had a dog before and wondered why his parents had never thought to get him one; it might have made all the difference and made it easier for him to come to terms with affection, or rather perhaps, the lack of it.

Buster ran with the dog down the length of the beach as usual, paused to play with some sticks and prepared for the return journey. Each way took him roughly fifteen minutes at a smart run and he was fine on the tide; it wouldn't be in for almost an hour. As he glanced at his watch, his eyes were attracted by something glimmering on the skyline. Ah … the usual inevitable car was parked far away up on the coast road. How long before the occupants would realise they couldn't get down to the beach that way, and finding no other, move on? But the car stayed. He got fed up waiting for it to move and started to run back along the same tidemark, amusing himself by stepping into his own fresh footprints which wouldn't disappear until the sea came in. From time to time, he looked up and saw the car was still there. It was a silvery colour, or was that just the sun? Who cared!

He made the return trip in one minute more than the outward. That wasn't bad – considering – but he was seriously out of puff. He sank down into the sand and allowed Mungo playfully to bowl him over. There was a lot of excited barking and he buried his head in his arms to avoid the thrashing black tail and enthusiastic licks. 'Get away, Mungo,' he yelled, 'That's enough, boy! That's enough!'

Suddenly, the barking changed, taking on a warning note. Then came a low-throated growl. 'Mungo!' said Buster sternly, not daring to open his eyes until he'd wiped away all the grit. He caught the dog by the collar just as he sensed it crouching to rush forward: the growl had turned into little whines. Then he felt the shadow cross his face as someone came between him and the late afternoon sun.

'It's all right,' said a soft voice. 'You can let the dog go. He knows me.'

'Catalina!' Buster struggled to his feet, blinking hard. 'How did *you* get here?'

She looked him up and down, amused. 'I might say the same to you!'

'Me! Well... I come here every day, with the dog – we have a run, you know! A bit of exercise – for the two of us.'

'Over the sand dunes?' she arched a disbelieving eyebrow.

'Well – er ... actually not. I've found another way...you probably wouldn't know, but er –'

'Actually I *do* know,' she retorted. 'You seem to forget, Buster Bloomfield, I have a boat. I know this coast like the back of my hand. All the paths and passages, even the tunnel! How do you think I got here just now, without breaking my leg or something?'

'Good God,' he said, 'of course! And I thought I'd been so clever.' He looked so crestfallen, she had to laugh: that long tinkling laugh that set his skin shivering with goose-bumps and making his loins – at least he thought it was his loins – ache with desire.

'You *have* been clever,' she said, surveying him. 'Not many know the way, certainly no *estrangeiros* that I know of. That's why it's the safest place on earth to meet you.'

'But how did you know I'd be here?'

'Because I've been watching you!' she laughed again. 'Does that surprise you? I've watched you here for the past three days, and you've always looked far too busy rushing up and down to be interrupted.'

'My God! You've been spying on me!' A sudden realisation hit him, 'Is that your car up there on the roadside?'

'Of course. Is this the first time you've noticed it?'

He nodded, momentarily dumbfounded. What a fool he was! He'd been so engrossed with his speed, his timing, his dog, he hadn't noticed, hadn't felt those eyes upon him – those eyes that he longed for, dreamed of every night, every waking moment.

She broke the magic with her next question, 'Do tell me, *meu querido*, what is that funny garment you're wearing? It's been puzzling me!'

'It's a tracksuit,' mumbled Buster, embarassed.

'I can see that,' she replied, a smile twitching at the edge of her full lips, 'but it looks prehistoric. All buttons, no zips, it must take an eternity to get into the thing – or out. Where *did* it come from?'

'It's a relic from my GI days... but look, Catalina,' he said, 'you didn't stop by to discuss my clothes. I still don't understand how you came to spot me – your house isn't on this road – what exactly were you doing driving along this lonely stretch?'

She twinkled at him disarmingly. 'I'm not telling! Maybe I've been looking into my crystal ball, at least I found you! Do you mind if we sit down? It's nice and shelterered round this rock here.'

She was squeezing her way round the edge of the cliff, where only someone familiar with the cliffside would think to venture. 'Careful, don't slip!' he warned, relieved to note she was wearing plimsolls. She threw him a look of utter disdain and disappeared from view.

He had no option but to follow, but his heart was thudding. Where was she going? What did she want? Somehow, he knew the next few steps would be irrevocable, they could even be life-changing. Round that rock and where next – a new life? Was this what he, Buster Bloomfield really wanted?

Of course he should have known it the moment he saw her. She was leading him to the tunnel, his tunnel. She had said nothing as she manoeuvred the cliff face, too concentrated on what she was doing and on each careful footstep. Now reaching the little sandy inlet that led to the cave within, she continued to move silently. He caught up with her and gave her his hand, but she was having none of it. 'Don't spoil things 'til we get there. Don't forget I'm a sailor, balance is everything.'

He knew she was right. Talking was taboo on exercise, you needed every faculty intact for the task in hand. There were still rocks to negotiate: she knew what she was doing. Finally, they were there. The whole exercise had taken less than a minute but a moment's lapse could make all the difference between a twisted ankle, a head split open or a safe arrival. She kicked off her shoes and sank down into the soft white sand at the edge of the dark recess. Tucking her legs under her, she spread out her jacket and patted the sheepskin lining with her hand. 'Now you can talk,' she said seriously, as he dropped down beside her.

'I asked you a question,' he said, realising it was unimportant, but playing for time. 'What were you doing driving along that stretch of road?'

'If you really want to know,' she said tugging at her scarf to free her wild, gypsy hair, 'I've been going to and from the peecture framer's for Jock. There's a retired fisherman in the next village who does the basic frames, mainly to protect the canvases on their journey to the UK, before they get tarted up for the exhibition in London. The last few days, I could not help noticing this rather striking figure of a man, dashing up and down the beach with a dog. After a while, I found I began to look out for him.'

'I see. You mean you stopped your car and watched?'

'Why not? Was eet such an awful invasion of your privacy?'

'I guess not – it just seems so strange. Why didn't you hoot, or come down, like today?'

'I was hardly dressed for rock climbing,' she said. 'Besides ... I wasn't sure if I was ready ...' her voice trickled out and she looked down at her hands folded in her lap. He noticed how long her eyelashes were. They threw shadows onto her creamy cheeks and there were tiny freckles he'd never noticed before dusting the bridge of her nose. She sighed a little, then said. 'Actually, I just enjoyed watching you. I did not really feel the need to come down until –' she broke off and he finished the sentence for her.

'Now?'

She nodded. 'But today, I planned eet. I knew it had to happen, so I dressed appropriately. Eet was more than an accident of fate. I chose to come.'

There was a long silence. She would not meet his eye, and he resisted touching her. He needed time. They were on a precipice, safe in the sand for another half-hour before the tide came in, but close to another edge, from which he knew there was no going back.

Doubts crowded in. Could he trust her? He knew she wanted him, but for him this would be no idle affair. It would be the end of the world he knew and a start of something completely different and foreign; he could not settle for second best. He started scooping up handfuls of sand. Wordlessly, he let it brim over his cupped palm and then trickle out slowly through his fingers.

'Did you know this sand is very special?' Catalina was saying. 'Here on the Atlantic coast we have more fossils per square metre than most beaches have per square mile. That's why it's so clean, granular and firm. I love its feel, don't you? Amazing to think what you're holding now dates back millions of years to when life itself began.'

She copied him and as he scooped, still silent, their two hands touched. Buster's chest went tight and he held his breath, as if under water. Her breathing continued evenly but he could feel the pulse quicken under her pale skin. He closed his fingers over hers and squeezed them hard, then harder. She did not snatch her hand away, yet he felt a thread of resistance. The knowledge made it exciting and there was no stopping his erection. Had she noticed? Their eyes met. It was as if she melted! In that fleeting second, he realised all restraint had left her.

Immediately, her breathing became fast and urgent. He pulled her to him. Oh! How warm and soft her body! Sun-kissed, his for the asking – was she? Could it be true? He had to be completely sure.

With his free hand he turned her face towards him and tilted her chin. He needed her to look him straight in the eye again. 'Catalina,' he said, 'Do you want me?' He wanted to say *do you love me?* … but something held him back. Even the first question scared him but he craved reassurance. There must be some sort of verbal commitment – now – whilst he was still strong enough to take it either way. She could easily say no.

Her whisper, when it came, was so quiet it might have been a breath of sea breeze. But it sang in his ears, like a hallelujah chorus. 'Yes,' she said.

He watched the wave roll in. His body was taut, pulsing with joy and the strength of his desire, and he wanted to savour every moment. It would never be quite like this again. He knew now he could take her – any time – but he wanted this wonderful moment of anticipation to last just a little longer. Golden clouds were floating across the blue vast, sunset was not far off and the softer, dove shades of evening were already creeping in with the changing light. The wave broke gently. Almost in slow motion. Frothy water ran up the shore, its lacy fingers almost touching them before seeping back into honeycombed hollows, as the sand shifted back to the ocean. It was getting late and the tide was fast approaching.

'Catalina,' he said again. He adored the sound of her name. Its liquidity and lightness wound itself around his tongue, captivating and mesmerising him – even though he was the author of the sound. 'What do you want, Catalina?'

She groaned and pressed against him. For a moment her hand lingered there at the crook of his thighs, then they moved up. In an instant, her nails were probing, tearing at the buttons of his tracksuit, feverishly pulling them apart, all the way down past his waist. 'I want *you*,' was all she said. 'I want *you*.'

'Now?' he knew he was dragging things out and couldn't explain why. It was all so momentous…it would be terrible to rush. 'Here?'

Her eyes flashed. 'Yes, here! Why not? It's beautiful!'

He pulled himself out of the offending garment and spread it round her. He felt oddly vulnerable, half kneeling in his boxers, but he needn't have worried. Her eyes were locked into his as she lay, hair spread like a mantilla, half on her jacket, half over him. She'd hitched her skirt right up around her waist and made no attempt to remove it. He gasped as he took in dark sepia stockings, and the whitest of flesh between the top of her stocking and a black lace suspender belt. She wore no pants so the rest was clearly meant to stay.

Never had he seem a woman so surrendered. He gasped at the sight and ripped off his shorts. Her shoes had been tossed aside. Mungo plucked one up and was happily guarding it. It was all so incongruous, the black underwear, the black dog. Buster wondered if he was dreaming. But this was no dream, and he heard his voice grunting with desire as suddenly masterful, he ordered her onto the layer of clothes underneath. He smoothed them out with his hands, wiping away every trace of sand. He had to enter her cleanly. 'Bend your knees up, Catalina!' he commanded. 'Let me arrange you.'

She complied easily, her pelvis arching up at him invitingly. He was looking into a dark forest, beckoning from within – and he wanted to go there – like nothing on earth. He knew exactly where he wanted to go.

There was little resistance as she opened to his touch, she was a rosebud – about to burst into flower – and he? Why – he was the hot, hot sun. And now that he had found her, there was no escape. He heard himself gasping – not just in desire but in gratitude – he was grateful to feel so contained. He had waited for this all his life. 'Oh my God…Oh my God… *Catalina!*'

She was full of laughter in her passion. It came bubbling out of her, wild and exultant. It served only to heighten his ardour and although his entry had been more powerful than he meant, it did nothing to quench the source of her frivolity. The thudding in his ears had begun slowly. He moved rhythmically, the sureness of his touch giving him confidence to take time, marvel at his potency. It had never been like this before.

But the noise in his ears was something else. Uncontrollable, it was getting louder by the second, taking him by surprise in its rush to besiege his temples. In no time at all it had reached such a crescendo that he had cried out in fear that the ocean was upon them – had slipped between the rocks to take them by surprise – the full tide in all its might! He heard her echoing answer come far away from the distance and to his immense surprise the most delicious sensation of warmth and fulfilment racked his entire body. He was drowning in a flood of his own making.

She lay quietly now in his arms. The laughter had died in her eyes and he could not make out the faraway, dreamy expression they held. He leaned over, suddenly anxious. He had to tell her now, to allay her fears. 'Catalina, darling. It's all right. I love you. I *love you!*'

But her eyes were veiled as she said, 'Do you?'

He couldn't believe she could doubt him. So soon after giving herself – giving everything – so completely. 'Yes, dearest love. A thousand times yes! I've loved you since…I guess …the first moment I saw you. Only – I just never dreamed that you could want me too. It seemed so utterly impossible.'

'Why didn't you tell me before?'

'You seemed so special, so out of reach. You were more interested in my wife than me! For a long time it seemed like I didn't exist – I'm not complaining, it's just…I never dreamed it could come to this!'

To his horror she suddenly rolled away from him and pulled down her skirt. 'Oh, Buster!' she cried. 'What have we done? I'm so afraid!'

'There's nothing to be afraid of,' he said, drawing her back and full of wonder, kissing her neck, her shoulders, her throat. 'Catalina, look at me and believe what I say.' He surprised himself again with the boldness of his voice, as he heard himself say, 'I'll take care of everything.'

'Everything?' she paused, dusting the sand from the tops of her legs, and reaching for her shoe.

'Yes!' the excitement rose in his eyes as carefully he thought about what he would, must do. After a moment he said, 'Look, I haven't worked it all out yet – but I will. First of course, I'll talk to Leah. She won't like it one bit, but she's always been the practical one – she may even understand. Then, we'll go and see your husband. It will be a shock but I'll break it to him gently… tell him how much we love each other…don't worry, I'll take all the blame and – '

'No!' she said with such firmness that he put his hand up to his face as if she'd slapped him. It was an automatic reaction to a massive blow.

Her voice softened then. 'Don't you see, darling, we must tell no one! Absolutely no one.' She took both his hands in hers. 'What you say is very admirable, but it isn't the way, not yet! Don't you see, *querido*, we have to give ourselves time. Time to think, time to play a leetle …' she hesitated as he frowned at this, then giggled, '…time to make love.'

He was bewildered. He took a hand away to rub his brow. 'We can't do that!'

'Why not?' her voice was sharp.

'I told you Catalina, I love you. Don't you understand? I don't want an affair – I'm not that kind of a guy. I want to live with you, marry you, never be away from you …'

'And so you may, my darling,' she soothed, kissing his captive hand and guiding it down between her legs again. They lay there silent for a time as he gazed up at the sky and thought. The tide would soon be here, yet how could he tear himself away? It was all so amazing, all so confusing – what she'd just said hardly made sense. She was playing his fingers over and around her inner warmth, and already his body was responding – blotting out his thoughts – fickle and excited. My goodness, so soon – he must be fit.

She lay over him and again he was filled with her scent and other smells too – forbidden, delicious. 'There!' she smiled as he groaned and clasped her once more to him. 'There my *querido*, no more foolish talk – this is what you need, this is what my Buster needs from his Catalina. My! What a man you are! One thing at a time… slowly, slowly… *there*.'

This time it was not a dream. The tide did come in and touch them. Catalina felt it first and shrieked as one of her shoes bobbed away. Buster was after it in a flash but it was Mungo who retrieved it. He barked loudly and proudly as she put it on. They got dressed just in time. Two minutes later and the cave behind them was filling with water. 'Come on!' cried Catalina, 'If we don't go through now, eet will have to be the sand dunes!' They scrambled over the rocks together and penetrated the tunnel as it led them away from the sea and back towards the headland. Hand in hand like truant children, they ran together, breathless, guilty and giggling.

'Oh honey!' Buster stopped for breath and cradled her face in his hands, 'How I love you!'

They had reached dry sand and the tide was behind them. At the exit of the cave on the other side, he leant her against the rock so that her hair fanned out against the yellow sandstone. From a barely discernible horizon, the dying sun bathed the line of her shoulders, the edge of her collarbones and the top of her breasts in pale gold. He took one last look then, reluctantly, fastened the last remaining buttons. A moment later he was pulling her towards him again. 'One last kiss,' he said, 'just to prove it really did happen.'

'It didn't happen! It was a dream!' she laughed.

'Don't say that.'

She pulled away from him then. Snatched up handfuls of hair and wound it back into a screw of wiry black, fastened it with elastic and then the silk scarf, so recklessly torn off only minutes before was neat and knotted again. Suddenly she was all practical and her voice had taken on a different tone. 'I'm sorry, Buster darling, but I must. I insist you treat it like a dream. Just for a leetle time. Pretend it never actually happened...'

'How can I, Catalina?' he burst out. 'How can I? You're asking the impossible.'

'No, I'm asking for what has to be – at this stage in time.'

'But I can't hide all that's happened between us. It's going to be too obvious to anyone that knows us. Besides, I don't think I've got the strength.'

'Then find it!'

He watched, a dumb expression in his eyes, as she pulled the sheepskin jacket close to her chin and prepared to walk up the sandy path, across the headland, back to the road ahead and the waiting car. Every instinct told him that this was wrong – yet he'd promised – in the after-glow of passion, she'd made him promise to wait. When he'd remonstrated with her, she'd only pleaded the more. Things would only 'work out', she said, if he promised to wait.

'Goodbye, my darling.' She held herself very erect. 'No, don't – ' she pushed him gently away as he bent to kiss her once more, 'don't make things worse – I must go now... and please, Buster,' she looked deep into his eyes, all vestige of passion wiped from her face, '... please do as I say, do eet for my sake. No, *don't* escort me to the car!' Her voice was sharp. 'Wait at least twenty minutes before you go for yours. It would be madness to follow me. No one must know we were together.' She turned then, and hurried rapidly up the track.

Long after she'd started up the Mercedes and he heard it roar into the twilight, he stood there – rooted to the spot – the place where she'd left him. Mungo came then. Put his nose into his hand and left it there, a cold, wet comforter. Buster shivered under his thin tracksuit and finally took a step forward. It was getting chilly. He shook himself, jogged on the spot, walked in small circles for what seemed an age, then thrust back his shoulders. 'OK Mungo, old son. I s'pose we'd better get going.'

Together they left the beach as smartly as they'd arrived.

'Hi! honey,' cried Leah as the door opened and Mungo bounded into the kitchen, covering her with his peculiarly appreciative, wet kisses. 'I was getting quite worried about you – it's late.'

Buster closed the door carefully behind him. He had been dreading this moment all the way back. It was all very well for Catalina to say 'pretend it didn't happen', but it *had* happened and the instant his wife set eyes on him, she would read the truth. How could she avoid it? After sixteen years of faithful marriage, it would stare her in the face and she would see his treachery for all it entailed.

Slowly, he turned round, his hand still on the door handle. He braced his body for the rain of blows – both verbal and physical – each as painful as the other, but deserved all the same. He screwed up his eyes as he remembered a beating he'd had as a kid, after telling his father a lie. 'Deception! It's written all over your face, Buster my boy. There's no hiding a lie, you know!'

Jeez – she was taking her time. Why didn't she come at him with her fists? He wanted to scream at her for torturing him like this – she must have noted the body language. He felt like a skunk standing there in the doorway. He would almost welcome a beating.

'Did Mungo behave?' her voice was calm. Heaven help him, she was going to goad him first with petty questions – the cow! He opened his eyes to see how the knowledge of his defection had affected her face and was astounded by what he saw. She had her back to him! She was rolling pastry... as if nothing had happened! He could not believe it.

'Wha- *what* did you say?'

'I said was Mungo OK? He didn't go chasing any more chickens like the other day with Benjie, did he?' She still had her back to him.

'Ah – er – no, he was fine...just fine...' His voice was surprisingly normal. Could it be? No, surely not – was there the slightest chance she hadn't sensed anything amiss?

'I'm glad to hear it,' she was banging up and down with her rolling pin now, showering the marble counter with flour. 'The Boys always make such a big thing about these misdemeanours. It just shows – with gentle discipline – most animals can be brought to heel. In fact...' she sounded wistful, 'they're really not much trouble at all.'

He walked up to her then. Catalina had said to say nothing, but he would have to show her. This deceit couldn't go on. She knew him too well. He opened his mouth to speak but she was still burbling on, '... if you love animals, if you're good to them, they repay you soon enough – unlike humans...they – er – harbour no secrets.'

So that was it. She had cynically chosen to make an example of him by comparing the human capacity for deceit to the innocence of a dumb animal. Oh boy! This was some conversation, some Virginia Woolf dialogue destined to bring him to breaking point. Again he remembered Catalina's words, but he was beyond caring. It required some extravagant gesture to bring it all out into the open. He took the plunge and put both arms tightly round her waist. Now she'd be left in no doubt, she'd look into his eyes, read his guilt and they could then face up to the truth together. With the physical contact, she'd feel everything. It was inevitable! She might even feel sorry for him, she was that kind of person. He could already sense her little speech.

'Oh, honey…' hardly surprising, she was unlocking his arms… 'You're a dear and very special person…' Holy shit, why must she begin like this? 'You're also extremely patient …' well this was different – a compliment – before a massive slap on the face? He winced. But she hadn't finished. 'For many years you've put up with me and my little whims…' (yep, she was dead right there) '…it hasn't gone unnoticed, believe me. Why! you even went against your better judgement and gave in about the party!' Ah – that's what this was all about. The tango! The start of his romance with Catalina: he might have guessed.

But she hadn't finished; he picked up some indistinguishable words about the geese. *Geese*! Buster put his hands to his ears. Could this be true? He'd heard of sadism mixed with so-called humour but this was too much. '… Then when Mungo dropped onto our doorstep, I never dreamed you'd be so supportive – especially when the Boys were so "anti" …' He clutched at his head to stop it spinning. 'I know it's demanding of me – but could you see your way just one more time? – after all, the newcomer's only a *cat*!'

'*What*!' Buster's hands fell to his sides as she whirled round to face him and looked him in the eye. '*What* did you say?'

'Yes dear, I knew it would come as a shock,' said Leah shame-faced and pale. 'But I promise it won't interrupt our lives. We've only gotten ourselves a little kitten.'

Buster stood stock-still and stared. He could not believe his ears. All the agony she'd put him through – the guilt, the fear, waiting for her to snap, rant at him, plead, cry – all the things he'd envisaged, had just withered away. And the culmination of it all was a godarned cat! Jesus wept! Bereft of words, he stomped across the kitchen floor and noisily flung off his sand-covered sneakers.

He made straight for the drinks cupboard. As he felt her anxious eyes following him round the room, he felt nothing but contempt. No fear, no remorse, nothing but a mounting irritation that only a very strong bourbon would quench. She was still talking. He wanted to yell at her to blot out the voice, but opened the bottle instead. 'I'm really sorry, Buster,' she was saying. 'I can see you're upset, but really there's no need to be. You know I'll take care of her. She's such a cute little devil, I couldn't refuse. She's thin of course, but there's plenty of spirit there. Oh, be a honey – and take a look!'

She hooked her arm into his and dragged him towards the boiler room. 'She's in a box in there. It's nice and warm for her and it will keep her out of Mungo's way until the time comes to introduce them. Aw, c'mon Buster, you've got to admit it – she's a darned pretty little thing!'

Buster peered into the gloomy depths of the large cupboard, his head reeling. Ah – there was the wretched animal – a scraggy looking scrap of a thing. He could feel Leah's breath hot on his neck and wanted to scream.

'Well? What do you think, honey?'

He turned slowly. She was begging for approval and suddenly he felt deeply and unreasonably mad at her. He'd been ready to admit everything. Despite his promise to Catalina, he was unwilling to live a lie. He would have taken the blame like a man – fair and square, on the chin – and they'd talk things through. He'd have told her it was all his fault and she'd be well shot of him. He didn't fit in here, Howard and Benjie would prefer him out of the way, and she'd do better on her own, anyway. Of course it would come as a shock, but together they'd have mopped up her tears and discussed the future. Once she'd come to terms with the truth, she would see his point of view and grant him his freedom. They'd go their separate ways. She'd always been so practical for a woman.

Yet now! What had happened? She'd robbed him of that moment of truth. The opportunity had been spectacularly lost. Somewhere deep in his bones, he knew it would not present itself so easily again. He was so choked with impotent rage he could not answer her.

She tugged again at his arm, 'Honey?'

'Yeah, yeah…' he could hardly bear her touching him. 'Yeah, well – that's it then. I think it's… er… great!' the words were spilling out of his mouth. 'In fact I don't think I've ever seen such a cute cat!'

She flung her arms round his neck and kissed him loudly. 'I knew you'd think so!' A second later she was flying back to her pastry board. 'Gee! I must get this into the oven before the Boys get back. Oh, you've made me so very glad. There's just one more thing!'

'What is it?' he said wearily, all the fight had gone out of him.

'You will stick up for our kitty, won't you?' she looked up from her work, a small frown puckering her brow. 'You know what Howard's like?'

'Sure,' he said, downing his glass of rye in one. 'Anything you say.'

25

Jock McKay entered the Anchor Bar with a sense of real relief. It had been a laborious six weeks preparing his main collection ahead of time, but in addition he'd just signed off three extra canvases which had stood untouched for over a year. If one didn't complete the work while the momentum was still there, it lost its appeal and it took real self-discipline to get the energy back. Today, however he'd forced himself and with a rare sense of achievement, he had packed the very last exhibit into the back of the car for Catalina to take to the framer. He now felt utterly drained.

The Anchor was busier than usual for this time of year. Some conference at the Maritimo had brought in a host of Canadians so there was a good chance of being swallowed up in the crowd. The London pub was the best place in the world for that. He loved the anonymity of the East End with its small cafes, cellars and watering holes, preferably within the sound of Bow Bells, frequented by people of every ethnic background and culture. Tonight, the Anchor could and should have provided such a haven, if only Johanna Vincent hadn't hoved into sight. Much as he liked her, he simply wasn't in the mood.

'Jock, darling!' she bore down on him, wafting goodwill and Chanel, 'How marvellous to see you! Rumour has it you've tucked yourself away and are working very hard indeed for that exhibition. Poor darling – you look exhausted!'

'I am, actually.' He hoped she'd take the hint.

Across the room he could see Maysie, hopping from foot to foot, to see if anyone interesting had come in, but Johanna stood squarely in front of him, slim and boyish in velvet jeans and a V-neck cashmere sweater. 'In that case you need a drink – and a decent one at that. Jerry – a double Scotch for Jock please – for my account!'

He was about to say he was off spirits, when as if by magic the drink appeared. She was one of the few women he knew who could order a drink across a crowded bar and get it immediately. Oh well, he'd have the one, then make his escape.

'And now you can do *me* a favour,' Johanna was saying.

'What's that?'

'Drink that up and get some colour back in your face! You look like a zombie darling – it's time we saw a sparkle again in your eye, Jock McKay.'

'I don't think I've much to sparkle about.'

'Nonsense!' replied Johanna, 'You've got plenty.'

He was struggling to find the right retort, but was rescued by the daughter turning to demand a cocktail. 'So Maysie – you're still with us! London must be missing one of her brightest stars,' he forced a tone of lightness into his voice. 'The place can hardly be the same without you!'

'Hardly, Jock,' the leggy blonde looked at him out of cornflower blue eyes and as usual taking him rather too seriously, 'but they're saying once the Vogue shoot's over, there's a good chance I'll get a screening – probably with Warner Brothers.'

'Following in Mummy's footsteps, eh?' said McKay.

'Certainly not,' said Maysie, 'I wouldn't go through all that rep and theatre slog if you paid me! It would have to be telly or films!'

'She doesn't change, does she?' McKay watched her flit away to greet some new arrival. 'I wonder if Katy will turn out like that when she reaches the ripe old age of twenty-five.'

'Heaven forbid!' said Johanna, 'though you certainly spoil her enough.'

'Do I? I didn't think I did. All I try to do is talk to her. Catalina isn't a great one for dialogue, at least not with her own child.'

'It's a pity you can't try for another,' said Johanna, 'a brother or sister would help.'

'Good God, Johanna, I can't even afford to house and feed three of us, let alone a fourth. Besides Catalina would never go through another pregnancy, she swears having Katy ruined her figure for ever.'

'Doesn't seem to put people off!' Johanna said, then smothered her mouth with her hand. 'Well, you know what I mean…' she ended lamely.

'Oh yes, I *do* know what you mean,' laughed McKay wryly. 'Believe me, I notice most things. And Catalina will never be short of admirers, whatever she does – I know that.'

'And you don't mind?' she could not help but ask.

'Mind?' McKay laughed, '*Mind*? Johanna, who am I to mind what other people do and think? I've made enough bloody mess of my own life, not to go round worrying about other jerks. No, my priorities are clear. Head down, work hard and regain all I've lost. If I can do that I'll be happy.'

There was a pause as Johanna looked into her glass. 'I take it you're still hankering after Scotland, but – are you really being realistic? I don't mean to be depressing, but after all that's happened – your determination to beat the system – what makes you think it will work this time? This castle of yours! These places eat money! You've a lovely home here, wouldn't it be safer to cut your losses, settle down and enjoy what you've got now – not far away in the mists of time?'

He swung round on her savagely. 'I take it you're not suggesting that I give up my life's ambition plus five hundred years of family history?'

'Yes! – because it's destroying you, Jock McKay!' she snapped.

'Ah … I see,' his eyes gleamed blackly, the skin across his upper lip stretched taut. 'You're advocating I quit? Clearly you don't understand the kind of man I am, the kind of family I come from. How little you know me!'

'Perhaps I don't, Jock,' she said, her voice softer and tinged with sadness. 'You scare me sometimes. All I know is that ambition can be a very dangerous thing.'

'Meaning…?'

For once she was lost for words and was glad of the background noise and laughter that filled the gap. Finally, she said, 'I think what I mean is that once ambition overrides common sense, it can be quite destructive. It can even cast an evil spell over one's life. I've seen it happen too much in the film world.'

He gave a little bow. 'And I thank you for your concern, dear madam,' he said, 'but as you know I have an exhibition coming up. So if you don't mind, I'll hold on to that ambition just a little longer and if it doesn't work – then by all means, you can lecture me again. You see I'm afraid I'm somewhat different from today's young ones – like your Maysie over there. Once I start on something, I mean to finish it. Whatever it takes.'

Jacqueline van der Stel bumped into Catalina in the main square. She had two baskets full of fruit and vegetables and it was all she could do to manage Bombita, her black poodle, on the end of his lead. The weather had finally broken. The sky was leaden and the late November wind cracked at the canvas awnings of the market stalls. At any moment it might rain. It was a good excuse anyway to drag Catalina off into the warmth of a café for a coffee, a cigarette and a gossip.

Catalina allowed herself to be dragged. She quite enjoyed the other girl and it amused her how Jacqueline, coming from a big city to a small place like Santa Felicia, had to make up for the lack of diversion in her life. She did this by making it her business to know exactly what was going on with everyone else's. They found a table and Jacqueline heaved herself into a chair. 'Thank goodness for that,' she said, 'these baskets weigh a ton!' and all in the same breath, she pounced upon the lurking waiter.

'I let Philismena do my shopping,' said Catalina, 'Why not do the same with your maid?'

'No fear, ' said Jacqueline, 'that would leave me with even less to do! Sometimes I think I'll go mad in this place. Don't you ever feel the same?'

'I can't say that I do,' smiled Catalina. 'My life is really very full indeed.'

Something about the complacent way she stirred her coffee irritated Jacqueline. 'Well, what *do* you do?' she demanded.

'Oh – the usual things, you know,' Catalina looked amused. 'Jock takes quite a lot of looking after, especially with the exhibition coming up. Then there's the child, shopping, and my fashion magazines. Once the winter's over, there's the boat and the beach – I never seem to stop, really ...'

'I've hear you do quite a lot of visiting too ' interrupted Jacqueline slyly.

'Heavens yes! Don't we all?' Catalina gave her famous tinkling laugh, 'provided one can make the time.'

'Which you obviously do! I have to say Leah Bloomfield seems a very different type from your usual friends.'

'It's nice to make newcomers feel welcome,' Catalina sounded smug.

'Oh hell! Come off it Catalina,' she gave the other's arm an impatient shake. 'You don't have to sound so pious with me – we've known each other far too long. But I must admit,' she added, 'I do feel the teensiest bit jealous – you rarely come by *my* house these days. So what's the big attraction about the house on the hill?'

'If you really want to know, it's Howard and Benjie,' tinkled Catalina. 'My only problem is – which one to choose!'

Jacqueline raised one well-shaped eyebrow and shot her a glowering look. 'You're becoming impossible, Catalina McKay. But just be careful you don't lose all your friends, and don't say I didn't warn you when none of us want to know you any more.'

This time Catalina laughed outright. 'Oh stop being so dramatic, Jacqueline! You expect everyone to see things the way you do and act accordingly. I tell you what – just to show there's no ill feeling – I'll give a lunch. What about next Thursday? A very select hen-party to say *au revoir* to all my girl friends before we leave for England. I'll give it in the *Cozinha Velha* and ask Fernando to think up something really delicious.' She clapped her hands in excitement. 'What fun that will be!'

Jacqueline brightened. She liked lunch parties and it would break the monotony of another winter's day. It did not occur to her that the last thing Catalina should be doing was spending Jock's hard-earned money. 'So who will you ask? Johanna for starters?'

Yes, of course, and Maysie… and probably the Neves girl and – er – Leah…'

'Leah! I thought this was to be a *select* little group?'

'Oh for heavens' sake, Jacqueline, I said it was for all my girl friends. Of course Leah must come. In fact it's obviously most important that she does and you all get to know her better. I'd like to think she has more people than me to rely on – one day she might need you.'

It was raining hard now and more people were coming in to shelter with dripping coats and umbrellas. They spotted Janine Baxter in a green sou'wester and she pushed her way through to join them. 'We'd better ask her too,' whispered Catalina, 'she's quite amusing when she doesn't drink too much and it will be a better balance – two Americans I mean.'

'Hi Kids! Talking about me by any chance?' said Janine, cheerfully plonking herself down beside them, uninvited.

'Actually, yes,' grinned Jacqueline.

'I'm giving a lunch party next week,' said Catalina. 'Would you like to come?'

'Where and when?' Janine's hat sent a shower of raindrops over the paper tablecloth.

'I've still got to check, but probably next Thursday – one o'clock at the *Cozinha Velha*.'

'Dear me, how grand!' said Janine. 'You just won the lottery or something? What's the occasion?'

'The occasion is to see all my girlfriends before Jock and I leave for London. And no, we haven't won anything, but I feel it in my bones – this visit will herald a turn-around of our fortunes, and what better way to give it a kick start?'

'What – no men?' bleated Janine, 'Fortune or no fortune, that sounds a bit of a drag to me.'

'You don't have to come.'

'If it's all British, I don't think I will. I don't mean to be nasty but you don't all half bitch about each other.'

'Surely, I don't have to remind you I'm a Portuguese national,' said Catalina.

'No-o, but you're European and that's almost as bad,' said Janine, dropping ash in Jacqueline's saucer.

'Well my dear Janine, you're in luck,' said Jacqueline sweetly. 'Catalina's planning to invite Mrs Buster Bloomfield Junior along too, so you and she can have a cosy *tête-à-tête*. I must say, I just *adore* these trans-Atlantic smoking habits, don't you Catalina?'

Catalina pretended not to hear. *I wonder what game she's cooking up now*, thought Jacqueline. *This 'everybody's friend' approach, is somehow deeply out of character.*

Leah was surprised when she heard the now familiar sound of the McKay Mercedes coming up the drive at teatime. Surely Katy came back from school at this time? She was on her way back to the house after dampening the goose-eggs, having read somewhere that this would help the hatching process, due in about ten days. With her hair scraped back in a bedraggled pony-tail, and her heavy gumboots and oldest apron impeding her progress, she turned to greet her friend in some surprise. Catalina, in contrast, looked ravishing in a smart red PVC mac which brought a flash of gaiety into the grey day.

'I'm not staying!' she cried, dark hair flying as she hurried across the gravel to get out of the drizzle. 'I just came to check you were still joining us tomorrow.'

'For the ladies' lunch?' Leah wiped her wet hands on her apron as they stood in the porch.

'Er…yes. Although it's turned into more of a farewell party now. You will come, won't you?'

'*Farewell*? But when are you going? I'd no idea you'd set yourselves a date?'

'We hadn't – until last night. But Jock's finished all his work now, the pictures have all been air-freighted out and he's just itching to follow them. You know how he is – restless and impulsive. He's booked us onto on the car ferry, leaving Bilbão this weekend.'

'This weekend!' cried Leah, aghast. 'This all seems terribly sudden … I mean, it's going to seem so strange here without you.'

'Without whom?' Neither of them had heard Buster come through the door behind them.

There was an awkward silence. Leah eventually filled it by clutching Buster's arm and announcing the news. 'Honey, it's ghastly! Catalina's just been telling me she and Jock are off to England in no time at all.'

'So I gather,' he shook her off irritably, 'I heard most of it.'

Catalina looked from one to the other, rueful and apologetic; the raindrops glistening on her cheeks enhanced her flawless skin. She made her eyes big as she said, 'It's just as sad for us too, you know. We've both enjoyed your company so much recently, it seems dreadful to have to leave you especially when Christmas is in sight. Jock was saying only the other day how he must – '

'This is hardly the time to trot out what your husband says in private!' said Buster shortly. 'If you're going, you're going, and no more to be said!'

'Buster!' Leah noticed he'd gone very white and was amazed.

Catalina gave her tinkling laugh and caught Leah by the hand. 'Husbands!' she smiled indulgently, 'They're all the same … like to be in on everything. I can see what's going on with yours. It's quite obvious!'

'What?' said Leah, unable to take her eyes off her husband, who was as pale as moonlight.

'Why, he's jealous of course! It shows a mile away! Anyone can tell he'd give his eye-teeth to go home for Christmas, and just because we are – and you're not – he's madly jealous.'

'But this *is* home!' said Leah.

'Don't tease,' Buster said in a low voice.

'You see!' Catalina was triumphant. 'I've touched a nerve. I knew I was right. And now of course, typical male, he's damned if he'll admit it. Isn't it funny how men *loathe* having their minds read?'And she tossed her hair back over her shoulders as her laughter pealed through the damp afternoon. She linked arms with Leah and they hurried across the wet forecourt to the car. As she bent to climb in, Buster could not help but notice that the tendrils of hair where it parted at the nape of her neck were beginning to curl with the damp. Just like they had – in the cold sea air, down at the beach – just over a month ago.

As he watched her rev up and make some parting remark to Leah, Buster did not stay to wave goodbye. He shut the door with a slam, then turned abruptly and went back into the house. He found Benjie in the kitchen putting cherries on a white iced cake. 'Hi,' Benjie said, 'Isn't Catalina staying for tea?'

'Nope.'

'Too bad! She must have been in some kind of hurry,' he said, probing in the jar for an extra large one for the centre.

'I guess.'

'Well, isn't that a shame – ah – here's the very one I want. I like seeing her around, she's always so *decorative* –' he was patting the final cherry into place.

Buster did not reply. He seemed engrossed in the rain which was growing heavier by the moment. Leah clomped in, soaked to the skin. 'Well, if that doesn't beat everything!' she cried.

'What's happened now?' Benjie arranged a doily and put the cake on a silver stand for all to admire.

'Catalina McKay! Just how casual can one get! And I'm supposed to be her best friend too…' she began to ease off her boots, quivering with supressed indignation.

Benjie looked up with distaste as clods of mud fell on the tiled floor. 'Can't you do that in the porch? Just what's she supposed to have done?'

'Done! It's what she hasn't done that's upset me.' snarled Leah, sounding more New York than usual. 'She and Jock are off to England for two months and she only tells me now, having already – it seems – informed half of Santa Felicia.'

'Is that all?' said Benjie. 'Hardly much to get in a state about, surely? We knew they were going this side of Christmas. They probably only just decided – wouldn't you agree, Buster?'

Buster grunted and remained at the window. His head was reeling; his insides had numbed themselves, turning into tight bands across his belly. Catlina had continued to visit but less so since Jock had become so busy and he'd never had the chance to catch her properly alone since that one incredible encounter on the beach. There had been snatches of conversation, stolen in those few moments between her arrival and departure when neither Leah or the Boys had gotten in the way, but it had been difficult. It was always the same: she would put her fingers to her lips in a shush-ing gesture and tell him to be patient. Everything would change in the coming year. She promised.

He was beginning to wonder if he believed her. His whole life had changed since that afternoon of passion, and with it, his entire psyche. He had thought of nothing else ever since. At night, she filled his dreams; by day, his every thought. Once or twice in his waking hours he had almost called out her name, and it shocked him how close he'd come to dropping his guard. One false slip and his defences would be tossed to the wind. He knew he wasn't a good enough actor not to capitulate if Leah were to guess outright and come onto him. He needed time. Time to recover and time to get his story and his feelings sorted.

As he struggled to control his face, his hands were shaking. How could Catalina continue to act so cool? To drop in today – with absolutely no warning – was unforgivable. He wondered what madness had driven her to such action. A ladies' lunch party indeed! It all sounded so frivolous. Was this her idea of being prudent? To allay suspicion by asking the wife of a man she'd recently fucked, out to a gossipy, girlie lunch? It was she who had made him promise not to give the game away; was this her way of testing him to the limit? To make sure he was indeed a man of iron? What did it all mean?

'Buster – are you joining us for tea?' Leah's voice suggested she had recovered. 'We're going into the library to sit by the fire. Benjie's made this wonderful cake.'

'I'll be there in a minute,' he said, anything to get rid of her.

'Well, mind you don't catch your death of cold standing there by that window. I can't think what you're looking at.'

'He likes the rain,' said Benjie. 'There's a certain type of person who is mentally stimulated by watching falling rain. Wally told me, it's good for some particular neurosis.'

'Well, that wouldn't surprise me!' she said, trundling the tea-trolley before her. Perhaps Buster did have feelings after all; for once they almost seemed in sympathy.

'It's wonderful you were able to come!' Catalina stood at the horseshoe-shaped bar of the *Cozinha Velha*, in a scarlet Yves St Laurent costume, greeting each guest with her own very individual brand of enthusiasm. She did it so well that each of the five women might have believed their welcome to be the warmest of all.

'How *marvellous* to get you at such short notice!' she greeted Maysie who arrived languid and late in high-heeled suede boots and a scrap of plaid mini-skirt.

'You nearly didn't,' replied that young lady with a preening action of her hand. 'I was supposed to be in Lisbon for lunch with the Da Cunhas' – everybody had heard of the family that owned the biggest retail chain in Portugal – 'but then I took one look at the weather and couldn't face the idea of flying.'

'Their loss is our gain,' said Catalina managing to nudge Jacqueline as she manoeuvred a huge jug of vodka and tomato juice in the newcomer's direction. 'Help yourself to a Bloody Mary to warm you up,' she smiled as they all gathered round, 'Fernando has spiced it up for us, specially!'

So far, the weather had driven away all passing trade and only two tables were occupied, one of which was presided over by Manolo Vaz Valqueiro and a couple of younger men. The three looked up with interest at the lively party, and Manolo raised a polite glass in their direction. Only Janine remained silent, the sight of Manolo having had an immediate and dramatic effect.

'I must say this is rather jolly, darlings!' said Johanna, cross-legged and elegant on her bar stool. As usual, she wore beautifully pressed trousers, the pale fawn of her roll-neck lending a youthfulness to a skin that enjoyed the most exquisite grooming. 'It seems years since I attended a hen party and what a quaint mixture of 'hens' we all are!' she surveyed them through a gold pince-nez held at arm's length. 'Whatever made you think all this up, Catalina dear?'

'That's what I was thinking,' said Leah, feeling slightly too formal in a fitted pinstriped three piece. 'You certainly took my breath away yesterday.'

'Oh, I love spur of the moment!' said Catalina. 'Jock and I only decided to leave this weekend once we secured a place on the ferry.'

'But why ladies only?' asked Janine, her back well turned to the tables.

'Exactly what Mummy and I were wondering,' said Maysie. 'Rather unlike you, Catalina, not to want the men too!'

'*Men!*' Catalina positively shook with feminine laughter. 'Who wants men around on a wet miserable day like today? There's only one place I'd go with a man right now and that's to the bedroom. Well, wouldn't you all agree?'

For once, everyone fell silent. It was well-known Johanna had a Portuguese lover in Lisbon, Maysie claimed to have a string of admirers worldwide, Jacqueline was head over heels with her husband, Janine was permanently love-sick – it didn't help the present victim was in full view – and as far as the others were concerned, only Leah was the unknown quantity. Leah felt her cheeks flush as she felt all eyes turn to her, particularly when Catalina rather pointedly added, 'After all, what better way to keep warm – surely?'

Since her last remark was addressed to Leah, silence fell. God, she's a bitch, thought Jacqueline as Leah half-nodded, clearly uncomfortable.

'You see!' said Catalina, triumphant, 'We're birds of a feather, Leah and I. We like sunshine and warmth and all the good things in life.' Leah smiled at this. For a moment she thought she was being put on the spot – but where was the harm? She thawed even more when Catalina slipped an arm through hers, almost a public declaration of their friendship.

'And what's more,' Catalina went on, 'Leah and I share something else in common; we've worked hard on our men and we've each got our husbands well and truly under control. They'll do anything for us! There's Jock, the old devil, carrying me off for a scintillating time in London – whilst clever Leah, has achieved her dream house in the sun! She can hardly wait to celebrate the festive season European style. So, with all that spoiling to look forward to,' she demanded – 'who needs men today?'

The spell was rudely broken when Johanna interrupted with some asperity, 'You rest on your laurels very easily, Catalina, darling. Be careful not to drag others less capable than yourself into unknown territory. Have you never read the poets? '*...a limbo large and broad, since called the Paradise of Fools, to few unknown...things fall apart; the centre cannot hold'*... W B Yeats: he was Irish – very knowing.' She ran a quick hand through her silvery blonde hair, 'I'm sorry to quote,' she smiled in a self-deprecating way, 'but the poets so often put things better than anyone.'

'Oh, Mummy! How *learned*! – but must we have a lecture just as we're all beginning to enjoy ourselves? I'm much more interested in what Fernando's prepared for us to eat!' said Maysie, whose ability to eat like a horse and still weigh nothing was legendary.

'I've chosen something traditional,' said Catalina, 'but I know you're going to like it.'

'I only hope it's not too fattening,' said Jacqueline.

'Yes, you might drop a pound or two,' said Maysie.

'I disagree,' said Janine, joining in for the first time, 'Twiggy went out years ago!'

Catalina nodded swiftly to Fernando who led them to their table before an argument ensued. She placed Johanna on her right, Leah to her left. Leah guessed it had to be that way around in deference to Miss Vincent's age. Catalina was always so correct. Janine plumped herself down opposite where she could glance sideways at the men without being observed but they were already making moves to leave. At the door, Manolo turned briefly to afford them all the smallest of bows, then he was gone. Janine covered up her obvious disappointment by spreading lashings of butter onto a large bread roll.

'What a simply marvellous meal, Catalina darling!' cried Johanna, as the waiter cleared away their first course of mussels with coriander sauce and replaced it with an enormous platter of partridge sauteed in olive oil, garlic and stewed apple. 'I just hope I can do all this justice – you know I eat like a bird!'

'I'll be very hurt if you don't,' said Catalina. 'Just think! It may be a very long time before we're all gathered together again under the same roof, peacefully eating and drinking at the same table.'

'Put like that it sounds as if you expect to be away for ever,' said Jacqueline, 'I thought it was only two months.'

'You never know,' Catalina replied whilst responding to Johanna's searching look with a brilliant smile.

'I must say Santa Felicia will seem quite odd without you,' Jacqueline continued. 'By God, I envy you going to London. If it was me, I must confess I'd think twice about returning.'

'The difference is – I never think twice!' said Catalina. 'But I do care about my friends, and sometimes you can't please everyone.'

'Oh, I wouldn't worry about us,' said Jacqueline, picking up a wing and attacking it with relish.

'I think Catalina's different,' said Leah quietly.

'They all turned to look at her and she tilted her jaw a little as she went on, 'There's a type of woman who prizes friendship above all other things. It can't be broken by constraints of time or distance. We Americans feel this very strongly because we're used to travelling thousands of miles to see a good friend. Geography just doesn't enter into it.'

'Geography maybe not – but what about history?' said Johanna.

'History?' Leah looked blank. 'I'm not sure I follow.'

'I didn't think you would,' replied Johanna, unmaliciously. 'I suppose I was thinking of relationships I've had in the past – in the theatre world, that sort of thing. Historically – things that happen during the course of a lifetime – often put a different slant on things. I always think it dangerous to open one's heart to embrace anyone too readily. Real friendships take years in the making.'

'You're full of moralising today, Mummy,' said Maysie, filling up her own wine glass and neglecting everyone else. 'Quite out of character for you.'

'Yes,' said Johanna in a lighter tone, 'I daresay you're right. My saving grace in life has always been my independence – Sagittarius is my sun sign – and knowing not to rely on anyone.'

'Your talking of history,' said Catalina, 'has reminded me of a game we used to play at boarding school – when it was raining and we had to stay indoors.'

'Like today,' put in Jacqueline, glancing at the rainswept window and shivering despite the warmth of the room.

'That's right...' Catalina paused, as if doubtful whether to continue. Then she pushed her empty plate away. 'We were about fifteen; that terrible age when everyone was man-mad and yet all of us had led too sheltered a life in the convent to have one iota of experience. We would make up wildly exaggerated stories about imaginary men, and the game I was referring to was pure fun. We each chose a character from history – someone we admired or were intrigued by – El Cid or Dick Turpin for instance. Then, the others would ask questions to discover the identity, but it had to be yes-no answers. I thought it might be amusing to play amongst adults and to judge if the men chosen bore any relation to their real life partners.'

'So we'd have to be honest about our choice,' said Jacqueline. 'In my case it would be no good choosing someone like Dante for instance. He may have had a brilliant mind but he'd have been far too virtuous and bookish! I like men of action. Henry the Eighth was very good looking when young apparently, so one might have had a bit of sport with him... provided he didn't knock one's block off in the meantime!'

They all laughed. 'You're giving everything away, as usual, Jacqueline!' said Catalina, 'it's no fun if you make it too easy.'

'I agree,' said Johanna, who loved games and often introduced charades at the end of her own dinner parties. 'I think I get the gist, you choose someone that genuinely fascinates, and if the jury guess, presumably they're allowed to give their verdict. This sounds like fun!'

Catalina beckoned to the waiter to clear the pudding plates away and settled deeper into her chair. Her cheeks were flushed from the red wine and the glow of candles and she was clearly excited. Coffee and *petits-fours* arrived and everyone waited for her to speak. 'So you all understand what to do? Just think of a man!'She clapped her hands with relish, 'Now who's going first? Janine! What about you?'

'Oh no!' wailed Janine whose thoughts were still full of Manolo. 'I can't possibly think of anyone who bears the slightest resemblance to my ideal man.'

'I've got someone!' cried Maysie.

'Good! Let's think, is he English?'

'Naturally,' said Maysie, 'one gone.'

'I don't see it's so natural,' muttered Janine.

'Last century?' asked Jacqueline.

'No, two.'

'Before the fifteenth?' suggested Leah.

'No, three.'

'Don't let's waste questions,' said Johanna, 'that leaves us somewhere in between. Was he a warrior?'

'No, four.'

'A man of the arts?'

No, five gone.'

'A politician?'

'I don't think so, six.'

'She doesn't want to give us a 'yes' answer,' said Janine, 'This is a stupid game if you ask me.'

'Was he an explorer?' It was Leah who asked the question.

'Yes! Seven.'

'Sir Walter Raleigh!' they all cried at once.

'Yes,' said Maysie, pulling a face.

'Of course,' said Catalina, 'it had to be. All that chivalry and stepping onto the poor man's cloak so as not to get your shoes wet...'

'But of course!' said Maysie, languidly.

'Jolly useful on a day like today!' said Jacqueline.

'I think Leah was the clever one guessing he was an explorer,' said Catalina. 'Now – what's everyone's verdict on Maysie's man? Do we all agree he's a suitable choice for her?'

'Absolutely,' said Jacqueline.

'I can't think why I didn't guess at the beginning,' smiled her mother, 'Good choice, darling.'

'I'm not so sure,' said Janine slowly. 'My history book seemed to say something about him only spreading his cloak out for royalty... not commoners.'

'Oooh-ey,' said Jacqueline.

Maysie shot Janine a strong look of dislike and Catalina interrupted hurriedly before tempers flared. 'Come along, I thought we agreed today there'd be no beetching. We've all decided Maysie's chosen aptly, so whose turn is it now? What about you, Leah?'

'If you insist. I've certainly got my guy all lined up!'

This is going to be interesting thought Johanna to herself. I only hope this game is as innocent as Catalina makes out. They guessed Leah's man at the fourteenth question. Her choice was Alexander the Great. Before anyone could say anything, Maysie had butted in, 'What an extraordinary choice!'

'Why?' Leah's voice was high-pitched and defensive.

Johanna tried to kick her tactless daughter under the table, but Maysie was not to be put off. 'But I never heard anything so ridiculous,' she said. 'Alexander the Great isn't your sort of man at all. Anyone can see that!'

'Just because Buster doesn't ride horses!' laughed Johanna, trying to make a joke of it.

'No, *not* because of that – '

'Maysie, I think Leah probably knows a little better than you do what she secretly admires in a man,' her mother cut in.

'I thought we were supposed to give a verdict!' Maysie swung round indignantly.

Catalina's face was a study. An enigmatic smile rested on her lips but for once her eyes were completely expressionless. She reminded Johanna of a tigress watching over her cubs. A lenient tigress, letting them fight and maul each other, unwilling to intervene in order to teach them a lesson about life. The trouble was, thought Johanna, someone might get hurt in the fray. Not everyone wore a shield of armour like her own daughter.

She intervened again, 'I think Leah's choice was very fair, but we're all agog to guess whom you've chosen, Catalina darling. Stop keeping us in suspense!'

'All right,' said Catalina, a glimmer of speculation lit her eyes. 'You'll never guess who my man is, but you might as well try.'

She was right. Nobody did. When she finally told, Jacqueline, who had grown exasperated with so many negative answers, nearly exploded.

'King Alfred, did you say? King Alfred! I thought this was supposed to be some sort of truth game. I never heard such balls in all my life!'

'I thought I would outwit you,' said Catalina, unperturbed at this blasphemous outburst.

'You can't mean King Alfred who burnt the cakes, can you?' said Leah, wrinkling up her nose in perplexion.

'That's exactly who I do mean – Alfred, the awkward one who burnt the cakes! Only, he went on to become a real man of action – but only afterwards! That's when he surprised everyone!' declared Catalina.

'That's not good enough,' said Janine. 'I knew this was a silly game from the start.'

'Personally, I think you're all rotten at this game,' said Maysie. 'I seem to have been the only person who's stuck anywhere near the truth. Can we order some more coffee now?'

Catalina nodded to the hovering waiter and their cups were refilled. 'Have a liqueur,' she said persuasively.

Johanna chose Grand Marnier and puzzled everything over in her mind. What *was* Catalina playing at? It was clear that something was brewing and the atmosphere had changed. No one seemed to have much more to say, so she picked up her bag and stood up. 'Well, it's been interesting, but I think it's time to go. Otherwise the day will be gone. Perhaps we can finish the game another time. It's been a delightful lunch Catalina darling. Thank you so much.'

They all followed suit, their chairs squeaking on the stone flags as they pushed them back. Catalina saw her guests to the door as they all poured out into the wet afternoon. The game was forgotten as they waved their goodbyes, thanks and greetings for Christmas less than four weeks ahead.

Only Leah hung back. 'Catalina, is this really goodbye or do we see you once more before you go? Can't you come back once more to the house – perhaps with Jock?' she added politely.

Catalina shook her head. 'I think it's better not, Leah. You see, I hate goodbyes and there's so much still to do and get ready. Jock really needs me every moment of the day from now until the exhibition.'

Leah nodded, trying to hide her disappointment. 'It's going to be kind of lonesome in Santa Felicia without you. I still can't quite bring myself to get really close to these other people,' she nodded her head as the last car moved off. 'Oh, they're nice enough,' she said hastily, 'but they don't seem like real buddies.'

'It's what I always told you,' said Catalina.

'I guess so,' Leah sighed and turned to go. Her hand on the door, she hesitated as a thought struck her; then she wheeled round excitedly, 'Good gracious, honey! What a dope I've been! I've just seen the light!'

'You have?'

'Yes! I mean about King Alfred! I couldn't understand it at first. I kept thinking you'd chose some great sculptor or artist – like Jock – I had Michelangelo in mind for you!   So when you said about King Alfred, I just couldn't see it. Now, of course, I do.'

Catalina was looking at her very curiously. 'What do you see Leah?'

'You gave it away just now when you said how much Jock needed – needs you – before the exhibition and so on. A great man, we all know that, but in the eyes of the person closest to him, quite a helpless one. Only able to function with the support of his woman and all that entails.' She nodded, pleased with her deduction, 'I'm sure that means the exhibition will be a great success – just as Alfred's campaign worked out for him!'

Catalina smiled and nodded thoughtfully. A moment later they embraced and putting up her umbrella, Leah stepped out into the street.

'Now, don't go getting wet, honey,' she called back, 'I'm OK. Just don't forget to write – you've got our address, haven't you? – the odd postcard from London would mean a lot.'

'Of course,' said Catalina, 'I've always liked postcards!' And with a wave of her hand, she stepped back into to the warmth of the restaurant, a thoughtful smile on her face.

No one appeared to have noticed a tall figure emerging from a doorway further up the street.

Catalina ordered herself another coffee as she went to settle the bill. It was cheerful and bright inside and she found herself putting off the moment for going home. Fernando came up to the counter to take her cheque. It had been agreed he would only pay it into the bank after *Senhor* Jock's Christmas exhibition was over. This was the kind of favour that was quite normal in their small community and certain trusted clients deserved no less.

'Do you mind if I join you for a cognac?' he said in Portuguese, reaching for an exotic looking bottle at the back.

She nodded graciously and replied in her native tongue, 'It was a wonderful meal, Fernando – please congratulate the boys in the kitchen. It was one of your best ever. The partridge in particular – *estupendo.*'

'And the American *senhoras*, were they happy too?' Fernando, ever the professional, took a genuine interest in the likes and dislikes of his international clientele, particularly when it came to local dishes or a new sauce.

'Most definitely,' she was saying, but the words froze on her lips. Instead of Fernando, the bulky figure of a man in a thin jacket and sodden trousers came to join her at the bar. A pool of water gathered round his feet and little rivulets ran from his hair down either side of his face, only to disappear from view under his collar. He was shivering with cold. She drew in her breath sharply. The slight sound seemed to bring Fernando, who'd been standing gape-mouthed on the other side, to his senses.

'What is it I can do for you, *Senhor*,' he said in clipped English, drawing himself up to his vast, burly height and peering through his shaggy eyebrows at the intruder with a degree of hostility.

'You can give me a double Scotch,' the nasal twang was unmistakeable.

'I am afraid thees is impossible, *Senhor*. The bar has just closed. Now if you will be so good as to – '

'Fernando, it's all right. You can give him a drink,' said Catalina impatiently, 'This is a friend of mine.'

Fernando looked doubtful, but obeyed. It was clear he did not recognise Buster, and little wonder. His bedraggled appearance and ashen countenance was very different from the smooth, urbane look he normally presented to the world. He took the whisky without a word and polished it straight off. 'I'll have another like that,' he said. Catalina watched, half in wonder, half in horror. So far, he had refused to acknowledge her. She waited silently, for once at a loss for words.

Buster was staring straight ahead. He wore a glazed look, but to her relief he stopped shivering when the second drink was placed before him. Finally, she could not contain herself. 'You ought to get out of those wet clothes immediately. You'll get pneumonia if you don't!'

He turned then and looked her carefully up and down. 'I guess it wouldn't make much difference to you if I did.'

'Oh don't be silly, Buster.' As she spoke she noticed that a huge drip was forming on the end of his nose. The situation was too absurd for words and she found herself laughing out loud – unsure whether it was with nerves or genuine amusement – probably a combination of both.

'Do you want to share the joke?' As he spoke the drip enlarged as water from a stray forelock swelled its volume. She watched, fascinated.

'Well?' He jerked his head up with impatience sending a spray, a myriad droplets all over her and the bar.

'Oh, Buster,' was all she said.

'Is that all you can say – "Oh Buster"?' He was angry. 'I've been standing outside for almost two hours waiting to see you – in the pouring rain – soaked to the skin, and all you can say is "Oh Buster."'

Shush,' she said putting a finger to her lips, with a warning glance at Fernando's expressive back as he washed glasses.

'No, I will not shush,' said Buster. 'Not before I've had some kind of explanation. Christ! I never thought it possible women could find so much to say to each other in all that time. Do you realise your so-called hen party lasted almost four hours?'

'Did it really? They were obviously enjoying themselves.'

'If I'd known!' he snorted, 'I'd have found myself some cosy taverna in which to while away the time.'

'So why didn't you?'

'I've been trying to explain, haven't I?' he pushed his glass away and lit a cigarette. 'I had to see you. Don't you understand? I was afraid if I didn't hang around, I'd miss you. I thought as soon as the party was over you'd be gone with the rest of them.'

'But why not stay in your car?'

'Because Leah had it of course. God, you just don't seem to think…or care – do you? If you really want to know I jogged to the bottom of our hill and then thumbed a lift into town with a passing farmer.'

'And then you just stood outside in the cold and the wet, hoping we'd soon be finished. Oh my poor, poor darling,' her tone had changed, 'I am so sorry.'

She took his hand under the bar and held it in both of her warm ones. It was a relief that Fernando had finally decided it was safe enough to return to the kitchen; she hoped he had not overheard too much. Soothingly, she rubbed some heat back into the chilled flesh just as she had done a hundred times before for Katy.

'Yeah,' he said wearily. It was as if her hands had drawn all the pent-up anger and indignation out from his very finger-tips. All he felt now was very tired.

'You shouldn't have come here, you know,' she was saying. 'It was risky and foolish, but –' she put up a warning finger as he opened his mouth to protest – 'I know you came because you love me.'

He nodded, 'Something like that, I guess.'

'Dearest Buster,' she continued. 'I know what you've been thinking. You thought I was going to leave Portugal without a goodbye, without a single word of explanation. Just sail out of your life for two months without even a promise for the future.' As he nodded again, she said again, 'You poor darling – what a beetch you must think I am.'

'I wasn't sure what to think,' he said in a low, flat voice. 'You were all smiles when you came to the house to ask Leah to lunch. You hardly looked at me. It was as if all that had happened between us, really hadn't happened. I didn't know what was going on.'

'But we agreed that was what we would do,' she said, lowering her eyes and peeping up at him sideways through her long lashes. 'I wanted to reinforce it, to make sure you saw how possible it is to play-act, to pretend. I wanted you to see for yourself. Did you not guess that?'

'Not really, it all looked too damn real. I had serious doubts about you. Lightweight, I think is the word … I've never seen you as a bitch. Only as a young, impulsive, passionate – oh Christ, Catalina, I've run out of descriptions – just a crazy young woman playing grown-up games and not realising the consequences.'

She smiled and squeezed his arm; then fell serious again. 'Sometimes I myself theenk I'm not to be trusted. It's often a mystery to me what drives me on. Look at today! How, without meaning, I've made you suffer. What sort of woman would have that effect on a man?

'A very beautiful one,' he said spontaneously, 'and the sexiest one in the world.'

'Oh darleeng!' she sat in silence for a moment and he watched her in wonder. How cool and controlled she seemed today, so calm and poised. If the memory of her fiery passion was not so fresh in his memory, he might have believed it all a dream himself. Where was that trilling laughter, that reckless throwing back of her head, the bared throat, the skirt pulled up hastily over her knees. Was this sophisticated, well-dressed woman really the same girl he had taken in the sand?

There was no laughter about her now. Nothing showed in that smooth, untroubled face. What was she really feeling? Were those kind words, the hand warming, the light touches of her fingers, just empty gestures? If only she would give him something to hold onto – some betrayal that her emotions were running amok like his! He needed some token of reassurance to succour him and bear him bravely through the barren months to come.

'Buster darling,' she was gathering up her things. 'Come with me to the door – I must talk to you where there's no risk of being overheard,' she whispered. She arranged a gorgeous silk scarf over her hair and called Fernando. Her smile was ravishing as he returned to the bar. 'Put these last drinks on my account,' she instructed in Portuguese, 'And a very happy Christmas to you and your family. Thank you again – *até a proxima*!'

'*Até a proxima!*' The man responded, looking after her wonderingly as she swept out of the dining room and into the hall. Buster turned to see the dark eyes harden as they rested on himself. He too saw the pool of water that he'd left behind on the polished flagstones. Oh, what the hell!

Catalina was looking out onto the street. 'Come,' she said. He came to her side and put his arms round her. 'There's not a soul about,' she whispered.

He was unprepared for the sudden rush of warmth as she suddenly pressed herself against his chest. 'Oh darling, darleeng, hold me. Hold me tight!' He caught the sob in her voice and held her fiercely to him. The thudding had already started in his head and chest but he did not care. Her fingers were reaching up round his ears and neck and she pulled his head down to kiss her parted mouth. He remembered the burning lips, whilst the soft sublety of her tongue brought back memories of other delights he had tried to hold at bay for weeks.

'Darling, darling!' she was gasping now and he tried to find her breasts but she stopped him. 'No! Oh what a fool I am!' she cried, 'oh, oh … No darling, *no!*'

He felt her pull away and he could not bear it. Hell, he thought savagely. Why must it be like this. Why, why, why? Why should he ever let her go?

'Buster darling?' Reluctantly he allowed her to unwrap his arms from her waist. 'Darling, are you all *right?*'

He took a long gulp of cold air – a cold shower would be more appropriate – before answering, 'Yeah – I'm all right – just.'

She looked at him ruefully and he saw the expensive scarf had fallen round her shoulders, her hair loose once more. 'I knew it would be madness to see you, and you see – I was right.'

One moment apologetic, next triumphant, he felt like a yo-yo, strung between her changing emotions. Next moment she was reaching for her handbag which had fallen to the floor. What was she after now, her lipstick? Christ! he watched her fumbling in its depths, what *was* she up to now? 'It's here somewhere, I swear I put it here this morning – for safety…' He stared, uncomprehending.

'The letter, Buster! I wrote you a letter. I would hardly do otherwise! The postboy – I gave him a tip – was to smuggle it to you. I wanted to read it once more, before he collected it – but I suppose I'd better give it to you now. Seeing as you've … well you know… forced the issue.'

She stood up and held out an engraved envelope of dove-grey, thick and expensive. Even as he held it, he could not focus. His attention was held by the design on her Hermes scarf. The classic script letters, carefully intertwined with horses' bridles, seeming to bounce upwards and outwards and fizz before his eyes. His head was aching, he put a hand to his brow, and still everything spun – as if the design was jumping out of the silk to bruise his eyeballs. It was all getting too much to bear. Suddenly, he wished she'd go.

'I've written it all,' she was saying. 'Everything I dared not say to your face is in this letter. You see I felt it better not to meet again before we left for London. I'd hoped you'd guess that, when I came to see Leah. I tried to catch her alone, then you came and, well – you almost gave us away. Don't look like that, Buster. Read the letter, and you'll understand everything.'

'But hang on, Catalina!' Even to himself, his voice sounded desperate. 'I don't understand!'

She patted his arm and withdrew. 'You weel, Buster darling. You weel. Goodbye my love, be patient.'

And with that parting quip, she stood on tiptoe and kissed him once, chastely, on the cheek. He watched as she stepped out into the shining street. She did not even turn to wave and he did not expect it.

It had stopped raining and the sun had peeped out, but she pulled the scarf up over her hair and began to run. As she disappeared round the corner to her waiting car, his lingering memory of her that winter, was the red, gold and black of the expensive silk, billowing in the wind.

A second later, he heard the roar of the Mercedes as she turned it up the hill.

26

*A*s he slooshed his way through the puddles, Buster had no idea or care for where he was going. It was a small town, yet quite possible for a stranger to lose himself in the maze that formed the poorer quarter. Once you lost sight of the sea, the narrow twisting streets with their archways and cul-de-sacs could confuse even the sharpest brain. It had started to rain again and the sight of a half-open door and glow of a gas lamp beckoned Buster to approach the humblest abode he had ever set foot in.

He was not sure at first if the peeling frontage belonged to a *taverna*, shop or private dwelling. He thought it was the former, but either way, it didn't matter very much; he could always feign ignorance. Pushing his way past strings of hanging garlic, he was reassured by the smell of tobacco and what he took to be a smile of welcome from a hunchbacked man behind a makeshift bar. A couple of barrels served for tables and glasses of all shapes and size were scattered everywhere. As well as the hunchback, he saw two clumps of cronies – all appeared to be fishermen. Most wore thigh-high rubber waders, a few of the youngsters, inadequately protected, wore half-boots, whilst one and all sported the check flannel shirt – the traditional 'uniform' of Algarvean boatmen. Oilskins and thick wool jackets lay steaming on the floor before an evil smelling stove.

Clearly the weather had interrupted their normal sea-faring. Instead, they were whiling away the afternoon with the local firewater, an undiluted spirit known as *medronho*, made from arbutus berries. There was heated discussion, the odd laugh and a constant scrape of chairs. Every head looked up as Buster made his way into the room, but none of their faces registered much surprise, just a relaxed acceptance of this *estrangeiro* in their midst, as they got back to their own business.

The hunchback scuttled round from the counter and pointed out a row of bottles, grimy with dust and fly dirt. There wasn't one label he recognised.

'Scotch?' said Buster hopefully. Then as the man looked perplexed, he tried again, 'Wiskee?'

'A-a-aar…' it was a long throaty utterance and the man shook his head firmly. 'Wiskee, *não – não temos*.' Probably too expensive, thought Buster, even on the black market. Instead the man had taken down a long thin bottle, half-full of some clear-coloured liquid and set it down in front of Buster. '*Isto! Isto e bom!*'

Buster was well beyond the point of caring. He pulled out the cork, sniffed it and nodded. 'OK.'

The hunchback beamed and took the bottle and a brandy glass over to a smaller barrel in a corner. He motioned for Buster to sit down. '*Isto e bom*,' he repeated, with a conspiratorial wink. Turning his back, he was soon deep in conversation with the fishermen. Buster got the feeling they might have been discussing prices or politics – so earnest were they – and he was grateful to be left alone.

He poured himself a measure and took a gulp. Christ! The fiery liquid leapt down his throat, burning all the way down – no wonder they called it firewater! He'd heard it could seriously light you up or seriously lay you flat. He'd better be careful. He tried again, this time a tiny sip… ah! that was better, but he would have to watch it. As he felt his strength seep back, he felt inside his jacket for Catalina's letter. Timing was everything with these things; only two minutes ago he was like death warmed up, now he could deal with anything! He wasn't so stupid as to believe it would last.

Carefully, he took a folded sheaf of paper from an unsealed envelope, spreading the crested parchment before him. 'My Darling…' it began; the childish hand that had made out the party list danced before him. That seemed an eternity ago.

'…Don't think badly of me but for the present I am going to disappear without a proper goodbye. One week from today we shall all be in England and the thought of leaving you makes my heart very heavy. For this reason, I cannot bring myself to see you again before I go.

'I am sorry about yesterday. I had hoped you would not be around when I came to talk with L. – that was why I came no further than the door. It was as horrible for me as it was for you – only I think I'm a much better actress!

'I shall only be gone eight weeks my darling, so be brave. The time will not be wasted, I promise you. I have so many thoughts and plans in my head for our future, it would amaze you if I divulged them now. But I will very soon. You must learn to trust me.

'Although we cannot see each other, we will be constantly in touch mentally and spiritually. I want you to write to me often to reassure me of your love. Write to me please Poste Restante, Kew Post Office – see address below. Please use my maiden name N-O-B-R-E (not McK) to be safe. By the way, it translates as 'noble' – which is what your love has done to my heart!

'In all that we do my Darling, we must be very careful. I cannot impress upon you enough how important this is. Believe me, if anyone were to find out about us now it would ruin everything and I am sure I would not have the strength to come back to you. So – let us observe Secrecy. Can you rent a numbered box at the post office here, then send me the number so I may write to you without fear of discovery?

'Think of me now and then my Darling. Remember the Passion we shared every time you look at the ocean. You know that was only the beginning – there is so much more to come. Next time will be even better and I promise to bring you delights you never thought possible – not in your wildest dreams.

'Now I must leave you. Be brave my Dearest One. C.'

'Oh my God,' groaned Buster when he had read it. 'Oh my God…'

'Senhor?' the hunchback had appeared at his elbow and was refilling his glass. 'O senhor chama-me?'

Buster shook his head as if in pain and bade the man go away. He read the letter again, then a third and a fourth time. Finally he screwed the two sheets of dove grey into a ball, placed them in the large metal ashtray that lay before him and put a match to it. 'Oh God,' he said again as he watched the flame flicker, then rise and fall, until it left behind a little pile of black ash. 'Having found you – how will I ever manage without you?'

He looked round to see if anyone was watching him but no one seemed interested. It was as if foreigners who talked to themselves burned letters in their midst every day of the week. He poured himself another measure and then another, and quite suddenly the bottle was nearly empty. The last gulp no longer seemed to have any bite to it and when he stood up, the warm, fiery feel in his chest had disappeared.

Swaying a little, he pulled out his wallet. The little landlord took an age to come. 'Quanto e?' he asked. It was one of the few phrases in Portuguese he had mastered.

'Vinte-cinco,' said the hunchback.

Buster drew out a wadge of paper and thrust the first note, blue for a hundred escudos, into the tobacco-stained hand.

The man shook his head and tried to give it back, helpfully trying but failing to extract a brown one instead. 'Cinquenta, melhor,' he encouraged. Buster was having none of it. He wished the fellow would go away. He snatched back his wallet and it fell to the floor. The hunchback picked it up, and gave it back with the blue note and a toothy smile.

'Oh Christ,' said Buster, 'why can't you leave me alone?' But the man was still hovering. In the end, Buster shoved the blue note into the ashtray beside the burnt out letter and lurched towards the door. Two of the fishermen rose to their feet, anxiety in their kindly faces as he lurched against a barrel and almost sent it crashing. One of them gesticulated to the effect of helping him home. Another pushed his wallet more firmly down his back trouser pocket. Buster shook his head. Why couldn't these people get off his back?

Eventually they seemed to get the message and he stumbled into the street. The rain had stopped again. It was a real pity, he thought. Now there'd be nothing to cool his burning face on the long trek home.

Catalina and Philismena were attacking the contents of an enormous wooded trunk full of winter and evening clothes as Jock wandered into the bedroom. A faint smell of mothballs hovered around, as McKay flung himself wearily onto the bed, avoiding a white chiffon evening dress. Philismena discreetly left the room.

'I'm tired,' he said, kicking off his old leather moccasins. 'Can't you stop that for a moment and come and lie beside me?'

'I'll only be a few minutes more,' said Catalina without looking up.

He watched her rounded fingers smooth over the creases in a tweed coat and skirt, then deftly tuck tissue into the sleeves as she transferred it to a smaller case. 'How did your lunch go?' he asked.

'I thought you were never going to ask,' she replied. 'You've been so engrossed all afternoon, I thought you'd forgotten.'

'Is it likely I'd forget when I'll have to foot the bill? How much do we owe Fernando?'

'Just over three thousand escudos.'

'I see.' His voice was expressionless. He hated having to ask her; money was such a sordid subject. He lay his head against the pillows, 'I hope it was good at that price.'

'Oh it was, Jock, it really was. Thank you.' She picked up the chiffon gown, hung it on a hanger, then came to perch beside him. 'Fernando really excelled himself. All the girls were most impressed and in tremendous form by the end of it.'

'Including you?'

'Including me!' she gave her tinkling laugh.

'You were quite late getting home,' he said.

'Yes, I know,' she smiled, nestling against him and unbuttoning his shirt just enough to rub her nose against the hair on his chest. 'Actually I stayed on a bit after the others had gone.'

'Oh?'

'Yes, it was rather funny,' she couldn't resist telling him now they were on the subject. 'Leah's husband, Buster came in. Quite a surprise! He and I had a drink together.'

'That creep?'

'Yes. You know, he made me laugh – he can be quite amusing – in small doses.'

'I hadn't noticed.'

'That's because you never allow anyone to amuse you, unless you consider them above average intelligence,' she said amiably.

'Maybe. What did you talk about?'

'Oh this and that – the usual small talk. I can't really remember,' she giggled and climbed off the bed as suddenly as she had got on.

'Sounds scintillating,' said McKay and closed his eyes.

She giggled again, unusually self-conscious, and returned to her sorting. Sometime later, she held up a gold coloured costume for him to inspect. 'Shall I take this?'

'Hmm, why not, might do for the preview. You know I like you best in solid colours, better with your hair.'

'I thought you might be tired of it. I've taken it two years running.'

'What's two years?' he muttered. Then in a louder voice, 'You realise, of course, that goon Bloomfield's in love with you?'

She did not reply for a moment, busying herself with the contents of the trunk. Eventually, she looked up and said calmly, 'I doubt he's any more obsessed with me than half the men in town.'

McKay shook his head. 'No, this time it's different. You mark my words. I reckon Bloomfield's the sort of geek that falls in love – you know the passionate stuff, the real works – only once in a blue moon. With that type it can go deep enough for them to get desperate.'

Catalina laughed, ' In what way, darling?'

'In his case, I'm not sure. Stop at nothing, probably. It will be interesting to wait and see.'

'Not much chance of that,' said Catalina, 'when we're off the day after tomorrow.'

'Nonsense!' said her husband. 'Absence makes the heart grow fonder.'

'What ideas you have!' she said and came back to the bed. This time she wriggled herself into his arms, moved her tongue around his ear and nuzzled his chest, but when she put down her hand to feel the usual quickening response, she was disappointed. Nothing had happened.

Buster arrived home in the dark to find every light in the house blazing, but apparently no one about. He came in by the kitchen door and was greeted by a baleful look from the kitten, esconsed out of dog-reach on top of the deep-freeze.

It was sucking at a most unpleasant looking piece of grey fish which Leah had obviously prepared. She had made a good job of weaning it and it was growing by the day.

He lumbered into the hall and then into the *sala*. Although a fire burned in the grate, there was nobody there. Someone had put on a stack of records which played softly in the library – but there seemed not a soul around to listen. Then he heard the sound of running water coming from the Boys' quarters and looking at his watch, realised it was much later than he thought. They were obviously all showering before dinner.

It had taken him almost two hours to walk the three mile journey from the centre of town. As he passed by the headland which led to the spot where only a month ago, he and Catalina had clung together, the force of the words in her letter came back to him. Despite the alcohol and burning the evidence, the words kept repeating themselves in his befuddled brain. *'Remember the Passion we shared every time you look at the ocean… you know that time was only the beginning… there is so much more to come.'* It was heady stuff.

As he realised just how drunk he was, the more insistent and repetitious the words became. He had reached a point when all he wanted to do was bang his head against the sea wall, to cry out for peace and quiet. Once, a passing workman had looked at him in concern and offered help. Shaking his head, he'd muttered 'Get a grip, Buster, keep moving for Chrissakes, man!'

Gradually, the exercise had paid off. He had jogged the last few hundred yards home, got into the rhythm of swing, push on, swing again, the diagonal nature of the gait renewing his vigour. The wind, which had chased the worst of the rain away, now whipped new blood into his face and dried off his clothes. His head was thumping less and he saw their driveway loom into view. Above, there was a sliver of new moon, like a thin slice of cheese. Above that, to the right, at about one o'clock to the orb, he saw the evening star. It was all incredibly beautiful and he wished Catalina was there to share it with him.

Relieved to leave the public road behind, he had stopped halfway up their hillside to bathe his face in the flow of icy water that came gushing over the rocks from a spring that had been dried up all summer. It was exhilarating. As he saw the beckoning lights of home, all the muddled thoughts in his head seemed to separate and clarify until they became crystal clear shafts of light within his brain. He was glad to be home. Now he could tackle and take charge of his life again.

There were things to sort out.

As he started to climb the stairs to look for Leah, he began to feel better than he had all day. He went along the landing. The bedroom door was closed. He opened the door quietly but was unprepared for Mungo who threw himself against his master, almost sending him in a heap to the floor. 'Leah!' he said, recovering his balance, 'Leah!'

But Leah was not there, although her clothes were – laid out carefully – on the Chinese silk counterpane. The door to the en-suite bathroom had been locked, probably to keep Mungo out. There was another door into it from the other side. He shut the dog in the bedroom again and made his way along the landing towards his dressing-room.

Usually she took a shower, but tonight she was in the tub. She had the tap running as he came in and there were soap bubbles up to her ears so she was completely oblivious. He stood there in his anorak, his hands dangling at his sides, watching her and never uttering a word. She had a pink plastic cap over her head and he noticed how bony her small knees were as they protruded out of the bubbles. Perhaps it was intuition that made her jerk her head up sharply.

'Oh, it's you, honey! You gave me a fright. I never heard you come in and it felt like a stranger. Where have you been all this time? We were getting quite worried about you.'

'I've been out,' he said. Even to himself, his voice sounded heavy and thick, but she didn't seem to notice.

'I guessed that, but why on such a horrid afternoon? And where? I had the car. I'd no idea you wanted to go out, or I'd have come back earlier. You should have told me.'

'I went for a walk.'

'Well, really,' she said, dipping herself down into the suds again, 'you might have taken Mungo with you. He's had a miserable afternoon with us both out, poor lamb.'

He said nothing but continued to stare in front of him as if he had not heard her. She began washing behind her ears with a candy-stripe face cloth. ' We girls had a great luncheon,' she said. 'Catalina was more than generous. And such fun too! Don't you want to hear about it?'

He came towards the bath. 'If you turn over, I'll loofah your back for you,' he said.

She looked up, a gratified smile on her slim, shiny face. 'Why thanks hon, you haven't done that in ages!' she handed him the loofah, kneeling in the water, then flipped over onto her stomach, obediently, expectantly.

He sat on the edge of the tub and began to run the loofah up and round and between her shoulder blades. Christ, she was thin; it was painful. There were moles too, he'd never really noticed them before, but they were hellish ugly. Why hadn't she kept her tan up? There was something repugnant about the fading yellowness of an old suntan. Why couldn't she have Catalina's rich creamy olive skin – deep skin that didn't need a tan – because it glowed from the blood and love of life, that pounded within? Why did she, his wife, turn him off so much? Why? Why? Why?

He let go of the loofah and watched it plop into the water. Suddenly he pushed. He couldn't help it. He just needed to. In that moment. Without thinking, he pushed again, hard! His hand felt strong and heavy, even to himself. He could break her willowy spine if he wanted. One snap would do it! Of course, he didn't want that – but she might be better out of sight, out of temptation's way. He pushed again and felt her go down. Into the deep tub. Under the soapy water. Much safer down there. Out of harm's way.

Her head surfaced once but she'd swallowed water and was gasping. 'Honey!' she cried. But only that one word – because now, his hand was on her neck and again he found himself pushing down, down, down…and it wasn't difficult to submerge her face in a couple of feet of bath water. Out of the way, best out of the way!

He was panting and excited and the heavy outdoor clothes lent a strength to his hands and a massive heat to his body. This was awesome. Suddenly she arched her back and bucked and he could feel the strength of her fight to free herself and breathe against his outspread hand. Ugh! These moles! They'd reappeared momentarily above the water and repelled him.

He moved his hand slightly so he wouldn't have to touch them and that gave her a second to regain ground. She flipped her ass into the air and got her elbows underneath her. Now she had some leverage. Christ, she might be slight, but she was tough. Stronger than he thought and how she fought! One had to admire the fight in her – it surprised him. He pushed again, even harder if that was possible. Then he felt her go limp.

Christ! Had he drowned her? Was this what he wanted? Oh Christ! There was no resistance in her back now and he quickly took his hands away. Then he heard the gurgle as the last of the water ran out. The foam and soap suds were so thick he had failed to notice. Somehow she'd pulled the plug out. She'd goddarned gone and saved herself! He walked out of the room, disgusted both with her and himself.

Leah coughed and choked and coughed again. She felt the soapy water spew hotly up her throat and out of her burning mouth. There was a rim of soap against her gums and again she coughed and then she spat and coughed again. She clutched at her throat and as she rubbed it, she felt terribly, dreadfully, painfully ill and it was a sensation like none other she had ever experienced. And she prayed to God that it could never, would never, happen again. There was soap everywhere. In her ears, in her nose, in her windpipe, her blinded eyes, somewhere deep in her lungs – and in every pore of her skin. And how it burned and scorched! And she wanted to be sick.

And having felt she'd coughed ten score times and ten, she pulled herself up off her belly and onto her knees. Tremblingly, she clutched at the taps like a lifeline, and would not let go. As the minutes ticked by, slowly, miraculously, she felt the strength return to her body as her lungs dried out.

The first time she tried to climb out of the tub, she nearly blacked out. She felt herself slither pitifully back, but then she tried again. To her astonishment, the second time she made it. She stood on the bathmat, naked and shivering, too weak to grab a towel and not daring to unbend her body and let go of the washbasin which supported her. It was some time before she registered that she was able to stand up unaided.

The towel she wrapped round herself became a friend, a comforter, a protective shield. With this armour about her, she summoned up all her reserves of strength and walked resolutely into the bedroom where she knew she would find her husband. Surprisingly, she was unafraid.

He was over by the window, his hands in his pockets. 'You've been a long time,' he said as she entered the room.

'Yes. I'm sorry. I got delayed. I almost drowned.'

He laughed harshly and wheeled round. 'No, you didn't! Don't you understand, you stupid fool?'

He had never spoken to her like this before in his life, but she did not flinch. Nothing could shock her now. 'I only understand one thing. You tried to drown me.'

'No.'

She shrugged. 'It doesn't matter what you tell me. I know what happened and what I felt. I've a good mind to call the police.'

'Don't be ridiculous. I know I went a bit far,' he said. 'I see now this was uncalled for. But you know very well I didn't try to harm you. It was a game that went wrong.'

'A game? So what were you doing – playing submarines?'

'I was proving something to myself and to you. I guess I shouldn't have wasted my time. You always misconstrue what I do.'

'Oh thanks!' she screamed at him. 'You try to murder your own wife, you bastard and then you have the gall to turn round and tell me you wasted your time! Because it went wrong, no doubt! Why didn't you finish the job? Why not go and get a knife from the kitchen and do it better? Go on, kill me! I don't care – I'm not afraid. Finish it off, why don't you? You'll have a bit of explaining to do, but at least I won't be around to see it!' She collapsed in a little crumpled heap on the floor then and began to sob. And as the sobs tore at her already agonised throat, she sobbed the more with the pain of it.

He came over to her at last and helped her to her feet. She was still weeping but quietly now so that her body no longer shuddered with the violence of her anguish.

'I think you should put some clothes on,' he said gently.

She gulped and nodded and he handed her the things from the bed. As he helped her into them, her weeping grew less and less until it was only a sniff. She still shivered, but her lips had lost that blue look. When, finally, she was dressed, he led her by the hand to the dressing-table and made her sit down. ' Fix your hair and your make-up,' he said, 'and you'll feel a whole lot better.'

'My tranquies,' she whispered, 'Where are my tranquies?'

He found a bottle of discarded pills far to the back of the medicine cupboard. She hadn't had one for months, but he knew this could save her – and him. He poured her a glass of mineral water, and handed her the bottle. She fumbled with the safety screw and in the end he took it from her and counted out two of the small blue capsules.

'Thanks,' she said and her teeth chattered against the glass as she swallowed them.

While she attended to her face, he began to strip off. He was filthy from his walk and stank of dried sweat and the mustiness of damp garments, but something stopped him from going back into their bathroom. Instead, he took a shower in one of the guest suites, then returned to the bedroom to douse himself in cologne. He pulled on a polo neck sweater and tweed slacks. The wool smelt sweet and fresh and brought a feeling of relief. He sank on the bed and waited for her to finish. She seemed to be taking forever.

She had pulled a turquoise turban over her wet hair and was stabbing at her mouth with lipstick. The tranquillisers were beginning to take effect. Her hand no longer shook and her heart had stopped that terrible racing. She began to wonder if she had imagined the whole thing. She swivelled round to look at Buster half-lying on the bed as if nothing had happened. If only he would speak – perhaps he really did have an explanation. He'd obviously been drinking, but why the violence? Usually alcohol made him goofy or merry. Had someone put something in his drink? She was ready now to accept anything. She chose her words carefully.

'You said you were trying to prove something?' she said eventually.

'Yeah.'

'OK. So I'm ready to listen now. Please explain.'

'I dunno what got into me,' he said. 'You looked so vulnerable lying there in the tub. Usually, you're so strong. It suddenly seemed to me how easy it would be to prove how strong *I* was … to show you *I* was in command – as simple as that!' He swung his legs off the bed and put his head in his hands, and she had to strain to hear him. 'And it was no good just thinking all this, I had to show you, to prove it to you – and to myself.

'Don't you see?' he got up suddenly and spread his hands out before her. 'Recently, I've felt so out in the cold, so ineffectual – while you called all the shots. Something in me drove me – to show you – with these!' He tensed his joints and jerked his outspread fingers in front of her eyes. 'Don't you see,' he said again, 'with these bare hands I had to show you!'

'Show me what?' she breathed.

'That I could take it all away from you, if I wanted. Only – only I didn't...' his voice subsided to a whisper...'I didn't, Leah. I realised how much I cared for you. I proved to myself how much you meant to me. I couldn't do it.'

She felt too weak to make her brain work hard and start unravelling the puzzle of words that cluttered her mind. And yet – she knew, she ought. There was something amiss here. She fell silent as she made the effort to think, remember. None of it really made sense, yet he seemed sincere in what he was saying. One didn't live with a man for almost two decades without knowing, surely, when he was telling the truth.

And yet...

There was a discrepancy in his story...she couldn't quite put a finger on it. She wished she hadn't had the pills. Her mind was already trying to oblilterate the scene in the bathroom and she didn't want to remember. Why should she? She felt so calm now, almost lightheaded, and the nightmare had passed. Why should she not just accept his story and forget it ever happened? It would be such a relief.

'But honey,' as she opened her mouth to reassure him, her brain jumped ahead of her mind and she could not stop the words as they tumbled out of her mouth. 'How can you say all that, when it was *me*? I saved myself! I pulled the plug out! It wasn't you who saved me at all...it was me, me, me!' Her voice was rising again and she bit her lip hard to stop the waves of hysteria that started in her tummy and threatened to engulf her, just as the water had done.

He came over to the dressing-table then and banged his fist on the glass top. 'No!' he shouted. She watched fascinated as a hair crack appeared and ran the length of the surface towards her. She saw his face in the mirror, red and angry. 'It wasn't the plug coming out that saved you! It was me! I could have gone further – I had that option – but I chose not to. It was me who took control of the situation. I saved you!'

Without waiting for a reply, he turned and went swiftly out of the room. For once the dog didn't run after him.

'What's happened to Leah?' said Benjie, opening the oven door for the third time in quick succession. 'If she doesn't come soon my casserole will be ruined.'

'She had a migraine,' said Buster, struggling to get ice out for his bourbon. 'She'll be down in a minute.'

Howard came into the kitchen looking annoyed. 'I don't understand it,' he said. 'I could have sworn I filled this decanter only two days ago, now there's only a few inches left. Also, we had two spare bottles of Four Roses in the larder and they've mysteriously disappeared.'

'Well, I've been using a little for my toothache,' said Benjie, wincing as he touched his cheek, 'but certainly not that much!'

'Toothache?' said Howard, accusingly. 'I never knew you had toothache.'

'No, I didn't mention it because I know how much you dislike illness in others,' said Benjie, peering into the oven again. 'Leah's been making whisky swabs for me and it's helped a lot.'

'I don't call toothache an illness,' said Howard huffily, 'besides, I resent that remark.'

'I'm sorry,' said Benjie, 'I retract it.'

'Well it doesn't solve the mystery of the bourbon,' said Howard, looking pointedly at Buster. 'But no doubt we shall discover the culprit all in good time. The annoying part is, this sort of thing puts our house-keeping budget quite out of kilter, and it hardly seems fair on the rest of us.'

'All right, all right,' said Buster. 'You're all looking at me, so I'll take the blame. It's true I've had a bit more than usual lately. I thought I felt a cold coming on, but don't let that worry you! In future, I'll start buying my own private supply – then no one need fuss.'

Howard pursed his lips. 'Well that's settled then. Now we'd better start looking for dentists for you, Benjie. We'll ask around – I don't somehow think we'll find what we're looking for here in Santa Felicia.'

Part 3

27

Thirty Years On – Portugal 2004

The next time she rang Michael, Kate only got his answerphone. Dialling through before breakfast, she'd been certain he would pick up. The Algarve Church couldn't expect him to work all day and all night, surely. When he didn't respond she felt surprisingly let down and hung up. He must get calls from English mobiles all the time – but she wasn't going to leave a message. Besides, she wasn't quite sure whether she wanted him to call or not.

It was the morning after Leah and she had gone to Casa Amarela, and as regards remembered places and background information, it had been surprisingly fruitful. From another aspect, it had been disturbing, and she really wanted to talk about it. The new owners of the villa had been gracious, accepted Leah's simple but truthful story that Kate used to come here as a child, and had allowed them to explore at will. They knew Leah slightly, and seemed flattered she wanted to return. 'It's been some time,' said Debbie Turton-Smith, the wife of the wealthy Mancunian builder who'd bought the place. ' Gerry and I have altered a few things, but nothing structural and we're only too pleased you want to take a trip down Memory Lane. Help yourselves, we'll be on the patio if you want anything.'

What no one had anticipated, was the emotional charge that bound the two visitors together. It came upon them as a bolt of electricity and passed right through them. A foot over the threshold and they were into another world – as one. It was as though Casa Amarela, the name now boldly embossed with ornate tiles on an exterior wall, had taken over. As they explored the various levels, little had been said. They started in the hall, and manoeuvred themselves onwards, silent and wondering.

From long ago Kate suddenly remembered the chandelier. It was extraordinary, she was sure she had never thought about it, but now it was no longer there – she missed it. Massive and glittering. Conspicuous by its absence. Leah told her she had sold it. It was one of the very few things left, she explained, and Kate had the sense to say nothing. Memory was a strange thing and the awareness of loss was happening all over again in the *sala* and it was uncomfortable. Suddenly Kate found herself looking for the grand piano; instead they were being confronted by a gigantic plasma TV, big enough for a private cinema, and it was such a let down. A chill had settled in the air, despite the heat outside.

The curtains were heavy brocade, traunched up with gold tassels against massive brass hooks, and she could sense Leah shrink away. 'There were oatmeal-coloured drapes here,' she murmured quietly. 'Light, bleached linen, almost cheese-cloth in texture; I used to love the swish of them fluttering in the breeze when I threw open the French windows. They weren't much good as curtains, 'cause they let in the light, but that – in my opinion – was rather the point.'

In the library, scene of the tango, it was equally dark and oppressive. A teak cocktail bar stood at one end where Howard's careful shelving had been ripped out and a heavy royal-blue Axminster stretched wall to wall, swamping the wooden floor. Their feet made no sound on the thick wool as they went to gaze out of the window, but Kate felt a sense of weight in Leah's tread as if constantly bracing herself against the expensive but dubious taste which awaited them in every room, every picture, each piece of furniture. Despite some banter scattering their conversation, Kate was only too aware of the silent disappointment this house could still inflict.

All this time, she, herself was struggling with her own demons. She tried to see her mother dancing here, but failed. She tried to see her father, leaning into a corner, dragging on a Gauloise and watching – in that way he had – one hip forward to support his weight over one leg, the other tilted back, casual, but proud. Only, he didn't fit here either – the image she imagined she'd seen was somewhere else – far away, in the mists of time. More like Scotland, she thought, as he waited for us to come home, poor devil.

They proceeded upstairs. Despite the flowery distractions, wallpaper, curtains, ornaments, she tried to conjure up the ghost of her mother sitting on the edge of the bed in the master bedroom and almost succeeded. 'We always gossiped in here,' said Leah. 'You know – girl talk, after lunch – when the men had gone back to the garden.' For a moment Kate pictured a kittenish, raven-haired temptress perched there, pouting mouth, glistening eyes, but in the next moment she had danced right out of sight, unreachable, untenable. Try as she might, Kate couldn't get her back.

What she hadn't expected, and what came as an unwelcome intrusion, was the stalwart figure of 'Uncle' Buster looming in almost every room. It was as though he had never left this place. How she wished he hadn't! First there was his voice, drawling, nasal and loud, but it was his physical appearance and the lack of clothes that shocked her the most. She had never, thankfully, seen him naked, but here she could see him, semi-clad with his toned muscles and tanned six-pack bulging above a pair of stylo bathing trunks – as clear as day. She shook her head to send him away, but all too often she would see and remember again. Why therefore was it so hard to remember what had happened to him in that other place – in the sea – that awful day?

They were back on the landing and the door to a bathroom beyond was wide open. Yellow tiles glistened on the walls and Kate could just make out shiny gold taps. She moved forward to grasp the handle and peer in.

'Don't!' Leah's voice was sharp, making Kate jump, 'I think it's a bit too personal round here for us to intrude.'

'Fine,' said Kate, 'I think I've seen enough up here anyway. I don't really remember any of this, only a few things downstairs. The kitchen most of all.'

'Stick with that, honey,' said Leah, 'I don't want you having nightmares as well as me.'

Kate looked at her curiously. She had a feeling it had something to do with the open bathroom, but she was not going to push. Back on the ground floor, they were coming to the end of their tour. The jumble of images and emotions that had flooded both their minds, seemed to cement them together. Occasionally, Leah had glanced or reached out to Kate, more often the opposite. The younger woman still felt guilty she had brought the American again to this place and every so often, had said in a quiet voice, 'Are you sure you want to go on?'

But true to form Leah had replied bravely in the affirmative. By the time they'd taken in the pool, wandered up the hill and to Kate's delight, discovered 'the wild bit' which was now surprisingly tame, two hours had passed. 'I remember the geese!' she said suddenly and was rather surprised when Leah did not enthuse at her recall. Changing the subject, the rockery was pointed out on the way down and it was a definite relief, finally, to take their leave. More coffee was offered by the hospitable Debbie, but neither woman wanted to stay.

'I've done it now,' said Kate as they drove down the now immaculate concrete drive, 'and I can't thank you enough. I'm so grateful and – er – ever so glad I came.'

'So am I,' said Leah, 'It's done me the power of good, particularly since now I dislike the place more than ever before. There's one more thing you should know. I couldn't bring myself to say it before. That bathroom – the one we stopped outside – can you believe?… he tried to bump me off there!'

Kate almost spun off the road, 'What?' she breathed.

'He denied it of course, he may even have regretted it – but he definitely had a go. Wally thought he must have gone off his head for a few minutes. So – unlike the rest – it wasn't premeditated. It just kind of happened. One of those things…'

'But…'

'We won't go into it now. I exorcised that particular ghost many years ago and now I'm fine about it. Only, I couldn't quite bring myself to go in there today.' Her voice changed; she was quite brisk again. 'Thank you for that, Kate! It's helped me reach a decision about *Caverna*. I'm going to sell – no hard feelings there, either. It's time to move on.'

They'd squeezed hands and parted. Leah would be tied up the next day and Kate returned to her hotel. After a thoughtful dinner, she realised how much she still wanted to talk to Michael. Leah's revelation at the end of their meeting had sent shivers down her spine and it brought back alarming thoughts of her own. She knew it would be hard to talk to James about such matters, but even just to hear his voice might reassure her. Besides, something in her conscience made her feel it was disloyal to ring a virtual stranger when her own husband was probably waiting to support her. In the end she wished she'd ignored that conscience.

It had been a ridiculously unsatisfactory conversation because James had been called to a meeting in Brussels and she'd had to wait until almost midnight before he'd got away from his clients and been able to talk.

When, after several attempts, she did get through to his room in the far-off Marriott hotel, he sounded tired and flat. Although he listened to all she had to say about the villa and its inmates, she could sense it was an effort. There were a few polite 'Goshes', 'reallys?'

and 'who'd have thoughts…?' but he seemed uninvolved and distant. Besides, he had a lot on his plate and she knew it wouldn't be fair to load him with too many grisly details now. Clearly, he still could not really understand why she had gone there and what it all meant to her – retracing her mother's steps and trying to see things for herself. As for today's visit, particularly Leah's latest disclosure, explaining any of this down a telephone would simply sound weak and pathetic. Soon, she was wishing heartily that the conversation would end.

'Uncle' B! What a ridiculous name, she thought as her husband related his own problems in Brussels. How she'd fought against calling him anything at all – and how Mama had chided her. 'You must show more respect, Katy,' she remembered her mother's dark eyes flashing over some minor misdemeanour soon after they arrived in South Africa. 'We've all been together quite a time now, and you're going to have to accept this is our new life out here! Uncle Buster's been very patient with you, so be a nice girl and be kinder with him. You'll only make things more difficult for yourself if you don't.'

How could her mother have put her through that? Sudden indignation bubbled up within her. There was outrage for the child she'd been, and sadness for the adult now – struggling to be understood and comforted. And yes, of course her emotions were raw, now that she'd come to this place and faced up! But she didn't regret it. Not for a moment. It was good she could begin to find excuses for her father, even in time perhaps for her mother – but it wasn't so good that all she was getting from the other end was an account of a thoroughly boring board meeting!

So, as she in turn muttered 'greats' and 'of course' and rathers' to her husband, her thoughts were elsewhere. She needed someone apart from all this, someone dispassionate. It would be such a help to turn once again to that tousle-haired young man whose breath she could still vaguely sense on her neck, whose smell was so clean and somehow innocent and who, in other ways too, seemed rather too inviting. And was that so bad, to want a distraction?

She would try him again tomorrow she decided as she made a brief kiss-kiss sound down the line to end the conversation. James was much too busy to be worried, but Michael would understand. It seemed to her he made such wise suggestions. The words, 'it's for you to judge Kate…' had swirled around in her head since their last meeting, and she wanted encouragement for having made a good start.

She slept fitfully, wondering, as she showered the next morning in the cramped bathroom, how James would have got on in this small hotel. Not for him cheap tiles with dodgy grouting, leaky tap or plastic curtain! His was a world of five star sleep-overs, sleek conference rooms and executive airport lounges, and it was little wonder he had become more and more removed from the sort of everyday life that other mortals faced. She did not grudge him this, he worked so hard and was always the first to don boots and tramp in the mud with the men around the farm at home… but that was different.

In a man's environment, he rarely had to deal with small but immediate crises, crippling self doubt, uncertainty and worry, encountered every day by women all over the land. Not for him the struggle to be there for the children, the old, their nearest and dearest, neighbours – all in order to preserve that precious status quo on which so many families depend. How many men out there could begin to understand the fragility of that other small domestic sphere and that it was the women who kept it all together in their efforts to make the world a better place? And couldn't James and other husbands or partners like him, see that juggling balls to preserve a reasonable balance at home came at a price for the juggler? And that reassurance and the odd word of praise came pretty high on their list of priorities?

With these thoughts uppermost in her mind, she dialled Mima Macrae far away by Fort William, hoping she was early enough to catch her boys before they were bundled into the school bus. The phone was picked up by Charlie himself and she found herself breaking into a wide smile of relief as she heard his breathless voice, 'Mum! I knew it was you! How are you? Where are you? What's the weather like! It's pouring here!' The words came tumbling out and she could see him now, in the much disliked school trousers, striped red tie hanging crooked, hair roughed up and spiky. 'Yep, Maurie's fine – he's out with Badger, you know – Mima's spaniel! – he'd better hurry, we're going to be late. Shall I call him?'

Some high pitched yelling, some closer scuffling sounds, dog and boy, squeaks on the floor and then an even more breathless voice as her younger son came on the line. 'Yeah, great, Mum, we're having a great time! Mima took us ten-pin bowling last night, we're going to the slide pool tonight! I miss you!'

The parting shot was so cheerful, she had to laugh as she put the phone down and picked up her make-up bag. She always wore some carefully smudged eyeliner and mascara, but hesitated as today, she found herself playing around with a box of eye shadow. Leah would be tied up with her Dutch partners but had arranged for her to meet up at midday with Benjie and Roger for a drink at the Anchor. Did she really need that blue, or the soft blusher for a casual appointment with two gays? And what about afterwards?

She jumped as her mobile suddenly buzzed out its familiar tune, slithering across the polished surface of the bedside table. As she retrieved it, the screen told her it was Michael Hargreaves. Was he simply responding as part of his job or did he know it was her? Why was her heart racing now as she determined she would let him speak first?

'Kate?' So he did know. 'Are you OK?'

She was suddenly overwhelmed with relief to hear his voice. 'Hi,' she said, making an effort to keep her voice light and breezy, 'Yes, I'm fine.'

'You rang, sorry I wasn't here – I had early morning communion to take.'

How foolish, she hadn't thought of that – not the best time to ring a budding priest. 'Oh yes, yes, of course.'

'Did you – er – want to discuss anything? Is it all going the way you want?'

'Well, there's a lot to tell,' she ventured. 'In fact, masses. I rather hoped, that is – if you could bear it – I could … er … fill you in a little?'

'I'm a bit tied up until four,' he said, 'But how about taking the boat out later on this afternoon? I'd love a lesson from you on how to manoeuver the thing, that is – if you felt inclined?'

Safety in a small powerboat, she thought immediately. Too uncomfy and exposed for kissing, and all hands on deck rather than anywhere else, sounding horribly practical. He's shrewd, our priest. 'Sure,' she said, feeling oddly disappointed and yet relieved at the same time. 'What sort of time did you have in mind?'

'How about four thirty?' said Michael. 'That's my time off for today. It changes like the wind, but hopefully it's a good time for the sea. It looks nice and calm right now and you can tell me all your news once I've learned to master the controls.'

'Fine,' she said and meant it. Carefully, she applied a soft blue colour to her eyelids and smudged in some darker beige behind. After adding the usual mascara, she felt ready to face the day.

Arriving at the cottage in the inevitable whirl of dust, Kate found Michael already outside, dressed in tee-shirt and baggy shorts with a hamper at his feet. Hoisting this to his shoulder got him out of the usual Portuguese greeting of a kiss on both cheeks, and he nodded pleasantly to Kate – checking first if she wanted to use the bathroom before locking up the front door.

'Don't worry about towels and extra sweaters and things,' he said, escorting her to the path that ran round the back of the house to the beach below, 'I've got all that here, plus some bottled water, cans of Coke and some gingerbread if you get hungry. One of the ladies of the parish seems determined to make me fat, I get a cake offering almost every day!'

'You're being well looked after, then,' said Kate, following meekly behind as he navigated the way down a steep incline. There was a rickety hand-rail that ran some of the way, but at the top of a flight of ancient looking wooden steps, there was nothing but tufts of thrift and prickly gorse to grab if one lost one's balance.

'Hang on a minute,' called Michael glancing round. 'I'll dump this at the bottom of the rocks and come back for you – it can be damn slippy.'

Kate was having none of it. If she was to teach him to handle a power-boat, it was important to banish the image of the frail needy female, as quickly as possible. Instead, she speeded up her stride and overtook him just before he reached the top step. 'Careful!' he warned, clearly surprised.

'I'm always careful when approaching the sea,' she said firmly. 'You learn a certain discipline long before they let you loose in a boat, so don't worry about me.'

She was down the steps in an instant, and as she turned to put out a helping hand for the hamper, she had the satisfaction of seeing Michael's greenish eyes open in surprise and could there be a glimpse of respect? 'I take it this is the boat,' she said matter-of-factly sweeping a long leg over the painted red bulwark and noting the name *La Bella* as she climbed in. It had been a needless question not really deserving of an answer because there was nothing else there in the tiny cove. It was obvious someone had only recently folded up the dew-damp tarpaulin which had covered it here in the lee of the rocks and which now lay drying in the sun. In silence she inspected the dashboard and controls and finally added, 'Looks OK, anyway. I presume you have the key?'

'Yes, ma'am,' he said in a mock American accent, 'to both questions.'

She wanted to smile, but desisted. He had set the scene the way he had greeted her and she was not going to try to woo him now by fluttering her eyelashes and breaking into the sort of smile that threw out all those subconscious signals that led to other things. That would merely be giving in to her femininity and if he could be disciplined, then so could she.

She nodded and turned her back to examine the boat more closely. It was a very average sort of power-boat, quite well maintained and no more than 21 foot in length. It was the perfect model, she decided, for your average punter; neat and handy and about five years old. The horsepower was modest enough not to get into trouble, but sufficient to enjoy a good run down the coast and back again before any weather set in. Its handling would hardly require a 'lesson' as such, but she could see that to a complete novice, knowing what button did what and which was the throttle and which the clutch could be daunting to someone without experience. Nevertheless, to your average sports person, particularly with a brain to boot, it would soon become obvious that once one had the hang of balancing the thing, there'd be little case for lessons, more a question of putting mileage or rather, knots, on the clock. The first prerogative was about acquiring the confidence to manoeuvre and to understand how to take the waves, especially on an approaching tide; bringing the boat ashore could be a little more tricky, but again most of it would be common sense.

'Have you ever ridden a horse?' said Kate, climbing back over the side and standing squarely to face up to him in the sand, glad of her thick trainers and the fact she'd tied them up firmly.

'No, glad to say not!' he replied, 'Are you teasing me Kate?'

'Not at all,' she responded. 'It's well known people who have good hands with a horse, generally do well on the ocean. It's all about power and balance and knowing how to channel the two.'

'One lives and learns,' he was smiling broadly, 'So having started off with that disadvantage, are you still OK about teaching me?'

'Of course,' she said lightly, and then more pointedly, 'And that's why I've come!'

Having got that out of the way, they proceeded to pull the slim vessel over and beyond her mooring of planked runners and down the beach. The land sloped away sharply and it was not very difficult. 'It's going to be hell to bring her up again,' remarked Kate.

'Don't worry, I've thought of that, there's a Portuguese guy who tends the garden at the big house as well as maintaining the boat. I've got his mobile and he said to give him a ring when we got back and needed a hand.'

A chaperone! thought Kate. Safety in numbers! He's clearly thought this all out…oh well.

The thought of their cosy conversation was slipping away and she felt a little cheated as the first wave came lapping up and with one final push, they heaved La Bella afloat and pulled themselves in. ' Sit in the middle,' she commanded 'and watch what I do to get her started'.

The engine ticked over sweet as a bird, and she breathed a sigh of relief as she brought it up to a roar and the smoky smell of diesel pricked their nostrils and made them run. It was obvious this gardening guy had looked after the engine and whilst La Bella might have looked even more 'bella' with a new coat of paint, it was good to know the main things actually worked. Easily, she turned the pointed nose into the waves and they were off, bumping at first in staccato manner against the tide, then gathering speed and starting to soar.

'I'd like to get the feel of her before I start any instruction,' she shouted back to Michael, her voice shrill above the resounding slap of water on the hull, her eyes fixed on the controls. Her blonde hair had taken off in the breeze, one moment standing up like a precarious golden halo, a second later whipping her ears. 'It's windier out here than I thought,' she called, reaching up with one slim arm to strangle it all together into a small cotton scrunchy. There was something vulnerable, he thought, about the soft flesh between her armpit and the underside of her sleeveless vest and he gripped the hard seat with his hands and determined to keep his gaze on the horizon.

'If you watch what I'm doing…' Goddamit, he thought, could she feel where his eyes were? '…you'll start to get a feel of when to act. Then you'll be in a better position to understand once I start explaining. Follow where my hands are! Lean in to me and look over my shoulder!'

The words were out before she realised the possible implication. The last time he'd looked over her shoulder was when he'd kissed her at the door, but hopefully he wouldn't notice. Her feet wriggled in the wet trainers and she had planned to take them off and let them dry in the sun, but decided against it. She did not want to catch his eye at this moment in time and even baring her feet might be seen as a sign of letting her guard down. This was a professional day for both of them; he had made her very aware of that the moment she'd arrived. Whilst she might talk to him a little about the visit to the villa towards the end of their trip, it would be to Michael the curate, not Michael the man who had caught her in his arms and made her heart leap.

They travelled in silence for a couple of knots and then she brought the boat parallel with the shore and started to head west. The white beach was now far away, the houses mere dots on the hillside and the big yellow cliffs of the Algarve coast seemed to intensify the depth and majesty of this ocean, surprisingly black and dense like thick olive oil now they were far away from the blue shallows. Kate shivered and pulled the proffered sweater over her head.

'The weather always catches you by surprise out here, I remember my mother saying. We all tend to think of the Algarve like a continuation of nearby Spain, but it's so clearly not. No balmy Mediterranean lake here! This is the big, wild Atlantic and it's cold and deep and can be very lonely.'

Michael was wrapping up too. He pulled on an old rugby sweater, whose faded feel immediately conjured up memories of sweat and pressure and the kind of physical activity in which he'd once delighted but seemed to have neglected of late. Now, here was an opportunity to be alive again. To throw away his books for a few hours and glory in God's amazing natural world … the Creation! The side of ministry we all forget, he thought. How could we? How neglectful! When it's all so awesome!

He felt elated by the sudden freedom, the relentless tugging of the wind, the sharpness of the air, the swish of the waves against the vessel as Kate let the engine idle before suggesting they changed places. Here, there was beauty and majesty all around – no beginning, no end, no Alpha or Omega. It was easy to imagine what drove the explorers on and on. They had to find where heaven meets earth, sea meets eternity. A timeless ocean – a place so vast, wild and uncharted – it made all their earthly worries, habits and ambitions seem meaningless and trivial. No wonder these men were prepared to risk all. Wow!

Carefully, they got up to swap places, swaying slightly to keep their feet as *La Bella* bucked over the bigger waves. Now seated behind him, intent, concentrated, Kate pulled her knees up to her chin, as she called out the different controls. But she was almost wasting her breath. He was a natural, diligently taking in the mechanics of it all; already aware of what was what and where each small knob or lever lay and in what position. Moreover, she sensed he had more than that, there was anticipation and an awareness of balance. Now all he needed was the confidence.

'It's just a question now of feel,' she said encouragingly, 'Back to what I meant when I mentioned horses. You have to feel your way, feel for when to increase the throttle, feel when to hold back. You know, you've got to be able to collect it all up and then let her go when you can feel her pushing against the groove.

'The other thing to watch is the tide. One can be happily following the coast and think one's holding a horizontal line, and then before you know it you've travelled further and further out without realising. Keep checking the shoreline and use your eyes! Get two landmarks in your sights.'

'I see what you mean,' he said. 'It can be deceptive, it all feels so great, so easy – you can't imagine anything going too wrong, but I hear what you say.'

They fell into an easy silence. Despite the disturbed memories of yesterday, Kate was feeling surprisingly at peace with herself. It was fun to have someone else drive the boat, which allowed her the luxury of leaning back and trailing her hand through the cool water, without having to focus on anything very much. She became aware that this was exactly what was wrong with her own life. That she never had *nothing* to do – nothing to think about – nothing to concern her. Always, there was something to be started, finished, got ready, be there for at a certain time, sort out, organise, do! She was a performing seal – always there for others, never having a moment, like this, for herself

And when she did think of herself it was always in relation to those others – principally her husband and children. Did she measure up? Do enough for them? Be all things to all men…the farm workers, the estate, her father? And maybe – just maybe – it was her concern for them and her lack of self-interest that had turned her into the neurotic mess she now felt herself to be. A stronger person would have been firmer – kicked all that self-doubting rubbish out of the window and concentrated on making space – for herself. She longed to tell Michael all this and to start again. But now was not the moment.

They continued peacefully along the coast, passing a small fleet of fishing boats heading for Portimão, for which Kate ordered a wide berth. 'They won't thank you for ruining their last catch of the day,' she replied in answer to his question about not trusting him. 'It's not like driving a car,' she added, 'There's plenty of lanes here for everyone provided you don't go really out to sea – then it all gets strict again with the big vessels, tankers and the like. Look, there's an empty beach, why don't we pull in close, rest the engine and have a swim.'

She stood over him, instructing as they bobbed on smaller waves and noted the shingle of a small shallow cove. 'Look, you can see the bottom now. With water as clean and pure as this, there shouldn't be a problem guessing exactly where the seabed lies. Eight to ten feet's probably ideal for taking a break and letting the boat stand.'

'Stand?' he said, 'is that what you call it?'

'No, the proper phrase is dropping anchor. But remember my mother was Portuguese and so she had certain little words which she thought described it nicely, but which other English people – particularly the sailing crowd – thought quite odd. They were her own inventions, of course, but they weren't to know that!'

He grinned at her, pleased with himself for arriving safely at this point; pleased with the fact Kate had been able to talk about her mother so dispassionately. It was talk of the sea and boats that had made this possible. This was the second time today she'd referred positively to her mother, no clouding of the memories with recrimination. 'Kate, you know, I think you ought to do this more often. Do you never sail or take a power boat out for fun in Scotland?'

'Too cold,' she said, and 'too essential. Don't forget every time I go to the mainland we have to get in a boat. It somehow takes all that fun side out of things.'

'That's a pity,' he said putting a towel round his waist as he stripped off his jeans. 'Maybe you should think about changing things.'

'What – change the weather or move to Portugal?'

'No, I mean – go off in a boat just for your personal pleasure. Around the islands or something, you're such a natural! It seems you waste your talent and since we've been out here, you've become a different person. It clearly suits you.'

'It's funny you should say that,' she said. 'We have friends who do sailing holidays right up the west coast and even up to Shetland and the Hebrides. I've often recommended them to shooting clients, but somehow never made time to go myself. We're always so busy at the farm.'

'You should make time,' he was struggling to climb into his swimming gear under a towel.

Kate was stripping off too. She'd had the forethought to wear a bikini under her clothes and laughingly pulled off her outer layers in a couple of swoops and dived straight into the water.

'That's better!' she cried, coming up for air at the side of the boat and clinging onto the tiny steel ladder. 'I guess you could be right…I'll think about it!' And with a whisk of her knotted blonde plait, she was gone, smooth and sure underwater as a seal.

Michael threw down the towel and pulled on his trunks. This over-modesty was silly and he felt annoyed with himself for not changing beforehand. He hadn't seriously believed he would make so much progress they'd be swimming off the boat. The whole thing was thrilling and a bit unnerving. Kate was a brilliant teacher, she'd been clear and careful in what she did, making it easy to copy. Diving in, the coldness of the water took his breath away. His first thought was to swim towards her, and catch her in his arms for warmth, refuge, love of life – he couldn't make up his mind about the motive – but he resisted. Instead, he forced himself to swim in the opposite direction round the starboard side and away from temptation. Out of the corner of his eye, he kept the anchored boat in view, safely bobbing in the bay.

The sheer velvet of the water was surprising. Here out of the wind, it felt voluptuous and all embracing, so different somehow from the thin, chemical feel of the swimming-pool at the *quinta* where he went of an evening, when the owner was away. The temptation to swim in the sea was of course overwhelming, but invariably he was running late with his church work and it was easier to head straight up the garden to the pool. Also, he was wary of going out too far alone. The big beaches where the tourists went were well attended by coastguards with flags that warned one when the tides were tricky. Here, in these small rocky inlets, there was nothing to tell you and the water could be deceptive. Michael knew he wasn't a strong enough swimmer to take too many chances and had frightened himself on his first day by going out beyond the surf and being unable to get back. In the end, he had given up struggling and let himself be carried by the current round the small peninsula from which he'd started, lucky to be washed up around the bay. A close shave and not one he would have cared to admit except to his Maker who he reckoned had given him a second chance.

He was back in the boat long before Kate. This gave him time to towel himself down and change. Had she stayed out longer on purpose? He wondered. She must be cold and weary by now and he felt bad he had made it so abundantly clear there was to be no close exchange between them with the body language all wrong. It was ridiculous really; they could still be friends and he must try to make it up to her. They could talk a bit on the boat, before restarting the engine and heading back. She'd been good coming out with him like this and he owed it to her to hear what had happened at the villa yesterday. It had been such a major thing for her to go there and he had promised after all. Dammit! – what kind of a priest was it, who wasn't there for the person he had promised to help?

As for that other thing, well – he could handle that too, surely? It wasn't as though he hadn't been prepared. Time and again, they'd been warned at theological college not to get sidetracked with other people's problems, confessions. There was the usual reference to the seedier broadsheets and how the British public had an appetite for 'Sunday stories' to match their love for sausages, bacon and eggs. How they revelled in a good scandal about vicars and sexy spinsters or priests and choirboys – even the great and the good. The thinking was it made the general population feel better about never going to church! Don't walk into that trap, lads, was how his own mentor had put it – no getting sucked in – unless of course, you want to be splashed all over someone's breakfast table! Keep yourself apart, pray for guidance, pray against temptation

When Kate swam back, he noticed with admiration she wasn't even breathless. She hauled herself into the boat, graceful, glistening and pink as she wrapped herself round in a huge blue towel which only served to heighten the flush in her cheeks, the sparkle of her eyes, elated and bright with achievement. 'That was marvellous,' she said 'I went further than I meant, but it's so calm here. I could have swum for ever!'

'Perfect conditions,' he agreed, 'I guess I couldn't have had a better day for my first run! It's not always so, though,' he was doling out a can of coke and some gingerbread. 'I got caught the other day.'

'On the receding tide?' she said.

He nodded, 'It can be tricky.'

'I'll bet,' said Kate, 'Mama would never let me swim unless the tide was coming in.'

They munched silently and finished the gingerbread. The evening sun was glinting on the prow of the boat and the water here in the little bay was smooth and silky. 'Did you want to talk?' asked Michael.

'I did,' she said, 'but funnily enough this afternoon's changed all that. I felt so disturbed yesterday, the villa was pretty vulgar and I kept seeing Buster's face everywhere, but my mother and father felt far away – and that cheered me up a lot. In fact since I've been out in the boat, only nice memories about them have come flooding back, so maybe it's best I go away with that and leave the analysis for another day. You see, I've got you to thank for that!'

'I'm really glad,' said Michael, 'I've been feeling a bit of a heel about things ...' he dropped his eyes and with the sun behind him, the long dark lashes shadowed his cheek and she thought how vulnerable he looked, 'Well – you know how it is. I felt I'd let you down and ... er ... one thing and another.'

'Don't worry,' she put out an impulsive hand and touched his bare knee. 'I guess we're both to blame, but now at least you know how to drive this boat and hopefully we can go for a spin again without either of us feeling guilty. Then we can have a nice dispassionate talk and put the world to rights!'

28

Portugal – 1973 to April 1974

As Benjie's toothache grew more acute over the next few weeks, it was decided that he, Howard and Leah should take a trip to Lisbon. Johanna had given them the name of her own dental surgeon – and they would combine the visit with some Christmas shopping. Howard, who would be footing Benjie's bill, was unenthusiastic from the start. Things changed, however, when Leah discovered there was a celebrated dermatologist who specialised in nervous allergies at the next door clinic to the dentist. Soon he was acting as if the whole expedition to the capital had been his idea in the first place.

Buster had elected not to come. In his own words, it was obvious someone had to stay behind – what with Leah's blessed geese, the dog and kitten to look after. Moreover, after six months on the waiting list, a date had finally been agreed with the only swimming pool firm in the Algarve. They were hoping to install the pool by April.

Leah was not sorry she was to go alone with the Boys. She was back on her pills which had helped push the incident in the tub to the furthest recesses of her mind, virtually convincing herself again that Buster's explanation was plausible. Despite all this, she needed a break. Recently she had found the house oppressive, especially when the weather was bad and her husband was confined indoors. She agreed with Howard, it would be fun to feel a city sidewalk beneath her feet again, and the Lisbon stores were reputedly sumptuous.

The appointment with one Dr Faustino Angelo de Serra, who boasted more letters after his name than in it, had been arranged well in advance. Benjie was to reconfirm by telephone, two days before. Thus, one sparkling morning early in December, Benjie set off in the Fiat, to make his trunk call from the post office in town. The fact they still did not have a telephone of their own was turning out to be a blessing in disguise. Unknown to his partner, Benjie had other missions to accomplish.

As he waited for the elderly telephonist to connect him to Lisbon, Benjie was fretful. Not only was the pain in his jaw getting him down, he also bore a load of guilt on his shoulders. The time was drawing near but there'd been no word from Roger Grafton about the return of the figurine. It must be very close to vacation time, but everything had gone strangely quiet.

Some weeks before Benjie had leased a numbered collection box at the post office. Whenever he was able to snatch the opportunity, he would unlock the box with his little metal key to inspect its contents. These secret sallies forth had been fun at first, fraught as they were with daring and danger. Invariably, he had been rewarded with a letter, its contents as delicious as the forbidden fruit it represented in Benjie's mind.

There'd been enthusiastic descriptions of Roger smuggling the figurine back to his rooms at college, real cloak and dagger stuff, his first encounter at the pawn-shop, the bartering, haggling, and eventually – Benjie had sighed with relief – successful negotiations. He had exulted when Roger wrote of repaying the pusher, getting rid of him once and for all, and giving up the 'weed'. Then came the jubilant letter when the promised birthday money had arrived and how without further ado, he'd been able to retrieve the piece of Dresden and take it safely back to college. Each letter had shone with his undying affection and gratitude, the words transforming Benjie into a giant amongst men, ten foot tall, a saviour!

Then had come the lapse. No letter, no grateful words, nothing! Benjie mused over it moodily. Of course no news could be good news … but, there was this feeling of unease. It seemed so out of character.

The telephonist interrupted his thoughts with frantic hand signals behind the glass. The call to Lisbon was through. Benjie darted into a cramped booth of old wood and brown cracking paint and picked up the receiver. It was hard to keep his voice normal as he breathed in stale tobacco combined with the reek of garlic. Fortunately, Dr Serra's secretary spoke good English. With both appointment and time confirmed, he came out thankfully to confront his private mail box in a long row with several others.

As he delved into in his jeans pocket for the small hard key, he became aware of another man, moving up beside him and doing the same thing. So what? This had happened before and there were several boxes. Nonetheless, it unnerved him. He kept his eyes front – one mustn't be furtive – that *would* attract attention. Boldly, he inserted his key, turned it and yanked the box open. His companion did the same. Some familiar gesture must have penetrated his peripheral vision. He jerked his head up. His companion did the same. He spoke out loud – he couldn't help it – 'Buster!'

'Benjie! What are you doing here?'

There was a nasty silence. Buster was the first to recover. He shoved what looked like a postcard into his jacket, then turned to Benjie with an amiable grin. 'I guess you could say 'caught in the act', eh?'

Benjie coughed, uncertain what to do. The flapdoor of his box hung open to reveal a slim blue airletter. It would arrive today of all days! He made a silent oath and waited for Buster to move away, but Buster stood immobile. 'I should take that out of there, if I were you,' he remarked. 'If you stand there gawping, you'll alert the whole of Santa Felicia. The last thing you want – surely?'

Benjie removed the letter and shut the spring door with a snap. 'That's the way!' mocked Buster, a large grin spreading across his face.

Benjie hurried out into the December sunshine, while Buster fell into step beside him. 'Now hold it, Buster!' Having failed to shrug him off, he swung on his house-mate violently. 'You're going to have to forget about this. I want none of your fancy jokes played at my expense, no chance remarks, nothing! I know you've got a twisted sense of humour, Buster Bloomfield, but this …' his voice had risen to a nervous pitch, '… this time I want to play no part in it. Do you hear me? No part, whatever!'

Buster looked at him sideways. 'You're still attracting attention, you know. Calm down! Whoever said I was going to split, sonny-boy? Not me! There's only one way I'd find myself telling Howard about that cosy little pigeon-hole – can't you guess?'

'What would that be?' said Benjie, relief, like a rush of water, sweeping over him.

'I think you already know the answer to that one – it's hardly rocket science,' said Buster. 'It would be such a shame to upset a happy household. Let's just leave it at that. I'm sure you agree in principle.'

Benjie did. Buster had as good as confessed his own guilt and it didn't take a genius to work out the cause was likely to be Catalina McKay. What a god-send, thought Benjie – who would have thought? He knew Buster had a massive crush, but things must have gone further than they'd realised. For Leah's bosom friend to be writing secretly, and without Leah's knowledge begged the question – why? He began to think their life in the sun was becoming more complicated by the moment.

They parted company not unwillingly. Benjie was glad of the refuge of the little Fiat which he'd parked in the shade of the acacia trees. He wondered if Buster had guessed about Roger. Nervousness overtook him again as he slit the letter open with a nail file, '*Christchurch, Oxford, December 8th, 1973. 'My Dear Benjie…*' Even before he took in the next scrawled paragraph, he was filled with a sense of premonition. Coldly, it worked its way up his gut, and he knew it was bad news. The knowledge made him shiver. Forgetting his toothache, he read on:

'*… You must think I'm an utter heel. Indeed, I feel like one and it's unforgivable of me not to have written before. I enjoyed your last letter so much, but for the past two weeks there've been so many lectures and essays, I've not had a moment. The exams come at the beginning of next term and if I'm not prepared, it will be curtains. I didn't do so well last summer after all – too much fun, hash and not enough work – and now I'm paying the price.*

'*Another reason for not writing was how to sort out the mess in which I now find myself. I was all set to fly back to Faro in three days' time, and was counting the days. Then, last week Dad rang to say he and Mum have decided to come back to England this year for Christmas…*' Benjie's heart missed a beat – what a foolish risk he'd taken… '*Surprise, surprise… we're now off to the ancestral pile I told you about – for the whole hols. It'll be kind of fun, hunt balls, parties and so on, but I'll miss you.*

'*I tried to get hold of a friend from Albufeira, to bring the figurine instead of me. Then thought about it. He likes his drink. What if he has one too many beers on the plane and drops the parcel on the tarmac? Could happen.*'

Benjie felt sick. He could just see Howard's face when the shit hit the fan and the papers got hold of the story. '*Customs officer retrieves damaged ancient porcelain, one of two surviving pieces in the world… mysteriously broken by rogue handler at Faro airport… how did it come into his hands? Read tomorrow's edition for update on this fascinating mystery…*' The story could run and run!

'*I decided you'd probably prefer I held on to it than risk such a fate.*' Too right! '*So here the holly girl sits safely, only – in the wrong country. But you can rest assured, I will be out at Easter – wild horses wouldn't stop me. Can you wait that long? I simply can't see a way round it otherwise.*

'I feel so badly about all this. Obviously, posting is out of the question. I'll be down in Gloucestershire after 13th December, my address: c/o Sir Arthur Grafton, Bute Park, Little Martin, Glos.

'I just hope this won't affect you too much and that if I don't hear you'll have a really Happy Xmas. Affectionately yours, Roger.'

'A Happy Christmas!' expostulated Benjie, 'a *happy* Christmas! I'll probably have a nervous breakdown before Christmas even gets started.

Catalina was in her element. They'd already been in England ten days, and finally the exhibition was almost upon them. A chauffeur driven car, courtesy of the gallery, had been sent to pick her up from the house in Richmond where they were staying. Now she was on her way up to London's West End, looking and feeling as if she owned the world.

Only that morning, before he left for the gallery to make last minute adjustments for tonight's preview, Jock had confided, 'This show, my darling, will make or break us. If it's not an even bigger success than the other years, I might as well go out and walk under a bus. At least then you and Katy would have the life insurance!'

Such a ridiculous thought! She smiled to herself at the memory of it as she adjusted a diamond earring and sat back against the rich tan leather of the Rolls Bentley. Hmmm! How she loved that smell of expensive upholstery! As for Jock's exhibitions, they were always a success: the critics found him quirky, but the public adored him. She had no doubts. The traffic was moving slowly; it was that time in the evening, but she did not care. It was pleasant to watch English surburbia unfold itself before being engulfed by the strong arms of the spreading metropolis. Over Hammersmith fly-over…she caught her breath a little …smarter cars were joining them, Jags, other Bentleys, other Rolls, the odd E-type, mothlike MGs, all heading like her for somewhere sophisticated, somewhere chic in central London.

As they squeezed into the Cromwell Road edging their way towards Knightsbridge, the lights became brighter, the buildings taller, the porticos more impressive. She felt the old familiar thrill at the throb, the pulse of London, as they entered that elegant hub. For her, it would always be the world's most exciting city. The usual cluster of lights at the turn-off for Beauchamp Place had slowed progress; by the Hyde Park Hotel, it would be the inevitable jam. Red, amber, green – stop-go; go-stop – continuously on five different sets, all designed to filter backwards, to narrow the overflowing lanes, as they passed Harrods.

Pavements surged. People were entering small bars and brasseries, businessmen impeccable in their pinstripes, alone or sneaking a quick drink with the secretary before going home. Others, more permanently coupled, were bustling to pre-dinner cocktails or the theatre. She craned her neck backwards, to catch a glimpse of the great store, which had been blocked out by a van. It stood resolute having survived that awful bomb – glittering unashamedly – a top-heavy ship crowning it over a sea of lesser vessels, the royal coat of arms shining in the lamplight.

They would soon be there. She hugged her thoughts to her and felt the dimples twinkle in her cheeks. She was glad she had chosen to wear the black chiffon. She had bought three possible dresses for this opening night, thrilled by the generous cheque Jock had handed over yesterday when she announced she had nothing to wear. After changing her mind a dozen times or more, she had finally settled for the black. It was by the young designer Zandra Rhodes and there was an amazing ruffle cut on the bias across the skirt, so you could see her knee and a daring slice of thigh if she sat cross-legged. Slimming and alluring, the dress had stood a rigorous testing as she stood in front of the mirror to examine it from every angle. Impulsive by nature, but rarely with clothes, in Mrs Jock McKay most couturiers recognised a very discriminating client.

And so tonight, Catalina was pleased. With her long dark hair coiled high on her head, she knew she would make an entrance the moment she entered the gallery. It was not her party, so she would arrive a little late. That was expected. Jock's patron would welcome the guests, she would create the buzz. Catalina was well aware that every eye would be on her, both men and women, and she relished the thought. Tonight, the world was her oyster. She, Catalina McKay could have anything or anyone she pleased.

As they entered Sloane Street and began the slow, halting trawl southwards towards the river, she thought again of the telegram. It had arrived at the post office this morning and now lay neatly folded and tucked away in her miniscule evening bag. The knowledge it was safely there only confirmed her power and her potency. What were the exact words? She could not resist taking one more look at it. She prised it out of its hiding place and read once more the message it contained – Buster's message – the words as gauche and as simple as the man himself. It made her smile how he had evaded a planned trip to Lisbon and was to have the house to himself for a few days.

He had asked her to ring him at the Maritimo tomorrow and she wondered how and to where she would slip away for this secret assignment. Perhaps the Savoy – she might as well conduct this affair in comfort – or perhaps the Dorchester – but no, it would have to be nearer the gallery, so maybe that nice new hotel, the Lowndes, hardly a taxi ride away.

Well, she had plenty of time to work it out … she thrust the cable back into her bag and the elation came bubbling up inside her again, turning the corners of her mouth up. Of course, so many of her future plans depended on tonight. As Jock had said, it was make or break time … but he didn't realise that for her that meant in more ways than one. She pulled her silver fox wrap a little closer about her and gave herself a little hug of excitement.

Jock McKay allowed himself a slug of neat Scotch as he stood back and took a final look at the forty-odd pictures he had produced over the last two years. It was the first time he had found himself alone in the room all day and it was a strange sensation. To be alone with his own personality and that of his pictures seemed a doubtful privilege. He reckoned he deserved the drink.

The gallery was comprised of small but expensive premises. Tastefully laid out on the corner of a busy road to one side and a quiet mews to the other, it lay just south of Sloane Square not far from the Chelsea Hospital. The neat three-storey building was owned jointly by the senior partner of a famous brewing concern and an extremely wealthy lady collector of modern art, Emma Cootes. Mrs Cootes, a Canadian by birth, was by far the most influential of the two, which was why McKay had made it his business to get to know her well, when they first met over a decade ago. Widowed back in the '50s, Mrs Cootes had been a serious collector of McKay's work from the very beginning. It was well-known in her privileged circle that she doted on the artist and called him her *protégé*. Although she was probably no older than he, he still referred to her, in public at least, as Mrs Cootes, and she to him as 'my Boy'.

As far as he knew, he was the only artist in London to exhibit his work there completely free of charge and he was quietly grateful. When, at the end of each viewing, other artists received a mere balance after all expenses and every commission had been accounted for, the only deductions made for him were for catering and drinks at the cocktail party. Even the artwork for the carefully laid out catalogue was sponsored by Mrs Cootes. He picked one up – works of art in themselves, they, like everything else in the gallery, were in exquisite taste. His pictures were too expensive to display any price tag – according to Mrs Cootes, that would be much too vulgar. Instead, a list of figures lay in a separate folder on top of a grand Baroque desk near the door. All an enquirer had to do was match the number to the title of each work and all was revealed.

Once the preview got under way, the imposing desk would be monitored by an equally imposing debutante chosen by Mrs Cootes especially for the occasion. Mrs Cootes' debs were well-known in art circles. The 'deb of the year' was usually snubbed by his patron as being too pretty or pleased with herself for such a role. 'We don't exactly want them detracting from your paintings, now do we, my Boy?' she would say. She also disdained those who were attending art college, 'Artsy-fartsy won't sell pics, dear Boy... we need someone with a head on her!' Normally a bright young thing would be produced, someone trusted to make intelligent remarks about the range of work on display, point out the investment potential, advise on export procedures and so on. McKay shrank from these matters, glad to have them taken care of.

Nevertheless, he had always viewed these clever-clogs creatures with some trepidation. Not only was it up to them to answer questions nicely, it required some considerable tact to make the four-figure price seem a mere trifle. Up until now, Mrs Cootes had never let him down with her choice of young woman, but he was always afraid there might be a first time. He'd often thought Catalina would be the best person to fill such a role: she could be very persuasive. Unfortunately, no-one would hear of it.

He polished off his Scotch and was about to pour himself another for luck, when the street door was thrown open and his patroness herself floated in. She reminded him of a large fluttering moth in an amazing creation of pale beige and lavender silk, with matching ostrich feathers that bobbed and beckoned over a beaming face.

'My dear, *dear* Boy!' She bore down on him with an elaborate gesture of her winged arms. For a moment the material got caught up on his top button as she clasped him to her scented bosom, but he managed to unhook it before she stepped back to present him with her choice for the evening, 'my *favourite* deb, Miss Pandora Aitkenhead!' who followed in her wake. Dutifully, he went to shake her hand, but at that moment his stiffly-laundered collar caught his Adam's apple, which threw him off balance. He tried again but instead of returning the compliment, she merely tilted her head and gave a curt nod, so that four inches of chestnut fringe obliterated her eyes. As she turned to settle herself at the desk, he noticed her hair was as short at the back as it was long in front.

'Pandora adores your work, dear Boy,' oozed Mrs Cootes, 'ask her to name twenty of your paintings and she'll rattle them off straightaway, giving the year and everything! Such a clever gal! That's why we're so-oo lucky she could come and join us this evening.' Pandora stared up at him out of a pair of sharp green eyes that looked altogether too close together for comfort. Having decided she was about the most unfeminine girl he'd ever had the misfortune to meet, with her tall, ungainly body and intimidating air, McKay looked away. Deep in his heart of hearts he'd already decided the exhibition hadn't a chance and went to pour himself another scotch.

It was almost time for the party to begin when the senior partner of the brewing firm, a red-faced colonel, arrived. He was closely followed by Catalina, who had been dropped off by her chauffeured limo. Mrs Cootes and Catalina had never hit it off, but fortunately Colonel Amory adored her and proudly led her in on his arm, pleasing those members of the press who had rolled up to snatch some early pictures.

'Perfect timing, my love,' said her husband.

'Hello, darling!' she bubbled back up at him, flushed and radiant with health and energy. 'Goodness, don't you look smart! I hardly recognize you.'

McKay's face softened momentarily as he in turn admired his wife and her dress. It was only as he bent to kiss her, he noticed that *she'd* noticed he was back on the scotch.

'And who's this?' said Catalina, determined not to let things show as she went in search of a catalogue. 'I don't think we've met before?'

'We haven't, I'm Pandora,' came the gruff retort. 'Mrs Cootes asked me to come because I'm an expert on McKays.'

'*Mae santissima…*' breathed Catalina in an amused voice, '…how absolutely splendid! I'll look forward to your advice then – you see I'm only the wife!'

'I know,' said Mrs Cootes' deb, the irony lost on her as she adjusted an article worn round her long, thin neck, that closely resembled a lavatory chain. Silence followed. To Catalina's immense annoyance, she realised she'd been dismissed.

She wandered back to her husband. 'How lovely it all looks,' she said. 'I know it's going to be a huge success, darling, so there's no need to look so worried. Only go easy on the drink, please… And, oh Jock – I do wish they'd chosen a more *simpatica* girl for the desk. The last one was sweet.'

'I know,' McKay said gloomily, 'this one's a real cow. I hope Mrs Cootes knows what she's up to.'

People started to arrive and it was not long before the gallery was bulging to the point of bursting with a handsome complement of the more illustrious names from London's art and business world as well as the usual *glitterati* from those of entertainment, sport and politics. Mrs Cootes' address book read like *Who's Who*, and McKay soon cheered up as he found himself being congratulated by the Home Secretary, whilst Adam Faith, the pop star, told him how his red landscape from the last exhibition, now adorned his dining room in Tuscany. Old colleagues and admirers were queuing up to have a word, and he was turning this way and that, eager not to miss a question or a hint that might lead to a sale. Ever so often, out of the corner of his eye, he would catch a fleeting glimpse of his wife. Constantly surrounded by admiring men, her rippling laugh, unmistakable above the chink of champagne glasses, rang in his ears. Coquettish and inviting, Catalina was the best promoter any artist could hope for – if only she was at the door.

From time to time, he would crane his neck to see what was happening at the big desk. There was no sign of Pandora. Perhaps she had her head down, sorting out cheques. Unfortunately, his view was partially obliterated by huddles of people and clouds of cigar smoke. Flash bulbs were going off for Maggie Smith and Joanna Lumley who had just arrived, and he thought he spotted Michael Caine on the sidelines. It was always hard at these events to get a feel for whether the evening was just a cracking good drinks party or had turned into something more serious. All in good time…

After yet another blinding picture had been taken by a persistent young lady from the *Evening Standard*, he heard Mrs Cootes' voice in his ear, '*The Harlequin*'s just gone to the Greek ship-owner who bought so much the last time, dear Boy. And I think *Pale Puce* is attracting that nice Dr Coles from the slimming clinic in Harley Street. Keep your fingers crossed!'

As she wafted away, she did not hear him say 'Only these two? No more?'

By seven forty-five, the crowd was thinning and McKay began to feel uncomfortable. So far, he'd counted only two of the little red sales stars in evidence, and *Pale Puce* was still unmarked. So was *Hot Horizon, Chapel, Potentate, Unearthed* and a host of others that Mrs Cootes had called exceptional. He managed to escape from one of the Sundays' critics, a man he particularly disliked and who'd never had a good word to say about his work anyway. Nonchalantly, as though lost in thought, he proceeded to pace out the room, round a couple of corners to the long viewing wall at the rear and then back to the main room via an archway. By the time he had completed the whole circuit, he was trembling. He just could not believe it. He poured himself another Scotch, again without soda, marched straight over to Pandora Aitkenhead's desk and thumped it hard. She jerked her head up from the paperwork before her and this time the red fringe flew the other way. 'Yes?' she demanded.

'What the hell are you playing at?' growled McKay. 'You've had your head down this last hour or so. I've been watching you. Don't you realise people buy on the way out? If they see some disinterested, half-baked creature not even bothering to look up, smile or show some respect, they're going to change their minds pretty fast. It takes acknowledgement and a few pleasantries to create a spark of interest! Make people think about what they've just seen! Why, I've just had to bang on your desk to get any reaction!'

'I was going over the prices,' she said defiantly. 'My feeling was they were over the top.'

'It's not for you to decide that,' he flew at her. 'You're supposed to be the friendly face on the way out. The idea is to attract the customer's attention *before* they leave!'

'It's not *me* that attracts,' she replied, her green eyes starting to flash. 'It's the artist's work. Let's face it, Mr McKay, you're just not up to standard this year. It was obvious to me from the start.'

'I *beg* your pardon?' his voice was ice.

'I'm not the only one that's saying it. Everyone is. The critics and half the private collectors. They think you've lost your… well *you* know…your flair!'

McKay glared at her. She did not flinch but stared back, equally angry. There was nothing in her face but frankness and he realised why, right from the start, he had found her so unfeminine. You could read her face like an open book – there was no mystery, no mystique, no invitation to discover more.

'I believe you mean exactly what you say,' he said with wonder.

'I do.'

'Then fuck you!' he half whispered between clenched teeth and turned on his heel. The gallery door closed quietly after him.

It was another of those sparkling winter days that come so often after a rainy spell and seem to bite, sparkling and joyful, into the subdued sleepy climate that the southern provinces of Europe may enjoy in the run-up to Christmas.

'A perfect day for travelling,' pronounced Howard as he gave the bonnet of the little Fiat a final dust with a spotted hanky. 'I must admit I'm quite looking forward to this trip. Are you sure you've got the maps, Benjie?'

'Absolutely,' said Benjie, 'and I've even got our route marked out so you can navigate for me. Johanna Vincent says don't touch the coast, it's prettier but it takes forever. We're to take the central route, cutting through the hills and winding up to a place called Ourique. Then it's hills, hills, hills and then plains, plains, plains. About five hours in all; Johanna's up and down to Lisbon every other week, to restock her shop.'

'Come on, Leah!' said Howard, looking at his watch. 'We ought to get going now!'

'Coming!' she yelled from halfway up the wild bit.

'What the hell's she doing?'

'Saying goodbye to her precious geese,' grinned Buster who had emerged in his dressing-gown to see them off. He was full of bonhomie this morning and couldn't wait to get rid of them.

'Honey!' There was a scream from up the slope, 'Hon-eeeeeee!'

Aw shit, he thought, she's gone and hurt herself. We can't have her not going…

'What is it?' He was scrambling up the path with undue haste. Howard and Benjie looked at each other and sighed. A moment later, Leah came hurtling down the hillside full pelt. She flung her arms round her husband's neck, then rushed onwards in her headlong flight and grabbed Howard by the hand.

'I'm sorry,' she said breathlessly, her eyes shining. 'You'll have to excuse me from coming. I can't possibly now! I think Cleo's eggs are beginning to hatch! There's a dark shadow and a tiny, tiny crack on one shell. Oh, I just can't wait to see it all happen!'

'Well, that's that,' said Howard, half-relieved, going to take her suitcase out of the trunk.

'Hey – wait a minute!' said Buster, as he moved to the car and put out a restraining arm. 'Leah's out of her mind. Of course she can't change her plans. She needs this break.'

'Oh, honey,' Leah bubbled up at him. 'It's good of you to think of me, but of course I must stay. My place is here now. I'd no idea those goslings were due to hatch so soon. Carlos and I had figured on another four days at least.'

'Now, wait a minute,' Buster's voice was firm as he patted his wife's hand. 'This is what husbands are for! One, to lay down the law and see their wife has a good time; two, to take care of things while she's away. Don't think I don't know I've a bit of making up to do. Let me do this for you. I'm just as keen for the babies to hatch as you, but it's a long process, I'm told. You can't hold back just 'cause one decided to come early, now, can you?'

'Come on, come on,' said Howard, growing impatient. 'Make your minds up!'

'Oh dear, put like that, I don't know what to say,' said Leah. She had taken a double dose of her pills that morning, and felt less able to think on her feet than usual.

'I think he's right, Leah,' said Benjie, who had reasons of his own for wanting her distracting presence. If he had a rough time at the dentist's, he could count on Leah's sympathy. Then there was the guilt thing; he was so afraid his worry over the figurine might show on his face so anything to divert Howard from noticing would be welcome. 'I've heard these things can be really protracted. How many eggs are there – half a dozen, ten you say? Oh well then – you can be pretty sure they'll still be hatching when we get back. We're only away two nights!'

'Oh, I don't know what to say,' said Leah, wringing her hands.

'Come here!' Buster said. Very slowly he wrapped his arms round her and gave her a warm embrace. 'Go! Please! For my sake – you really need this break and it will mean a lot to me if you go. It's more important than you think … Please!'

Her face, already flushed, now softened. So he did care, after all.

'OK, honey,' she gave him a peck on the cheek. 'I'll do as you say.'

'Good, that's fixed it then,' said Buster releasing her quickly and helping her into the back of the car.

Howard climbed heavily into the front passenger seat while Benjie switched on the engine. It was cold and needed a lot of revving. 'Honey!' Leah was shouting above the din and trying to wind down the window.

'What's the problem now?' said Howard testily.

'I'm sorry,' said Leah, 'but I must just warn him what to do.'

'Switch the engine off, Benjie. I can't stand this noise!'

Leah craned her neck out of the back window. 'Look, promise you'll check on those eggs every few hours or so. It's very important someone keeps wetting them. This is the crucial stage and if they're allowed to dry out too much, the little ones may not have the strength to break out of their shells. Carlos knows, I've told him what to do!'

'Sure!' said Buster, 'we've been through all this before. Now don't go worrying, it'll all be fine.'

'Yeah, but promise me, honey, you'll keep checking?'

'Look, I've got it babe! I'll do everything you say.' He winked at Benjie, 'You'd better switch on again.'

Benjie did and a moment later, they were off. Buster waved to them until they had rounded the bend. Then he disappeared swiftly into the house.

'I wish he'd promised,' said Leah, more to herself than anyone else as they reached the main road. 'He said he'd do it – but he didn't *promise.*'

29

Buster dressed with care. Yesterday he had approached the manager at the Hotel Maritimo to explain that he was expecting an important business call from England. Since Casa Amarela was still waiting for a line, would it be in order to receive this at the hotel? 'With pleasure!' *Senhor* Ignacio meant it. The four Americans had been good patrons in the early days, and still frequently dropped by and spent money. He would happily offer *Senhor* Bloomfield the facility of his own office if it would help. Heroically, Buster said that would not be necessary but he would present himself at the front desk the next morning.

Despite burgeoning tourism, Santa Felicia still possessed remarkably few lines in the Portuguese cable and telegraphic network. Even in Faro, capital of the south, things were not much better. It could take from twenty minutes to a couple of hours to book or receive an international call since everything came via Lisbon and much depended on patience and luck. Buster was prepared for a long wait. He'd planned to arrive at eleven, which meant ten in England – the time suggested by Catalina who, knowing the system, hoped they might speak by midday. To while away the time, he would take a couple of *Time* magazines. Not much of a reader, this would be a good opportunity to catch up with current affairs. Not that he would be able to concentrate…too much else occupied his mind.

Even dressing that morning felt different – a frisson of excitement ran through his lean body as he perused his wardrobe. Finally, he disdained the usual polo shirt and bomber jacket and recklessly put on a long sleeved shirt and a silk cravat. He even made a little ceremony about tying it. And why not?…he asked the reflection in the mirror as he struggled into a navy blazer. This was a special occasion and he had no doubts in his mind about it. He could see Catalina now in her smart London hotel, dark, appealing, well-dressed as she charmed the reception staff and sat cross-legged and elegant in some luxury padded booth.

Nothing had been left to chance. Her first letter from England had been dynamite; she was prepared to commit to all he wanted – a permanent future together – but only under the terms she had sketchily outlined. He had not totally understood these, but what did it matter? The fact all he had ever dreamed of was suddenly within reach was enough. It made his head reel and his heart sing. Any feelings of guilt he had pushed hard to the farthest recesses of his mind; he knew in his heart Leah would be better off without him. They had both changed since coming to live in Europe and he could not be responsible for his own behaviour if they stayed together. He would be doing her a service, really.

There followed a shorter note, promising this call and the need to talk. Finally, yesterday's postcard confirmed the time and yet again, exhorted him to secrecy. He wondered if this was her way of testing him, before she took things further. *'Can't you see…. if J. were to guess in any way, he would immediately become high-handed and impossible. He might even remove me and the child from Santa Felicia once and for all. As for confronting him openly –as you originally wished – please, my darling, never think of such a thing again! He would either broadcast it abroad and make you a laughing-stock, or shoot you dead! I'm not joking… with J. there's no in between. Neither can he bear to lose face. For this reason he would never ever willingly let me go…'*

Buster had thought about those last lines many times and was beginning to admit to himself that perhaps she was right. After all, who was he to judge this proud Scottish guy? Catalina was right to say he hardly knew him, and he recorded only too well the night of their dance and the grim, inscrutable look in the other man's eyes. On the question of Leah, it was harder to be convinced. At first he had thought Leah would be a push-over. Since the episode in the bathroom, he wasn't so sure. He still did not know what to make of that night himself. He had been horribly drunk – that he knew – but something dark and primaeval had invaded his system; it had scared him more than he cared to admit.

He was reminded of those long-ago days in Korea: when in dealing with the enemy, instinct took over and the body acted independently of the mind. *Each man for himself.* They were scary times. He remembered scaling a slippery slope, cold, cut off from his mates, where a clod of earth, the smallest pebble could betray his position. There was no time to wait for orders, no time to think. You simply took your chance. And in that moment, you might find yourself doing something you'd never done before. Would never, ever have done in your right mind – only – you had no choice. And only after the event, did Buster Bloomfield find out he was capable of, indeed surprisingly efficient at, snuffing out the life of another human being.

Of course, the thing with Leah was different. It had started as a game, a kind of dare – to prove something to himself. But he knew, as he'd confessed, it had been close. Damned idiot that he was! The brutal fact was there'd been no warning bells, no anticipation, no thought of harming her. But it was she who had sparked something off within him. She'd gotten in his way, like those enemy troops… and it had just happened. And this time he did not have the excuse of fear and self-defence. He remembered the court-martial, when a bunch of them had been made to explain themselves over one rather questionable massacre. They'd got away with it. But what if he'd gone too far this time? It did not bear thinking about.

So Catalina was probably right. Give nothing away, don't rock the boat, protect his wife from the truth and hold your own counsel – at every turn. The only difference, Catalina's views on Leah were entirely at odds with his own. In his experience Leah could be stoic, determined and surprisingly tough. In Catalina's eyes, she was gentle and vulnerable. Only by limiting the damage to her 'dear friend' argued Catalina, could she bear to continue their liason.

It was such a selfless, noble letter, he had to read that part again – even although he felt she was misguided. *'I have studied Leah…'* Catalina had written… *'in a way that only a woman can, intuitive and insightful. Do not forget my Darling, that Leah and I have shared a close and rewarding friendship. It is because of my understanding of her as a woman, that I feel* by acting in the way I shall divulge to you, she will come out of this, unhurt, unscarred and able to cope…'

There had followed more protestations and concerns which he skipped over. He didn't need to be reminded about his wife's little traits, they'd annoyed him for too long… 'If however, my Darling, you were to act against my wishes by breaking the news to her suddenly or even with half-hints about the love we share, I will not be responsible for the consequences. I fear Leah might have a complete breakdown and this will upset me so much, I fear it would destroy all the pleasure in each other which we now share…'

OK, Catalina! He'd give in. Not a word. Not yet.

Because he knew it would please her, he had parked the car some distance away from the hotel, just off the main *praça*. Tongues might start wagging if it were observed boldly parked outside reception for half the day. '*Bom dia, Senhor*,' said the porter in his blue and gold uniform, opening the door with a respectful little bow. A blast of hot air rose up to meet him, as he sauntered into the foyer. There was no-one familiar about the place, only some very pale American tourists, hovering anxiously round their luggage. Buster nodded to them in a superior way, thinking, Jeez – I guess I once looked like that!

'*Bom dia, Senhor*,' beamed a plump man at reception, adding in English, 'It's Mr Bloomfield, is it not?'

'I'm expecting a telephone call from England some time this morning,' said Buster carefully, fingering his cravat. '*Senhor* Ignacio knows all about it.'

'Ah yes, I have the note here. Perhaps the *Senhor* would like to wait in the lobby or the bar? I will send a bell-boy as soon as the call comes through. We have a telephone kiosk available for our guests in both rooms.'

'*Obrigado*,' said Buster, walking on air.

He settled himself down in the lobby. Here again, there was no one he knew. Luck was with him all the way today. He opened his *Time* magazine and ordered a double *espresso*.

The call did not come through until just before one. Time had passed remarkably quickly. Coffee, a couple of beers and Buster had surprised himself with his restraint as he read his magazines from cover to cover. Nevertheless, he was on his feet before the bell-boy was halfway through the door, installing himself in the kiosk as the telephonist transferred the various plugs from her switchboard.

'Hello, hello!' his voice was breathless, eager. After an eternity, he heard her milky, honeyed tones coming through clearly, 'Buster?' His heart missed a beat.

She did not waste time with preliminaries. She came straight to the point and despite the adrenalin rush, he listened carefully as she described the events of last night. There was no hint of emotion and he admired her for it. She sounded like a reporter… 'a wonderful start'… all the right people came… and then – disaster! Only one picture actually paid for, another in pipeline, and that was all… in Colonel Amory's words 'all pretty dire' Exhibition scheduled to run another five days but everyone knows it's a flop… reviews, all except one, worse than imagined… appalling girl at desk did not help. Jock on verge of breakdown… drinking heavily, feels a failure…'For the first time in our marriage,' she concluded, 'he really needs me.' Buster's heart missed a beat. What could be coming next?

'There is no doubt I must not even think of leaving him until he has had sufficient time to recover.' She was talking in full sentences again, and he let his breath out; he'd held it all that time. 'But do not worry, my darling, the delay will be a good thing, as now we shall have time to plan things properly.'

To Hell with the planning, he thought, but she hadn't finished. 'Please, Buster, let us not be irresponsible about this. I have already started packing things away for our future together…' This was more hopeful. 'Before I left I sorted out my various clothes for Portugal, and then there's my English wardrobe too and my little luxuries. Remember, darling, I'm a creature of comfort,' it was the first time the tinkling laugh was allowed to escape, 'and I cannot do without those luxuries. Jock has always understood that, I hope you will too.'

'Yes, Catalina – I know, but it may be difficult at first.'

She laughed again and sounded amused, 'Not if we plan carefully, my darling. I see no reason why we may not arrange a little slice of paradise for ourselves –' he started – that sounded like Leah! He wished she hadn't chosen those particular words. She was still talking and her tone took on a more serious note – 'but it's important we organise ourselves properly and set things in motion while we have the time.'

'But Catalina –'

She brushed him aside, 'Obviously – as in my marriage, so in yours – we must have accumulated many lovely things which mean something special to us and us alone. There will have been things shared, and things which we regard as particularly ours – pictures maybe – I am thinking of my knick-knacks, ornaments, a special rug, artefacts from our travels, silver. Don't forget we shall need everything we can lay claim to, for our new life together.

'Of course,' she continued, 'I would never dream of depriving Jock of anything that he sees as 'family'; but things we bought together, and which I chose – well then, that's a little different. Wouldn't you agree? Jock would have no further use for them anyway, it must be the same with Leah. In such a case, we should feel no guilt about taking things. But still, we must preserve secrecy, my darling, until the day comes for the truth to be revealed. You do see that, my Buster, don't you?'

'Yes,' he said doubtfully.

Her voice lightened as she went on, 'It's so wonderful to me to have this strong, *strong* rock to lean on at such a time. My own personal Hercules! So solid, so protective! Now I've been thinking – could you do something for me, for us, darling Buster?'

He brightened, longing for activity. 'Just tell me!'

'I wondered if you could go on a tour of exploration,' she giggled. 'It would be best to go inland, off the tourist beat. Might you find us a disused barn or garage on some remote farm or holding, and rent it? Again, no one must know – there must be no inkling. Use a false name and give the owner a generous tip to keep his mouth shut. Do you think you could do that?'

'My Portuguese is non-existent, but I could give it a try. But Catalina, I don't really understand. Why?'

'My sweet darling, don't you see? This will be our very own hiding place. Our little store. Our Aladdin's Cave! Here, we can start to build together our own modest cache of possessions for our future life. We must have *somewhere* to put them, after all? It will be such an adventure. Taking things there and watching it grow! Who knows, we might even make love there… if it's cosy enough! Oh, how exciting this could be! Don't you think it's a brilliant idea?'

He could hear the catch in her voice, almost feel her breath at the end of the telephone.

'Where are you ringing from, Catalina?'

'The Lowndes hotel. It's beautiful – and discreet.'

'Oh Christ, I'm missing you,' he said. 'Santa Felicia's a morgue without you.'

'Poor Buster!' she said. 'Now – do you understand what you're going to do? So while I'm away, you'll have something to work on?'

'Yes, but –'

'But *what* Buster?'

'I dunno. Everything seems to be happening in such a different way from what I'd hoped. It all seems so drawn out, devious…'

'Buster!' The distance did not muffle the sharpness of her voice. 'I thought I'd explained all that. We're doing this to protect – them *and* us… If you wish to back out now, only say the word. I shall try not to hold it against you.'

'No, Catalina! No, darling, I'm sorry. It's just your way of thinking is so different. I like to tackle things head on, you know – up front, get them out of the way! I guess… I guess you're just much smarter, that's all.'

'Not smarter, Buster darling,' her voice was liquid honey again, 'just a woman, with a woman's instincts. A mother hen! I can't help planning and wanting to arrange a cosy nest for us both. It's in my make-up.'

Buster could think of no one less like a mother hen. 'I guess, I guess.'

The three-minute pips sounded for the sixth time in succession, and he heard her catch her breath. 'I must go,' she said. 'I'm due at the gallery in half an hour.'

'Catalina!' He could not bear that she was going to ring off without some intimacy. 'I love you, Catalina. I love you.'

'Me too, darling Buster, and do you know what?'

'What?' he felt suddenly breathless.

'We're coming back earlier than we thought. I'll be back in your arms by the New Year. Jock says we can't afford to stay longer. Since the preview – everything's changed.'

'Catalina! That's wonderful! You kept the best news to the end!"

'Of course,' she said demurely.

'Oh, honey…' He became aware he'd been clenching his free hand into his chest and had difficulty in releasing it to punch the air, '… I just can't wait.'

'Nor can I,' she said in a very measured voice, 'In fact, I'm counting the hours unteel I feel you inside me again. Goodbye!'

Without waiting for his gasping answer, she rang off. He stood there inside the booth, the sweat suddenly trickling off his brow and splashing onto the receiver. He had a sudden huge urge for sex, right there and then. The telephonist's voice came booming down the line, 'Have you finished your call, *Senhor*? Have you finished speaking?'

'Yeah,' he said faintly and put the receiver back on its hook.

He hurried through the marble foyer to escape out into the sunshine, only to have the under manager block his way. 'Ah! *Senhor* Bloomfield! your call from London came through, finally? Loud and clear I hope, we try our best here!'

Buster forced a smile, irritated to have his thoughts disturbed 'Oh – yeah, yes – thank you. It was fine. Very – er – kind of the hotel – to er – allow me...' He was already backing away when he was arrested by a soft voice in his ear.

'A call from London, eh?' How awfully exciting for you!' Maysie Vincent's sharp blue eyes were laughing into his, as she hung on the arm of the young man they'd seen her with in the *Cozinha Velha*.

'Oh! – er – hi there. I didn't see you. Yeah – well, better get going!' Buster coughed and found himself backing out of the impressive glass doors, dutifully held open by the uniformed porter. Damn these people, he thought as he felt Maysie's eyes following him all the way into the street. You can't as much fart in this place without the whole town knowing about it.

He went to collect his car. The adrenalin-charged excitement which had been rising in his groin now crept upward to grip his entire torso. He could feel the blood coursing under his skin and knew his reactions were now razor-sharp. Off flew the cloak of middle-age, suddenly he felt young again. So this was being in love! It was like being reborn.

Buster sped out of Santa Felicia, away from the main exit to the north, heading west. He drove focused and very fast. Soon he was rounding the familiar point, past the beach where Catalina and he had walked together, past the cliffs that harboured the cave where they had made love. He did not even look up as he swept by the eucalyptus at their own entrance, with its long twisting drive. There was no pleasure to be found in an empty house. Besides, he had business to attend. He was not sure how far he would have to go or how long it might take him, but he would not rest happy until he had succeeded with at least the first part of Catalina's plan.

The more he thought about it, the more he liked her daring. He wasn't convinced about removing things from Casa Amarela; that would need some thought. But he was all for buying the odd piece of furniture here and there. Gradually, he could fill their store with pretty things. The first purchase – he grinned to himself – would be a bed; a great big king-sized one. Now where were those black satin sheets he'd once bought Leah? They must have brought them over from the States, but they'd never used them since Leah announced she couldn't stand black. Buster had hoped they might spice up their sex life and had been disappointed when they were firmly put away; then typically, he'd forgotten.

Jeez! he remembered them now all right – he'd bet his bottom dollar Catalina would go for them in a big way too. He could see her pale olive body, arranged lynx-like, naked and inviting, in their folds. The feel of the satin beneath her butt would make her squiggle and squirm with delight. She'd love it! *To think she'll soon be mine, all mine...* It was hard to take in.

Whistling tunelessly, he drove on. Through small villages and hamlets, the car plunged sharp right away from the coast and onto an inland road heading for the Roman town of Silves and thence north to the Alentejo. He had never explored around these parts before and although he had a rough idea of where he was from his tourist map, it was all excitingly dramatic and unknown. He began to enjoy the drive. It was a beautiful day now that the sun was high, more like September than December.

The countryside grew greener and more verdant the further inland he went. Buster began to wonder why the coast had so charmed them, when really – these softly rolling hills and snug villages held captive and unsullied the real spirit of the Algarve. He had not passed another car since leaving the sea, but numerous mule waggons and donkey-carts had trundled past. He passed through a copse of stringy-barked gum trees and the tiny breeze made by his car set up a rustling all around which transposed the leaves into shoals of leaping silvery fish.

He looked at the dashboard; he had already driven twenty-five kilometres; soon he could start looking out for a lonely farm or smallholding. He was approaching a staggered crossroads. There were no signs, but a couple of sandy tracks intercepted the tarmac on either side and looked well worn by cart and what might have been tractor wheels. The left hand one wound up a hillside towards a couple of whitewashed, sailless windmills standing sentinel over a valley of fruit trees. Romantic, but too exposed, he decided. The other ran through fields of stubble to a cluster of cottages about half a kilometre away, from which a curl of smoke issued faintly. Nicely off the beaten track! He could just make out outbuildings behind the cottages, and decided to make these his goal.

He turned down the right hand lane and was surprised how well the Opel rode the pitted terrain. Dust rose up on either side as they lurched forward and he wound up the windows of his car. As he approached the cottages, a bevy of dogs came running toward him, barking and yapping. A miniature sandstorm enveloped them and then an even more motley flurry, this time of children, from the back of the dwellings. Before he had even left his car, a woman in a ragged headscarf with a baby in her arms appeared in the doorway of the first cottage. She eyed him with silent suspicion.

He smiled broadly, eager to reassure, and threaded his way through the huddle of animals and children to climb a whitewashed step into a scrap of garden. 'Bom dia, Senhora,' he managed to say, careful not to tread on the few frail sproutings that might have served for vegetables, scattered close to the path. She did not return his greeting but continued to stare with hostile eyes. He tried another smile but it had as little effect as the first. This wasn't so easy after all.

He had had the forethought to pop the Portuguese pocket dictionary they always kept in the car into his jacket and struggled for it now. His expression of friendship was making his face ache as he thumbed its pages, cursing himself the while for his inability to speak the language. The word for 'husband' might be useful. If he could talk to the man of the house, everyone might relax. He dropped his gaze for a moment…'hurricane, hurry, hurt – husband!…marido or esposo…' he read. The children were standing on tiptoe to peer over his shoulder and giggled amongst themselves. The dogs were now sniffing his legs; at least they had stopped their racket. Relieved but flustered, Buster shut the book with a bang and addressed himself again to the woman. He would try both words, 'Marido?' he asked, a clear question in his voice. 'Esposo?'

It had an effect. She shook her covered head and looked away. For the first time, Buster noticed she was clad in black. So many were, in the countryside. Oh Christ, he thought.

That war of theirs, Angola – or was it Mozambique? So many of them had lost loved ones…dammit, he thought – I would go and choose a goddarned widow.

He rummaged in the dictionary again, not looking forward to the prospect of negotiating with this miserable female. It wasn't his fault, after all. 'Barn?' What was the word for barn… 'barley, barm, barn…' – he seized on it… *celeiro, granja, estabulo* – shucks! Which one to try? He plumped for the most prounceable, it sounded like 'stable'. He cleared his throat and looked up – the word framed on his lips …*es-ta-bu-lo*…but the woman had gone! Disappeared with the baby back into the gloomy depths of the cottage behind. He was left alone at the top of the step. Feeling foolish and rather cross, he looked round for the kids. They too had disappeared but they were there all right. He spotted one, peeping round a corner grinning from ear to ear of its grimy little face.

This was useless, a sheer waste of time! He shoved the dictionary back into his jacket, got in the car and drove back the way he had come. He had had no idea the task Catalina had set him was going to prove so difficult. The countryside was so very different from the coast. Everyone there spoke English.

Catalina idly stirred up the dying embers of the evening fire with a poker and observed her husband light his sixth cigarette in succession with the butt end of the one before.

'This new smokeless fuel as they call it,' she complained, 'it gives out no heat at all. There's no heart to it like our fires at home, but I gather it's compulsory.'

He nodded. 'We're on the edge of London, they're getting very strict nowadays.'

'Well eet's horrible,' she said. Despite the central heating which she'd turned up full blast, she still felt the cold. The last few days in London, it had been only two or three degrees above freezing and everyone was talking of a white Christmas.

They had just got through the fourth day of the exhibition and only one more painting had been sold – a small harbour scene, the cheapest there. McKay had discussed the option of slashing the prices, but Mrs Cootes remained adamant. 'No way, my Boy. The moment you do that, you might as well give up for good. They'd never forgive you. No one likes an artist who has lost confidence in himself as well as his public. I'm afraid it's the economic climate to blame, there's a recession and everyone in the retail world's been badly affected. I was more or less prepared for this. But I had hoped with your luck and your charm, we might just get away with it.'

His luck! McKay had blanched at this but there'd been no point in disagreeing. Her mind was made up. It was all very well for Mrs Cootes, he thought now with some bitterness. She could afford to cope with the odd failure. He could not. It was as simple as that.

He had already made up his mind that they would leave the house in Richmond as soon as the exhibition was over and move down to Somerset to spend Christmas with his cousins. He had not the heart or the inclination to go to Scotland and it was already costing them too much money to stay in Richmond. Although they had the use of the house rent-free, there was the housekeeper to pay – a monstrous fifteen pounds a day – not so long ago it had been fifteen pounds a week. In addition there was Katy's 'holiday camp' – run by the local prep school, babysitting in the evening, and even food – all seemed double the price in this expensive part of the world.

Catalina had taken it surprisingly well when he had told her of his intentions to return to the Algarve as soon as Christmas was over. 'I know you'll miss the end of your gay London season, darling,' he'd said, 'and all the New Year parties and theatres, but for once we must be stringent and think about how to get though the year ahead. Thank God we at least have a home to return to and there's no need to worry about the cost of heating or transport. If needs be – I daresay we can live on fish for a year – there's always something going cheap in the market!'

Now as he dragged on his cigarette and gazed dolefully at Catalina's despised fire, he wondered what sort of reaction they'd get from their so-called friends in Santa Felicia. Word would soon get round that Jock's work was no longer fashionable and that the old days of Catalina's famous dinner-parties, and Jock's opening a bottle of bubbly at every opportunity, were gone for good.

He thought of those cranky people who lived in the yellow house on the hill and the wife who'd taken Catalina so possessively to her bosom. Would they still be so keen to know them? Would the husband still be as hotly in love with his lovely *Latina* once he noticed the droop of discontentment hovering around her lips? Perhaps if he, Jock, could no longer keep her supplied with the clothes and luxuries she constantly demanded, the besotted Bloomfield would. Then his little wife's mouth would turn up charmingly and the irresistible pouts and dimples return.

'Is Bloomfield as rich as they all say he is?' he spoke his thoughts out loud and Catalina stared at him in surprise.

'*What* did you say?'

He repeated the question and she looked thoughtful for a moment before answering. 'I believe they have a considerable fortune between them, but I always got the impression it was Leah's business rather than his, although I did hear something about joint accounts.'

'I see – then that way, it would be pretty easy for one or other of them to put their hands on the lot. One spouse would only need to hold the other's power of attorney, the kind of thing one often does in any form of land transaction, and they'd be away!'

'Er– yes, I suppose so,' she murmured and went back to her task of stirring some life into the fire.

He said no more on the subject but eventually announced his intention of going to bed. 'Aren't you coming?' he said, getting up to stretch wearily.

'I think I'll stay here a little longer,' she said. She looked like a small dark animal, curled up artistically on the pale sheepskin rug.

'All right, darling,' he kissed her absently on the top of her head and made his way upstairs. He called in on the way to see if Katy needed tucking in again. From the landing light he could see her eiderdown had slipped off the bed and he tiptoed in to retrieve it. Her hair was spread over the pillow like a thin gold cloud and she slept with her thumb in her mouth. He kissed her too and was just creeping quietly out again when she called him, 'Papa!'

'Hush, darling, go back to sleep!'

'I love you, Papa,' was all she said, then snuggled down again with a small contented sigh. He lingered there in the doorway, his face as soft as it had ever been. Within seconds, she was asleep again. In that silent moment, he longed to sleep the sleep of the innocent.

Buster had almost given up hope of ever fulfilling his mission as he drove up to the small farmhouse which stood on the edge of a scrubby looking wood.

It was almost dark and he was hungry and thirsty and very disillusioned with his ability to get around and make himself understood. He had never experienced any problem with the language barrier in Santa Felicia itself, or indeed anywhere along the coast. Even those who didn't speak English were marvellously adept at guesswork. Until now, it had never really occurred to him to try to learn more than a few words and he often laughed at his wife for trying so hard.

Here in this rural landscape, it was a different story. He had been amazed just how poor and primitive some of these people were but when he had produced his wallet in the hope of evoking some form of reaction, they treated him with real suspicion or an almost haughty indifference. It was all very puzzling.

He had tried at five different homesteads now, all without success. This, the sixth, would be the last for the day as he did not fancy exploring any more unmarked roads in the dark. Some ran on for hours without sight nor sound of human habitation, others fizzled out in fields, and there were a host of others where it was impossible to turn. These were the worst, where one was forced to reverse for yards between deep ditches or high banks.

The dwelling he was approaching now was the most unattainable of all he had seen to date. He had followed the lane for over two kilometres and would have given up long ago, had he found a place to turn. From down low in a sandy valley, he was relieved to see a clearing ahead and the double-storeyed farmhouse that rose up before him looked reasonably prosperous. He noted a cheerful glow of light behind half-shuttered windows so at least someone was at home. Buster's spirits lifted; he had a feeling about this one.

Stiff from driving, he clambered out of the car. Determined to take the upper hand, he strode up to a newly painted front door and rapped a knocker in the shape of a bull's head. Almost immediately, the door opened and a short, thickset man of about his own age stepped briskly into the gathering dusk. A pair of sharp brown eyes ran all over Buster and the car, and finally its owner allowed his face to relax into something resembling a smile. '*Sim?*' he encouraged.

This was better thought Buster. He started his well rehearsed patter; no point in beating about the bush. '*Estabulo?*' he began, '*Estabulo aqui?*'

The man looked at him with singular curiosity. 'You're Eenglish?'

Buster could hardly believe his ears. At last! 'I'm American,' he said eagerly.

'Ah!' said the man, knowingly.

'You really speak English?'

'Some English, some French, some German. I spend twelve years working een Canada.'

'Well that's a start,' said Buster, 'then perhaps you can help me.'

'Maybe yes, maybe no,' said the man. What ees you want?' His accent was an extraordinary mixture of west Canadian and Portuguese, but to Buster it was music in his ears.

'I'm looking for a barn,' said Buster, plunging straight in. 'A big barn – one I can hire – with a good, stout door on it. Do you have such a thing?'

'Barn?' said the man, looking puzzled.

'Yeah, you know, barn, shed – no better than that, a store – somewhere to lock up things.'

'Ah, yes…you mean an *armazem*!'

'Er no – not according to the translation, er… I think it's an *estabulo*?'

The man swept him aside with a wave of his arm, 'No, you mean *armazem*,' he said firmly. 'Yes, naturally, I have such a theeng. We farm here. In fact…' there was a note of pride in his voice … 'I have two,' he held up his fingers, '*dois armazems*. You wanna look, see?'

'Sure!' said Buster, amazed at his luck. Happily he followed the man round the back of the tall house. Here, they found themselves in a large, concrete yard with a huge open-fronted barn, a dozen or so rabbit hutches, an aviary and a hen coop. Outside a kennel, a thin, yellow dog dragged its chain along a stretch of wire stapled into the ground, barking furiously.

'Don't worry about the dog; heem tied up,' said the man, nevertheless giving the animal a wide berth, which Buster copied.

He led the way past the chicken coop, through a narrow gate and out onto the far edge of the woods. Buster could just make out the dim outline of another enormous whitewashed building, similar to the one they had just passed, shrouded amongst the trees.

'My best *armazem*!' said the man, proudly.

They went up to the long-fronted building and walked around it. One half, partially open to the elements, housed a stack of straw bales piled high to a pan-tiled roof. The other, bricked up in front with a small upper level window, boasted aluminium double doors. To the back was a lean-to made of wood, from which came the comfortable sound of munching and Buster made out the dark shape of a large animal moving about in the straw.

'Him my *mulo*,' said the man, again the hint of pride in his voice.

'What do you do with this closed in part?' said Buster, touching the tin door with his toe.

'I rent. My friend, him keep his tractor here. You wanna see? I go, getta key,' the man said obligingly.

'Steady on,' said Buster, 'There's no point getting the key if the barn's already in use. I wanted an empty *arm* – *armer* – er… barn. I may have some stuff to put away here.'

'How much you pay?' said the man, getting the message amazingly quickly.

'It depends,' said Buster, 'I haven't seen inside yet.'

'I go get key,' said the man firmly and disappeared. Buster could hear the dog creating again in the yard behind.

When he returned, he had brought a torch as well as the key. He unlocked the door and they went inside. A light switch was found and he heard a generator in the distance start up. White light from two long tubes flooded the building. It was much bigger than Buster had imagined – a good forty feet square and a high new roof above their heads. 'Does it leak?' said Buster.

'Leak?'

'The rain – does it come in?'

'Oh no, no – watertight, very watertight. All new tiles.'

Buster looked at the tractor dubiously. There was also a trailer, enveloped in plastic sheeting, some boxes, cutting equipment and what might have been a motorbike in a corner.

'What about these?' he said.

'All belong to my friend. He steel in Canada.'

'Can you get rid of them?' asked Buster.

A crafty look spread over the man' face. 'You pay good money, then I send them some place else.'

'I see,' said Buster. He wished Catalina had given him some idea of what he should pay in terms of rent. He had absolutely no idea. 'What were you thinking of?' he said carefully.

'Two thousand *escudos* – a month,' said the man.

'That's too much. I'll give you half that,' said Buster.

The man shook his head and made to go out.

'Just a minute,' said Buster. 'OK – you're on! I'll pay it but only with conditions.'

'*Sim?*'

'First, I want this place thoroughly cleaned up. No oil on the floor, no cobwebs in the corners.' He walked round, inspecting the whitewashed interior. It wasn't bad, but there were a few stains where machinery had been laid against the walls. 'I'd like all that painted over,' he pointed. 'I want it better than this, I want it immaculate.'

The man nodded, 'No problem.'

'And secondly,' said Buster, spreading open his legs and folding his arms firmly in front of him. 'I want no one to know about this. Do you understand? No one at all. Not even your friend in Canada. If you tell anyone about an American coming here and renting this *arm – arm –* barn, I'll –' he fixed the man with his eye and ran his finger sharply across the front of his own throat. The man understood perfectly. He nodded delightedly.

'I don't tell no one,' he said. 'I keep the mouth shut, all secret. Even my wife won't know, she away, in Azores. The *Senhor* need worry about nothing.'

'OK,' said Buster. 'Just one question. Can I get a car up to the door?'

'*Sim, sim,* how you think we get tractor in? There's a road come round other side of my house. There! You see?' he was pointing into the dark.

It was too obscure to see but Buster took his word for it. He took a thousand *escudo* note out of his wallet and handed it to the man. 'That's an advance,' he said. 'I'll be back tomorrow after midday and I want to see the tractor out of here and all the rest too.'

The man took the money and held it up to the light. Then with a grin, he folded it carefully and tucked it into his hip pocket. '*Sim Senhor.*'

'Fine!' said Buster.

It was only later as he was driving homeward that he realised that he didn't know the man's name. Neither had the man asked him his. Oh well, he shrugged, it was probably better like that.

It was pitch dark when he got home and it seemed strange going into the empty house – well, almost empty. There was a frantic scratching at the door as Mungo heard him fit the key in the lock and Buster was surprisingly glad of the excited welcome the dog gave him. 'Poor old boy, did no one walk you then? Never mind, I'll take you with me tomorrow,' he promised. He fumbled for the light switch and far away, his own generator kicked into action, sounding twice as loud as the one he'd left behind.

God, he was tired. He let the dog out, then went straight to the decanter. As he poured himself the last of the bourbon, he made a mental note to buy a couple more bottles tomorrow otherwise there'd be hell to pay when Howard and the others got back. He cast his eyes round the kitchen. Maria had been in as usual to clean and had obviously fed the animals for there was an empty bowl on the floor and the cat was lying in its usual place on top of the refrigerator with a half-eaten fish carcass in a saucer at its side. He wondered what Leah had left him to eat. She'd said something about a casserole but he'd been so busy making sure she and the other two got off, he hadn't paid much attention. He opened the fridge door and saw a delicious-looking stew in a Pyrex dish. He lit the gas oven, put the dish on the top shelf and settled down to relax in his favourite chair. Good old Maria! The library fire was still burning; she must have stacked it well.

Propping his feet on the brass fender, he thought about the day's events. Everything was happening so quickly now. Until this moment, he had not had time to register exactly what effect these plans would have on his life. He looked round the room, already feeling removed from it. He'd be leaving this house for good – that was clear. Sad in a way when he'd seen it through from the plans on the drawing-board to the present, but it had always been Leah's creation. He'd played his part but he was not bound to it, like she was – or even the Boys. He doubted even if he'd really miss it. It was a grand house, a beautiful house, but there'd be others out there. And anyway, how could a house have soul if you didn't share it with the right person?

He thought about the Boys. If Leah hadn't been around and he'd been a single man, would he really want to bring Catalina back here to share her life with him, with those two in the background? He decided he wouldn't. No way! He wouldn't want to share his Catalina with anyone. It said something surely about his relationship with Leah, that he'd entered into this whole crazy sharing thing in the first place. They'd all be so busy planning, they'd never really stopped to think about it.

He would never make those mistakes again. In fact, did he really need a big house after all? Even with all the money in the world, it was a luxury he could do without. He hoped Catalina would feel the same. Better by far, he reasoned, to get a small cosy place together. A house that breathed and lived, far from the tourist trail. A retreat! A love-nest... wasn't that the word she had used on the phone? Something about a nest, or lining a nest? It all came to the same thing.

He wondered where they might go – Spain, France, Italy? Or would she wish to stay in Portugal? She was after all Portuguese. They said the north was very beautiful – somehow that appealed. They could buy a little chalet up in the mountains, far from the madding crowd – with a view of the famous lakes perhaps or overlooking the Douro and its rich, fertile vineyards. He wondered if she'd like that.

He thought again about the bed. Tomorrow he would go into Faro and arrange for one to be delivered. Making love in a barn! What a crazy idea... would she really be willing? Logically, of course it would be more practical than the beach ... sand got into everything! But women were not always ruled by logic. He'd have to make that bed mighty inviting to compensate for the lack of romance. He started to smile... this was getting crazier by the minute. He shut his eyes and wriggled his toes in front of the fire. A vivid picture of the black sheets was gliding before him... he really hoped they had not been left behind in the States.

He was almost asleep when the sizzling aroma of stewed beef assailed his nostrils. He pulled himself up and stalked though to the kitchen – hmmmm…delicious! – but a few more minutes would do no harm. Black satin sheets, he couldn't get them out of his head; he must satisfy his curiosity. Imbued with an energy he did not recognise, he leaped upstairs two at time. There was a large walk-in linen cupboard between two bathrooms. He opened the louvred door. This was Leah and the Boys' domain – he'd never been in here since the move. Christ – there was a lot of stuff! Towels, tablecloths, pillowcases, blankets, sheets! There were shelves of it all, enough to bed a battalion! He began to examine them carefully. White Irish linen, crisp and fine like good parchment, Egyptian cotton, colour co-ordinated for every bedroom, lemon, moss green, apricot, pink, duck-egg blue – that's Leah! Then came piles of patterned stuff he didn't recognise, why on earth did they have that? – guest rooms perhaps.

And finally, Eureka! At the very bottom of the last pile, there they were! Masked by some psychedelic drapes – Benjie in the sixties? – suddenly, he saw them. Black satin sheets! – still in their package, pristine and new. This was a real stroke of luck! Why had he doubted? He might have guessed Leah wouldn't leave anything behind – she was much too careful for that.

He extracted them carefully. No one would ever know. While he was at it, he might as well remove the red flowery ones – and the pillowcases – they went with nothing, so they'd never be missed. But no – hang on a minute! He couldn't quite see Catalina accepting such lurid taste, she'd be all for lacy and white, frothy and pure – in contrast to the black. Well, surely, they had enough of the Irish linen not to notice one set gone? She deserved it, that girl of his. It would show how thoughtful he was; that against the naughty black, he appreciated her fragility. She was, after all a woman of contrasts. I'll take you at night and I'll take you in the day, my love!

He was feeling romantic now. He was just about to switch off the light when it occurred to him that they might get rather cold on their new bed with just sheets. They needed something to snuggle under. Better take a few blankets too – there were plenty of those – he could take his pick. He did; the cellular ones were the lightest and the warmest. Perhaps a couple of towels would come in handy. There'd be no ocean to leap into straight after their lovemaking.

As the pile gathered on the floor around his feet, he deliberated the towel situation. He had no idea they were so spoiled for choice. It was an Aladdin's Cave! He eventually selected some dark crimson bath sheets to go with the black satin and some fluffy white to accompany the Irish linen. There was a matching white terry bathrobe as well, Catalina would look such a doll in that – vulnerable, virginal and appealing.

He tidied everything up into neat bundles and took them downstairs, ready for his expedition the next day. He now felt ravenously hungry, so he sauntered back into the kitchen humming a little tune of satisfaction. It had been a good day. By now his casserole was just how he liked it, singed on the top, the gravy bubbling merrily over thick slabs of stewed beef with carrot and onion. In no time at all, Buster was tucking in.

It was only several hours later when he was in bed, sleepy from a large meal and good red wine, that he remembered. He sat up with a jerk. The geese! They had started hatching today and he'd forgotten all about them! He swore silently. Should he get out of bed and go and check up? No, surely that was unnecessary? Carlos would have been there all day to see to everything. Yet Leah had asked! Didn't she trust the guy? For heavens sake, what did they employ him for? He knew far more about birds and such like than he, Buster. It was all ridiculous, another little ploy of his wife to make him feel involved over her growing animal collection, no doubt. Well, he could do without it – at least for today. Yawning, he rolled over onto his side and in no time at all, had fallen asleep.

30

She had never seen Lisbon look so beautiful. It was six o'clock in the evening and as dusk fell, the streets were alive with the bustle of shoppers. Down the Avenida da Liberdade, into the crammed streets of the Baixa and up the hill to Camões, the whole of the fashionable shopping area was ablaze with gorgeous fairytale lights. Shaped like stars, they spanned the main streets and squares, shimmered over the heads of passers-by, and found their own reflection in the plate glass of the great stores.

Leah and Howard had set forth from their smaller hotel just behind the great Tivoli, to do some late shopping while Benjie had been left behind – packed off to bed with antibiotics and a couple of sleeping pills. The ordeal at the dentist's had proved even more unpleasant than anticipated, but at least they had got to the root of the problem and the offending abscess treated. He was due to return in twenty-four hours' time.

Meanwhile his travelling companions were determined to enjoy themselves. 'I feel sorry for Benjie,' said Howard, 'but it won't help his recovery, if we mooch about ourselves. Come on, Leah, let's celebrate being in a city again. I'll buy you a hot chocolate and one of those famous *pasteis de natas* if you take a trip with me up the Rua Augusta.'

This was the busiest hour of the day in the capital. Afternoon shoppers, laden with expensive carrier bags and beribboned boxes, still lingered before magnificently gilded windows, loath to tear themselves away and return home. There was too much magic about, too much warmth and colour. Even now, offices and nearby government buildings were disgorging their employees at the end of another long day. Coming alive in the cold air, they emerged in scattered throngs, chattering gaily and laughing as they swelled the crowds on the wide mosaic pavements, then spilled carelessly into the street causing the drivers of cars and cabs to throw up their hands in despair, hooting in protestation as traffic was brought to a standstill.

'It could be Madison Avenue,' said Leah enthusiastically, picking her way over the well-worn cobbles. 'It may not be so big, but they've done it every bit as well.'

'It's prettier, actually,' said Howard. 'I'm always surprised how much style you find in Lisbon, the women are so sophisticated, look at all those shoes and gorgeous hats! '

'It's certainly a world away from the Algarve – that's for sure,' said Leah, 'Manolo told me some time ago, Portugal's the only western country that can still match its currency in gold reserves! Did you see the jewellery on that young girl in the leopard skin jacket?'

'It makes the Algarve quite primitive!' replied Howard, his attention on an older woman in an elegant tweed suit trimmed with mink. 'Look at the makeup, Leah, and the coiled hair! – she could be Ava Gardner!' he sighed appreciatively as she swept by. 'So is minerals what this colonial war's all about – defending their African diamond and gold mines?'

'Don't ask me,' said Leah, 'Catalina would know though, why don't you ask her.?

'I'll do that,' he said, 'when she returns. People seem quite nervous to mention politics here, but now we're all settled, I'd like to know more about what actually does go on. I can't believe it's such a taboo subject as everyone makes out. Say, why don't we do a bit of Christmas shopping now – tonight? Window shopping's all very well but for once I'd like to surprise Benjie. Generally he comes with me and we choose gifts together, but the unexpected is a bunch more fun.'

They set off and found the expensive leather goods shop Howard had in mind halfway up Chiado. Leah stood happily to one side as tray after tray of expensive crocodile and snakeskin belts were pulled out. She was amused and touched by Howard's scrupulous examination, seeming to know by the merest slide of his fingers over the skin which were the best. When he wished, Howard could be extremely generous and he never once compared the outrageous price tags. Eventually, the choice lay between two crocodiles, one a dark tan, the other ebony, both with spoon-shaped gold buckles. 'What do you think, Leah?' he turned to her, 'I'd appreciate your advice.'

Flattered to be asked, she made the final choice and was rewarded by a rare smile as they waited for the purchase to be gift wrapped with the customary Portuguese bows and flourishes. 'I love the way they can turn the most humble present into a work of art,' he said. 'We could never get this quality of tissue paper in our country. It used to drive me mad.'

'There's a lot about this country I like, ' said Leah, 'as you said, quality is everything.'

'Yeah, it's interesting. They may be poor out in the sticks judging by the drive through the Alentejo, but oh boy – do they know a thing or two about elegance in this city.'

'Shame Benjie's missing all this,' said Leah, 'never mind, when he receives that present, he won't grudge it one inch. You're always so generous Howard, he adores your presents.'

'I'm not so sure,' said Howard. 'Since we moved out here, the things I do for him seem to interest him less and less. Lately, I've felt him remove himself to somewhere distant and he's become edgy and irritable. It's puzzled and depressed me.'

Leah felt a sudden rush of sympathy for the big man whom she ought to know so well after so many years, but who lately had also been a stranger to her. This was the closest they had been for months, but perhaps that was as much her fault, as his. After all, she was always so busy – the house, the garden, her friendship with Catalina, the animals. Perhaps she too in her way had made herself unapproachable. They all had their problems and it was possible Howard's gruffness was the only way he could show the insecurity that lurked beneath. She began to wonder if early retirement had been a mistake for him. He had always seemed so content, despite the pressures of his monolithic decorating empire. It was not so much Benjie who had changed, she reflected, it was Howard who now had the time to notice.

She made a sympathetic noise and tucked her arm through his as they left the shop and headed downhill towards the main Avenida. It was properly dark now and Chiado was full to bursting; it was a struggle to leave. Policemen with loudhailers did their best to keep the impatient traffic moving but it was a thankless task with horns blaring furiously, the screech of brakes and militant shop commissionaires whistling for taxis which held the heaving streets up even more. Everywhere was the smell of rich food in the *patisseries*, expensive clothes and cars, beautiful women in mink coats, elegant men with dark handsome looks and money. It was always like that in Chiado before Christmas.

Buster was awoken very early the next day by a persistent tapping on his door. He woke instantly and, naked, leapt out of bed to pull back the curtains and let the sunny day flood in. Then he climbed back into bed, pulled up the sheets and called 'Sim!'

'Aiee! – Meu Senhor!' It was Maria the maid who stood there in the doorway, tragedy in her voice, her face wretched. She held a tray with the customary breakfast cup, their small cafeteria and a jug of hot milk, but would come no further.

'*Entra, Maria!*' said Buster, waving her in, amused to think that the long face and hesitation was due to the fact that for once, she was entering the bedroom of a man on his own.

She shook her head and bit her lip. '*Meu senhor,*' she said again croakily and did not budge an inch.

This was ridiculous, thought Buster. If he got up stark bollock naked and took the tray from her, she'd probably hand in her notice. He'd heard how prissy and religious these old peasant women were; but at the same time she was clearly too shy to edge any nearer. If he did not act now, he'd be waiting all morning for his coffee. Silly old fool!

'Put the tray down there!' he commanded in English, pointing at the floor where she stood. He had often told Leah if you were firm enough in your own language, they generally understood. She was hesitating, still unsure, and looked at him pleadingly. 'Yes! Down *there!*' he nodded vigorously. Finally, she seemed to understand and placed the tray carefully on the carpet. Then, with a sob in her throat, fled from the room.

Half amused, but also exasperated, Buster padded over to retrieve it. He was halfway through his coffee when there was another tap at the door and without waiting for a reply, the boy Carlos burst into the bedroom. 'Senhor!' he cried. '*Os gansos! Estão todos mortos!*'

'What the hell? *Que?*' began Buster.

'*Os gansos – os bebes – estão todos mortos.*' The boy's face was glum as he stood before the bed in his hobnailed boots.

'Oh Jeez!' One did not have to be a linguist to guess the meaning of the word *morto*, and he'd already been indoctrinated into the Portuguese for goose – *ganso* – by his wife. 'Holy shit!' he said, slopping the tray with coffee as he put down his cup with a bang. Ignoring the boy, he climbed out of bed and into some clothes. A few seconds later he was striding up the path to the wild bit, with Mungo leading the way and the boy following at a safe distance.

There was a hiss as he pushed at the door of the goose-house and bent his head to go in. '*Cuidado!*' yelled the boy in warning, but it was too late. The gander, a handsome bird with a black stripe down his snaking neck came at the man, his weasel head lowered, the beak menacingly open to reveal two long strips of razor-sharp teeth, the dark tongue raised. Then the wings came up with a terrific rush of sound and before he knew it, Buster felt someone had punched him very hard in the chest, knocking all the breath out in one violent blow.

He staggered backward and put out a hand to save himself. The gander was less than a yard away, its beady eyes darting at the intruder struggling to regain his balance. Up ruffled the feathers, the neck thrust forward and swelling to twice his normal size, he made as if to come at the man again, wings out-spread like some monster flying bat. This time Buster did not wait; half-backing, half-stumbling he was out of the door in a trice. The moment his feet touched earth, he slammed the door in the creature's face, finding himself beside Carlos, who was pale as a sheet. 'Holy shit!' he said, 'I never knew they could be like that.'

'*Zangado!*' said Carlos, indicating the creature's fury.

Buster eyed him up and down and felt a surge of uncontrollable laughter bubbling up within him. He let it gurgle out, knowing as he did so, that he would be released from that moment of panic when for a horrible moment, he felt the gander might do for him. Some of the pallor had now left Carlos's face but he looked shocked. Back in control again, Buster reassured him. 'I'm OK,' he said. '*Senhor Buster OK! Compreende?*'

Carlos nodded despite the mangled syntax and held up a finger. '*Momento,*' he whispered and disappeared into the hut. Again there came a faint hissing but almost immediately it subsided. Silence followed. Anthony and Cleopatra clearly knew the difference between friend and foe.

Buster dusted himself down and waited outside. His chest still stung from the forceful lash of the bird's wings but otherwise he was unhurt. Of course, he should have known better than plunge straight into their house like that. They were funny birds and who knew how they might behave with young around – that was if there were any. He hoped he'd mistaken what the kid had been trying to tell him. Leah would go mad.

But there was no mistaking the pathetic little bundles that lay in the boy's hands when he returned. In one hand lay a tiny gosling, perfectly formed, a ball of yellow and grey down, its beak stretched open; in the other, a half-cracked egg, curiously dark in colour with a telltale beak half-protruding from one side. Clearly it had given up some time ago to die half-born, still trapped by the rock-hard shell. There was a glimmer of sorrow in Carlos's limpid brown eyes as he peeled off pieces of shell, to reveal the same yellow and grey down, still sticky from the membrane.

Buster looked on, sickened. 'Are they all like that?' he wondered aloud.

Carlos seemed to understand and nodded. '*Estão todos mortos.*'

Buster turned on the boy, suddenly angry. 'And where the hell were you yesterday? Why weren't you here to save them?' He spat the last insult, 'What do you think I pay you for you stupid Portuguese peasant!'

If he did not understand the words, the boy understood the accusation and the sneer. Hurt surprise filled his face; then a hint of contempt came into the eyes and he stared at Buster with a kind of pity. Only then did Buster remember. Yesterday was Wednesday. No wonder Leah had asked him to check. It was the boy's day off. Disgusted, he turned away and walked back to the house.

Maria was in the kitchen bent over the sink. When Buster came in she straightened up, wiped her soapy hands on her overall and shook her head. '*Tenho pena, Senhor,*' she said and went off into a gabble of unintelligible dialect. Buster ignored her completely and made himself another cup of coffee. There was nothing more depressing than someone whining away in a foreign language. You'd think it was her geese that had snuffed it. These country folk either took their animals too seriously, or did the opposite – as with Mungo. There was no balance in the matter and he refused to get drawn into the hand wringing. He wished she'd get back to her sink.

Although it burnt his throat, he downed his coffee in one. He *had* to get out of the house. In the last 24 hours he had sensed an atmosphere of overbearing repression and this, mingled with this morning's disaster, gave him claustrophobia. He could not wait to get away.

Whistling to Mungo, he picked up the bundle of linen and blankets he had stashed out of view in the big French armoire in the hall and went out to the car. He shoved everything swiftly into the boot, just in time. Maria had heard the door bang and was peering out to see what he was up to. Nosy old thing, thought Buster as he settled into the car with the dog and drove off. Lucky she didn't see my parcel, or she'd be telling Leah in two twists of a monkey's tail. I know how these servants live for gossip.

He arrived in Faro just as the shops were opening. He had decided to go to the capital for his shopping because it was bigger and more anonymous than anywhere else on the coast. He cruised round the harbour, past the hotels, cafes and gardens full of business men taking coffee before going into their offices. Searching down some improbable one way streets, he finally found a parking bay. He could see a large shopping precinct in the distance. A few moments later and he was in one of the most vulgar furniture stores he had ever seen. At least there'd be no danger of bumping into Miss Maysie Vincent or her inquisitive mother here!

'*Bom dia, Senhor*!' An obsequious man with flaccid lips and loud suit came up to greet him, happy to see an *estrangeiro* in his shop so early in the day. 'Please, what may we do for you, *Senhor*?' he added in perfect English.

'I've come about a bed – a double bed,' Buster believed in coming straight to the point.

'Yes sir, *uma cama de casal* – indeed sir, I think we can arrange that,' the man beamed. 'Won't you come this way?'

Buster and Mungo followed him through a baize-covered door into a cavernous store at the back of the shop. Whilst the main shop housed smaller pieces, occasional tables and chairs, lamps and pedestals, the heavyweight stuff was crammed into this second chamber. He saw everything from gothic chests to mammoth sofas, carved dressers to four posters. Mostly dark and over-ornate, there was not much to choose between the pomposity of the furniture and the manager's suit.

'Here is our most popular *cama de casal*,' the man's teeth gleamed as he patted a resplendent monstrosity with a black headboard of carved wood. Complete with bolster, it even boasted an rosary hanging from one of its many knobs. 'Beautiful craftmanship, lignum vitae, a masterpiece!' The man's smile faded as Mungo lifted a half-hearted leg against one of its legs. 'Twenty-five thousand *escudos*,' he snapped.

Buster was rubbing his horn-rimmed glasses as though unaware of the dog's misdemeanour. 'It's not the type of bed I had in mind,' he said. 'Have you nothing a little simpler?'

With less enthusiasm, the man led him into another section where a number of modern divans had been piled one upon the other, the headboards leaning against the wall. 'That's better,' said Buster, running his eye over the uppermost one. 'Those others were like something out of the Arabian Nights, not my scene at all.'

'These are much cheaper,' said the manager disapprovingly. 'There is no craft or technique in these at all. Mass produced, I fear.'

'They look OK to me,' said Buster, prodding the springs, wanting to add, just leave the technique to us. 'Can you fetch one out?'

There was a reluctant nod, then a whistle and a boy shambled into view. Together, they pulled out a double divan plus mattress for Buster to approve. Buster laid himself down unceremoniously, rolled over a couple of times, then sat up again with a jerk to pronounce, 'It's fine!'

The manager tore off the price tag, added something in biro – 'for tax'– and came swiftly to his conclusion, '*Seis mil.'*

'OK. And I want it delivered to a place near Messines,' said Buster getting out his wallet. 'Will that be included?'

The man shook his head. Buster noticed the whole of his mouth seemed to wobble. He must have ill-fitting dentures. 'How much more then?'

'Messines is a very long way,' said the man. Finally, they settled on a figure and Buster whistled to Mungo, who had disappeared on a small tour of exploration of his own. With the shop's telephone number on his receipt, Buster had already decided he would let his new landlord deal with the delivery of the bed. On his way out, he noticed quite a pretty whitewood dressing-table with a matching chair and chest of drawers. In a moment's mad impulse, he decided to buy these too. He could just see Catalina seated at the dressing-table, combing her tousled hair after a particularly wild bout of love-making. With the extra purchase, the manager became all smiles again and even threw in a shiny pink cushion for the chair free of charge. 'Pink for a lady,' he said ingratiatingly as Buster grunted.

His business done, he was now in a hurry to leave. He nodded curtly and strode out into the street again. For a moment he could not remember where he had left the car. There were at least six other narrow streets, all looking the same and all intersecting the one on which he now stood. He was certainly carrying Catalina's secrecy advice to the letter. It was most doubtful anyone they knew had ever set foot in that area or that particular store. As for buying from there – why, they'd probably all run a mile!

The McKays were to move down to Somerset four days before Christmas. Although tempted to leave before, McKay knew he must hold out in London until the exhibition officially closed on the 20th. If he did not stick it out, everyone would say he had lost face, and although things were moving at snail's pace, Mrs. Cootes had already been proved right. By not dropping prices, and by his continual presence at the gallery, acting as though nothing had happened, sales had rallied – slightly. A few more pictures had been marked down for sale. Nothing would be delivered until after the exhibition had closed, and although in former years it was the exception to find a picture without a red star at this stage in the proceedings, seven sales were nonetheless better than two. McKay could at least be grateful he would not now have to worry about the cost of their sea passage back to Spain and thence to Portugal.

He had been amazed by Catalina's reaction to the whole ghastly saga. He had often asked himself what would happen if failure struck, experiencing as he did, a sneaking sensation of doubt. Notwithstanding his lack of faith, she had remained up-beat all week and in addition to her high spirits, he'd observed a new sense of excitement and purpose. This had puzzled him, since he had already explained that their situation on returning to the Algarve, must be one of restraint, even semi-retirement from the old gaieties.

Gone for them the moonlight picnics with expensive speedboats moored on private beaches. The shopping trips to *Sevilla* and *Lisboa* must simply cease; so too the dinner parties, the restaurants and the private rooms. The merry-go-round could continue to whirl, but without the McKays, and someone else could buy the caviar and champagne if his young wife really craved it. He tried to tell her all this as matter of factly as he could; and matter of factly, she seemed to accept it. How strange!

On this particular day – it was a week before Christmas – snow was falling lightly on London. Both the gallery staff were down with 'flu, so he and Catalina had held the fort for two days. She had spent the morning dusting imaginary specks of dust from every picture and frame, in between making innumerable coffees in the little kitchen at the back of the show-room as she chattered interminably about this and that. Since this was so out of character and from anyone else would have annoyed him, her words became somehow enchanting and lifted his own heavy spirits.

If anyone ventured over the threshhold – there had been a few that morning – she would move elegantly forward with her most ravishing smile and a catalogue. As they perused the pictures, she would hang back, but never too far. It was as though her own energy could add impact so that the viewer felt drawn in and included within an intimate orbit of appreciation for the art on view. Once enmeshed, anything seemed possible.

Jock himself kept tucked away in the background. It did not do for the artist to push himself forward. Only if a customer asked for him, would he appear with genuine reluctance. Today looked as though it would be another of those barren mornings of no sales or even half-promises. Suddenly, without warning, a middle-aged man in a rumpled but well-cut suit burst into the gallery just before lunchtime. He wore no overcoat although it was snowing hard now and he looked round, cold and abstracted, for somewhere to place his dripping umbrella.

'Here! I say, you look *frozen!*' McKay looked on amused as Catalina flew to the man's side, eyes and voice brimful of concern. He allowed her to take his umbrella and when she gently removed the sodden bundle of newsprint from under his arm, he nodded gratefully. 'Oh yes, my *Financial Times*...I'd...er...quite forgotten it was there.'

She bore everything off to return a moment later with a 'What can we do to warm you up?' The newcomer found himself looking into a pair of wide apart ebony eyes, that shone with obvious distress. How lovely he thought, was the face in which they were set. He blinked and seemed not to hear, so she repeated the question, 'What *can* we do to warm you up? A coffee, a cup of tea, what about a – er – wiskee?'

'Oh – er – I'm all right m'dear, thank you so much,' said the man, biting back a shiver from lips that had turned quite blue. 'Silly really, I left my coat in a taxi on my way to the City this morning. Second time I've done that this year. It gets rather tiresome after a while, what?'

'Oh, it's just the sort of thing, I'm always doing,' said Catalina untruthfully, ignoring McKay's raised eyebrows across the room. 'But you know, if we don't do something about you, I'm afraid you'll catch your death of cold. What about some really steaming coffee with a dash of brandy in it? It won't take a moment to make.'

'I wouldn't dream of asking you – it's – much too much trouble.'

'I won't take no for an answer,' said Catalina firmly. 'Why don't you have a look round the exhibition while I make it? I won't be long, I promise. Your family would never forgive you if you caught the 'flu at Christmas!'

'I dare say they wouldn't,' acquiesced the man, whom McKay had judged to be a stockbroker and not a very successful one at that – if he was as scatty as he appeared. He began to study his surroundings and as Catalina whisked past to the kitchen, added, 'Most awfully kind of you, m'dear.'

Nodding vaguely to McKay, he made a beeline to the radiator which stood against a central pillar. As he positioned himself with his back to it, he found himself in full view of McKay's own favourite – an abstract of racing with horses' heads and jockeys' colours just distinguishable through a vivid blur of speed. It was the most expensive in the gallery and McKay believed it to be one of his best ever; that was, until the opening of this exhibition. Named '*Challenge*', it had scarcely raised a single comment.

Steam was pouring out of the stockbroker's pin-striped trousers in an ever-expanding upward stream to which he seemed oblivious. After what seemed an interminable pause, he turned to McKay with an apologetic air, 'Er – forgive me for asking – but it *is* racing, isn't it?'

McKay glanced up from the pen and ink with which he'd been tinkering in a corner. Without getting up, he muttered, 'Well – that's what *was* in my mind when I painted it, yes.'

At that moment, Catalina chose to come back with an enormous mug shrouded in a napkin and handed it to their visitor. 'You must drink this while it's hot!'

He thanked her and clasping his blue hands round the mug, continued to study the painting. McKay noticed that the steam from his bottom had lessened and he winked at his wife. She stood again beside the fellow, but this time volunteered not a word. He drank his coffee, shook his head and said 'By God, m'dear, that had a kick!' He was smiling for the first time since he'd arrived. Then he returned to his silent perusal.

McKay watched the small scene before him, fascinated. No one said a word, and no one altered their stance. He was beginning to get bored and about to interrupt the whole charade when he heard the words, 'I'd like to take this painting now, will you accept a cheque?'

McKay opened his mouth to explain all cheques had to clear before they could part with anything, but received such a look from his wife that he shut it again. She went to the desk, picked up a folder and returned to the stockbroker, still rooted by the radiator. 'That will be four thousand, two hundred and fifty pounds,' she said, as though it was forty-five pence.

'Right, m'dear.' He wrote out a cheque there and then and wordlessly, Catalina lifted 'Challenge' off its hook.

'If you wait a moment, I'll wrap it up for you,' she smiled.

'No need for that; I'm dry now, thanks to you,' he nodded cheerfully. It was not a large picture and he took it gently from her, undid his jacket, tucked it underneath and picked up his still dripping umbrella from a stand near the door.

'Thank you so much for the excellent coffee, m'dear. Good combination that!' and with those parting words he went straight back into the street. 'Taxi!' they heard him cry and a moment later he'd disappeared from view.

'My God!' cried McKay, 'if he can leave his overcoat in a taxi, what's to stop him doing the same with over four thousand quids' worth of picture?'

'Nothing,' smiled Catalina, and handed him the cheque. It was from Coutts' bank, the Queen's bank, Mayfair branch. This reassured him so much, he did not look at the name; instead he whirled her almost off her feet, clasped her tightly round the waist and they danced a wild kind of polka round the gallery, the cheque fluttering between their outstretched hands like a pennant.

'We're mad!' he cried, changing the tempo to a Scottish jig. 'Do you realise what we've done? We've broken all the rules! Mrs Cootes will have a fit!'

'Let her,' said Catalina.

'But you didn't even ask him for a banker's card, my sweet. I trusted your judgement of course, but even so –'

'There was no need. Don't you know who that was?'

They ground to a halt and McKay looked at her curiously, 'Tell me, my darling.'

'Just the Earl of Newmarket.'

'That absent-minded boffin?'

'I thought he looked familiar when he came in,' said Catalina. 'Don't you remember, he was on a sports programme the other night. But what confirmed it for me was this!'

She delved into the wastepaper basket and retrieved the wet newspaper. 'I couldn't help notice when I took it from him. Look – stamped across the top – "House of Lords" – and scribbled underneath "Newmarket".'

McKay smoothed out the pink paper and shook his head. 'Well, I'll be damned,' he said, 'The absent-minded peer! Who'd have thought?' As he scrutinised the signature on the cheque, a rare light shone in his eyes, 'My God, that's one of the biggest names in racing today! Not only does he have one of the finest studs in England, he's loaded!'

Catalina beamed. 'Then you're not cross I broke the rules?'

'Hang the rules! If you hadn't given him the picture there and then, he might easily have changed his mind as soon as his trousers had dried. You never know with these rich buggers, they invariably act on a whim!'

'That's exactly what I thought.'

McKay hugged her hard. 'You're a clever little witch, aren't you? Tonight, we'll go and celebrate! And darling – you don't need to worry about Christmas any more. You and the Catkin will have no cause to complain when you open your stockings on Christmas morning.'

Her eyes flickered. 'I wasn't so worried about *that*, Jock – there was one thing, though …'

'What's that? '

'I hardly like to ask,' she bit her lip, then out it came in a rush, 'I had hoped to spend a few hours Christmas shopping and wondered if I might do so this afternoon?'

'I thought you and Katy were all booked up for that tomorrow in Harrods, after her carol service.'

'Er – yes,' said Catalina, blushing. 'Only, I had some private shopping I wanted to do. What I'd hoped for – was some cash.'

'Of course! How thoughtless of me.' He took out his wallet and counted out some twenty-pound notes. 'That was to have lasted until we left London,' he said ruefully. 'Now thanks to my clever darling, our luck's changed for once. Why don't you go and blow it all, before I change my mind!'

'Are you sure?' She was already putting on her fox coat and fluffy matching cap which made her look more warm-blooded and desirable than ever.

'As sure as ever I am of anything,' he laughed recklessly and patted her on the shoulder. 'Run along now, pretty woman. And take your umbrella. It's snowing again!'

'Good!' she cried and went swiftly into the street. People swept past, their collars pulled up, faces half-obscured by mufflers and scarves as they hurried west towards the tubes or leapt onto buses caught at the lights round each corner of Sloane Square. Catalina stood quite still amongst all the activity, bright of eye and fur-clad, like some young woodland animal just emerged from its hole. McKay watched her raise a gloveless hand and was about to reply with a similar gesture when he realised she was not waving at him, only catching snowflakes.

31

*I*t was not yet ten o'clock when Buster drove out of Faro. He pulled into a lay-by just off the main highway and debated what to do. The long-awaited appointment with the swimming-pool engineer, an Englishman called Roper, was at midday. He would be home in less than an hour but he had no wish to hang around the house until the man rolled up. It seemed empty without the others and he had visions of a weeping Maria and long, accusing looks from the boy Carlos over the fate of the baby geese. He would have liked to cancel the appointment with Roper, but that would be a risk too many. Retribution from his wife was one thing; that of the Boys quite another. They were both desperate for that pool.

Acting on impulse, he ignored the Santa Felicia turning when it came up; instead he kept on going west until he spotted the right hand fork which would eventually lead him to Messines. It would be ironic if he couldn't find the goddarned farm again, he thought to himself. He was cutting it mighty fine, and gambling on Roper's being late. As he drove, it struck him that he was less equipped to play Catalina's game of anonymity than she supposed. It had been too dark to take in many landmarks, but fortunately, his natural sense of direction kicked in and soon he was passing the first entrance that had resulted in failure – with the woman in widow's weeds. Cheered, he drove on, knowing he had miraculously found the right road.

When finally he almost shot by the entrance, it was satisfying to realise the sunken track he had travelled down really was sunk. Even the farm buildings were obscured in a hollow. It was the lights that had drawn him before; now it was hard to know they were there at all. He marvelled at his own luck. Before pulling in, he checked in his mirror that no one was behind. It was unlikely, but not impossible, that someone like Johanna Vincent might use this as a short-cut to Lisbon, which would ruin everything. Now, as he checked to right and left, he wondered just how familiar this rough and rutted trail might become. How long before he and his lover would be together, not just for a few snatched hours at this hidden outpost, but as a proper couple – open and defiant to the outside world – forever?

The Opel bumped over the last few ruts and he changed into neutral and freewheeled over the last rise and down into the yard. Everything looked different in the sunshine. The house was no more welcoming than the night before, but he had been right about the door; even in the light of day, it had a prosperous air. The roof had been newly tiled and the windows were modern and well-fitted. There was even a brand new Citroën with French number plates in a shed next to the house which he had failed to notice last night. He could not help wondering what purpose the mule served, when so much on the farm was mechanised. Clearly, this man was on his way up in the world.

The Opel was still moving gently forward over the sloping ground and he let it coast round a curving track which ran behind the house and the garage to meet up with a larger tractor lane leading in from a ploughed field. Here the farm steading gave way to 'his own' whitewashed barn, bordered by dog kennels to one side and the straggly copse of wood at the back.

The red soil underfoot was still soft from the recent rain, and it was evident that his new landlord has been as good as his word. He noted fresh thick double tyre marks on the ground, as well as a single track made, he hoped, by the departing motor-bike. Buster smiled, pleased with his detective work, and wondered where they had taken everything. A neighbour's farm perhaps, another property owned by the same guy? He was still examining the evidence when his acquaintance of last night came quietly up from behind, an aggrieved expression on his chubby face. '*Bom Dia*, my friend. You come very early. Me not expecting you thees time of day. You say later, much later. Me thought thees afternoon.'

'I know, I'm sorry,' said Buster, keeping a watchful eye on the yellow dog which had bounded noisily into view, having apparently had its lead extended. 'I just wanted to check everything was OK.'

'Eet's OK,' said the man, 'but nothing ees ready. My women clean inside now.'

He stood between Buster and the half-open door of the barn. Neither he nor the yellow dog made any attempt to allow him to pass. Buster was consumed with curiosity to peer inside, but sensing an unwillingness on the part of his new landlord, resisted the temptation. Instead, he delved into his pocket and brought out the card of the furniture shop. 'I came to ask you a favour,' he said. 'Would you ring this number and arrange for the manager to send through the furniture I bought this morning? I want it delivered here.'

The man's face was impassive as he studied the card. 'What kinda furniture?' he said, again with that incongruous mixture of rough Canadian and Portuguese.

To his intense annoyance, Buster found himself reddening. 'Er – there's a chest of drawers, you know, and a dressing table, a chair, and – er – a bed, and I guess that's about it.'

'I see.' The man smiled suddenly and unexpectedly. 'Well now, that's not so much to ask,' he said. 'You wan' I do this today?'

'Well, if you could ring the shop before lunch, they said they would deliver tomorrow morning.'

'It means going up to town,' said the man. 'There's no telephone here, Mister. No line, you see. This ees Algarve, not *Lisboa*.'

Buster was ready for a little reluctance. He pressed a thousand *escudo* note into the man's hand but was was surprised when the fellow shook his head. 'You keep that money, Mister,' he grinned. 'If there's more business, we talk about it later,' and he winked. 'Now you go. When you come back, everything be ready, you see!'

With another wink, he retreated through the half-open door into the barn. The yellow dog tried to follow but someone from within hit it with a broom and it ran, yelping miserably, back to the yard. Mungo growled in the back of the car and Buster felt suddenly gloomy as he backed out of the yard, round the building and headed off back down the sandy track. There was something he didn't care for in the man's behaviour today. He'd put his confidence in him, but those continual winks were aggravating and might spell trouble. He only hoped he was wrong.

Buster arrived home only seven minutes late for his appointment but as luck would have it, Roper was already there. 'So much for Algarve time keeping!' said Buster, by way of an apology. 'Everyone I meet says take it easy – time doesn't count here – but it looks like I've kept you waiting.'

Trevor Roper eyed his new client up and down and held out his hand. 'Depends who you are,' he said, baffled when it wasn't taken. Some people had no manners. 'I've been in business for over six years in these parts and if I didn't stick to a tight timetable, I'd have gone bust long ago. Some of us have to work for a living,' he added, unrolling his plans and spreading them out on a knee, as he balanced one foot on a rock.

Buster was about to retort that he'd worked hard enough too and didn't need a lecture, then decided against it. A month ago, he'd have thrown heart and soul into this project; now it was all he could do to concentrate on what the man was saying and give intelligent answers.

'I take it you're still happy with this spot? The architect filled me in over the change of heart, but I have to admit this new site is much better. Apparently Mrs Bloomfield was concerned by the lack of shelter; I only wish all my clients were so sensible.'

Buster nodded – it was always Leah who got her way – but what did it matter? Now, as the man rabbited on about levels, his mind was wandering again. It was shocking in a way – he really could not care less about the whole shebang. Let the guy get on with it and have done.

The plans back in a canvas bag, they walked round the area together. Roper was still trying to explain technical issues which would make the final location ultimately more expensive despite its suitability. 'Are you sure you're OK with this? The fall of the land at this point does require more shoring up and then there's the matter of soakaways, but it will be well worth it in the end.'

'I understand,' said Buster.

'And you appreciate, Mr Bloomfield, we'll have to dig out more of the rock-face otherwise we could hit real problems when the drains go in?'

'Look, we've been here before, haven't we?' said Buster.

Roper frowned, taking his irritation for a misunderstanding over the price involved. 'You do realise that rather bumps the figures up?'

'Yeah, yeah,' said Buster.

'Of course, you could always settle for a less ambitious pool,' Roper said earnestly. 'That might balance out the figures as regards the extra excavation costs.'

'What's that?' Buster was screwing up his eyes against the winter sun which hung low in the sky. He'd noticed Catalina's ebony hair had a reddish tinge when silhouetted against the sun.

'What I'm trying to say,' Roper passed a weary hand across his brow… he was beginning to think this man was seriously obtuse or was he simply thick? 'The pool you and your wife – oh, and er – Mr McDermott have chosen was of course our very top of the range. That's why the total bill will be rather more than I would have hoped. We do have a considerable choice of smaller, more modest pools – take this kidney shape for instance – we'd have to re-approach the planners – but it's very popular. I completed installation of one of these only two days ago just the other side of Albufeira. If you like I could take you there to have a look – I'm sure Baron von Oöstermann would not mind.'

Buster assured him testily that the price was no object and that the largest Olympus, their original choice, was still the one they wanted. 'The bulldozers can come in as soon as New Year's over. When can we expect the pool to be ready to swim in?'

'Provided all goes well, and there are no nasty surprises, you should be swimming by the end of April.'

'What do you mean nasty surprises? Are the men likely to go on strike or something?' Buster could not understand why the guy kept trying to under-sell himself, he'd have fired him long ago if he'd been working for them in New York.

'Good God no!' Roper smiled despite himself. 'Forgive me, Mr Bloomfield, this is Portugal! We never have strikes here, not like back home – ' he tilted his head back over his shoulder, ' – wish they were illegal there, too. No, I was merely thinking of something unexpected like hitting an underground spring – that sort of thing – or the weather, of course. We can't dig if it's seriously wet and Algarve labourers don't function too well in bad weather. There's a different work ethic in the south.'

Buster grunted and was glad when the interview came to an end. The Englishman drove off to his next appointment, and he was left once again to his own devices. Maria had gone home for lunch, having left him a plate of cold chicken and salad for which he felt no appetite. More for lack of something to do, he picked at the food idly before lighting up a cheroot and pacing round the room. He'd forgotten to replace the bourbon and grudgingly, polished off a couple of beers. Instead of mellowing his feelings, the drink inside him only heightened the impatience that had been gnawing at his stomach all morning.

What was he to do to kill time between now and returning to the farm? He felt it prudent to give them as long as possible to get the place shipshape. It must have looked over-keen to have appeared so early that morning and he had a sneaking feeling it would be foolish to put himself in the fellow's debt. The understanding that seemed to have been reached by the rejection of his very large tip had not settled his mind at all.

He wandered onto the terrace but at present the view held no charm for him and he looked at his watch for the third time in quick succession. This was getting ridiculous! He'd never had to watch the hands go round before, so why was he doing it now? He stubbed out the cheroot angrily. What he needed most was action! A moment later he was back in the house, springing upstairs, two steps at a time.

He entered the master bedroom; pausing on the threshold, his eyes swept over the array of ornaments and pretty things laid out on chest tops and Leah's dressing-table. No – he could hardly remove anything here without its being missed immediately. She was an observant shrew, his wife. He wandered down the corridor, shuddering slightly as he passed the open bathroom.

The memory of that strange occurrence flooded back to him more vividly than ever before – he'd tried so hard to forget it. It was a relief to enter the linen cupboard. This time, instead of working out what would suit Catalina and wouldn't be missed, he helped himself indiscriminately to blankets, pillows and towels. It had become a standing joke between the four of them, they had enough stuff to furnish a hotel! As he pulled out the last of these, something dark and heavy fell to the floor with a loud clatter. He bent down.

There on the floor lay what looked like a mini filing-cabinet, three boxes hinged together with an outer skin of navy blue leather. He fingered an ornate silver clasp which kept it all together. What the hell could it be? Even as the words framed in his mind, he remembered. Of course, the Georgian silver! Leah must have hidden it here amongst the bedlinen as it was too big to fit in the safe. Well, what a stroke of luck! They had never used it, so it was unlikely to be missed. Catalina would adore this and it was a crime to leave it festering amongst the sheets and pillows.

He remembered back to a winter's day in New York. The canteen had been brought into their showroom by a little old Jamaican lady. She had struggled with the weight of the thing and something about her demeanour made them think she might have been somebody's housemaid. She had spun them a story about having fallen on hard times, and her reluctant desire to sell this – a family treasure – which her grandfather had been given in return for many years of hard service on a British plantation. Neither Buster nor Leah were convinced by her explanation and had been loath to give her any money just in case, at some later date, the silver proved to be stolen.

In the end, they agreed to accept it, get it valued and would give her cash if and when they could find a customer. She'd taken her receipt, agreed with alacrity and almost run out of the shop, as though relieved to be rid of her burden. That had been more than seven years ago and was the last they'd seen of her.

They'd held onto the silver, in case she ever returned, but by the time it came to move to Portugal, it was easiest just to bring it with them. 'If all else fails, we can sell it in Europe one of these days,' Leah had smiled …' a nest-egg if we run out of money!' In the meantime, it had lain there, unloved, unclaimed as before. Buster was sure Leah had forgotten all about it by now. Both they and the Boys had their own sets of cutlery and even for the party, there'd been enough to go round. Pleased with his find, he set off to add it to the growing collection in the car.

He arrived at the farmhouse just before five. He had shopped en route to refurbish the drinks cupboard before the others returned; he was in enough trouble without that. There seemed no one about as he parked, although the yellow dog was creating as usual somewhere out of sight. Glad to be alone, he made straight for the barn which had been left unlocked. To his delight, he saw that the furniture he'd bought that morning had already been delivered a day early. All neatly stacked against the wall where the motorbike had lain, he noted to his satisfaction that not a speck of grease or dust remained. If there was one thing the locals here were good at, it was cleaning up. At home, Maria and her various minions from neighbouring cottages kept the villa spotless. It was the same here; the floor and the walls well scrubbed. He touched one and it was still damp, but as he took his hand away he realised that the whole barn had been newly white-washed too. No wonder it looked and smelt so clean! With a smile of satisfaction he began to think the farmer wasn't such a bad guy after all.

He went out to the car and started to fetch in the things. First the heavy canteen; he mustn't forget to lock that up, it had a key inside and he didn't want the farmer putting his greasy paws all over it. Then the armfuls of soft furnishings – Jeez! – once out in the open, it all amounted to quite a haul! Catalina would hardly believe her eyes when she saw this little lot.

When he had finished unloading, he stood back and admired his booty. The door had slammed behind him but he was pleased by how much light the one high window afforded although it irked him to see the bed up on its end against the wall and the mattress still tied up in brown corrugated paper. Impulsively, he turned everything the right way up and began to drag the divan over to the corner which he'd already envisaged as the perfect site. Now it was the turn of the mattress. Unlike their heavily sprung ones in the villa it was lightweight and manageable – after all this was only temporary. He cut at the strings in one swoop of his knife, whilst his finger-nails tore into the thick brown paper. It was coming off in handfuls and within a moment later he was hoisting it triumphantly aloft on his shoulders to place on the bed.

He looked at it for a moment, squared it up with reverence until it was perfectly aligned to the base, then threw himself down on top. A long shiver of anticipation was running down his spine. How surreal was this? – to be lying there, his heart thudding, on a newly bought bed, dying to take his woman in a whitewashed shed in the middle of the Portuguese countryside!

In this one single act, he had conjured up and crystallised all his thoughts, longings and ambitions for now and for ever. It was unbelievable and ridiculous and yet wonderful! And it all boiled down to one thing – and one thing only. He was in love! And the girl of his dreams would soon be in his arms again – on this very bed.

It was all so unlikely he began to wonder if the whole thing was pure fantasy. He shut his eyes and thought about her and was rewarded by the usual delicious sensation creeping up his trunk and enveloping him all over. Life was a strange thing. If someone could have filmed his activities over the past two days and they'd been flash-backed to him a year ago while he was still in New York – he just would not have believed any of it. Absolutely no, siree!

He leaped to his feet, tickled with the idea, and started to move the dressing-table. It was not a heavy piece of furniture, but it was long and awkward. By the time he had got it into position only a few feet away from the side of the bed, he was sweating profusely. The triple sided, high-backed mirror was effective in obscuring most of the bed from the curious gaze of anyone entering the barn. This pleased him. Not that they would get a chance! He'd buy his own large padlock so even the owner was excluded. But ambience was important, perhaps a screen would help. Women were funny creatures; if something didn't look right, they were easily put off. And then they froze up – he'd come across it before.

He began putting the linen away. The long drawers of the dressing table were perfect. Sheets here, towels there – he felt like a housewife, and was enjoying himself. Finally, he came to the black satin sheets and scrunched the material sensuously, between finger and thumb. There was only one place for them, and that was on the bed itself.

Half an hour later – everything was done. Despite its plain surroundings, the bed looked quite sumptuous with an abundance of blankets and cushions. All it needed was *her*! He was just wondering what to do next when the door was pushed open, and the farmer strode in. 'Good afternoon my frien– ' He stopped dead and looked at the arrangement in the corner of the room in amazement. Then he let out a long and expletive whistle. 'So-o!'

To his annoyance, Buster found himself reddening. 'As you can see, I just finished arranging everything. I guess I should thank you – I found it all very nice and clean – and – er – you fixed the furniture for me.'

'The furniture?' said the man, 'oh yes. I think I've been a little…how you say?…slow?… about that. I did not realise exactly what to expect.'

'But I told you,' said Buster, his voice rising, 'I told you what to expect.'

'*Sim*, you told me there is a bed and a chest and a chair and I say OK, but you not explain you want to use thees bed, thees chest, thees chair. You play dirty with me. You say you want a store, not an apartment.'

'I don't want an apartment,' said Buster shortly. 'I haven't played dirty with you. I have no intention of staying here, if that's what you're worried about. It's just temporary – until I move it to – er – our new house.'

'So you arrange the bed for what?' said the man, his face quite expressionless.

Buster felt the palms of his hands beginning to sweat. He had allowed himself to get carried away. Originally, it was true, he'd had no intention of renting a barn for anything other than a store, just as Catalina had ordered. Then, there was that remark she had made. Had she been joking? Somehow, circumstances had got the better of him, and oh, shit! What a darned mess he was making of this.

Before he could think of a reply, the man said smilingly, 'I told you there would be more business to discuss. Look, I'm not a difficult person. I am just a simple man, but I like things straight, see?

'Now why you and I not go into my house and have a dreenk, hm? You like whisky? I gotta new bottle of Johnnie Walker Black Label. Top quality, you know eet? Then we have a leettle drink together and then we talk a bit more.'

He suddenly shot his hand forward to shake Buster's. 'You can call me Chico! Everyone in Canada, they call me Chico. Here,' he jerked his head backwards, 'they call me Senhor Gonçalves, biggest house in village you understand' – but you – different – you can call me Chico, yes?' He allowed his eyes to roam over the glimpse of shiny black sheets appreciatively, then winked. 'Now, we go and have a leettle drink and a leettle talk, OK?'

'OK,' said Buster dubiously and fingering his wallet, followed Chico towards his house. After all the elation, there was a sinking feeling in his chest.

Leah found herself nodding off in the back seat of the Fiat. It was odd she felt so sleepy with all the bumping and twisting. The last hundred kilometres were definitely the worst. They were returning by a different route and she had been unprepared for range upon range of steep hills, most thickly covered by eucalyptus and most deserted by man or beast. There was an unyielding sameness about them. How anyone had ever built a road at all was a miracle, and the only cottages they passed were poor and solitary – and with no sign of power or telephone in sight, they seemed medieval. She was beginning to understand why the Portuguese referred to the fertile plains of the Alentejo and Ribatejo and north to Oporto as 'the kingdom', but to the Algarve, as a foreign country. This endless expanse of thrusting hillsides, carved by so many Ice Ages, effectively sealed everything off. Would they – could they – ever build a motorway here to link the two? Surely not in her lifetime!

They had been driving now for almost four hours and she was feeling car-sick. Normally, a good traveller, the constant ear-popping and relentless twisting in a small car, combined with the delayed action of last night's sleeping tablets, were not agreeing with her. Wally had sent a new brand of pills for 'emergencies', and a strange bed in a noisy capital city seemed a valid enough excuse. Leah's nerves could not afford to be deprived of her correct quota of sleep.

The atmosphere homeward-bound was not proving as amicable as the one going north. Earlier this morning, while checking out of their hotel, there'd obviously been a tiff. Ever since, her companions had preserved an ominous silence and Benjie's white-knuckled hands on the steering wheel were a bad sign. She had tried chatting brightly with both in turn, but when eventually Howard had snapped that he could not bear 'forever gibbering away like a monkey', she lapsed into hurt silence.

Still, she reflected, having rudely awoken over a bad pothole – it was scarcely surprising. Howard had tracked down the 'famous dermatologist' but after two hours in the waiting room, the consultant had offered little advice other than a 'clearing of the blood'. Two thousand *escudos* later, a prescription for six weeks' dose of expensive suppositaries was the last straw. As Benjie untactfully put it, 'Who would have thought to sort out one's hands from that end!'

Leah had tried to soothe ruffled feelings. 'I'm all for giving something a chance – there's got to be a first time!' This was received with such a black look, it took away all the pleasure she had derived from a wonderful meal and the *fado* singing they had so enjoyed in the Baixo the night before.

They had now reached the highest point of the highest range, marked out with a tourist viewing point. 'Oh, do let's get out and stretch our legs,' said Leah, but then regretted it as the two men stood silent and moody despite a stunning 360 degree view over so many peaks it was impossible to count. As they began the long descent towards the far-away coast, a surprisingly bright winter sun beamed down on the green and yellow landscape far below, causing it to shimmer like a long, flat mirror. Leah craned her neck so as not to miss a single inch of the spectacle, surprising herself with the fierce pride she now felt whenever she thought of the Algarve. She never ceased to wonder at its beauty and variety and the feeling of belonging that she had so craved was getting closer by the moment. 'It's just so pretty,' she cried out loud, forgetting her resolution not to speak again until they arrived. 'Look at those wild gladioli! Who'd have thought?'

Even Benjie was sufficiently moved to slow the car and comment. It was a particularly beautiful roadside stretch, thick moss and violets at the verge, competing sporadically with thyme, oregano and heather against a straggling stone dyke. Overhead, a line of blue-grey eucalyptus swayed majestically, dappling the scene in changing half-lights as a breeze rippled down the valley above a fast-moving stream. 'I guess it will be good to get home,' he said quietly. He ventured a hand gingerly to his mouth and finding that the gummy gap held no more pain, put his foot down hard on the accelerator to cover the last lap home in record time.

They arrived in the early afternoon and poured out into the soft Algarvean sunshine. Buster came out to meet them with Mungo at his heels, who rushed straight to Leah and covered her pale blue suit in muddy pawprints. 'It'll brush off,' he replied to her cries of protest, glad of a distraction for he was dreading the next question.

'The geese!' she cried. 'Have they hatched? How many?'

Even Benjie stopped in the act of unpacking the car to hear the answer. He knew it meant a lot to Leah.

'Er – you'd better come inside, honey and I'll explain what's happened.'

'What!' she screamed, and there followed a deadly silence. Howard joined in to listen too.

'It's a long story,' began Buster awkwardly. 'The fact is, honey,' he cleared his throat and looked up the hill, 'It appears all the eggs were addled.'

Leah went white. She dropped everything. 'Addled! It's impossible!' she cried. Then she turned where she stood and in her high-heeled shoes flew up the treacherous path to the wild bit.

Howard looked at Buster. 'That seems a great shame. When not raving about the journey, she's talked of nothing else but getting back to the geese.'

'It's not my fault, is it?' said Buster.

'That's something only you know, presumably,' said Howard going inside. 'Come on, Benjie!'

Buster stood at the top of the drive, unsure whether to follow his wife, wait or help with the baggage. In the end, he waited. When eventually she rejoined him, her voice was very tight and quiet, 'I'd like to see the eggs.'

'Oh – I guess they got thrown away.'

'What do you mean, you "guess"? Don't you know?'

'Carlos disposed of them,' said Buster, hoping the lad would have the sense to shut up and keep quiet about the whole affair. He cursed himself now for not priming him – but he'd been too busy motoring half the length of the Algarve to give the situation much attention.

'Then I shall ask him,' said Leah, her voice pure ice as she picked up her own suitcase, brushed past him and swept into the house.

Five minutes later she had emerged, changed into denims, an old sweater, and the inevitable gum boots. With Maria at her side wiping her gnarled hands on her apron, they set off purposefully towards the vegetable patch. Buster watched them go from the patio. He supposed they had gone in search of Carlos.

Carlos had been mending a water pipe which drained rainwater off one part of the hillside and diverted it down onto a more fertile slope. Here, they had been experimenting with different varieties of young fruit trees, later to be transferred to the main garden, and Buster had been proud of the progress made. The youth looked up as they approached. He observed the *senhora* had already learned the news and the shadow of shame crossed his face. He felt nervous.

'Don't be afraid,' the *senhora* said in her broken Portuguese. 'I know it's not *your* fault,' and she touched his arm.

He looked up at her grateful, but wary. He had caught a strange look on the face of Maria as if warning him of something – but of what, he could not be sure.

'Come with me, Carlos,' the *senhora* was saying, 'I want you to show me where you put the eggs.'

He nodded eagerly and caught another look from Maria. Now he was puzzled. The *senhor* had said nothing about concealing them. He did not see any harm, and better surely that she understood.

They all turned up the hillside together and Carlos beckoned the *senhora* to follow him to the back of the outhouse where they kept their firewood. Here, Benjie had started a compost heap for their herb and rose garden. Lying on top of the rotting vegetation and grass were the eggs, some broken, some still intact. They were no longer whiteish grey, but a dark, fetid colour. Despite a sickening smell, Leah picked one up, examined the small beak protruding from the chipped shell, then put it back gently. She had seen enough.

Carlos and Maria stood aside to let her pass but she did not seem to notice them. Without a word, she stumbled away from the scene and to their surprise took the cliff path to the upper reaches of their land. Only when she got to the old fisherman's bench did she let the tears fall. Buster had lied to her. She had known it rightaway. It had all been so unnecessary, she thought. So very, very unnecessary.

'Have you heard the latest?' said Jacqueline van der Stel to Maysie Vincent as they sat in their jackets, taking coffee together on the sun terrace in front of the Maritimo.

'Depends what you mean by the "latest"?' said Maysie, pulling up her collar, as with eyes closed she turned her face heavenwards to keep up her tan.

'About the American burglary,' said Jacqueline.

'Burglary? Good God, no. What got pinched? Money?'

'Oh no, that's it. The most extraordinary things! The police have drawn a complete blank. Apparently none of it makes sense, so they're not treating it very seriously. I think they take the view the stuff got left behind in America. But Howard and Leah are adamant.'

'So what's the story?' Maysie was now sufficiently interested to open her eyes.

'Well, apparently –' Jacqueline lowered her voice confidentially, 'It was Howard who discovered the first missing item. They were putting up their Christmas decorations – they seem to do things awfully early in the States – and when he went to get the centrepiece for the dining table – by all accounts some fabulous bit of Meissen or some such – there was the box intact, but no Meissen inside! I gather he nearly did his nut since that particular piece was very rare indeed and worth hundreds, no thousands of dollars.'

'But what a funny thing – keeping a valuable bit of porcelain just as a Christmas decoration!' said Maysie. 'Mummy's got a pair of Meissen swans and she has them very much in evidence in her glass cabinet all the year round. They're always being admired!'

'Ah, but I think in this case, this particular piece had something to do with Christmas, perhaps a nativity or something.'

'Who would take that?' drawled Maysie, returning to her sunbathing. 'Was that all that went?'

'No, that's just it!' said Jacqueline. 'According to Janine, who happened to be there the day they made the next discovery, all sorts of linen and stuff was taken too. Sheets, blankets, towels, cushions…you name it! Maria their maid started to complain she couldn't find matching sets for the bedrooms and it seems someone's been in, raked around and helped themselves!'

'It sounds to me like a practical joke,' said Maysie. 'When there's so much real loot around, why should any thief concern himself with soft furnishings! I've never heard anything so ridiculous in my life!'

'It's certainly odd,' said Jacqueline, 'and what's really annoying Howard is the lack of activity on the police's part. He personally thinks it's either the maid or the gardening boy, but although the *guarda* interrogated them both, they're taking no action. Also Leah's convinced they're innocent and Benjie supports her.'

'And what does darling hubbie think?'

'Well, you know how laid-back Buster is. He doesn't seem concerned either way, but as Gloria says, it wasn't his bit of valuable china that got stolen. He's saying what the police thought – they probably lost a crate or two during the move – or some tramp's been in and helped himself.'

'Can't see a tramp picking out a bit of Meissen,' snorted Maysie, 'Talking of Buster – such an amusing thing happened in the foyer here, the other day!' She regaled Jacqueline with details of their chance meeting, adding thoughtfully, 'Of course – suspicious me – I couldn't help wonder if it wasn't a call from Catalina!'

'Oh Maysie, you do jump to conclusions,' said Jacqueline. 'It was probably something terribly innocuous, like his stockbroker or something.'

'Somehow I don't think so,' said Maysie. 'He had such a guilty look on his face.'

'Then I dare you to tackle him about it!' said Jacqueline. 'We'll be seeing them all tomorrow night at Manolo Vaz Valqueiro's Christmas party.'

'Does this bow-tie look all right?' Benjie wanted to know, going into Howard's room.

'I suppose so, though you know I don't care for these made-up ones.'

'But everyone wears them nowadays, and besides, you can't buy the other kind in velvet,' Benjie fingered the plush material, 'at least not to my knowledge.'

'I suppose not,' said Howard, smoothing out his own silk one which had taken over twenty minutes to tie. He put the finishing touches to his sparse head with a tiny whale-bone comb and they went down to the library where Benjie had set up a tray for their dry martinis.

'There!' said Benjie with a last flourish of the shaker and popping in an olive. 'I must say you look superb tonight, that burgundy coloured cummerbund really suits you! I'm glad we're going out under our own steam, the others are bound to be late – there's been another argument and the atmosphere is getting really quite acid – so sad at Christmas.'

'Buster and Leah aren't the only ones who don't feel jolly. I can't stop myself brooding over the holly girl. It's sickening. Why, we've had her out every year since we've known each other. Christmas won't be the same without her.'

'I know,' said Benjie soothingly, putting on some festive music, 'It's horrible for you and no one could be more upset than me.'

'You're a good boy, Benjie.'

Benjie smiled, 'Well I'm sure some people would argue with that – but I am *sensitive* – I do *feel* things for people, and right now, I'm really hurting for you – more than you'd think.'

'I bought her when I was just starting *Maison Parfaite*,' said Howard. 'Every inch of capital had gone into the business and I could scarcely afford to dine out once a week, let alone buy priceless pieces of china. But I'll never forget the day I saw her. It was about this time of year, and New York was under snow. I walked past a shop window in 75th, cold and keen to get home, when – there it was! Such a beautiful thing – and so reminiscent somehow of Ireland, the ragged girl with her bunch of holly – I couldn't take my eyes off it. I *had* to have her. I didn't dine out after that for almost a year!'

'I've a feeling she may turn up – even yet.'

'You think so?'

'I've a kind of hunch – deep in my bones. The police aren't as stupid as everyone makes out.'

'I hope you're right,' said Howard, sounding a little comforted.

They put on their overcoats and went out to the hall. 'We're off!' called Benjie shrilly, from under the chandelier. 'See you at the party!'

'If we ever make it!' Buster yelled back from upstairs, a sarcastic ring to his voice. Benjie looked meaningfully at Howard and shrugged. 'What did I tell you? A singular lack of Christmas spirit in that quarter.'

They set off, Benjie slipping behind the wheel, as usual. What a difference to his feelings tonight, compared with those on the long journey to Lisbon the other day! He grimaced at the memory of the abscessed tooth; it was doubtful which was the harder to bear, the excruciating pain or the gripping guilt and fear. The spectre of discovery over the porcelain's disappearance had loomed darker and more formidable with each passing day.

And then the miracle! How it had happened, he could not begin to imagine, but it had! Some sort of burglary had taken place – as if by magic – to distract and take attention far beyond the holly-girl and onto to another whole level. An extraordinary level which involved Leah and Buster and their servants too, and visits from the police and other possibilities. And although none of the evidence gleaned had made much sense, he knew now for sure that he had been saved. Suspicion had fallen on others, and would never – in this present climate – couldn't possibly – fall on him. He was liberated, safe! Saved by Fate! Maybe there was a God, after all.

32

$\mathcal{A}$s they drove through the centre of Santa Felicia, out into the country and finally down a small private road to the brand new golf course where Manolo Vaz Valqueira had leased his villa, Benjie felt in high spirits. With the curse of the porcelain lifted from his shoulders, there was nothing to stop him enjoying this evening. With Manolo as host, it would be a sophisticated and lively party. Parking as directed on the rough grass at the ninth tee between a Lotus and a Ferrari, he found himself humming *I'm Dreamin' of a White Christmas* as they climbed out into the cold air. Was that a shade of a smile on his partner's lips? After all the upset of the last few days, the brightly lit villa could only bring cheer at such a time.

Within minutes they were part of it all, brimming glasses and melt-in-the-mouth canapes being pressed upon them by long-legged girls in Bunny suits. Augusto and Corinne Neves edged up smilingly, having struck up quite a friendship at one of Johanna's little supper parties. Benjie winked at Corinne as Howard buttonholed Augusto, eager for news of Wall Street and other broking matters. He was now positively beaming with appreciation at someone who talked his own financial language.

There was a stir when Johanna and her stunning daughter Maysie were sighted. Both nearly had their entrances overshadowed by the arrival of the Bloomfields who were equally late. In contrast however, the American couple were throwing out so much negative energy, Benjie shuddered and turned away. 'Right at this moment, I feel it's important we don't appear as though we live in each others' pockets,' he hissed, steering Howard in the opposite direction. 'Buster looks ready for a fight!'

Despite a slinky black cocktail dress, Leah appeared haggard. Johanna, by contrast, looked even more beautiful than ever in a holly-berry red gown of light cashmere that billowed out gracefully from a fitted bodice. As she moved, it swirled round her long legs and she clearly knew she looked gorgeous. Her daughter, in a shimmering gold halter-neck should have eclipsed her, the same fine bone structure and large eyes a photographer's dream, but her air of weary aloofness drove most prospective suitors away. Even the Portuguese stood back. What a waste, thought Benjie – someone should tell her to smile once in a while.

'My dear Leah,' Johanna was saying, 'I haven't seen you or your husband in an age! Are you quite well, my dear?'

'She's on top of the world,' cut in Buster, 'and she's going to have a ball tonight.'

'Well, that's a relief,' said Johanna, amused. A moment later, she was being greeted by Manolo – as if she were some goddess – thought Leah, as they all drifted up the long *sala* together.

For once the party was not dominated by ex-pats. On the cutting edge of development, Manolo was an avid networker and Leah recognised their notary, two local lawyers, the mayor and several minions from the town hall. Judging by the official car with its Lisbon number-plate, flag and chauffeur at the top of the drive, he had even managed to lure the Minister for Tourism from his city haunts. Normally, Leah would have been enthusiastic about such an opportunity, but tonight she felt inadequate to the occasion. Everyone looked so glamorous and in fine form except her. The house too was stunning; an enormous Portuguese fir stood in the hall whilst artfully arranged garlands of fresh holly and ivy trailed the picture rail. What a waste of an evening when she felt so low!

The chief of police, a constant presence in their town, recognised her and lumbered up. When off duty he enjoyed his drink and despite her throbbing brow she caught a strong whiff as he inclined his boar's head towards her. *Cabo* Fonseca prided himself on his grasp of English, all picked up in his dealings with the ex-pats. When he'd started in the force as an under-paid *guarda*, Santa Felicia boasted few international visitors, but he made it his business to keep tabs on every new resident and had surprised himself with his linguistic skills. Now, 30 years on, he was a force to be reckoned with. Fonseca kept things clean, ordered and on a tight rein. He exercised discipline. He had a head for names and faces. He knew every single inhabitant of the town, local and *estrangeiro* and kept a watchful note of their comings and goings. Rumour had it he was in daily contact with the dreaded secret police and he was always the first to know of impending trouble.

Partially feared, definitely respected, the *Cabo* sitting behind his huge desk in the police station at the top of the town was a familiar sight to most ex-pats. Not only could he open the door to achieving residential status, the precious licences upon which every business depended could be given or taken away at one swoop. Without his last say in the matter, there could be no work permits, no long-term place for a foreign car and no trade. For a man who exercised such slavish adherence to the state, he had a surprisingly entrepreneurial eye for opportunity. As people grew to know him they became aware that Fonseca knew exactly how and where to distribute largesse – or the opposite – all within the law. In sharp contrast to turning a blind eye with some, he took a draconian attitude with others, his own compatriots proving no exception especially where drugs were concerned. He was particularly allergic to students down for the holidays from the universities of Lisbon or Coimbra – hot-beds of evil and insurrection – he often remarked.

Whilst Leah was streetwise about local authority, she also knew how to butter up bully-boys; there'd been plenty of those in New York too. Just prior to returning to America for the last time, she had gone to the police station to collect a bundle of forms for their *residencia* and he'd called her into his office. 'Everytheeng OK, *Senhora* Bloomfield? Getting ready for your beeg move, very soon, ha?'

'Oh, yes, we can't wait, quite frankly!' She was only too aware of the rows of files, lined up like neat soldiers in the guard room. She knew there was already a file on Casa Amarela, but she had nothing to hide, so what did it matter?

'Anytheeng more I can do for you?'

'You'll keep an eye on our place, won't you sir,' she had smiled as they shook hands and pressed a five thousand note into his waiting palm.

As he turned to see her out, his heavy grey uniform and winged breeches seemed to slow him down, and she wondered if it wasn't enough. 'You good lady,' he said thoughtfully. '*Cabo* Fonseca like people like you. Santa Felicia need good residents. Solid peoples… not reeff-raff.'

She guessed he knew she knew the rules of the game. From that day forth, and over the months that followed, there seemed a mutual understanding between them.

Clearly tonight there was no ulterior motive in his warm hand-shake, but even so. It amused him to see a muscle twitching at the side of her mouth and he fancied it was his own importance that had this effect on her. But this was not the time for discord. It was the festive season and tomorrow was the Feast of *Natal* so he could afford to be generous. 'And how ees the *Senhora* Bloomfield tonight?' He wore his most reassuring grin as he squared up in front of her.

'Oh – er – as well as can be expected, thank you, *Cabo* Fonseca.' The smell of his breath as it washed over her, a mixture of brandy and garlic, made her want to throw up, but she managed a weak smile.

'We steel see no sign of those meesing objects,' said the policeman cheerfully. 'But my men – they work on it, steel. You may rest assured.'

'Yes, I well realise you're giving it your best attention, *Cabo* Fonseca. We all appreciate what you're doing – very much.' She backed away, but he merely took a step closer as he repeated the question she had heard too many times before.

'You are quite, quite sure, *Senhora* Bloomfield, that a friend does not play thees theeng they call the 'practical joke'? For me, it seem like the – how you say – inside job!' He raised a crooked eyebrow.

Leah shook her head emphatically, but the nervous tic at her mouth had intensified. He looked at her shrewdly and she found herself flushing as she replied that it was quite impossible that anyone should do such a thing. Yet… even to herself it sounded feeble.

'Very well,' he said, 'then I and my men – we continue to search for thees – er – thief. Stealing is a serious crime, *Senhora* Bloomfield. Santa Felicia not a place where thief get away. Not with *Guarda Nacional Republicana!*'

'I hope not,' said Leah, relieved as he drew back and fresh air assailed her nostrils again.

'And now, I wish you the Merry Chreesmas,' he said and appearing satisfied, withdrew his presence to melt into the throng.

Buster had not reappeared and Leah was just wondering whether or not to get her own drink when Jacqueline van der Stel bounced up to her. 'Manolo sent me over with this!' she said, handing her a steaming glass of punch. 'It's his special Christmas brew and he said you were to drink it up rightaway and then help yourself to another one. Seems to think you need pepping up! Crikey!' she said, breaking off in full flight, 'Are you all right? You look simply awful!'

'That's all I need!' said Leah, clasping both hands round the hot glass so that Jacqueline wouldn't notice the tremor in them.

'I saw old Fonseca with you just now, no wonder you're shaking! He always makes me feel guilty, even though I've done nothing wrong! Was he giving you the third degree?'

'No, he was just reassuring me about the robbery. I don't think he believes it was a theft though. I could tell by the look in his eyes.'

'Yes, they're horribly expressive,' said Jacqueline. 'I'll never forget the way he looked at me when he discovered I hadn't had my passport stamped for over sixty days. For a moment I really believed he was going to put me behind bars. I said to myself – there and then, I must –'

She was still talking when Leah's goblet fell to the floor with a clatter; a moment later she was lying at Jacqueline's feet. 'Oh my God!' she cried, helpless and staring, 'Someone do something! Quick!'

Within seconds, they were surrounded. Jacqueline's own husband was already taking charge, clearing a path through the hushed and muttering bystanders. Within seconds, he and a tall Portuguese boy had carried the inert, crumpled figure of Leah towards the patio door and fresh air. Another Portuguese, a kindly middle-aged man with greying hair, pushed forward with the magic words, 'I'm a doctor...' and with a relieved look on his face, Manolo indicated a room where Leah might gently be laid on a bed to recover.

Jacqueline was still rooted to the spot when Karl came back and put his arm round her. 'She's all right,' he said. 'She's already come round.'

'Thank God for that,' said his wife, close to tears. 'She looked so terrible and I stood there like some dumb idiot and did nothing to help. I've never seen someone go out like that before! One moment we were talking, next moment she went straight down! It was horrible.'

With the drama now removed to another room, the hum of voices soon rose to normal levels again and as Karl led his wife back to the centre of the party, he noticed to his surprise that Buster was at the bar. Clearly he must be oblivious of what had happened. He pushed Jacqueline in between Johanna and Maysie Vincent, whispering something in the older woman's ear, then strode over to Buster to break the news. 'You'd better go out there, mate,' he said, nodding in the direction of the hall. 'Your wife's been taken poorly – she passed clean out.'

'You don't need to tell me,' said Buster belligerently, 'I've already been called out there once.'

'But –' Karl was both puzzled and surprised, 'aren't you going to take her home?'

'Aren't I hell!' said Buster. 'The doc says it's best she lies still for a bit. Why should I miss a good party? – we'll go when I'm ready.'

Something in Karl's expression egged him on, 'It's not my fault, you know. The reason she passes out like that is because she's taken too many of those goddarned pills again. Tranquillisers she calls them! I wouldn't be surprised if she doesn't tranquillise herself so much she never wakes up one morning.'

'Well! If – er – there's anything more I can do, let me know,' van der Stel drew back, oddly embarassed. 'If you want any help getting her out to the car, just come and find me.'

'Thanks for the offer, buddy – I'll do that!' Buster jerked a thumb at him.

Manolo, thrown by the events of the last few minutes – he was used to 'everything' he told everyone, 'except people fainting' – decided to bring on the food before the whole party atmosphere ground to a halt. Uniformed maids had replaced the bunny-girls and scuttled cheerfully to and from the dining room. In no time at all, their host was gratified to see his guests tucking into the traditional Christmas Eve dish of 'bacalhau à brás' – dried codfish cooked in an exotic way with eggs, onions, olive oil and fried potatoes sprinkled with chopped chives.

'I've always thought this sounded disgusting,' said Maysie, toying with a miniscule portion of white fish and forking it into her mouth. 'In actual fact – it's really quite tasty.'

'I told you,' said her mother. 'I wonder how poor Leah is now?' She turned to Jacqueline, 'I feel quite guilty for not having given her more sympathy when we arrived this evening. She was obviously in dire need of some support.'

'Yes,' said Jacqueline, who had lost her appetite. 'I believe she's had a rotten week. First, you know, she lost all the goslings she'd hoped to hatch, then came the robbery, and lastly I believe Buster's been giving her a hard time.'

'Oh really?' said Johanna, interested. 'Oh look! Here come the Boys, perhaps they can tell us more.'

The two friends advanced then separated to stand one on either side of the famous actress. 'You look *gorgeous!*' they said in one accord. Johanna fluttered with pleasure before asking coyly what was going on at the yellow house on the hill, that one of their community should pass out so dramatically on Christmas Eve itself.

Howard's face clouded over, 'I'm not a bit surprised,' he said. 'Personally, I've suspected Leah to be heading for a nervous breakdown. Ever since the McKays left, she's been odd – then we had the crisis with the geese – we all blame Buster for that, he behaved in such an irresponsible and heartless way – much as I dislike the creatures,' he added hurriedly.

'Can't say they're my favourite bird, either,' said Johanna sympathetically.

'You know it's really odd,' Howard continued, 'The atmosphere in the house used to be so cheerful, so motivated, so full of – oh I don't know – a kind of promise for the future. There was a tempered excitement, we were all so agog with plans, ideas and schemes for improvement…the realisation of a dream come true! And now –' he paused for breath, almost embarrassed by his sudden burst of eloquence –

'Go on,' said Johanna.

'Well, it was exciting! Challenging! But now – something seems to have gone badly wrong. It's as if a rot has set in, taken hold, entered our lives. In a way it reminds me of Benjie's abscessed tooth – sorry, old guy,' – he squeezed his companion's arm – 'I don't mean this personally, but it's a good comparison… the poisoned tooth affecting everything and everyone.' He broke off and forked some food into his mouth. 'Pardon me, folks,' he squinted round at them from behind his pebble lenses, suddenly embarassed. 'I guess I've talked too much. It must be Manolo's punch – or something.'

Catalina opened an eye and peered sleepily around the unfamiliar room. It was still dark but she could just make out humps of large furniture until her eye finally rested on the small travelling clock her husband had placed on the dressing-table the night before. Its luminous hands pointed to what looked like half-past six. Oh well – a good hour at least to go – provided Katy did not wake too early. It was always such an onslaught on Christmas Day. First the invasion of their room, creeping uninvited into their bed, dragging half her stocking behind her, repressed anticipation for more presents off the tree – Jock insisting that the bigger gifts were only handed out *after* the Queen – what did it matter, for heaven's sake? And then, driven to distraction with all the unwrapping, there were the usual impossible questions – which chimney had Santa Claus come down? Had he eaten the cake they'd left out? How did he know how to find her? Why no reindeer prints? And all the rest.

For how long would it go on? Catalina couldn't help but wonder. She still remembered her own bitter disappointment when – at the tender age of seven – her mother informed her it was all just a story. Years later, when she hurled a host of recriminations at her parents in a typical teenage row, the subject had come up again. Her mother's response that she felt it wrong to lie was not good enough. Catalina thought it a poor excuse. In her opinion, it was OK to lie in a good cause and she said so. Besides, it was fun! Despite the nuisance of it all, she hoped the magic of belief in a real Father Christmas might stay with Katy until the child found out for herself. After all, it made it more entertaining for the adults too!

The air in the room was biting. She never could quite get used to Jock's barbaric practice of sleeping with the window open a crack, no matter how low the temperature. It was one of the few matters on which he insisted on having his own way. He was still sound asleep, breathing quietly, with his back turned towards her. She snuggled into him for warmth and tucked her knees spoonlike into the crook of his. She knew she would get no more sleep now; she too was excited and the thrilling thoughts of what lay ahead today, tomorrow and the next day, were already pounding away at her brain. But it was cosy lying here like this. She felt as snug and protected as a young squirrel in its nest. She also had a feeling that if Jock woke up and felt her here so close, he might want to make love to her. That would be a nice start to Christmas morning.

It had been their third night in this draughty old house. She had not been looking forward to the move from fashionable Richmond down to rural Somerset, but had surprised herself by adapting to country life quite easily. They were kind, Jock's cousins – sensible, unimaginative people whom she fancied were slightly in awe of her. They travelled little, had no time for the theatre or the arts and their main preoccupation in life seemed to be dogs, horses and getting their feet muddy whenever humanly possible. To Catalina's relief, the mud this year had been replaced by a firm carpet of crunchy snow which delighted her daughter. In front of the kitchen porch – no one seemed to use the front door, a pity since it was rather impressive – stood a long line of wellington boots, yard boots, riding boots, walking and hobnailed boots, and every manner of outer footwear imaginable, stretching for eternity.

Even Katy was forced to join the boot brigade. Susan, Jock's first cousin, an angular wispy-haired woman in her late forties, had marched the child into their local market town on the first day of arrival. Triumphant, they'd come back bearing some very smart red wellies, which Katy had lived in ever since. Susan and Geoff had no children of their own – Catalina doubted they'd ever made time to initiate such a process – but it was probably a blessing when one considered all the four-legged dependents that made up their family. Feline, canine and equine, all were given top priority – especially the latter. Soon Katy was being sucked into this pattern of life, so much so that she eagerly accepted Cousin

Susan's invitation to stay on until the end of the holidays, even after her parents returned to Portugal for New Year.

Jock was stirring in his sleep and turned towards her. His arms came round her neck and she guided his fingers into the cleavage of her breasts and pushed her rounded tummy against his flat one. He edged towards her and she moved in tighter, marvelling as she did, how well their bodies fitted and how he still turned her on. Soon, he was growing hard against her and a smile of anticipation lit her lips. They had not made love since that disastrous time of the telegram – it seemed like an age – and the worry and pressures of the exhibition had clearly killed off all desire on her husband's part. Now, if she was careful not to disturb this sleepy state too suddenly, they could have a delicious time and he wouldn't start thinking logically or worrying about their predicament until it was too late.

Scarcely daring to breathe, she entangled her arms and slipped down the bed, humping the heavy covers up and over her shoulders to engulf them both in their heat. She knew exactly how to arouse him from his sleepy state, her tongue roving easily around the smooth ridges of his length, preparing him, tempting him for what must happen next. Before he had time to protest, she had pushed herself up with her elbows and come gently down onto his growing desire. Coming up for air, she gasped with delight – then pushed down harder to check all was secure. Only when they were snugly locked together did she allow herself the luxury of a chuckle. Slowly, slowly she began to move her buttocks in a rotating rhythmical motion, the urgent heat of her stomach drawing him into her own rhythms, cyclical patterns of craving and warmth. Just as she'd planned and done a hundred times before, he was taken over by the spontaneity of his own strong body matching hers. They took a long, slow time but as usual he waited for her to come first, and it was all utterly divine.

Later, lying back against the pillows, damp from their mingled sweat, McKay stroked her hair and felt an overpowering sensation of protectiveness. There was something so childlike about his wife, even though he recognised in her the most manipulative woman he'd ever met. 'I feel a new man,' he said, looking up at the ceiling as the slow streaks of dawn changed the room from black to milky grey. 'It's an awful old cliché, but it happens to be true.'

'It was my Christmas present,' Catalina was looking up too, 'or rather, one of them.'

'Are there more?' he asked, kissing her bare shoulder.

'Mmmmm – you'll have to wait and see,' she stretched luxuriously.

'When may I know?'

'After breakfast.'

'I suppose I can wait until then. Just let me know... hello! Did I hear someone at the door?'

'It's the child,' Catalina could just make out a pale face peeping round the lock. 'I've told you always to knock!' she called.

'Yes, but it's Christmas!'

'Come back in ten minutes' said Catalina sternly. Then in a kinder tone, 'and we'll all have breakfast together, and you can show us your stocking!'

Leah awoke early. Her head was clear but her right elbow ached. She put an explorative finger around the joint and discovered a bruise the size of an orange. She hadn't been aware that she'd banged it when she collapsed last night.

She slipped out of bed. Buster was sprawled diagonally across two-thirds, snoring his head off. The room was stuffy and she found her fluffy mules and went to open a window. She poked her head outside and listened to the wakening sounds of birds, frogs, crickets and far away in the distance a donkey braying, followed by the soft muffled clanging of its bell. She inhaled the sweet air deeply. As usual her lungs and nasal passages felt instantly cleansed by the tangy saltiness of the Atlantic air. The gift of the ocean to all of us lucky enough to live here, she thought. Delicious! Who could ask for more on this Christmas morning?

Leaving the window wide open, she crept back into the room, pulled a robe around her and stepped silently onto the landing. All was quiet on the Western front. As usual I'm the first one up! Oh – and it's our first Christmas in the Algarve! How blessed we are to be here, she thought. Perhaps with the advent of this special day, last night will be forgotten and everything come right again.

Full of optimism and pleased that she could think clearly after all that had happened in the past week, she proceeded downstairs to the kitchen. She would make the most superb festive breakfast ever, lay the table for four, light the fire and the candles, put on some music and when it was all ready, she would call each one of them to come along and share in the Feast.

How surprised they would be – especially after last night! She had not seen Benjie and Howard again after she'd fainted and reckoned they'd kept away on purpose. It was their kind host Manolo, who finally tracked down Buster and persuaded him to take her home. The Boys had stayed on – who could blame them? The trouble was, she'd caused a scene. She knew Howard hated scenes and Benjie would always stand by him, quick to condemn if occasion demanded it. But, after all, it had been an accident! A quirk of Fate, pure and simple…surely they would be persuaded to see that in the cold light of a new day? Christmas was for good cheer and putting the past behind you. This festive breakfast must surely wipe the slate clean and put everyone in good spirits. She was convinced of that.

As she opened the kitchen door, Mungo threw himself at her with unexpected pleasure and she found herself gripping the wall to steady herself. 'Down boy, *dow-own*!' Why was her voice trembling? This was ridiculous! She switched on the light, cursing herself as she did so, in case the sound of the generator roaring to life woke the others. She pulled out a kitchen chair and sat down heavily. It was all so silly. A moment ago she had felt fine, now – somehow – her legs had turned again to jelly and the old panic feeling was threatening to take hold. As she felt her heart thumping under the thin bathrobe, she wondered whether or not to take a tranquie. No, better not, she told herself.

Buster had railed at her last night; told her she was no better than a junkie and that her pills were to blame for everything. 'As for your fainting act – why you had to draw so much attention to yourself like that, I shall never know,' he had said bitterly as they'd driven home. 'You wanted sympathy because of a few upsets which should have been left behind – and so you decided you would get it – and in your own way. And *what* a way! I tell you I was ashamed.'

She had felt too fragile and weary to have yet another blazing row with him, but tears had come and she hated herself as she recognised the self-pity. Leaving Buster to console himself with the bourbon bottle in the library, she had gone to bed. It had come as a surprise when later, despite the alcohol, he'd clambered under the covers and slowly and deliberately had sex with her. It had taken a long time for him to climax and all the while he lay on top of her she felt used and miserable, knowing there was not a trace of love in his advances. For an awful moment the thought struck her she had now become a mere receptacle for his gratification and that any self-respecting female would have pushed him off. But it was easier, somehow, to give in. Nevertheless, as he plundered his way – without even uttering her name, or an endearment – she felt the hot tears prick her eyes and wondered how it was possible their marriage had come to sink so low.

Now as she sipped black coffee and concentrated her mind, she wanted to believe her compliance last night had not been in vain. Sex was important to Buster and if she could use this to shore up the rift and bring them together physically at a time when frayed nerves, tension and coldness had driven them apart, it was worth persevering. She braced her back-bone and gave herself a little shake – determining in her head that last night's visitation could herald some pleasanter future state – acquiescence, tolerance, acceptance. Anything would be better than the sensation of alienation they had both endured, one with the other, over the past few weeks.

Soon she was back on her feet. The caffeine had kicked in and she needed to be busy. Christmas lunch was scheduled for three in the afternoon but this year Benjie and Howard had elected to do the turkey so there was nothing to be done there until they decreed. Neither was there any tidying up. It was a public holiday throughout the land so Maria had the day off, but since they'd been out the night before, the work surfaces looked immaculate. Then she remembered, she'd eaten nothing! No wonder she felt so wobbly and weak, it wasn't the tranquies, it was lack of food! Feeling happier, she spread a piece of toast with maple syrup and planned her next move. What would she give them? Eggs, sausages, mushrooms, tomatoes? – oh and corn cookies – she'd stashed a supply in the freezer. Out came the cereals too – puffed wheat for Howard, muesli for Benjie. Who could resist a good American breakfast on Christmas Day in the morning?

As the bacon she was frying separately for Howard and Buster began to sizzle, she took time laying the table. The *sala*, library and dining-room where lunch would be served, were already liberally adorned with holly and the festive garlands they'd brought over from America whilst a tall silver tree stood sentinel in the hall. Apart from strings of cards, nothing much had been done in the kitchen. This she felt deserved something different.

It was Mungo who gave her the lead. He scraped at the door and as she poked her nose outside and waited for him as he disappeared into the emerging dawn, she had it! A memory tugged at the back of her brain. Yesterday, when she'd gone out to her wild bit to feed the geese as usual, she'd spotted it. A particularly pretty blossom – a fragile pinky-white flower on a prickly bush – which she'd never noticed before. She was almost sure it was arbutus. What better way of celebrating Christmas Morn than by bringing some wild blossom into the house and setting it in pride of place on their breakfast table! Without waiting for the sun to come up, she seized a pair of shears and followed their dog out into the cold morning. It was time to bring in her own particular offering.

The three of them sat up in bed together, warm from the closeness of their bodies and from the delicious farmhouse breakfast they had just eaten. It was a rare treat for this small trio to eat, laugh and whoop together. Cousin Susan had borne in the breakfast tray, her brown eyes merry as she observed the large patchwork quilt strewn with Christmas wrapping, silver paper, tangerines and nuts and all the debris of Katy's stocking.

'Breakfast in bed! Good Lord!' Jock had cried, 'What spoiling! Let me help with that tray.'

'No, don't get out,' his cousin said firmly. 'You'll only upset the applecart. Stay put and make the most of it!' and she set the tray down on their collective lap and swiftly withdrew again, chuckling to herself.

Now, as the last delicious morsel of sausage and scrambled egg had disappeared, with not a drop of tea remaining in the pot, Catalina addressed her daughter, 'Time for you to go and get dressed now, darling. Aunt Susan will be wanting a hand with the animals no doubt.' As the child left the room, she turned to her husband still leaning against the pillows and obviously savouring the luxury of the moment. 'And now it's time for your present,' she said, an air of importance in her tone.

'But we usually do this later,' he replied, 'mine are all downstairs, under the Christmas tree.'

'And so are mine, but this is an extra one. I wanted to give it to you when we were on our own.'

'How mysterious!'

She shot him an enigmatic look and climbed out of bed to fetch it from her suitcase, a compact, curvaceous figure in a clinging coffee-coloured negligée. She came back to bed with the tiniest of packages. As she watched, he unwrapped it to reveal a small leather box. Out fell a ring. For a moment he said nothing. He stared at it; then stared at her. Her face gave nothing away.

He looked at the ring and was puzzled. A surprise knot started to tighten in his stomach. He hated rings on men and she knew that. Only his father's old signet ring with the family crest was allowed. This he wore on the little finger of his left hand, but even this, he often forgot. He remembered telling her on more than one occasion that whilst European gentlemen might wear a wedding ring on their fourth finger, in Britain it was considered naff – at least in his circles. No officer or gentleman of his generation would dream of wearing such an adornment, unless it was a ring of office – a member of the Church – or the Royal Family.

Very aware of the niceties of etiquette, Catalina had listened carefully and taken it all in. Sometimes she berated him for being old-fashioned. Other times, she would nudge and comment, especially if she spotted a wedding ring on another ex-pat. So why this? What *was* she up to?

Still unable to speak, he turned it over and examined it. All the time he felt her eyes upon him. It was obviously an expensive piece of jewellery, soft gold of the highest carat, he suspected, inlaid with jade which ran in a narrow band around the centre. The whole thing was slim and discreet. If one liked rings, it was by no means offensive, in fact it was austere and rather beautiful. But try as he might, he had no desire to put it on.

He could feel his own silence weighing heavily between them. In the end, he simply said – 'Why?'

She lowered her eyes so that her long sooty lashes shadowed her cheeks demurely, but he was not taken in. This was no maidenly blush. All his instincts told him it concealed an ulterior motive which, for reasons best known to herself, she did not wish him to read in her eyes. He knew her too well. Finally she composed herself and with eyes wide-open and bland, replied 'Don't you realise what it is?'

'It's a ring,' he said, whilst the knot tightened inside.

'But what kind of ring, darling?'

'I've no idea,' he said shortly. 'You know I don't do rings.'

'There's no need to sound so cross,' she said. 'I don't expect you to wear it.'

'I see,' he said, not seeing. 'Then, what precisely do you wish me to do with it?'

She sighed as if he was being particularly obtuse. 'Keep it,' she said, 'That's all.'

'That's *all*?' he repeated.

'Jock – please – don't you understand about signs and symbols? It's an eternity ring! I know you won't wear it but you must keep it – as a token. Don't you see? A token of me – for eternity.'

'OK…that's great. I'll do that…er, thank you very much…indeed.'

He felt cross now. What a fucking waste of money. This little number was no Christmas cracker trinket; the box said Cartier! He did not mind pranks, but this was crazy and so unnecessary in their impecunious state. If it wasn't Christmas, he would have spanked her bottom very hard indeed. As it was, she had already ruined his day.

'You're not pleased, are you?' she said.

'Not very, but never mind. I dare say I'll get over it. It's Christmas, after all.'

'Darling – please,' this time her mouth was wobbling and for a moment he thought he spotted genuine tears. 'I know you think I've been silly, wasting your money on something you'll never wear – but I mean what it symbolises. It's an eternity ring – for you to keep, and remember… for ever. It's important to *me* that you have this.'

He sighed inwardly, but kissed the top of her head. 'Well, the timing's very odd. But OK. I'll put it in my studbox and it will always be there. Does that please you?'

She nodded and then without further ado, got out of bed. 'I think it's time we got dressed now,' was all she said.

33

Christmas had merged into Boxing Day and an uneasy peace settled on the yellow house on the hill. Everything had passed off smoothly enough. Leah's breakfast had been appreciated and the Boys excelled themselves at lunch with their sixteen-pound turkey and three kinds of stuffing. The Christmas pudding blazed its way obligingly all the way from hob to table and the brandy butter, made with Portuguese cognac, was pronounced the best. To finish off, a box of orange peel coated in chocolate from Lisbon, and marzipan fruits, took precedence over the usual *marrons glacés* and that was before they moved to the fireside when Buster brought out a vintage Dow.

Before lunch on Boxing Day they held open house for all the other Americans living in the Algarve and by the time that was over, champagne bottles strewed the garage floor, and wrapping paper was ankle-deep. The only discordant note to the holiday atmosphere had been the noticeable absence of the Dresden holly-girl, a matter which Howard pointed out to every guest, every visitor and every helper in the forlorn hope that someone might have seen her – plus the fact that Buster had completely forgotten to buy a Christmas present for his wife.

To Leah's credit, she had laughed it off in laudable manner, but as Howard had observed later to Benjie in private, it showed how swiftly the marriage was breaking down and he wondered not for the first time that week, how any further fracture in relations would affect them.

The last few days of December passed quickly and uneventfully. Work started again in the garden and they all seemed to fall into the old routine of taming the land, building, improving and creating. There was one noticeable difference, thought Leah, wondering if any one else had noticed; instead of working as a foursome, everything now seemed to happen in shifts. It was the same in the kitchen. All summmer and autumn, she and Benjie had seamlessly shared their culinary tasks and although Benjie could be possessive over a particular recipe, generally they worked in harmony. Now, all that had changed. The day after Boxing Day, he asked pointedly, 'Are you cooking tonight, or shall I?'

From then onwards, they took things in turns. Vanished were the small volunteers over side dishes and salads, and when she offered some support on 'his night', it was politely declined with a bland smile, 'No thanks – I'm really much better on my own.'

Increasingly, the Boys were getting asked out, often without the Bloomfields. Johanna Vincent's small dinner parties were typical and when Leah remarked on this to Janine Baxter in the market place one morning, her fellow countrywoman laughed in her face.

'But of course! Whatever their leanings, they're two spare guys, for heavens' sakes. With so many single women round this god-forsaken place, it's little wonder they're in such demand!' Such a thought had not occurred to Leah. It should have made her feel better, but instead she continued to worry that she and Buster were being slighted on purpose. Only the Neves seemed keen to see them, although even those visits had slackened off once the tennis season was over.

On the morning of 29ʰ December, she was cheered enormously by a heavier than usual delivery of mail. There were dozens of delayed Christmas cards from America, mainly old staff and business associates, but the news that really excited her was an *aviso* for a telegram. It was addressed to her personally, and for some reason she had a hunch it just might have come from the McKays. She had missed Catalina more than she could say and had heard on the grapevine that Jock's exhibition had not gone well. In fact, reviews in both *The Times* and the *New York Times* seemed to have been positively dismal. Could it be they might be returning home, ahead of schedule? She would hurry into town and find out.

The cable had come from Spain; how very strange – she had been hoping for one from England. As she opened it up, her heart raced. It *was* the McKays… but they were already on their way! The message was perfunctory.

'*Arriving Algarve on 30 th. Will ring you at the shop at six! Can you be there? – Love Catalina X*'

It had been sent off from Burgos the day before. This meant the McKays would now be heading through central Spain. She wondered at which frontier post they would enter Portugal. They could already be in the north for all she knew, or they could be heading down to Andalucia. Whichever route they took, it would be a long, wearisome drive and they would need cheering up. She and Buster had nothing planned for New Year's Eve, so with any luck they might be allowed to welcome the returning couple home. Leah could have hugged herself with delight. She would be ready and waiting for that call.

So far, the subject of any festivities had not been discussed in any depth. Howard and Benjie had indicated they were off to a party; where to and whose, she had no idea. She was certainly not going to ask. They were discussing their plans over breakfast that morning but when she'd sauntered in with Mungo after his walk, they closed up like clams. They had become so secretive nowadays, it really hurt.

Contrary to her Christmas hopes and expectations, things with Buster were not much better. She had hoped the recent sex would lead to a warmer relationship. There were no more desperate rows, but she felt him growing daily more distant and no matter what she did, she could not seem to reach him. On several occasions, he had gone off with the car for no apparent reason and when she asked him why – he replied, 'I just like looking around.'

One day, when the air held the promise of spring, she saw him getting ready to drive out as usual and asked if she might join him. 'It would be kind of fun to explore,' she said.

'Oh,' was his reply, 'then you better take the car.'

'No, you dope – not on my own! I wanted to join you!'

She saw the irritation leap across his eyes but he opened the passenger door and said, 'Jump in then.'

She got in and as they bumped their way down the hillside, he said, 'Where to?'

'Where do you go? I only want to go where you go.'

He tightened his lips and set off in an easterly direction through the villages that led towards the main road and Faro. 'I just drive around,' he said more to himself than to her, 'me and the dog. And if I find a good walking place, then we get out – if not, we come home.'

It had been a disastrous afternoon. Words were sparse and she felt his growing resentment loom between them, building a wedge. The scenery on this eastward side was less interesting, and they scarcely left the highway. She vowed never to try to join him again.

Now the only bright spot on Leah's horizon was the return of Catalina. It would be fantastic to see her friend again, laugh with her, giggle, feel that warm soft hand squeeze her arm, oozing sympathy and understanding. She hurried home full of news to tell her husband. He was out at the swimming pool site, talking to Roper. Buster ignored her as she came up. Roper smiled politely and stood aside to let her join them. Only when she thrust the telegram under his nose, did Buster take any notice. 'What's this?' he asked sharply.

'It's the McKays!' she said, breathless with excitement. 'They'll be back here tomorrow night.'

Roper looked from one to the other and was curious. The one normally pale and earnest, now looked flushed and exhilarated from her scramble down the hill; the other, whom he could have sworn was ruddy-cheeked a moment ago, had grown quite pale. He wondered if the McKays – whoever they were – meant bad news, but it was not his business, so he kept quiet.

'Well, aren't you going to say something?' the wife was demanding.

'What do you want me to say?' the husband was quick to regain composure.

'But don't you think that's the greatest news we've had this side of Christmas?' her pale blue eyes were shining.

'Yeah – sure, it'll be good to see them again.'

'Is that all you can say?' cried the wife, 'I tell you I just can't *wait*.'

She flounced off, exasperated but happy. Roper looked after her, then back at the man with whom he was doing business. He somehow sensed the news the cable had brought was not as inconsequential as his client made out. Somewhere, Roper smelt trouble. He hoped whatever it was, it wouldn't interfere with the completion of his contract. He also wondered for the hundredth time, if he wouldn't be wiser in future to insist his clients paid everything up front.

They had decided to spend the last night of their journey in Seville. Normally, after the voyage from England, they would cut diagonally across northern Spain to enter Portugal halfway down at one of the mountainous passes such as Guarda. This time however, Catalina begged her husband to drive directly south and into the warmer climes of Andalucia first.

'It would be wonderful to spend our last night in Sevilla,' she had said persuasively. 'Then we can head straight through to Ayamonte, on the 30th take the ferry across the river to Vila Real and be back home in time for tea!

He had agreed. It would be their last extravagance. The city held a special significance for it was here, not long after their marriage, they had taken part in the Holy Week celebrations as guests of the great Alvarez family. Jock had been at Harrow with Don Luiz, one of the biggest sherry exporters in Spain, and his magnificent town house with its retinue of servants was put at their disposal. Catalina, caught up in marital bliss and all the excitement following their wedding had remained wide-eyed and thrilled throughout the fever-pitched week of fiesta. It was her first experience of life in a European nobleman's house and the whole atmosphere of processing through the streets, the gilt Madonnas, the cathedral, high-stepping horses, bullfights, *flamenco* and all the while socialising at the private *casetas* and restaurants acted upon her quicksilver mind like a double shot of adrenalin.

Spellbound, she had become as loving and romantic as if she were playing the heroine in some medieval drama. Young Katy had been conceived in that week, and for Jock that week in Seville was remembered as probably the happiest of his life. They had made several pilgrimages back to that stunning, radiant city and both regarded it as their own special place.

Now on their homeward journey, Catalina seemed desperate to return to her *Sevilla*. McKay felt curiously touched and despite the extra expense, determined to make it their last carefree night before grim reality set in. In a moment of madness, he telephoned in advance and booked a room at the Alfonso XIII, arguably the finest and grandest hotel in the Peninsula.

To her credit, Catalina was clearly surprised when they left the hurtling traffic behind to turn in at the imposing gates. Their last three nights had been spent in small inns and *pensiones* and she put a hand to her mouth as he parked in front of a great flight of steps and a turbanned boy not much taller than Katy opened her door. 'But darling!' she cried in wonder, 'You never said a word!'

'A small pub I know,' grinned McKay, loving the moment and wishing there could be more. 'Come on, jump out! I need you while we check in – you've got the passports.'

She pulled her skirt down and slid out of the Mercedes, obediently following into the warmth of a bright, marble foyer. The Mercedes was already being driven away by a man in uniform, someone else had placed their cases on an elegant trolley, and the concierge was opening the register for Jock to fill in their names and address. As one in a daze, she scrabbled in her handbag for their documents. Buried deep under a host of lipsticks, pens, purse and powder compact, she dislodged a small package as she drew them out. It was a tiny square box but it rolled with a life of its own and disappeared out of sight under a sofa. Horrified, she dropped the passports on the counter and bent to look for it – only, one of the young men behind the desk was quicker. 'Allow me, *Senhora*!' he retrieved the package and with a flourish, placed it on top of the register.

Before she could recover it, McKay had picked it up. 'Cartier!' he read in wonder on the outer wrapping. 'Haven't I seen something like this before? Catalina – what in heaven's name?'

'If the *Senhor* would just sign here, *por favore*...'

'*Si, si,*' McKay took the proffered pen, but his hand felt unsteady and there was a sick feeling in the pit of his stomach. Catalina snatched the package and snapped her handbag shut. The concierge seemed oblivious and was explaining about keys for the room, keys for the mini-bar, keys for the safe. But McKay was not listening.

'What the devil was that?' he turned to his wife who stood frozen to the spot on the marble floor.

'Sir, madam! – the boy will escort you to your room. You follow him – please?'

A bellboy waited, his hands gripping the handles of the shiny brass trolley as though it was carrying the crown jewels instead of two rather battered overnight bags. Catalina made to follow him but Mckay was having none of it. 'No, you don't!' his eyes were glittering and his voice was low. Catalina knew that voice and shuddered. 'Tell me what's in that package.'

'Nothing!' she managed a laugh and he seized her arm.

'Don't,' she said, 'You're hurting.'

'I want to know,' his voice was even quieter.

'It's nothing, nothing at all.'

The bell-boy had changed his gaze from one of indifference to barely concealed interest. McKay dug deep into her arm with hard fingers, 'Stop lying to me.'

'For God's sake, Jock, you're making a scene,' her voice was tremulous. 'I'll tell you – if you just let go of me.'

'You'll tell me now.' There was a look in his eye which frightened and thrilled her.

'All right,' she whispered, 'Only – please, let's just get to our room.'

Twice the lift had arrived and gone and the boy was recalling it a third time, persisting with the button. Now the grilled doors were parting and McKay strode in, pushing his wife ungently in front of him. The bellboy and their cases were in the service elevator. He had programmed their lift for the fifth floor and they reached it first.

'I want no more lying from now on,' McKay hissed in her ear. 'Do you hear me?'

'I thought this was supposed to be a romantic last night to our holiday,' she tried to sound flippant as she stepped out.

'Holiday! *Holiday*! That's so typical of you, Catalina! We've been in England on serious business – an exhibition if you recall – but to you it's just another holiday. All life's a holiday – a time for partying and fun and the receiving and giving of expensive presents. I must have been mad to think of stopping here! I wanted to recapture something from our past. How bloody wrong – and how foolish – of me!'

The bell-boy had re-appeared. They walked down a corridor, the carpet thick under their feet. He was unlocking their door. McKay braced his backbone and stood rigidly by as his wife went ahead. He heard her gasp as blinds were pulled up and the full beauty of the suite became apparent. The room faced west and a red winter sun was setting far away over the cathedral tower.

'*Es muy bueno?*' the boy had opened his mouth for the first time.

'*Es bueno,*' said McKay shortly, fishing a note out of his trouser pocket and dismissing the lad with one curt tilt of his head.

On their own again, he threw himself down on the royal blue brocade of the king-size bed. 'Christ, it is *muy bueno*, isn't it *just*? What a fool I am, what a fucking waste of money.'

Catalina tried to brush past him on her way to the bathroom, but he caught her elbow and pulled her back. 'Come here,' he said roughly and before she knew it, she'd been dragged down, next to him. She was a hostage.

He rose up then and towered over her. Suddenly vulnerable, she tried to sit up but he held both her arms away from her sides, and pulled them upwards and back and over her head. Her breasts pushed up and she felt the nipples grow hard. Pinned down by the weight of his hands, she tried to struggle but found she could do little. Then she tried a half-hearted kick and he merely laughed unpleasantly. 'I always knew you were a clever little cow, but I never dreamed my wife could be such a bitch.'

'You haven't let me explain,' she said.

'I'm not minded to hear now,' he replied, his eyes devouring her. There was a change in his demeanour and she wondered what was coming. 'I'm after something else first – some form of atonement for all the trouble I sense is coming my way.'

She stared up at him, her eyes troubled. This was a Jock she did not know, and he had not even had a drink. She wondered, but already knew what she'd suspected. There was a curious light in his eyes, and it wasn't love.

'You're making a big mistake, you know.' But he seemed not to hear. He was unzipping his trousers and out of round, aghast eyes, she recognised real lust.

'I don't make mistakes over that sort of thing,' he growled, ' I just couldn't bring myself to accept the truth.'

He was pulling off his shoes and stood there in his stocking soles. She remained where she was, free now to move away – only she didn't. He would probably only seize her arms again and in a way she wanted this. It might relieve the awful tension between them.

Fully erect now, he was breathing heavily but he hadn't finished yet, 'If I was to get your handbag and take out that parcel, do you know what I'd find?'

She said nothing, her breath too was coming in gasps. She wondered why he looked so much bigger and stronger than she had ever noticed before. Why didn't he get on with it?

'I'd find a package, marked Cartier!... only it wouldn't be for me. Oh no! I've had mine. This one's much more signficant. It would be for him! *Him*!' he yelled.

'No!' she cried, knowing he knew that she was lying, and wondering as she did so why she had bothered. She stared again at her husband. He seemed huge.

He slapped her then. Not hard, but enough to sting. She did not flinch. She had asked for that. And now he was upon her, pressing his mouth hard against her lips, pushing up her skirt, tearing at her underclothes, strong and unusually insistent with his hands... and as she looked down at this man who was her husband, she felt all resistance leave her body.

And it was a curious feeling. Despite the anger – she wanted him. Yet love had fled! They were both lusting for each other in a frightening, unholy way. She wondered if for him this was closer to rape. Had jealousy and suspicion turned him on? For her, it was like watching a film in which she played the central character. It was an exciting film, with loud background music and plenty of action and she found it incredibly, unbelievably thrilling.

Afterwards, when it was all over, and they lay there silently, strangers again, she touched her cheeks. She wondered at the tears she found there.

They set off for Portugal early the next morning, not even enjoying the luxury of the five -star breakfast so carefully laid out in their room. 'I wish we hadn't left Katy behind,' said Catalina as they swung out of Seville and onto the dual carriageway that would eventually take them to the Huelva roundabout. 'If she'd been there, we'd never have had that row.'

'You should have thought about that long ago. Just like you should have thought about everything else,' said her husband.

Little more had been said about the night before, but there was a lingering atmosphere of resentment in both their hearts. Each blaming the other for their actions and each knowing that what they had done was wrong. Clearly, things would never be the same again.

They were approaching Huelva by eleven o'clock. 'Do you want to do some last minute food shopping?' said Jock, 'everything's a bit cheaper here and there's more choice than in Santa Felicia.'

'I thought we were too broke,' she said bitterly.

'I've got a few pesetas left,' he replied, stung by the remark. He had never known why but whenever she referred to their impecunious state, it hurt him to the quick – as if she were casting aspersions on his manhood. Perhaps that was why he had done what he had last night. He had been severely provoked – in so many ways.

'No, let's get back.'

'OK.'

They pressed on, past the Huelva exit and onward to Portugal. There were signs looming up for the frontier at every roundabout. 'Funny how it's one of the few countries where the spelling's the same in every language,' said Jock. Unlike Spain now – *Espanha, Espagne...* always small differences. Portugal stays constant, in French, English, Italian and Spanish.'

'I can't wait to get back, said Catalina, her eyes bright with homesickness as they swept over the countryside. The horizon dazzled before her, turning the road white and radiating heat as the midday sun bore down. It was a searing welcome to all those who followed in its path.

'Don't tell me you missed home for once?'

'Well, I have. Home and friends are more precious than one would think.'

'Especially friends?'

'Possibly.'

'So you mean to go on with this farce? Even though you know I know?'

'I thought you'd worked out the answer to that last night. Wasn't that why you hurt me so much?'

'Oh come off it – you've always liked a bit of rough and tumble.'

'I didn't mean that, and you know that Jock.'

'But you can't cope with the fact I now know we've reached the point of no return – or put it this way, that it's out in the open.'

'It's not that,' she said.

'Then what is it?' his voice was surprisingly mild.

'I can't tell you, I can't explain. Only – something's driving me on and somehow I think you yourself hold the answer. And yet you're making me take all the blame.'

'You talk in riddles,' he said.

'But I think you understand all the same,' she said quietly.

'Not really.'

She managed a laugh then, a pale imitation of her usual tinkling peals. 'Well, maybe that's the beauty of our relationship – if you can call it that. We try, but we never quite understand each other. But in that lack of understanding – we accept – and we do what we have to do.'

'This is much too deep for me,' he said. 'I'm an uncomplicated man.'

'No you're not, Jock! You're incredibly complicated … ask anyone that knows you. They all say the same – you're a real enigma.'

'Why should they think that?'

'Because one side of you is – well, like you say – simple enough. But it conceals a deeper, stranger side. I mean, if you'd wanted to stop all this before, you'd have let the straightforward side take over and put an end to it all. But you didn't. Your strange side, came into play. It was almost as though you were too curious to put an end to it all.'

'I've always liked to see where Fate takes me, that's true,' he said. 'But you can't pin your own bad behaviour at my door.'

'Oh Jock!' she said wistfully, 'What a crazy beautiful mess we're in. Me – with my impulsiveness – you with your curiosity. Most people would think we were mad.'

He drove on, concentrating hard as the traffic increased and the state of the road worsened. She began to talk of complexes and people's psyches and as she chattered by his side, he paid less and less attention to her words and more and more to his driving. Two jeeps overflowing with Franco's armed police had overtaken and he was aware of their possible presence all the way to the border. From bitter experience, he knew how easily one could pick up a severe fine, even be hauled up to the guard room if the slightest detail was found amiss with one's documents.

Only when they reached Ayamonte, the last port of call on the Spanish side of the Guardiana which separates Europe's mainland from the Algarve, did he drop his guard as Catalina dropped her bombshell. Jock had just overtaken a parked bus on a narrow tree-lined avenue, when a taxi cut him up. At the same time Catalina let fly with one of her chance dagger remarks and the result was a skid which took them within a hair's breadth of losing a lot of paint, and a certain fine. McKay raised two angry fingers to the taxi and complained coldly to his wife about her timing.

'But it's true, isn't it?' she said, unapologetic.

For once he was at a loss for words. She darted in again, 'I've always known it gave you a kick. That's why I felt no hesitation in leading him on in front of you. And last year – don't you remember when Terence O'Connor invited us to dinner and the van der Stels were there too? You got as high as a kite and I knew you knew he had his hand on my thigh the whole evening. There was a look in your eyes which told me you found it exciting. Not that different from how you looked last night.'

His knuckles, he noticed had grown white on the steering wheel. What was she saying? Could it be true? Had he, Jock McKay grown into some sort of pervert – now that he was past his prime and with a young temptress for a wife? Was there some truth in her accusation?

She hadn't finished. 'And when we got home, don't you remember, you were mad for me? And as you undressed me, you kept asking, if I'd done it with him? Even when I said no, you went on, asking and asking, and all the time you got more excited – and you made love to me like it was the last thing on earth!'

They were approaching the docks now, following the file of cars, many with foreign number-plates, all waiting their turn. Soon they would mount the ricketty planks that led onto the bobbing vessel. If they had not been so near, he would have stopped at the first bar. Now, as he paid for their tickets and straightened up the wheels, his sobriety paid off. They had safely left the quay and were firmly on board. The gangway between the boat and the harbour's salty depths was surprisingly fine. Much the same as his life, he thought wryly as he prepared for the crossing to Portugal.

Within an hour of entering their house, Catalina was on the phone. The guttural voice of the storekeeper answered, as he called the *senhora*. Thank God, it *was* Leah! Catalina was half afraid Buster might have collected the telegram and taken matters into his own hands. It would be just like him and she didn't feel ready – not quite yet.

'Hello! We're back! Did you think we were never coming?'

At the sound of her lively voice, Leah felt she had shed ten years. 'It's *wonderful* to hear you, honey! I've missed you so much. We were hoping we'd see you tomorrow night. You will spend New Year's Eve with us, won't you?'

Catalina had half expected this. The Bloomfields were nothing if not hospitable. A fine *cabrito* – a whole kid, fresh from the hillside of the Alentejo – had been bought; it would be roasting slowly on the spit. There would just be the four of them. She found herself agreeing.

McKay had gone up to the studio and did not hear the arrangements. When Catalina broke the news, he merely shrugged. From now on – nothing would surprise him. Already the last few weeks had taken on a dreamlike quality, like being under gas in the dentist's chair. The present, was the grim awakening, complete with the pain that followed. He would learn to live with that pain. He had done so enough times back in the past.

Philismena, despite her gift of Andalucian nougat and a new shopping basket, greeted them as serious as ever. She attacked the car, brimful of cases, boxes and bags, and bustled around unpacking. Without Katy to attend to, she could spend more time on her mistress's needs, and within an hour no one would have known they'd been away. Everything was back in place, travel-stained clothes and suits borne away to the laundry room. The house had a pleasant smell of wax and newly cut flowers, and all the debris of the journey had disappeared.

Catalina was putting the finishing touches to her hair, which she would wear full and loose this New Year's Eve, when she saw Jock's face behind her in the mirror. 'Shouldn't you be changed by now, darling?' she said without looking round, 'I said we'd be there by eight thirty.'

'I'm not coming.'

'Don't be silly, darling,' she put out an arm to catch his hand, but he was out of reach. She let it fall again as the other busied itself with the comb, 'Of course you are!'

He said nothing but turned away. With a sigh, she got up from the dressing-table and followed him. 'For God's sake Jock! It's Hogmanay! And you're a Scot!'

'In which case I shall be quite happy celebrating at home in traditional fashion – with a bottle.' He was pulling off his shoes as he spoke and replacing them with his old leather moccasins which Philismena had thoughtfully laid out.

'Jock!' she cried reproachfully, her eyes growing moist with dismay. 'You can't mean it. You couldn't let me go alone, surely. Husbands and wives are supposed to be together at this time of year. We've always done that.'

'It's your choice to go out, not mine.'

'But – ' her lower lip wobbled and she held up her hands imploringly.

'Look,' his face wore a resigned look, 'you run along if you want. We had our own special celebration – if you can call it that – in Seville. If you want to join these friends of yours – that's fine with me. Only don't expect me to be part of it.'

She wanted to weep, but did not allow herself the luxury; her make-up had taken the best part of an hour. 'You can't mean it,' she said feebly, knowing in her heart that he did.

'I do, ' he was already out of the door.

This was a blow she hadn't expected. Tonight of all nights, she wanted Leah to feel secure – but without Jock, the prospect of Buster mooning over her with sheep's eyes might prove difficult to stave off. She ran after him and tried again, but it was no use. His mind was made up. No, he was not jealous – anything but! He simply saw no point in wearying himself with two people in whom he could find little in common, amusement or charm.

The evening turned out to be far less awkward than she had feared. Leah's bubbling spirits manifested themselves into non-stop questions and expressions of delight which overrode any possible undertone of suspicion. Even when a rather merry Buster kissed Catalina full on the lips at the stroke of midnight, with something very akin to passion, Leah merely clapped her hands, grateful that for once her husband shared in her intense pleasure at being reunited with her friend. Not daring to tempt Fate too far, Catalina took her departure soon afterwards, truthfully saying she felt tired after the journey.

She was triumphant too. During Leah's several sorties to attend to the cooking, Buster managed to convey most of his news. Their next meeting place had already been arranged. They had planned it two days ahead in the fishing town of Portimão. Catalina often went there to shop, so anyone catching sight of the Mercedes would suspect nothing. From there she could join Buster in the Opel, as he transported her along the little known back roads, to the special hideway he had prepared for her, deep inland.

'I was wondering, would you and Karl be free for dinner on the last Saturday of February?' Johanna Vincent was behind her desk at *Estrela*, perusing the Christmas trade figures while Jacqueline van der Stel thumbed her way through a pile of cashmere sweaters.

'Goodness!' she said, 'that's far enough ahead! Is it something special? I don't think Karl's away that week, but I'll have to check. We always do our damnest to get to *your* parties – whatever stands in the way!'

Miss Vincent smiled. After a pregnant pause, she said, 'I've got rather a special guest coming – a new face, at least to Santa Felicia. Quite a catch for some woman, I fancy.'

Wishing she could afford it, Jacqueline put down a pale apricot cardigan and looked at her curiously, 'Meaning you, Joey?'

'Oh no, darling. I don't play the matrimonial game any more. I leave that to you young things – at least not you exactly – you're well and truly wedded and happy with it – but other hopefuls, Maysie included. There's many a singe girl who'd give their eye teeth for a good-looking divorcé, despite the age difference – and of course, there's the title.'

She let the last word drop from her lips and looked quite pained when Jacqueline pounced upon it. 'A title, Joey – a proper one? None of those faded European ones… Count this and Count that?'

'A proper one – a good English barony, if you want to know!'

Jacqueline gave a whoop of excitement. 'Cunning cow Joey! Who is he and how did you meet him? Are you *sure* he's not your latest?'

It was well known amongst her inner circle that Johanna had only just returned from a weekend in Lisbon with her heavily married Portuguese *amour*, although no one quite knew who he was. Despite a respected family background and the fact his practice had prospered under both Presidents Salazar and Caetano, Johanna said little. Their infrequent meetings were arranged far away from ex-pat eyes, which ruled out the resorts. Rumour had it Pat Weaver at The Anchor enjoyed a lucrative hotline to the gossip page of a Sunday tabloid back home and any hint of scandal was anathema to the former actress. She'd had enough in her life to last to eternity.

'No, I'm sorry to to disappoint you, darling, he's *not* my latest. Nevertheless he is quite charming and an excuse for a dinner party. He seems rather shy and it seems a shame to let him waste away up in the outback.'

'Outback? What do you mean?'

'Well I gather he's got a farm somewhere in the hills between Monchique and Messines where he trains horses. I suspect he's quite a private person. I don't know very much more,' she admitted, 'other than his name's Crompton. We met at a Consulate party and apart from the horsy talk, I found him fascinating.'

'Well I can't wait to meet your lord,' said Jacqueline, returning to her cashmere. 'I think on the strength of the company we're about to meet, I'll go mad and have one of these after all. We need a touch of class around here. Who else will you ask?'

Johanna doodled with her figures, turning eights into fat ladies, 'I thought the McKays, Contessa Spritziani, the Graftons – they can talk horse – the Boys and one or two of Maysie's more glamorous friends.'

'You *always* have the Boys,' pouted Jacqueline, writing out her cheque. 'I say – don't I get a discount?'

'I've taken off ten per cent. But they're extra males, darling and they are amusing. Benjie tells a singularly good story after he's been wined and dined.'

'This Lord Whatisname may find them a bit colonial,' grinned Jacqueline, 'But I guess the McKays are interesting and I suppose that old dragon from Italy keeps up the cultural side – that's if one wants to hear about her sinking palace in Venice!'

'Sinking or stinking?' said Johanna and they both giggled. 'My only worry is Jock,' she was suddenly sober. 'Last time we met he looked terrible. It's no secret the exhibition was not the usual success – we all read the reviews – but I'd no idea he was taking it that badly.'

'I'm convinced it's Catalina that's upsetting him – not the exhibition,' said Jacqueline. 'She's forever heading out of town in that car of theirs. I see her when I'm out walking Bombita, and sometimes coming back too. Lateish. I had thought it was the Yellow House that was attracting her, but according to Leah, she's hardly seen the girl since New Year's Eve. She was complaining bitterly in the supermarket the other day.'

'Nothing about Catalina surprises me these days,' Johanna folded the cheque into her cash box. 'Her behaviour at that lunch party she gave before Christmas was positively ominous.'

The visits to their 'country retreat' – as it amused Catalina to call it – were becoming more frequent. The first time Buster had taken her there, she had sat in the small car beside him, stiff with apprehension, wondering what horror lay in store. He had spent most of their journey apologising. He warned her about the dirt track, the house, the man Chico, the yellow dog, the melancholy mule…everything. 'Don't worry, darling,' Catalina had soothed. 'We're not going to live there, are we? It's only a store for our little nest-egg, isn't it?'

Buster swallowed, his eyes fixed on the road – 'I had hoped – we might…I – er – bought a bed. And there's sheets and cushions too. It's all ready…you see…' his voice trailed off. He wanted her so much – it had been a long time.

To his surprise Catalina went into peals of laughter. She chuckled all the way up the bumpy road and when they drew up at the barn and there was no sign of Chico or the yellow dog, just a twitching of curtains from the house and some muffled howling a long way off, she leant against Buster helplessly and began to laugh all over again. By the time he had fumbled with the key in the huge aluminium door and twice bungled it, she was almost hysterical. Thus the 'retreat' was renamed the 'happy, crazy place' and later, she even pronounced it 'madly romantic'.

In truth, Catalina was impressed with Buster's ingenuity in finding such a remote spot. He had carried out her instructions to the letter and she was confident that no one would ever discover their hiding place, until long after the need for secrecy was required. Of course, she reflected, it would have been more comfortable to rent a small villa or apartment together – but altogether much too risky. There was be bound to be paperwork and where documents existed in Portugal, officaldom followed. Besides, one had acquaintances or friends of friends, everywhere. It only needed for the pair to be spotted by one person, leaving or entering a building together, and the tale would be around the Algarve like wildfire. 'We told you so…it was bound to happen…surely you must have guessed there was something between Jock McKay's wife and the Bloomfield husband – remember that party!' Catalina knew only too well how scandals spread. Even with this safe haven, they would need to move swiftly. Early suspicions had a habit of growing.

So for now, they must lie low. The incongruity of the place only heightened the appeal of her plan. It was daring beyond belief! She had worried their trips to a dreary destination might dull her excitement about the whole affair; instead the uncertainty of what they might find at the whitewashed barn – Chico, the dog or some other unknown quantity – lent an edge of romantic skulduggery to the enterprise. Catalina was now charged with a physical and mental excitement that surprised even her.

To Buster, it would always be a squalid place. He did not tell Catalina of his private arrangement with Chico over the bottle of Johnnie Walker. As he had guessed, his new landlord's mercenary mind had reckoned the price of silence to be far higher than their original rental agreement. His one consolation was the knowledge that Chico had no qualms of conscience and that even under pressure, he would have no hesitation in lying. As for his prize – his love of this woman knew no bounds. Of that he was more sure than of anything else in his life. And despite his distaste for their surroundings, once he held her in his arms, he could lose himself in her warmth for ever.

From that first irrevocable step behind the aluminium doors, life for the two of them took on a wholly new aspect. For Catalina, they were not only lovers, but schemers, plotters, bandits even. Sometimes, she imagined she was being held prisoner in this empty barn. Then Buster, strong and mighty, would set upon her, like the leader from a marauding gang, and take her for his own. Apart from that last time in Seville – which she had tried to blot from her mind – his love-making was in sharp contrast to that of Jock. Where her husband was a sophisticated lover, drawing things out, unselfishly desiring her pleasure before his own – Buster was a mere boy. He loved her with such a passion, the actual act could be perfunctory – but in accepting this – she found a new source of delight. More than the climax, she loved the feeling of invasion – the excitement of this big athletic man possessing her so utterly. If everything exploded too soon – so what? The delicious aftermath of his offering was a turn-on in itself.

The point was the excitement. It was flattering to be taken like this – to be so desired he could not wait. Never had she felt more feminine, more in control of the whole situation. She could play games with Buster, which her husband would not have relished. It was fun sometimes to tease and push him away – and make him try all over again – which he did with gusto, like a clumsy puppy dog. It was the element of surprise that made up for the finer techniques she took for granted in her marital relationship. Jock was a practised lover – but there was nothing like predictability to take away the fun.

When finally, they had had enough, she would curl up cross-legged, wrapped in a large fluffy bathrobe on the divan, watching him drag on a cigarette. Then they would plan the future. Often she amazed herself at the audacity of her ideas, and she had discovered a new accomplishment – which added another thrill of power to her lively mind. By murmuring vague hints of what she wanted, he would seize upon these, turn them over in his mind and then produce a concrete idea, truly believing it was his own in the first place. On several occasions, she found herself congratulating him on his clever iniatives and he lapped it up. 'If only Leah had done that,' he once said. 'She was always made me feel she was in control.'

Catalina hugged herself and smiled a secret smile. 'We Latin women understand men,' she murmured. She would never speak against her friend but there were ways and means of sowing seeds. Her own husband would have pounced on any hint of mind games immediately, but Buster was different. It was as though she only had to think something, and he would do it. She marvelled now as she thought of the amazement in people's minds during the aftermath of the Plan – and its successful execution. The time was drawing near, and it was becoming more of a reality with each passing day.

She shivered uncontrollably at the thought and slipped under the black satin sheets as she buried herself deep into the pillows. Buster mistook her trembling for passion and pulled her deep into his arms once more. 'You hot Latin woman,' he murmured fondly in her ear, 'you gotta give a man a few minutes to recover!'

34

With the frequency of these visits to their country retreat, Buster's confidence grew. Now he could laugh at himself when he thought of his former shyness, the quick betrayal of his feelings, the spontaneous blushes whenever he thought of Catalina. For the first time in his life he knew the meaning of fulfilment through a human relationship. The bond he had never felt with his mother had been compensated for by something altogether better.

Any sense of self-worth derived from sport, work or after a particularly exciting manoeuvre paled in comparison to what was happening to him now. Never before had he been touched in this way, deep down in his soul. This was new and thrilling and with it came a sense of purpose which gratified and surprised him. He had recognised this driven quality in other men but suddenly it was his for the taking. He became more resourceful, not only with his beloved but he was now capable of bringing order to his home-life which – until recently – had lain in chaotic rags.

An actor had emerged from the old Buster who was playing his part in their domestic existence like a professional. He laughed as he thought of all their faces. Howard and Benjie … Leah … so bland and unsuspecting! Who would have guessed? The relief when they saw the old happy-go-lucky, don't-give-a-dime Buster back in their midst, was palpable. Instead of holding himself tightly lest a stray fuse snapped, he could shamble round the house, attending to jobs, supervising the swimming-pool with apparent enthusiasm, scattering amiability in his wake. Meanwhile, he hugged his true inner spirit to himself – only to be let out in the presence of Catalina. The elation this play-acting afforded him was heady.

Catalina had given him a gold-and-jade ring. A token – for power and protection, she had said. 'To make you do anything you want. To give you the world … and me!' she had added, modestly. He wore it in her presence, and otherwise kept it in his money-belt. Back home, he would rub it in the privacy of his dressing room. Like magic … his own secret talisman … the mask of the actor slipped away as he savoured the ease of it all – sensational!

Just occasionally he could keep up the pretence no longer. The desire to laugh aloud could catch him at odd moments and he'd make a dash for the lavatory and let the silent laughter bubble up in his throat like bile. How he was taking them all in! Who would guess that even now he was conducting business far away in another country which would ultimately affect all their lives? A plan so daring, hatched under their very noses whilst they remained blissfully unaware. He could not wipe the smile of satisfaction off his face.

Alone, he would study himself in the shaving mirror as he let go of the grin. When all was as it should be again, he scarcely recognised his own reflection. His face had tightened and toughened in the last few weeks. He knew it was not just imagination – he had changed. He had finally become master of his own destiny and instead of leading this lax life of luxury which Leah had tried to impose upon him, he was up and running; on the move again. It suited him best. And it showed.

This was the Buster he could admire – more akin to the Buster he had left behind in Korea. The chin was more resolute, the hazel eyes inscrutable. The mouth, for all its mirth had grown hard, more determined. Even his bone structure seemed more prominent, his tan skin stretched across the cheekbones, tight as a drum. He recognised he was reaching the zenith of his life. Everything he wanted – could ever want – was within his grasp. There were few men in the world who could ever hope for such a state of personal achievement.

Catalina had been right to tell him to wait. He had been a fool to be impatient before. What was a little waiting compared to what lay in store? He unzipped his belt and took out the ring. He pressed it to his lips, then composed his face, and put it back. He flushed the john and strolled back to the kitchen. He beamed at his wife who was cleaning silver, 'I'm just on my way to the pool. Call me when it's time for lunch!'

He ambled out to watch the three men left permanently on site tackle the rocky ground with their pick-axes. The bulldozer had gone as far as it could, now the work was largely manual. Once the drains were laid, the main structure could begin, starting with a concrete seal at the base. By mid April, the whole thing should be nearing completion.

A van drew up and Roper himself arrived. 'Morning!' he called, striding across the churned land. 'Glad to catch you, there's a small problem come up – and I'd be glad of your opinion.' Buster noted the slight figure, normally bristling with energy, looked distracted.

'What can I do to help?' he was all amiability.

The engineer was momentarily taken aback. Was this the same tetchy fellow who grudged any form of discussion? 'Er – it's a question of the liner,' he began tersely.

'Go on.'

'Well – as I think I explained before – we get all our liners flown out from the UK. It used to be a simple thing; we'd put in the order, wait a month or so, then once we knew which plane to meet – drive up to collect from the commercial depot in Lisbon. Things have changed however. Recently, Customs have been delaying things – we don't know why – but the machinations of this government are hard to understand and one can't ask too many questions. But the fact remains. With the last few consignments, we've had liners held up for two, even three months at a time. When they finally release them – a huge duty gets imposed. The amount bears no relation to the value of the liner and seem wholly unwarranted.'

'I remember you told me something about it – you said you couldn't quote for the liner until ours had cleared Customs.'

'That's just it – cleared Customs. Today, I've just heard from my agent fellow in Lisbon, that our latest consignment – which included your liner – has been rejected and sent back to the UK. I think there's some kind of competition going on here and they're trying to force us to buy from a firm that's started to manufacture them in Setúbal. Trouble is – I don't trust them, I'd rather stick with the goods I know. The hassle of replacing a liner that could be faulty is just not on.'

'I can imagine,' said Buster. 'So what's to be done?'

'Well, being the sort of impatient bloke I am – I've already thought out a solution. It will however require a certain amount of trust on your part, and I'm afraid a little time.'

'Fire ahead.'

Roper brightened, 'I can get your liner flown into Spain – as a special order – that's no trouble and there's very little duty. Where you come in is this. Would it be beyond your scruples to motor over to Seville for a couple of days – pick up the liner personally – and stick it under the back seat of your car? You'd then cross the water and drive back via Vila Real de San Antonio, but being such a small frontier, the customs there rarely check foreign-owned cars. The moment they see your passport, you'll be waved through – the Algarveans know how much their economy depends on tourism. Even if they do find it, I doubt they'll impose duty – not like the Lisbon boys.'

'It seems kind of a sweat,' began Buster, 'I thought we paid you to figure these things out.'

'You do – and I have. But, as I explained, this is a new thing we're up against, and if you want that swimming-pool finished by the end of April, it would seem the easiest…'

'Wait a minute!' the American slapped him so hard on the back, Roper almost went spinning into the pit amongst his men. 'I – er – yep! Of course, we'll go for the liner. That's a brilliant idea! Just the ticket! I couldn't have worked it out better myself!'

Roper, ruefully rubbing his back, had the distinct impression that this man must be a schizophrenic of some kind – one moment, tricky – now over the moon with excitement – all over a bloody liner! Better pin him down before he changed his tune again.

'So I can take that as definite, Mr Bloomfield? I can make arrangements with the firm in England for the liner to be sent out in your name? And you personally will collect it? As long as the goods are for private use and your passport matches the name on the order, it's all perfectly legal. And you don't mind driving to Seville Airport? It's on the outskirts of the city and not hard to find.'

He felt he was speaking to a child, but he need not have worried. 'Sure, yeah, great! But – er…' Oh dear, Roper sighed at the hesitation, and wondered what was coming.

'I think – to be on the safe side – we won't put the goods in my name,' the fellow had sweated up and was breathing hard; now Roper knew he was mad. 'Put it in the joint names of Mr McDermott and Mr Liebermann. I guess they'll be the ones we send to pick it up.'

Roper squinted in the sun. One didn't half find 'em in this neck of the woods – sometimes he wondered why he'd ever left Essex. 'Are you sure of that now?' he said patiently. 'It's rather important that whoever picks up and signs for the package shares the name on the paperwork to accompany it. The Spanish, as I said, are fine about liners, but they do like their documentation correct.'

'Oh sure, sure,' said Buster, 'only it's better you put it in their joint names – then they'll both have the pleasure of producing passports, eh? '

Roper looked at him. This whole scenario was taking on a surreal quality. But the man hadn't finished. 'What I'm trying to say is – they're real good guys,' he winked and nodded back at the villa – 'but – er – like many folk – they're apt to get jealous sometimes. If you send the goods in one name only…could cause bad feeling. Make one feel more important than the other and all that. We don't want that. Better make sure the two names are there!' He winked again, 'I'm…er…sure you see what I mean?'

'Perfectly,' said Roper, shutting his file of papers, a glazed look on his face. 'Well, having settled that, I'll be on my way. Thank you for your time.'

Walking on air, Buster returned to the house. Roper had just solved for him the most problematical part of the Plan yet. It must be heaven-sent. Not that he believed in that sort of thing, but Catalina did. She'd be off to Mass if he wasn't careful.

They had arranged only a short meeting that afternoon. Catalina was bringing some more things from her own house to add to their growing pile and it was agreed Buster should delay his return while Catalina dropped in at Casa Amarela, to visit Leah. The fact she would call when Buster was still out, should satisfy Howard and Benjie's suspicious minds. Catalina had noticed some knowing looks between the two of them at recent drinks parties, 'You can't afford to drop your guard for a moment,' she had chided.

Despite all, Buster ate an excellent lunch, excitement only strengthening his appetite. 'Excellent quiche this!' he jerked his fork in the air in a gesture of appreciation. 'Who's the cook today?'

'Me,' said Benjie.

'Thought so. You can tell by the pastry. Did you know all the finest pastry cooks in the world are men? Go to any big hotel and ask. Something to do with the handling of the raw material and shaping it up. Bet none of you knew that now?'

They all smiled politely. Leah was beginning to feel warm and secure again. She was still taking tranquillisers but no longer irresponsibly. Her husband had put a stop to that. He really did care after all and only the other day he had told her he wanted her to take a trip back to New York to spend a few days with her shrink.

'It's all very fine you're living a rural life on top of a hill with your sea air and pretty view, honey,' he'd said, 'but the fact is – it's taken a lot out of you adapting to this new system. It's been hard on us all. I myself went through a tricky time before Christmas, but I got it sorted by going off on my own each day for a little break – it's done me the power of good. I think Howard and Benjie have had their problems too. No wonder Benjie got that poisoned tooth…all the shit had to go somewhere!'

Leah hadn't thought of it like that, but said nothing.

'The fact remains we three have shrugged our troubles off, whilst you're still much too dependent on them little blue pills and I'm not so sure Wally won't want to change your regime. I reckon he'll be prescribing a whole new range of drugs when he sees you – something to give you support, but not the highs and lows that you've been prone to.'

She'd listened meekly, but he hadn't finished.

'What you need – if you don't mind my telling you hon – is a few sessions with him on the couch again. Then you can get it all out your system. And come back to me cleansed and refreshed. I tell you I'll be a happier man when you jump off that plane with Wally's report! That way, I'll know for myself how to handle you. I feel I've let you down a bit lately, but it's not too late for us all to sharpen up a bit, is it? I just need Wally to tell me how.'

She had put out a hand then, realising as she did so, that they were all vulnerable. But Buster was right. The change had taken its toll – she admitted that now. Fainting that evening at Manolo's party had frightened her. But not enough to help her reliance; if Wally could prescribe something that would let her down gently – she could learn to be free again! She might also earn back the respect of her house-mates again.

Thus when Buster promised to write to Wally himself, she agreed. Mid-April seemed a good time, 'It'll be warmer for you in New York then, honey. No point arriving in a snowstorm – a contrast after the Algarve sun is the last thing you need! You'll enjoy yourself seeing all the spring fashions and no doubt you'll want to restock your wardrobe. I'll hold the fort here and make sure work on the pool progresses. Who knows, it may even be ready by the time you fly back!'

It was good to let him organise her for once. All her life, Leah had organised everyone and everything, but if it suited her husband to take on the mantle of responsibility – why not let him coddle her for once? The unaccustomed sensation was rather pleasant. Now, all they had to do was wait on Wally. As soon as he responded with a date, Buster would book her ticket.

He was getting up from the table now. Pushing back his chair noisily and wiping pastry crumbs from his chin, he snapped his fingers for the dog. 'I guess I'll be off now,' he said, 'So where's our Mungo?'

'Sleeping,' said Benjie. 'He must be dog-tired after all that exercise you give him.'

Buster looked at him sharply. Catalina had been right – as usual. He was glad she would drop by later.

'See you then folks,' Buster aimed a husbandly kiss somewhere near his wife's mouth. 'Be good!'

'You too!' Leah slapped him gently on the butt and watched him go, the dog at his heels. She gave a small sigh. It still hurt he never wanted to take her too, but at least he'd explained why. Clearly, despite its size and scope, the house gave him claustrophobia. He blamed it entirely on Benjie and Howard, who he claimed had put pressure on their marriage. 'I never guessed it would upset me so much,' he had said, 'but seeing them day after day, wears me down. Yeah, yeah – I know we went into all this before we left the States and that's why we built such an enormous place. But reality often turns out different to supposition; I guess I made a mistake about this sharing game – it does affect me.'

'But what can we do?' Leah had been close to tears. 'We can hardly change things now – too much has gone into this house. We're in for good now. And it was my idea in the first place – you must blame me for that?'

'Shush! You've got me all wrong, honey. I like the house. I like the situation. As long as I can have my space, I'm OK. That's all I ask. It ain't much, is it?'

'No,' she twisted her hands pathetically.

'And the time's put to good purpose,' he grinned. 'As well as me, it keeps the dog happy!'

How easy it was to lie, he thought now as he remembered the well-rehearsed words. Well, part of it was true anyway. And it kept them all quiet. He waved with carefree abandon as he reversed the car, and made off down the hill, scrunching tyres over gravel. The excitement at seeing his beloved was already mounting somewhere in his groin.

The Boys got up to clear the lunch things, but Leah stopped them. 'I'll do it,' she smiled. 'I need to get on with my silver cleaning and I'll only make a mess of the table again, so don't worry.'

It occurred to her, as she watched Benjie's neat bottom in a pair of skin-tight faded jeans depart to the garden, that it was a while since Buster had made love to her. Not since Christmas Eve, when she'd been so poorly – almost a month now, which was wholly out of character. Maybe it was all that physical exercise.

The almond blossom was bursting out in riotous profusion all along the road to Portimão. How different the fragile almond flower was from the heavier waxier orange blossom that came later! Today, even Buster was affected by the sheer glory of the sight to which people flocked from all over the world. They called it the 'Miracle Spring' – but in fact the scene seemed more wintry than springlike. Every time the breeze stirred, the shimmering petals wafted down like snowflakes with parts of the road completely white. It seemed sacrilege to drive over that delicate blanket of frosting.

After Roper's visit, Buster felt as though the last weight from his mind had been lifted. The pieces of jigsaw now fitted together – at least, almost. Certainly, they were no more gaping holes. The last one, for which the missing pieces had presented a real problem, was filled by this morning's meeting. Strange, he thought, how Fate weaves her mysterious ways.

He wondered how Catalina had fared in Portimão this afternoon. She was a compulsive shopper and at their last meeting he'd given her three hundred dollars to buy a porcelain dinner service she fancied. This was prompted by the canteen of Victorian silver which he'd produced as a surprise. Proudly, he'd unlocked the drawers to show her all three tiers at once. He would never forget the expression on her face. Her plump white hands had flown to her mouth and her face had lengthened into an unusual expression of worry and dismay. 'Darling B…' – her new name for him – 'should you have taken that? I mean it looks terribly valuable. Are you sure Leah won't be upset? I couldn't bear to deprive her of something personal. Are you sure it's as much yours – as, er – hers? I thought you would only take what is yours, by right?'

'Honey,' he sounded sharp; it was time to stamp out these ideas once and for all. 'Everything in that house, I have a right to. Now remember something –' how could he make the words acceptable to her Catholic sensibilities? '– when the time comes, and our plans are put into action – the final part I mean – Leah will be laughing. She'll have the house for a start! And she'll be shot of me! What more will she want?'

'Oh B! You make it sound dreadful. Sometimes I wonder –' she buried her face in her hands.

As usual, when she had those moments of anguish, he wrapped his arms around her and held her. Her weakness seemed to strengthen his own resolve. Her concern for Leah was touching, but it made him all the more determined to take, for Catalina, whatever he wished. Leah had more than enough. Often she seemed quite uncaring about their priceless antiques or works of art, fussing more over her darned geese and stray cat. She had changed so much since leaving New York; the old silver was a good example. After the move, it had remained untouched, unlooked at, unappreciated – not dissimilar to their own marriage – until now. Yet the pleasure it would give his Catalina was deep and genuine.

They met today in their usual place and she came running towards him down the narrow street, wrapped up warmly in a camel coat, the collar turned up to hide her face. It was cold out of the sun and a sea breeze tugged at her mane of hair. A square of red silk at her throat matched the flush of excitement that coloured her cheeks, and he held out his arms to her and kissed the top of her head. He had never known such a sense of protection, at times it was overpowering. 'Hmmm, you smell so good,' he said.

'You too.'

They linked arms and went back to his car. All the way to the farm, she chattered about the china. 'It won't be ready for a week. I've seen samples and ordered it and they're sending off to the factory rightaway. It's simply beautiful. *Vista Alegre*, former suppliers to our old royal family, the best in Portugal.'

Buster was swinging out to turn sharp left. Suddenly, there was a shriek of rubber on tarmac and they felt and heard the scrunch of tearing metal. Catalina gasped. Buster pulled into the verge and got out. He let forth a diatribe of angry and unprintable language. Someone else had got out of their car too, and a quiet, educated voice said in English, 'I know, I know, you're probably quite right. I'm sure everything you say is correct. I like your choice of adjectives – quite original! Yes, it probably *was* my fault – I always think I own the road in these lonely parts – but I'm sure we can settle this without too much ado. In the meantime – let's see the damage. Is the lady all right, for a start?'

Catalina looked out of the passenger window to find herself face to face with an elegant figure in a tweed jacket and a pair of well-cut but mud-spattered riding breeches. The face which surveyed hers was a curious mixture of concern and appreciation, and the eyes were definitely twinkly. 'I'm fine,' she said, getting out and straightening her skirt, 'It was only the noise that scared me.'

'I'm sorry about that,' said the stranger before Buster pushed in between them to examine the wing. 'Don't usually see people around these parts, I'm thankful it was my *car*, not my horse!'

'Horse?'

'Yes, I ride these lanes as well as drive.'

'Hmph ... well it could have been worse,' Buster said grudgingly, rubbing his hand over the scraped metal. 'But you should watch where you're going, Mister. I did indicate – and you almost ran into me once before. That car's too big for these country roads – maybe you should stick to the horse.'

'You're probably right,' said the Englishman, 'you can either send me a bill for the repairs, or if you like I'll settle now. Not worth bothering the insurance company, is it? The damage can't be more than a couple of *contos* at the most.'

'OK ... I'll settle for that,' said Buster, relieved that names and addresses hadn't come into it. The Englishman held out two large notes and he pocketed them without a smile. ' I hope we don't run into each other again – we might not be so lucky next time.'

'I sincerely hope not too.' The man in riding clothes smiled, nodded his head in polite salutation to Catalina and strode back to an enormous battered Ford, which now bore the marks of yet another near escape.

'Shit, shit, shit!' said Buster angrily as they turned down their now familiar track.

'Don't be upset, B darling,' Catalina put out a soothing hand. 'It's unlikely we'll ever meet him again. He's probably only a visitor, anyway.'

' Dressed like that? I don't think so for a moment. Besides, this is the second time he's seen me turning off the public road. The last time was when you were still in England.'

'Even so,' said Catalina, 'I've never seen him anywhere on the coast before, and it's highly unlikely he knows anyone we know. He's probably a farmer and keeps himself to himself.'

All the same, she was worried and the afternoon was spoiled for them both. For once they didn't make love, and despite Buster's telling her of Trevor Roper's visit that morning and his subsequent idea, she felt heavy-hearted and irritable. It annoyed her that such a chance happening could throw her off balance; she had thought herself so completely in command of the situation that nothing could daunt her. She would not tell Buster, but in order to reassure herself, decided she must find out more about the strange Englishman and play it from there. He seemed an attractive character and it would be a challenge to think up some ploy and swear him to secrecy. With her feminine intuition, her wits and sex, no doubt she would get her own way. Having taken that decision, she felt better about facing the visit with Leah.

When Catalina arrived at the yellow house, she was surprised to see Howard and Benjie setting off in the Fiat without so much as a wave. The door into the kitchen was wide open and she found Leah sitting in a huddle, white as a sheet at the kitchen table. ' Leah!' Catalina rushed over to the other woman, 'What is it?'

Leah shook her head, her hair a cock's comb where she had raked it up with agitated fingers. She looked more vulnerable than Catalina had ever remembered. 'I dunno,' she seemed to be talking to herself. 'They've either been at it again, or it went the first time round. I never thought to check. But who'll understand that? As usual, they'll be all questions and why didn't I notice before?…and so on and so forth…but who would have thought? I mean – *who* would have thought?'

On the table before her, a little heap of soiled rags, a half empty jar of silver polish and a brown chemist's bottle with the lid off, stood forlorn. Catalina noticed there were only a few blue pills left in the bottom.

'Leah!' she said sharply, 'I don't know what you're talking about but how many of these have you taken?'

'You're as bad as Buster,' Leah got up, vaguely attempting to smooth her hair back from her forehead and laughed. 'Don't worry, Catalina honey – not enough to do any harm.'

She began to tidy the table but Catalina put out a restraining arm. 'Sit down again! I'm going to put the kettle on, we'll have a good strong coffee and then you'll tell me all about it.'

'I'm all right! Honest!' Leah smiled sadly, but remained seated like an obedient schoolgirl. ' I guess I just got a shock, that's all. Howard and Benjie have gone for the police.'

'Police?' Catalina wiped the table with a cloth and laid a tray.

'There are cookies in the tupperware,' said Leah absently.

Coffee was made and they sat in uneasy silence for a while. Finally, the older woman took Catalina by the hand. 'I don't know what I'd do without you, honey,' she said. 'You always have a knack of turning up at the right moment. I always feel better when I see you, it's kind of crazy, huh?'

'So what's upset you this time?' Catalina said, her eyes wide.

'It's some Victorian silver,' there was a catch in Leah's voice. 'It's been in that cupboard ever since we moved, and today – well, I decided to have a spring clean and tackle the stuff the maids never get around to – so up I go, knowing exactly where I'd hidden it – and no canteen! The silver just ain't there!'

'It's probably been put somewhere else! Have you really looked? Even if you didn't move it, Maria might have – or what about Buster?'

Leah shook her head. 'Maria's been with me all afternoon. She was there when I discovered it had gone. She's been through every nook and cranny, and we both know that canteen was where I'd left it. That was until recently.'

'Did you use it at Christmas?'

'Nope.'

'Well, I'm sure there's a simple explanation,' comforted Catalina. 'It's my guess Buster may have moved it.' Popping in a few pearls of truth made the lying easier, she thought.

'Buster! You must be mad, honey! Buster never lifts a finger in the house. He's an outdoor guy – you must have noticed that.'

'Well, I must say it is odd,' Catalina was warming to her theme. 'No doubt the police will have ideas. Do you think it was taken when those other things went missing – when we were out of the country?'

'That's the trouble – I just don't know. Since I haven't checked for a while, anything's possible.' Leah began to pace the room and was close to tears. 'What I can't understand , honey, is why it's always our things that go. Apart from that figurine of Howard's, everything that's disappeared has belonged to us. It's as though we're being spied upon – but who by, Catalina? Who by?'

Catalina bit her lip, 'I don't think it can be like that, Leah –' she began and broke off thankfully at the sound of a car. 'It's Howard and Benjie!' she ran to the window, 'I wonder if the police are following them?'

But they weren't.

Howard came storming into the kitchen full of indignation. 'They were almost rude to me at the *Guarda*,' he exclaimed, plucking a cookie out of the plastic container and crumbling it into pieces with his nervous hands. 'I described the silver in some detail as you'd told me, I explained how old and valuable it was – and do you know? – they just looked at me. More or less, in disbelief!'

'In the end Howard got angry,' said Benjie. 'He banged the chief's table and said 'aren't you going to do something?''

'And do you know what he did?' Howard continued, incensed. 'He winked at me!'

Catalina dug her scarlet nails into the palms of her hands. She had an irresistable desire to giggle. Everyone looked so serious. Howard reminded her of a stranded whale, puffing and blowing. Summoning all her self-control, she said in a subdued voice, 'Sometimes I feel ashamed of my own countrymen. You must think we Portuguese are hopelessly inefficient…I am so sorry.' She hung her head.

Leah ran to her at once, brushing away her own tears and cried, 'Of course not, honey – we love your country and your people – but police are the same the world over – a race apart. There's no explaining how they're going to take things.'

Benjie said, 'A few notes were taken and they asked for the insurance photographs, but when we asked if they would come and check for finger-prints, they laughed in our faces. It was most insulting.'

'They probably thought having done it once, there was no need again,' said Leah. 'We can't really blame them.'

What a mess she looked, thought Benjie. Tear-stained, ruffled, she had let herself go in every sense of the word and yet here she was defending the police! He did not even feel sorry for her now. He and Howard had done their best and that was that. Their responsibility ended there. As they left the room, he turned back to say, 'Why don't you go and bathe your face, you've got gobs in your eyes and a dirty mark on your chin.'

By the time Buster arrived home, the excitement had died down. The Boys had gone out to another cocktail party, and the two women were sitting in front of the fire, with a bottle of red wine for comfort. Catalina told him matter of factly what had happened while Leah sat between them on the sofa, nodding assertion. She felt too weary to explain again herself.

Buster took it all surprisingly calmly. 'Don't worry, hon,' his voice was full of sympathy. 'There's no good reproaching yourself – it sounds like the silver went with the first lot of things. There's always the insurance I guess.'

Leah nodded. There seemed no point in dwelling more on the subject, but she was more upset than she let on about the canteen. Perhaps because it strictly hadn't belonged to them – that poor little lady, it was all rather sad.

'Catalina's been so kind staying here with me till you came back. The others weren't very sympathetic. Why don't you stay on to supper?' she turned to her friend. 'I know Buster would like to see something of you and I took a Virginia ham out of the freezer this morning.'

Catalina shook her head. 'Sweet of you, but I must get home. Katy flies back the day after tomorrow and I want to reorganise her room this evening.'

'So I'm to miss the lovely Catalina's company yet again!' said Buster. 'I hope you're not avoiding me?'

He looked so hurt that Leah flung her arms around him. 'You silly goof! Of course she's not, but you know you get bored by women's talk.'

'I guess so. Well, at least I can see the lady out,' he escorted Catalina to the door and Leah remained by the fire as they disappeared into the dusk. Feebly, she shifted a log with the poker and watched, as a stream of bright sparks harmlessly showered the hearth.

Thank God for Catalina – she thought again. Buster was right, the house had grown claustrophobic and he was right about the cause too. Howard and Benjie! Ex-pat life was going to their heads, they probably regarded the adulation of all these silly older women as their due. They probably made comparisons between her and the sophisticated Vincents and their set, and despised her for what she was. It was hard to put these thoughts into words even in her own mind – let alone try to explain them to someone else. It would be good to see Wally again. He knew Howard and Benjie on a social level but his loyalty lay with her. With him, she could really unload all the pain and hurt she had stored up over the last few months– and he'd tell her how to deal with it.

She'd like also to explore the incident in the bathroom – but that might take a little longer. She wouldn't tell Buster though – he would be less keen to encourage this trip if he thought she'd spill the beans. She had thought she was over it, but the truth was otherwise. There came a point when one had to be honest to oneself too.

Buster came back into the room and pushed back the piece of wood she had just moved. 'I've been thinking, honey,' she said, 'everything will get better after I've been to the States. This last piece of bad luck hasn't helped of course, but at least it's convinced me it's time to see Wally again.'

'Well that's a good start,' said Buster, settling down into an armchair and lighting a cigar. 'As soon as we hear from him, we'll book that ticket for you.'

It was after seven when Catalina got home and already dark. Despite her long absences from the house during the day, she had been careful always to return in daylight – which in some extraordinary way salved her conscience. It meant her husband could never accuse her of spending romantic evenings with Buster and he rarely asked what she had done with her day.

She knew the house was empty before even she pushed open the unlocked door. Philismena had retired to her basement flat for the evening and although she could smell cooking, she could feel the lack of a physical presence with a surprising force. Was it only Jock who radiated nervous energy to such an extent that when it was removed, the atmosphere felt bereft and drastically flat? Or was it all men? Catalina had asked herself this question many times before. Somehow, she couldn't imagine walking into a room and feeling the lack of Buster quite so palpably. And what of other men?

She decided Jock was unique and sighed. All these things that she took for granted were soon to be changed. She was not altogether sure if she would manage. The feeling of doubt grew as she mounted the stairs, and when she entered the darkened studio, her heart felt full of gloom. She went round the main area, switching on lights and when that didn't lift her spirits, put on a record with the volume turned high. As usual the fire had been carefully stoked up for the night, the table set for two for dinner. Philismena never forgot anything. Downstairs, their dinner was timed for Catalina to take out of the oven at eight; timing was the one solid thing in their household.

So where *was* Jock? Catalina jigged to the music and climbed the tower to see if he had started some new masterpiece with which to impress her – but no. The clock on the mantelpiece struck the hour and she meandered downstairs. Perhaps Philismena would know where he had gone.

But the old servant knew nothing. *Senhor* Jock had left the house just as dusk was falling, but she had presumed he would return for dinner as normal. He had certainly left no message to indicate otherwise. Had he had a drink? The old woman shook her head, no curiosity or hint of sympathy in her voice as she relayed the simple fact that there were no dirty glasses. The role of a good servant was never to question and she had long ago ceased to be surprised at anything her employers said or did.

At eight-thirty, Catalina took dinner up on a tray and ate on her knee. She was ravenously hungry but for once the food tasted of nothing. In the end she pushed it away and sat gazing into the fire, debating what to do. Guilt, doubt, hurt and anger lined up in turn to confuse her thoughts. By the time she had finished a half carafe of wine, she was full of self-righteous indignation. She determined she would sit up until her husband returned. She had no doubt it would be late and that he would be very drunk. She was almost looking forward to the prospect of an altercation. They had been silent and secretive with each other ever since their arrival home, and it was time to try to clear the air. At least, as much as they ever did.

She was just rehearsing what she would say to him, when the telephone rang. It made her jump and she wondered for a fleeting moment if he were ringing to apologise for missing dinner. Even before she picked it up, she knew that would be out of character.

'Catalina darling! It's me – Joey!' the musical voice brought momentary life to the room. 'I rang to remind you about tomorrow – you hadn't forgotten, had you? It was such ages ago we fixed it … I thought I'd better just call to remind you.'

Catalina had forgotten; she hadn't checked her diary for days. 'Of course not! How could I?' she lied, 'we're both looking forward to it!'

'Splendid darling! Look your prettiest, won't you! Is everything all right, darling? You sound a bit muffled.'

'Eveything's fine Joey,' Catalina fibbed again.

'See you tomorrow then – eightish – bye!'

She heard the click at the other end, but stood there, nursing the receiver. Why hadn't she told Johanna? She could have trusted her. Why couldn't she tell her everything – instead of pretending to be interested in some silly dinner party – and wondering how she was going to humour her husband into going? What did it matter anyway? Why did she care about not letting Johanna down tomorrow? Why did any of these trivialities matter when what she was about to do was so huge, so terrible? If anyone guessed, it would rock the whole stupid dinner-party establishment to the core. Things would never be the same again.

She picked at the telephone flex and tried to unplait it. Under her arm, the machine complained loudly. The whole thing was too ridiculous. Life was ridiculous. She hadn't told Johanna about Jock because she hated the idea of talking about him behind his back – at least about his drinking. They all knew he did it, but from her it would seem like a betrayal. And yet? This was nonsense. Hadn't she already betrayed him time and time again?

Suddenly she hurled the receiver across the room as hard as she could. It took the cradle with it as it flew off the table, crashed onto the floor, and bounced against the skirting board, which tore the flex out. Finally, it rolled over onto its broken back with a screeching stop. Without a backward glance, Catalina threw herself onto the chaise-longue and burst into hot, angry tears. 'But that's different! That's different! That's different!' she screamed at the top of her voice. 'And anyway, Jock,' she sobbed, quieter now, 'none of this would have happened if *you* hadn't made such a mess of things.'

Several hours later, Jock McKay came rolling crookedly down the *Esplanada* firmly escorted by Karl van der Stel. 'Now, you sure you're all right?' Karl was helping him fit the key in the lock. 'I think I'd better come in with you. You don't want to go crashing up those winding stairs waking Catalina.'

'Fuck her!' said McKay grinning, as he lolled against his shoulder. 'I'sh shkeep telling you, I'sh perfeshly all right!'

'Sure, sure,' Karl helped him up the step and propelled him gently into the hall. A table lamp glowed on the side and he saw the open door of the morning room ahead. He went in, switching on the overhead light, and looked around. 'Look, why don't you sleep here tonight, mate?' he nudged McKay forward before he attempted the stairs. 'We'll make up a bed on that couch and then you'll be none the worse.'

With cushions for a pillow and a large overcoat for a cover, McKay was fast asleep even before Karl removed his shoes. 'Poor bloody chap,' he remarked as he tiptoed out, turning off the lights as he went. He wondered what sort of reception he himself would get. Jacqueline had always disapproved of drinking with the boys – especially at three o'clock in the morning.

Instead of the confrontation she had been looking forward to the night before, Catalina had greeted her husband with quiet equanimity the following morning. No explanation had been given for his having spent the night in the morning room – neither did he remark on the smashed telephone. It was a beautiful warm, sunny day and they lunched on the terrace together in pleasant silence. Only after coffee, did Catalina venture to mention their engagement for the evening ahead.

'Oh, I hadn't forgotten,' said McKay squinting out to sea and counting the sardine boats. 'Karl reminded me last night. Apparently Johanna's got some peer of the realm coming along.'

'So it seems,' said Catalina relieved. 'I think I will go and have a rest. I have a slight headache.'

'That makes two of us, ' muttered McKay and arranged himself on top of the rubber lilo they kept in a locker on the terrace. Perhaps the sea air would blow away his own peculiar cobwebs. Katy was coming home the next day and he hated the thought she might smell alcohol on his breath at the airport. The poor child never got much of a welcome from her mother; if he couldn't control his own drinking, for God's sake, who could blame her if she grew up totally dysfunctional? He determined to hold himself in good check tonight.

35

*T*hey were the last to arrive at Johanna's villa that evening. Judging by the cars, a carefully selected cross-section of Santa Felicia's society had gathered within those elegant walls. Despite the sadness he carried in his heart, it still brought a smile to McKay's lips to see his wife's chin lift a good two inches as they were shown into the drawing-room.

The two van der Stels stood on the fringe, Karl looked somewhat sheepish, Jacqueline animated but possessive…no prizes for guessing why, thought McKay. McDermott and Liebermann, tanned and tuxedoed were swarming round the Contessa and another regal lady whom he thought he recognised as the celebrated French playwright, Madame le Buthaud, an old friend of Johanna's just arrived from Sintra. The youngest there, Lucie and Sebastian, added colour, she in an orange Indian dress, slit to the thigh, he in shredded blue suede, faded like denim. Gerald and Christabel Grafton had divided forces, one to help with the drinks – anything to get away from his wife – the other to talk in a loud and overbearing way with a military looking man of about his own age. He seemed the most likely candidate for the guest of honour and it amused him that the more Christabel enthused on her chosen topic, the more the man tried to edge away.

On the other side of the room, he spotted the Neves couple, Senhor Gonzalo, the British Consul and Wing Commander Eustace Stacey who had apparently just flown in from North Africa. Around them loitered Maysie in a white pyjama suit with a couple of accolytes from London, all equally thin, blonde, decorative and monosyllabic.

Champagne was flowing, the waiter from the Maritimo having difficulty keeping up with demand and Johanna herself held a bottle in her hand as she hurried forward to greet the newcomers. 'Darlings!' she cried breathlessly, 'At last! Divine to see you! Come and be introduced. I think you know everyone except Eloise Le Buthaud and Jasper Crompton.'

Introductions made, McKay could not help but admire the way Johanna had conjured up such a broad diversity of guests. Writing, the theatre, fashion, music, the aristocracy were all represented as well as seven different nations; despite being off-season, it promised to be an amusing evening. Christabel's tenacious monopoly of the hapless peer made McKay sorry enough for him to break things up. It surprised him that Catalina, normally so keen to support on these occasions, had melted away into the crowd and was nowhere to be seen.

'… And so you see, with Tom Tucklebury as Master – you'd know him of course, good with hounds but bloody with people – all horn and nothing up here – there wasn't much chance of them pulling themselves together that season. So what with all the antis and a feeble hunt committee…' she paused for breath, and McKay seized his opportunity.

'Nice to meet a new face in the village. Are you on holiday, sir?'

'No, I live out here,' the man before him looked positively thankful at the interruption, 'but I rarely get the time to come down to the coast. Animals and too much work get in the way.'

'Animals?' McKay was genuinely interested – it made a change to meet someone who actually did something in the country, other than feed the tourist industry.

'Yes, apart from all the waifs and strays that come my way, I have a small farm and breed horses.'

'Ah! Right – Johanna told me …'

Christabel Grafton was interrupting again, 'And I said to Gerald "how very strange Lord Crompton and I have never met before. If a horse coughs in the Algarve, I'm the first generally to know about it."'

'Maybe it's because my horses don't cough,' said Crompton drily. Good fellow, thought McKay, she deserved that. It was not long before they'd managed to change tactics and found a common interest on the subject of deer management, a subject with which Crompton seemed equally familiar. After that of course, Lochaig and death duties came up and for once McKay had the impression he was talking to a man who could really understand.

'So what's up with you?' Maysie was tackling Catalina who looked as white as a sheet.

Catalina took a deep breath and blinked before answering, 'Nothing, Maysie, thank you – nothing at all. Now, why don't you hand round those canapés you keep waving under my nose? They really do nothing for me at all, and I can see *Senhor* …, your Consul looking very hungry over there.'

'There *is* something wrong,' Maysie scrutinised her through narrowed blue eyes, 'And I mean to find out. I have a feeling it has something to do with Mummy's guest of honour this evening. Is he an old lover of yours or something – I know you're into older men? No, it's all right – no need to bite my head off! I'm going! But you needn't think I shan't discover more!' She wafted off with her silver dish of goodies to be pounced upon by the Consul, delighted to have her within range.

'Ah, the charming Miss Maysie returns to our midst,' he beamed in appreciation as his plump fingers selected a sausage on a stick. 'You know, Commander, you ought to employ this beautiful young lady to make – how you call it? – the publiceety for your environmental schemes. The health food, and so on – 'ere we have the perfect feegure to launch it all. Everyone will want to grow carrots in their back garden! '

'My dear Consul, you may be a diplomat, but your understanding of what I'm trying to achieve does you no credit,' Stacey interrupted. 'I have not been talking of health food for this past half-hour, but of agricultural reform and self-sufficiency on a grand scale. Take Portugal! If you were to lose your precious colonies of Angola and Mozambique – how the hell do you think you would make out? None of you have the faintest idea of how to capitalise on your inheritance. You have ideal conditions and yet driving through the central plains, it looks third world! Your resources are wasted, and all that Angolan gold which could have been poured into modern agricultural equipment, building dams and producing your own power, is frittered away on out-of-date weaponry for an out-of-date war!'

'Hush! Old chap!' The Consul's little piggy eyes swept round the room, momentarily worried. 'I know we're among friends, but walls have ears and you don't know what you are saying. Besides,' he brightened at the appearance of more sausages, 'if you had a colony that produced half as much oil as our beloved homelands in Africa, I swear you too would still have the conscreeption and the word independence would not have entered the peecture.'

Dinner arrived and people began to move towards the dining-room where a hot buffet awaited them on the sideboard. Johanna had set out three round tables laid for six, with elaborate hand-painted name tabs conveying the seating plan. The room looked out onto a long verandah through French windows and since the evening was warm and balmy, she had opened up the middle section with an arrangement of flowers and candles to draw the eye to the small lake beyond.

Admiring glances were rife as people helped themselves to the first course. Johanna preferred parties with an air of casualness. Not for her waiters behind each chair, still to be found at some of her friends' great houses, nor the lurking presence of a butler. Anything which restricted conversation and gossip was, in her opinion, a crime. The point of a party was to throw off reserve. Often she would introduce charades or other harmless games to liven things up, so that under her roof at least – people did not just meet, they also had fun.

'These are your seats for the first course,' she announced. 'Then I want all the men to move up a table to the same place. That way none of us will get bored with each other!'

Catalina, who had been hanging back from the main throng, was one of the last into the dining-room. Most people had settled down with steaming plates of seafood risotto, but she was in no mood for food. A quick glance had shown her she was to sit on Lord Crompton's left and again she felt the blood drain from her face. There was no way out now – in a moment she would be exposed. As she took her place, with eyes lowered, she wanted to be anywhere on earth rather than at this man's side.

She could almost hear the words '... why, hello again! what a pleasant surprise! I still feel badly about that Fiat of yours ... is it repaired? I'm afraid I badly shocked your husband! No, that can't be right – your husband's over there! Er – your friend ... he –er – seemed quite cut up about it ... such a narrow stretch of road ... you won't be wanting to venture into those parts again ...' And so on, the agony would be awful and prolonged.

And afterwards, all the questions from everyone else! Maysie would dive in first, backed up by Jacqueline, ever thirsty for gossip. As usual, Joey would be delightfully curious. And all the time her own husband would maintain an impenetrable silence. He would let others do the donkey work, waiting until the end before moving in for the kill. If she was clever, she might just lie her way out of the whole thing, but Benjie and Howard would be eavesdropping and see her discomfiture as she made up some story. No doubt every single word would be repeated to Leah, who from then on would be on her guard. If that happened – the entire Plan would be ruined.

Lord Crompton had stood up to help her settle. On his right sat the elderly Contessa but they had already exchanged many words and now he turned his attention to the Portuguese beauty on his left. If he saw the chin lift, the throat swallow hard and the burning intensity of pleading in her eyes as she forced herself to look at him, he gave no sign whatsoever. Instead he smiled and said, 'This looks jolly nice, doesn't it, perhaps we ought to make a start before it gets cold.'

Catalina picked up her fork. 'Joey's a wonderful cook,' she managed to say.

'Yes,' agreed her companion, 'It seems she's one of these people who can turn her hand to anything. Whatever they do is a success.' He turned back to the Contessa with a deprecatory grin, 'Wish I could say the same about myself!'

'No doubt you are modest, Lord Crompton,' she gave a little bow. 'How pleasant it is to see a new face in Santa Felicia. Apart from our hostess, had you met any other guests here before?'

Now it was coming. Catalina stiffened, then violently coughed and dropped her napkin. She made feebly as though to retrieve it, but the guest of honour had already bent down. For the second time that evening their eyes met. 'Please,' she implored in a whisper. A trace, half of amusement, half curiosity flitted across his face but it was gone by the time he sat up and returned her napkin. There was no mistaking however the small wink he had given her from under the table.

Relief flooded over her like warm rain and she felt the colour creeping back into her cheeks. Even if she had not heard him apologise to the Contessa for the interruption and confirm that apart from the British Consul, everyone else was a stranger to him, she knew that from then on she was safe. At least for now. No one else seemed to have noticed the small drama she had enacted beneath the tablecloth, and even Howard planted on the other side of the Contessa seemed too engrossed with his food to allow his eyes to wander in her direction.

The table next door to them was headed by Jock who was on his best behaviour. A lively conversation was in progress between him, Madame le Buthaud, Augusto Neves and Eustace Stacey on the commander's favourite subject – politics. For once Jock seemed to be enjoying himself and as he remarked later to her at home, it made a change to talk to educated, intelligent people. The subject swung from England and France to Portugal, and was picked up by Gerald Grafton who sat on Catalina's right. He left the table in no doubt that he felt the morale of the Portuguese army, particularly in the lower officer ranks, had sunk to an all time low.

'These are the chaps who get blown up at the drop of a hat, while the old generals and brigadiers sit at their desks all day and are scarce fit enough to tie up their own boot laces. Caetano's making a big mistake not to give the military a shake-up. Those old boys should be pensioned off – they look like relics from the Peninsular War if you ask me, and they need some new blood and a bit of brain in the decision making. If the young 'uns don't get a chance of promotion soon – I can see trouble ahead. Don't you agree?' he barked at Howard, 'You ought to know – you went through conscription, didn't you?'

Howard went pink and pulled down his cuffs, 'Er – well, no actually.'

'No! Why ever not?'

'Er – health reasons.'

'Ah.' The single word spoke volumes and once again the diplomatic Lord Crompton saved the day by changing the subject. Secretly, he was congratulating himself that he did not live amongst these people on the coast.

When the main course was over, Johanna insisted that they all change places before pudding. She had endured a heavy time of it with the British Consul and Karl. The British Consul took himself very seriously indeed and had monopolised the conversation from beginning to end. Instead of being his bright, supportive self, Karl seemed unusually hung over. Now, with Jasper Crompton moving into his allotted place between Maysie and herself, it promised to be a more entertaining evening.

Meanwhile Karl slipped into Gerald Grafton's chair and put a brotherly arm round Catalina to ask if she'd been behaving herself lately. In reply to her pout and moue of innocence, his eyes searched hers and he said, 'I brought your husband home last night. He wasn't in good shape. Don't push him too hard, my dear, or you may come to regret it.'

She was careful not to rise to the implied criticism and instead managed a placid smile, saying she would not dream of doing so.

'I'm glad of that,' said Karl. 'He drank like a demented man last night and I sometimes think he's got a monkey on his back.'

'A what?'

'Don't you know that expression? It means he's got troubles, demons – you know. But seriously, Catalina, I've been worried about him for some time. You must be too.'

'He's always liked his liquor,' she said somewhat coldly. 'He's no worse now than he's ever been.' But even to her, the words sounded hollow.

'Sure,' said Karl, 'forgive me!' He removed his arm and lapsed back into silence.

She turned to Eustace Stacey on her other side who was wearing a splendiferous emerald green *jellabia* and looking disappointed to have lost his previous audience. 'You do look smart this evening Commander,' she said pleasantly. 'Where do you find these amazing creations?'

'Depends, depends…' he patted his ample stomach. 'I think this one came from Agadir; I fly in and out of Morocco quite frequently. I tell you – after all the city suits one has to prance about in the City of London, one feels a lot freer – not so restricting round the girth! Tell me, my dear,' he helped her to cream, 'have you seen the rave reviews on my latest book?'

It was not until they'd moved into the spacious drawing room and dancing had started at one end by the stereo, that Catalina had a chance to thank her benefactor of the evening. She had just finished jiving with Sebastian with his flapping hair and shredded suede jacket when Crompton came to claim her for the next dance, a slow number. With some foreboding she accepted and for a few moments they did not speak as they concentrated on the beat. 'I'll try my best not to tread on your toes,' he grinned, holding her lightly.

After a pause, she said, 'I wanted to thank you.'

'Whatever for, Mrs McKay?' the look of amusement came into his face again and she thought he must be one of the most attractive men she had seen for a long time.

'For not giving me away.'

'You need hardly have gone to all that trouble to warn me. I recognised you of course the moment you walked in the door, but as you were introduced to me with your husband, it didn't take too many brains to – well, let's put it this way – I wasn't born yesterday!'

'Thank you anyway,' she smiled demurely and allowed her body to relax against his. The lights were low and she leaned her cheek against his shoulder. Suddenly, she looked up at him again and said anxiously, 'You promise not to tell anyone – ever?'

'Mrs McKay, what an extraordinary request. Do you think I would? I'm not a marriage breaker. What sort of people are you used to around here?'

'Troublemakers and gossips,' she said bitterly. 'None of them would hesitate to – but please, please, won't you just promise?' Very gently, she eased her pelvis against his and moved her hips in time to the music in a circular swaying action.

There was no doubt he felt it. He looked at her, but her face was averted now so he only saw the perfect profile and the length of dark eyelashes that threw a shadow on the smooth porcelain cheek. For a moment he swayed there with her, the rhythm simulating sex as the song writer had intended. Then, as if suddenly awoken from a dream, he held her gently away. 'Mrs McKay,' he said, the voice beautifully intoned and even. 'When I say something, I mean it. Promises are only made to be broken, which is why I never make them. When I said I was not a marriage breaker, I meant it. You have a very beautiful body, Mrs McKay. Don't throw it away on the wrong person.'

He felt her tense immediately, but they finished the dance and when he returned her to her place, he said 'I enjoyed that. Thank you.' Once again, she fancied she caught the tiniest of winks as he bowed and walked away.

February passed seamlessly and by the time they were into March, the pool area was taking shape. They were glad to have allowed time for its landscaping. With last year's shrubs now bursting forth and emerald spears of healthy grass emerging on the lower slopes in front of the house, the land no longer looked so raw and naked. Whilst Leah busied herself with more planting, the two Boys had relaxed during these winter months to enter a hectic social whirl of activity. This involved travelling further afield, including visits to Sintra and Estoril – the result of connections made at Johanna Vincent's party.

During this period, Leah had managed to reduce her intake of pills, but still worried quietly that their house had been entered by a criminal and that they were no nearer resolving the mystery. She had tried talking it through with Buster, but finally gave up. He always said the same thing – the police will find the culprit – these things take time! It was disappointing but she had gotten the distinct impression he had dismissed it from his mind.

How different they both were, thought Leah. Whilst she liked to bring things out into the open and tackle them head-on, he seemed perfectly content to bury his head in the sand. She guessed it had always been like this, but where in the past, these differences had actually complemented their business relationship, now it worried her. She had tried discussing these concerns with Catalina, but on this subject, even her best friend was of little help, other than to make soothing noises and platitudes. It was for this reason more than any other, that she could hardly wait to return to New York. There was so much to unburden, discuss and hopefully let go, she began to feel she would burst if held up much longer.

The letter from Wally finally arrived on March 22nd – exactly a month from when he looked forward to welcoming Leah as his house-guest for a few weeks. He apologised for the delay in replying, but he and Melinda had been in Miami for some winter sunshine. Now he felt *'refreshed, revitalised and capable of handling the zaniest of cases!'* Leah giggled; she was reading the letter aloud to Buster.

' *"It sounds like these Europeans have placed one helluva chip on those little slight shoulders I remember so well,"* ' she went on, ' *"but a few days of Wally's couch will sort that out and all the other wayside naggings too"* …What else? …oh yeah, he says… *"Your pill intake is disastrous. Throw away the blue tablets or you'll set up an allergy to them and plug yourself in the meantime with Vitamins B and C until you get here. You can continue with 2 sleeping pills at night, and a valium in emergencies… but I mean to have you totally unhooked from everything by the time you leave New York"* …Wow! Do you really think that's possible, hon?'

'Anything's possible,' said Buster. 'All you need is a little motivation. What else does he say?'

'That's all really, apart from news about Peggy and Belle, both of whom are still going to him. I'm glad at least I'm not the only one of the old crowd … say, honey! – ' her face lit up like sunshine and for a moment he almost saw the Leah he had married, 'I'm quite looking forward to this trip after all.'

'The twenty-second of April then, is it?' Buster pondered. 'I had hoped he'd have you a little sooner. Oh well, I guess it's as good a time as any – only a month to wait! I've got to go out today. I need to see Roper about something and will drop by his office. I can order your ticket in Faro at the same time.'

'That's sweet of you, honey, you're so good to me these days.'

'Wasn't I always?' he looked at her with some curiosity.

'Oh sure hon – but recently you've looked after me like you never did before. Don't you remember, I was the one who set everything in motion for you! Fly out to Venice, next stop Cairo, then on to Goa – you just went with the flow, didn't seem to care very much where or how. Even on the home front, you shied away from crunch decisions, leaving the final confirmations to me – remember? It suited me that way of course, one of us had to take responsibility – but after all, the company was originally mine of course, so you probably felt more comfortable that way and I never dreamed…'

'Stop talking that way!' he said roughly. 'Listen to you babbling on! What are you trying to say? That I had no part in it?'

'Oh no, honey!' she was amazed at this outburst. 'I never meant that. I'm so sorry, as I said, I thought you didn't care that much –'

'Well, I do care and I did care. I let you think you had the upper hand because it kept you happy. You and your neurosis, your sleeping tablets, your gee-up pills, your mama's little helpers… and all the rest of it. If I hadn't played second fiddle to you all that time, who knows how and where you might have ended up!'

'And what precisely do you mean by that?' she stared at him coldly.

'What I say. By playing the underdog, I preserved your morale. I didn't mind, it worked! Good for you, good for me. It saved you turning into a junkie years ago!'

'Thanks very much!' she snapped, white with anger. 'I'll have you know, Buster Bloomfield, that if I had to do it all over again, I could! And I wouldn't need you there playing underdog – or second fiddle!'

'I'll remember that then,' he said and went out slamming the door.

For once she did not burst into tears. She was too stunned; too angry. It was the first quarrel they had had for weeks, and such a horrible one too – as unfair as it was unexpected. There was so little truth in his words that for once she wasn't wounded, only amazed and furious at the injustice of it all. Damn! The row had started off one of her migraines. She must go and lie down. Slowly, she mounted the staircase, her head hurting more with every step she took. She found her migraine tablets, took two and lay down on the bed. Try as she might, she could not lie calmly and longed for the solace of the blue pills. But no, Wally had said no more and it might be harmful to mix them anyway. Instead she just lay there and suffered.

Buster's harsh words resounded in her ears, 'Second fiddle, underdog... I let you think you had the upper hand...' Could it be, she wondered that all that time in business he had resented the fact that it was her business and that she was in command? The thought worried and gnawed at her for the rest of the morning. She had never even considered the possibility before, never had reason to doubt him.

She tried to analyze him as a man, and drew a blank. How could you analyze your own husband? Especially someone like Buster, someone so outwardly relaxed, happy-go-lucky, easy-come, easy-go! Or was he? He had changed. Certainly, he had changed of late. Did she know this man at all?

The questions hammered at her head and she put her hands to her temple. If only she could ease the pain – searing white pain which pounded behind her eyeballs – desperate to get out.

In the end, she climbed out of bed and padded downstairs to the kitchen. She looked guiltily at the cat who was watching as she disappeared into the pantry, where she'd pushed the bottle to the back of a shelf, out of sight behind a row of bottled preserves. She'd hidden it there for emergencies. Well, this was an emergency – if no one else did, the cat at least would understand. She popped two blue pills into her mouth and gradually the tension eased. The awkward, unpleasant questions which had troubled her so only a few moments ago were slipping away. As she got back into bed, the floating peacefulness that she had sought was spreading itself around her. Now it fluffed itself up and seemed to lift her up like a soft bed of cotton wool. Now she might sleep. When Buster came back, she would tell him she was sorry she had lost her temper and all would be well again.

Benjie was in a quandary. He had gleaned from Gerald Grafton at Johanna Vincent's last dinner party that they were expecting their son Roger back for Easter. 'In fact, he may appear on the scene any time – the young rascal,' said his father. 'His last letter gave the impression he had done enough work, attended enough lectures for this term and would catch the first available cheap flight out.'

This statement merely confirmed the letter Benjie would shortly collect from his private pigeon-hole the next day. Roger would be back at the end of the month and he swore that this time he would not let Benjie down. The figurine would safely be returned. But this posed a new problem. How could the porcelain suddenly reappear in their midst without causing further suspicion and possibly another police visit? The whole thing was turning into a nightmare; it should have been a time for rejoicing. Questions would be asked. Did Benjie trust himself to deal with them without giving something away? Howard would never forgive him if he found out the truth.

He was lolling on his bed after lunch a few days later, still puzzling the thing out, when Howard came into the room. 'Guess what? We've been asked out to dinner tonight by Buster and Leah. A rare treat! Do we want to go?'

As usual, he took no decision without first asking Benjie's opinion. It was precisely this trust and dependence that Benjie had no intention of losing – Roger or no Roger. He tore his mind off his own predicament, and weighed the pros and cons of the subject in hand. 'What's brought this about?' he asked suspiciously.

'I can't think,' said Howard. 'But judging by Buster's air of excitement, I have a feeling he's up to something.'

'I've had the feeling he's been "up to something" for many a long month,' said Benjie. He had never voiced his suspicions before, but recently Howard had begun to notice certain things for himself. Besides, Benjie was convinced Buster had too much at stake with Catalina to risk spilling the beans about other people's private lives.

'It's odd you should say that,' Howard sat down heavily at the end of the bed and regarded him seriously. 'I don't pretend I'm psychic or anything, but I reckon I can smell trouble and it's Trouble with a capital T. I tell you, Benjie – I don't like it. Something is going on and it's coming to a head. What worries me is I'm very much afraid it's going to affect us all. Has it ever occurred to you, that if Leah and Buster break up – we're going to be left high and dry in Shitsville?'

Benjie had never thought it would come to that and said so. Howard was worrying at his hands again, 'Don't!' he said petulantly.

Howard shook his big head. 'I try not to, but they get worse when I'm agitated. It's this feeling I've had. It affects me in every way – my hands get bad and sometimes my heart gets fluttery too. I suppose I'm carrying too much weight, which doesn't help,' he sounded despondent.

'Oh, cut the crap, Howard! Food's one of your real pleasures in life – you can't deny youself everything. Besides, you'll soon lose a few pounds once that pool's been installed.'

Howard smiled; Benjie always managed to say the right thing, 'Does that mean you want to accept the invitation?'

'Depends where they're taking us? If it's the *Cozinha Velha*, yes, yes, yes! We haven't been there in ages and the crêpes are so good. It'll cheer you up, Howard! Then, over dinner, we can try to find out what the guy's up to. A neutral venue is often so much better for dissecting situations and getting at the truth.'

They set off to the restaurant in two separate cars. They were to meet at the bar at seven. In their greeting, they were almost formal with each other. Had they become total strangers?

Leah wondered, as she sipped her vodka. She caught Howard's eye resting on her; a little sad, perhaps. She put out a hand and squeezed his arm. 'This is nice,' she said. 'I'm so glad you could come. You're both such social butterflies, it's rare to share a meal together these days.'

Howard nodded. 'Things have changed, haven't they, Leah?' he spoke in a low voice and Leah had to strain her ears to catch the next sentence. 'When we were all in America and we spoke and dreamed together of this new life, I used to think how wonderful – such an idyll – we shall build together. We shall have purpose, our friendship will grow and perhaps we shall achieve some sort of perfection.'

She nodded eagerly, 'that's how I felt too. It was great.'

'I see you speak in the past tense,' said Howard. 'And, like me, you know it has turned out differently. We're no more together than we ever were – in fact, despite living cheek by jowl – I'd say the opposite. More and more we've gone our separate ways. Benjie, me; you and Buster. I used to think of you two as a unit – now you're two separate, very different people. Buster, I can't fathom… the confident Leah I used to know so well – has fled from our midst – I only hope she returns…' He swallowed hard and half-raised his glass to her.

It had been a long speech for Howard. Leah resisted a sudden longing to hug this funny fat man who had been such a friend and advisor in days gone by. When there'd been problems with the business, she had confided in him, when he'd come to her in desperation for a particular picture, artefact or wall decoration, she'd oblige. There were times when she had thrown her arms round his plump, hunched-up shoulders – both in victory and in despair. Theirs had been a friendship that thrived on honesty and trust. She'd never had to impress or falsely reassure. They both did their best for and respected each other.

Now he looked vulnerable. For all his brusque ways, Howard was a genuine and basically kind human being. Behind those pebble lenses, the rather vacant stare, lay a sensitive soul. In contrast there was Benjie and there was her husband. Outwardly easy-going and pleasant, you could never quite tell what they were thinking at any one time or another. Look at them now! They were eavesdropping on a group of Portuguese, one of whom was Manolo Vaz Valqueira – who seemed to live in this restaurant – and Buster had a crafty look in his eye.

She was close enough to hear they were talking politics. It surprised her they spoke in English and then she realised why. It was rumoured the secret police were all around, ordinary looking people in ordinary clothes who worked under-cover whilst going about their normal business lives. They could pose as a waiter, a teller in a bank, a telephonist – and they had ears, but the lower orders were less likely to pick up on English – especially spoken as fluently and rapidly as these men. She had never paid much attention to these implications, since politics left her cold even in her own country, but one never knew. It worried her that Buster was showing too much interest.

'What d'you say the name of this guy in the military is?' To her horror, Buster was loud enough for most of the bar to hear.

'Spinola!' said one with a sense of recklessness as though he had decided they were safe in this company. Manolo's eyes narrowed and he looked over his shoulder. It was interesting, thought Leah, he remained a little apart from the group, out on the fringe. She supposed it was natural he did not wish to seem involved. He probably had too much to lose.

Benjie had edged up to talk to one of the younger men, handsome but hardened by war, guessed Leah. She was right. 'Yes, I'm recently back from Guiné,' he was saying in perfect English. 'The rebels trapped me in a shoot-out and I got taken hostage. They tried to make an example of me – about to cut my ears off and – er – probably worse – ' he said with a grin, 'luckily a platoon of our men turned up in time and they got me out.' Despite the grin, he was deadly serious.

Benjie was staring open-mouthed. 'Where did you say this happened?'

'*Guiné*, on the West African seaboard, a tiny place north of Angola and Gabon, but the most feared by our men. They seem to breed a particularly nasty type of guerilla there and we certainly get the worst casualties per capita. You could say I'm lucky to be here.'

'So you got to know this Spinola guy well?' Her husband had turned to an older man who might have been a major; he was very upright, moustached and oozed under-stated authority. As usual, Buster was talking too loudly and Leah felt an urge to kick him. Would he never learn to be discreet?'

'Oh no, I just heard him speak. We all did – *amazing*,' the man said quietly, 'that was before he brought out his book…' his words trailed away as though he had said too much.

'You have a copy of this book?' Buster had just ordered more drinks and included the four Portuguese. There was an uncomfortable pause filled by the barman manoeuvering glasses. The group of men all looked to Manolo. For the first time since Leah had been listening, he spoke. 'The book's been banned,' he said firmly. 'Our government does not consider it suitable reading.' Everyone knew Manolo's brother was a cabinet minister and that they didn't get on.

'But you have it?' said Benjie, eagerly.

Again, they all looked at each other. 'Thank you so much for the drinks,' was all that was said. Buster was getting bored and turned back to his wife, 'Have you guys ordered yet? I'm getting hungry.'

Only after the main course, did Buster divulge his plans for Leah. 'She's flying out from Portugal on April 24th and will spend a fortnight in Manhattan with Wally and Melinda. You guys may have noticed for the past few months, Leah's been living under a load of strain,' he grasped her hand across the table and his wide attempt at a sympathetic smile enveloped them all, 'haven't you, honey? In fact, it's my belief she's been heading for a breakdown.'

If she is, thought Howard, then it's your fault, you oaf. But he remained silent.

'Now it's my opinion that Wally will safely help Leah with her dependency problem but she needs proper help. We're both optimistic about it, and I think we can promise you guys, that any atmospheres you may have noticed in the house of late, will vanish – by the time she returns of course. In fact, I can safely promise there'll be a real change!' He raised his glass, and steadily surveyed the three of them. 'Shall we drink to that?'

As they politely sipped their wine, Buster's eyes were burning with a deep elation and the expression took Howard by surprise. Perhaps after all, the man really did care. Clearly the successful outcome of Leah's visit to her shrink was important to him. Had he completely misjudged the guy?

'While we're here,' Buster was eating again and talking rapidly between mouthfuls, 'there are one or two other things I'd like to say. It mainly concerns the new swimming pool and this is where you two come in,' he waved his fork at Howard and Benjie. 'As you know – I took on full responsibility for the building of the pool. I've been out there in all kinds of weather, planning with Roper, watching the men, keeping an eye on technicalities, getting knee-high in mud, that sort of thing. I think we're all agreed things are moving on nicely – even if a bit slower than we might have liked – mainly because of the weather. There is however just one thing I'd like you two to see to.'

Uh-huh, thought Benjie… I knew he wanted something out of us. Must be big to go to all this trouble!

'I had a meeting with Roper yesterday afternoon in his office in Faro, and there've been problems with the liners. I think I mentioned the details to you only the other day.'

They all nodded. 'He's very fussy, Roper, will only deal with this one firm he trusts in England – says all the other liners are crap. In the end I gave permission for Roper to go ahead and get the one he wants flown direct to Seville as a special order. That way it avoids a large amount of duty. However, as luck would have it, it arrives the very same day I have to take Leah to the airport. Only problem is – the liner arrives at ten in the morning, Leah's connecting plane isn't until midday! If only it was a day later, I could have picked the liner up myself!'

He had finished eating and wiped his mouth with a napkin. Benjie noticed there were little beads of perspiration shining on his forehand. 'I guessed you would not mind, but I had to make a decision there and then. I told Roper to go ahead and have the liner arrive in the name of McDermott and Liebermann. We had to make a swift decision to book the order – otherwise several weeks would have been wasted. The firm only sends out once a month.'

Howard was frowning, 'I see – er – go on.'

'Well, I guess it's kinda selfish of me – wanting to drop off Leah myself – but what else could I do? I couldn't call you, obviously – and Roper's agent was hanging on the telephone to the UK to catch the consignment, so it was really the only option. I was sure you'd understand. Apart from the odd party, your diary is not exactly choc-a-bloc, but the trip to New York is a big one for Leah and I couldn't allow a darned plastic liner stand in her way! Is it really too much to ask you two to take a trip across the border and collect the liner yourselves? Seville sure is a pretty city, by all accounts.'

It was a perfectly reasonable request. Howard was already feeling mellow from an excellent meal and several glasses of a very distinguished Portuguese burgundy. He wondered therefore what made him hesitate before assenting. He looked sideways to catch his partner's eye, but Benjie was already perched on the edge of his chair, staring straight ahead, excited and happy. It was as though the unexpected prospect of a trip to Spain had uncorked him! Suddenly he was gabbling on about the proximity of the place – less than two hundred miles – across the river too – so romantic – and Johanna's recommendation of marvellous shops and heavenly sidewalks. 'Plus of course,' he added, 'all that Moorish art and architecture… which I'm just *dying* to explore.'

'That's enough, Benjie!' The sharpness of Howard's voice surprised even himself. Benjie stopped in mid-flow and gaped.

'I'm sorry,' said Howard, as they all stared at him and even the tourists at the table next door had turned round, 'I just like to think these things through before coming to a decision.'

Buster had ordered some more wine, 'Sure, you do. Perfectly reasonable. I guess if it's not convenient, they'll just send the package back and we'll have to try again – at some later date. It'll delay the pool by weeks of course… but I for one can easily wait. Sorry if I jumped the gun.'

'It's not that,' said Howard. 'I just – er – ' his voice trailed off and he began to worry at his hands. He did not know what it was holding him back, and for once was at a loss for words. He felt Benjie's hurt eyes upon him. He had been so attentive lately and he'd been ill in Lisbon – why not give him a treat? It would be fun to go to Seville – for both of them! He sipped his wine, but still something prevented him from agreeing to it. Then Leah made up his mind for him.

'Please, Howard,' she implored. 'If you don't go for the liner, I'll insist Buster goes. I know how much you've been looking forward to that pool. Only… it does seem a little sad he won't be there to see me off. You may think it's silly – but to me it would mean a lot.'

Howard looked at her. She rarely asked him for anything these days. He felt he had been mean and difficult. 'Of course we'll go,' his tone was businesslike again, 'I'm sorry for the delay in deciding.'

'Well that's mighty good of you,' said Buster. 'Kinda takes a big weight off my mind. Now!' his voice was brisk, 'Who's for *crêpes suzette*?'

36

The next few weeks flew by. Catalina came often to the house and as many times Leah would say, 'I wish you could come with me to the States. I'm going to miss you so much.'

'I would have loved it too,' her friend replied, 'but I daren't leave Jock. He's drinking heavily every night now and sometimes he comes back so bad he can't remember the next morning where's he's been or who he's been with.'

Leah's eyes grew round with horror, 'you don't mean other women?'

'Oh no!' Catalina regarded her almost scornfully, 'I mean the other people in the bar. He talks to people when he's drunk, about Lochaig and losing his money, and – oh well – you know! He obviously feels so sorry for himself he has to unburden. But the following day…' she pulled a face, 'he's no idea to whom he spoke! It's very humiliating when some virtual stranger reminds him and he can't remember at all.'

Leah sighed in sympathy. She knew it was true, she had heard from a number of people. Jacqueline van der Stel and Janine Baxter in particular.

Howard and Benjie were in the market choosing vegetables when Benjie caught sight of Roger Grafton. He was wandering around aimlessly with a big golden retriever on the end of a long lead, a stray lock of hair falling over his face every time the dog sprang forward and jerked against his hand. Howard was engrossed with prices of pumpkins, and Benjie made a muttered excuse about needing something from the chemist. 'I'll be back in a minute,' he said and hurried round the corner of a café, out of sight of Howard but hopefully into Roger's path – provided the dog didn't change tack.

The red hair flew up, as the youth stopped dead in his tracks. Even the retriever looked surprised. 'You!' he exclaimed. 'Oh, Benjie! – how absolutely marvellous!'

'Sh-h,' said Benjie, trying to suppress the warm excitement rising up from his chest. 'Howard's just around the corner, I've only got a moment. When am I going to see you?'

'I've got the figurine,' said the boy, grinning triumphantly, 'did you get my letter?'

'Yeah, yeah – thanks. Now, about that, can you hold on to it a little while longer? I haven't yet worked out how I'm going to get it safely back, but I will do…I'm working on it. Can you hide it in your house, somewhere really safe…where your mother won't find it,' he had a sudden dreadful vision of Christabel whooping a tally-ho at such a discovery and telling the whole of Santa Felicia.

'Yes of course,' said Roger, noting a shudder. 'It's safely locked away in a drawer in my room. Mother never goes in there and even if she did, only I have a key. I'm so sorry, Benjie, I've caused so much anxiety. I was worried sick about it all Christmas holidays.'

'You needn't tell me,' said Benjie with feeling. 'Now look, kiddo, I must go. I'll communicate again – in a week or so. Howard and I are off to Seville for a few days next Monday, but as soon as we're back, we'll get together. How about that?'

'Fine,' said Roger, playing with the dog's long, silky ears. 'I'll look forward to it. Everything's all right with me now, by the way,' he said, 'thanks of course to you!'

'I'm glad to hear it,' said Benjie. 'Now! I must go! Bye-ee!' He scurried across the street back to Howard. He felt lighter of heart than he had done for some time. It was nice to have done some good for another human being with absolutely no ulterior motive.

Buster and Catalina met at the retreat on the morning of Sunday, 21st April. It was to be their last meeting before Buster's Plan of Campaign was put into action. Catalina looked svelte and sophisticated in a sober grey suit and black patent shoes when he picked her up. 'I'm supposed to be at Mass,' she explained in answer to his whistle.

The atmosphere between them was tense as they drove out past Messines. 'We don't want to go seeing that farmer again,' said Buster. 'Three times in a row would be too much.'

Catalina agreed. She had decided not to tell him who he was or of their meeting at Johanna's. Life was complicated enough as it was at present, without stirring him up further. It was strange she thought how the giggling, flirting and lovemaking had recently ceased, as though by mutual agreement. They were nearing the day that had been set aside for the first part of the biggest scandal Santa Felicia had ever, would ever, know. She was all too aware of that fact and even now terrified in case it did not come off. No wonder she felt no desire! She guessed he too felt the same.

Only three more days! The date loomed up in her brain – outlined across her mind – large capital letters scrawled with a huge black pen. On Wednesday the 24th of April 1974 – one mammoth, irrevocable step would take them into the unknown. Suddenly the confidence that had driven her to this point felt a weak and fragile thing. Did Buster feel the same? He had told her the Plan could not fail – but was he as frightened about it all as she?

They arrived at the farm. He helped her out of the car and noticed how pale she was, teetering on her high heels across the rutted yard, while the dog as usual barked and strained at its chain. Only when they reached the sanctuary of the barn and he had carefully locked the door behind them, did the colour gradually seep back into her cheeks.

He got out his notes from the trunk under the bed and they sat down side by side to go over everything one last time. They both knew the movements by heart now, but as Buster said – a good campaign commando always checks, double-checks and checks again. The build-up to the moment of attack and its timing must be perfect. There was no room for the smallest error of judgement.

He had some last moment amendments to make. He showed Catalina, and went over and over again with her each small point. She knew it all backwards but he was not satisfied. He had become stern and unrelenting and she eyed him with the obedient respect of a young student, being prepared by a trusted but tough tutor for her final examination. Yet again, he was making her reel the whole thing off – without any reference to their notes. As before, she did it perfectly, word for word, but he gave her no acknowledgement, no praise.

She swallowed hard and burst out 'I remembered everything! You know I know it! Why are you torturing me like this?'

I'm not,' he said shortly. It's just I want you to be sure. I need to be sure. I want to know you're totally prepared! Things are different when one's under pressure.'

'I'm at my best under pressure,' she retorted. 'The point is – are you?'

He laughed then, 'Oh boy,' he said, 'You should have seen me in Korea – especially under fire. When it's all over you'll thank me for this.'

When finally they got up to go, he stopped her at the door. 'This is the last time you'll see this building like this. Next time, it'll be transformed – not necessarily to your liking. Do you realise that, baby? We've been happy here – don't you want to take one last look?'

She shook her head and refused to turn around. 'This is a past that one day I shall want to forget. The future will make this a pale, shadowy thing. I am already theenking only of our future.' She stepped into the bright sunlight and spread out her hands to the elements. 'One day I will forget that this place ever exeested!'

On Monday, the 22nd April, Howard and Benjie set off in the Fiat for Spain. They were to make a little holiday out of their mission – much encouraged by Catalina who had raved about the last time she and Jock had stayed in *Sevilla*. They would stop overnight at one of the great government run *paradors*, and on the Tuesday head for the airport to meet the morning flight from London and pick up their precious cargo. Buster had organised two tickets for a special flamenco show at a famous restaurant overlooking the Guadalquivir that evening. 'I didn't want you rushing back,' he explained with a disarming smile. It's good of you to go in my place and you might as well enjoy the trip while you're over there.'

'Oh we mean to,' said Howard, surprised and touched. Things were certainly looking up. For the first time in years, he and Benjie would be sharing a suite and he'd planned to take time exploring the city. First the romantic sights, via horse and carriage; the great cathedral with its Tower of Gold, reflected in the winding loop of river below, the Giralda with its incredible views over landscaped gardens and the Alcazar, vibrant with mysticism, myth and mystery. Culture absorbed, they could then shop; first, the *Calle de las Sierpes*, for pedestrians only with its narrow, covered ways offering shade and romance, and the largest department store *Galerias Preciados* a must, not forgetting a visit to the elegant Loewe in the Plaza Nueva. Another day, they might drive out into the countryside, visit some *bodega*s and sample some really good sherry before returning home to Santa Felicia around the 27th.

'I can't wait,' said Benjie blithely as they waved the Bloomfields goodbye, 'they say Andalucia is magic! You may never get me back again!'

'Be my guest,' said Buster, 'I can easily hold the fort here if you do decide to dawdle a bit.'

It was another beautiful spring day. Leah and Buster saw them off from the top of the drive, their arms about each other's waists looking for all the world like a thoroughly devoted couple. Only when the Fiat was out of sight did they turn indoors. 'Do you realise, honey, this will be our first night alone together – ever – in this house?' said Leah, 'I feel it calls for a celebration. I know! I'll bake your favourite sweet for dinner – angel cake! How do you like the sound of that, honey?'

Buster said he liked it very much and wondered how he was going to get through the long day. Until now, there had been so much to do, so many loose ends to tie up, last minute calls from the Maritimo – some to New York, a couple to Zurich, instructions to a firm in Beja, and some last minute calls to Chico. He'd been juggling these complicated negotiations since New Year, but he needed to reassure himself they were still ahead of the game. There had been so many last details to carry in his head, he'd hardly had time to think.

Now all that had been taken care of, the prospect of a day of doing nothing filled him with dread. There was one last task – how to keep his wife happy and suspicion-free for just 24 hours? And that might prove hardest of all. Thank God he would soon be freed from the farcical character he felt he had acted forever. Thank God, the comedy would shortly end.

Leah was busy with her creatures up in the wild bit, so he spent the early part of the morning studying the stock market report in the *Herald Tribune*. It might be a week old, but things couldn't have changed that much. It seemed as good a time as any to complete what he had set in motion, and he felt no qualms about it. He wasn't used to sitting still and it wasn't long before he found himself snoozing in front of the fire, waking up with a jerk when his wife entered the room with a cup of coffee. 'Why, honey!' she said, 'this is rare for you?'

'Can't think what came over me!' he got up carefully and stretched. 'I oughta wander down to the pool and see what those men are up to. They're just about ready for that liner, but they need to tidy up the concrete – there's a lot of rough edges which could do damage. I guess I'll have to kick ass to get it perfect.'

After lunch, it became so warm Leah suggested they went out to the patio for some sun. Buster took off his shirt and lay on a lounger. It would suit him to snatch some extra sleep, he needed all the rest he could grab between now and D-day. Leah sat by his feet, uncomfortable and squeaking as she fidgeted, on a rubber airbed. Eventually, she complained of being too hot in her jeans and disappeared to change. He was just drifting off into another delicious doze, when she reappeared. 'Hi! How d'you like this? It's new, Johanna's shop!' she twirled in front of him.

He opened an eye. She was standing between him and the sun, stealing the warmth from his face and chest. Resisting a rude retort, he counted to ten and observed her. Jeez, he thought. She was in a red polka-dot bikini which was too generous in the upper storey and did nothing for her. 'You look great,' he said eyeing the stiff pointed cups which she only half filled. 'Isn't it a little on the big side?'

'Trust you to notice – but I'm determined to put on a few pounds … after I kick those pills,' she slapped him gently on the shoulder. He winced, not in pain, but repugnance. Luckily she did not notice. She had turned her back to him and was settling herself down on the lilo again, this time on her stomach. He caught sight of the moles between her shoulder-blades and the awful memory of the scene in the bathroom flashed before him. The unexpected moment was so overwhelming, he felt physically sick.

'I thought it was time to get a tan on my back,' she said unnecessarily. 'I can't be all white for Wally's examination.'

'I thought he only examined your mind,' said Buster.

'He does a full check-up. He's a proper physician as well as a psychologist and he likes to be aware of one's physical condition before he prescribes anything. I'm glad he does.'

'Well, apart from losing weight, you seem in pretty good shape to me.' Buster wished she would let him return to sleep.

'I guess you *will* be all right on your own honey?' she sounded concerned, 'I always hate leaving you.'

'Oh sure! I was OK last time, wasn't I?' Immediately, Buster regretted that as there was a long drawn out sigh and a small 'hmmm' as they both remembered the geese. However it was her next remark which almost caused him to fall out of his chair.

'I told Catalina to drop in on you. With the Boys away, I felt you needed some company and she's such a doll – she agreed at once! Why, she even said she'd cook you a meal which seems quite unnecessary, I told her there were plenty of prepared dishes in the freezer.'

'Did she now!' he recovered sufficiently to say, 'Well, I'll look forward to that.'

'To be truthful, I didn't know she could cook,' said Leah. 'From what I'd gathered, Philismena always does their cooking.'

He was silent, thinking. Maybe she'd have to learn! Who cared, he could cook for them both to start. It might help keep him out of her bed, at least some of the time!

He heard his wife shifting about on the airbed and the rubber squeaked again. Settle down woman, for fuck's sake…settle! Eventually she did, now on her back. 'I don't know how these girls you see on the beach lie for hours on their stomachs,' she said. 'It's so uncomfortable. My hips, or are they pelvic bones? – anyway, some bone or another always seems to get in the way.'

He grunted. This conversation was going nowhere. How could he have lived with this woman so long? Presumably because they were always working…and rarely forced to be together for any length of time.

'I know you always say I'm way too thin, but it must be worse sunbathing if you're fat,' she prattled on. 'Think how you'd sweat! You wouldn't like me really to put on weight would you Buster? *Buster*?'

There was no reply. He was fast asleep. She sat up to look at him. 'Honey?' she whispered, 'Honey Bee?'…that was a nice name, funny she'd never thought of it before. Oh well, let him sleep if he wanted to. No doubt he needed it.

That evening she laid a trolley in front of the fire. It was surprisingly cold during these long April evenings, but she was glad, for it made them cosier. She had prepared a simple meal of hamburgers and coleslaw, followed by his favourite angel cake and fresh cream from the farm down the road. A bottle of claret fetched up from the cellar stood on a stout log by the hearth. On the trolley, she'd placed a pair of Georgian candlesticks complete with scrolled red candles left over from Christmas. It all looked romantic and inviting. She went through to the library and put on the stereo – classical music tonight – Rossini – something light but elegant should do the trick.

He came into the *sala*, suave and smelling good after his shower and headed straight for the drinks cupboard. 'You sit down, honey!' she commanded, stopping him in his tracks.

'You need to preserve your strength for all that pool work. Put your feet up! I'll fix your drink.'

She beamed at him as he took the bourbon and ice from her outstretched hand. She was determined that nothing would spoil this, their last night together. Everything was prepared, she'd done all her packing, and now all she had to do was run and change herself. Then, it would be time to savour each other's company before she made the long journey back to the States. She would fly to Lisbon from Faro, BEA to London and then a direct TWA flight to JFK. It was important to her that he remembered tonight in a really positive way – a good light – until she returned to him, renewed and restored.

'I won't be a minute, honey,' she slipped from the room. 'I'm just going to freshen up!'

He groaned inwardly. He had a niggling suspicion she would don something romantic and sexy to complement the tone that had already been set for the long evening ahead. It was all too obvious for words. He was right! When she re-appeared she was in a long black tie-around garment, angora and cashmere, which on anyone else would be irresistable to touch. Instead of the usual screwed-back ponytail, she had brushed out her hair so it fell away from her face in a shiny curtain, just touching her narrow shoulders. She wore more eye make-up than usual; Catalina had shown her how to smudge and kohl her eyes instead of the hard liquid eyeliner she normally used and the effect was softer, more mysterious. She waited for her husband's reaction.

'Gee – well look at you! You're – er – dressed up quite special tonight, huh? Let me get *you* a drink!' He was on his feet as she was about to arrange herself on the arm of his chair, and was relieved when she settled elsewhere. He poured a massive slug of vodka on the rocks, and added the tonic with a flourish. 'Cheers!'

'Chin-chin! To us!'

'To your trip!' he said.

'OK – to my trip! And I'll come back a new woman, you'll see!'

'I'm sure you will – and I'll drink to that too!'

A silence sprang up between them. Suddenly, thought Leah, there seemed nothing to say. Was it so long since they'd spent an evening together where the words came easily, where the gaps – if they ever existed – had no significance? Where you could just talk or not talk but it didn't matter? Did they nowadays rely on the Boys to divert at every turn? Good or bad – there were always things to say about them! But now, what *was* there to say?

She went to turn up the Rossini. When she came back, she noticed he had topped up both their glasses again.

'D'you feel anything strange?' she ventured.

'Like what?'

'Well, d'you notice anything?'

'The trolley looks nice. There's a good smell coming from the kitchen.'

'No, not that sort of thing, you dope,' she said.

'I don't know what you're trying to say,' he said, biting back the exasperation from his voice.

'I thought how odd it was the silences between us. As though we no longer knew each other and were awkward left alone together.'

'It's this house,' said Buster quickly. 'It's so big, it awes us.'

'That's the second time you've spoken against the house. If you had to do it all again, would you rather not build it? Do you regret it?'

'I regret nothing.' He peered stolidly into the fire and she felt a wall come down between them.

She brought the food in and they ate on their laps. 'This is good,' he said. 'You always were a good cook.'

It was a rare compliment and she felt pleased. 'It's something you either have or haven't' she said, 'it's called flair. Good entrepreneurs often make good cooks.'

'Yeah,' he said, 'Is there more coleslaw?'

She heaped the salad onto his plate and watched him eat. There was something primaevally satisfying about watching a man – your own man – eat. It made her feel maternal too. She must remember to jot this down in her diary to show Wally. Recently she had made notes – tiny analyses of her feeling and thoughts – ever since she'd known she was going back to the States. Sometimes the notes contradicted themselves... *'Tuesday: Buster masterful, over-anxious about my departure, made me feel very cared for... Wednesday: Buster in a dream, felt my own protective feelings springing up. Sometimes he acts like a wayward child, I want to guide him; do I have a kid complex? I don't think so, but these feelings come and go a lot... Thursday: woke up feeling happy, light as air. Then he goes and ruins it – really short tempered and a hard look in his eyes when I ask him something. Friday: happy again, no need for pills, Buster great in morning, good feelings increase. Later got into an argument about business. Buster really angry, shocked me a lot. Left questioning and doubtful... Did I give him a complex – all those years ago? More important – what about now... ????'*

She hoped these scribblings might give Wally more insight into her current problems. Benjie and Howard were mentioned too, but to anyone perusing her diary, her moods were entirely affected by her husband – a point which she herself had failed to see.

He whooped with delight when she brought in the angel cake. She was delighted. 'There'll be enough to keep you going for a couple of days, hon. Lucky the boys aren't here to devour it. You know what a sweet tooth Howard's got. I wonder how they'll take to Seville? Do you remember I used to make a lot of trips there in the old days? Mainly to buy all those lovely church chests, altar rails and so on and all those magical Moorish wall hangings?'

'Oh, did you? I'd forgotten.'

'Oh honey,' she looked at him helplessly, 'You forget almost everything.'

She could see the romantic farewell evening dwindling before her eyes. Buster was in one of his vague moods; he had probably drunk too much and was already yawning. Oh well – perhaps it would be just as well to have an early night. She would have to be up at the crack of dawn the following morning if they were to get off straight after breakfast. It just seemed such a pity not to have taken more advantage of having the house to themselves. She rather fancied the thought of making love in front of the fire – not remotely possible of course in the past – in a penthouse apartment – but now – a rare opportunity? Only, too late... he was already leaving the room, without a backward glance.

She remained where she was, reluctant to leave this haven of warmth and peacefulness. She looked round at the beautiful room again – shadows and firelight competing with each other for supremacy on the walls. She needed a memory like this to take back to the States. A memory of her little slice of Paradise – her birthchild, her creation. Her eyes skimmed over the priceless furniture, the rare pieces of china, originals of pen and paint, framed *petit-point* on the walls, rugs from Afghanistan and Persia littering the floor. She was drawn back to the fire – the flickering but soon to be dying fire.

What was a room, however beautiful, without a fire – without a soul? When the fire went out, the *sala* would become a cold shell of aesthetic beauty but with no life. Was that the trouble with this house? A wealth of treasure, but lacking a heart? Could it be the people in this house were like the dying embers of the fire? They lacked sparkle, warmth, had no heart? She gave herself a little shake. These thoughts were ridiculous! She was so ashamed of them, she would not even write them down for Wally.

Eventually, she got up. She resisted the temptation to clear away the trolley – let Maria do that in the morning, there were no Boys to disapprove. Still, deep in contemplation, she climbed the stairs to their room. Buster was already asleep, his clothes strewn across the floor, a pair of loafers carelessly dropped, almost causing her to trip. She undressed, disappointed. It was of course her own fault for remaining by the fire – but even so – he might have waited.

It was so rare she wanted sex. Those thoughts by the fireside had been pure fantasy – but why not? They had stirred something within her and she remembered a film, long ago in New York – *Women in Love* from the novel by D. H. Lawrence. In it, a dark, sexy English actor, Oliver Reed had taken his woman by the fireside and it was all so erotic, so urgent, it had blown her away. Despite that, she'd long ago accepted that she was probably under-sexed. There had rarely been anything romantic in their own love-making and even in the early days, Leah had often faked desire. Only tonight, for some reason, she had felt her body stir. Perhaps it was just the doubts in her mind, making her flesh crave physical reassurance – she couldn't be sure. Nevertheless it would be nice to be held.

She climbed into bed naked and holding up her tiny breasts in her hands, pressed herself into the warmth of his back. She could feel his muscly butt against the parting of her legs and a frisson of excitement ran up her spine. She held her breath and listened to his steady breathing. Once he swallowed. So he wasn't asleep after all. Would he turn and take her in his arms? She willed him to, and waited. 'Honey,' she whispered, pressing closer still and slanting her pelvis into his. There was no reply. 'I know you're awake, honey.' She pressed a little more, 'Honey, I really *want* you.'

Buster moaned a little and rolled away. She bit her lip and listened to the silence of the dark. Funny, that advice of Catalina really hadn't achieved very much, after all.

37

They arrived at the airport sharp at ten the following day. The parking lot was only five minutes from departures. Without a word, Buster picked up the two cases, declined a taxi and walked purposefully to the small, utilitarian building as Leah struggled to keep up. The sun was already high in the sky and she could feel the heat rising up from the tarmac.

'It'll be a shock leaving all this, the casualness I mean and flying into JFK,' she remarked. 'Just think back to the days of meters and multi-storey car parks. I won't know what's hit me! Thank God Wally's agreed to pick me up. I doubt I'd find my way around any more.'

'Don't be crazy,' he said, 'you can't have changed that much in a year.' But she had.

Her one hour flight from Faro to Lisbon was scheduled for 12.05. She would board the London flight at 2.45 but later at Heathrow would have to collect her luggage as she changed terminals. Her TWA flight to New York did not leave until early evening. She'd be settling down to a flight supper just as Wally and Melinda were preparing for lunch. Her arrival at JFK some seven hours later, would be supper for them and night for her. What did a few hours difference make? – there'd be so much to catch up on – she couldn't wait.

They proceeded to the check-in desk behind a long, straggling queue. Maysie Vincent was checking in for the same flight, and so were the Neves. It was extraordinary how the simplest act always seemed to involve half their social circle. Buster felt irritated. Could you do nothing in this goddarned place without the whole world and his brother being involved?

Tickets in order, Buster nudged her ahead. The others seemed in no hurry to go through passport control until the last moment. 'It's Portugal, not Heathrow! Come and join us for a drink,' called Augusto but the Bloomfields were already out of earshot.

'Come on hon,' he said, 'I'm not having my Leah rushing for her plane – these guys don't know the meaning of punctuality. I'll see you safely through the gate now – then you can settle yourself down with a stiff vodka and tonic on the other side.'

She felt protected as he marched her firmly to security, stood sentinel as she scrabbled around for her ticket and kissed her goodbye, full on the lips. If only he'd done that last night... never mind! There'd be plenty of time to make up – when she came back, whole and refreshed. She beamed at him, and tried to catch at his hand, but an officious looking woman in uniform was trying to examine her handbag and they were separated.

He waited behind the barrier as several more stamps were added to her passport. The Portuguese didn't half indulge in these signs of officialdom – kept some people in a job, he reckoned, wishing they didn't have to make such a meal of it. Leah noticed the strained look on his face – could it be he was worried about her? Suddenly, she wanted to rush back to give him one last hug. But it was too late and she was firmly ushered through. Both their hands came up simultaneously in a feeble farewell and that was the last she saw of him.

Long before the hands on the terminal clock showed midday, Buster was driving out of the airport. He was heading straight to Faro, where the biggest hotel on the square boasted an efficient telex service. He had checked it all out weeks ago. The Maritimo was not up to what he had in mind and it was too close to home. With four messages to send, he was not convinced someone wouldn't take a peek. There was time to kill so he ordered himself a coffee. He read the messages again. They merely backed up the four business letters he had sent abroad some weeks ago.

It was annoying having to hang around, but he couldn't afford to act until he knew his wife was air-borne. An unnecessary precaution probably – but just in case – one could never be too careful. He had given the girl in the telex room a 500 *escudo* tip, plus the written requests but had told her on no account to send them off until he gave her the nod. He needed confirmation that flight BEA l56 had taken off. The telephonist at the switchboard on the other side of a glass partition was in the picture. She disdained her hundred *escudo* tip but promised to ring the airport at 12.15. At 12.10 he was on his feet.

He checked again in the telex department. The girl was looking bored and painting her nails. His carefully written messages lay unopened beside her machine. He marched round to the switchboard. The older woman curtly told him they had agreed for five minutes later. Was she to ring now? Why not, he said, it generally takes time for people to answer.

A second later, she was shaking her head. The airport was engaged. Another line? No – this wasn't Lisbon – the *senhor* should know! At Faro airport there was only one general number – for the public that was. Maybe … in another few years … when more tourists came? The suggestion was left hanging in the air.

The girl from the telex, hearing voices, popped her head across the barrier to see what was going on. She held both hands outspread so as not to smudge the nail varnish. It was a bright purple colour. 'You wan' I send everything now?' she asked in Americanised English.

Buster shook his head, as the telephonist tried again. 'No – I said – I'll give you the signal.'

Looking relieved, the girl returned to her desk. Tapping out messages was not the best thing with newly varnished nails. She decided to risk a second coat.

The woman at the switchboard was still trying. Twenty minutes later, she got through. 'They're preparing for take-off,' she said, a relieved look in her eyes. Buster told her to hang on. She hung on. A further ten minutes passed. The man was '*loco*'; the call would cost him a fortune. She knew just how much the hotel added on for every single unit spent, and it was considerable. She could hear the meter on the wall clocking it all up by the moment and hoped he would pay the bill.

'They've taken off,' she said finally, at 12.40. She was in transit - yippee! Buster wiped his brow. It could have been much much worse. The connections he'd organised allowed for such delays. Indeed, they were destined to take as long as possible. Provided there wasn't a major incident at Lisbon or London, Leah would soon be winging her way across the Atlantic with hours to spare. Buster looked at his watch. It was early morning in Wall Street, a good time to send a telex ahead of all the other business of the day. He bounded back to the telex section. 'Send the messages!' he instructed. The girl examined her nails and sighed with satisfaction. With maddening slowness she tapped out his messages.

Buster waited, then paid. 'Now don't forget,' he said, his eyes like slits. 'At nine o'clock this evening, I will call back for the replies.' The girl told him it would be another operator. 'I know that, but *you* are going to prime her,' he placed another five hundred *escudo* note on her in-tray. 'We've been through this before. I want the replies ready and waiting. This is very important. Do you understand?'

She did. She nodded her dark head and without a backward glance, he left the building. Once she'd finished her job, she grimaced at her companion through the glass, '*Loco*,' she said, folding the money carefully away in her handbag.

By two o'clock, Buster was back in Santa Felicia. He and Leah had left the house as the swimming-pool men were breaking for coffee; now they were finishing their lunch, hunched over small braziers where lay the remains of sardines, on roughly fashioned wire grilles. Each man had his own modest carafe of wine at his side and they looked for all the world as though they were taking their time. This wasn't in the plan – he'd specifically asked Roper to give them the afternoon off. He saw their delapidated motorbikes still propped up against the wall, and held up two fingers. 'Two o'clock! *Fora! Imbora!*' he said, jerking his head towards the bikes.

No one moved. The boss had said to leave early, but they were worried about their wages and had worked on. Now they would finish their wine and their cigarettes. They had earned them. It was all very well for this fine *americano* – he wasn't paid by the hour. Who cared what he did whilst they sweated in the pit? If he wanted them away because he had a woman to screw, let him get on with it – there was nothing new about that, they'd seen it all before. They regarded him blankly as again he pointed to the bikes and made a shooing gesture with his hands. *What was it with these people?* A vein drummed painfully in Buster's temple – he couldn't take this hanging around. For the second time that day he began pulling notes out of his pocket. Within a few seconds, all the motor-bikes were gone. They could move when they wanted to, he thought wryly as he headed for the wild bit where he knew he'd find Carlos pottering about near the geese.

Thankfully, this wasn't so hard. Carlos was beginning to understand a smattering of English, and he managed to convince the lad that with the *senhora* away, he wasn't needed for the rest of the afternoon. Carlos wanted to ask who would put the birds to bed – but decided against it. There was a determined tilt to his boss's jaw which he saw no point in upsetting. Besides it would be good to have some time off and the tide was just right for some unexpected fishing.

By the time Buster reached the house, the clock in the kitchen showed 2.25. He could hear Maria fussing round with her duster on the staircase. He went into the hall, trying to compose his face. Time was marching on and it worried him. 'Maria!'

'*Sim, senhor!*' she hurried down to him. It was rare that he spoke to her. Generally, she took her orders from Leah. There was no point now beating about the bush, thought Buster. He pointed to the door, and in his most commanding voice said, '*Fora!*'

'*Fora?*' she repeated the word as though he had sworn, and frowned. She understood it, but it clearly upset her. It was the word she used when she put the dog or the cat out.

'*Sim Maria, fora. Esta tarde!*'

'A-ah …' she seemed to understand a little better. It was his lack of language. Only for this afternoon – what a relief! She had thought he was dismissing her. '*Sim*, OK!' she smiled obligingly, pleased with the expression she'd picked up from the television in the local taverna. '*Maria, fora esta tarde, sol.*'

She picked up her duster and placidly continued her work on the bannister. She'd been well taught; always finish what you've begun, before you leave a task. The work ethic in her family was very strong and she was proud of that. The *senhora* had commended her so many times for her thoroughness.

'Maria!' the *senhor* sounded angry now. He was rapping at the glass on his watch with an agitated forefinger. '*Fora!* Now!' Hell thought Buster, this darned dialect, why did these ignorant peasants never understand him? Didn't they read body language? 'Now!' he yelled, but still she didn't understand. Her dark eyes had clouded again and he thought shit – she's going to weep or something – the last thing I need. Where was his dictionary? What was the word for 'now'? They looked at each other, servant and employer and Buster thought this is too ridiculous for words. Foiled by a single word. Then he had a brainwave. '*Maria, carro!*' He knew that! '*Maria – carro, senhor – carro, Maria – casa!*'

He would give the silly woman a lift down the hill to her cottage. She seemed to twig and went to get her coat. He started the Opel and held the door open for her. Still disconcerted, she got in. It occurred to him on his way down the hill that he had no idea where she lived. He hoped wherever it was, she could not see their house from her window. She couldn't. When eventually he dropped her off, it was down one of those innumerable sandy tracks that wind their way towards the beach. It was on poor, low lying land hidden between the sand dunes, a picturesque but humble dwelling, once used by fishermen. The best thing about it in Buster's opinion was it offered no view at all.

It was three o'clock when he got back to the house. In less than an hour stage two of the Plan would swing into action. He hoped to God, this – the trickiest part – would run on schedule. He would have to fly to get ready for them. He resisted the temptation of a cold beer and instead grabbed a hunk of bread, some cheese and salami and raced upstairs – he would need to keep his strength up for what lay ahead. A moment later he was tearing hangers off the rail in the closet, bundling those clothes he used the least into two large sturdy trunks brought up from the basement. These would be put in store for now; the everyday stuff he'd take with him.

He heard the first truck come up the hill at 5.15. Good, it was early; he had Chico to thank for this having drummed it into the man there'd be a handsome tip if they arrived on time. It was still light, but he wasn't too worried, it would be dark by the time they departed. The vans were modest enough not to arouse too much interest even if they had been observed. They could be something to do with the swimming pool, Roper's lorry came frequently, or a delivery from the builder's merchants. Buster had demanded they came singly – half an hour in between – again to allay suspicion. What was one more truck on a drive that was in constant use?

He went out to meet the driver and his mate. The older man at the wheel would be the boss, Jaime Diaz, and he'd spoken to him on the phone at least a couple of times. He'd also been warned what to expect.

Sure enough, the most cut-throat looking character alighted from the cab. Not only was he big, his face was as scarred as a well-thumbed map and his attitude was hardly reasssuring. Chico had warned him he'd been in trouble with the police already and wanted no more '*problemas*'. He might take a little convincing that Buster was the owner of the property, as he didn't do stolen goods any more. He was from the Alentejo – an anonymous town near Beja – and he spoke passable English. Buster had been insistent that whoever was hired could communicate with him, his altercation with Maria being a vivid example of how easily things could be delayed through lack of understanding.

'*Senhor* Diaz,' he held out a hand.

The man pushed out his chest, gave him a hard stare and declined it. 'Thees your house, *sim*?'

Buster nodded. He was prepared for this. 'Bloomfield's the name. Come inside. Look around.'

Diaz entered and looked. He saw the chandelier, the space below it and all around and his lips tightened. It was obscene for just two people. He wished he didn't have to do this job but the money was good. Wherever he looked, he saw foreign type furniture, foreign carpets, foreign pictures on the wall. It all looked very expensive and it made him feel uncomfortable. He walked into the *sala*. He took in photographs on polished tables, a silver framed one of this foreigner, portrait pictures standing on a desk. Others too. He picked up one of an auburn haired woman and with the other hand, a group picture of them all taken in front of the house, this same house. 'My wife!' said Buster following his eyes.

'And them?' the man peered at the images of Howard and Benjie.

'Brothers…' said Buster, momentarily taken aback, '…my brothers. They come here for holidays.'

The man nodded, but seemed unconvinced. Buster beckoned him into a study and picked up a handful of letters. 'If you need evidence that I live here,' he said, 'Take a look at these. Read the name and address!'

Diaz looked but was still not satisfied. 'Passport!' he said.

Buster began to feel irritated, but held himself in check. Chico had said once he accepted there were no hidden catches, Diaz would do it well. He just needed a little reassuring, but he was the best in the business – at least for what the *senhor* wanted.

His passport was in his breast pocket. Reluctantly, he withdrew it. There was something infinitely annoying about not being totally believed. He opened the photograph page, but held onto it. He was not going to put it into anyone's hands until he reached the Spanish border.

'OK,' the man nodded. 'I understand.'

'Right,' said Buster determined to establish the upper hand, 'That's settled then. Shall we get to work?' Diaz nodded again and dropped his shoulders. It was a sign of acquiescence.

It took the three of them precisely an hour and a half to fill the first lorry. The second one took longer. Meticulously they went through the whole house. The only rooms left unscathed were Howard's and Benjie's. Buster had had the forethought to lock these. When they came to clear Buster and Leah's own bedroom, Buster said 'Take everything! Except the bed.'

For the second time that day Diaz looked troubled. 'You say before … you leave the lady's things. Chico tell me you leave wife – don't touch nothing of her.'

'That's right,' Buster was annoyed to feel a slow flush rise up from his neck; you'd think he'd be better at lying by now. 'Don't you worry! All her stuff is locked away in those two suites I pointed out – the ones we didn't touch.'

Diaz scratched his head. 'Me no understand. We do rooms downstairs. Everyseeng you point and say "this ees mine – take; this not mine – leave"! Half peectures, half furniture … all – how you say – divided? Now bedroom – you no want I leave 'alf. You want I clear all … except for one bed. I want no trouble you understand … 'alf and 'alf seem fair, maybe wife go to *policia* if you not fair. Then trouble for Diaz.'

It was a long speech but a meaningful one. The man was standing there on their white bedroom carpet, arms akimbo and not moving.

Buster thought quickly. 'OK – leave the bed and – er – the dressing-table.' He pointed to the glorious French piece with its ornate mirror and sighed. He had so looked forward to seeing Catalina sit before this glass, powdering her pretty pert nose. The cheap whitewood imitation he'd taken to the farm had irked him beyond belief.

'Yes,' said Diaz firmly, 'this for sure lady's thing. Thees we leave.'

He went back to work. Gradually, the second lorry was filling up. It was seven o'clock by the time they started on the glass and silver. They were the packing experts so Buster did not help with this, merely supervised as their stubby fingers with blackened nails moved deftly, quickly wrapping, packing, stacking into tea-chests lined with wood shavings.

'This stuff,' Diaz was carelessly grasping two crystal decanters with silver tops round their delicate necks. 'These too?'

'Er – no, those are my – er – wife's,' said Buster, wishing he had a collection of decanters as fine as Howard's. 'But those thistle ones, these are ours – I mean – mine – these can come.'

His head was throbbing again. He longed for a bourbon. He had resisted a drink all day as he knew the alcohol might make him over-confident, even rash. In the end, he compromised and poured a beer for himself and the men. They had almost finished. Diaz was checking his list as the second driver and their mates started to tidy up the lorries, make sure everything was firm and tight, pulling back the canvas awnings, drawing up the rope ties to prepare them for their journey. Forty-five pieces of furniture, sixteen boxes and two trunks. 'Are we done?'

'Looks like it,' said Buster, 'but I'll take another walk round again before you start up.'

The two of them were standing in the hall once more. They had left the chandelier. Although it belonged to the Bloomfields, it was much too delicate and complicated a thing to waste time dismantling. Also, he doubted he and Catalina would ever want such a huge piece hanging over their heads in a new villa – it would remind them too much of this one. As the two men drew on their beer, there was a pregnant silence. A stale stench of sweat hung in the air and the accusation of unspoken thoughts dividing but at the same time somehow binding them together in a way both found uncomfortable. If the man beside him only *knew*, thought Buster.

Suddenly, he felt it incumbent upon him to make some explanatory remarks. How empty the house looked, it was as though he had to make amends for this… supported by a few words. 'Er – I guess you must be thinking it odd my – er – moving out like this,' he said.

'People move out all the time,' growled the man, 'Not everyone take theengs. Thees I find – how you say? – not usual. Here in Portugal – men walk out, women stay. Women keep all.'

'Yeah… well my wife and I have an arrangement. Half an' half – ' he lied. 'It's always been that way. Things are different in America.'

Diaz said nothing, but Buster didn't care for the look in his eyes. Did the man despise him?

Was it the beer that made his next words come out in a rush. 'Yeah – as a matter of fact I've been more than generous. She'll keep the house – in its entirety – and er… of course…' – he was beginning to resent the need to lie '… there's all her stuff in those two suites – so you see – she'll be just fine!'

Diaz looked at him straight between the eyeballs. 'Look, you give me a job. I do the job. I don't want to hear nothing more. Thees *your* business,' he said and started back through the kitchen to the yard. 'I leave you to make final check.'

Buster stood. It was the last time he would see this room. The *sala* – as they'd named it – their pride and joy. Now that he had a moment to look, really look, he was horrified. The whole place seemed desecrated, vandalized – there were pale marks on the wall where he'd removed his and Leah's pictures – dirty footprints on the floor. But it was the emptiness that got to him. In this half-furnished state, the room suddenly seemed even emptier than before they'd moved in. Howard and Benjie's pieces were dotted around like lost ships on the horizon of a huge ocean, incongruous in their isolation. All the binding effects of a variety of art, artifacts, furniture of different periods and styles, of woods, colours and textures had been lost. Justifiably, you could call it a rape! The rape of an elegant and once grand room.

He had stood there so long, Diaz reappeared. He cleared his throat. 'It's almost eight, Mister. You said we must be on road by then!' He hoped the American wasn't having second thoughts. He was damned if he was going to hump all of that stuff back into the house again. Personally, he thought the man must be mad. Chico had indicated as much. The fellow had a Portuguese mistress, he'd explained, was leaving his *estrangeiro* wife to run off with her. She was quite a piece! Who could blame him? – the one he was leaving behind probably one of these cold business types. He'd come across them in Canada.

Half the contents of the house were to be removed, half left – that was for the wife. Chico thought it was crazy but then most of these *estrangeiro*s who lived around the coast generally were. Look at their villas! They had more money than was good for them. If he,

Chico, did not want his wife any more, he would boot her out and lock the door. That would be the end of it. Diaz felt it would depend – he liked to think he would play the gentleman. Theirs was not to reason why, however. For him, it was just another day's work and a highly profitable one for them both – so why complain?

'OK' said Buster, pulling himself together. 'You're right – better get going. I'm relying on you to get to Chico's place by 9.30. Then I want everything unloaded and in that *armazem'* – he had finally mastered the word – 'by the time I get there. And stack it carefully. Don't break or lose a thing! Chico will show you where to put it all. And don't forget I have a list!'

Diaz looked at him contemptuously. What would he do with this stuff? It was all *estrangeiro*! It would stick out in his world like a sore thumb. Now if there'd been a few television sets, that hi-fi, or something like that … well, *then* they might have been talking.

It was 8.15 when the lorries rumbled their way down the hillside. Buster stood at the top of the drive, watching them go. If anyone observed them now in the dusk, it would hardly matter. There was nothing very remarkable about them – no name or address written on the side, no shining chrome or bright paint. They were singularly ordinary vehicles, of uncertain age, make and colour – something between a grey and a dirty blue. They had the usual fold-down wooden sides for cattle and a removeable, waterproof canvas roof. They could be made to do any job, and suit any purpose. They were as different from the sleek removal vans which had delivered their goods and chattels from the Lisbon docks as chalk from cheese. As they rounded the S bend by the prickly pears and disappeared from sight, Buster couldn't help but congratulate himself for having thought of all these small but important points.

He checked his watch again with the clock in the kitchen. He had left himself just 45 minutes to finish his own packing. That shouldn't take long. He'd already cleared all the rails, it was just a case of emptying the drawers willy-nilly into all the small suitcases he could find. The Opel couldn't cope with big packages but at least he had no passengers this time.

Mungo had clung to his heels all afternoon and totally out of character now climbed onto the bed in the middle of their empty room, regarding him with sorrowful eyes. Buster had remembered to feed him before the vans came but felt heavy-hearted they would soon be parting. 'I'm sorry, old guy!' he said, 'you're about the only thing I'll miss in this place, but you'll be OK. Really you will! I wanted to take you, but border guards don't like dogs like you and sadly you don't have papers. I can't risk it.'

He walked round the top landing once more. There were a couple of prints he didn't much like, so he'd left them. Next it was the turn of the public rooms downstairs. Since he'd ejected Maria before she had time to light fires, the dining room and library seemed damp and cold. It was almost dark now. The far off chug-chug of the generator only emphasized the emptiness he encountered at every turn. How eerie it was … the emptiness of the tomb. He had to force himself to enter the *sala* again. To walk round, to check in the cupboards and cabinets to ensure that not one piece that had ever belonged to him and Leah remained, was a real effort. And as he made his final reconnaissance, he felt the ghosts of the past at his heels.

It seemed he had left nothing. They had been thorough all right. The room looked and felt ghastly. He must try not to harbour any qualms of conscience – it could soon be brought back to life. He had left the kitchen intact so Leah would still have something to sit on. Besides, Howard and Benjie had far too much furniture stashed away in their respective quarters. They could move some of it into here and the place would soon look lived in again. It would give them something to do again, he thought wryly; their artistic imagination needed a little stretching.

On the way out, he passed Howard's pair of whisky decanters again. This time he poured himself a slug of bourbon. He reckoned by now he needed it. He almost regretted not letting Diaz wrap them up after all. But of course, that would have been foolishness itself. Not one single thing, not one iota must he take from the McDermott-Liebermann partnership. If he did that, he knew he could be accused of a criminal offence. He did not fancy the idea of the Portuguese police on his back for theft. No, siree! Strange how that figurine of Howard's had vanished. That could have proved the louse in the woodpile, although he had an idea that Benjie knew far more than he was letting on. Oh well, none of it was his problem – any more.

Now that the moment had come he was almost reluctant to leave. The kitchen was the only room, he would really miss. Maybe because Mungo's day basket was there – under the table, the pine table he liked to eat at … homely and welcoming. Would the others ever eat there as they had before? A threesome was not quite the same as two couples.

It was 8.42 and he was still just ahead of schedule. On a moment's impulse he sat down at the table for the last time, to scribble a note. He had originally decided to write a proper letter from Spain but now this seemed an unnecessary delay and besides, did they really want to give their whereabouts away? No, it was safer and perhaps fairer to leave a few short lines to greet the Boys on their arrival home. He needed to leave instructions about the dog after all.

The short missive did not take long to compose. He put it on the unlit cooker, weighted down with a flower–pot, so it couldn't blow away. With this final act of drama, he felt happier about leaving. He let the dog out for the last time, put him back with the bribe of a biscuit, into the utility room which was warmer, and closed the door. As he turned off the kitchen light, the generator went silent. In the dark, the house rose up like a great hulk before him. Bricks and mortar, that was all, in truth, he was leaving. Best to think of it that way. There must be no regrets. He was about to enter the most wonderful and exciting phase of his life. How could he ever regret it?

Silently, he turned the keys in the lock and slipped them into his pocket. It was unlikely he would ever need them again, but one never knew.

Jock McKay poured himself another scotch. Catalina had said something about an early dinner, but he did not much feel like eating anyway. He had done no work all day, very little the day before, and none the day before that. This one day on, one day off system, was becoming too much a thing of habit. He despised himself for it. Just like he despised himself for drinking. The trouble was the exhibition had dented his morale and he felt none of the old zest and excitement in his work when he picked up the palette. If that cow at the exhibition was right about last year's work not being up to standard, he wondered what she'd have to say about what he was producing now.

Katy came rushing into the studio, pink and damp and smelling of roses, for her goodnight kiss. 'I've just had my bath!' she said triumphantly. 'Good night, Papa!'

He put down his glass and held her in his arms. She leaped into them, one slipper falling off as she did so, full of love and confidence. 'Goodnight my Catkin!' he held her tight and kissed her hair. He did not want her to smell the whisky on his breath.

She stayed there, pressed against his chest, not wanting to let go. 'Don't be sad, Papa,' she said.

He drew in his breath sharply. What made her think – ? 'You're always sad now. Since I came home.'

'It started long before you came home, my Catkin,' he said, his chin in her hair. He saw no point in lying to the child. He never had. 'But you're not to worry about it any more, it's just to do with grown-up things, like money and stuff… But it will all come right. It will come right in the end – of that I'm sure. You'll see!'

'Will you be happy again then Papa?' she asked.

'A good question,' he said. 'But remember one thing, my Catkin, I'll always be happy with you beside me. You're the best daughter any man could hope for.'

She wanted down then and hand in hand they descended the short flight of stairs to sit by the fire. As he took her on his knee they said nothing for a while, just savoured the moment. Finally, she said, 'When will you be happy Papa? When will it come right?'

'One day,' he said, 'soon – I hope.'

'Tomorrow?'

'Well, maybe not tomorrow, but very soon.' He felt himself crossing his fingers under her dressing-gown.

'It's my painting lesson tomorrow,' said Katy. '*Senhora* Oliveira says I'm the best in the class and it's because of my Papa. I *love* painting, Papa.'

'I know,' he said. 'I'm pleased.'

They lapsed into silence again, watching the fire. He'd always appreciated those silences; she was a dreamer like him. He'd have hated one of those over-chattery children, never still for a moment. At length, Philismena came to take her to bed. As he watched the flaxen head bobbing alongside the stalwart figure, he had a sudden longing to call her back. To take her on his knee again and have her here in the warmth, just a few minutes longer. But he didn't. It would upset the routine and Catalina would moan that he had made dinner late. Instead he went to the whisky bottle. A few minutes later, he heard the dinner gong in the hall.

Buster arrived at the hotel in Faro at 9.20 and marched straight across to the reception desk. There was no one at the telex machine but a plump girl with frizzy hair manned the evening switchboard, engrossed in a piece of crochet. '*Boa noite*,' said Buster loudly. She jumped. Then her slow face spread into a wide buck-toothed smile. 'You've come for the telex messages?' She had heard all about the wonderful stranger who left tips of five hundred *escudos* a time.

'That's right,' said Buster thanking his lucky stars that for once someone seemed on the ball.

'I go get them for you, *Senhor*,' she beamed, moving from her section into the area next door with amazing alacrity. Buster gripped his hands, willing everything to be in order.

She came back with a sheaf of papers and handed them to him. 'They are all here,' she said, flashing the teeth again.

'Thanks,' he said, trying not to snatch them. He was about to march out of the building as quickly as he'd come in, when something about her expectant air made him stop. He felt in his back pocket for a tip and shoved down a hundred *escudo* note. She stared at the note, then after him. The buck-toothed smile vanished as quickly as it arrived...'*Cabral*,' she muttered at his departing back.

In the sanctuary of his car, Buster read all four telexes under the bright glow of a street lamp. A slow smile of satisfaction spread over his face. Everything had gone according to the Plan. He turned the car and headed off to pick up the road for Messines. He must be careful over the cobbles, with all that precious cargo in the back.

By 9.30 they had finished eating and Catalina was stacking the plates. 'I've a splitting headache,' she said. 'I think I'll go to bed early tonight. I hope you don't mind if I don't sit up with you. I presume you'll be going down town later.' It was a statement, not a question, and since he never varied his routine he did not bother to answer. As he helped her clear the table, he remarked 'It's not like you to get a headache – what brought this on?'

'Maybe I had too much sun at lunchtime,' she said. 'It was hot on the verandah, more than one would expect in April. I should have worn a hat.'

'You usually do! I often think we Brits are much hardier in the sun.'

'And all your women ruin their complexion,' she said. '

'An early night will do you good,' he said. 'It's cold now, shall I make you a hot-water bottle?'

'Yes please, Jock,' she smiled at him and there was something wistful in her glance.

When he arrived in the bedroom, she was already under the covers. She wore a red viyella nightie and her face seemed very pale against the vivid colour. 'Would you rather I didn't go tonight,' he said, tucking the bottle in around her feet.

'I'd much rather you did go,' she smiled. 'Then at least I know you're happy for the time being, instead of pacing around here, filling the house with a doleful atmosphere.'

'How dreadful to be "doleful",' he said. 'What a bore I seem to be becoming. Even Katy's noticed it.'

'Things will get better, darling,' Catalina said, forcing a lightness into her voice she didn't feel. 'You mustn't give up now. You won't, Jock, will you? For the child's sake?'

'Give up what?' Unconsciously, their hands had slipped into one another's as he sat, rather uncomfortably on the hard edge of the bed.

'Give up hope,' she stroked his long artist's fingers. She was full of tenderness tonight, he thought wonderingly, and that always brought out the best in him. If only they could be like that more often.

'Promise me you won't,' she was saying again, rather more urgently.

404   *Sylvia Loch*

'OK! I promise – for what it's worth,' he said, getting up. She snuggled down in the pillows and looked up at him.

'That's good…' she smiled up at him, 'And take your time, my darling, I always sleep better when I know you're enjoying yourself.'

'You are a funny one,' he said and kissed her on the brow. A moment later he slipped from the room, pulled a windcheater off the peg in the hall, and stepped quietly out into the cobbled street.

He set off at a brisk walk. Catalina was out of bed and at the window in a flash. She watched him go. How distinctive he was from behind, she thought proudly. That arrogant swagger, those small fluid hips in their tight jeans, the broad capable shoulders, and the mane of silvery hair, curling over his collar. He was almost round the bend in the road now. Would he look back tonight or would he think she was too sleepy to remember?

She caught her breath. He had stopped. Slowly he turned and she saw his up-tilted face, gently tanned even in the pale street lamp, expectant, waiting. She fumbled with the casement catch, and threw wide the window. Eagerly, she leaned out. And waved. He waved back. Pretty white hands, he thought – white fluttering doves. So she'd come to the window after all – even when she wasn't feeling herself.

It was 9.45 when McKay pushed open the swing door of the Anchor. As usual the place was bursting at the seams. There were several faces he knew. Within minutes he had got his drink and was swallowed up into the crowd.

At 10.30 Buster drove into the darkened farmyard at the retreat. No lights showed from the road, but when he turned the gable-end of the farmhouse, the back yard seemed alive – headlights from Chico's parked jeep, a lamp in the back porch, another burning above the entrance of the *armazem* and a chink of fluorescent light gleaming from within. He was able to make out the deep ruts the lorries had made where they turned; no sign of them now. What a mercy – it had been as quick as he hoped.

Chico was waiting for him, a loud-checked cloth cap pulled low over one eye which gave him a sly, conspiratorial look. 'Everytheeng OK,' he announced, rubbing his hands with obvious satisfaction at the night's events.

Buster nodded, 'Open the doors right up!' he said shortly.

The man pulled the big aluminium doors apart. Buster whistled. The barn was choc-a-bloc. Stacked high to its tall roof with their precious antiques all covered in dust sheets, it presented a very different sight from the last time he'd been there. Only their small corner remained uncluttered – as instructed.

He pulled his list from his pocket and began to count the hulks of furniture – their identity sometimes given away by protruding clawed or Georgian turned feet. Since there was little room to manoeuvre, he could not be sure of everything…nonetheless, it looked promising. He lifted the lids of those chests within reach. All seemed well, they were packed to the brim. Chico watched him with a bored expression and folded arms. 'I tell you Mister, they honest men. You plenty OK with Diaz. He don't want more trouble, learned his lesson. They take nothing. Open not the mouth. They friends of me!' He grinned and stuck his thumb in the air, indicating that all was right with the world and wasn't Bloomfield a lucky fellow to have him and his mates as allies.

'Sure, sure,' said Buster. 'But I already told you, buddy – I don't take no chances.'

He turned on his heel swiftly, 'Now, it's just this lot to get unloaded,' he said pointing at the car, 'and mighty smart too. I want everything out – yes everything. We've a lot more to pack into this.'

Chico nodded and set to work with a will. He laid down everything at the barn entrance while Buster removed various items to place in the corner where the bed still stood. He wasn't going to have the fellow tramping all over his sanctuary at this late stage of the game. The short man came struggling in with an armful of heavy clothes. As Buster took them off him, the coarse hands rested momentarily on an antelope jacket and his eyes looked longingly. ' Very fine,' he said and there was admiration in his voice.

'You can have it,' said Buster, suddenly rash. Why not? He rarely wore it. The guy was a rogue, an expensive one too, but he had done his work well and the more he was in Buster's debt, the better for the future. More than anything, Buster knew he could rely upon him to keep his mouth shut in the weeks to come. They had a deal.

As for the jacket – a present from Leah – if it kept the guy happy, it was being put to good use. Chico's face lit up in animated delight. He escorted Buster back to the now empty Opel, running alongside, full of hero-worship, like a schoolboy for the captain of cricket. 'Now don't forget,' Bloomfield instructed, 'I'll be back here around midnight. The *senhora* will arrive first, and you're to unload the car for the second time. We must give the *senhora* time to sort out what she wants to take. Then I'll appear. You will load the luggage we're taking into the new car. The rest stays here. I want the loose clothes taken care of. I want them wrapped in polythene and stored away in those chests and wardrobes over there. I don't want the moth getting at them.

'Finally,' he patted the roof of the Opel before climbing in, 'I want this hidden and out of sight before I leave here tonight. Don't forget, I shall take the keys with me and the *cartão*. If anyone sees this around, we are lost. Your hay shed is the ideal place. But keep her well-covered. Once all the fuss has blown over, and I've got the furniture away – I will send you the documents. What you do with it after that is up to you. It's a good little car – not bad for one night's work – and keeping your mouth shut, eh?'

Chico knew this, they'd negotiated for the car, but the jacket too! That was an added bonus. His luck was running high and it was in his own interests to do everything the American demanded. He also understood that the man must be *loco* – to go to all this *carga de trabalhos* just for a woman. But who was he to quarrel? '*Sim Senhor*,' he reassured. ' No worries I promise. Everyseeng stay hidden. You can depend on Chico.' And so he could. It was just like the films! 'You don't worry about nuzzing,' he smiled again. 'Chico take care of everyseeng.'

'You better had,' said Buster darkly as he drove off. It was just after eleven o'clock when he left Chico's yard. Time was getting tight.

Contrary to her husband's suppositions, Catalina did not climb back into a cosy bed after waving him goodbye. Instead she got dressed again in a hurry. She put on a bare minimum of make-up and ran a comb through her hair. She looked at her watch. Buster was due just before midnight. She had more than two hours in which to do her packing and organise

Katy. It was more than she had dared hope for; sometimes Jock did not leave until ten. Good, things were going well.

The first two cases she packed carefully; the contents of these would have to last her for at least a month or more, although Buster would be keen to top up her wardrobe as soon as they were settled somewhere. He had already spoken of a trousseau and she hadn't argued. She worked quietly and methodically. She carried the cases into the hall and put them neatly side by side: smart pigskin – their only good ones – hopefully Jock wouldn't miss them too much. After that, she flew round the house, grabbing a print here, an ornament there, a favourite footstool, a box of records she'd already set aside, the odd book, a small canvas of a sunset by Jock – one of his least modern ones and more in the style she liked – an Indian rug, a cushion and, because it reminded her of home – Jock's leopard skin from off the sofa. She couldn't bear to leave that behind and prayed he would forgive her. All the time the mound in the hall was growing. By the time she added her clothes it would be a mountain.

She crept into Katy's room, cocked an ear and listened. The breathing was so quiet she had to stop breathing herself. So often when Katy was a baby, she'd panicked for this very reason. But she needn't worry now. The child was clearly fast asleep and she'd leave her like this to the last minute. She would have packed for her before but hadn't dared. Old Philismena was quick to spot the slightest thing, so for now she must make do with the most basic of clothes and then they could buy more en route. The child was growing so fast, it wasn't worth taking much. Satisfied with the bare essentials, she returned to her own wardrobe. Suddenly, it didn't seem to matter very much about how she did it – time was of the essence – and she fancied she could hear the minutes ticking by. Is this what was meant about panicking?

She found herself tearing silks, satins, furs and tweeds from their hangers and dumping them into plastic bags. How different from the ceremonious folding and packing she and Philismena had conducted between them for the London exhibition. Poor Philismena – the old servant would turn grey at the sight of Catalina's lovely couture clothes being handled like this. Silly old trout – she fussed far too much anyway. She smiled as she stuffed a lynx jacket on top of an Yves St Laurent shirt. Then felt the smile fade as she thought of the servant's face when she saw the empty beds. What about Katy? How would the old woman take that? She hoped it wouldn't give her a heart attack.

She shoved the thought to the back of her mind and hurried on. What else? Boots, shoes – done! Make-up, toilet things – done! Heated rollers, she couldn't live without these… where were they? Done! Curling tongs…?

Finally she zipped up the last bag and surveyed the hall. Would all of this plus the three of them truly fit into one car? Thank God Buster was picking up another – much bigger – for the journey itself. She'd tried to persuade him to bring it here, but he said it was most important it wasn't seen in Santa Felicia. The police were far too sharp. A new car like the one he'd ordered would stick out like a sore thumb!

No – that was the whole point of The Plan! They would cross the Border in a car no one else knew about, no one had ever seen before. And meantime, everyone would be on a wild goose chase, looking for the Opel! She hugged, herself – he had thought of everything!

She looked at her watch. There was only one more thing to do.

'Darling! Katy – wake up!' she switched on the overhead light. 'Wake up darling! It's Mama!'

The child opened her eyes and blinked. She brought a sleepy fist up to block out the brightness and would have fallen asleep again but Catalina took her firmly by the wrist and gave her a little shake. 'I said wake up, darling! No, don't go back to sleep again! We've things to do!'

The child sensed the urgent ring to her voice, and sat up. 'What is it, Mama?'

'You're to get up darling. Yes, I know it's dark outside, but listen to me. It's a surprise! We're going to get you dressed and as you put on your clothes Mama will tell you what's happening. Now out you get! Out of bed!'

The child obeyed. It did not take very long to get her dressed in a pair of warm corduroy trousers, a Shetland sweater and some sturdy shoes. 'Where are we going Mama? Where's Papa? Why isn't Philismena here?'

'Choose a doll,' Mama was saying. 'You can bring two favourite dolls with you. What about Lily and Pooh? Wouldn't you like them?'

Katy nodded. She was puzzled and wrinkled up her small nose in bewilderment. 'But where are we going Mama?'

'We're going on a sort of holiday,' said Mama. 'A surprise holiday, darling – for Easter. It's Easter very soon you know.' She was packing Lily and Pooh away in a small red suitcase that looked surprisingly full. She noticed Lily's dress was sticking out. Suddenly Katy felt very uncertain and afraid of something she could put no name to.

'Where's Papa?' she said again.

'You'll be seeing Papa later,' said Catalina. Well, it would be later… some time. It wasn't a complete lie. 'Anyway, we're going with Uncle Buster to start with and then, maybe we'll meet Papa in Spain. He's not quite sure when he'll be joining us. He has lots of work to do. You know Papa. But it's very exciting. I know how much you like Spain and you missed our last trip!'

'But Papa – I don't want to leave him behind. I don't want him to come later!'

Katy's small face, pale at the best of times, had gone even paler. She started rocking to and fro with distress and Catalina snapped at her. 'We haven't got time for this, Kate! Stop fussing now, pull yourself together. The car will be here soon.'

Mama was closing up the suitcase but having difficulty with the locks. Lily's dress was still sticking out, but for once Katy didn't care about this. 'But I haven't said goodbye, Mama! And Papa didn't say goodbye to me!'

The case was snapped shut. Catalina turned to her daughter with very sharp, very black eyes. 'Darling, I thought I said you weren't to fuss. Now that's quite enough. Papa will understand. Now here's Panda, he wants to come too,' she thrust a shabby soft toy under the child's arm and led her by the hand out into the hall. 'Now you wait here,' she commanded, 'and don't make a sound!' She plonked the child down on top of a hold-all and rushed upstairs again to the studio. A moment later she was back, a couple of small framed photographs tucked into her coat pocket.

'Uncle Buster will be here very soon,' she said.

'Where's Philismena?' Katy started to make a wailing noise that threatened to spill into tears.

'Hush darling, I said not to make a noise. Philismena's in bed darling. She wanted to say goodbye, but she's very tired. I told her to stay in bed. You know how old she is, it wouldn't be fair to go waking her up.'

Mama seemed more flustered and was talking more quickly than she had ever seen. Again, the feeling of fear crept coldly around Katy's heart. If only Papa was here. He got cross sometimes but he always made everything calm again. Especially with Mama. She clutched at Panda and stared at the mounds of luggage around her. There was even more than when they went to England. It must be a long holiday. She was not sure she wanted that.

Mama was looking at her watch again and Katy could feel the tension like sprung-wire all about her. 'It's almost time now,' she said. 'Uncle Buster will be wanting us to hurry. Now where's your coat? You're to put it on.'

There was the lightest of taps on the door, and the child felt her mother jump. 'It's him,' she said, 'Come on darling! We're off!'

Katy remembered only glimpses about the rest of that night. Often in the months and years to come, she struggled to piece together those untimely events, to relive it stage by stage. But try as she might, the sequence was askew: there was always a piece missing or something didn't make sense. Even when she was older and could look at the whole picture with the benefit of hindsight, there was the horror of disorientation; the nightmare of uncertainty and fear of the unknown could still grip at her heart.

Odd things stuck out. The discomfort of the journey through the back streets of Santa Felicia. She was in the rear of the car, squeezed between a multitude of cases and bags, the smell of leather and plastic making her claustrophobic and queasy. Uncle Buster had driven at extraordinary speed, bumping hard over the cobbles so that the springs of the seat rose up and prodded her small bottom at every turn. She'd clung tightly to Panda, wishing the sharp edge of the suitcase on her right wouldn't keep bumping her side. Under her feet were more bags, so she had to turn her knees sideways in a cramped position.

She remembered Mama's head and neck, stiff and expressive from the back, and how – when they'd gone down one of the main streets where the lights were brighter – she had crouched down in the passenger seat and told Katy to do the same. 'It's to keep things a secret,' said Mama, 'you know how Papa hates the whole of Santa Felicia to know what we're doing. People might be jealous we're going on holiday. We must do what Papa wishes darling.'

She'd asked again about Papa. Would they see him soon? Uncle Buster had put a hand out to Mama then and when Mama had answered, 'Yes, darling – all in good time,' she saw his hand moving up her leg. Under her skirt and high up – somewhere near where it joined her body.

After that – she couldn't really remember too much. It had been so dark and so long, maybe she'd slept. But she remembered Uncle Buster getting out at a place that might have been a garage and Mama gave her a drink and insisted she ate a sandwich, even though she wasn't hungry. Then they were on their own – which seemed a little better. Now Mama was driving and she was sitting in the front beside her, stretching and wriggling her legs to get the life back into them again.

They seemed to go a long way together like this and she kept hoping when they got to where they were going, there'd be no more Uncle Buster and only Papa. But it didn't work out like that. She must have slept again, because when she did wake up she felt cold and stiff and the seat belt, done up too tightly, was cutting into her. She was just about to ask if they were in Spain, when suddenly a man with a funny hat was helping her out of the car and they were in a big building with very bright lights. Mama was bending over a suitcase which was on top of a bed and there were clothes everywhere. Her own red case had been left at the entrance and Lilly's dress was still sticking out. She had asked then for Lilly, but Mama had said no and kept looking out anxiously to see who was coming.

She was taken to the loo in a strange house, then back to the building for more packing. Mama said she might wander about but there wasn't much room and a moment later a big car roared up and almost backed into her. There was a strong smell of petrol as it stopped with its rear in the building and all the doors, including the hatch were opened. Uncle Buster had climbed out to talk to the man with the funny hat who kept touching her hair, and saying '*Bonita, louro!*'She cried then and buried her head in Mama's skirt and wished that Papa would come…that part was very hard to bear which was probably why she'd forgotten most of it.

Her only other memory was seeing a sofa from Aunty Leah's house, sticking out sideways – under a sheet, half up in the air. She tried to point this out to Mama in case Aunt Leah had lost it, but a second later she felt Uncle Buster's muscly arms about her and she was being lifted into the new car. It seemed enormous after the other one and she was in the back seat again, this time on cream leather, covered with clear shiny plastic.

'There you are my little pet,' Uncle Buster was saying, 'Now you'll be more comfortable! Look – you've got bags of room. You can even stretch those long, long legs of yours!'

Mama was getting in the front. Uncle Buster was outside again, talking to the man who had touched her hair. Mama turned round then and took Katy's hand. This bit Katy would never forget.

'Darling, this will be a long night for you,' her eyes were tender with concern, 'Try to sleep in the car a little. Here,' she handed her the tartan travelling rug, they always took on holiday with them. 'Wrap this round you.'

Katy seized the familiar plaid and held it up to her chin. It was soft and comforting. 'Papa's tartan,' she murmured, 'McKay.'

'Yes, darling,' said Mama. 'Now you must try not to go on too much about Papa. You'll see him soon enough and it's rather hurtful to Uncle Buster who's doing his best to look after us 'til we get to Spain. We're not going the usual way, darling. Not the ferry this time – so there'll be more driving, but I know you'll be a good girl and not complain. You've got Panda and your rug and you can snuggle down when you want to sleep.'

'Whose is this car?' she had asked.

'Why ours, darling! Our new car! It's nice isn't it?' Katy wasn't sure. She felt Mama trying to take her hand again, but she had them both firmly tucked into the rug. For some reason she couldn't bear to let go of the rug, the rug with her family tartan. Papa had told her that she was a McKay too and it was her tartan as well as his, and this seemed very important.

Mama gave up trying to take her hand. Instead, she rested both elbows over the back of her seat and rested her chin on her hands. Katy would never forget the look on her face as their eyes met. Mama's face was pale as china, and there were dark blue rings under her eyes, but two bright spots of colour burned in her cheeks. These made her eyes seen bigger and blacker that Katy could ever remember them. She was almost whispering as she said, 'This is going to be the biggest adventure you and I have ever had in our lives, darling. You must be a good girl and help Mama all you can. Papa will be very very proud of you when we see him. You're a lucky girl to be going on an adventure like this and I know you won't let me down. Don't forget you're a McKay, and McKays are brave and strong.'

She paused, and lowered her eyelids so Katy could not see the expression that lay behind the next words. 'Remember what I said about Uncle Buster. He's a kind man and you're not to upset him... Ah...' she broke off and turned away. 'Here he comes, darling, the adventure's beginning. Now try to settle and rest all you can.'

She handed Katy a bar of chocolate. It was as though with the chocolate, she was handing away all that care – she'd just shown – a moment ago. In her chest – or was it her tummy? Katy felt a new sense of dread that was to haunt her again and again in the days to come. But at that moment in time, all she knew was that Uncle Buster had climbed in the car. And in that moment, Mama no longer had time for her. For the first time in her life, she felt utterly alone.

38

The new Saab nosed its way out of the farmyard at 1.30 am on Thursday, 25rd April. The driver dropped three sets of keys into the lap of the passenger sitting next to him, with one terse instruction. To take care of them. There were two sets of car-keys, and a couple of stubby brass keys. The latter looked as though they might belong to a couple of very stout padlocks, but no one offered any explanation. There was too much at stake for idle conversation.

The automatic engine purred as softly as a contented cat, and no one heard or saw the sleek dark beast as it slunk its way round the sunken lanes of the *campo,* gathered strength on the flat plains, then growled with more energy to ride the rolling hills, as pleasant pastures gave way to dark forest. As they reached the summits of Monchique and headed north, the tone was more subdued. Each tortuous twist and sudden turn concealed a hidden drop. Black rock above them and below, some running with water gleamed in the headlights, others spouting a miniature cascade, made the going treacherous. The driver revved, hooked back with the brake, then held the car on an upward spurt of energy on each bend to put the miles behind them. The car was eating up the road and soon the Algarve was giving way to that no man's land that separates the south from the kingdom, as the Alentejo unrolled before them with remarkable rapidity. The driver was totally focussed.

It was 3.30 when they crossed the long, low bridge of Alacaçer do Sal, and not a soul was about to see them. The men from the red-roofed homesteads, who laboured all day in the wheat fields that stretched to either side of the winding river, were still abed. Even the pack of pie-dogs from the market place, up all night to scavenge and thieve, were settled in an ungainly heap by the boathouse as they passed through darkened streets like silent ghosts.

At 5.15 they were wiggling through Coruche. The tree-lined streets of the prosperous market town were deserted, apart from a drunk, lying in blissful oblivion on a wide mosaiced pavement by the traffic lights. The dark-green car slid silently down the main boulevard and out again onto the road for Almeirim which lay to the north-west before it crossed the great River Tagus.

Jock McKay had left the Anchor some time between half-past two and three o'clock. He wandered home, taking his time to stop and gaze out to sea, hoping for inspiration or a reassurance he did not feel, for his future. There were many boats out there tonight. One line, far to the west, had become a string of irradescent pearls against a black velvet drape of ocean. Nearer to shore, hovering lights from the squid boats held a different enchantment – fairy-lights Katy called them – as they bobbed and lured and beckoned.

The sky was murky tonight. No moon and even the bold Orion, his birth sign, had vanished. Sometimes he saw a shooting star and made a wish. But not tonight, you needed a frost for that. It was childish the way he looked for a signal from the heavens, but it did not stop him believing in something out there – an innate goodness that might come to his rescue at times like these.

He had enjoyed his visit to The Anchor. O'Connell had been there with a small party of Scots from his big hotel near the airport and they'd got talking. McKay had little in common with the golf fraternity, but these Edinburgh business men also fished and knew some of the salmon rivers where his father had taken him as a boy. As they spoke, he remembered the thrill of the quiver of the rod in his hand, and despite the wave of nostalgia for peaty waters, the heather and the silver birches, he determined not to drown his sorrows. Instead he would let his half-glass last a little longer , chat cheerfully and walk home a sober man.

Looking back, he was surprised that nothing in his subconscience had prepared him for what was to come. Neither in the bar itself, nor on the way home, or during his relaxed gaze out to sea was he interrupted by a single premonition. It was as though Fate had kicked him in the back teeth by loosening his reserve, and allowing a certain lightness of heart to creep into his demeanour. He did not even have the anaesthetic of booze to protect him from the horror of what lay in store.

Even as he found his key and turned the knob of his own front-door, he suspected nothing. Despite the rumpled rush matting, as though a herd of elephants had traversed the hall, there was no moment of foreboding. He merely prodded it down with his foot, in case his wife might catch one of her high heels when she ventured forth in the morning. It was only as he pushed open the bedroom door that he began to sense something was different.

There was no breathing. He had not consciously stopped to listen but he knew immediately there was no one in the room. He switched on the light and saw the empty bed. It had been disturbed and the top sheet and blankets were pushed back, but it was obvious she had not slept in it. So she had come to the window and never returned. How strange! What was she up to?

He went back to the darkened studio and switched on the lights. There was something odd about the sofa – it looked threadbare and naked – stripped of its leopard skin and the Spanish shawl from the chaise-longue – where had that gone? In that moment the light of truth flooded his brain. He knew without looking further that she had left him. Had his subconscious mind already registered the missing coats from their hooks in the hall, the outdoor shoes from the rack by the backdoor, the cushion from the piano stool, and the photo of Lochaig? And now here in the studio, blank spaces on the wall – oh heck! His favourite portrait of Katy and the orange sunset that Catal– Oh my sweet Christ… Katy!

He flew across the landing, through their own bedroom and down the little corridor to the small bedroom that jutted out over the verandah, behind the eaves. It was happening again! Before he had flung himself into the room he could hear the silence. No breathing.

He snatched at the blankets and scrunched the sheets between both fists. They were cold. They had taken her away some time ago.

My little girl! My little girl! Oh Christ, oh Jesus – help me! He could feel the sweat gathering on his brow, dripping down, under his collar, coldly bathing his chest and neck. Oh God, let me find her. Where can she be? Where have they taken my little girl?

He did not even know what he was looking for. Clues? A hair-ribbon dropped, a chalked message on a mirror? A part of her she'd left behind? Or what? He did not know. He flew around the house. And there was nothing! Nothing to tell him where they'd taken his baby. The tears started to course down his cheeks, fear gripped his heart and he went back to her room. It still held something of her but the desolation was growing by the second, and soon there'd be nothing of her left. No smell of roses, no fragrance on the pillow from her hair. He looked on the shelf by her bed. Even Panda and Lily had gone. Oh Christ!

He sank to his knees and tried to push away at the tears with the rough sleeve of his jacket. It was no good – let them fall. What did it matter? What did anything matter now? He buried his head in the cold sheets of the empty bed. Such a small bed. Such a small person. Here she knelt at nights to say her prayers and often he would hear them. Should he pray? *Could* he pray? It had been a long time. But maybe…where to begin? 'Please God, let me find her. Let me find my little girl. Please…' Oh dear.

His voice was croaking. Would God ever listen to such a dreadful croaking voice? Catalina had called him doleful. Was this what he'd become? Was this why they'd left him?

He tried again. Cleared his throat and struggled with the words, 'Please, oh please God – just let me *find* her – I'll never ask for another thing. I'll be content with what I've got. Only, please let me find my little girl.' He began to get up, then from all those years ago – remembered what his mother had taught him – so stumbling, he added …' For Jesus' sake. Amen.'

Once on his feet, he was filled with new impulsion, new activity. Was it God? Or was it adrenalin? He was also filled with a new hate for whoever was responsible for this dreadful thing. He already had his fingers round the car-keys on the hall-table and a moment later was starting up the Mercedes with a roar that would have awoken the dead.

Soon he was roaring up the cobbled street, out of the town and onto the coast road as though he was in league with the devil and the inmates of Hades were at his heels, pushing him on and charging the Mercedes with their fiery fuel. He arrived at the house on the hill with a screech of brakes and a hailstorm of gravel as he abused his tyres on the sweep of drive outside the porch. He had never seen a house look darker or deader, but then the cackle of geese on the hillside rose up in the still air and he knew he wasn't quite alone.

It was a waste of time really going to the windows and peering into the blackness beyond. He could have spared himself the cut hand by getting a cloth to wrap around it as he picked up a lump of concrete from the builder's skip round the back, but he was beyond caring. Thus armed, he broke into the place in the time-honoured way of the amateur burglar. The bump and the grazed knee, as he leaped over the window sill and came into sharp contact with a carved bench, were all unnecessary aggravations to his cause. It was a relief to reach the light switch without further mishap and to hear the generator cut into the silence, bringing some sort of life to this empty shell of a house.

But what a house now! He had never known it intimately but he could sense the desecration before he even looked. When he did, indignation and outrage was screaming out of every corner. The house had its own *persona*. Even though he'd never much liked it before, he'd felt its energy – now he felt its loss. It was horrible! Howard's collection of Louis XV chairs stood about scattered and bewildered in a room which lacked co-ordination and grace. There was a sudden vulgarity about the consoles that stood in isolated grandeur on either side of the fireplace. Without the binding effect of soft furnishings, tapestries and carpets they seemed inappropriate and out of place. And those empty spaces…everywhere the telltale marks of what once had been – but were no more. Despite his own loss, he whistled.

If he had not seen the house in all it glorious, luxurious, cluttered heyday, he wondered if the shock of discovery would have been so great. But as he searched for the lights in the hall, he knew it would. Even here there were signs of abuse. Shelves that he remembered covered in porcelain half stripped. Chairs gone. Somewhere, not far away, a dog was barking. That wretched cur of Bloomfield's – in the kitchen no doubt. He'd leave that room alone; no point in adding to his injuries.

He bounded up the marble staircase, two steps at a time – the continued presence of the chandelier giving him hope. Was there still – just a chance? The vague hope that even now he might not be too late added wings to his feet. Catch them *in flagrante delicto* before they made their escape? Forlorn hope!

He arrived in the matrimonial quarters and here the physical actuality, or lack of it, hit his stomach with a force that knocked him sideways. He clutched at the frame of the open door. He saw a bed, a dressing table – and that was it. Great armfuls of nothingness. An empty sepulchre, the grave of a marriage! Heaven help Leah!

Sickened, he returned once more to their drawing-room. The large desk he remembered had gone, but there was a small walnut escritoire tucked away by the entrance to the library. With faint hope in his heart he made for this, turned the small brass key in the lock and pushed back the rolltop. What was he looking for – a note – a proclamation that the birds had flown? He should have guessed: the desk belonged to McDermott. There was no note, only a bundle of airmail envelopes, a box of embossed visiting cards and some stiff monogrammed notelets. Not one personal document, letter or diary to be seen.

He sighed and replaced the lid. The mantelpiece was bare. There were no drawers to investigate, no other obvious places of note in which to leave a message. It seemed to him the Bloomfields owned all the practical furniture there'd even been, the Boys only the decorative. It was time to go. Nothing more could be gained here.

He let himself out of a side door. Switched off the light; no point in letting the generator run out of *gasoleo* – thus adding one more problem to McDermott and Liebermann's surprise homecoming. He supposed it was the police station next – but all the way back to town he deliberated driving in a fury to the Spanish border to give chase.

He was almost into the cobbled quadrangle outside the dimly lit *Posto da Guarda Nacional Republicana,* when he remembered Philismena. Christ! He'd forgotten all about her. Would she have gone too? He resisted the infinitely more appealing option of turning round, returning home and waking the old servant to see if she could throw some light on the matter. They could weep on each others' shoulders. They could search for a letter. Surely she'd left him something? He chose instead to brave the police.

He mounted the wide stone steps which ran in an L-shape from the yard into the guard room above. The door was open. Heavy-hearted he crossed the bare wooden boards to the desk where the *Cabo* himself sat slumped. Heavy with fatigue and a late night dinner at the fisherman's tavern, the big man was still on duty – just. At 4 am when the clubs closed, he would knock off.

'*Boa noite, Cabo,*' McKay went forward gingerly and shook the enormous hand, brown with liver spots. Then he stood back, at a respectful distance. This man held more power and jurisdiction in the palm of that hand than the Civil Governor of the Algarve himself. McKay had enjoyed several small skirmishes with the policeman, but they had always ended in smiles and camaraderie all round, much helped by the *Cabo*'s partiality to a rare malt whisky.

Cabo Fonseca surveyed McKay rheumily through tired eyes. His right eyebrow had been split by shrapnel from an Angolan grenade many years ago. The resulting scar gave him an almost comical appearance when frowning, as he was now. One half arched down in a half-moon towards the bridge of his nose, whilst the other rose up to disappear under his hairline. This was an odd hour to call even for that hard-drinking Scotsman. The policeman could see that this was no social visit, but with a heavy bout of indigestion, he was hardly in the mood to be disturbed. It would have to be a good story, to get much action from him at this hour.

'*Pois?*' he said, not bothering to conceal a large belch which rumbled forth as he pulled himself up in his chair.

Standing erect and rigid, almost to attention, McKay told him. It was a short concise story. With each passing second the policeman saw the tension build up in the clenched white knuckles, noted the hate leap across those unforgettable eyes. He also observed a desperate, greyish tinge to the tanned complexion.

When McKay described how he'd broken into the yellow house on the hill and found half the things gone, or more, Fonseca gave a bark of triumph. 'Ha! I knew it. It ees as I thought. A domestic theft. I had the hunch.' He burped again, and banged on the table with his fist. 'No one believe me, and yes – I had some doubts – no proof you know, just a *Cabo*'s ... how you say? ... *Sensibilidade.*' He went off then into a gabble of Portuguese and McKay had difficulty pulling him back to the subject in hand.

'Fonseca – you've got to help me. We must stop them. I need you to get Interpol involved before they reach the border. They may be there very soon ... if not already. We must give it our best shot – it may not be too late. Bloomfield would never dare risk staying in Portugal with the *Guarda* and the *PIDE* after him. Also – myself – he knows I'd kill him gladly. Fonseca, I need your help! We must act now! Before it's too late.'

The policeman looked at him impassively. McKay came forward, the bubbling anger still held in check, but near the surface. Formality set aside, he gripped the other man's hands with both fists and leaning over the official desk, looked him straight between the eyes. 'For fuck's sake, Fonseca, don't just sit there. Pick up the telephone. And do something.

You have your friends in high places, your contacts on the frontier. My wife and child will be into Spain in the twinkling of an eye and if I only knew which frontier post to aim for, you can bet your bottom dollar I would be there first.'

Fonseca, completely unmoved by this outburst, looked at him pityingly. '*Senhor* Jock,' he said, 'I am your friend, I like you. But what do you think I can do? The facts are thees.' He held out his hand and struck off the stubby fingers, one by one.

'First, your wife has taken your child. Whose passport is the leetle girl on?'

'My wife's,' said McKay, starting to pace the room.

'Precisely,' said the *Cabo*, 'and the wife has the free will to leave Portugal with whoever she chooses. Child or no child.'

'But – ' Fonseca hadn't finished.

'Two – this Meester Blookfield, he clear out the house. But only, you say, he take the theengs of him. Not of the other two gentlemen.'

'Him and his wife,' said McKay with heat. 'She clearly had no idea what he was about to do.'

'*Sim, sim, Senhor* Jock, I understand. But who is to say what is hees, what is hers? That is a matter for divorce court, not for *Guarda Republicana*. Not for Algarve police. Three! ...'

'Stop! Stop!' cried McKay, highly agitated. 'I see you don't mean to help me despite everything, despite my losing my family to a scoundrel, despite ...'

Fonseca's next words cut him short. 'As far as I can see *Senhor* Jock, the only person who commit a crime is you. Breaking and entering I believe you call it in Eengland.'

McKay swung round, his face twisted and white with anger. A tirade of words, quite undistinguishable to the recipient, cut the night air. When he had finished he sank down onto a wooden bench and put his head in his hands, spent and drained of all emotion.

'Look *Senhor* Jock,' the big man chose to ignore the outburst and moved round to his side. 'I am your friend. I told you. And I would like to help you. *Sim*, really. Now you come to me again. And you make statement. You accuse thees Blookfeld of stealing something of yours – not your wife, not your child – think of sometheeng else. Then I may contact the PIDE and they stop and question your wife and ... her lover,' – McKay flinched – 'at the frontier. Now – give me the details of their car. Have you the number? No wait, it will be here in the file. I get the guard to check it out. A red Opel, isn't it?'

'Yes, probably travelling in convoy with a large furniture van – if they've got any sense. He wouldn't want to leave all that loot behind, having taken so much trouble to get it, I mean.'

Fonseca nodded. By the time McKay had given him a full description of his wife and daughter, he was becoming intrigued – despite the hour. It wasn't every day a man stole someone else's wife and cleaned out a huge villa all at the same time. It would look good if he could catch the culprits, even if the law was still on their side. 'And now this Blookfeld, the gangster,' his eyes sparkled at his own wit, 'I need descreeption of he, too – brown eyes or blue?'

By the time McKay had filled in the missing blanks he was pacing the floorboards again. 'Time, *Cabo* Fonseca, time!' he was pleading. 'With every minute they are getting further.'

'*Senhor* Jock, I don't have to tell you, surely. They cannot cross ze frontier until ze morning. Now, *por favor*, we have almost finished.'

Finally, he seemed satisfied. McKay signed a statement which they both knew to be false to the effect that Bloomfield had stolen valuable antique pictures from the McKay household. They had reason to believe these were being smuggled out of the country. Even if they were not in convoy with the van, this information alone should be enough to detain them until the local *PIDE* moved in. There would be questions of course, but at least it should give *Senhor* Jock sufficient time to catch up with the runaways and retrieve his wife and child. As long as there was no trouble…no shooting, no fighting… *Cabo* Fonseca was insistent – a satisfactory result should be obtained. *Senhor* Jock might have a little explaining to do, but as long as he stuck to his story, no one need get hurt.

Was *Senhor* Jock able to do this, stick to his story and promise not to kill anyone? He would? Then he, *Cabo* Fonseca, would contact the – er – his voice always hushed a little – the International Police. He put his hand on the telephone and stifled a yawn. It had been a long night. It was strange: there seemed no tone when he picked up the receiver, but he was used to line problems. It would be fixed soon enough. He indicated for his visitor to depart.

'Now you leave, *Senhor* Jock. I see you later, yes? You come to the guard room about midday, *sim*? Then maybe, I have some news for you. You give the word you stay here in Santa Felicia unteel then? Maybe the PIDE will need to interview you. Thees is the best way forward believe me.'

McKay nodded curtly and got out. He knew when he was not wanted. He made a mental note to go to the bank before he returned to the Guard Room.

McKay reached his home again as dawn crept in a silvery slipstream across the Atlantic. At the same time, columns of soldiers, some marching all night, others arriving by tank, truck and armoured car, had surrounded every government building in the centre of Lisbon. The airport and radio station had been seized. The Salazar Bridge was in the hands of the army. Troops with machine guns had stormed the military stronghold of Dr Marcello Caetano, the prime minister, and his ministers. Police headquarters were about to fall.

On the parade grounds of the barracks at Mafra near the coast, more men were being assembled. Those who had not yet left the barracks further inland at Santarém, where the movement had started, awaited their summons. The revolutionary song of the Movement of the Armed Forces was now playing on every radio. All over Portugal, Madeira and the Azores, people were waking up to the strains of a new tune. *Grandola*, the marching song of the workers and of the glorious Revolution, was stirring. The all-male voice choir was convincing and strong. At the end of each verse, a commentator was proclaiming the end of the *Estado Novo*. Who could it be? Could it be true? If the radio said so…it must surely be! Throughout every town, village and homestead, the people learned that the long years of dictatorship were over. They were asked to be calm, remain peaceful and to stay at home.

Unaware of all this, and in no mood to switch on the radio, Jock took his own vengeance out on the car. Arriving at his own front door with a screech of brakes, he remembered he had left the key on the inside. It was one of those self-locking Yales, and it was the last straw. He hammered on the heavy front door, oblivious to the neighbours in the half light. How to wake Philismena, below stairs, was the next problem. He hammered again, wishing it was Bloomfield's head. Then he remembered the bell – it was wired through to the basement – which was how she was able to answer the door first when people came. Was he going mad that he had just bloodied his knuckles unecessarily?

He pressed it. And waited. It was 5.25 – normally she arose at 6.30. Would she hear him? This was getting ridiculous; might he now have to break into his own house? He pressed again. Just as he was giving up all hope, the door opened a crack, held on the chain. A small face under a frilly cap peeped cautiously out. '*Senhor* Jock?' As she undid the catch, he half stumbled over the step, a smell of candles and floor polish assailing his nostrils. Suddenly all the strength had gone out of him and he sank down heavily on a chair, his head on his hands. She took one look at his face and headed straight for the brandy bottle.

He waved it aside when she brought the glass, muttering to himself that if he had had less of 'the juice', they might not now be in the mess they were. But one did not argue with Philismena, and in the end he accepted it meekly and felt the better for it. As gently as he could, he broke the news. She accepted with amazing calm the fact that her mistress had gone although there was a tightening of the old lips and a frosty look in her eyes. He paused, accepting her awkward sympathy and platitudes which neither of them believed, that there had been some mistake.

When he got to the bit about Katy, it became clear that the thought of her going too, had simply not occurred. She cried out then – a wild, shrill 'Aieee…' – her hand flew to her brow and the silly lace cap fell forward at a rakish angle. For a moment he thought she would faint. Now it was his turn to fetch the brandy bottle.

Impatiently he thought – all this is wasting time. As I get comforted, they're heading further and further away, now I'm doing the comforting, they're getting even further. He began to regret he hadn't given chase immediately, but by which route? – that had been the problem. It might still prove to be the stumbling block. Would Fonseca's contacts really check every border, every car? He hated this inaction on his part and despised himself for it.

A thought occurred. If he had been planning this elopement, would he not have tried to put the other party's car out of action? Then why had Bloomfield not tampered with the Mercedes, or at least let the tyres down? It seemed almost an insult that nothing had been touched, as though they never expected him to follow them! And how right they were! How they must be laughing! With three or four roads out of the Algarve to choose from and seven exits from Portugal to Spain, no wonder they felt confident. Let him chase after them! Chances were the old bugger would choose the wrong route and merely make a fool of himself. He could see Bloomfield smiling as he planned it all. What a mockery the whole thing was!

But there again, thought McKay, as he waited for their old retainer to recover… she was hunched into herself, bent and speechless, dabbing at her eyes with a small handkerchief as silent sobs wracked her body. Christ, they liked their dose of drama these simple people, but he was grateful, all the same, for her show of emotion. Perhaps – after all – they were not making for the border. He was sure they must, at some stage – Bloomfield would scarcely feel comfortable in the same country as himself – but maybe not right away. Perhaps, to throw them off-scent, they had decided to lay up for a time. Hide away in some remote village inn, or even a slick Estoril hotel, well camouflaged by the tourists, until the hue and cry were over. Somehow though, he thought this unlikely.

It was more probable they were bound for the border. But all he could do now was pray to God or the Devil – he knew not whom he served at this particular moment – that Fonseca's message would be passed on in time. The frontier police were a funny lot of coves. They could be highly efficient, or remarkably lax. It often depended on the time of the day. He reckoned the odds were no more than fifty-fifty. Probably less – fuck it.

Philismena was recovering slowly. How incongruous she looked, poor old thing, in her worsted nightgown, her tired fat ankles poking out at the hem, swaddled in bedsocks. She hadn't even had time to put on a pair of slippers, poor thing. Suddenly, she was all excitement, and was catching at his sleeve. '*Senhor* Jock! *Veja-la!*'

How he had missed it, he never knew. For there, behind a vase, not far from where his car-keys had lain, was a letter. A large plain envelope addressed to him in Catalina's familiar purple writing. It said '*Jock*'. And it struck him how bald his name looked on that expanse of dove grey, as if stripped of dignity, bereft – like him.

In a strange way it also reminded him of the yellow house on the hill. You're going nuts, he told himself as he picked up the letter with all the care of someone handling a loaded gun. He left Philismena and with a heavy heart, carried it wearily upstairs. He needed to be alone for this.

'*Darling Jock,*

'*I hope one day you will forgive me. I am running away with Buster because I feel it is the only way. I am only a burden on you and the longer I stay, the more difficult things become. I feel you will be better on your own once you get used to it. You will then be able to concentrate on the things that matter without me to worry you with my constant demands. I hope also with me gone, you will no longer have an excuse for drinking so much.*

'*Buster is a decent man and I shall be happy with him. You must not worry about me. He has also promised to be a good temporary father to Katy though he knows he is hardly a substitute for her real Papa. Katy will learn to cope and at least she won't have to cope with mood swings and the crises which seem to have become a feature of her parents' life. Perhaps it may not need to be so long, before you are reunited with her. In the meantime however it would be very wrong of you to try to see her. And of course, we shall make that impossible, for everyone's sakes.*

'*I hope therefore you will be sensible darling and understand that I have to do this. It will be for the best in the end and one day you will understand and be happy again. Please believe me – I mean this with all my heart.*

'*I also hope you will not try to follow us as it will be a waste of time and frustrating for you. Katy sends her Papa a kiss and I embrace you.*

'*Your ever loving Catalina*'

'My God!' he cried aloud. He screwed the letter into a tight tight ball and threw it violently across the room in the direction of the fire. It missed and bounced off the fender and onto the hearthrug. Later, he wished that it had burnt the first time, for through the hours to come he was to read the crumpled page again and again. Each time, the calculated deliberation behind the message hurt more and more. So did the veiled accusations. To be reminded in words of his own reprehensible behaviour and the hopelessness of his situation, with such crystal clarity, brought the pain level to a new threshold.

Each time he read it, it hurt more. And so it continued with each reading, until finally he saw sense and stoked the thing into the dying embers of last night's fire. He had considered saving it for his lawyers, but the shame was too great. He felt better once it had gone, but there was an odd feeling in the pit of his stomach and he remembered that he had eaten nothing since the glass of brandy and that for him the grape had never combined well with the grain. Not long after that he went into the bathroom and was very sick.

Leah had awoken on the 24th April to a glorious New York spring day. She had slept extraordinarily well the night before. The relief of getting there at last was immense. It was so nice, she thought, to be with normal people again. She immediately felt guilty then and checked herself. After all – wasn't her own household, her husband, Howard and Benjie, pretty normal – deep underneath?

Wally and Melinda had given her such a welcome last night. The plane had come in on schedule and the two of them had been at JFK to greet her and drive her uptown to their Claremont apartment. As she emerged from customs, Melinda spotted her amongst the arrivals, rushed forward and hugged her warmly. 'Welcome home, honey! We've all missed you so! Now let's take a look at you and see what Europe's done for that delicate complexion.' She stood back, both hands on Leah's shoulders and studied her.

'Oh well, honey,' she said after a moment's hesitation, a tiny frown appearing between her eyes. 'You're just a little tired from the journey. New York will soon put you right again – in no time!' She laughed gently and bore Leah off towards the car park, leaving Wally to deal with the luggage.

They had a light supper. Leah tried to forget it was three o'clock in the morning and that Buster and everyone would be sound asleep. She had managed to snooze on the plane, but was nevertheless glad when they packed her off to an early bed with a dose of Mogadon in her hot milk. Melinda sat up with her husband until the late night movie had finished and said – 'Well, what do *you* think?'

'She's in bad shape, poor kid,' he said. 'I had my doubts about that venture of theirs right from the beginning, and from what she's let drop so far, I wasn't far wrong. It's not *she* who shouldn't have left the States, Leah's a person who'll make good of most situations. Put her on a desert island and she'd make the best of it. It's the others who are the problem – particularly that bone-headed husband of hers. He's the one – if my guess is right – who's turned her into the physical wreck we're looking at right now.'

'Will you be able to help her, honey?' Melinda's voice was full of concern.

'Sure, I'll help her. We'll get her off these drugs, and straighten her out. But the moment she goes back to that rarified atmosphere, who's to say the strain won't prove too much and she'll start off all over again.'

'Poor girl,' said Melinda, and meant it.

At first there was little traffic on the road north of Coruche. The region of the Ribatejo was agricultural, all vineyards and cork, cattle and horses, but there was a big barracks at the old Roman fort of Santarém and Catalina had warned the bridge over the Tagus might be busy. You had to go all the way to Vila Franca to find another crossing before Lisbon so even at this hour they might be delayed.

Buster was congratulating himself on the time they were making as they approached the bridge when the Ford Cortina he had been trying to overtake applied its brake lights, and out came a warning hand to slow him down. A moment later they were at a standstill to allow a column of army trucks full of soldiers in camouflage uniform to rumble past. There were thirty trucks in all, and two great Crusader tanks brought up the rear, manned by two very young looking subalterns with a couple of sergeants. They were saluted and allowed to proceed and Buster thought how disruptive to start men on manoeuvres in peacetime at such an uncivilised time of day.

In the town itself, all was activity. As they passed the enormous barracks, there seemed to be some sort of parade in progress, as more soldiers came spilling out of the grey dawn, assembling in large numbers on the tarmac. Catalina remarked on the unaccustomed sight through open gates and thought the army must have changed from the days she remembered, when her cousin had been drafted up and everything took place behind closed gates.

Once clear of the city centre, there was less traffic to impede their progress. As they drove north out of the fortified city, the ancient walls gave way to plane trees and the solitary Saab roared up a steep incline that meant they were safely heading for the old university town of Coimbra. When they made it there, just before eight a.m., some students were already going about their business. The Saab slid in through the old city portals and shared a procession of traffic lights with the inevitable VW Beetles, the odd sports car and a multitude of bicycles. Suddenly, there was a strange feeling in the air, and several people were hooting their horns and winding down their windows in the middle of the street. In front of them someone did a sudden U turn with no warning at all, and instead of apologising, the occupants of the car hung laughingly over the door and whistled as they threw flowers over their bonnet. Another driver was jangling a rattle.

'What the devil?' began Buster indignantly.

'Don't worry, darling,' said Catalina, 'It's obviously some kind of *carnaval* – you know what students are like! The sooner we get out of here, the better. Look, there's a sign for Viseu, that's the road we want before we head off for Guarda.'

They had decided to take the country route to the border to avoid any chance of being spotted. When Buster read out 'Only 168 Kilometres' with a hint of triumph in his voice, he was unaware of just how countrified their chosen route really was. In her usual optimistic way, Catalina had failed to point out that most of it consisted of hairpin bends, narrow bridges over gorges, plus precipitous drops at every turn. They were about to cross the Serra da Estrela.

'We'll stop for breakfast half way up,' said Catalina firmly. 'There's a little place at the summit where they serve coffee and cakes. Katy's still asleep but I suspect she'll soon wake with all this twisting and winding and we don't want tears – or sick. We'll need to wash and freshen up and I for one need to stretch my legs.'

'I'm not sure that's quite wise,' said Buster, 'I'm anxious to get through to Spain just as soon as we can. There's no knowing what your husband may be up to, so if we can hang in there 'til the border, I'd feel happier.'

McKay was grey with fatigue when he reported once more to the guard room in Santa Felicia, but he felt a little better than he had earlier. Philismena had cooked him an egg and bacon breakfast and had stood over him until he'd eaten. Washed down with several cups of steaming black coffee, the meal gave him the heart to face the day even although he hadn't been able to sleep a wink. He had bathed, shaved and changed his clothes before visiting his bank earlier that morning to withdraw a sum of five thousand *escudos*. Only the bank was shut. Strange! Must be one of those religious holidays… never mind, he'd make up for it later, provided the *Cabo* was successful. Surely, that would be the case! Luckily he had a *conto* note in his jeans pocket. It would have to do for starters.

With the brightness of the spring day, the beauty of the sea view spread all around him as he crossed the old part of town on foot to the police station, McKay began to believe that success *had* to be his.

Mounting the familiar stone steps, lighter of heart than he dared to hope, he knocked. It was strange the door was closed, but people were there because he could hear low voices. He also heard the distant chime of the church clock, resounding through an open window as though beating time to the conversation within. No one seemed to have heard him, so he knocked again.

There was the tramp of heavy boots across the floor boards and a young, red-faced policeman opened the door and blocked his way. McKay knew most of the younger ones, but this surly faced youth he did not recognize. '*Cabo* Fonseca?' McKay made to pass him, but the man blocked his path.

'*Não esta*,' he said dourly.

'Then I will wait,' McKay replied in Portuguese.

The man shook his head stubbornly. The *Cabo* was sick, he was told. There would be no point in waiting.

McKay brushed the remark aside. 'You don't understand,' he said impatiently. 'I have an important appointment with the *Cabo* for midday. I was with him early this morning, at three forty-five to be precise and if he's got sick, it can't be too much. He is expecting me – urgent business. No doubt he will be here soon.'

The policeman looked at his boots. The red of his face had spread to an ox-like neck and two large jug-handle ears. There was a sullen resentment in his voice as though he'd been caught in the act of something he should not have done. Again he replied in his native tongue but with less care, 'I tell you, he will not be coming. We are closed today.'

To McKay's shock and horror he turned on his heel and shut the door in his face. Once again, he heard the low voices coming from within. Most of it was muffled, but the words '*presidente*', '*republica*' and what might have been '*militar*', floated out of the window. Then everything became indistinguishable once more.

Angrily, he went back out into the street and marched off at high speed in the direction of Fonseca's private house.

'Sit down,' Wally ignored the couch in the surgery and pointed to a high-backed armchair. Leah obeyed and waited. She had undergone a brief medical earlier that morning, the results of which were still unknown to her. Now it was time for the psychotherapy – in her opinion, the real thing. She had half looked forward, half dreaded this first session for weeks. There was so much to say, but she wasn't ready to spill it all out yet. Wally seemed to sense this and was in no hurry to press her. 'There's some magazines there, help yourself!' He was at his desk, scribbling in a leather-bound notebook. 'I'll be with you in a moment.'

Leah picked up a copy of *Home & Garden*, but it remained on her lap unopened. She gazed round the room looking for inspiration. She had no idea how or where she should begin. How tastefully Wally had organised this place, she thought. It was new to her as he had only recently taken on the lease of a second apartment for his practice in the same block as their home. In the old days the surgery had been in the flat and Melinda was always complaining it was an invasion of their privacy. Not all their patients had become close friends like Leah.

Now, they had a chic reception room and office with efficient secretary in tow, and a large bright surgery. The sun streamed through half-open Venetian blinds casting shafts of sunbeams over a collection of rubber plants. A big bowl of cream and lavender-coloured hyacinths stood on a round table in the window. The walls were covered in a restful shade of smoky blue hessian, with clean white woodwork and a prettily corniced ceiling. Dark- and pale-blue Mexican rugs adorned the pine floor, framed opera programmes hung on the walls, and the whole place, like Wally himself, presented a healthy, pleasant picture of organised wholesomeness.

Wally finished his notes, made a couple of calls from one of the matching blue telephones that lined his flat-topped desk and finally gave her his full attention. 'You must be wondering why I said the chair and not the couch, Leah,' he said. 'The truth is our session today is going to last five minutes only.' He leaned forward and looked at her intently. 'You could say I'm taking your money under false pretences, but I'm going to stick my neck out.

'Today, I want you to take a walk around Central Park. Have a look at the lake, then the trees. It's the trees I want you to study. Examine them closely. Remember their features. Imagine they're important people, clients of yours, whom you may meet again in a short space of time. It wouldn't do for you not to recognise them. You may meet them in a different environment, so you've got to remember their most obvious attributes – right? I'd like you to go all round the park and when you've had a good look, chose the six that appeal to you most. Tomorrow,' he made a sudden note in his book, 'I'll want you to describe each one of those six trees to me and why you liked them. Do you understand?'

Leah nodded gravely. Nothing that Wally said ever surprised her.

'Secondly. You'll go to your favourite beauty salon and have the works. Hair, face, manicure, pedicure, waxing – the lot! When you come out of there, buy yourself some new outfit, a suit maybe, a dress – designer of course. I know you can afford it! It's very important you don't feel guilty about it. This is all part of the therapy. There'll be plenty of time later for lying down over there,' his eyes slid over the couch, 'then we can get on to the nitty-gritty.'

Leah was about to speak when he hushed her. 'I don't want to hear another word out of you for the moment. Now off you go – or you won't have time to fit it all in. The walk in the park involves more brainwork than you might think. Oh, and Leah!' he called her back as she made obediently, for the door. 'May I suggest you may want to visit your bank first!'

She laughed then, they both did and for a moment, her face lost its anxious look. 'I was thinking the same thing myself!' she called as she walked towards the elevator. She took a cab to her bank off Madison Avenue. It was a heavenly spring day and almost reminded her of the Algarve – and yet how totally different it all was. Even if one took away all the buildings, road signs, neon-lights, sidewalks, bus-stops and store fronts, and concentrated only on the natural things – you could not compare the two places. Why even the grass was different, the birds, the trees. The trees! She found herself peering upward as they whisked across the lights at Columbus Avenue and wondered about the task Wally had set ahead for her.

There was something noble in a tree, certainly in these trees, tall, slender beautiful creatures constantly scanning the sky bringing moisture and oxygen to a fume-filled city. Did people appreciate them? Had she? How many looked at those strong arms, opening their buds and throwing their fortune to the wind as they embraced the sun. 'Think of these as important people...' he had said. Did he hope she would discover herself in their springtime flourishing, that yearly miracle which each one of them performed so graciously, so silently? She could not guess. It might only be Wally's clever way to get her mind off of herself and to relax for a moment. Oh well... either way she would give it her best shot. Now where was the bank! She yelled at the cab driver, he was going down the wrong street – typical – treating her like some unsuspecting tourist to earn another dime! She jumped out at the junction of 5th to get some air. A few minutes later she was walking into her bank.

It seemed desperately cold after the mild air of the streets. She'd forgotten how unused she was to air conditioning. She only had two cheques left in her cheque book, and half her credit cards were out of date. She decided to draw out a substantial sum of money and order a new cheque book to be forwarded to Wally and Melinda's as soon as possible. Everyone in New York was so paranoid about carrying money these days. But she wasn't. When she had the business, she sometimes went round with a plastic carrier bag that harboured literally thousands of dollars in the bottom. Swung casually, as though it were a bag of potatoes, it never merited a backward glance. It was handbags and brief-cases that crooks went for, not cheap plastic carriers from the drugstore.

She smiled at the teller, a sober young man with a crewcut and horn-rimmed spectacles, not that different from Buster at that age. Poor honey, what would he be doing now? Would he be coping on his own with the Boys gone? Oh well, she'd left him plenty of goodies in the freezer. 'Er...' she hesitated over her cheque – how much should she take out? – 'oh well... one might as well be hung for a sheep as for a lamb! It's for rather a lot,' she smiled self-consciously, 'I may have to transfer some money from our deposit account, if there isn't enough in this one.'

'I'll check on it, Mrs Bloomfield,' said the young man reading her name off the cheque and adjusting his spectacles, as he went off to consult a computer. He was back a moment later. 'You're right, there isn't enough. Would you like to make out a transfer slip?' He pushed a form towards her and disappeared once more to consult another machine for details of her deposit account. Leah filled in the form for five thousand dollars, and waited for him to return.

He came back frowning. 'Mrs Bloomfield,' he was fiddling with his glasses again, 'I – er – think there must be – er – some kind of mistake here.'

'Oh?' Leah decided the glasses did not suit him at all. Horn-rims looked much better on Buster, who had a nice square jaw to balance them … or was it the low forehead? The young man looked again at her transfer slip and bit his lower lip. 'I think perhaps you should have a word with Mr Straker, the manager.'

'Why – sure,' said Leah, unperturbed. 'If it's really necessary. I thought all this was pretty routine.'

She had already decided the young man was new at his job and was bound to make a mish-mash of it anyway. It would be a relief to deal with someone more senior. Who was Mr Straker? It was Mr Robinson last time she was here. But of course, that was well over a year ago. It might, after all, be a good idea to meet the new incumbent.

'Will you come this way?'

She found herself being escorted into a small plush office next door to the tellers' department. Mr Straker would be there in a moment, she was informed by a hovering secretary, who seemed reluctant to leave her alone in the room. It had certainly all changed since her last visit. 'What did they do with the panelling?' asked Leah.

'Pardon?' the woman seemed surprised at the remark.

'Did they rip it out? If they did, it's a great pity ' said Leah. 'I'd have offered mega-bucks for that panelling. My west coast clients would have given their souls for mature oak of that period.'

'I'm sorry, I'm new here,' was the reply. Leah thought she looked anything but sorry.

'It seems that everyone's new here,' said Leah drily. At that moment a stocky, forceful looking man of about her own age came briskly into the room. He pumped her hand, dismissed the secretary and had crossed the room all within a breath.

'Mrs Bloomfield! What a surprise!' he was settling at his desk, and beckoning at a chair opposite. 'We thought you were in Portugal. We are so glad to meet you. Now won't you sit down and we can discuss your problem?'

It wasn't often that Leah took an instant dislike to someone, but something about this stolid little man's officious manner upset her and she replied, cold and unsmiling, 'I wasn't aware I had a problem.'

'Uh-uh.' Mr Straker regarded her keenly for a moment as though coming to an important decision. That made, he said 'Are you trying to tell me, Mrs Bloomfield, that it's normal to close your main savings accounts one day, and then come in to draw a considerable amount of cash from it all in the same week?'

Leah's heart missed a decided beat, if not two. 'Can you repeat that, Mr Straker?' Her voice sounded strained, even to herself.

Straker obliged. He had not taken his eyes off his client since he'd sat down.

After a long silence, Leah said, 'I think there's been some terrible mistake.'

'No mistake, Mrs Bloomfield. The first letter arrived … just a moment.' He switched on the intercom, 'Sheila? Have the Bloomfield file sent up from Extinct Savings Accounts. I want the last few letters received from Portugal, plus yesterday's telex please.' He turned back to Leah, 'You'll see for yourself in a moment … early February, I think it was and a follow up in March.'

'You said something about a telex?' He had to lean forward to catch the whispered words.

'Yes, that came through yesterday. It merely confirmed – as you'd said it would – what had already been discussed and agreed. It gave us the go-ahead to forward the money forthwith. It was a pretty large sum as you'll recall – well over a hundred grand, or was it two?…from the Gold…and rather less from the Instant Access – we can check in a moment. As I thought, it seems your main accounts closed with our offices here at 5 pm yesterday afternoon.

'Ah – here she is, good gal!' The secretary came in without knocking, dropped a sheaf of correspondence on the desk in front of him and disappeared again without sparing Leah so much as a backward glance.

'Yes, now here we are!' he got up and brought a handwritten letter round to Leah's side of the desk for inspection. 'As I thought February 7th, PO BOX 66, Santa Felicia, Algarve, Portugal.'

'PO Box! You've got the wrong person mister, we don't use a PO box! We've got a perfectly good address. It's Casa Amarela, Estrada –' Her voice faltered; her heart seemed to leap from its normal position behind her ribs and drop downwards into a state of collapse, somewhere deep in her stomach.

For the first time a look of concern crossed the bank manager's florid face. The woman was obviously confused. 'I don't think so,' he said pleasantly, 'wasn't that your old address and then you wrote back in – er – here we are, December - to say mail was getting lost and it was safer to use a numbered box in future?'

Before she could answer, he was hurrying on; he had an appointment in ten minutes' time and this was a tedious delay; but clearly it must be dealt with. 'We are thorough here, you know. We naturally changed the records and were quite happy with the signature at the bottom. It matched the specimen held here in our records. We always do an electronic scan when customers instruct us by letter. It's done by computer – fail safe!'

As the woman before him did not utter a word, he hurried on to fill the uncomfortable silence. 'There's still your current account, Mrs Bloomfield for any immediate needs … how much have we there? Ah, only eight hundred, but it's a start if you want to rethink further investments. So much easier to open new accounts when there's an existing one in place. I really don't think you need worry, Mrs Bloomfield, your husband obviously had his own good reasons for having the money forwarded; no doubt he has a programme of profitable investment all arranged in Spain. I hear the economy's pretty buoyant there.'

'Spain!' The words shrieked out and she sprang to her feet. 'You're telling me our funds have left here and been moved to Spain! How many accounts are we talking about? What the hell is going on around here? Isn't someone going to tell me what's happening?' She was getting shriller and shriller. 'I tell you I don't understand. I just don't understand!'

Straker eyed the stricken face and for the first time believed that he might have misjudged the woman. Her surprise seemed genuine and she seemed on the verge of hysterics. Was it possible the various instructions he had received had been done without her prior knowledge? Could it be that the husband was pulling a fast one? Surely not! If she did not trust him, they would hardly have all these joint accounts together. Neither would she have granted him a Power of Attorney over everything they owned!

He moved his chair round to her side of the desk and went through the documents one by one, relieved that she had subsided into silence once more. When it came to the telex, he said, 'You can see, Mrs Bloomfield, why I was surprised to see you here. This was received yesterday, very early in the morning, from Portugal. You can see the time here 1.30 in the afternoon their time, 7.30 ours. It therefore seemed extremely odd to us when less than 24 hours after that telex was sent, you should appear in person asking us to transfer five thousand dollars! Young Mr Philipson was quite agitated when he discovered that you had no credit to transfer. Can you see that now?'

The woman seemed not to be listening to him. 'Can you do me a favour,' she asked in the same quiet tone she had used before she went ballistic. Straker nodded and sighed. He was already late for his other client and none of this was doing his ulcer much good.

'I want to call my accountant,' Leah was saying in a very even voice, 'and I'd appreciate doing it from your office.'

'Very well,' Straker acquiesced somewhat grudgingly. He hoped they did not have a serious problem on their hands. 'Sheila!' he called into the intercom.

39

*I*t took patience and what seemed interminable minutes of banging to get a response from *Cabo* Fonseca's whitewashed doorway. At last a woman with enormous hips but a sweet and pretty face ventured out into the narrow street and shut the door behind her again swiftly. McKay immediately recognised Rosalinha, the *Cabo's* wife and mother of seven grown-up children.

'*Dona* Rosalinha, I'm sorry to disturb you at home,' McKay began in the rough Portuguese he had learned from the fishermen, which was so different from his own cut-glass English, 'but I need to see your husband right away.'

'*Não é possível,*' she muttered, avoiding his eye.

'But I'm sorry – I must!' The anger had subsided but there was no mistaking the desperation in his voice. Rosalinha was about to deny him again, then saw the anguish in his face and decided to trust him.

'*Senhor* Jock, you had better come into the house,' she said in dialect. She turned abruptly and almost pushed him up the steps. He only just had time to duck his head under a low stone lintel. Again the door was shut firmly and to his amazement, she turned a key in the lock. 'You must wait a moment,' she showed him into what was obviously the best room in the house – the front parlour – rarely used but a must in every self-respecting burgher's house. 'I will try to persuade my husband to come. He's in a poor way. If he will come for anyone, it might be you, *Senhor* Jock. It's possible, you of all people, he will trust.'

She bustled away. Why in hell does he need to trust me? wondered McKay, puzzled and bemused as he fingered the single crisp note in his back jeans pocket.

By the time *Dona* Rosalinha had returned he was heartily sick of the front parlour. With its artificial flowers, it was stuffy and had an overpowering smell of leather furniture although he forebore to open a window. 'He will see you,' she announced. 'He is preparing himself. Only a few more minutes,' she grimaced, 'can I offer you something?'

He shook his head, shuddering at the thought. If anything was destined to make one feel ill it was a glass from one of those highly coloured liqueurs that people who owned front parlours exhibited proudly in their display cabinets. Other trappings included heavy carved chests and side-tables, antimacassars and ornate lace cushions. He wanted to expostulate that Fonseca had bloody well not keep him waiting much longer, when he realised Rosalinha had slipped from the room again. Was something up? Even through his own misery, he remembered that her normally cheerful face had looked drawn and almost fearful. What could have happened? Perhaps the *Cabo* really was ill?

He was spared considering the dubious merits of the highly embellished carpet at his feet, by Fonseca's sudden entrance. No handshake, no preliminaries, he just stomped into the room and slumped into one of the leather armchairs. It groaned under the weight. Since they'd last met – less than seven hours ago – he had aged ten years.

'You know of course!' he said.

'I know nothing,' said McKay, 'why do you think I'm here? I'm waiting for you to tell me!'

'I'm not talking of *that*!' Fonseca waved Buster and Catalina out of his mental vision with a scornful gesture. 'I mean the uprising! The revolution!'

'*What*!' For a moment, McKay forgot his own predicament.

To his astonishment, the man broke down. McKay had never seen a policeman weep before and the sight did not sit easy on his own shoulders. He felt acute embarassment and a depression of the deepest sort which was in no way connected with his own troubles.

'Revolution!' he repeated. 'Here in Portugal? You can't mean it?'

'It has begun,' said Fonseca, taking out a large folded handkerchief and unashamedly wiping away real tears from his sagging cheeks. 'In a few hours the world will know – if they do not already have an understanding. The television and radio, they have fallen. *O Presidente* – ' again the tears were flowing copiously, 'they do not tell us yet where they take him. Maybe house arrest…maybe worse. But I theenk,' he shook his head, choked with emotion, 'he is being held somewhere – together with our first Minister, his excellency, *Senhor* Caetano. Who knows what will happen to them.'

McKay stared at him in horror. He had lived in this strict but stable country for almost a decade and could scarcely believe his ears. The bottom was indeed falling out of his world – and this man's too – but what about those million of others? Not only in Portugal, but in the vast African colonies and the islands. How could something so grave, so far-reaching, happen so suddenly?

'But who are 'they', Fonseca?' he managed to gasp. 'Who is responsible?'

'I not know for sure. But we shall learn soon enough. They call themselves the MFA. I theenk it is the young officers of our army and air force. They are impatient, greedy, *loco* for power. They go to fight the wars in Africa, the Communists, the guerillas…and there they listen to propaganda – trouble makers who want to make problems for Portugal.

'There is a man; he is called Spinola. He – governor-general in Guiné – much influence with young officers – write a book and everyone is reading it. He make speeches, everyone is leestening. Our government do not like what he say, he say bad things against our Presidente, that war in Angola and Mozambique is too expensive. Yes, we have nearly 140,000 overseas – but he forget one thing! We defend our people, our business, our commerce…Portugal always good in Africa – we no make apartheid, we share and our people inter-marry and mix. But Spinola say all is wrong, Portugal cannot afford, war is not the way, government must change. And young officers, captains – they go on listening. Think thees man is clever…' He dabbed ineffectually at the tears again. All the time, his eyes remained downcast, as though studying the terrible carpet.

McKay sat on the edge of the sofa, riveted but aghast. 'I think I've heard of this man,' he said, 'I thought he meant well.'

Fonseca shook his head. He went on in his broken English, stammering over the words, not so much from lack of fluency but because he was having tremendous difficulty in speaking at all. 'Our Presidente, he send for thees Spinola. He say I strip you of your position. You are dangerous, you make trouble with our troops – please! No more speeches, no more book. He ban book here in Portugal. We, Portuguese,' he looked up and finally met McKay's eye for the fist time since he had entered the room, 'we no like insurgence.'

'I can see that,' said McKay without a trace of irony . 'I don't much care for it either.'

'But the grain… how you say? *Semente* …?'

'Seed,' supplied McKay.

'*Sim*. The seed is sown. All people in the military, they are talking of politics, of change. It is forbidden, but they are getting bold. Our police, our special branch – the *PIDE*, they listen, they watch. Some peoples, political peoples, trouble-makers, they go to prison. But it ees a disease – a cancer – this politic thing. It spread. Not everyone we catch. And now!' he flung up his hands in the air and heaved himself to his feet. 'Portugal! *A minha terra*! Our *Presidente*! Our government! They are falling. Where? How? I do not know. No one knows. Many people have been taken, our secret police – ' he turned to McKay again, his hands outstretched, the normally sharp brown eyes clouded with dismay, 'this morning – early – they are all arrested. I hear it on the radio just now. That is why, *Senhor* Jock, I cannot help you.'

'My God, I see! But your border guards – are they gone too? Are your frontiers now open to all and sundry? It's hard to take in… when did all this happen?' McKay put a hand to his head and felt his own shoulders slump, just like the policeman. It seemed so unreal.

Fonseca was pacing the room. 'Look, when I see you last night… I theenk all is normal, all is – how you say? – as it should be. That is why, after you come to me *Senhor* Jock, I pick up telephone – remember?'

Jock nodded. He remembered well.

'And so I try, but line is dead. We are cut off. In Algarve, we are always last to know. And no one come to tell me. And so I go home. It is getting late, I try on my phone in house. This time I get – what you say, the noise?'

'Tone.'

'*Sim, sim* – but it take a long time. Finally, I speak with one man, not a friend but… I know he is a *PIDE*. He say little, he very strange with me. I tell him about your wife, your *filha*, the American gangster. He say he make report – tell frontier police – yes, yes – no *problema*. He say 'I call you back.' I wait. I wait all night. I keep my promise to you. I do not go to the bed. Sometimes I sleep a little in my chair… but always waiting. But he no telephone,' he paused.

Again McKay felt a strange strickening in his throat as he watched this man who had always appeared so powerful, struggling now to finish what he had to say. The inevitable breakdown of self-control was probably just around the corner.

'At six o'clock it is getting light, and steel I wait. No call. At seven, I telephone to him again. This time,' he passed a gnarled fist over his stubbled chin and pushed at his lower lip as though to support his voice – 'this time I speak with wife.'

'Yes?' said McKay eagerly.

'She tell me they have come to house and take him away. Soldiers come at dawn with guns and a *camião* – they put him inside. She not know where they take him.' He shook his head again. 'I do not believe. I think – ah – there is some mistake. I telephone to others. Everywhere it is the same. They are all taken. Only we,' – he tried to puff out his massive chest, but failed – 'Only we, the *Guarda* of the *Republic*, the police who protect the *presidente*, are left. Maybe soon they take us too. I do not know. I do not leave. I wait.'

He got up then, the tears coursing down his craggy cheeks. Before he lumbered from the room, he said. '*Senhor* Jock, I have failed you. I have failed my country. I am *nothing*.'

McKay found himself alone. A solitary figure rooted to the spot in an airless, opressive room. He could not believe what he had just heard. What was happening here in this country he had grown to love? It was like some dramatic but make-believe Hitchcock movie on some over-exaggerated Hollywood set.

Dona Rosalinha came back into the room. She had been crying too. 'I am sorry *Senhor* Jock. It is better you go. My husband says if they come for him, it is dangerous for you to be here too. He says he is very sorry he could not help you.'

She turned to go, but he caught at her sleeve. '*Dona* Rosalinha, give him this,' he tried to press the note from his pocket into her hand. 'Don't say no. You might need it.'

She looked at it and shook her head. 'No *Senhor* Jock, it is kind of you, but no. Money cannot help us now.'

Roger Grafton had set his alarm clock for 5.30. There was no need for the burst of shrill ringing and he switched it off quickly. He had already lain awake for hours and it was a relief to get dressed. Ablutions done, he was out of the front door as silent as a cat, his rubber-soled sneakers moving soundlessly over the tiled floor. Onto the pavement and down the deserted streets, he wondered if he would meet anyone on the way. Not that suspicion would be raised. He already had his excuses worked out, 'Glorious day! Just perfect for an early run on the beach!'

But there was no one around. As he left the town behind and followed the coast road to the west, a stream of mule-carts rumbled along, market-bound, laden with fruit and vegetables. There were no foreign cars. Why should anyone bother anyway with a teenager clad in the usual jeans and tee-shirt? The small back-pack between his shoulders was normal too. You saw them all over the place; there was nothing special about this one.

It took Roger less than an hour to reach the bottom of the dirt road that led to the yellow house. He looked at his watch. He hoped to God it was safe. What if the servants had decided to go in early? Benjie had said 7.30 for Maria, an hour later for Carlos and the swimming pool men. Buster rarely descended before them. He slept like the dead, assured Benjie, and all the bedrooms faced the other side of the house.

Besides, the task was simple. He had his key. All he had to do was slip through the door, leave the parcel on the kitchen table, and nip out again – locking the door carefully after him. The whole thing would only take two minutes – probably less! What could be easier?

Roger had forgotten how steep and long the track was. He arrived breathless and paused to rest on a convenient boulder on the last bend before the sweep of gravel. The memory of that first clandestine meeting with Benjie at the prickly pears was still fresh in his mind. So too was his kindness and patience; it had been overwhelming.

What a nuisance he had been! And what a fool to hope, during those long winter months, that Benjie might be tempted to walk out of the yellow house and join him in England.

By giving his saviour super-hero status he had overlooked one thing. Whatever passing attraction might lie between them, Benjie's devotion to his partner overrode everything. They had never spoken of it, but just as he depended on the good favour of his parents and his trustees, Benjie was probably equally reliant on Howard.

It was silly of him to have day-dreamed otherwise. He had fallen in love with an idea. Fashionably dressed, artistic, well-travelled Benjie, with his easy-going urbane manner, might not be his own master. Roger sighed. He knew now that Benjie's kindness to him had not only been an act of generosity, but rather more than that. By taking those risks, first the loan itself, then the renting of the mail box, the trips into town, the communications sent, he would have assuaged his own personal pride. By helping another human being, Benjie had asserted a modicum of independence, and with it no doubt a greater sense of self-respect. No wonder he had taken the risk. No one likes to feel totally tied into a situation, however cushy, and Benjie would have relished those moments of freedom, especially now that it had all turned out so well.

Roger jumped off the rock and hauled himself back onto the path. Life was full of surprises. Appearances deceiving. Had he suddenly grown up? He pondered this as he drew level with the sleeping house. Good! Nothing seemed disturbed, although there was a distant barking. Benjie had said not to worry about this. The dog generally slept in the freezer-room – just off the main kitchen. He was always barking. No one paid much attention.

As his foot scrunched the gravel underfoot, he started. It hadn't registered before, but now it was all too obvious. There was no car! Where was Buster? Was he already up and out? Heaven forbid – he might return at any moment. There were skid marks too, and it looked as though some extra heavy vehicle had been trying to turn, just under the kitchen eaves. Oh well – his was not to reason why. Better get the job done as quickly as possible.

Taking the key from his pocket, he crept to the kitchen door feeling rather like a burglar. It slipped in easily and he turned it twice; it had been double-locked. Into the kitchen in a trice, he took off his back-pack and pulled out its precious cargo. Gently, he placed the parcel on the table.

Now that he was rid of it – he felt quite sorry. He had grown fond of the holly-girl although the responsibility of her safekeeping, preyed on his mind all through term-time and the winter vacation. Now he could shrug off that burden and be free again. Not like poor Benjie – it looked like he would never be free.

Strangly enough, now he was in the house, he no longer felt anxious. He had been afraid that his hands would tremble or he might fall over something, bringing an irate Buster charging downstairs, heavy on his heels. But there was something so utterly dead about the place that he took his time. Only that poor dog, locked away somewhere, scraping and whining. He wished he had the courage to let it out, but that would really give the game away.

He was about to leave, when he noticed the ants. They were moving in a purposeful line across the floor and up the table leg. He realized then that the table was covered in the remnants of a meal and it seemed sacrilege to leave the figurine amongst the crumbs and what might have been a discarded piece of German sausage as the little red army moved in. He decided then and there to clean the table and remove the porcelain from its wrapping.

It did not take him long to wipe everything down with a cloth he found in the sink, and find a pair of scissors, hanging with the knives on a strip of metal over the cooker. Carefully, he cut the knotted string and started to peel back the protective covering. Only a moment longer and he would be done. It occurred to him as he unwrapped the holly-girl carefully and slowly, that this must be rather like undressing a woman … gentle hands and smooth co-ordinated movements, so as not to alarm her. The brown paper came away easily and he was down to the white tissue paper stacked around her more fragile parts – like frilly underwear.

There was a muffled bang from next door and he almost dropped her. Christ, what was that? Better be quick. He felt the adrenalin surge into his limbs and his hands were clammy as he removed the last vestige of paper. That was better; at least whoever came into the room and found her would now realise what it was. A parcel could get tossed aside – at least now, she'd be picked up with reverence. After all her travels, she deserved that at least.

There was another bang; the dog was barking again. It was time to leave. 'Goodbye, holly-girl, thank you!' he tiptoed to the door and looked back at her once more – erect, alone but home again. The ants seemed to have moved off to pastures new. As he left the house, carefully locking it behind him, he became aware that the banging was coming from the exterior of the house. It sounded like an unfastened window. Oh well, he would never know. He dusted his handkerchief over the lock and round the door handle – just in case. No sleuth had ever done it better. Pleased now that he had managed it all, he set off down the hill again at high speed.

The sun was climbing higher in the sky and the sea shimmered in a blue haze with the promise of a hot day ahead. There was no one about. No one had seen him come or go. Only a nanny-goat with two capricious kids broke the early morning silence as she moved about the hillside, her bell gently chiming as she searched for the lushest grasses. Roger leaped down and over the last bend as agile as a goat himself. As he took a shortcut across the springy turf to the coast road, he felt happier than he had for a very long time.

'But you can't have! How *could* you? You can't have sold *everything*! Why it's impossible! … I just don't believe this is *happening!*'

The hysteria was rising as the woman grappled with the phone and Straker looked at his secretary, shrugged and spread out his hands appealingly. 'What's that? No, I simply don't believe you could *do* such a thing. I'm *finished*! Aren't I? … What? No, you'd better talk to my bank manager here. And talk sense for heavens sake! I just don't understand a word you're saying. I don't understand! Did you hear? I don't under – ' she handed the receiver to a bewildered Straker and wheeled round to face the secretary.

'Honey, it's my broker! I think the man's gone ape. I can't understand what's happening … in fact I don't understand any of it, do you read me? I don't *understand!*'

As the hysteria increased in tone, Straker, who was attempting to talk to the person at the other end of the line, gave his secretary another sharp look which said quite clearly 'Get her out of here!'

'Come on, Mrs Bloomfield, we can talk about this. Why don't you come with me?' Sheila

Wilkins took Leah firmly by the wrist and headed for the door. She had not expected to meet such resistance. Leah's feet were still firmly planted in the same spot and were going nowhere.

'I tell you the man's gone ape! He *can't* have sold! It's impossible! I tell you I don't understand!' Again the voice was rising, shrill and protesting.

Straker was shouting now. 'I can't hear you, sir! Look – I'll call you back when things are quieter. Your client's taken sick.' He slammed the receiver down. 'For God's sakes Sheila, can't you *do* something!'

The manager was by nature a tidy man, whose life was an ordered round of bank, bridge and golf. All three facets slotted nicely into the filing cabinets of his mind and all his life he had kept at bay any form of distraction which could interfere with these three things. Predictability and routine were important to him; he found them in his wife, his daughter and his work. What he saw before him now filled him with horror. This was definitely one of those messy, emotional situtations which other people had, but which he'd always managed to avoid so expertly in the past. The fact that it had manifested itself here in this office, his inner sanctuum, filled him with deep dismay.

The woman was now pacing up and down, gabbling at the top of her voice, the same phrases over and over again. She had not yet wept – he dreaded this – but she shuddered alarmingly as shock racked her slim frame in ever-increasing spasms. A trickle of spit ran from the corner of her mouth in a snail-like trail to her chin, and as she prepared to rant against her broker yet again – Straker had a sudden urge to clamp his hands over his ears. Damn this woman, breaking into his peace like this. His other appointment had given up waiting and he could feel his ulcer threatening to erupt.

It was the secretary Sheila who put an abrupt end to the tirade by releasing the woman's wrist and slapping her very sharply on the cheek. The noise stopped. It was as though a tiresome radio had been switched off. Calm crept back into the room and Straker sighed with relief. Thank the good Lord above for sensible secretaries.

Sheila had led the woman back to her chair. 'Sit down!' her voice was sympathetic but very firm. She put a hand on the woman's knee. 'Mrs Bloomfield, is there anyone I can contact – someone you're staying with perhaps – who can come along and collect you?'

The woman shook her head, but to Straker's relief, only once this time. She made little moaning noises through her fingers and a tear plopped into her lap. Another eruption couldn't be far from the surface.

'Mrs Bloomfield. Just give me a name and I'll look them up in the directory. There must be someone you know.

Straker watched, half fascinated. He must remember to raise Sheila's salary some time. She really was surprisingly able for one so young.

'Mrs Bloomfield,' the girl didn't give up easily. She was forcing one of the rigid white hands away from the woman's tearstained, puckered face. 'You must listen to me. I'm sure everthing is going to turn out fine. Now I must have the name and number of some friends of yours. Think now,' she coaxed. She's got the patience of Job, thought Straker.

The fog cleared in Leah's brain momentarily. She closed her eyes and thought. In a shaking voice she murmured, ' Ring Wally. Wally and Melinda Murray. The number's in my bag... They live at Claremont...'

'Thank you,' said Sheila. 'Now I suggest we leave our Manager to do his work and go together into my office. Shall we do that?'

It was like talking to a four year old. With masterful persuasion, the secretary led the still shuddering woman into the next room. Mission accomplished, Straker closed the door thankfully behind them. He returned to his desk and poured out a medicine glass of brandy from a flask he kept in the bottom drawer. Immediately, he felt revived.

Strange business, he thought – domestic of course. Their file was still open on the desk in front of him. He flicked through. As he thought – all the requests for the movement of money in the last few months, had come from the husband. Not content with the cash, it now appeared he'd sold every single bond plus stocks and shares too. Their broker had seemed adamant. Not nice! But it only proved what he'd always said. Trust no one but yourself. This woman had obviously made one big mistake somewhere down the line.

'What are you trying to tell me?' Howard's voice rose a petulant octave which could be heard all round the marble foyer of the Seville hotel. A group of English tourists choosing picture postcards whilst awaiting their coach, looked on in mild interest.

'...Only that you won't get into Portugal today,' said the reception manager with a shrug. 'That is why I suggest you might like to remain here until the frontiers open again.'

'When will that be?'

'Who knows,' said the man. 'Such a thing has never happened before.'

'But it's preposterous! I have a house there. Engagements to attend. I must get back.'

The man shrugged again. 'You can try, *Senhor* McDermott, but already thousands of Portuguese nationals trying to return home have been refused entry. Tourism has ceased completely – at least visitors in. Those already there can't get out! All airports held by the rebels.'

'I can't believe this,' Howard turned to Benjie for support, 'In Portugal! They always said it couldn't happen there.'

The reception manager said a little smugly, 'we had our revolution in the thirties – now it is their turn!'

'Oh my God,' said Benjie, 'You're not suggesting it could turn out like the Spanish Civil War, are you?'

'I'm not suggesting anything,' said the man, stroking his small moustache, 'but of course one never knows.'

'Oh Jeepers,' Benjie was clutching at Howard's sleeve, 'This is scary. Don't you remember all those Hemingway books? Spain was in massive turmoil after their revolution, the war dragged on for years and years. You don't think it could be like that, do you?' he was turning to the man again, 'you know – bloody – people being hacked to pieces?'

'Who knows,' came the sage reply.

'Come on, Benjie,' said Howard, irritated by the man's manner. 'There's no good hanging around here. I think we'd better make our way to the American Consulate and get some proper answers.'

'So, you'd like we keep the room, sir?' the reception manager called after him.

'Oh – er – yes,' said Howard shortly.

'It is fortunate we can make this favour,' said the man, looking down his nose at the register. 'If it had not been for a cancellation – caused by the border closing – you would have had to look elsewhere.'

'Yes, very well, fine,' said Howard, straining to go. 'Er – thank you.'

'You will just sign here please,' the voice was supercilious. Feeling that he had definitely scored a point, the reception manager watched them go. Ungrateful people! No wonder revolutions started in countries where people took everything for granted.

Howard had arrived at the street entrance, cursing. 'Why did you let that cab go?' he snapped at Benjie.

'What cab?'

'One dropped off someone here a moment ago. We've lost it! Goodness knows how long we'll have to wait for another.'

'I'll get the porter to order one for us,' said Benjie, turning back. It wasn't his darned fault there'd been a revolution.

Howard stood morosely in the morning sunshine scanning the busy street. The package tour's coach had arrived and with much ado, dozens of them streamed past him, noisy as a gaggle of geese.

'Did you bring the instamatic, Bill? I reminded you before we left?'

'Have you got those pills for the runs, Mum? I don't think I'm going to last the day!'

'Move over Ron – that's *my* toe you're treading on!'

'Did you 'ear all that about Portugal? That poor gentleman seems quite upset!'

'Glad we didn't choose Estoril after all. The lad at the travel agents tried ever so hard to push it on us – d'you remember? It was ever so expensive.'

'Jimmy Martin went to Madeira. That's Portuguese, innit?'

'Never!'

'It is, I'm sure!'

'Don't argue with Dad, Mabel...'

And so it went on, their flat vowels carrying clearly over the rumble of traffic. Howard looked on disapprovingly. The Algarve tourists seemed a cut above these ones. Still, no cab in sight. What *was* Benjie up to. It should be easy in the middle of a city.

The coach moved away with its noisy cargo. Some jolly soul waved out of the back window to Howard. He did not reciprocate. Benjie appeared. He had someone in tow with him. Howard's lips tightened. He had a wonderful way of picking up strangers. It was annoying.

'Howard, this is Mr Blair. The porter introduced us – thought it might be helpful. 'He's from Portugal too.'

'In the same boat – as it were!' A thin man in his middle thirties, with a loudly striped tie, pressed a damp palm into Howard's hand. 'Ken Blair, pleased to meet you.'

Howard nodded, but was quick to drop the contact. Everyone in this hotel seemed to be British and over-familiar.

'Bad business this,' Ken Blair was shaking his head. 'I'll lay two to one we don't get through for at least a week – if then,' he added darkly.

'I find that hard to believe,' said Howard. 'Did you fix a cab, Benjie?'

'No, I told him not to bother,' said Blair. 'Just ordered one for myself – I can drop you off on the way. I'm going to the British Consulate. Great minds think alike!'

Howard looked annoyed, but said it was good of him.

'Don't mention it, mate, we all have to stick together during troubled times. Bit like the war, eh? Before my time of course, but my parents always drummed into me about looking out for each other. You might remember of course?' He raised a quizzical eyebrow but luckily the taxi arrived before Howard could make a squashing retort. He hated it when people made assumptions about his age.

'I may be over-worrying of course,' Ken Blair was quite oblivious to the effect he was having as he held the door open, with a 'Be my guest! But your friend here, Benjie – isn't it? – said you owned property in the Algarve. That would be of real concern to me. Case for long faces, if you ask me.'

'I'm not!' said Howard primly, 'I'm reserving judgement until I've heard what our Consul has to say.'

'Shouldn't think he'll know any more than the hotel people. In fact in cases like this, the officials are usually the last to know. Sit on their backsides all day in plush offices, go out to big lunches, and fall asleep at their desks after the port. Tea brought in by a secretary – usually a dragon in sensible shoes – then home to the official residence and then the drinks begin all over again!'

Benjie began to laugh but was quelled by a stern look from Howard. 'I've no doubt it's all a storm in a teacup. The Portuguese are far too sensible to revolt. Why, the *escudo* is one of the most stable currencies in the world.'

'Famous last words,' said Ken Blair. 'Anyway – I'm not worried. I'm on expenses and the night life here in Seville's a damn sight better than where I'm based.'

'Where's that?' asked Benjie.

'Oporto – bit puritanical for my liking. Now don't laugh – I'm a sales manager in gents' underwear. Care to see a sample?' he reached for his briefcase.

'No thank you,' said Howard quickly.

'Didn't think you would,' said Blair, unoffended. 'Bet you didn't know there was a booming textile trade up there now, did you? Thought it was all port wine and fish, I bet! We reckon the manufacturing of cotton garments will be Portugal's biggest export in a year or so. Goodbye Lancashire mills! Your actual Mr Marks and Mr Spencer will be ordering from here – or rather there!' he cocked his head in what was destined to imply a north-westerly direction as he withdrew a pack of cheroots from his breast pocket.

'Care for one?' he asked Howard.

'Neither of us smoke.'

'Oh well, your funeral!'

He puffed in appreciative silence for a moment. Howard could feel the itching start on the back of his hands, and rubbed them under the fold of his jacket, so no one could see. It was one of the few things Benjie was allowed to nag him about – but he didn't want him starting now. 'Surely, it can't be this far?'

'Oh, we've a way to go yet, mate. Know this place like the back of my hand,' grinned Blair. 'The American consulate's right up the other end of town, not far from ours. You'd be surprised what you find in Seville…' he gave them a knowing wink, 'spent a lot of nights here. It's on my rounds you see. El Corte Ingles, the Gallerias…they've all ordered from my firm at some time or another. Actually I was half-pulling your leg. It's not just underwear, we do tee-shirts, socks, overalls, casual shirts, pyjamas, the lot. As long as it's ready to wear, we're ready to do it! That's my slogan! What's your line of business, then?'

'Interior design,' began Benjie obligingly and received another look as Howard cut in.

'We were,' he said. 'I'm retired now. That's why we came to Portugal and bought some land.'

'Real estate, is it? Always fancied a go myself, but the opportunity never seemed to come my way.'

'No, not real estate,' said Howard firmly. 'I don't buy and sell. We merely own a villa with a fair amount of land round it. For our own private use and pleasure.'

'Nice,' said their new friend. 'Oh well, let's hope it's still yours when they allow you back in. I say!' he was pointing out of the window, 'That's the Alcazar – well worth a visit sometime.'

'We know, we've been there.' Howard resisted a sudden urge to be very rude indeed.

They travelled the rest of the way in silence. An embarassing exchange took place outside the Consulate amidst thick mid-morning traffic, when Howard refused to get out of the cab until Blair accepted his share of the fair. Blair was equally adamant and would have none of it. 'I told you I was going this way anyway, mate, what's a few pesetas? – it all goes down on expenses. You're the one who should be watching his pennies.'

The traffic was building up behind them, but Howard remained, one leg in, one out. 'I insist upon paying,' he looked in vain for a small note in a wallet stuffed with travellers' cheques. Benjie sighed from the edge of the pavement.

Everyone had started hooting and Howard grew pinker and pinker, 'I know I've got a hundred pesetas somewhere, I noticed before we left.' Their driver turned round, letting forth a torrent that was anything but complimentary. He started to move away and Howard almost fell into the road. He was highly indignant.

'You can buy me a pint in the bar this evening!' Ken Blair stuck his head out the window and shouted after him.

'Oh no!' said Howard, 'don't say he's staying on too!'

The visit to the Consulate was not a huge success. Instead of the immediate and intimate tête-à-tête Howard had warmly envisaged with the representative of their great country, they were shown into a small waiting-room. To his dismay this was already crammed with people of all nationalities and tongues and it was clear they were very much at the end of a queue.

Howard made two attempts at walking off in a purposeful manner down a corridor, past various offices, towards what he supposed might be the inner sanctum of power, only to be firmly turned back by an official in military uniform. An impassive face was turned to all Howard's protestations and entreaties to talk to 'someone senior', at least. In the end he had to be content with giving his card to a very junior secretary, with the promise that 'when the time came', it would find its way onto the consular desk.

While Howard was on his fact-finding mission, Benjie eyed the company around him with interest. As far as he could see, there were few other American nationals like themselves, but as no one had opened their mouths since he and Howard had entered the room, he could not be sure. Across the room, three hippies in dirty jeans and even dirtier sandals, sat sprawled and silent. The rest of the gathering looked predominantly Spanish, with a scattering of Chinese, a Nordic couple, a trio of Jews with skull caps and two families that might have been from Ghana or Nigeria. The Spanish chattered noisily amongst themselves, the Africans snoozed, the Chinese seemed mute and so far he had not heard one word of English spoken.

When Howard returned, flushed and disgruntled, Benjie could not resist saying in a loud voice, 'You sure we're in the right building, Howard, there seem to be remarkably few Americans around here as far as I can see.'

One of the African families came to life then and the man said in a deep southern accent, 'You be in the right place boy, I'm an American – fourth generation.'

Benjie had the grace to blush and they all subsided into gloomy silence once more. After about an hour, as numbers were called and went, a bespectacled woman bustled into the room. She had a New England accent and they couldn't help but notice her sensible shoes. 'Will all those still waiting for news about Portugal, please come this way.'

To their surprise, only the hippies and the Norwegian couple moved forward. They all followed the secretary into her office and she told them that she was very sorry indeed but the Consul was completely tied up all day. However the news from Portugal was so uncertain and incomplete that for the time being all their Embassy could advise was for them to remain where they were. As soon as news concerning the re-opening of the frontiers filtered through, the Consulate would advise them if they cared to phone in to a special designated number. There would also be announcements on Spanish radio and television and they were advised to keep checking. She very much regretted that for the time being, that was all that could be done for them, unless they were suffering some extreme hardship – in which case they could remain if they wished, to be put in touch with one of the support charities here in the city.

'Are you trying to tell us that this so-called 'revolution' is for real then?' Howard had grown quite pale as he began to take on the seriousness of the matter. He had not allowed himself even to consider the possible truth before.

'We know there has most definitely been a coup orchestrated by the armed forces,' said the secretary studying a piece of typed paper in front of her. 'It says here, *"fall of government, resignation of prime minister, discussion amongst military and political leaders"* what else? … *"all public services, radio, television and media in hands of militia … some arrests"* … doesn't say who or what … *"advice to foreigners to stay at home for next 24 hours …"'* she looked up and passed a harassed hand over springy grey hair. 'I'm afraid that's about all we can tell you for the time being. It's obviously very worrying for those of you hoping to go there.'

'But we live there!' Howard sat down on the nearest chair. No one else looked very concerned.

The hippies moved off in dispassionate silence with neither a goodbye or a thank you and the 'Norwegian' girl who turned out to have a Boston accent said to her equally blond partner, 'Well, that's settled then, let's cancel the Portuguese side of our tour and move on down to Marbella. It looks every bit as fun as the *Al*-Garve. Thanks for the info!'

Howard and Benjie were left with the secretary. 'Was there anything else?' she asked. 'If not,' she went on smoothly, 'I'm afraid I must ask you to go. People are coming in or phoning endlessly at the moment and we just don't have the room or the staff to do more than we're doing. I hope you understand.'

Howard looked as though he did not, and pressed their hotel name, address and room number into her unwilling hands. 'I've already passed my personal card onto someone. Perhaps when the Consul sees it he may wish to telephone.'

'I'm afraid that's most unlikely,' said the woman. 'The Consul is working under great pressure at the moment and as your case doesn't directly concern Spain, there would be little point his responding to questions beyond his control.'

She bustled them out and a moment later they were looking for another taxi. Howard's hands were bright red, erupting with the worry and frustration. He was working himself into a frenzy with his scratching as Benjie looked on helplessly. 'I don't know what we're going to do,' he said. 'I thought going to the airport and picking up the pool liner would be taxing enough, that was *nothing* compared to this! If only there was a telephone at the house and we could get through to Buster to find out what's going on down their end. It's all quite ghastly!'

At that moment, Benjie had an inspiration. 'Johanna's got a phone. Why don't we call her? If anyone can advise us, it'll be her.'

'Good idea,' said Howard, 'We'll get back to the hotel immediately and book the call.'

40

By the middle of the afternoon of the 25th April, everyone in Santa Felicia knew something had happened. Those who did not own a radio heard the news boomed out in the market square or open street. 'Where's it all coming from?' they wanted to know. Overnight, a well-known shop-front had been transformed with red banners and posters – somewhere from deep within, a loudhailer proclaimed their good fortune. Near the beach a former ice-cream parlour had gone through a similar make-over. It was the same everywhere – overnight a transformation – Portugal was free! The Armed Forces had brought liberty for the people. Again and again, the same words, the same exhortation to rejoice and be happy.

Whilst there was celebration and dancing in the streets amongst the young and the very poor, the attitude among the local bourgeoisie was more conservative. 'Let's see what happens!' was the cautious response of many. Others were greeting their neighbours with broad smiles, forming spontaneous groups and suddenly talking politics without looking behind their backs.

The tourists found themselves caught up in the general mayhem. People were taking flowers off the market stalls and handing them to strangers, students were leaping about, cigarettes and sweets given away, for some there was kissing on both cheeks. Jauntiness hung in the air and a sense of it really doesn't matter what we do! In some ways, it felt rather surreal.

Only those who had held great authority were fearful, plus one or two foreign residents who allowed their imaginations to run away with them. The remainder of the *estrangeiros* greeted the news with genuine excitement. The fall of the regime could only mean less taxes, less corruption in high places, more free enterprise and above all else an end to the tiresome practice of bribery. Those who ran small businesses, the car hire people, the small pubs and restaurants, the launderette, the disco, the English supermarket were full of optimism. Now they could apply for the correct documents without a massive tip.

Johanna Vincent proved the most informed amongst her small circle. Early that morning, she had received a telephone call from her Portuguese lover to warn her about the public announcement. He had also insisted that in no way should she panic, be frightened or worry about the outcome. 'Lisbon is in Carnival! There is jubiliation all round! The soldiers are handing out *cravos* – red carnations – government offices, the *quartel* are festooned with flowers, there are banners everywhere and people are taking to their cars to follow the liberation forces round the city. It's crazy but it's peaceful. No one has been hurt.'

'But won't this lead to civil disorder?' said Johanna. 'I heard on the BBC world service they'd broken into the jails to let all the prisoners out.'

'No, the army have freed most political prisoners,' he replied. 'Anyone who ever dared to question the former regime. I have friends amongst them, liberals and journalists who spoke out against the dictatorship and got locked up. Don't believe all you hear, instead, my Johanna – rejoice with me! It is the most marvellous day for my country,' his voice was buoyant. 'Now at last we Portuguese have a chance to begin again! To establish democracy, to choose intelligent, decent people to be our leaders and to forget for ever this crumbling structure of incompetence we've put up with for so long.'

'So it's not a left wing take-over, darling?' Johanna had asked.

'Far from it. You need have no fear of that. This is a rebellion stirred up by the cream of our young, thinking militia – mostly captains – though naturally a few more senior officers are involved too. They were sick of the promotions within their ranks bought with money and influence. Those who rose through their own merit will always be revered, but those ancient brigadiers and generals who refused to step aside, can now be pensioned off – and good riddance!'

She listened carefully as more details emerged, but it was his last remark that struck her most forcibly. 'It is so wonderful, my dear, to be able to talk to you on the telephone knowing I can say what I *want*, and without – how you say? – repercussions.'

'You mean you never could before?' she was incredulous.

'Come, my darling. I thought you knew that! A man in my position was always being monitored. There was the constant danger of being…you know, I must take care not to say the wrong word… 'bugg-ed'… is it not? I hope I got it right?'

'Yes,' Johanna chuckled at the thought of the word he had managed to avoid.

'And so, always I had to guard the tongue. Over everything – think before speaking. Everywhere, in all circumstances. Walls always had ears…terrible! But all that is gone – ' she caught the jubilant catch in his voice. 'At last we Portuguese can enjoy freedom of speech! You took it for granted, we did not.'

She was to think back to that speech of his many times in the months ahead. She supposed they had been naïve to believe it would all work out as they hoped. Could anyone have foreseen the rapidity with which the coup grew sour? How overnight, Communist headquarters supported by Cuban and Russian money would appear in every village, every town all over the land? How in cruel rebuffal of all their efforts, those idealists who had made the revolution possible would shortly be ejected from power?

Within a year Amerigo, and many like him, would be forced to leave all they held dear, and flee. The Communists were organised; the democrats were not. As civil war broke out in Portuguese Africa and the mother country began to flood with refugees, people had nowhere to go. With just a knock at the door, land, houses, hotels and family businesses could be sequestered. In those most militant areas, animals were taken, crops destroyed and buildings burned. For some, lying low with shuttered and bolted doors became a way of life. For others it was prison. With much of the country in thrall to Marxist activists, the new regime brought suspicion and fear to many households throughout the land.

But no one could have imagined any of these things on that bright sunny day of April 25th. The people could only think of a glorious future as with passion and hope in their breasts, they pinned on their *cravos* to the Revolutionary Song, *Grandola Vila Morena*, which pumped out from their car radios, or blared across the land from wherever they were.

After she had spoken to Amerigo, Johanna felt it her duty to pass on the good news she had just received to those closest to her. For several days ahead, there might be confusion, so the sooner she set her friends' minds at rest, the better. First, she rang Jacqueline and was pleased to find Karl at home, for she was quite sure it would all have gone over his young wife's head – politics not being her forte. Karl, on the other hand, might be seriously worried about his job and now she could him set him straight. Tourism should not be affected, neither should building projects, she assured him. On hearing this good news, Karl was clearly delighted. 'You're a brick, Johanna,' he said gratefully 'I'll admit I was worried. Come round this evening and we'll celebrate. I'll put the champagne on ice.'

Next, she tried the McKays. Jock had had enough bad luck lately without having to dwell anxiously on this unexpected development and he was bitter enough about politics and the aftermath of socialism in their own country, to think the worst. She could imagine him trying to drown his worries in a bottle of whisky by the radio and being scolded by his young wife. She rang several times throughout the day, but only succeeded in talking to their old servant who gabbled hysterically at her. Despite trying to calm the woman in her moderate Portuguese, there was just no sense to be made of her... she kept droning on about some child or other who'd been taken. Clearly to her a Revolution meant kidnapping and cloak and dagger stuff, so Johanna might as well give up until Jock or Catalina picked up the phone themselves.

By the evening she had spoken to the Graftons, Jerry and Pat Weaver who were doing their best to calm stranded tourists cramming their bar for information, Eustace Stacey and many others. Eustace was particularly enthusiastic.

'Splendid, splendid news! I've quite a mind to get in on the act and fly myself up to Lisbon. Spread some of my self-sufficiency propaganda about. If the colonies are to fall, as I hear they might... someone ought to educate them on how to handle the ensuing food crisis. Only problem is – I heard the airport was under military control – don't want them thinking I'm an escaping right winger, do I? They might shoot me down if I start distributing pamphlets from the air, what?'

'Probably not a good idea, Eustace,' said Johanna, tactfully. 'Things may get a bit out of hand during the next few days and there are bound to be arrests. The Graftons told me the British and American embassies are advising everyone to stay at home for the next few days or so. I believe the frontiers are still closed, so it's probably the sensible thing.'

Satisfied with her day's work, she bathed and changed into her favourite 'uniform' as Maysie called it. Black velvet jeans, a black silk shirt, a huge buckled Mexican belt round her slim waist and her favourite Russell & Bromley slip-ons. Putting the finishing touches to her make-up, she frowned a little into the mirror, and worried anew about Jock McKay. She had felt unhappy about him for weeks; now, as she prepared to go out, the nagging doubt had enlarged to an indefinable but unquenchable concern. The maid's outburst, although clearly inappropriate, had intensified her worries. Philismena was hardly the type. In Johanna's experience, the temperament of these old peasant women was generally much too wise to be moved by political manoeuvrings. They had seen it all before and had little to lose themselves, so why the hystrionics? She looked at her watch; she was already late for the van der Stels…but no matter. She would try the McKay number once again.

This time she got Jock. She knew at once something was very wrong – had the Revolution affected him in some more personal way? What could have happened?

'What is it, darling? You sound terrible.'

A pause. She heard him strike a match and light up. She heard him drag long and hard on his cigarette and then somewhere down the wire, as though a system of mind-reading electrodes was at work, she sensed it. The loss, bewilderment, desolation all came streaming back at her, along the line. At last he spoke. His voice, a croak – 'Johanna, I don't know what to do. Catalina's left me.'

She should have been prepared for it, but she wasn't. She and Jacqueline had several times discussed the possibility of Catalina's one day deserting her older husband – but now – of all times! Nothing could have been further from her mind. There was no need to put the shock into her own voice. She already felt it – more keenly than she would have thought possible. 'Jock! Surely not! I mean – surely it can't be true!'

'It's true.'

'But it seems… so – oh my poor darling Jock – it seems so impossible. You and Catalina, why you were always the golden couple – at least in my eyes – so alive, so glamorous. How can it have happened? It just can't be…' Her voice trailed off. Words had never seemed so ineffectual.

He seemed to guess at her thoughts. 'There's no need for suitable noises…words of incredulity, my dear. It's happened, right under my nose and I've been a fool. You see – ' she heard the catch in his throat, 'they've taken Katy.'

'Oh my God!' she thought rapidly. She must go to him. Help him. Go swiftly before some further tragedy occurred. She would ring Karl – put them off – they would understand. 'Jock? Jock darling – listen. I'll be round there immediately. Do you understand? Immediately.'

For a moment she thought he had hung up. At last he whispered, 'Thank you. I'd like that.' This time he did hang up before she had time to say goodbye.

She rang Karl. Jacqueline answered and was full of dismay when she heard Joahnna could not come. 'But we've got champagne, Joey,' she wailed.

'It will have to wait darling. Something's come up. Desperately urgent. I can't tell you right at this moment. I'll call you back later. I'm sorry.'

She rang off, grabbed her jacket and keys and was half-way out of the door when the telephone rang. It was Karl. 'You're not in trouble, Johanna, are you?' his voice was all concern.

'No I'm not. But someone is. I'm sorry about this evening. I'll ring you later.'

'Johanna – you are not to drive out of Santa Felicia, do you hear me? Don't forget there's a revolution on and amongst the revellers, some strange people about. It would be folly to go out of town. You know that yourself, don't you?'

'Yes darling,' she smiled, despite her whirling emotions. There was command in his young voice. 'Don't worry about me. I've no intention of setting foot outside this small town. I give you my word.'

'All right,' he said. 'But call us if you want us. We shall be here all evening.'

She double-locked the front door, thinking it was good to know there were people who really cared. Out of the dozens and dozens one collected in a lifetime, only one or two were always there for you, no matter what. And they were the ones who mattered; the ones to cherish. She was walking away from her villa, across the old paved patio, when she heard the telephone ring again, dim but unmistakeable. This time she did not turn back. She was quite sure Jock McKay needed her more than whoever it might be.

'Drat and damnation,' said Benjie coming out of his booth. 'She's clearly not at home.'

Howard made an impatient noise with his tongue. 'Just our luck,' he said. 'We wait all this time to get through and probably miss her by a hair's breadth. Well then – it had better be Catalina – though she's bound to dramatise everything. You've got her number too, haven't you?'

'Yes, but we haven't booked it yet. It could be midnight before they manage again. And what about dinner?'

'They can page us in the dining room,' said Howard. 'Hurry up, book the call and let's get going. It's driving me crazy all this hanging about.'

Benje returned obediently to the hotel switchboard and gave the new number. 'I can't promise anything,' he was told in good English. 'The lines to Portugal are completely jammed. It was a miracle to get through the last time.'

Morosely, they made their way to the dining room. Howard had intended eating out tonight and the prospect of a hotel menu with no *à la carte* did not enhance his mood. They had just sat down when a loud voice said in their ear, 'Mind if I join you?'

Before either had a chance to reply, their acquaintance of the afternoon had pulled out a chair from their table laid for four and settled himself comfortably next to Benjie. 'Well, what gives?'

'I beg your pardon?' Howard blinked behind his thick lenses and wondered how to get rid of the man.

'What's new on the Western front? Any success at the Consul's? I thought you two would be bursting with news,' Ken Blair passed a hand through his sparse hair sending a small shower of dandruff over the crimson tablecloth.

'Look,' said Howard firmly, 'My friend and I want to eat undisturbed tonight. Neither of us are feeling very well, and I wonder – er – if you would – er…'

'Piss off?' said Ken Blair cheerfully. 'Why sure, I know when I'm not wanted. No trouble at all!' He scraped the chair back noisily and stood up. 'I only came over because I thought you'd be all agog to hear the latest bit of info re dear old Portugal over there.'

'You mean you know something?' said Benjie eagerly.

'Why sure, wouldn't have butted in like that if I didn't,' said Blair cheerfully. 'Oh well, I'll be off now.'

'No, wait,' said Howard. It was a command not a request and Blair merely cocked an eyebrow at him. 'I'm sorry, I didn't mean to sound inhospitable. We owe you a drink anyway. Perhaps you'd like to have dinner on us instead?'

'Well, if you insist,' Blair esconsed himself again with remarkable alacrity. 'Glad you're feeling well enough, after all.'

It turned out their companion had had more success at the British Consulate than they had at theirs. The official statement had given little more away, but he had had the good fortune to bump into a journalist friend who was hot with news.

'Course he wouldn't give out much – saving it for tomorrow's big broadsheet,' said Blair, 'but I wriggled this much out of him – Tomás and Caetano are being exiled to Brazil – not sure if they've left town yet, all very hush-hush…'

'Hang on a minute, which is the president?' Howard looked confused.

'Tomás, you nut – how long have you lived here? And Caetano's the prime minister… anything more you need to know on that front? Well, as I was saying – that's got rid of them – so to speak. No one seems too sad. As for the others, things are not so cushy…'

'What do you mean?' Benjie's eyes were on stalks.

'I mean all the old members of *PIDE*, the secret police, you know – well, they're being hunted down like rabbits, out of every nook and cranny in the land, and then being carted off.'

'Carted off where?'

'Jug, I suppose.'

'Jug?' said Howard, who'd retired behind the menu, offended by the 'nut' remark.

'You know *inside*, clink, jail – whatever you like to call it.'

'God,' said Howard, despite himself. 'But why? They were only doing a job!'

'You tell that to the political prisoners – who've now been released,' said Blair. 'They were hated, don't you know? Feared and hated. Now the people will get their own back – you'll see.'

'It sounds bad,' said Howard. 'We only moved here because we thought it was one of the safest places in Europe.'

'Well it is, really,' said Blair. 'And this was bound to happen sometime; it's been expected by those in the know. Better now than later, in my opinion. It will soon settle down again.'

'No one ever talked politics in Santa Felicia,' said Benjie. 'I did hear some mention of a special branch, but we have the FBI, CIA back home and no one cares too much.'

'That's 'cause you kept your nose clean, presumably.'

'But who *were* they?' Benjie was genuinely interested now.

'I can't tell you that because I don't know. The Ports seemed to know though. It was often whispered round the office that so-and-so was a member, and it would be quite an ordinary sort of 'bod' with a very ordinary sort of job. Then there were the informers. They were everywhere. We had several, it was rumoured – at the factory.'

'I had no idea it was like that,' said Benjie. 'What a lot we still have to learn.'

Food came and they ploughed their way through some tired tapas and an indifferent steak. Ken Blair attacked his as though he had not eaten for days. Howard picked; he was worried and depressed about their situation and annoyed with Benjie for treating the whole thing like a big adventure.

'The other thing he told me,' said Blair, through a mouthful of chips, 'was that a Communist HQ has opened in several towns and villages in the Alentejo.'

'What!' Howard and Benjie were unanimous in their horror.

'Strange, isn't it, when they've been outlawed for the last forty years? Looks like they'd been pretty busy underground all the same – in fact bloody well organised from all accounts – by Cuba, probably. Any ketchup around here?' he snapped his fingers for a waiter. Howard was far too eager for more to disapprove of this breach of etiquette.

'You don't mean this is a Communist take-over, do you?' he said pushing his plate away and looking a little green.

'Oh I shouldn't think so,' Blair replied. 'It's just the price you pay for democracy isn't it? There'll be political parties of every type springing up all over the place from now on. You mark my words!'

'Sometimes I'm not so sure I like democracy,' said Howard gloomily.

'Did your friend have any ideas about the frontiers re-opening?' asked Benjie.

'Yep, it's rumoured in about three days' time. They'll want to catch all the *PIDE* first – stop the last stragglers slipping into Spain. Reckon it'll take that long to round 'em all up.'

'I see, so we're stuck in this hole until the end of the week.' Howard shook his head. The situation had taken on the unreal quality of some ghastly nightmare. It was not helped by having to entertain this terrible man with his terrible tie and dandruff at their table. The thought of having to spend another three nights under force in this strange city had become an anathema. Overnight, stunning Seville had taken on a sinister role in his mind, not helped by the poor meal, mediocre wine and indifferent service. Worst of all was the worry for the future. Would everything still be the same when they got home? Would Santa Felicia be changed? Would all that they loved, together with the familiar easiness of their place in the sun, be gone forever?

If only the call to the McKays would come. Then at least he would know the worst.

The menu was before them again and Blair was ordering ice-cream and hot chocolate sauce. 'Got a sweet tooth,' he grinned and Howard noticed a gaping hole in one of his molars and looked the other way to hide his distaste. He ordered two coffees before Benjie had time to accept their companion's invitation to 'join him in a nice ice'.

'I feel very concerned,' said Howard, determined to get his money's worth out of their guest. Now that the man had established himself with them, he seemed less inclined to talk than before. 'Does your friend think there'll be problems over property for foreigners?'

'Depends, doesn't it?' said Blair. 'I mean if one's been a good boy and been nice to the locals, no doubt they won't start making problems. It's those who've gone snidling up to the authorities in the past, that won't be so welcome. You know, there's always a certain type of ex-pat who's as corrupt as the fellows in high places themselves. Always a ready hand in the pocket, bestowing and then reaping – special favours.' He grinned. 'Mind you, I'll admit I've done a bit of the old bribery myself. In small doses – I reckon it's all right – it's the big fish they'll be hard on. You know, the property developers, investors in big complexes and so on, who've paid literally tens of thousands to people at the heart of government to get their planning permissions whistled through. Don't s'pose you come into that category though, do you?' he eyed them, speculatively.

'No,' said Howard.

'And I take it you were always nice to the *people*?' Blair looked as though he was enjoying every last scrape of his ice.

'What people?'

'You know – The People! It's always called 'The People' after a revolution. Surely you know that? Here in Portugal, they call themselves *o Povo*!'

'Hmm…as far as I know I've offended no one,' Howard found he had begun to sweat and his hands were giving him hell under the table.

'Don't be so sure,' said Blair, stirring it.

Howard was at a loss for words. He'd managed to sneak in several good scratches without anyone spotting him.

'No, we like the Portuguese,' said Benjie firmly. 'Howard's done his best to learn the language which is more than can be said about most ex-pats.'

'Few people master it,' said Blair, snapping his fingers in the air again, 'mind if I order another of these?'

Howard grunted an assent, thinking he had a nerve. The man was horrendous but at least they were gleaning some information.

'Course it's attitudes that count,' Blair was warming to his theme. 'If you've been a bit over-bearing, snobby like, you know – chances are you're in for a difficult time. Some of 'em have a chip on their shoulder, the working man does anyway, feels he's downtrodden and all that. If people have behaved all high and mighty, it's as like as not, they'll get their own back.'

His second ice had arrived and he attacked it as though he was beginning – not ending – the meal. Howard and Benjie looked at each other helplessly. They longed for him to go, yet here they were hanging on every word. And he knew it.

'If you ask me,' Blair was summing up now. 'Those who have been *simpatico* – so to speak – will probably be left alone. Those who haven't …' he paused dramatically and folded his napkin into a neat square, '…they'll no doubt find out soon enough.'

'So that's that.' Wally Murray put the phone down and looked across at his patient.

'Tell me,' she whispered. She seemed amazingly calm now. The moment he had got her into the car, she had stopped. The tears dried, the rasping tortured gasps gave way to a steady regulated breathing, the sobs were replaced with the odd sigh and the face took on a new resolution. Now, she wore the set look of the determined, even the fanatic. As he turned to tell her the rest of the bad news, he realized the blue eyes were shining with an intensity hitherto not encountered. It frightened him a little and for a moment he wondered if she was verging on the border of insanity. Should he give her a shot to spare her from the void of horror beyond? Before he had time to weigh up the matter, her calm voice stopped him dead in his tracks.

'It's as I thought. I suppose I knew the truth, the moment that young man in the bank queried my credit. Only I refused to believe it then. It all had to be spelt out to me – in black and white. The file! First the manager, then my accountant, then our stockbroker and now you – on the phone – to my insurance broker. Four separate institutions, all duped by that man I call my husband!

'There's no reason why you should have guessed,' Wally said. 'Who would have thought he could be so thorough? The bank accounts yes, even the investments – the stocks and the gilts – I guess. But to have the brass-necked cheek to contact your insurers and convince them to trade in your life insurance – the way he did... Well, I have to say that took some doing. Has it occurred to you we're almost dealing with a criminal mind here? Not just one driven by greed or lust...'

'...or love,' supplied Leah. 'That's the problem, Wally, I'm beginning to think he may have had a girlfriend and that's what made him do things that were totally out of character. All those trips out in the car – perhaps he was meeting up with one of those Americans that live down the coast. There was a blonde at our Christmas party – I had the feeling they'd met before. Oh – who can tell? But it was a new Buster in the latter months. One that we didn't know at all. I can see it all now. He'd been swept off his feet, re-invented himself. That's probably why he tried to drown me. The old Buster wouldn't have done that... but the new one would have no compunction.'

She said it so matter of factly, he felt a cold shiver pass down his spine. What was she talking about? This was a new piece of drama and it sounded rather too real for his liking. But...? No, he'd rather not take her there now. As he'd said before – she wasn't ready for the couch – yet. Better to stick with material things, for now.

'Whatever his behaviour,' he tried to brush over this new revelation, 'We need to find him. But it's hard to know what to do right now with this coup in Lisbon. The information coming out is not looking good for us at the moment. The whole system has collapsed and as far as one can make out law and order now resides in the hands of the military.'

'I'm surprised he didn't have a hand in that too,' said Leah drily. 'He was always mad about the forces.' He hoped she was being facetious but didn't press it.

'It's such a shame we can't contact him by telephone. Not that he'd answer, probably, but your maid or someone might give us an idea of his movements.'

Leah shook her head. 'It would be a waste of time,' she said. He noticed she was sitting bolt upright on the edge of one of the easy chairs in his surgery, her hands white and still in her lap. 'The telephone wouldn't help, even if we had one. No, he's gone.'

'We don't know that, Leah,' said Wally, wishing he sounded more convincing.

'Oh yes, all that secrecy, the correspondence to a numbered box – and never a word. I should have guessed before of course. He always liked Spain, you know. Right from the beginning, he said 'Why Portugal? – I prefer Spain.''

'Your bank manager thinks he may have had wind of the coup in Portugal and chosen Spain for investment purposes. Events in Portugal have sent prices rocketing in Madrid. It would be a shrewd investment move.'

'I daresay that's what he's done,' said Leah. 'But not for us both – for him.'

'What makes you so sure?' Wally still thought there was a slim chance she might be mistaken – only very slim – but worth pursuing in the interim. The other alternative was so self-defeating.

'He's hated us all lately. He – as I said – changed. The house became oppressive to him – and all of us in it. Even the geese upset him…the cat… Howard and Benjie…only Mungo he put up with – as long as he served a good purpose.'

'Mungo?'

'Our dog. He went off with Mungo in the car. Said they went for runs together. Sometimes I wondered. Near the end, Mungo was getting fatter rather than thinner – even Catalina agreed.'

'Catalina?'

'My best friend out there, married to the artist, Jock McKay.'

'Do you want to ring them.'

'I'd like to,' she said, 'but no thanks – maybe in a day or two, when I feel stronger. They've got enough troubles of their own – and what with this revolution and so on…' She looked down at her hands again, composed and bleak. Wally found himself growing more and more uncomfortable at her stillness.

'Go on,' he said.

She was back in the past again. 'After the bath of course – I should have known.'

It was the second time she'd eluded to it. 'Bath?'

'Yeah. If I'd faced facts then and there we need not have had this. Only – silly me – I was too much of a coward. I couldn't bear to contemplate the truth.' She gave a small laugh and continued. 'I guess I knew then that he had grown to hate me. That he wanted out.'

Wally had picked up his note pad and was making surreptitious squiggles with an elongated ballpoint pen. Leah said 'Write away – if it helps. It won't help me now. We're too late for that.'

'I think we may be over-reacting,' said Wally. 'We know nothing definite yet. We may have completely misjudged your poor husband. He may have done all this because he got wind of the revolution and saw a way of making a killing.'

'Killing!' laughed Leah. 'The only person that man would want to kill is me! '

'Have you never considered,' said Wally, not to be put off, 'that Buster found the fact that it was you who started the business, built it up and made such a success of it, hard to bear. The very fact you took the decisions, handled the finance and were so good at it all could well have dinted his male ego?'

'Yes, I have. We had a row about it.'

'There you are!' said Wally eagerly. 'So now he gets some tip-off about the coup in Portugal, realises the Spanish stock exchange is about to soar and decides to show you just what he can do! Rash, I know, to move so much money at once – but that would be Buster's way. If he really knows there's profit to be made, I can just see him getting the bit between his teeth and taking a snap decision. Then, when you return, he can say – 'Look at me! I increased our investment by twenty-five per cent – or whatever! I did it on my own!' And then he hands it to you on a plate. It would really restore his feelings of manhood. He'd feel fulfilled, clever, indispensable.'

'No,' she said quietly, 'I wish what you said was so, but I don't buy it.'

His face fell, he had half-believed what he was telling her himself. 'Why not, Leah?'

'Because of so many things that have happened. Little things… insignificant. He was very careful. His only big mistake – which gave him away – was the bath.'

'Tell me about it,' said Wally, giving in and preparing himself for a long, long afternoon. He beckoned her to the couch and to his surprise she went to lie down meekly. He put a blanket over her; she was as white and cold as snow. He held her lifeless hand and waited for her to settle. 'Tell me about it,' he said again.

She looked around her. The white and blue of the furnishings were merging into the colour of ice. A chill had settled over her heart some time before. Only her toes felt vaguely alive; she wriggled them under the blanket, determined to be lucid, to make sense. What a comfort this man was. A real friend. She'd tell him about it … she'd been bottling things up for so long. Really, it would be a relief. Slowly, methodically she began her story.

Much, much later as he waited for NBC to give them an update on Portugal's revolution, Wally repeated her story to Melinda. Leah had asked him to – she treated them both as equals. 'Poor kid,' she said sympathetically, 'do you think it's all true, Wally, I mean that he really meant to do it?'

'Who knows,' he said. 'He'd been drinking, so he may have just gotten himself out of control for a moment or two. I expect he wanted to give her a fright.'

'Kind of sadistic,' Melinda said with a sniff.

'Sure, but I always reckoned that guy had seen some things in Korea and had built himself a hide like a buffalo.'

'Protective for him, no doubt, but hard on others,' said his wife. 'I'd like to hear what Howard has to say on the matter, he's a shrewd cookie.'

'He didn't know about it, neither did Benjie. She never told a soul – not even this Portuguese girlfriend of hers.'

'They must have noticed something amiss.'

'Well, it's a bit late now, if they did. If what she suspects is true, and there isn't another account or another policy hidden away for emergencies, then Buster's cleaned her out. And I mean that. How it will affect the two Boys is anyone's guess – they were all in that house together and things could get very awkward. But my main concern is Leah herself. She tells me she's only got seven hundred odd dollars in her personal current account. Everything else was in their joint names, so overnight she may have gone from millionaire to pauper.'

Melinda whistled. 'It's iniquitous. I can't believe it!' She got up and switched off the television and began to pace the room.

'Hey, put that back on! We want the news!'

'Oh blow the news. As Leah says, the political situation won't make a dime of difference now to her – not if she's in the mess, she thinks she is.'

'Maybe not, but at least we'll know where we stand. One of these days, she'll have to go back there and face up to her responsibilities. It would be a help to know what's happening and her chances of tracking down Buster,' Wally pursed his lips and switched on the machine again.

'Well you can hang about and see. Shall I go check on our patient – I presume you gave her a sleeping pill?'

'I knocked her out, good and proper, poor kid.'

'Thank God, I'm knackered,' said his wife, making for the door. ' I reckon we'll need all our energy to deal with tomorrow. You realise, honey, if what we all imagine is true – Leah won't be able to afford your services any longer?'

'I realised that the moment I spoke with her broker this afternoon. Do you think it makes any difference? We're not all shits around here.'

'I know, honey,' Melinda smiled at him around the door, 'Thank the Lord for that. I, by the way, think you're just great and she's darned lucky to have you.'

41

Johanna Vincent arrived in the dusk at number 9, the *Esplanada* and was surprised to find Jock McKay quite sober. Philismena had let her in, dramatically pointing to missing objects en route to the studio. In the hall, and again halfway up the stairs, she explained between sobs that they were gone – gone forever. Johanna knew the 'they' actually stood for a lot more and it was depressing.

McKay did not hear her enter the long room. He was lolling on Catalina's chaise-longue, one foot on the ground, one propped up. His arms were clasped round his knee, his chin resting on his hands in earnest contemplation. Johanna coughed gently. He sprang then to his feet and came forward, leaner than ever, his normally tanned face gaunt and intense.

'Johanna!'

She held out her arms and he came into her strong grasp, tall man that he was, stooping a little to rest his head against the softness of her neck. She held him for a long moment and stroked the fine pepper and salt hair.

'Poor darling, poor, poor darling.'

He said nothing. Then, as if by mutual consent they drew apart and he went to the drinks cupboard, his back carefully turned as he said, 'I've no champagne, will vodka do?'

'Yes, on the rocks, darling. What about you?'

'I haven't had a drink since I got home last night.' He waited for her to sit down, then flung himself back onto Catalina's favourite perch. She noticed a gaping hole in the button-back upholstery and saw that the leopard skin which used to cover it had been removed. 'Drinking helps nothing. If I hadn't been so wrapped up in my own problems and drinking to nullify them – none – ' he threw out an arm in a gesture of despair – 'of this need have happened.'

'Just what has happened, Jock?' Johanna said gently.

'As I said, Catalina's gone. She's taken Katy. She left me a note. It said "I've pissed off with Buster..." or words to that effect. "Don't worry about us and don't try to find us – 'cause you won't..." That's about it!' He averted his head again and the quick brush of his sleeve across his eyes was not wasted on her. She got up and poured him a scotch from the decanter.

'Have that!'

As he began to protest, she shook her head and said 'Don't be so damned stubborn, darling. You may be right, if you hadn't drunk so much, this might not have happened, though personally I doubt it. I doubt it very much. However, one drink now when you really need it won't make a shred of difference. So don't play the high horse with me, unwind a bit and then, maybe, we can sort something out of this mess together. Now,' she said turning away from him as though she had not noticed the tears, 'where's this note you were talking about?'

'In the fire.'

'Oh – well, no doubt a fitting place. Can you remember *exactly* what it said?

'Word for word.' He sipped fitfully at his whisky and told her.

'I see. Looks like Spain then, doesn't it? You obviously reckoned the same yourself.'

He told her about his visit to the police, his relationship with Fonseca and the painful visit to his house. He missed out nothing. 'If only I hadn't hung about,' he ended, 'If I hadn't wasted time – I might have caught up with them. Oh God – it's unbelievable! So utterly impossible, a million in one chance! Portugal's first revolution, my wife's first elopement – the dates colliding at the very same time! A day earlier and I could have had them stopped at the border, a day later, they wouldn't have got through. Who would ever believe such odds?'

'Truth is stranger than fiction,' she mused. 'Are you *sure* they got through, darling?'

'No, I'm not. That's what's tormenting me. But if they're here, how and where do I begin to look? With a virtual curfew covering the whole country, I daren't risk being slapped into a jail by causing a nuisance. Since I saw Fonseca, I haven't exactly been idle. I 've been onto Scotland Yard, and they've been on to Interpol but with the current situation, they're not much help.'

He got up to get his cigarettes and lit one for her before puffing on his own, 'My story centres on Buster being a fine arts thief. That'll only stack up if they've got the furniture in tow, so if they dump it it's going to be harder,' he gave a dry laugh. 'I told them he was hanging around at my London exhibition and we had been warned. I'm quite good at fabricating a story when I put my mind to it! With all that gear in tow, they'll hopefully think the worst and hold him at customs. Then it's up to Scotland Yard.'

Johanna was screwing up her eyes and looking confused. 'Now steady down, Jock, I'm not with you. Philismena pointed out a few empty spaces on the way up, but you still look pretty well furnished to me – what do you mean 'all that gear they've got in tow'?'

'Oh my God,' he groaned and polished off the whisky, 'I forgot to tell you that part. After I got home, found them gone – I hadn't seen the note at that stage – I jumped in the car and drove hell for leather up to Bloomfield's villa. It was all dark, no one there. I thought then – that's it – the birds have flown. But – just to make sure, I broke into the house.'

'Jock,' she said breathlessly, 'You don't hold back, do you?'

'Well, would you?' he said. 'No! I didn't think so...' Forgetting his resolution, he topped up both glasses. 'It was only then I realised I was up against something big,' his voice hardened and he faced her squarely, all trace of tears gone. 'This was something well planned. I knew it the moment I switched on the light. Every stick of every piece of furniture that the Bloomfields had between them, had been removed. Pictures, mirrors, carpets, rugs, desks, chairs, tables, sofas, porcelain, silver, the lot! Gone!'

'My God!' It took a lot to shock Johanna but the colour drained from her carefully made up face and for a moment her jaw dropped open. In that moment the years she concealed so carefully from the outside world, were revealed in one cruel blow. She blinked, took a gulp of vodka and regained her composure almost instantly. 'What an *extraordinary* thing!'

'Not extraordinary,' said McKay, 'Wicked! Criminal! It just shows the mind of a man like Bloomfield. If he could plan such a thing, what else is he capable of? And he has my child!'

'Then this is no ordinary escapade, no flight of fancy – this has been planned for a long time?'

'I reckon so – for sure. He's not taken a few baubles, Johanna, the villa's been cleaned out. Sure, some of the Boys' stuff has been left – most, no doubt – but the place has been effectively trashed. It'll never be the same. What has been going on beneath my very eyes must have taken weeks, if not months of planning, and Catalina's had a hand in it. In fact I can see her now, working it all out, whilst playing her two roles – the solicitous wife and the duplicitous lover. That's what hurts so much.'

'Surely not,' said Johanna. 'Of course we all … er … thought,' she paused, embarassed and fiddled with an ashtray.

'Yes?' his eyes were very green as he looked into hers.

'Oh darling, I don't know how to put it – you must have known too – it was all pretty obvious, that Catalina was … well … amusing herself with the Bloomfield husband. I can't believe you didn't notice it – '

'You're right. I did notice. Only I …' he bit his lip, '… was too conceited, too egoist if you like – to believe she could really – ' he got up and gave himself a shake ' – go through with it. Oh, what the hell , Johanna! What matters is – it's done! Fool that I was not to see she really could betray me. I never imagined for a moment … God, how wrong can you *be*? And now! And *now*?' he turned to her, suddenly boyish, helpless, 'What do I do? Where do I begin? I've got to get my daughter back.'

Johanna joined him as his restless pacing began all over again and threaded an arm through his. 'I think you've done all you can for the time being, darling. There's a revolution on, and we've all been told to stay at home. It will do Katy no good at all if her father gets arrested – as you said. And if there's to be any news – it will come here first. A wild goose chase over the countryside will achieve nothing.'

'But at least I'd feel I was doing something. It's this waiting … why, I haven't even slept yet, but how can I?'

'I realise that, it's soul-destroying – but you don't have much option. Wait a minute whilst I put on my thinking cap.'

Together they paced the length of the studio and a silence fell between them only broken by the sound of their feet on the marble and the sparking of the fire. A solitary desk lamp burned and their shadows moved along the walls in the firelight, like huge, gliding ships upon a red-painted sea. Eventually Johanna said, 'Come back and spend the night at my place. No, I won't take 'no' for an answer … blow my reputation! You can have Maysie's room and I don't sleep walk, I promise! I'm going to cook you a late supper, pack you off to bed and then I'll get on the phone to our man on the spot in Lisbon. If anyone can get things done – he will. He has contacts everywhere and with any luck by tomorrow we'll know which frontier they slipped out of – if any.'

They had stopped in front of the flickering fire. Jock put his hands on either side of her well-defined, oval face. 'Johanna, how I wish you'd been twenty years younger when I met you. I'd have married you, you know. You're a woman in a million.'

'Well, I wouldn't have married you, Jock McKay!' she retorted. 'I've never fancied cradle-snatchers and you'd soon be trading me in for a younger version.'

'I asked for that,' he said, and she noted with satisfaction that he was actually grinning.

Philismena was called; a hold-all packed. They were just leaving the house when the telephone rang. 'I'll take it,' said Johanna firmly, pushing him through the open door towards her car, before he changed his mind.

'Hello! Yes? A call from Spain?' her heart raced. She was just about to call him back in a sudden wild hope, when Howard's unmistakeable flat Brooklyn voice came over a crackly line.

'Catalina? Is that you Catalina? It's me, Howard McDermott. I'm in Seville – it's a very bad line.'

'I can hear you, can you hear me?' Johanna cried. 'It's not Catalina, it's Johanna Vincent.'

'Who? Who did you say?'

'Jo-hanna! Vincent!'

'Oh go-od – this is *so* lucky! We've been trying to call you all evening. We're an hour ahead here and we'd almost given up. It was actually you we wanted to talk with. Do you hear me, Johanna?'

'I hear you!' she made a face at McKay as he came back into the hall and made a thumbs-down sign. 'It's Howard,' she said.

McKay began to wave his hand furiously, 'Tell him to look out for them! You never know, they could be in Seville, even in the same hotel! Tell them what's happened. Tell them just to find Katy – that's all I want. Just my daughter! Please!'

Johanna swallowed hard. 'Howard, listen to me. Something's happened since you've been away.'

'We know,' he sounded impatient, 'the Revolution, we know all about it. We just want to know they haven't taken our house. The revolutionaries, I mean! Is Buster in control of the situation? We keep hearing rumours but we need to know! They say foreigners' property is safe – but I've been worried sick. Just tell me the Commies haven't taken our house!'

'Howard, shut up and listen to me!' Johanna's crystal-clear voice cut in sharp as a chisel. Despite the bad line, it had an effect; the monotonous drawl ended abruptly. 'That's better, now if you want news of your property, keep quiet and allow me to finish. Something terrible's happened here. Buster's run off with Catalina McKay. They've raided your house and taken little Katy. Jock is accusing Buster of theft and has Interpol onto them, but he thinks it was too late to stop them crossing the border. They are probably in Spain although we don't know for certain. This means that far from looking after your property Howard, Buster has walked out of it – for good – by the looks of it.'

She had made her voice purposefully dramatic and paused. There was a long hush on the other end, and for a moment she was afraid they had been cut off.

Eventually, Howard's voice no more than a whisper came over, 'You can't mean this, Johanna. My God, you can't!'

'It's true,' said Johanna. 'I'm very sorry for all of you. Now listen Howard…' a burst of expletives gathering noise and momentum came down the line and she held the telephone away from her ear with a rueful look at McKay. '…if you don't quieten down – I can't tell you what to do to put this right again, can I?'

'I'm sorry,' the voice went faint again – as though the unusual outburst from this quiet, buttoned-up man had left him short of breath and emotion. Johanna felt desperately sad and almost guilty about the lie she was about to deliver, but needs must – she had to help Jock. 'There's only one chance, Howard, of ever seeing your stolen things again in my opinion. That is for you and Benjie to scour southern Spain for Buster and Catalina. Jock thinks they would have crossed over at Beja or even Castro Marim – the quickest exit by road. He can't see them taking the boat to Ayamonte – too many people would remember them. You can describe the Opel can't you? And it's possible they had a furniture van in tow – unless they left that behind…who knows. The point is Katy with her flaxen hair would have stood out a mile at one of those interior crossings; they're not used that much by tourists.'

'Johanna – what exactly have they taken?' Howard's voice was tremulous. Johanna could almost see his double chins wobbling, at the end of the line.

'Darling, who knows? I haven't been up to the house myself, but Jock has. It appears they've cleaned the place out – at least some things were left – but an awful lot appears to have gone, pictures, ornaments, carpets as well as furniture.

'My God!'

'Yes, it's dreadful. I would never have thought they could have gone to such lengths, to rob you *all*…' she crossed her fingers under McKay's nose – an old childhood habit to excuse herself from lying…'I'm really so dreadfully sorry.'

'My God!' said Howard again. He seemed to have run out of words.

Johanna seized the opportunity as McKay whispered urgent instructions in the other ear. 'I suggest you leave immediately for the road north west to Merida. There's a good *parador* there – you know – government run hotel. They may well have holed up there on their first night. It's as good a place as any to start and then you might start enquiring at all the petrol stations – Jock says they are few and far between – and they'll have needed to fill up somewhere along the line. By the time you're ensconced yourselves further north, we can talk again. As far as I can make out most of the Lisbon telephone exchange has walked out to join the crowds in the streets, so there's no way I can ring you – but you should get through to me – there must be someone still working. Try me at home around eleven tomorrow morning and I may have more news from this end. You've got my number?'

'OK,' said Howard, sounding uncertain. 'But I can't – oh God – I can't promise a specific time. It took me four hours to catch up with you this time…this is a nightmare…'

'Well, *try*, darling. Book the call at dawn – or something! And remember, the *child* is your biggest clue – people will remember –' There was a loud buzz, 'Hello, hello…damn – we've been cut off.'

McKay picked up the machine and shook it impatiently but the thing had gone dead – not even an engaged tone. 'You didn't say he was to grab Katy,' he said accusingly.

'Darling, first things first. Give the man a chance to locate them. Howard's no fool. He won't rush in, and frighten the birds away. No doubt if he finds them, he'll plan it carefully. He knows you've got Interpol on your side. If he's any sense, he'll go to the nearest police station and leave the Civil Guard to arrest them. You know how formidable Franco's police can be.'

'*If he's any sense…*' said McKay gloomily. 'Bet he bungles it and they get away. Forewarned is forearmed.'

'Oh for heavens' sake – you pessimist!' Johanna was suddenly tired. 'I've done my best. It was a miracle he rang at all. Now, let's get going.'

As they left the house in the dark and walked across the street to her car, she wondered with a sudden sinking feeling in her chest, 'I wonder if anyone's thought to tell Leah?'

Edward Vaughan Parker Boddington Junior hung his bowler hat carefully on the stand in the hall and followed Melinda with misgiving in his heart. 'Shhhh…' she hissed outside a closed door. 'I'll need to see if she's awake first. If she's not, you'll have to wait. She mustn't be woken suddenly – Wally says it's very important – what with her breakdown and everything.'

'I've an appointment at five,' he said, disliking her proprietary manner. This was his father's client, his father's account and his father's business but – nervous breakdown or not – he was determined to see the affair through. It wasn't his fault his father was in the Bahamas. It wasn't his fault this woman had a double-dealing husband. It wasn't his fault that she'd given him an all encompassing Power of Attorney. Neither was it his fault that all the portfolios were in their joint names. He had all the facts and figures in his briefcase. The sooner he had showed them to her and cleared his own impeccable name and that of Edward Vaughan Parker Boddington Senior too, the better he would sleep that night.

'She's awake!' the Murray woman was saying, glaring at him in the accusing manner he had found so uncomfortable when he'd first arrived at the apartment a few minutes earlier.

'Good!' he said and assuming his best broker's manner, went straight into the room.

The blinds had been pulled down, successfully cutting out the springtime sunshine but he could just make out his client in a ridiculously large bed on the other side of the room. She was huddled, ghostlike, against cornflower blue pillows, shrouded in a bedjacket laced up to the throat. The face that peered out at him was greyish in pallor, but he was disturbed by the intensity of the eyes – they put the blue of the bedlinen to shame – there was an ethereal, burning quality about them.

The young man hesitated for a moment. Was he expected to sit on the bed? But no, thankfully the Murray female had leaped in to proffer a chair. As he sat down and arranged his briefcase carefully on his knee, she whispered fiercely in his ear, 'She's been very ill indeed. Be gentle with her.'

As if he would be anything else! This was a delicate matter and he had handled several delicate matters in his twenty-eight year old life. It was a relief, nevertheless when the woman left the room. He cleared his throat and was wondering how to start when a voice from the bed said, 'Don't look so worried – I shan't eat you. I really appreciate your coming like this. I gather your father's out of town.'

'That's right,' he mumbled. This was different! Startled, he looked up to find the disturbing blue eyes fixed upon him, an expression almost of sympathy hovering around the lips. 'I – er – it was no trouble, no trouble at all, Mrs Bloomfield,' he began. 'Mr Murray said it was urgent someone should come. He said – er – that you wouldn't settle until you knew – er – all the facts.'

'Well, that's strange,' she said, 'I think I know them already. I've never been afraid of the truth, you see. It's lies and deceit…' she shuddered so violently under the bedclothes, he thought she might have a seizure, but she recovered '…lies and deceit that I hate – and fear.'

'Quite,' he said, wishing the interview was nearing its end rather than just beginning. 'Well, I guess Mr Murray just wanted confirmation of the facts.'

'Oh yes,' she said. 'He would. Like all these mind people,' she smiled ruefully, 'he thinks I won't accept the facts 'til I see it all in black and white. But actually that's the problem, I have accepted it. But it doesn't mean I like it…' there was another shudder but less violent. 'The truth is – I don't like it at all.'

The last few syllables had changed in tone and he waited for the anger to spill over. The blue eyes were still intense, but the sympathetic look had been replaced by one of bleak despair. He'd encountered despair before – but less quiet and controlled. He cleared his throat to fill the gap and hurried on. 'Well, I have here in my case all the papers relevant to your and Mr Bloomfield's affairs. Photocopies of holdings, stocks, interest gained, closures, re-investmests… er… and sales.' He hurried over the last word. 'As well as our firm, your accountant has copies too. It's all in order. There's several files, but I can leave them here for you to peruse at leisure. There's no need to return them.'

'I only want to glance through,' she held out her hand for them. 'There's no reason why I should keep them now. No reason at all.'

'Very well.' He fussed with the combination lock of his briefcase, and got up to hand her a sheaf of neat stationers' files, bulging with documents. She glanced through them, as though barely interested. He noticed how blue the veins stood out on the back of her hands as she fingered the papers at random. His discomfiture increased as he noticed everything in the room seemed blue.

'Would you like me to explain these to you?' he offered, noticing a frown gathering at the bridge of her nose as she examined one particular column of figures.

'I've been reading accounts since you were in short pants,' she said, tracing her finger down the margin. After a further silence, she said 'Can you tell me the exact total sum of the full portfolio, the day before you received my husband's instructions?'

'Yes certainly,' he said, busying himself in the briefcase again and bringing out a calculator together with a small black notebook. 'Well, gilts came to three hundred and eighty thousand, government bonds –'

'I'm sorry, I'm only interested in the *total*.'

'Ah, just a moment,' Edward Vaughan Parker Boddington Junior withdrew a gold ballpoint from inside his jacket and made a few hasty notes in the black book. The calculator was then referred to again and a figure arrived at. He kept his eyes firmly fixed on his notes as he said, 'Two million, six hundred and eight-five thousand, four hundred and twenty seven dollars at current prices, not including interest for the month of April,

1974 – and of course that wouldn't include any annual interest due – the dates of those varying with each account.'

She seemed to absorb the information, then nodded her head as though satisfied. 'Thank you, Mr Parker Boddington, it's roughly as I thought. And now please,' again he felt the burning blue eyes upon him, 'I would like to see the letter you received from my husband in January, plus the follow up telex, instructing you to sell these bonds and where to telex the money in Madrid.'

'Certainly. In point of fact there were three in all – one dealing with stocks and shares, the other dealing with sundry investments, plus a further confirmation, you must understand. A further file marked 'Personal' was produced and he drew out three shiny photocopies. The slight figure in the bed disengaged itself from the mountain of pillows and leaned forward to receive them.

'Where are the originals, Mr Parker Boddington?'

He drew himself up a little before replying. 'In point of fact, Mrs Bloomfield, they are with our solicitor.'

She sank back against the pillows and closed her eyes. Then she opened them tiredly and shook her head. 'You and your father were afraid that I might try to sue, Mr Parker Boddington?'

He took time with his reply. He had been well taught by Edward Parker Boddington Senior, that you must take all the time in the world if a difficult question came your way – because once you had said the wrong thing, the word was out, the damage done. 'Frankly, in view of the extenuating circumstances, Mrs Bloomfield, the answer to that question is – er – yes.' Even to himself the words sounded pompous and he had the grace to blush a little.

'You are cautious people,' she said, 'and I respect you for it. But if it sets your mind at ease a little, your firm has nothing to fear from me. In any case, surely you know I haven't a leg to stand on in the eyes of the law.'

'One must always be careful,' he muttered.

'How right you are,' she said and closed her eyes again.

He wondered whether there was anything else and said so. The photocopies of the letters signed by Bertram Roache Bloomfield had slipped from her fingers and fluttered onto the floor. Glad of an excuse for further activity, he rescued them and replaced them on the bed, wondering if she had fallen asleep.

'You can take them all away with you,' she said in a sudden harsh voice, making him jump. 'I've seen all I want.'

'Very well Mrs Bloomfield,' he said, taking less care than usual to repack his case. He couldn't wait to leave.

'Just one thing,' she said as he prepared to say goodbye.

'Yes?'

'What was the number of the post box in Santa Felicia you replied to?' He had a photographic memory and recalled it immediately. 'Why, one hundred and sixty-six,' he said.

'Ah yes, the same as the one the bank used. Everyone seems to have had that number – except me of course. One way or another,' she had turned away from him towards the wall, 'there must have been quite a lot of coming and going from that little pigeonhole.'

Melinda came in at that moment and the young man wondered if she'd been listening at the door. She bustled over to the sickbed and straightened Leah's blankets. 'I hope you haven't tired her out,' she said giving him another of her sharp looks.

'I'm just leaving,' he said gravely, "Will that be all, Mrs Bloomfield?'

But there was no answer from his former client. She had fallen asleep with her back to him.

With a sudden longing for some fresh air, no matter how polluted from the city's rush hour fumes, Edward Vaughan Parker Boddington Junior was halfway out of the door, when Melinda Murray bore down upon him again. 'I'm sorry,' she said. 'I did want to catch you before you left. Did everything pass off quite smoothly? No hysterics or outbursts – or anything of the sort?'

'Nothing like that,' he replied. 'I can't think why she wanted to see me. She hardly looked at the papers and even the copies of her husband's instructions, she only brushed over. I offered to leave everything with her, but she declined.'

'It's this seeing is believing,' said Melinda. 'My husband thought it would help. You see although one side of her already knows and probably accepts what has happened, just seeing the papers will make all the difference to her recovery. It was the same yesterday with her insurers – just to see it all in black and white. It's not so much the content of the letters or the details of the figures, it's the physical reality of holding the papers, touching them – making sure they're real and not some awful nightmare.'

'I suppose it's understandable,' Parker Boddington nodded his head and for a moment felt genuine remorse for the woman he'd just left. Now it seemed likely there was no court case to fear, he could afford her a little sympathy. 'If you don't mind my saying,' he ventured, 'the husband sounds a real bounder.'

'He's a shit!' said Melinda. 'Do you know what caused the breakdown though, made her almost lose her mind? It wasn't so much the money – though that was bad enough – it was what came through the post last week. Wait there a minute!'

'I really must be going,' Parker Boddington looked at his watch, 'In point of fact I've an appointment at five.'

He was collecting his bowler hat, when she came hurrying back. 'Take a look at that!'

She thrust a picture postcard at him. It was of a sunset over a long golden beach. He looked mystified. She flipped it over in his hand and he noticed a Portuguese stamp. She jabbed a finger at the written part.

'I'm sorry, this is really none of my business, I have an appoi–'

'Read it!'

For once in his life Edward Vaughan Parker Boddington Junior gave in to feminine pressure. He did not have a wife, his mother had died young and he only took instructions from his father. Unwillingly, he read the simple message in large childish handwriting … it was written with a purple pen … how very bizarre …

'No time to write more than a card. We leave here in less than 24 hours and you'll know all about it soon enough. I just wanted you to know I never expected B. to take all those things from the house, just a few bits and pieces... but not like he did. I'm really sorry about that and just hope one day you may forgive me. I always liked you such a lot. I never meant it to turn out like this – I really didn't – but it just sort of happened. Try to understand. I hope you get better soon and can get on with your life. C. x'

'I'm sorry,' the accountant shook his head, he had been foolish to linger, 'this means nothing to me. I must go.'

'Just wait, young man!' Melinda's voice rang out with such authority, he stopped in his tracks. She was close to tears. 'Your firm's made enough money out of that poor sick woman in there, you can spare a few seconds more. You'll hear me out. That postcard arrived for Mrs Bloomfield, just a week ago. It arrived when she was at her lowest ebb – not long after she'd been to her bank. It very nearly killed your client. That postcard is from the *creature*...' her voice shook with emotion, '...who stole her husband and as you know, a lot more beside. Now it appears her home's been turned over too. Did you ever hear of such wickedness? The person who signed this card – was supposed to be your client's best friend!'

Boddington Junior blinked. He had seldom seen a woman so angry. She hadn't finished. 'I hope you realise if it hadn't been for this, your client – I should probably say ex-client – would not be in this sorry state. If it hadn't been for the writer of this card – well,' she paused for breath, 'even now, Mrs Bloomfield might be giving you instructions for further lucrative transactions and... instead of resenting this visit, you'd be leaving here with a swing in your step!'

Boddington Junior swallowed twice. 'I'm very sorry indeed for her, Mrs Murray. It's a tragic affair. But we acted in a purely professional way, we were not privy to her personal relationships...'

'Oh shut up!' snorted Melinda, 'I'm not blaming you! All I'm asking for is a little *humanity*. Does no one in this money-grabbing world care about *people* any more?'

He made another move towards the door and this time she let him go. 'Obviously you do, Mrs Murray,' he said with the ghost of a smile. 'Now I must be going – I have an appointment at five o'clock.'

He stepped into the lift and was gone. Bowler, briefcase and all. Melinda Murray remained on the empty landing. The tragedy of life's truths weighed heavily on her shoulders. 'Sometimes, it's a bloody, bloody world out there,' she said withdrawing into the apartment, slamming the door behind her.

One of the first people to fly back into Portugal after the frontiers re-opened was Maysie Vincent. She had only meant to be away two days for a photo-shoot and was missing her latest boyfriend. May 1st had seen crowds of over a million crowding into Lisbon to celebrate Labour Day and her mother had advised her to stay in London until all the mayhem was over, which she did resentfully. Finally on the weekend of May 4th, she took a British Airways flight back to the Algarve.

'I can't tell you how ghastly it is to be kept out of your own country when you're all prepared to come,' she complained to her mother as they drove away from the airport.

'Hardly your own country, darling. Think how much worse it's been for Portuguese people who have no other home. There've been an awful lot stranded.'

'Well, they were horrid at passports. Instead of the usual polite smile and then you're through, they looked at us highly suspicious and pretty hostile. It's like the Portuguese have really changed.'

'Well, the officials have. We've got to face up to it, a lot of the people one used to deal with and recognise have either fled the country or lost their jobs. No one's really quite sure what's going on, so I suppose everyone's a bit nervous.'

'Oh dear,' said Maysie, 'I hope Santa Felicia's still the same… Good Lord!' she broke off as they whisked by a group of normally spotless white-washed cottages newly daubed in red paint. 'Is graffiti allowed now? Not a very good boost for tourism,' she wrinkled up her nose as they passed a mammoth hammer and sickle, incongruously painted the wrong way round. 'I thought you said the country had gone democratic, that looked strictly Marxist to me.'

'Democracy means everyone has to be allowed to express their own views,' said her mother. 'Unfortunately, it seems rather to have gone to everyone's heads and defacing the countryside has become a sign of liberty. I suppose after years of not being allowed to say a word, you can't really blame them,' she added glibly. She was not going to tell her daughter that there were already rumours of a Communist take-over in high places, and those who had shared in the jubilation of the coup, were now concerned that Cuba and Russia were much more involved than anyone had guessed. Such suspicions were only at the murmuring stage, but the sight of so many Communist signs and slogans littering the coast, was hardly destined to raise spirits. A pity, she thought, on such a perfect spring day.

'Well, I think it's beastly,' said Maysie settling back into the doubtful springs of the beach-buggy's only passenger seat. 'Goodness, what a lot has happened since I left! Catalina and Buster! Who would have imagined they'd ever really do it! And what timing! Do you think Catalina – being Portuguese – had an inkling there was going to be a coup?'

'No, I really don't,' said Johanna. 'Even those with their ears close to the ground were taken by surprise. Poor old Fonseca's had the boot. His family have all gone to the Azores, they felt so unsafe in the aftermath. Besides, Catalina wasn't a very political animal. You know her, darling, her life revolved round clothes, parties and social life. Even her lovely boat never got used very much.'

'Of course I knew they were having it *off*,' pronounced Maysie. 'Only I never thought she'd run away with him. Such a provincial sort of man – I thought she had better taste! I thought she'd just keep him dangling on her sleeve, and from time to time indulge in a quick roll in the sand.'

'You make it sound most uncomfortable, darling,' said her mother.

'And what's happened to Leah – that's what I'd like to know? No one's mentioned a word about her.'

'I'll tell you about that when we get home,' Johanna's face clouded visibly and for once Maysie had the sense to realise that for the moment, this subject was taboo.

They had turned off the N125 and the sign to Santa Felicia loomed ahead. 'You know I think I'd like to get a job, Mummy dear,' said Maysie. 'Things have come to a bit of a halt in London and I wouldn't say 'no' to something amusing in the sun.'

Johanna looked curiously at her daughter. 'I wondered why you'd chosen to come back so soon. Does that mean your money's running out? I thought you got well paid for the Vogue job.'

'Oh, Mummy, I did – but you know London. It costs money just to breathe! Besides I found someone who was prepared to rent my flat for double what I pay, and I thought it would be worth having a change of lifestyle for a time, whilst I...'

'...whilst you live free at your mother's, is that it?'

She blushed again and was about to make a swift retort, when Johanna said, 'I doubt if you'll find any jobs in the Algarve this summer. Since the coup, tourism has taken a knock and if anyone's to get jobs, it will be the *retornados* I imagine.'

'The *who*?'

'The people who'll shortly be flooding out of the African colonies and other outposts of the empire. General Spinola is determined they should be looked after before all else, and they'll be hungry and needing work. In any case, the new authorities are no longer so thrilled about the Brits, Germans and Scandinavians running all the touristic things down here. Portugal's now about the *povo* and they come way ahead of us ex-pats.'

'God...so things really have changed!'

'Hmm... quite a bit. No matter! You can help me in the boutique if you like, in return for your board and lodging.'

'Mummy!'

'I can't afford to pay you a salary, darling. I had quite a lot of money on the Portuguese stock exchange and with that frozen, I have to be really careful. Also, with tourism so shaky, the shop is bound to suffer. You'll have to pull your weight for once.'

Her enthusiasm already dampened, Maysie looked around her at the familiar landmarks as they drove through the town square. There was more writing on the walls, and even the petrol pumps by the café had received their fair share of daubing. 'What does CDS stand for?' she asked.

'*Partido Centro Democrático*,' replied Johanna, 'they're fairly conservative, about the only ones – similar to the Christian Democrats in Germany.'

'And PS?'

'*Partido Socialista* – they're middle to left, similar to the left of our Labour party.

'Well that'll be the end of Portugal – if they are,' said Maysie, 'sounds the same to me. I suppose PCP is Communist something?'

'Yes, darling, *Partido Comunista Português*.'

'Charming!'

'Oh don't *you* start!' said Johanna and there was an unusual frost to her voice – a rare thing indeed.

It was only after they had got home and Maysie had unpacked, that the subject of Leah was broached again. Jacqueline van der Stel had descended on them and stayed for a snack.

Maysie was relieved by the intervention. Her mother was decidedly edgy, she felt and she wondered if it was a mistake to return.

'Have you heard any more from the Murrays in New York?' Jacqueline was asking and it was obvious to Maysie they had been discussing Leah. She sat quietly, all ears.

'Yes, Wally rang me last night. It appears she's a little better.'

'Thank God for that. Do they know when she'll be able to fly back?'

'Not yet. As soon as they do, he'll ring again.'

'It's awful,' said Jacqueline, 'to think we treated the whole thing as a joke – Catalina and Buster, I mean – and none of us very sympathetic. Remember that time she passed out at Manolo's? We should have realised then she was suffering and in need of real help.'

'I could kick myself,' said Johanna. 'We were all thoroughly thoughtless.'

'I wish you wouldn't keep saying that Joey. If anyone's to blame, it's Howard.'

'No, he thought I'd taken charge at this end. I was the one who informed him about Buster and at the same time took Jock under my wing. He also knew I'd instigated further searches at the frontiers through my – er – connections... whilst they went on their man-hunt. Of course I should have made it my business to find out where Leah was too and tell her what was happening, but I never thought. For her to find out the truth in that awful, terrible way – on the back of an apparently innocent postcard – almost tipped her over the edge. She was there in the Murrays' apartment on her own at the time – at her most vulnerable and completely unprepared.

'But I thought she'd found out most of it when she went to the Bank.'

'She found out about her money, but she did not know for sure Buster had vanished – even though she suspected. Neither had she allowed herself to believe her best friend had gone with him. I think she hoped he'd gone off on a tangent of his own or met some fellow American who'd taken his fancy – but that it would all fizzle out. The point was she trusted Catalina – even if she didn't trust Buster. So to have it all presented like that – in black and white as it were – from the perpetrator of all her grief, must have been terrible. '

'And she really had no idea?' asked Jacqueline thoughtfully.

'It seems not,' said Johanna.

'But I still say Howard should have rung her first – or cabled her at least. He knew where she was – you didn't.'

'I think he was so preoccupied ...' she swallowed hard, 'it just didn't occur.'

'And you had Jock on your hands,' said Jacqueline, 'You couldn't be expected to do everything, don't you agree Maysie?'

'I hardly know anything,' said that young female self-righteously. 'Mummy hasn't told me. I'm only vaguely beginning to grasp the bare bones of the situation now.'

'After all,' went on Jacqueline, 'Howard was Leah's lifelong friend. Poor Joey,' she put an affectionate arm round the older woman's shoulder, 'don't blame yourself – you never had much time for Leah anyway.'

'That's the problem,' said Johanna, 'And I was a fool. A thoughtless fool, in every respect. I assumed ... and Howard assumed ... she had got wind of it. We didn't care enough to think it through. If only we'd all stopped to *think*.'

'Oh stop saying that! It's just one of those unfortunate mistakes, Catalina and Buster are the real villains here. What can have possessed them?'

'Greed, lust – that's probably enough,' said Johanna.

'But to take all that stuff!' expostulated Jacqueline, 'I'm amazed they had the nerve. It must have taken a whole heap of planning.'

'I think that's what's upset Leah the most,' said Johanna. 'The fact that her best friend didn't just run off with her husband and her money, but that they plotted and then desecrated her home as well.'

'Is that why Howard and Benjie are taking so long to come back?' said Jacqueline.

'I expect so,' said Johanna, flushing a little. 'They're obviously anxious to find out where their possessions have gone as well as helping Jock find Katy.'

'Will someone please put me in the picture,' came a plaintive cry. Maysie was fed up with being excluded and whilst her mother left the room to make coffee, she couldn't wait to plague Jacqueline with questions.

For the first time in her life, Johanna was feeling seriously depressed. She had never imagined that someone else's troubles could weigh so heavily. Even when one of her greatest admirers – a fellow actor – had died of lung cancer, she had managed to stay up-beat – convincing herself that these things happened in life and what must be, must be. She had been brought up in the school of Stiff Upper Lip where – no matter what – the show must go on.

But this was different. The planned elopement with its devious ramifications, the stealing of Jock's little daughter, the rapid way in which Portugal was changing in the aftermath of the revolution, and now the arrival of her curious daughter, was all getting to her. She disliked too the fact she had lied to Howard. Granted, it had had the desired effect and kept the two Boys in Spain, long after they could have come home … but to what end? So far there'd been no sightings of the runaway trio and the longer the Boys remained away, the longer she had to keep up the pretence. How would she explain that she had thought all their things had been stolen, when quite obviously they were still safely there? Her only consolation was they would soon be home and she would simply plead ignorance. But would they be convinced?

It was different for Jock. The longer the Boys remained in Spain, the more his hopes were kept alive. Nevertheless, even those were beginning to fade. If nothing turned up soon, he would soon go demented. He spent half his life on the telephone, other times driving around the Algarve, had made a couple of trips to Lisbon – all to no avail. In between he wanted to meet for a coffee, have dinner together, unload generally. Since he was now firmly on the wagon, she hated herself for beginning to thinking him a tie she could do without, even a bore. Jock with the booze was interesting; Jock without, frustrated and grief-stricken, was not. Apart from this, she feared his dependency. If there was anything in life that Johanna prized above all else … it was her freedom. It was bad enough dealing with her own daughter; to have Jock on her heels tagging along for comfort and support, was more than she could bear – but again, she felt guilty for thinking like this.

As she laid the coffee tray, she switched on the radio. It was permanently tuned to the World Service and the situation in Portugal figured constantly as the main topic. Rarely mentioned before the Revolution, one might be forgiven for thinking the country didn't exist – as far as the BBC were concerned. She hoped tonight the news of the escalating civil war in Angola and Mozambique might be explained a little better. Where on earth were all these fleeing refugees going to be housed? They were already coming in by the boat-load. She had visions of the bigger houses in the land being requisitioned and felt glad the Algarve was a long way from Lisbon. Perhaps Amerigo would ring and give her some news. She seemed to need his reassurances every day now – in her own way she was getting as dependent as Jock. She liked herself for this even less.

'You mean to say the first Leah knew of everything was when she received Catalina's postcard?' said Maysie, enjoying the excitement of the scandal.

'Yes,' Jacqueline was nodding vigorously, 'she'd trusted her – don't forget. We may have had our suspicions, but clearly Leah had no idea. It was a huge shock.'

'Then she must have been blind!' said Maysie contemptuously.

'Love usually is blind,' said her mother, putting the tray down between them.

'Yes, but she must have guessed something – especially after her visit to the bank.'

'Apparently not,' said Jacqueline, sweeping her dark hair back from her pretty forehead. 'She knew Catalina was voluptuous, a flirt and all that, but she truly believed she was a friend. An exceptionally loyal and adoring friend. Don't you remember how Catalina was always sucking up to her? That girls' lunch party was typical – she always had a special smile, a secret word or two for Leah.'

'What a snake!' said Maysie, 'but surely Leah saw the effect she had on Buster? That stood out a mile.'

'Leah knew he admired her, but again – she trusted them both. She basically encouraged the friendship, she thought Catalina with her sophisticated ways was good for Buster.'

'How naïve can you get? I always reckoned she was a bad one though,' said Maysie.

'Well I didn't,' said Johanna, 'and I used to think I was a good judge of character. Oh, I know Catalina was naughty, cunning and extravagant, but she had good points too. I never dreamed she could actually carry out something like this. To tell you the truth, I still can't understand it. I could have sworn she was still madly in love with Jock.'

Maysie snorted. 'Now you're just being sentimental, Mummy. How could she be in love with Jock to do what's she's done? Pinch his child and then go off with another man – get real!'

'I know, I know. It doesn't make sense. Even so, I could have sworn Catalina McKay was, is, and probably always will be, in love with her husband.'

'Well, she's a funny way of showing it,' said Maysie. 'What else has happened?'

'Apparently there was a second postcard a few days later. That one came from Spain – somewhere in the interior that no one's ever heard of! That's been the main reason for the Boys continuing to search.'

'So they did get through!'

'No one's quite sure when though,' said Jacqueline. ' It was dated after the 25th April, but the fact that no one's seen sight nor sound, and there's no record of their car registration since your – er – mum's friend's had people checking at the frontiers – it seems they may have got away before the Revolution broke.'

'That's where they had so much luck,' said Johanna. 'They raided the house and took little Katy on the evening of the 24th, the coup began on the morning of the 25th, but some of the borders did not close until much later on in the day. It's very likely they got out, with the furniture in tow, just before that happened. This all points to their having left the country at a fairly southern location – otherwise they would not have made it in time. Then they'd have gone flat out into some obscure rural location with a head start on any vehicle that might have been following – Jock for instance! They might never even have realised at that point they had left their country in a state of Revolution behind them. They'd have been in such a hurry to get out.'

'Crikey,' said Maysie, 'the luck of the devil. I wonder if they're still in Spain?'

'Could be,' said Johanna, 'but it would be like looking for a needle in a haystack. My bet is they may eventually head up for France, somewhere in the Basque country would be a good place, or around Marseilles – a favourite hideout for criminals!'

'But it could be anywhere, couldn't it?' said Maysie, speculatively. 'Who's to stop them going anywhere in the world?'

'That's just it!' said her mother, 'now you can see what a hopeless situation it is. Poor, poor Jock. He just doesn't know where to go from here.'

42

*T*he crossing over the River Guadiana back to Portugal was a sombre occasion compared to their earlier embarkation. Originally, they had planned to take the land route from Badajoz and south through the Alentejo, but reports of demonstrations by Portuguese farm workers sounded so alarming, it seemed prudent to return home via Huelva. At least they knew the way.

Nothing prepared them for the queues at Ayamonte docks. It seemed the world and his brother was returning to Portugal and already a long line had gathered. They were nearly all Portuguese nationals, some of mixed race and a few Spanish. Apart from one very blond family who might have been Scandinavian, there were no obvious tourists in sight and this, not so long after Easter seemed odd indeed. The ferries were small and could only take fifteen or so vehicles at a time so it was doubtful they would make the first one. To pass the time, they started up a conversation with the blond family who turned out to be German, living further down the coast at Lagos. If Howard had hoped to have his spirits raised by some up-to-date information about the state of their adopted country, he was in for a disappointment.

'Things are looking tough,' said Dieter, the father. 'We've just come over to Spain for the day to buy some provisions. The shops around us are running out of imported goods, things like decent coffee, tins of fruit, chocolate, tobacco, and prices already are soaring. Now, we wish we hadn't bothered. Apparently, Customs are taking everyone's car apart on the other side and I hate that level of officaldom. That's why we left Germany! It just isn't worth the hassle.'

Howard and Benjie looked at each other and their hearts sank. The first and second ferries came and went – crowded to the brim – but finally, after what seemed interminable hours, they squeezed themselves into the queue for the fourth, and purchased their ticket. Unsmiling men were beckoning them aboard. Nervously, Benjie manoeuvred the small car up the noisy ramp, soon to be packed in like sardines. Howard's mood wasn't helped by the fact he almost got stuck climbing out. A grim-faced bosun' came to tell them they were holding up the boat and to hasten quickly to the passenger lounge.

The galley was packed. As well as car owners, dozens of foot passengers were coming aboard in work-clothes and overalls, whether from farm or factory, it was hard to tell. There were families with very old in tow, others with very young – there was much wailing and little laughter. Most looked tense and no-one made eye contact. Perched on a hard wooden seat Benjie worried about their liner. The extended trip through Spain had used up all their travellers' cheques and they were low in cash. What if an outrageous amount of duty was slapped on and they couldn't pay it when they finally got there? They had been so busy looking for Buster, they hadn't given it much thought and now it was too late to ditch the wretched thing.

Things were not going their way at all and the atmosphere on the boat itself seemed in such contrast to their outward voyage, they were filled with dread. It felt as though everyone had something to hide, including them.

The moment they disembarked, they were into another queue. Two Portuguese cars at the front were taken apart. Documents were checked repeatedly and a heated exchange took place. Finally a small van was allowed to proceed, a smart BMW held to one side. Next it was the Germans. To everyone's surprise they were waved through swiftly, coffee, tins of *pâté* and asparagus, Spanish cigarettes and all! 'It helps to have kids,' said Howard morosely as Dieter swept off, a hand of triumph waving back at them. With only one Portuguese car and a Spanish now ahead of them, they became more apprehensive by the moment. Both were being thoroughly scrutinised and a lengthy exchange and examination of papers was happening all over again. Another hour passed. Finally it was their turn.

'*Americanos*,' sniffed the Customs officer, who looked new at the job as he peered through their passports which had been duly stamped, 'Anything to declare?'

They had decided to point out the liner rather than risk being handcuffed for conspiracy to smuggle but the man looked disappointed. 'Camping!' he said in a tone of dismissal as Benjie obligingly pointed it out on the floor. Clearly he had no idea what he was looking at and without further ado, he nodded them through. It was almost an anticlimax. 'It seems they're only interested in their own people,' said Howard, wiping his brow with a large spotted handkerchief. 'And how on earth would you camp with that! Did he think it was a ground sheet?'

'More likely a marquee,' said Benjie, 'but let's not hang about to argue the point!'

He put his foot down and they were off, narrowly missing a mule and cart on the long dusty road that would lead them west. 'You'd think they were bothering more about who was leaving the country, rather than coming in. I wonder why they were so hard on the BMW?'

'Well if this is a people's revolution, that should be fairly obvious,' said Howard.

'But then why so easy on us and the Germans?'

'Because we bring money into the country, you dolt. They may resent us, but they need us.'

They drove on. Benjie's eyes were smarting with all the driving over the past several days, and his shirt stuck to his back. The afternoon was hot and hanging about at frontiers had not helped. 'Well, it's a mighty relief to get through. All I can think about is getting home and having a shower…but I'm dreading it as well.'

'We agreed not to talk about that,' said Howard shortly. 'It may not be as bad as everyone makes out, but if it is – I shan't rest until I've retrieved every single piece that I've lost. Buster must know that. I'll seek him out to the ends of the earth.'

'As long as I don't have to drive through Spain again,' said Benjie. 'I've never enjoyed myself less. All those mountain passes, those hidden villages and hairpin bends! Looking for petrol stations that don't exist… how they manage for gas in these parts, I shall never know! After all that driving, we only ever did find five – apart from those in the city of course.'

'You'd have liked it under normal circumstances,' said Howard. 'The scenery was awesome and the people quite helpful on the whole.'

'Except near the border,' said Benjie. 'I don't think they believed us at Rosal de la Frontera and they were positively hostile at Badajoz.'

'Well, they weren't getting much support from the police. One side was looking for escaping Fascists and one side nervous about harbouring them. As that ghastly Blair guy pointed out, they might share political sympathies but Franco would not want the embarassment. Did you see the looks of contempt when we asked about Katy and her blonde hair? Stuff the blondes, was the attitude, we're more interested in brunettes at the moment.'

'So you're saying it's all been a waste of time!' said Benjie. 'Well, really! You might have told me. My eyes feel like grit and I could have done without half that driving.'

'I didn't care for it myself,' said Howard, 'but we had to try! The whole thing's been a complete nightmare. Perhaps there'll be more clues when we get home. Johanna said there was a postcard waiting for us – from Spain it seems – to make us feel thoroughly useless.'

'But why should they do that?' said Benjie. 'I mean why give away where they've been?'

'God knows,' said Howard, 'unless they think that'll make us believe they're stopping there.'

'You could equally argue it would show us they had passed through?'

There was a silence. '*I* know!' Howard suddenly sat up and thumped the dashboard hard. 'What if they'd decided to stay in Portugal, but crossed the border to post a card just to throw us off scent? Now wouldn't that be the clever thing to do, and let's face it – Buster's not short of a brain or two when it comes to going in and out of countries? I well remember how he operated in the antiques business. Canny and devious to a fault!'

'Well, there's a thought,' said Benjie. 'But if that's the case, we might as well give up. This revolution business has certainly put a spanner in the works and until that settles down, I just can't see how we can get anywhere with the authorities.'

They settled back into gloomy silence as the long flat marshland gradually gave way to cultivated fields and pasture with cattle grazing. 'Oh no!' groaned Howard, as they passed over a small whitewashed bridge. 'Did you see that? Writing on the wall! Things have changed around here, no one warned us of this!'

They were approaching a hamlet. All around slogans appeared – on garden walls, buildings, even a telephone kiosk. Red paint, black paint – some carefully written, others scrawled; familiar landmarks despoiled. A moment later, Howard clutched his sleeve. Fighting lack of sleep, Benjie almost hit a parked taxi, 'Hey, steady on,' he protested.

'You don't know what I've just read – stop the car. Look back!' Howard was pointing desperately to a long church wall with the usual whitewash, plus the addition of well defined lettering. '*Trabalhadores portugueses não querem mais exploracão de consórcios americanos! O Algarve para o povo!*'

'I get the last bit, what's the rest all about?' said Benjie, rubbing his eyes and longing for some food.

'Don't you understand anything?' said Howard, 'it's quite pernicious. It says the Portuguese worker wishes no more exploration from US firms. That means they're getting anti-American. I don't like the sound of this at all.'

They passed on and caught sight of their first hammer and sickle. One could hardly miss it – it stood out in white and red right across the centre of the tarmac. Underneath was 'PCP'.

Howard tutted as they drove over it. 'I don't think this bodes well, Benjie. I wish Johanna had warned us. She tried to make out everything was fine... ' *don't worry darlings! – everyone's just so-o-o excited at their first touch of democracy!*' he gave a fair imitation of Johanna's cut glass English and lapsed into gloomy silence.

Benjie's eyelids were getting heavier and heavier. 'I need a slash,' he said. 'Can we stop for a coffee? I don't think I can drive much further.'

'OK. We'll stop at the next village. I wouldn't mind one of those delicious little Portuguese pastries. With all these nasty shocks, one has to keep up the blood sugar.'

They stopped finally in the market town of São Bras de Alportel. There were several cafés on either side of the main street, so they parked and looked about. Everywhere seemed full and there wasn't a foreigner in sight. Feeling uncomfortable, they strolled into the town square, hoping to see a tourist or two – something they had always taken for granted in this, *their* Algarve. Under a bright awning, freshly painted tables and chairs stood empty in the late afternoon sunshine. There was also a postcard stand to one side. This looked more promising so they went in to order.

The bar was packed. There were no other foreigners and no women either. Everyone turned to stare as though they'd descended from another planet. Men and youths were congregated everywhere, talking in small groups, earnest and gesticulating. As Howard and Benjie approached the counter, a sudden hush fell over the crowd. Every eye was upon them. Benjie made his escape into the lavatories at the back, Howard was left to order coffee.

'*Dois cafés, faz favor,*' he said wishing his Portuguese accent was not so abysmal, and he pointed to a plate of custard tarts under a glass cover. '*E dois destes!*' The man scribbled it down on a pad as Howard indicated an outside table where they would sit. Anything must be better than eating and drinking amongst this motley crowd.

The surly looking bar tender nodded and Howard hesitated, unsure whether he was supposed to go or carry it out himself. How different this town seemed from the multi-cultural Santa Felicia with its English speaking barmen and waiters, always ready with a lively quip and friendly grin. Here, he felt something menacing in the air. The men seemed rough and darkly brooding, caps pulled low over furrowed brows, a singular lack of welcome in the body-language. Their eyes too were inscrutable, taking in a lot but giving nothing away.

Pulling himself together, he moved back into the sunshine. He wished Benjie would hurry. Some soldiers had settled at the next table, drinking beer and smoking. There was something different about them, thought Howard. Was it a sudden lack of discipline, a carelessness or what? He tried to recall the attire of other soldiers he had seen here in the past, but could not put his finger on it. Did one only notice things when they were wrong? With a rush of recognition, he knew what it was. Never before had he seen a single Portuguese in uniform drinking or smoking in public; not a policeman, not a customs official, not a soldier. Yet here were these five young men, their legs stretched out, leaning back in their chairs, as though they had all the time in the world. There was idle laughter, cards were brought out, a lot of scraping of chairs and re-ordering drinks and somehow – through it all – a complete lack of respect.

It had been the same at the border, as they'd searched the Fiat. A cigarette had drooped from the lower lip of the man who'd examined their liner, spilling everywhere. His long moustache had also drooped, his whole demeanour sloppy. By serving in a new democracy, did it not really matter any more? He remembered the words from his history book – *Laissez-faire* – and shuddered. Was this how it would all turn out in the end – for each one of them?

Benjie reappeared. 'No coffee yet? I'm going to die if I don't have something to keep me going.'

'Well, either die or go and find out what's happened to it.'

Disgruntled, Benjie wandered off. He came back with two large white cups which had slopped half their contents into the saucers. 'It wasn't me,' he said as Howard opened his mouth.

'I was merely wondering where our cakes had gone.'

'Oh, I didn't realise! I'll go back and get them.'

'This coffee's filthy,' said Howard not waiting for his cake and getting up. 'Come on let's get out of here, I don't like the atmosphere at all.' The card-playing soldiers seemed to have lost concentration on their game and now appeared more interested in them. There was jeering and barely concealed laughter, interrupted by the odd hawk and sound of spitting. Howard had gown pink, his glasses misted up and Benjie suddenly thought how vulnerable he looked, despite his stature.

'Oh, all right,' he said, gulping back his coffee, 'but I could have done with that cake.'

He got up and followed his companion making purposefully for the car, parked beyond the other side of the square. There was a shout behind them and the bartender came running out – waving a piece of paper. Benjie had a wild instinct to flee, then stopped himself just in time. 'Oh hell!' he cried, 'we haven't paid the bill!'

'Fool,' said Howard, turning to see half the people from the café spilling into the square to join the fray. Mostly in their late twenties and thirties, he noted for the first time that more than half were dressed in black. Those who didn't, wore black hats or armbands or both. Together with their black hair, dark faces and black moustaches, they might have been a company of Moors, protecting the Alhambra. Again, the instinct to run, but with great presence of mind, Benjie stood his ground and waited for the shouting man to come up to him. 'I'm sorry,' he said in English, forcing a smile and bringing out his wallet. 'I forgot.'

To his surprise, the man half grinned, '*Parlez-vous français?*'

'Uh – *oui, un petit peu,*' Benjie managed to say.

'*C'est bien. Vous me devez quinze escudos.*'

'*Pardonnez-moi, monsieur,*' Benjie pressed a fifty escudo note into his hand. 'Er– *est OK, c'est tout!* – and uh – *guardez le change!*'

Out of the corner of his eye, he saw the café's inmates had already got bored and were trooping back inside. Only the five card-playing soldiers were still watching. 'Er – *obrigado monsieur – pardonnez- moi – encore une fois.*'

'*Merci beaucoup, monsieur,*' the little man gave a bow as they got into the car, then – as though remembering – raised a sturdy hand, clenched tight, '*Vive la revolution!*'

They drove away and did not look round to see if the soldiers had taken up the chorus of that much exploited phrase.

'That could have turned nasty,' said Howard as they rounded the corner and were out of sight. 'I never dreamed I should feel so unwanted in a civilised country.'

'Maybe it's not so civilised at present,' said Benjie, more shaken than he cared to admit. 'Lucky about the French – a lot of them near the border seem to have worked in France. He was really quite OK once he saw the colour of my money. Anyway, I'm sure things will be better once we're in familiar territory again.'

'The way it looks, things are getting worse,' said Howard. They were now heading towards Faro and the slogans were more liberally interspersed and varying in content. There were no more references to *americanos* until they passed the turning to the airport – when Benjie managed to distract his companion to look the other way. Another long epithet had appeared by the roadside, but he was damned if he was going to try to translate it.

Both their hearts were heavy. For the past twenty-four hours, they had studiously avoided mentioning the dreaded homecoming. Now that it loomed so close, it filled them both with foreboding. Benjie glanced across at his passenger. Howard would be sixty in another few years – today he looked a decade older. The face that gave away so little, with its thick-lensed glasses, its rolls of fat hiding the lines – little marks of character – seemed suddenly stripped. The sun came out from behind a cloud and lit up the smooth plump flesh exposing a facade that was as weak and helpless as a baby. In that moment, Benjie felt infinitely superior. In that moment, he himself had grown in stature, taken command. For Howard, he no longer felt awe – just a deep sensation of pity.

Driving through Santa Felicia, they were relieved to note a smattering of tourists. Nothing like the usual crowds after Easter, but at least some hardy souls. Several shops had been shuttered up, some with boarding and to Howard's horror, he spotted a red flag proclaiming that the old stationers' shop had become the town's new headquarters for the Communist Party. A few doors up, another red banner furled and unfurled in the breeze – this pronounced the office of the Socialist Party. They were both now closed for the night. 'My goodness,' said Howard, as he worried at his hands. 'Wasn't that a shoe shop? Is this the same town?'

There was no one they knew out there on the streets, but the Anchor Bar was still there and the door stood open. Crowds of men hogged the street corners, there was an absence of local women and they passed more soldiers. These ones were dressed in combat gear as they lounged outside an ice-cream shop eyeing the traffic. A bright beach buggy flashed by on the other side of the square. 'That was Johanna,' said Benjie, 'thank God for one familiar sight at least!'

They travelled the last two kilometres to their villa in silence. Apprehension lay heavy between them as they turned away from the coast road to climb the hill. There was no one about on the swimming-pool site which looked much the same as before, but the house was there all right. Not a trace of red paint anywhere! This had been Howard's greatest fear, he later confessed to Benjie, and he breathed a small sigh of relief.

They'd hardly got out of the car, when the door flew open and Maria came swiftly to meet them. She was preceded by Mungo who rushed toward them – then slunk away disappointed. Clearly, he'd been looking for Buster. To his surprise, Howard found himself hugging the woman. She promptly burst into tears and stood there, unashamed of her emotion, making helpless gestures with her hands.

Howard felt a lump in his throat. He was afraid to go indoors. 'Go in, Benjie,' he said. 'Go in there, then come out and tell me the worst. I'm real nervous. I can't do it.'

It was the first time he had ever admitted such weakness. Again, Benjie felt flushed with a new sense of command. Howard really needed him. The worm had turned. Elated, he pushed open the door and walked in. He was surprised to find the dog at his heels.

He was gone about ten minutes. Maria stayed with Howard who shuffled aimlessly round the gravelly parking lot. He could not bring himself to wander onto the lawn or notice the buddleia which had suddenly burst forth in their absence, even to cross onto the terrace. Maria's tears had abated and she was trying to tell him about the geese, the cat, the dog – where had it gone? – all of which were fine. She wanted him to know she'd held the fort, and done her best – under the circumstances. It had not been easy.

Howard squeezed her arm. It was all beyond words. He must simply hold himself together a few more minutes and wait.

Benjie came out again. There was a weak smile on his face. Howard looked at him in wonder, the dog was close at his heels and both of them looked relieved.

'You won't believe it, Howard! None of our stuff's been *touched*! Not a single piece –at least, not as far as I can see. It's simply fantastic! Johanna obviously got it wrong – didn't know what belonged to whom – why should she? But I tell you it's all there – all our stuff is safe. I can't see one thing missing! It all looks simply ghastly of course, but that's because everything's just been *left*! Like, he's removed all their pieces and ours are stuck there, abandoned but intact. Oh – and you'll never guess, old friend! Such a *very* strange thing … the holly girl's back!'

Whilst Benjie would always remember that initial step inside the ravished house with a sense of raw excitement – an almost sensual anticipation of his new status in their lives – for Howard there was nothing but outrage. Nothing would ever blot out the memory of his own shock. The horrendous visual impact – when all they had worked for, all he had dreamed of, all they had achieved together, had been mutilated in such a way – was soul-destroying. All that which had been held so dear, so balanced, so perfect, had been swept away – in one foul, selfish act. The feeling of waste seeped into him with all the relentlessness of a tidal wave.

Quite still, he stood in the once great, grand *sala*, taking it all in. For once his hands were quiet at his sides, the round vacant face which so rarely showed emotion, crumpled and wobbling with an uncontrollable grief. Benjie was at his side, barely able to conceal his own excitement. He moved from foot to foot, waiting with ill-disguised impatience for his companion to recover. 'I tell you, it's not too bad, Howard. It only seems bad because there are so many gaps – but we can soon rebalance it, fill the spaces up. In some ways, I can't help feeling we may even make it... er ...nicer. I sometimes felt it almost too much before, overcrowded...you know... personally, I always thought–'

'Be quiet, will you?' the softly spoken words had more effect than if he'd been told to go to hell. Momentarily taken aback, Benjie abated his chatter and found solace in a wet black nose whose owner now clung to his side.

After an eternity, Howard said, 'You realise this house will never, ever, be the same again? It was conceived and built as a dream. A dream house. A dream villa. But the foundations were clouds instead of concrete. The clouds have burst, the rain has fallen, the house has collapsed like a pack of cards.' He turned away and went outside.

Benjie went after him – but not too hurriedly. Howard was leaning against the roof of their car, his head buried in his arms. Benjie watched, learning anew all the time. When at last Howard raised his great walrus head, Benjie said, 'Our bedrooms are just the same – absolutely intact.'

Howard nodded. 'I daresay. Look – er – I need to be alone for a bit. You go and unpack.'

He wandered off up the headland, stumbling a little in his city shoes over the rocks and tufts of wild thrift. The geese set up a loud cackle as he reached the wild bit, but he plodded on, puffing now, but relentless in his desire to put distance between him and the house. Benjie watched him go and noted the resolute set of the shoulders. There was something extraordinarily lonely about the figure as he disappeared from sight.

He waited a moment longer, then turned to unload the car. He could do with a willing pair of hands. 'Maria!' he called. There was a new, imperious ring to his voice.

Katy woke up crying. She put her fingers to her eyes and tried to block the tears. Mama would be cross if she woke her again. It had happened too many times now. If only Papa was there. He would not have minded. He would have held her 'til the crying went away. The more she thought of Papa, the more the tears came. It was all so difficult.

She reached out in the dark for Panda and immediately felt better. Dear Panda – at least he was always there. She hugged him and told him everything would be all right. Poor Panda! So often, he was sad now too. Perhaps if she told him a story – ever so quietly – they would both feel better. She began in the way Papa had taught her, 'Once upon a time ...' and whispered into his ragged ear under the blankets, so that no one should hear except Panda. She simply must not wake Mama again, neither would it do for Uncle Buster to hear her story. It was for Panda's ears only.

'Once upon a time,' she began again, 'there were three bears – a big bear, a middle-size bear and a baby bear. They were a family!'

After a few moments, she stopped. 'Panda!' she said fiercely, 'You're not listening. Please be a good boy and listen to me. Then you won't be frightened any more!'

But Panda trembled against her chest and she knew it was no good going on. She stroked his threadbare head and pressed his nose against her cheek. Button-cold, but comforting. Panda always understood, no matter what. And he never scolded her...or she him. At least they had each other.

She tried to picture Papa now. Papa as she'd last seen him, when she'd sat on his knee and he'd squeezed her – much as she was squeezing Panda now. He had been sad that evening, her father. Did he know then he was going to be so ill? Poor Papa! If only she could go to him now and help. But Mama had said no. He was being well looked after. Besides, Papa had some illness she might catch.

She had asked what it was. Was it measles? A boy at school had had that last term. 'Like measles...' Mama had said, only it wasn't. It was something worse. Much worse! Katy could not imagine anything worse than measles, the boy had been off sick a long time. And when he came back they said he had been very ill. Poor Papa to have caught something worse than measles. And in Spain too – not in Portugal! That was something Katy could not quite understand.

They had been going to go to Spain – leaving Portugal – on their way to meet up with Papa, Mama had said, for the holiday she'd been promised.

Then something happened. Uncle Buster had been made to stop the car. They had had to get out, show their passports. Then back into the car, it had all been quite quick. Uncle Buster had gone very white and Mama had grown very excited and argued with some men in Portuguese. Fast Portuguese which even Katy found hard to understand. Such long words and words she'd never heard of! Mama had sounded upset, very upset, almost shouting. It was difficult to remember all she'd said to the men and all they'd said to her. But Katy remembered what they looked like. That was very clear.

They were soldiers and they all held big guns, slung across their shoulders over a green coloured uniform. They seemed cheerful – 'polite and really quite helpful...' Mama had said later to Uncle Buster. One of them gave Katy a stick of chewing-gum and grinned at her in a friendly way but later Mama had made her throw it away. The soldiers insisted they all turn round in the car and travel back along the road they had just come. Uncle Buster had been furious. She remembered noticing the tips of his ears had gone quite white. Like so many other things on that journey, it stuck out as odd...particularly when the back of his neck was so red.

Mama had put out a hand out to him then – on his leg – like she seemed to do a lot these days. She had told him it would be all right. 'We shall think of something else,' she said. 'All is not lost.'

Katy had wondered what they could have lost and worried for her. She could tell that despite all she said, her mother was very upset because she kept tossing back her head in that way of hers, then catching at the hair which fell down her shoulders, and winding it round and round her fingers. Katy knew that was never a good sign.

After that, she could not really remember. She had cried once because Mama had said they would not be meeting Papa after all that day. When she had asked why not, Mama had blamed the soldiers. When she couldn't help herself and asked again, Uncle Buster became cross and told her not to upset Mama. It had been so muddling – she had never meant to upset Mama. She was just worried about when they would see Papa – for Mama's sake as well as hers.

The journey after that had seemed endless. She thought it was days, but perhaps it wasn't, for night never came. Just sun and more sun and she had grown sticky and tired. A lot of the road was the same as they'd driven down before. It twisted and turned and there were mountains on every side. Eventually they passed by a place they'd stopped at much earlier to have breakfast but she wasn't sure if that was yesterday or today. She would have liked to stop there again, but she heard Uncle Buster telling her mother 'no way – that would be a big mistake.' He said someone might remember them. There was an argument then and Mama gave her lemonade and a chocolate biscuit which melted in her hand and somehow got all over her trousers.

At one point, they got out to wash their faces in a brook and Mama bathed her face with her own hanky. She was made to go to the loo behind a bush and didn't mind that but she did mind getting back into the car. And she did mind that Uncle Buster drove so fast and sometimes on the corners, she felt quite sick. Again, she must have slept and when she awoke she felt a little better. Everything around them looked very green and the grey granite of the mountains had been left behind. If she hadn't been so miserable about Papa, she might even have enjoyed this part of the trip. There were bands playing in town squares and a lot of people about and they heard some marching music – always the same tune – wherever they passed through. Soon there were great trees lining the road; not the Algarve eucalyptus and olive, but oaks and beeches, and other huge trees – like in England. She told Uncle Buster that Papa had taught her their names. He said nothing.

They had stopped at last in a small town full of towers and spires with church bells ringing a welcome in lofty domes. She had almost dropped off to sleep again but the bumps over the cobbled street they were climbing jolted her awake and she opened her eyes to see her mother fling her arms round Uncle Buster and say 'Darling! Let this be our refuge! It's beautiful. Here we shall stay until everything dies down and here we can plan the future. Do you know! I think in the end, the revolution will prove our friend! I feel it in my bones.'

Katy had kept as still as a little mouse while Mama spoke. Somehow she knew it would be wrong to let them know she had heard. Now Uncle Buster was speaking. 'I'd have felt happier in Spain – knowing they couldn't touch us there. But,' he sighed, 'maybe you're right. With the country in turmoil and everyone looking for another car and guessing we made it to the border – who will ever dream we stayed in Portugal all the time!'

He laughed suddenly and soon he was pulling the car up in front of a small white hotel. Suddenly, he leaned across and Katy watched him kiss her mother. Such a strange kiss – long and hard and on the mouth. There was something not quite right for just after, he made a sharp movement and swivelled round in his seat to look at her. Immediately, she clamped her eyes tight shut and there was a strong feeling of guilt – but for once, she knew it wasn't her who'd done wrong. She felt him looking at her for quite a time. Nothing was said, but later when they all got out of the car, he was ever so jolly with her. Only, from then on – she felt a deep misery – somewhere low down in her tummy. Something was very wrong. She could not name it. But it was something to do with Papa – and them being a family.

The couple registered as Mr and Mrs Roache remained in their hotel at the small provincial town of S. Miguel de Figueira until the end of May. During this time, Mr Roache made a number of forays across the Spanish border to procure finance. He would only deal in cash during these troubled times – and was relieved to find the *peseta* was standing up well against the *escudo* – so he actually benefitted on the rate of exchange when there were bills to pay. He also had cards to buy and to post back to Portugal, something he had failed to disclose to his partner who seemed worried about further upsetting those left behind. It must be her Catholic faith struggling to come to the fore, he smiled indulgently to himself. Well, it wouldn't get her very far with him around which was another reason for moving out of here as soon as possible. Too many church bells, shrines and reminders. He made sure they busied themselves with excursions, generally west into rural Portuguese Estramadura, as this seemed the quietest, most underpopulated area to scout for a possible house for rent.

The child, to be known henceforth for purposes of security – 'because of the Revolution darling' – as Katherine Roache, was sent as a temporary pupil to the local school. 'A blonde-haired child in the back of a car is bound to be remembered in these tricky times, best she's out of sight …' insisted Mr Roache and her mother agreed. When Katy remonstrated about a new school and the change of name, her mother explained that people of property were not safe in the country any more. 'By going to this school where no one knows us, you'll be much safer,' she said. 'We don't want you kidnapped, do we?' The little girl had heard enough from the other pupils about people disappearing to believe what she had been told and with a heavy heart, had tried to settle in as best she could under her new *alias*.

On June 2nd, after several enquiries had been made and after much deliberation, a house in the wine-growing region just inland from the medieval isthmus town of Obidos was chosen. This would serve as a suitable base until such time as the couple could reclaim their belongings. The next move would be to South Africa…the Roaches would in the meantime ship out all their goods and chattels, move their money from Spain to Switzerland and start a new life. There would be no more hiding away, no furtive securing of safe houses. They could be themselves there and no one could touch them.

But that was all in the future. And, as part of the Plan, it always had been so – despite the unexpected delays.

The whole country was in a state of upheaval. Foreigners and nationals everywhere were coming and going. Daily, mixed race, black and white refugees from Angola and Mozambique swarmed off boats and planes to swell Lisbon's sweltering pavements with ever increasing numbers of homeless people. Despite the crowded cities, the countryside was partially deserted and there were many homes up for rent. While ducal homes and palaces were being taken over by the workers and many stripped of their contents, other more modest establishments were being let out to new entrepreneurs and local government people. Suddenly, homes which had once earned valuable income for their propertied landlords could be had for a peppercorn rent and a new class of tenant was springing up.

Around the coast at glamorous Cascais and Sintra the old order and the wealthier ex-pats clung on, but the countryside was for the *povo*. Thus no one raised too many eyebrows when a modestly dressed woman from Oporto and her quiet American husband and child moved into the stone-built farmhouse at the end of one quiet village. The incomers had been at great pains to make sure there were no other *estrangeiros* in the vicinity and word had spread around that the man was a writer and they needed peace. Despite the expensive car, their neighbours in the village were reassured of the couple's sympathies with their cause. The woman had said as much at the school gate and again in the shop. Attractive, under the head scarf she always wore and obviously well educated, she wore a secret smile around her lips and there was a definite twinkle in her eye. Quite unlike their local landlords, she appeared to have no airs and graces.

The old Portuguese family who owned *Quinta da Cruz* were thankful about the let. Many similar houses in the district had already been closed up, their friends losing out on long established contracts with foreign agents for lucrative summer lets. As they muttered between themselves, they rued the fact that no one, except of course the *retonardos*, was venturing to this part of Portugal from abroad these days. There'd been too much bad publicity. The workers were getting out of hand. And what would become of them all when some left wing colonel in the MFA was already boasting of taking over all five star hotels like the Lisbon Ritz and the Tivoli in which to house the latest wave of refugees? Where would it all end?

43

Early June, 1974

By coincidence, on the same day that the new occupants moved into *Quinta da Cruz*, a pale-eyed, pale-skinned lady with a new auburn rinse in her prematurely greying hair, stepped off a TWA plane at Lisbon airport. Soon she was boarding a half-empty domestic flight to Faro, to be met by a fellow countryman at a quieter than usual airport on Portugal's southern sea-board.

The lady's passport was checked and rechecked by an official in army uniform who stood at the side of the immigration officer in charge. Finally, he gave her a curt nod and said in Portuguese, 'You are permitted to pass, Mrs Bloomfield. Welcome back to a new Portugal.'

She passed through Customs unmolested and came face to face with Howard. He saw a painfully thin, twitchy woman who looked as though she had lost her life-blood itself, let alone everything else. In turn, she saw a heavily overweight man, no longer middle-aged; his colour and general level of unfitness suggesting he might be heading for a cardiac arrest. She also noticed his hands were red raw and the eyes behind the perpetual glasses had a wounded look.

'Where are all the people?' was the first thing she said to him.

He took her two cases. 'We don't get as many tourists these days. It must seem strange to you, but we're gradually getting used to it. I guess they'll all come back in their hordes one day but not ... er ... for now.'

They went out in silence to the car park. So much to talk about, yet so momentous, neither knew where to begin. As the white heat glanced off the concrete and rose up to scorch her eyes, Leah fumbled in her bag. She put on large tortoishell sunglasses which seemed no longer to fit. 'I'd forgotten just how hot it gets,' she said.

They had reached the car and he began to load her cases into the trunk. His movements torpid, he was breathing hard – she had never seen him look so large. Some time way back, she seemed to remember him saying he ate more when he was unhappy. So other people were suffering too ... what a strange old world it was.

He helped her into the passenger seat and seemed to be apologising for the weather. 'This, actually, is exceptional. It's been the same for ten days now, not a breath of wind – just searing heat. It's dried everything in the garden, but don't worry too much – it'll get better.'

'How's the pool?'

'Good, practically finished.'

'So you got the liner out OK?'

'Oh yeah. In the end, that was the least of our worries,' his face was expressionless as they headed slowly out of the airport to be confronted by the first of the anti-American signs. So far she had ignored the daubing. She had read all about it in the papers back home.

'I guess you get used to this sort of thing too,' she said eventually as yet another hammer and sickle loomed ahead.

'Not really,' said Howard, 'but we have to live with it. Most of the Portuguese round us are as horrified as we are … it's the students and out of work that are doing it mainly. Or, er … people with a grudge to bear.'

'How's Maria?'

'She's been a doll. All the time we were stuck in Spain she looked after the place on her own money. Buster had left her with nothing. She fed the geese, the dog and the cat – even filled the fridge for our return home and you know how modestly these people live. She's been so loyal. Carlos I'm afraid has gone, he went up to Lisbon to join in the festivities and never came back.'

'I guess the young people think it exciting.'

'Some, but not all. I was talking to one of Roper's men the other day and he's determined to keep his job and go on as before. I think he's already disillusioned. When they threw half the top bankers into prison, the *povo* – sorry, people – thought there'd be cash rewards for everyone. A few gullible ones even queued up outside the banks for free hand-outs! Of course nothing happened. Now, the price of living's shot up and no one's better off than before. Some are worse. If you kick out the boss, the business may fall.'

'I guess,' was all she said.

He looked across at her. She seemed disinterested. He wondered if her brain had been affected by her break-down and this was the new Leah they would have to live with. A person who spoke in phrases, syllables. Someone without energy, a pale shadow of her former self. And how was she going to manage without money? None of this had been discussed; he had hoped for some explanation in her letters. Would she, could she work? Had she got some scheme arranged as to how she would support her share of the house?

'How's Wally and Melinda?' he said hurriedly, guilty suddenly for having mentioned money quite so soon after her arrival.

'They've been so wonderful,' for the first time there was some animation in her voice. 'I've gotten the feeling they're the only true friends I have in the world.'

'I thought I was one,' Howard sounded hurt.

'I guess Buster's altered all that.'

'What do you mean?'

'Money,' she said. Now it was out! He felt uncomfortable as he felt her glance across at him, unreadable behind the dark glassses. Yet somehow in that moment he became aware that after all, her brain was as quick as ever. Meaningfully, she repeated the word. 'Money … huh? Don't think I didn't sense it coming between us the moment I stepped off that plane.'

He was taken aback. 'Nonsense,' he said unconvincingly. 'We've plenty of time to discuss all that later. The main thing is to see you settled back into the house … and er … to take it from there.'

'No, you know that can't be the case. But I just want you to know, there's no need for you to worry. At this moment, I've a thousand dollars in my purse – a loan from the Murray's – but I mean to get a job immediately and you can rest assured I will take up my responsibilities again as soon as I've gotten myself organised.'

'There's no need for you to talk like this,' Howard was turning off the main road and forcing a note of cheerfulness into his voice. 'No rush for anything. Say!' he tried to change the subject, 'you haven't said much about the aftermath of the coup! Not exactly a pretty sight, is it?'

'I'm sorry,' she shook her head and looked around. 'To tell you the truth it's much as I expected and I'm trying to let it all drift over me. There's nothing we can do – just like there's nothing I can do about my lost stuff, so what's the point of dwelling on it.'

'So you don't mean to pursue Buster?' Howard was incredulous.

'A waste of energy,' said Leah. 'Wally's lawyer – I can't afford one – chased up the bank in Madrid where all the cash was sent. It took days to discover anything, he had to go through a Spanish lawyer, but apparently the account was closed a week after it arrived, and he'd clearly made arrangements to move everything on.'

Howard whistled, 'He doesn't hang about, does he?'

She grimaced, 'He never did when he wanted something.'

'And everything else?'

'It's just as hopeless. Besides, who's to say now what's mine and what's his? Even if there was a decent legal system here at the moment – which clearly there's not – I very much doubt I'd achieve very much … and it would rumble on for years and cost more in legal fees than the whole lot put together.'

'Oh, come now,' said Howard, 'some of your art was seriously valuable.'

'In the right place, at the right time … but here! You don't know Buster, he'll have it smuggled away somewhere and may even now have sold half of it.'

'You seriously think …'

'I seriously think. Please,' she put up a hand. 'I don't really feel strong enough to talk about it at the moment.'

'No, no of course not.' They were approaching the last few bends in the road before entering the square and her next words – coming out in a sudden rush – took him by surprise.

'D'you know, I'm not sure I can bear to show my face here. Should I crouch down? Oh – it's so awful, does everybody know, the Portuguese, the shopkeepers and everyone?'

'Leah – honey,' Howard's gruff voice was kind as he put out a hand to steady her round the last twist in the road, 'I'm sorry to say the revolution rather eclipsed your and our personal tragedies. Scarcely anyone knows, and if they did, I doubt they'd care. Just behave as normal – that's the best advice I can give you. It's the only way you'll survive.'

So she did not hide her head after all, just stared morosely out at a street which was filling up with the usual market bustle, donkeys and carts and a few vans. There were no foreign faces about and none of the usual hire cars squabbling for parking spaces, but otherwise it all looked pretty much the same.

'I don't know how I'm going to manage, Howard,' she said. 'It's facing the other ex-pats that terrifies me – people like Johanna, Jacqueline, Maysie, Gloria – all that social crowd.

In a way, it sounds selfish, but it would help me to see they've had a bad time too – with this revolution I mean. It would put us more on a level – if you see what I mean.'

'Well, there's Jock for a start. He's been crucified!' said Howard, 'and they've all been touched by his plight – Johanna in particular.'

'Sure – but they've not much else to do with their lives…and people like to be needed. But they're hardly going to feel the same about me – and I wouldn't want them to. They probably think I got my just desserts anyway – and blame me for what happened to Jock! Oh my God, it's going to be hard from now on. I don't know if I'm strong enough to cope. Do you realise, Howard – I'll have to start again? It's amazing, isn't it? She laughed. 'Start *again*, Howard! In my forties, when I've worked like stink all my life! Do you think I'm strong enough for that, Howard?'

Leaving the square behind them, they pulled up the last cobbled hill. Soon they were past the fishermen's cottages, past the new villas that had been started, now abandoned on the headland – daubed with graffiti – over some unfinished road with open drains and finally they were round the point and dropping down onto the familiar coast road that would meet up with the bottom of their drive.

They were almost home.

Howard put out his indicator and his hand to turn right. You never knew when some Maserati wasn't steaming up behind ready to chance an over-take, so a double signal was prudent…except – that was pre-revolution – he had momentarily forgotten! He hadn't seen a smart car in weeks. She tugged at his sleeve almost causing him to graze a boulder as he turned in between the dusty cacti.

'Stop here. Just for a moment, Howard. I must talk. I won't be long. Just for a little before we see Benjie. I don't think I can bear to face Benjie before we've talked a bit more.'

With a sigh, he pulled up. Plonk in the middle of their rutted track. He turned to her, 'I've told you to take it easy,' he soothed. 'Take your time…adjust. It's very simple, no one will put demands on you. But by all means talk if it will help.'

'Thank you.' She sat quietly for a moment, then opened her mouth to begin.

But no words came.

After about half-an-hour, she agreed he might proceed. Howard drove a dry-eyed Leah up and onto the sweep of gravel that lay in front of the yellow house on the hill. She had found nothing more to say. All he could think to tell her was – they'd made up a room.

Late August, 1974.

Johanna had invited Jacqueline and Karl to attend Jock McKay's last evening in their midst. She would have liked to ask the Boys too, but then that would have meant asking Leah, and Jock couldn't have stomached that. So in the end four of them sat down to dinner.

She had done her best with the table to jolly it up – almost as though it was someone's birthday – putting out rather more flowers and candles than usual. Anything to distract her from thinking her most interesting friend was about to leave their circle. It was a relief

Maysie was back in London. After a few days of boredom, she had declined the job at her mother's boutique and Johanna had taken on Leah instead. She was first-rate and even did all the accounts.

The business was actually doing rather well. It was one of the few places left that sold imported goods and a new class of purchaser was springing up in the wake of the very wealthy Portuguese who were her former patrons. These newcomers were keen to be in touch with London, rather than Paris or Rome, and eager to be guided. This made it much easier for Johanna to concentrate on fashionable but affordable designs similar to those produced by shops like Biba and Monsoon and it helped that Leah had a flair for knowing which range and just how much and when to order, and when also to move on.

All this left Johanna time to continue with her poetry. She had already received an advance on a book from her agent, which was just as well as she'd caught a serious cold on the *Bourse*. She was amazed how disciplined and time-consuming serious writing had to be and how it consumed her energy. It would be hard to make the deadline that had been set, but at the same time she was determined to do it. She did not really have a choice.

Fortunately, it was most unlikely Maysie would be back to disturb her peace – at least until Christmas. Her daughter's life revolved round the availability of rich, eligible and exciting young men, and as soon as she discovered the Revolution had put paid to her former Portuguese *beaux*, she was on the next plane back to London. Luckily for Johanna, Maysie had become involved with a wine merchant who worked in Mayfair, so all was thankfully quiet on that front.

Now, as she put the last finishing touches to her table, Johanna wondered how badly Jock's imminent departure would affect her. The truth was she would miss the old fox. He had hung around her rather too much after his wife's elopement, not in a romantic way, but simply because he was incredibly lonely. She had watched him go through several stages, first the angry phase, then the self-pitying one – coupled with a more or less successful attempt to give up alcohol – and finally the frustrated one, from which he was still suffering.

Throughout it all, she had done her best to support him, but it had not been easy. She too had gone through crises of confidence which had not been helped by the departure of Amerigo and his family to Brazil. As Portugal leaned more and more towards extreme socialism and those who still had property or business feared a totalitarian regime of Communism which lay just around the corner, they had got out whilst the going was still good. This left Johanna in a vulnerable position and when one day Jock had come to her and talked about returning to Scotland, she felt deeply bereft. It meant the two people she cared most about in the country would shortly be gone.

But she was too much of a trouper to drop her defences – either to the world at large or to Jock. 'I think that's a very sensible decision,' she had said. 'You can't afford the rent here any more, so you might as well live in your own house – even if it is – as you say, falling to pieces around your ears. I'm sure too your picture sales will pick up if you're more available for interviews and press conferences – maybe even radio, you're still a celebrity, you know! You may well find you're in a better position, also, to keep tabs on Katy, hopefully through your solicitors.'

He nodded earnestly. 'That's sort of what I thought too, Johanna. But I can't thank you enough for all you've done for me. The birds have clearly flown…but as you say, with a reliable legal system and a decent Foreign Office at the end of a phone, I've got more chance of locating their whereabouts from home shores, than I have staying on in this place. For me, the spirit's gone out of it.'

She didn't add that it had for her too, but at least she had her work. Now with these thoughts in her mind, she waited for the doorbell to ring and hoped it wouldn't prove too sad an evening.

As usual these days, it was Jacqueline who bounded in first. 'Hi, Joey,' she said, 'Wow! Look at your table! I hope you don't mind, I brought Bombita with me, Karl's still at home filling in some wretched forms for the *camera* but he'll be here shortly. It's just...' she hesitated, '...in these troubled times I don't like walking up the street alone.'

She unleashed the poodle and he sniffed round their legs before settling down on one of Johanna's cream coloured sofas. 'Bombita!' his owner cried, horrified, 'you'd better get off there!'

'Leave him,' said Johanna, 'he may be black but he never leaves a hair, it's the shaggy varieties like collies and retrievers that do the damage. I used to have a little curly poodle myself and may get one again – it can be lonely here and you're right to have a dog.'

Something wistful in her voice made Jacqueline look at her closely. It hadn't occurred to her before just how dependent their friend had become on Jock. 'You'll be sad to see Jock go then, Johanna.'

'I will,' came the short reply. 'But I know it's for the best. Especially for him.'

'And how's the poetry going?'

'Well, actually, and all thanks to Leah. D'you know she could run that shop single-handed? I'm not surprised she's hoping to open up her own business next year. She's such a natural!'

'But you'll miss her – it's given you a real break from all that ordering and fussing about with invoices and stock-taking and the like.'

'It has – and I needed that – to finish my book. But I don't think I could stick it as a writer for too long – too many long hours and too many lonely early mornings. So once the book's published, I'll be ready to go back. I miss the buzz of the shop.'

The bell went again. 'Help yourself to a drink, darling – the white wine's over there,' Johanna called as she moved swiftly towards the door. But McKay had already let himself in. He looked taller, brighter than the last time Jacqueline had seen him and she hoped the evening would be happy and not too introspective.

He was holding a bottle of Moët under his arm and Johanna exclaimed in delight. 'Where did you get that, you sly thing?' she beamed. 'Since my little 'crash' I haven't touched a drop of bubbly, and I don't see much of it appearing in the supermarket these days.'

'Aha!' said McKay, 'it was one of the few things Buster didn't pinch. The Boys gave it to me and said to use it for a special occasion. I guess this is special enough.'

'Rath-*er*,' piped up Jacqueline, disdaining her white wine and disappearing into the kitchen for some champagne flutes.

'Where's Karl?' McKay wanted to know.

'Finishing paperwork,' said his wife. 'It's all so difficult nowadays. Bureaucracy has taken a turn for the worse and the clerks at the town hall – who are actually now the chiefs

– don't have a clue what's going on. Karl thinks his company will *just* about finish their present development, but with great difficulty. Then the whole caboodle's moving across to Spain. Near Cadiz is where the action's going to be for the next ten years at least.'

'Oh, don't say I'm going to lose you too,' said Johanna.

'No fear of that,' said Jacqueline. 'Karl's being left in charge here for the foreseeable future, but eventually we'll probably go back to London.'

The champagne was opened. Even McKay had a glass. 'It's strictly the grape only,' he told them, 'and just one glass. I'm being very careful. The doc says I'm not an alcoholic yet – but I was pretty close to it.'

'But you're going back to the land of the barley,' said Jacqueline.

'Yup, but the barley's not having me. There'll be too much serious stuff in my life on which to concentrate, and fortunately there's no handy little watering hole near where I live, and you know me – I don't like to drink alone.'

'So that's that,' said Johanna briskly, 'and if Karl doesn't turn up soon, we'll eat dinner without him!'

But Karl did come and they settled down, the candles lit, the French doors wide open and the birds still calling from the garden. It was a soft, still evening.

'I'll miss this place,' said McKay, 'it's still one of the most beautiful places in the world.'

'I'll second that,' said his hostess, spooning out beef stroganoff, served with fresh asparagus from her garden on a side plate.

'This is yummy,' said Jacqueline, drizzling the emerald spears with melted butter.

'I think they're the best I've ever had,' said McKay. 'I must say you've spoilt me a lot these past few months, Johanna. I'll miss you, but I might miss your cooking even more!'

'Thanks a lot,' she said, grinning from ear to ear and thanking her lucky stars that he was in such a good humour. She wondered if she dared to ask the question that had been hovering around them all for the past ten days or more. Then decided, it could do no harm, not with the van der Stels there to dispel the eruption – if it came.

'I've been meaning to ask you Jock – I know you've got quite close to the Boys, making statements to the police and so on, but have you managed to make your peace with Leah, yet?'

There was a silence. Jacqueline squeezed Johanna's hand under the table, Karl prodded his wife's leg with his foot. They all waited.

'I'm not sure if you would call it a 'peace', as in everlasting – and all that,' he said. 'We've met and we had a coffee together and I said what I wanted to, and she said her bit.'

'Oh?'

'Well, I told her I couldn't understand how anyone could have been so insane as to encourage those two in the way she did. I also told her she should never have left for America without putting her paperwork in order first.'

'Meaning?' Johanna raised a quizzical eyebrow, relieved there'd been no explosion, but choosing her one word phrases carefully.

'Meaning, anyone in their right senses would never have left an open ended power of attorney over every single account, share or policy they ever owned. She had signed that document back in January last year, for one purpose and one purpose only – the signing of the *Escritura* – the registration of their house here. But unfortunately, she did it in America which gave it status there too! The moment that was done, any normal person would have revoked it. She simply never bothered! If it hadn't been for the Boys sharing the house with them, no doubt she'd have lost that as well! I mean, how could anyone be so careless? I told her – she basically threw temptation in their way.'

'Well, that was decent of you darling,' Johanna couldn't help herself, 'you could call it rubbing salt in an open wound.'

'Well, I wouldn't! I would call it summing up the reason for *all* of this happening.'

'But – ' Johanna wanted to say he could have done more to discourage Catalina from her expensive lifestyle, her expectations and her greed, but she wasn't sure how to say it.

'I won't accept any 'buts',' he went on. 'Oh, I know what you all want to say,' McKay was starting to get that familiar glint in his eyes that meant he was close to a tirade, 'but that's quite different. Yes, I agree I spoilt my wife, yes I agree I gave her a little latitude in her life … but that's about freedom of choice … that's called trusting someone and not making them a prisoner in your marriage.'

'But …' this time Johanna plucked up her courage, '… did Leah really do so much worse, when you've just admitted you allowed Catalina her freedom?'

'Oh yes, she *did*!' said McKay and thumped the table, making the plates jump. Jacqueline noticed he was starting to bare his teeth now and getting back that lynx-like look for which he was famous.

'Like what?'

'She virtually gave the wretched man, that husband of hers, a blank cheque! She popped it right under his nose! And being the sort of man he was – a wheeler-dealer Howard used to call him – he took it!'

There was a silence. There was really nothing more to say. Even Johanna was at a loss for words and while his wife felt sorry for Leah, Karl quite obviously agreed with Jock. The subject was finally changed to politics as it always did these days and the evening all passed off successfully enough. When the others had taken their tactful leave, McKay lingered on at the table for a last cigarette.

The two of them smoked in companionable silence, McKay now calm and drinking ginger ale. Johanna fiddled with her long cigarette holder, he puffed on his usual Gaulloise. 'So you can see – can't you? – why I can never bring myself to be close to Leah,' he said. 'Really, in my opinion, she's beneath contempt. But I'll do my Christian best to *try* not to loathe her.'

'Well, I hope not,' said Johanna. 'She's suffered every bit as much as you and – '

'I beg your pardon,' there was steel in his voice.

'Sorry,' she coughed. 'I agree she didn't lose a child, but –'

'Thank you,' he interrupted coldly, 'that's all actually that matters to me – that and Lochaig – and I mean to get them both back.'

'Good,' she said, realising she'd blown it. But she was *not* going to regret what she'd said. Whatever he thought, Leah had suffered beyond belief and her own natural sense of justice had kicked in at the wrong moment for them both. In a way it was better like this. She could let him go now without too many regrets. He was too prickly by half and like so many men she'd ever known, he could only see his side of the story.

'Well,' he was saying, pushing back his hair and straightening his collar. 'Best I get going. It's an early start tomorrow. I drive to Bilbão and catch the ferry the next day from Spain to Folkestone. Two nights at sea, then a night with friends at Carlisle and I'll be halfway home on the Road to the Isles. I should be ensconced at Lochaig by next Monday at the latest.

'You're all organised, then?' She knew he was, but suddenly the conversation had gone polite rather than intimate.

'Yes,' he said, equally stiff. 'My furniture will follow once it gets clearance. It may take a while, with this damned new administration, the filling in of forms and trying to prove it was imported originally has been ridiculous. Luckily however, none of it's very valuable, so I can't see them wanting to hang on to it for too long. It's the people with the posh stuff that are suffering. All those Portuguese *dons* trying to take their family heirlooms to Brazil and do a runner – poor buggers ! They haven't a hope in hell. Everything of worth's being stopped at the ports or at the border and impounded, so I hear. The people have spoken!

'But why are we leaving, Mama? If we're not going to see Papa, I don't see why we have to go.'

Katy had decided she didn't want to help pack another suitcase yet again and she wasn't sure she wanted to go on a long sea journey either. Mama had said it would be exciting, and she'd always loved sailing in the past.

'But we weren't leaving Papa,' Katy wailed, starting to rock forward and back on the edge of the hard little bed she had claimed as her own. 'If we have to move, why can't we go back to England? I liked it there with Aunt Susan and the dogs and the horses too. Why can't we go there instead – now?'

'Because it's impossible darling,' said her mother briskly, folding up her meagre belongings and ticking them off on a list. 'You'll love the house we're going to, it's beside the sea – a beautiful piece of coast – we'll be able to swim again, collect shells and go out in the boat. You know how you like that.'

'So why can't we just go back home?' said Katy, 'then we can do all those things again and see Papa at the same time. And then 'Uncle' B can go and see Auntie Leah and we'll all be happy again.'

'You're forgetting everything I told you, Kate,' said her mother, snappily. 'Now sit up straight and stop doing that silly childish thing. I've explained I don't know how many times about the Revolution and how everything's changed. You know that yourself, you've seen all those horrid slogans, you've seen the people marching through the town. It's time to go away, Katy…the Communists are coming. Everyone's saying so. Papa wants you to be safe. So do 'Uncle' B and Mama. We're going to another country where we won't have to hide any more and we can all go about normally. You should be pleased about that.'

'But I love Portugal! I don't want to go to another country.'

'Katy, one of our oldest friends was put in prison the other day. All the people we used to know are leaving. I've already explained – your father's gone. We no longer have that house in Santa Felicia. It's hard for you to understand, dear child, but everything around is changing. We have to go. So you might as well get on and accept it. Now are you going to help me with this suitcase or not? I need you to find your toys and pack them, and anything else you can think of. What about your drawing things? There'll just be room if you put them in a neat bundle.'

Later that night, with her daughter finally asleep in bed, Catalina curled up on Buster's knee and rested her dark head against his shoulder. 'I'm absolutely exhausted,' she said. 'The child's been particularly obtuse, all the time I was packing and getting things sorted, she kept asking me why her other friends at school weren't leaving. I had to really overdo the Communist threat – luckily, she's heard lots of mentions from the other children. Even the locals are getting scared. But then – she really threw me by asking why we couldn't go to England. It was hard to find a reason.'

'You shouldn't have to give her one,' said Buster, putting the wine goblet they were sharing between them, to her lips. 'She's making your life hell at the moment.'

'It's not been easy on her,' said Catalina. 'She was just beginning to make a few friends and now we're uprooting her again. It's a pity we've been forced to stay here so long.'

'Yeah – that wasn't at all in the game plan – and we've wasted all this time trying to get our furniture without success. I feel I've let you down, baby.'

'It's not your fault, honey-bee,' – it had been easy to adapt Katy's 'Uncle' B into her own endearment. 'At least we've now got all our clothes and personal things. I'm sure the rest will follow once things settle down again. But in the meantime…what a *sheet* this revolution and its aftermath have been! They've left us in such a mess.'

'A real shit,' said Buster, squeezing her hand, 'and it's not been for want of trying!' he sighed. 'The crazy thing is, I had all the copies of the original import documents in order. But no one from this regime will accept or even recognise anything from the old regime. God knows how long things will take for people moving house legitimately!'

'But isn't that just the problem?' said Catalina. 'All those rich Lisbonians trying to make an exodus with their family antiques. I can just see those revolutionaries wanting to hang onto everything. They'll be seeing it all as 'national treasure' – a bit like Russia under Lenin. And even though your stuff came in the other way round, they won't have the brain to get their heads round that. We're being treated just like everyone else, it's not fair!' she swallowed hard. The disappointment was almost too much to bear.

'Actually the last official I saw in Lisbon did seem to see my point,' he was trying to comfort her now. 'I showed him the evidence and he's kept copies of everything, and says they'll look at our case. But he's warned me it could take well into next year – they've got too many other pressing matters on their hands and I suspect we're a long way back in the queue. Of course in the old days, a few thousand notes distributed here and there would have shoved us up to the front, but you risk being arrested if you try that now!'

She shivered, 'I hope you didn't even try?'

'No, I'm not that mad. I've begun to get a feel for these guys – they'll real hostile to any form of flattery, joke or nicety. But if you're patient and earnest enough they do respond. Everything is dead serious of course – everyone's equal – you've got to watch your words and that you don't come across as patronising. I bet they just love sitting there in those gracious government buildings with rich carvings and coats of arms emblazoned all over the place, while they puff away on their cigarettes in their blue jeans and open necked shirts! You have to act real nonchalant, like one of them!'

'I told you to wear your scruffiest jeans, didn't I?' she said, cheering up at her own cleverness.

'Yeah, as usual you were spot on, my sweet. Anyway, as a result – I've told Chico just to sit on everything. He and Diaz were going to organise a container at Lisbon docks, but since it's now obvious that won't be happening this side of Christmas, he's happy to retain it until such time as I give him the word. I've told him that very soon he can sell the car – so that's kind of made up. He wasn't going to get the documents until the furniture had arrived in South Africa.'

'I wish Katy was as easy to deal with as Chico,' said Catalina. 'At least she now believes me that her father's left. In the end, I had to make up a very complicated story about him having a rare disease.'

'Well, he has,' laughed Buster, 'Alcohol!'

'I wish you wouldn't say these things,' she said. 'Also, I wish I didn't have to lie quite so much – but I don't see another way out. Unfortunately, she's getting to that age where she won't be fobbed off so easily as before. I hope it won't be too tricky in South Africa.'

'She'll forget all her troubles when she sees the lovely place we've got out there. Hand me the details, let's take another look.'

'Buster, you're such a child yourself – how many times have you studied that already?' she teased, handing him the glossy real estate brochure which had been sitting on the coffee table ever since the deal went through. The company name and logo shone out in emerald green letters across the top; at the bottom it read Luxury Cape Properties, Hermanus. 'You must know every room and its exact measurements by now.'

'I guess I do, and d'you know what pleases me the most?'

'The location of course, the fact we overlook such a stunning bay – where the whales come in for shelter – Katy will love that!'

'Nope, been there, done that – well not the whales exactly – but the bay. Course it's important ... but the thing I'm really looking forward to – is?'

'The climate? It's not much different from the Algarve, but there's probably more to do in their winter.'

'Nope!'

'Oh I give up – you're always talking in riddles these days.'

'The fact it's all on one level! I really went off the idea of going up and down that massive staircase all day and all night. Sure it looked grand, with the chandelier and everything – but I dunno, maybe after all, I'm a simpler kind of guy than I thought. It was Leah and the Boys who thought it was oh so swell. Towards the end – I was getting fed up with all the showy stuff and I began to think hang on – what are one's priorities in life? To have a great flash house or be comfortable with the girl you love?'

'Oh Buster, you say the sweetest things,' Catalina held the glass up for him this time as she nuzzled his ear. 'And today of all days, when everything's gone so badly for you down in Lisbon.'

'Yeah – that's not been so good.' He polished off the wine and gazed into the fire. 'But I did one good thing,' he chuckled to himself as though it was a private joke.

'What's that?'

'Well, I had time to kill between government departments, so I took myself off to the airport and buttered up a few passengers at check-in!'

'You what!'

'Yep. It came to me in the night. You know those plain white cards Katy had drawn faces on for her school project the other day? She'd left a couple lying around and I thought how perfect for the job – no printing on them, no give-away telltale signs as to where they'd come from…well, I couldn't help myself…I scribbled on the back of them and addressed them to Leah. Then I found a queue of people checking in for London and asked an approachable looking couple if they'd be kind enough to post one from Heathrow after they'd flown in.'

Her jaw dropped, 'Buster, you didn't!'

He grinned. 'Then I couldn't help myself, I passed another queue – all Portuguese – smart looking people lining up to check in for São Paulo. Finally I found a young student, serious sort of type, who spoke English, so I asked him if he'd do the same in Brazil. He was delighted when I gave him some American dollars – with lots to spare – to pay for the postage!'

'Buster – are you mad? Whatever for?'

'To throw them off the scent again, of course!'

'But – why two locations? London and Brazil!'

'Don't you see? The London one's bound to get to the Algarve first, so my clever wife and the Boys will get all excited by that. By the time they get the second one, they'll realise we've been in transit ever since we left – which is kind of true – except in the opposite direction!'

'And Leah's bound to forward them on to Jock – oh dear, Buster, I'm a little afraid seeing those drawings by Katie might unhinge him. Was it really wise, do you think?'

'I think it's very wise. You don't know my wife!' he added darkly, '…you can bet your bottom dollar she'll have been turning herself inside out to look for clues. So, if she was getting close to that furniture, hopefully now she'll call off the chase.'

'What on earth did you write?'

'On the first, that we were on the move, sad to leave London behind – but much looking forward to our new home together in the sun. On the second, how great it was to reach our final destination and how we would soon be re-united with all our furniture again!'

'Oh dear God,' said Catalina, 'those people must have thought you were mad!'

'I explained it was a family game we played, and my daughter had done the pictures. I said that the more foreign stamps I could send home from foreign places and the more original the messages – the more points for Daddy! I don't think anyone was bothered… they were open cards, so they would have seen no harm in it.'

'Buster, there's no end to your talents,' said Catalina gravely. 'Sometimes you scare me a little.'

'You've turned me into something I didn't know I was,' he replied. 'I had hints of it in the military but being a lazy sort of bugger, I kind of lapsed back into happy go lucky mode.

But you've changed all that – you've awoken something powerful in me – as well as my cock!'

'Well, let's hope not too much,' she said. 'But I sort of see your point. You were obviously worried about leaving our stuff behind and this should hopefully work. But do you really think you can trust Chico, not to sell it all behind our backs?'

'He wouldn't dare. We've agreed terms. As I told you, he gets the car, buckshee! But – and it's a big one – I'm only sending on the keys and the papers when I receive his signed contract. It was put together by his lawyer, under my direction – and if he breaks that, we can sue him and he knows that.'

'What if he flees the country, like so many others seem to be doing?'

'Are you joking? A man in his position! This revolution's made for people like him. He's a future entrepreneur, our Chico, tomorrow's new rich. All he has to do is sit tight, let the old order pass away, get himself on a few local councils and committees and he'll be away! He's not stupid, our friend Chico, and he won't want a court case on his hands – not when he's trying to keep his nose clean and work his way up. I have every confidence our belongings are safe with him.'

'But they would have been so stunning in the new house – single storey or not – it's very spacious. I can't help feeling desperately disappointed.'

'Look, babe, me too. I had all that French stuff earmarked for you – and the pictures would have looked great on those long white walls. But … we'll make do. At least all the money's intact! We'll get some reasonable modern stuff, to get started. Then, when all these politics have died down and people are being sensible again, we'll get our stuff shipped out. Don't you worry. I reckon this Communist thing is a flash in the pan. Portugal's part of Europe, for Chrissakes. They'll see sense soon enough and probably end up like the French. The democratic process will prevail.'

'I hope so,' she nuzzled him again and flicked her tongue around his ear. Soon she was re-arranging herself over his knee as she felt his erection push up under her. Lord, even in adversity, this man wanted her! He seemed never to have enough. She stood up suddenly and looked at herself in the mirror. She was flushed from the wine and the fire, but her eyes were as shiny as they'd ever been and it made her giggle to see the desire in her own face. She pulled his hand away from his lap and he leaned forward to follow her grasp which took his fingers up and under her skirt. A moment later he was on his feet – 'You want me now, here? On the rug? Are you sure the child's asleep?'

She nodded and giggled again, her breathing coming in short, urgent rasps. Why did he turn her on so? They were both such animals!

And as they rolled together in the big farmhouse sheepskin rug, she thought, 'This is what I need right now, but one day I'll make sure I get all those things – and the house to go with it! And nothing, *nothing* will ever stand in my way!'

Part 4

44

Portugal – 2004

It was Kate's second meeting with Benjie and Roger. The three of them had got on so well at drinks two days before, she'd been invited to lunch at their village house which lay some ten kilometres inland near old Loulé. It was a different world she entered as she stooped under the lintel of a low doorway, then drew herself up and opened her eyes wide. Where the feel and contents of Casa Amarela had offended her senses in every way, here she felt immediately grounded by a welcoming atmosphere of warmth, good taste and serenity.

She had stepped from a narrow cobbled street straight into their living room. Greetings dispensed with, she looked around and was momentarily over-awed. It was a silent moment, an unconscious reaction quite obviously anticipated, judging by the two expectant faces at her side. A huge fireplace fashioned out of stone, with a thick polished oak beam for a mantelpiece, harboured a mass of warm ash on which burned sweet-smelling logs – 'Cork!' smiled Benjie before she even asked the question. 'A smell to die for, I couldn't burn anything else even if you paid me!'

There were other fragrances besides: jasmine, rose, myrtle, thyme and lavender. Overflowing bowls of pot-pourri liberally scattered stunning surfaces and jostled for scent-supremacy with six large, carefully placed beeswax candles on an ancient refectory table where the room narrowed away to form a diningroom. Kate threw back her head and her nostrils flared appreciatively.

'Hmmm...delicious!' she proclaimed.

'I once knew a little girl who sniffed like that,' said Benjie, suddenly. ' She'd come into the room as if led by her nose! Her mom used to get mad at her!'

'I suppose she would,' said Kate, hurriedly warming her hands at the fire and praying they wouldn't notice her burning face. There was no mistaking whom he remembered; her father used to tease her about it, years later.

Until this moment, she'd been enjoying the fact she rarely saw houses like this and that in her world these two men were rare birds whom she'd be unlikely to encounter again, so why not make the most of it. Stay cool, Kate, she told herself and composing herself added casually, 'I guess we're all a bit like that. Smell is very important to me; it can be incredibly nostalgic too. Your house reminds me a little of Liberty's in London, gorgeous fresh-smelling fabric and lovely antique wood, everywhere you look.'

Benjie nodded, pleased with the simile and she was glad there were no piercing looks as though she'd jogged his memory further. As for Roger, he seemed far too self-absorbed to notice and after checking and altering his button-down collar in the mirror twice, had moved across the room to exchange the pleasant CD of classical guitar for a long rendition of *Bohemian Rhapsody*. 'Hope you don't mind,' he said to Kate, 'Benjie will go in for that repetitive stuff. I bet you prefer Queen, don't you?' She noticed he didn't wait for an answer.

Once again however she managed to divert attention after an awkward moment, this time by crossing to the window and asking about Loulé. Benjie joined her by the leaded casement and spun a tale of travellers and inns, Spanish horsemen returning from the Peninsular war and heading for the Guadiana, cavalcades of gypsies, warlords and retreating Moors. For centuries, the Poço Geraldo, the well at the bottom of the hill by the old convent, had provided a resting place, a haven for animals and people alike, even as it did today.

Where Leah had talked sensibly and matter-of-factly about the Algarve and all its natural beauty, her new hosts made her feel she'd entered a world of visionaries and seers. There'd been a sighting of a dead Crusader at the churchyard on the hill, someone else had dug up a holy relic and a child from a nearby hamlet had been born with twelve fingers. Once in a thunderstorm it had rained frogs and Roger swore there was a poltergeist in the barn next door. There was mystery and energy in the air, which now seemed present in this simple room. Thick walls, humble surroundings, exotic contents all made fantastical by a magical hand – everything in its place, yet so well juxtapositioned one to the other – each object assumed an importance and vibrancy quite irrelevant to its actual fashioning or design.

Like the smells, the colours too were designed to assail the senses. Red next to purple, mustard merging into orange, green combating steel-grey and black jumping into bed with pink. Stones, wood carvings, rugs, porcelain, tapestries, old prints… suddenly she could see with amazing clarity why Benjie had chosen this ancient spot and even more, why he had been so pursued as a designer. With such talent, how could he have borne to be uprooted, to give it all up? More important – how on earth could he have allowed himself to become a mere companion in that brash new villa amidst a world of ex-pats?

She thought back to Santa Felicia and how it had developed. Once a simple fishing village, the transformation had been swift in coming and in the early seventies, the foundations for the fleshpots of the new millennium were being laid with alacrity and abandon. The materialist lifestyle, the burgeoning development, must have been suffocating to many a soul – especially its oldest inhabitants or to someone sensitive and artistic like Benjie. No wonder the musicians had left in their droves at the end of the '60s

As for people like her father, well at least he had his studio and his deadlines ; he may have drunk too much, but the pressure of exhibitions and work kept him sane. What did Benjie have to ground himself and keep him on track? Once the house was finished, there was the garden, but was that enough? In the words of the great Presley, he must have felt 'caught in a trap!'

Did this explain why he did not rescue Leah at the time she most needed friends? Why could he not have warned her what was obviously in the air? Had their life of luxury – Johanna's parties and the high life in Estoril – destroyed his sense of balance and proportion, so that the man who shared their house and would ultimately bring it down, was allowed to blunder on, unchecked? Kate found herself shuddering at the thought and wondering what dark skeleton had lain in Benjie's cupboard which had allowed him to succomb to such a fate. Or had he just been too self-preoccupied to notice?

She accepted a glass of *vinho verde* from Roger as Benjie busied himself in the kitchen beyond but found herself struggling to make conversation. After all the superlatives about the house, the furniture, the décor and so on, she was conscious of asking only the right questions, as it would be all too easy to blow her cover. She wondered how much of the truth she would get back in return. There was something about Roger which she found a little devious. He could not have been more than a decade older than herself, forty-five-ish? – but somehow he seemed younger. He had an insouciant but veiled look in his eye which could turn out to be deceiving. She asked him about his parents, knowing quite well the background but interested to see what he would say.

'Did you originally come to the Algarve on holiday?' she asked innocently.

'Oh no,' came the languid reply, 'My parents moved to Portugal in the early sixties. Bought a house in the centre of Santa Felicia. It's rather grand and now the mayor's residence. I was at boarding school first, later at Oxford, so I wasn't here that much.'

'So how come you returned?' said Kate.

'Oh I had friends,' smiled Roger, 'Benjie for a start and although we rarely saw each other, we would correspond. My parents went back to the UK six years after the Revolution – about the same time as poor Howard died. They were horrified at what had happened…too much had changed – a different type of tourist, they said – and so many of their old friends had left. Father's dead now too, mother's still hanging on by a thread in Gloucestershire. She finds it 'most odd' that I've come back here, but I wouldn't leave it for the world. Much prefer things now to how they were before. Everyone minds their own business, gets on with things. In the old days you couldn't move a whisker without the whole Algarve knowing about it.'

Kate had heard her parents say much the same. She wondered what Benjie would do if he found out who she was. Leah had absolutely forbidden that. 'You've no idea what harm you might do,' she'd told Kate fiercely. 'He's a lovely man, Benjie, but he and Howard suffered financially too. For a start they couldn't sell the villa until we knew Buster was out of the picture and that gave them years of heartache and real financial deprivation.

'Fortunately, under Napoleonic law it became clear your mother could not make claim to the title. With me alive, she could not even play the part of a common law wife even though she'd got away with that in South Africa when… er…Buster died. Nevertheless, what happened here made the practical running of the house desperately hard for the Boys. Until I started earning again, they had double the bills to cope with and even now, our Roger would be the first to point this out.'

'But,' said Kate, 'if you really feel we owe them something…'

'You don't! It would cause more harm than good raking up the past for Benjie and playing the trauma card. What would that achieve? You would feel even worse about what your mother did than you already do and you'd never hear the end of it! You ought to know Roger used to have a drug problem which got worse before it got better and Benjie's had a terrible time trying to get him clean. The past is best left alone for both those two.

For Benjie's peace of mind – he's been so stoic – and for Roger's future. It would be awful if he used this as a temptation to get back on the drugs again. The less you say about yourself the better.'

At this point, Kate had been all ready to abort any idea of further communication with Benjie, but Leah was adamant that more useful insights should be encouraged. 'Look sister! You're halfway there…why duck out now, just when you're getting to the end of the road? I think you owe it to us both to see this through. Blow the cobwebs away, like I've had to. It's important you understand about the Revolution too – not just from the history books – and Benjie's the one who can give you that. After all, I wasn't even *compos* by that stage…since that was the week,' she gulped ever so slightly…' it all happened.' And it was at this point she concocted Kate's cover.

She was to play the role of a budding writer and had come to the Algarve to research the ex-pat society of the seventies, and how the Revolution had affected them, for a magazine article. The beginning part of the story was true – 'But you *are* researching, honey!' she'd insisted – 'it's the truth and you've got nothing to lose! You've also got much to gain by finding out exactly how it was – as seen through the eyes of these two men – although in those days they weren't together of course. Remember!' she added, 'I, myself, was in no state to record the political events of 25th April. Benjie however was stuck on the other side of the Spanish Border, so you'll get some good background there which will help you understand better what you and your parents had to go through. Then it will become clearer why they were forced to stay in Portugal so long before you all went to South Africa.'

Kate had shuddered with the deceit of the whole thing, but Leah had said 'You're hurting no one! Benjie loves explaining the politics – most people sweep the revolution under the carpet.'

This had decided her, even though posing or lying was not in her nature. Once she got going however, she could not help but savour the duplicitous buzz the deception gave her. As she watched Benjie lay the table and Roger amble round the room in his wake, about as useful as a decorative butterfly, she wondered what Michael Hargreaves would think of her now.

The contrast between Leah's approach to historical events and that of the two men had only served to highlight all that he had warned her about. Michael had also pointed out that once the information had been gathered, any judgements made must be hers and hers alone. These people could only tell her things from their point of view, as it happened at the time. The overview and the sifting out of the truth and its consequences was her responsibility.

She could already see herself settling down on the spotted deerskin in front of the fire after lunch and hearing their stories. She suspected they might make those Revolution years seem like a Grimm's fairytale and it might be hard to separate truth from fiction. Oh well…as Leah said, what was there to lose? It had all been so long ago but it would be good to round off her understanding.

'So Communism only lasted about a year?' she ventured to say after her second helping of *açorda* – a delicious local dish made with bread, garlic, chopped coriander and prawns.

Benjie had been holding court for almost an hour and she'd learned more in that short time about the country of her childhood than she'd ever gleaned in any book and particularly from her own mother.

'Well, in name – but perhaps not in effect – the country was in a ghastly muddle for almost a decade,' said her host. 'It all went wrong for the democrats in November 1974, by which time a lot of our friends had wisely got out – I don't suppose you remember the Neves, do you, Roger? – or Manolo – or maybe even Jock McKay?'

Kate invented a coughing fit as she felt the scarlet rush to her face again, but luckily Benjie was far too engrossed with Roger's inability to jog his memory to notice. 'You must remember some of them, for God's sake, Rog … they were always around – at all the parties!'

'Ya, but you seem to forget I was at Oxford in between,' said the hapless Roger, 'and had troubles of my own,' he winked across the table at Kate. 'Hey, Manolo – that name seems familiar – and wasn't Jock the guy who got wronged by a naughty wife, lost his child and then went half off his head with grief? Wasn't that the reason he then broke into your villa around the same time I went there on my little errand?'

'Oh, you are so hopeless, Roger,' said Benjie exasperated, 'you know it was. You also know he was a great friend of our joint friend – or at least your parents' friend – Johanna Vincent. He was also a great artist … we've got one of his pictures hanging here, for God's sake. Were you so out of it, you'd forgotten?'

He turned to Kate, who appeared to be struggling with her napkin, 'We sure had some characters in our midst in those days! Can I take away your plate? Hey, are you all right? Sorry, we've lost the thread – we had this massive scandal going on here all around the same time as the Revolution – but that wouldn't interest you. Now where was I? Ah, General Spinola!

'As I was saying, he got chucked out pretty quick, but then, backed by the more conservative faction – indeed the ones who actually started the coup – he tried to regain power from the extremists when things started to go pear-shaped. Unfortunately, it all went horribly wrong in November '74 and Spinola got booted out for the second time. Then there was a really nasty atmosphere all through '75 when some of us began to think we might even lose our homes. The Algarve was never as bad as the rest of the country, but it was quite uncomfortable living here. No one trusted each other and with so much anti-American feeling about, even going to the bank was unpleasant. You were often made to feel unwelcome and sometimes the word *capitalista* might be scrawled over your car.'

'It must have been very tricky,' said Kate. 'You'd never think, looking round the Algarve today, that such a thing could have happened. I've never seen so many luxury cars, hotels or development.'

'Too much,' said Benjie, 'that's why Roger and I have retired to the hills. The kind of property I handle is far removed from all that concrete lego-land. Luckily there are still some marvellous areas quite unspoilt, particularly inland, and I think the present Social Democrats are being much more careful. Luckily we've had political stability now for almost two decades, and being part of the European Union is probably the best thing that could have happened to Portugal. Everyone's really well integrated and we've got brilliant roads now. You can get up to Lisbon in well under three hours whereas it used to take forever!'

'So, would it be true to say the ex-pats are just as welcome again here as they were pre-Revolution?' she asked, remembering her cover story.

'Oh absolutely, they're an important part of the fabric of society now,' said Benjie. 'The thing that was different about my day was, we all knew each other so any new face was exciting and new. Sometimes it went to people's heads…hence the scandals! Now, there are hundreds of new faces. People come and go all the time and it's hard to tell who's tourist and who lives here. As Roger says, many people prefer it that way. There's anonymity and probably far less bitching than before. Quite honestly, I don't think people have the time for all that. Things have changed, everyone has to work and get on nowadays.

' Before the Revolution, labour was cheap and we were all very spoilt. Of course today – there's still the odd super star around, a few top footballers and people like Cliff Richard for instance! But wherever they choose to live, the celebrities enjoy a rarified atmosphere, and the Algarve's no different in that respect from anywhere else.'

There was a pause, as he refilled her wine glass. 'Do you think that will give you enough fodder for your story?'

I'm thrilled with that,' responded Kate, truthfully adding, 'Thank you, Benjie. I think you've painted a better picture of how it all was than anyone else I've spoken to.'

As she took her grateful leave of them after coffee, she could not help mentioning that she had decided to drive inland to Messines to take a glimpse of the interior. Leah had furnished her with a map of the farm where the barn had finally been discovered long after it was emptied but she saw no harm in asking if her hosts knew of a shortcut to this largely agricultural region.

She was unprepared for their reaction. 'Messines!' cried Roger, coming surprisingly to life. 'That's a boring place to visit, it's pretty flat there – none of the usual rolling scenery – and there's little to see other than maize factories – at least I think they're maize – something dreary anyway, and the railway running through. I'd give it a miss and go west to Silves. That's got real drama, built by the Romans, it's on the river and the hillside castle played a strategic role in the battle against the Moors. There's a mammoth statue of some gorgeous warrior king just as you go in the gates!'

Kate smiled politely, then was struck by Benjie's silence. Finally, he said, 'Who recommended you to go Messines?' It wasn't Leah – was it?'

Kate regretted she'd said anything. 'As a matter of fact, she may have mentioned it,' then added hastily 'and I'm sure she said Silves too. It was only after I told her about my family's – er – farming interests, that she thought I'd like to see how they manage the land around there. I gather there's some good vineyards. If it's too dull, I won't bother,' she added untruthfully.

'I can't believe Leah's still hankering after these places,' said Benjie, more to himself than anyone else. 'She's crazy, that woman, she pretends not to care…but sometimes I wonder. Forgive me…' he pulled his shoulders back and gave her a reassuring smile, 'there's no reason you should know, but when there was that scandal I talked about, some stuff got stolen. Poor old Leah's things ended up somewhere near Messines. Only…she never found out about it until years afterward – and by then of course, it was much too late – it had all been dispersed.'

'Oh dear,' said Kate, growing more uncomfortable by the moment. 'I heard a lot of people suffered during the coup.'

'Yeah, the landed and professional families the most,' said Benjie, 'and the very poor, but not so much those in between. Funnily enough, the Portuguese guy who spilt the beans about Leah's furniture turned out to be the same person who'd harboured it all – for years and years. Only he didn't know it was stolen.

'In fact he tried to sell Leah a piece for one of her shops which she recognised. Kind of ironic isn't it? Unfortunately the main bulk had already been sold, because the guy who – er – originally – er – pinched it, couldn't get it out of the country.' There was a pause, as he appeared to struggle with his words, 'All that business didn't seem to do the Portuguese guy too much harm though. He became very powerful in local government but when he found out who Leah was – at least ten years after the revolution – he was anxious to get the past off his chest!'

'Heavens,' said Kate, not sure what else to say.

'Yeah – it was a tricky time for many …' said Benjie, a far away look in his eyes, 'and really such a terrible, terrible waste. Too many suffered quite needlessly.' A moment later he was brightening up again as he got out the map to show her the back roads.

'There you see! you can go to Boliqueime from here, wind around the hills, there's some real pretty villages – see this one called Purgatorio! Isn't that a wonderful name? – and Paderne – with its old castle – a bit crumbling I'm afraid. Then you can make your way inland to Messines, take in your vineyards and on to Silves where the castle really is spectacular.'

Not long after, she was taking her leave of them. She had asked to use their bathroom first, hoping to get a glimpse of her father's picture on the way, but this time her luck ran out. It must be upstairs; there was no sign of his explosive art in the downstairs part of the house and it would have been rude to delay longer.

It wasn't until she left Loulé, followed Benjie's instructions to the letter, and finally rejoined Leah's original route, that Kate realised she had been hyper-ventilating hard. That last revelation had been a little too close for comfort. She'd so much wanted to ask more questions but hadn't dared. She had a feeling Roger's inquisitive eyes might see more deeply into her soul, than he'd let on. She drove on slowly and thoughtfully, careful to look out for important landmarks.

What a waste, she kept thinking to herself. Do I really want to see the place where the furniture, Panda and Lily and I, all got bundled together at dead of night?

Deep in the countryside, far from the coast, it was easy to believe how her mother and Buster had escaped being spotted for so long. Where now a new series of motorways criss-crossed the landscape, the outlying towns and villages were still remarkably unspoilt, slumbering still as the roar of traffic, coast or city-bound, passed them by on high bridges and viaducts built by European Community money.

Yet, down in the valleys, the same sand tracks, the same small *caminhos*, remained much as they ever had. High, leafy vines, thickets of bamboo, screens of pampas grass, all combined to protect the deep red earth, the hidden farms, the outlying hamlets. It was a tranquil secret world that spread before her, beckoning to be explored.

Finally, she found the turn-off that would lead down the track to the famous hide-out and wondered anew about that long forgotten journey in the dark. Fleeting moments came to life – the relief when 'Uncle' B had vacated the passenger seat – she'd thought he'd gone for good, Panda's button nose, cold and comforting, against her cheek, and finally, getting out of the car, all hot, sticky and cramped, to stretch her legs.

Now that she was here, she couldn't recall this place, this turning – it had been dark for God's sake! But she did remember coming to a jolt in a rutted yard and being herded by her mother, tense and anxious, into a huge white building, full of crates and boxes. She could almost see it now, the tubular lighting harsh on her eyes, making her blink. And then the bed! There'd been a *bed* – covered in clothes – standing in a corner! But the worst thing of all was the smell. It suddenly came upon her now – a mixture of chickens and diesel. Ugh!

These latter were new images, new sensations…ones she must have buried deep down, all this time. Did she really want to enter that building again? Was she really ready to awaken and embrace more painful memories?

The farm now bore a name, proudly painted on a new sign at the end of the sunken road. *Quinta d'Areia*…Farm of the Sand – appropriate enough. She paused by the entrance of the track and debated. Far away in the distance, low in a dip, she could just make out the hint of red roof and a chimney stack, and was that a tin roof glinting in the sunlight?

And at that moment a vision of a plump, foul-smelling man who kept pinching her on the cheek, hove into view and she decided she'd gone far enough. Chico was best left alone. No matter how important he now was in the local community, the thought of even shaking hands with this man who'd colluded with Buster and who'd touched her face all these years ago, brought a sense of nausea and dismay.

And so it was Kate left that part of the past behind her. Instead of turning down the track, she went carefully past, then backed the small hire car between the newly painted posts, and retraced the route. She would drive back to the coast as quickly as she could. The clean open sea – her haven, her friend. And only when the blue of the ocean came into sight, and the panicky feeling had left her chest, did her breathing even out.

And it was then she stopped by the roadside to text her husband. *'All well here,'* she tapped out, hoping to God it was. *'Finding out more by the day. Fascinating! Soon be home. K. X'*

45

*I*t was Kate's last full day in the Algarve. She had said goodbye to Leah the night before, having insisted on taking her out to dinner at the American's favourite restaurant, a quiet fish bistro much frequented by the Portuguese, hidden behind the old Roman bridge. Never one to mince her words, Leah had insisted that Kate's last 24 hours in the Algarve must be for chilling out.

'That's what you need, honey,' said her guest over coffee, keen eyes searching Kate's face as they brought the evening to a close. 'You've done what you came to do. You've met the few people left connected with that time – you've seen Casa Amarela, your father's old studio and your own home, the famous Anchor Bar where so much of the gossiping took place, and you've travelled again the road to the barn. Chico's an old man now but I don't blame you at all for not going in.

'You've heard my side of things and a little bit from Benjie – and you've put two and two together. More importantly, you've got a feel for the atmosphere – the intrigues and – yes – the temptations of that era. The build up, the developments, the plot – and,' she paused '– the inevitabilities – right through to the climax, itself. And then it didn't just stop there – the saga itself. The way it ran, and ran. You knew that already of course, but now perhaps you can understand from a different perspective. It was the '70s…yes, all past history now …but I can assure you, heady stuff at the time.'

'But that doesn't *excuse* them!' Kate suddenly felt real anger on Leah's behalf, ' – the things they did – my mother and your husband! It's hard to believe they could have carried such a thing out and worse – got away with it!'

'That's what we all thought – but you have to hand it to them. It sure was bold! The truth is they might well have been caught if it hadn't been for a number of things. I call it the 'What if?' factor. What if – your father had turned back instead of staying on at The Anchor? What if – Lord Crompton had appeared back in our midst and told us about the barn? It was years before Johanna caught up with him again and discovered he'd seen Catalina and Buster near Messines all that time before. We might then have guessed about the hiding place and at least recovered some of my missing stuff! What if – someone had spotted the new car and taken their number plate? What if – well, the biggest one of all, obviously… the Revolution hadn't happened at the precise moment it did? If *Cabo* Fonseca and his cronies had continued in office just one more day, I still think the Portuguese secret police might have caught them at the frontier. We were only 12 hours too late!'

'If I was to sit down and write a story about all of this,' said Kate, 'no one would believe me. No wonder Mama was always so secretive. I've been thinking – she must have felt guilty all those years, Leah, terrified I'd find out the truth about how she left my father and what she did to you. No wonder I never got close to her.'

'To be truthful, I can't see Catalina ever being terrified … or guilty,' said her companion. Nevertheless, I do think she didn't mean for Buster to behave quite in the way he did. That postcard that caught up with me at Wally's – the one that almost sent me off my head – I think it was genuinely regretful. But only momentarily… she was far too busy going with the flow, following her dream and enjoying Buster's slavish devotion, to think she might still have reversed things.'

'I wish I'd met Johanna,' said Kate. 'I gave up on my mother's sense of morality years ago, but I somehow sense Johanna would have told me more about my father's. I've always clung to the belief that one of my parents at least was honest – and I reckon she'd have known for certain how it lay with Papa.'

'You're right there,' said Leah. 'I know he confided in her a great deal, not just after the coup – before too. It's too bad she's no longer with us, a shrewd cookie that one – in every respect – and always ahead of the game. You'd have found in her a sense of fun as well as a mine of information. She delighted in observing from the sidelines and was a great judge of character. I know she not only liked, but respected your father. Years later, after I'd worked for her and gradually we became friends, she told me she blamed herself bitterly for not warning me. She could see the way the wind was blowing but kept it to herself. The day of that infamous lunch party was the first wake-up call, in her opinion. But even then – no one could have guessed the extent of their cunning, and at her own admission – even Johanna was taken in.'

'Kate fell silent. 'And Maysie?' she mused. 'I presume you had your reasons for not introducing us?'

'That would have spelt more trouble. First, she's not a patch on her mother, second she couldn't really care less what went on – she was always tripping off to England in between and even when she was around, her mother chose to divulge very little. Third, she was and still is – totally self-absorbed. She's been divorced three times, you know, still has dubious boyfriends and continues to flit in and out of the place. Quite honestly, I would never recommend you talk to her. She's quite a stirrer and I suspect you'd have ended up more muddled than before. Apart from all that, she doesn't lower herself to talk to people like me – and unless we'd blown your cover, I doubt she'd have talked to you!'

'I could see that,' smiled Kate, despite her feelings. 'So what happened to all the others?'

'I'm afraid most are dead and gone. Dear, eccentric Eustace clung on for a bit, dabbling in politics and popping in and out with his plane – but even that got difficult – so he moved to Morocco and went native. I gather a bit of money-laundering went on – perhaps to pay for the politics, but he finally wrote a book – rather impractical I fear – on green issues. The last thing I heard was he'd died quite peacefully at his home in Tangier.

'Manolo Vaz Valqueiro, whose family supported the old regime, fled to Bahia where he married a beautiful Brazilian girl. They eventually came back to Portugal in the late '80s after the Social Democrats were well established, and he was able to regain some of his old property and set up in real estate at Luz Bay. I heard Manolo stayed dapper, charming and sexy to the end, but life eventually caught up even with him. The beautiful people…'

she gave a little sigh, 'they're just as vulnerable really as the rest of us. I heard he died of an unexpected stroke only a few months ago.

'Terence O'Connor went to manage a huge hotel in Hong Kong, but screwed around rather too much, from all accounts, which lost him his wife and family. He was only fifty odd when he died of a heart attack…such a waste! Janine Baxter surprised us all by marrying an Angolan *retournado* and has about five mixed race kids and is very happy. She pops into the shop occasionally and we have quite a laugh about the old days but unfortunately they're in the Gambia at the moment. Not that she could have told you any more. As for Jerry Weaver and his wife – he wan't such a bad old stick, you know, and they were kindness itself after the coup although they didn't much like your dad! Anyway, they sold the Anchor Bar to one of the big new Portuguese beer companies and live in happy retirement near Bognor Regis.

'Augusto Neves, as a highflyer, had to flee from Portugal straight after the Revolution and settled with his tennis-playing wife in New Zealand – theirs is a very happy story, their eldest son did well in the Australian Open and is now a hopeful for the next Olympics. I still get Christmas cards from them.'

'That's nice – are they your only links with the past?'

'Just about,' said Leah thoughtfully, 'You certainly find out who your friends are when things go wrong. Not that I blame the younger ones so much. The disco kids, Lady Lucie Prescott-Adams and Sebastian were never much interested in us anyway, and saw their business dive after the revolution so they sold up and went back to the UK. Same went for the van der Stels; Karl's company couldn't put up with all the red tape as one administration fell after another. His development was still only half built, when finally they pulled the rug from under him and sent him back to London. Pity! It would have been worth a fortune now – but like most companies at the time, their Dutch shareholders got cold feet. Jacqueline kept up with me for a year or two but let's face it, she and Karl and the disco kids were all protegés of Johanna's and much more interested in seeking her good favour than bothering with three rather pathetic Americans.'

'Three? Oh, I see what you mean – you and the Boys – struggling on at Casa Amarela afterwards. It must have been really hard.'

'It was,' replied Leah, 'and I don't really want to think about it now. For a time Howard and Benjie could hardly bear to talk to me. It was so hard on *all* of us – Buster doing what he did – but at least they didn't throw me out.'

'But you were working!' said Kate defensively.

'Oh yes, but I wasn't paying the cheques like in the old days!'

'No I suppose not, but even so.'

'We worked something out,' said Leah, 'and in the end things got evened out after Buster's death became official and we were able finally to sell. But that's all far away now – back in the mists of time,' she smiled a little wistfully. 'So you see!' she was changing the subject – 'We've come full circle so I hope you feel a little more informed and relaxed about the whole thing?'

'I can't think why – but actually – I do,' said Kate. 'It's helped most of all to talk to you and to know the damage wasn't completely irreparable. But that's all down to your strength of character which makes me feel doubly in your debt. Also I'm regretful that we couldn't have helped when you needed it most.'

'But you weren't to know,' said Leah. 'Things might have been different, if I'd had children and there were dependants and so on. Then it would have been much harder to pick up the pieces and start a business all over again. Happily, I had no real ties at all. Perhaps the very fact I didn't want children with Buster shows how incompatible we were. Funny that… I've only just thought of it. You see, Kate, without realising it, *you've* made me feel better!'

Kate reached across the checked tablecloth and squeezed her wrist. 'You're such a generous person, Leah, even now after all this raking over things, you can find a positive thing to say. As I've said countless times before, I can't thank you enough.'

'Aw, shucks! – spare the violins,' grinned Leah. 'Go on, take a real break tomorrow and spend some time on the beach. Lay the ghosts to rest and realise once and for all that you'll never know all the answers. That's not what life's about. It's doing the best you can out of the circumstances and then getting on with things. You need to concentrate now on your own life!'

'I know,' said Kate, 'And you're a shining example of all that. I really will try and do what you say. And I promise I'll keep in touch. You'll send me your new address, when the business is sold, won't you? The Silver Coast north of Lisbon sounds nice, I think it could suit you well. I just hope you won't regret leaving Santa Felicia after all this time.'

'No, now I've made up my mind, I can't wait to go,' said the older woman. 'You see in a funny way I needed you to come to focus on my own needs. I thought I could never leave this spot, there must have been that little tiny part of me hankering to cling on – which I hadn't quite acknowledged. But now that last thread's broken, there's a great sense of relief.'

Kate drove her back to Santa Felicia, parked outside her hotel near the main square and escorted Leah on foot to her studio flat. The squid boats were out in the bay, small lights bobbing over the waves, the glow of the sea's natural phosphorescence lighting their path. 'Stunning,' said Leah, as their heels clacked on the marbled paving, 'But I don't want to be around when the last one goes. There used to be two hundred of those boats out there of an evening, now you're lucky if you see more than a dozen. It'll be nice to go to a part of Portugal where they still fish like they used to and where you can go into shops and they all speak Portuguese!'

They parted under the lamplight of the *Esplanada*, just outside *Caverna*. Kate watched as Leah mounted the little iron staircase, and waved at the top. There was a black cat arching against her legs in greeting as the slight figure slotted her key in the lock. Black cat for luck, thought Kate as she held up her hand in farewell and silent thanks. Then she walked down the street again towards her hotel, her mobile phone tight against her bottom in the back pocket of her jeans. As soon as she got back, she would send Michael a text. She knew he knew tomorrow was her last day. He would be expecting a word, at least.

The meeting with Michael was arranged for lunch. Kate was surprised and appreciative when he rang back early in the morning to invite her. 'I thought you'd be much too busy,' she said, still in bed rubbing the sleep out of her eyes.

'I am, but I made time,' she could almost feel his grin at the end of the phone. 'I haven't asked for much since I've been here, and the least I can do for my sins is to be allowed to cook lunch for the most beautiful girl in the Algarve before she goes home. I told this to one of the ladies on the vestry, and she's insisted on providing us with some of her home-made gazpacho. Nevertheless, I'm afraid it all comes with a price tag!'

'What – the time or the gazpacho?' she said, glad he could not see the flush that covered her face ear to ear. She wasn't used to compliments so early in the morning, especially since she had a sneaking suspicion he might have meant it. She wondered what was coming.

'Both!' he said.

'So what's the deal?'

'Well,' he sounded a little sheepish. 'I've discovered this stunning cove,' he said, 'and I want to explore it. You see, your lessons have been invaluable or I would never have discovered it. I've taken the boat out a couple of times but I haven't got the confidence to bale out on my own and leave her 'standing'. What I'd really like to do is snorkel over the area, it's alive with unusual fish and the water's so clear you can see these fantastic rock colours and variagated seaweed. In fact, I've never seen so many amazing colours before in my life. But how to do it? The engine's been playing up lately, she's fine once started, but I'm a little reluctant to turn her off whilst I abandon ship.'

'In case you can't get started again! I can see that…' she laughed. '…so, you were hoping for a minder?'

'Er – yes!' he sounded embarrassed.

'Well that's fine, I've done my fair share of snorkelling. You swim and I'll mind the boat for you.'

'Are you sure you don't mind, on your last day?'

'Not at all, but I might want to talk a bit as well.'

'I was expecting that, and feel a heel about the last time.'

'No hard feelings, I wasn't really ready then anyway.'

'Great, one o'clock then for a g and t?'

'Fine!'

She laughed at herself as she leapt out of bed, ran down the stairs and poked her head out of the door before going in for breakfast. Not only was she lighter on her feet but she felt lighter in her heart than she had for months. Is it this lovely pure Algarvean air? – there was a light breeze whipping in from the west and she sucked in a really tangy scent from the sea – or, is it the thought of lunch with Michael Hargreaves? In which case – better beware, Kate!

It was 1.15 when she arrived at Michael's cottage. She had been stopped for speeding on the *auto-estrada* by smartly dressed, breeches and epaulettes, traffic police, but after inspecting her documents and licence she was allowed to proceed. After that she crawled like a snail and felt highly relieved to have been let off the hook. She had also been impressed by their English. They had pointed out that 'since we are in Europe' she could have got points on her licence, but perhaps aided by the fact she had made no effort to play the feminine card, and had replied politely in Portuguese, they decided to let her off 'this time.'

'I ought to have warned you,' said Michael, pouring out drinks into two glasses full of ice and lemon. 'They're pretty hard on anything like that down this end of the coast. I guess they get mightily fed up of our blue-eyed lager louts and ladettes, so hire cars are obvious fair game.'

'Pops used to slip them a twenty *escudo* note,' she said, settling down into a canvas chair outside the tiny kitchen where a table had been laid on a small patio, 'but that was in the day of the *Guarda Republicana*. I suppose if you tried that today, you'd end up before the courts for bribery and corruption.'

'Yeah, I guess some things about being in the EU are good,' said Michael.

'And others not,' she said. 'I'm afraid my father would disagree all the way down the line. He's not been back since the Revolution!'

'Europe's done a lot for Portugal particularly as regards roads, services, the airport, bridges. But people are very quick to forget, ' said Michael, 'I was talking to an elderly Welsh resident last night, whose enjoyed all the benefits of the excellent Algarve hospital and day-care centre that makes life good for him and other British pensioners in the area. Yet, he still persists in talking of your parents' time with rose-coloured spectacles. So on that note, have you dug out all you wanted to know about a time when Portugal still had an empire, when bribery was rife and the ex-pats and the rich had it all their own way – not to speak of people playing havoc with other people's lives? Not that they don't today – but as far as it affected your family?'

She looked at him quizzically wondering at the note of sarcasm in his voice. Having decided it wasn't directed at her personally, she proceeded to tell him all the things she had been saving up since the day he'd almost kissed her. Drinks over, they moved on to lunch. The gazpacho was mouthwatering, he served fish, fresh baked *cherne* with a delicious salad of which he was clearly proud, and still she was talking. She had reached the story of the Revolution as seen through Benjie's eyes, and it was at this point her own memory took over as she described arriving at the frontier, only to be turned back by the soldiers and the eventual move to South Africa.

'How long do you reckon you were holed up near Obidos?' he asked before disappearing through the open door to fetch cheese and fruit from the larder.

'A few months probably...' she said as she piled plates together and made more room on the table. She screwed up her nose at the memory – or was it the sun – he couldn't be sure? As he spooned out some very runny sheep's cheese, he thought for the hundredth time how attractive she was, the dusting of freckles across the bridge of her nose drawing attention to the fine chiselled cheekbones. '...I have to say Mama was amazingly dismissive, when I tried to pump her later. I don't think she enjoyed that time – none of us did. I hated changing schools again, I missed Papa dreadfully, and she and Uncle B were getting impatient. I vaguely remember the house we rented – it was very old-fashioned but homely. It seems they had planned to ship the furniture to South Africa at a later date, but even then things didn't work out as planned.

'Leah had sent out descriptions of every piece through Interpol but the whole security system was in disarray. With everyone trying to get things out, the risk of having it impounded, never to be seen again, was huge. Fortunately for them, Buster had lots of contacts – probably black market ones – in the world of antiques. In the end, they left it all behind but a few years later, when things settled down, Chico helped him shift it out piece by piece through various channels into France and Spain. It was too complicated apparently to send it on to South Africa, but systematically turning valuable pictures, carpets and furniture into hard cash swelled their coffers even more,' she gulped. 'I expect they got far less than they hoped, but nevertheless…I'm glad it never caught up with them!' She swallowed hard and looked away, 'I simply couldn't have borne to have Leah's furniture at Lochaig after all that.'

'And what about the Americana money – poor Leah's life savings?'

'The capital was sent to Spain according to Leah – then almost immediately Uncle B – I mean – *that man* must have moved it to Switzerland where it brought in good interest. No wonder my mother had so much to spend at Lochaig when she and I finally arrived home. It paid for the roof, the central heating, re-electrifying the whole place, amazing décor and then of course new *objets d'art*. I think Mama bitterly regretted the loss of the American stuff, so she hung around Sotheby's and Christies for years – every school holidays I remember being dragged along to auctions – to make up. Little was ever said when another new piece arrived home. I don't think my father liked it one bit… and maybe it was around this time that disillusionment set it. He was so withdrawn in my growing up years.'

Michael held his breath, waiting for her to go on.

' I always wonder – even if Buster hadn't had the *accident*,' there was still an emphasis on the word, but Michael noticed with satisfaction there was no shudder this time, 'if she wouldn't *still* have returned to my father. I can't believe she ever stopped loving him – not judging by the way they were later – and from a lot Leah let slip.'

'As you yourself admitted when we first met – you'll never know all the answers but it does look as though you did right to come, Kate,' he said gently. 'At least you can talk about it more easily and the guilt has evaporated…I hope. It also sounds as though you can see things more clearly now. You look so much more relaxed about everything.'

'I wouldn't say *everything*,' she said, her grey eyes serious. 'But I feel more at peace with myself. No one out here seems too affected today…except my poor father…which in an ironic kind of way makes me feel better. It certainly explains a lot about his recent behaviour and why he just won't talk about things. Leah is amazing, as we all know, and it seems there have been less casualties than I had imagined. Having said that, I can't help feeling poor Howard may have been hastened to an earlier death than he deserved.

'As for me – I still don't know the answer to the big question, did my parents plan it all or not? I may never now know the answer to that, but it does sound now as though my father was genuinely broken hearted, so how could he have?

'Seeing what I can through Leah and Benjie's eyes, the plot – if you can call it that – was probably something that developed of its own accord, you know a whirlwind of events hastened on by its own energy and emotions. I think my mother was bowled along by a chain of events, that gathered its own impetus and swept her into something she could not resist. Flattery, the glamour of it all, my father busy with his work and then leaving her alone whilst he went to London, who knows what she was thinking? Every time she arrived at the yellow house, it must have been like entering a stage set. Day after day as Leah herself admitted – she was being encouraged – by all of them – to play the role of princess amongst a willing court of admirers and sycophants. How she must have loved it! No wonder she got swept off her feet and into an affair with a man hungry for her love! I think the fact that Buster and Leah had never felt any real passion for each other must have had a lot to do with it.'

Michael nodded but held his tongue. She was on a roll now and he was glad.

'Buster must have gone mad for my mother. And she in a way with him, the slavish devotion with which he treated her would have gone straight to her head – especially at a time when my father was down, crippled with debt and self-doubt. Mama has never liked weakness in other people, she would have seen Uncle B like a knight in shining armour – with all his money, virility and bravado! I can just imagine it all, she must have thought he was the answer to everything.'

It had been a long speech, and Michael smiled sympathetically. 'You've been very brave, Kate,' he said. 'You've come through the storm and out of it. I'm just so pleased you've been able to put it into words for me today. In a way that will crystallize it more in your own head and give you the confidence to put it behind you and get back to life at home, your real life – the here and now.'

'I'm still slightly dreading that,' she confessed.

'Of course,' he said lightly, 'it may take a little time, but you'll be fine. If not, then it might be a good idea to talk to a professional, but I have a feeling you'll get there yourself. You're strong-willed too, Kate, like your mother. You don't need me to tell you that. Now let's go out to *La Bella* and have that last spin together. You're going to be amazed at the colours and contours of this particular little bay.'

'Sounds good,' said Kate, pleased to be on the move again. They had been sitting there too long and she'd probably drunk more red wine than she had meant. It would be good to feel the cold wind whipping round her face as *La Bella* got going and in fact there was quite a breeze already. They had moved away from the sunny sheltered part of the cottage to prepare for the trek down to the beach and she noticed clouds scudding aross the sky which hadn't been there before. 'Looks like it could be gusty! Are you game for a bumpy ride?'

'Sure thing,' said Michael picking up a bundle and the usual hamper he'd left at the top of the rise. 'I've brought some extra jerseys and drinks – anything more you need?'

'No – and I think if we're going to go, we oughtn't to hang about,' said Kate, outstripping him as before on the well-worn path before climbing more carefully down the wooden steps.

La Bella looked as inviting as she remembered and it occurred to her that Michael ought to get the engine looked at it, if there really were problems with starting. What if it cut out when he was on his own and he didn't have the experience to beach her without an engine? Oh well…it was her last day, she wasn't going to worry about that now. If they were meant to go out, the boat would start – if not…they could always go back into the cottage and talk a bit more. She didn't want to bore him, but it had been such a relief going over the events of the last few days with someone so detached and unjudgemental. It really had meant a lot.

They dragged the boat down to the water's edge. It wasn't so hard this time since she had been left closer to the tide-mark and someone had dug some of the sand away from the runners which made it easier to push her into the water. 'Shall I – or will you?' said Kate, as he handed her the key.

'You're in charge today, captain,' he grinned. 'Only remember, don't switch her off when we get to the cove.'

They were up to their knees in cold water and then into the boat in a trice. 'You can tell summer's coming to an end,' said Kate, 'are you sure you want to swim?'

She tried to start the engine, but it spluttered feebly once or twice, then failed. 'Use the choke!' said Michael, 'as long as we don't flood the engine, it's OK.'

She started it on the third attempt and soon they were away and out to sea, as the beach receded before their eyes. 'Go out not quite as far as we did last time,' called her host, 'and then turn right … er … starboard – direction of Lagos! Then I'll tell you when to slow down and start heading back towards land – it's a kind of natural harbour, but easy to miss. There's a huge rock sticking out, which makes you think it's part of the mainland – but it's not. It simply acts as a very good decoy for what lies behind – a hidden cove!'

They scudded along for a good six knots and she kept her eye on the sky. Michael, sitting behind her, seemed oblivious, but the weather was definitely taking a turn for the worse. The black clouds she'd noticed were still hovering well away from them, hugging the western peninsula at land's end, but they would eventually head their way with the wind behind blowing in hard from the open Atlantic. It was a pity they had taken so long over lunch. Clearly, she decided, he would have to make do with a shorter excursion under water than he had hoped. There was no point taking a risk.

He had climbed over to where she perched, and was shouting and pointing. She couldn't hear a word he said over the roar of the engine, the crashing waves and the wind, but she saw the rock he had described. True to type, the sandstone in this part of the Algarve took the form of crumbling yellow cliffs, often undulating outrageously so you never quite knew what lay hidden, both underneath and behind. Upright like a sentinel, just as he'd described, this particular rock seemed part of a spit of land which reached its amoeboid arm far out into the ocean. It was conical in shape and about the size of small church, complete with tower – in the form of a twist at the end, from centuries old frozen lava.

If he hadn't told her, she would never have believed it was cut off from land, but as she began to turn the boat coast-wards, she saw what he meant. Dropping a gear and slowing down enough to manoeuvre, she caught a glimpse of water behind the rock and a row of teeth like projections coming up between the promontory and the rock itself. It was bizarre yet beautiful but she knew they mustn't get too near. Now, they were no longer against the wind, but heading into a small enclosed bay. Even so, it was still surprisingly cold and gusty. The water looked very deep and in places oily black. She doubted he'd see very much today, it was far too overcast.

'Do you really still want to swim?' she shouted to Michael.

He nodded. He was already stripping off – his large goggles, flippers and snorkelling apparatus at the ready. She wanted to say she would drop anchor, and despite keeping the engine ticking, not move from the spot – but before they had discussed where she would pick him up, and how long he should be, he was over the side. Typical! she thought, just like a man and does he realize how heavy that anchor weighs? I don't think I'm going to risk doing my back in, by lugging it over the side myself. I'll just cruise around – gently in this bay – making sure I don't get too close to those rocky teeth over there – or get sucked in on the tide.

Ten minutes passed quickly. She had been going over in her mind all the events of the last few days and twice she caught a glimpse of him, a hand wave, and then he was gone. On a calm day it would have been easier to follow his progress but the water was too choppy to be sure where he'd gone next and she wondered how much he would see of these beautiful colours he'd described. For someone who was used to handling boats on a Scottish sea loch, it was funny the way she was disturbed by this weather. Most of the time shafts of sunshine still streamed down on them, then all of a sudden a dark cloud would pass across the patch of light and she felt a little shiver pass down her spine. The problem was, these were unknown waters and the rocks were lethal. It was all very unlike her smooth Scottish shingled beaches with their well-worn rounded stones and sloping edges. Here it could go suddenly very deep or very shallow and in some places, where it looked like safe water, there could be an underlying spike of sandstone which might catch her unawares. She was now travelling at about .5 knots an hour, and hoping Michael would pop up beside the prow at any moment, to call it a day.

The problem was, he didn't. *Where are you, Michael?* she thought, as another ten minutes passed. *Please don't do this to me. The weather's turning and we ought to be heading home.*

It was true, the wind had really got up now and the sun was hidden again as more and more of the scudding clouds she noticed earlier came hurtling past. The waves were bigger too. The wind whipped across the water, stirring them up, and she wondered how bad it would be out on the open sea. Or was it just this bay? She wasn't so sure she liked it. What Michael had failed to explain – perhaps he hadn't noticed – was the curious inbalance brought out by its being sheltered down one end, and open at the other. On a good day, this wouldn't be problem. Today however, a kind of vortex had been created and just beyond where she coasted now, away from the yellow rock, there was a whirlpool effect as the wind got harsher.

She decided to move the vessel closer to the open end of the bay, further from land but safer. She tried roaring the engine a little to indicate where she was, so he would follow. But there was still no sign of him. Then, as she pulled right away from the dragon's teeth, she saw him. He was waving. Would he swim towards her? – no! he was riding the big waves with a grin on his face and beckoning her to turn back towards him. She looked at the sky again; it was blacker than before and she felt suddenly afraid.

She wheeled the boat round; *La Bella* felt heavy in her hands. Without the impulsion given by speed, she seemed awkward and cumbersome. He was far too near that whirlpool but clearly he hadn't noticed. If he would just keep clear of that and come towards her – she indicated again – and then suddenly it happened. The engine cut out. And in that same moment, she saw his arms come up…

She saw them flailing. The wind was high and the waves were pushing him back against the rocks. He was struggling, treading water but then a wave reared up and hit him in the face and he seemed to disappear. Her mother was pale and anxious. Struggling with the wheel, it seemed she wasn't trying hard enough, but maybe she was. The boat was like a slug – a slug without limbs, no legs, no arms to pull itself along – just a heavy, torpid body that seemed to bump and slither this way and that, unable to move forward of its own accord, only going where the sea took it.

He was calling... she couldn't make out the words, the wind carried them away... but she could see the shape of his lips in a gaping O shape... and then his arms came up again. They looked white and helpless, no longer bronzed and powerful like she remembered them last night when she went to say goodnight and he was cradling her mother with that look in his eyes, by the fire. And now those same arms were flapping, broken – like wings – like the seagull she'd found on the beach that couldn't fly and Mama had said there was nothing she could do for it. And she had made her walk away in the opposite direction and forbade her to look back.

And now they too were turning away. Or were they? 'I can't reach him, Katy!' cried Mama, 'I can't get that close. It's too dangerous, we're almost on the rocks. Why doesn't he swim, why can't he get to me? Let the tide carry him... if only he'd stop fighting against it... let him come to me!' And she'd leaned over then, and screamed out of the boat to him... 'Buster! Buster! Swim... Come to us darling... SWEEM!'

But he did not seem to hear them. Or if he did, he did not try.

And Katy leaned too and saw him and hated his arms and his broken wings and the fact he didn't, couldn't try. And she screamed back, 'No, no, no! We can't come! We'll all drown. Stay away from us!' And she clung to Mama's back and pulled against her wet suit, and sobbed, 'don't go back for him, I'm so afraid, don't go back! Please Mama! The rocks! The rocks! Don't go back for him Mama, we're going to die, we're going to die. I wish he'd go away!'

'He'll come!' insisted her mother, 'I'll hold the boat here for him, if we wait long enough... he'll come...' but her voice was trembling and she was wrenching the wheel this way and that, trying in vain to steady it against the tide and they were getting nowhere. 'Oh my God, Katy,' she was sobbing ... 'I think he's got cramp... he's not coming! Oh dear God – I don't think he's going to make it. Try Buster, try!'

Mama was screaming now and Katy looked back, waiting and fearful. And from far far away, across the waves, close to the black rocks, flapping and flailing, Buster seemed to look at her. And she saw his eyes like black boot buttons in a white frightened face piercing into hers and the mouth had become a hole. And it was all so different from the Buster she knew. He was desperate and he was pleading, calling out loud, but the sea took his words away. He seemed so near and yet so far and she could only just make him out when the stern of the boat dipped right down and Mama tried to control it. And in the next moment it bobbed so high it seemed like a bucking horse and she couldn't see him. And it was a relief because she hated him in this moment – she hated him for terrifying her so and for putting them at risk in a boat her mother seemed unable to control – and she buried her head in her arms so she might never have to see him again.

And after what seemed an age, Mama managed to turn the boat around. And cried hysterically, 'Katy! where's he gone? Where's he gone?'

And she knew in her heart he was no longer there. And because she'd wished him gone, he had vanished. Gone! Forever! And she was glad. And all she'd tried to do was to save herself and Mama. Because it wasn't fair that they should all die and she wasn't ready for that. Besides, she'd promised herself that one day she would see Papa again and it wasn't fair on him most of all. And Mama knew that and shouldn't have even tried. It just wasn't fair.

514   *Sylvia Loch*

So she said nothing. Just sat there in the stern as her mother sobbed and struggled with the boat and they circled around. Only they were going nowhere and it all seemed to Katy a huge effort for nothing. But Mama wouldn't give up. Between sobs, she kept talking as though everything would come right. She said she wasn't sure where Buster had gone but he was either safe on the rocks and they'd send a helicopter or he was swimming underwater towards them, like he had so many times before. And on and on she went, all the time talking, all the time struggling with the boat. Until finally, with a gasp, she wrenched the wheel about, and sat down heavily. And breathed more to herself than Katy – 'I think he's gone – oh my God – what shall we do?'

And in that moment, she realized that if she didn't do something quickly they were going to crash. The yellow rock like an outpost was very close and the next moment, she felt a lurch and braced herself for the impact just as a strong hand came around the wheel, trying to force the nose to one side. And it was Michael, dripping wet and blue with cold at her side, desperately pulling out oars and shouting at her, 'For God's sake Kate, get a grip and stop us from ramming as I try and get this bloody engine going!'

And now she was fighting again for her life but this time with the oars and all her physical strength, as the man at her side crouched over the wheel and fiddled with the key, as the waves got higher and the tide pulled them in closer to the line of teeth … when suddenly – La Bella leapt into life. And at that point Kate fell sideways as the power shot through the boat and they missed the jagged teeth with inches to spare as the vessel hurled itself towards the shore. And she came to her senses and screamed 'Aft!' but Michael was quicker still.

He was at the wheel turning it hard, and the slug had become a bird, and now they were skimming towards the safe open side of the bay. Suddenly they were riding breakers head on but with a real roar in the engine and this time there was no mistaking La Bella's superior impulsion. This was what she was built for and she had suddenly come into her own. They were going full throttle. And in that moment, Kate realised she had taught Michael well and that he was a natural like her and this time – this time, she would be safe.

And it was at that point that she sat down on the hard wet seat and allowed herself to cry. As she'd never cried before.

She woke up and wondered why it was dark outside. She could see the sky through the half-drawn curtain and wasn't that a star twinkling far above? Where was she? She sat up with a jerk and looked at her watch. It was almost ten o'clock! And she was in Michael's cottage. At least, she must be! There was no other explanation.

She lay back on the pillows. They smelt a bit of mothballs, but they were soft against the back of her head. She also felt snug and warm. There was a hot-water bottle at her side. It must have been against her tummy as there was a warm patch round the waist of her jeans. Hang on they weren't her jeans … she was wearing a pair of grey tracksuit bottoms she did not recognize. They must be Michael's.

Realisation and other memories began to kick in. She cast her mind back to that nightmare journey in the boat. Had she blanked out, had she knocked her head on the side? How come everything had turned into that awful day – in South Africa? She could remember it all now. As clear as day. The thing that was more difficult to remember was what had happened here, in the Algarve – today. How had Michael got to the boat in time? How had he rescued her? What had she done? What had she been playing at? How could her mind have played tricks like that so that her own natural caution had been thrown to the wind? She was an experienced sailor... after all.

She lay there, looking at the low ceiling, counting the bamboo canes and hugging the tepid hot-water bottle to her for comfort. Don't force it. Let it come back slowly.

There was a timid tap at the door. Had he been here before? Was that what had awoken her a few moments ago?

'Come in,' she was too tired to lift her head. Funny, for once she wasn't embarrassed at being caught lying down. Even at home, no matter what, she always sat up.

'How's the patient?' he said. He was carrying a steaming mug that smelt good. 'I've brought you some soup. Sorry – it's not home made like the gazpacho – just good old tinned cream of chicken. But I thought it might warm you up.'

'I'm really cosy,' she said, 'but I'd love it.'

She pulled herself up on the pillows and held out a hand, gratefully.

'I can't quite believe I've slept this long,' she said. 'What time did we get back here?'

'Around five thirty, we were out in the boat less than two hours.'

'And – er – did I go straight to bed?'

'Yep... more or less. I helped you out of your wet things, you were a bit shaky. Then you got into some of my gear and then you – well – you simply crashed out.'

'Ah yes,' she said, 'I'm beginning to remember. I don't want too many more bouts of amnesia. It's beginning to be a habit.'

'I wouldn't worry about it,' he grinned. 'You've had a bit of a traumatic time. But I think you may find once you can put today behind you, everything will sort itself out.'

He was standing awkwardly, looking down at her. But the compassion was unmistakable. She put down the soup, put out a hand and pulled him towards her. This was something she had missed all her life. Compassion, understanding – a whole new experience! God! Why had she never thought about it before? Demanded it! But there'd been no one to give it. Not her mother, not her father, not her husband, not her kids! She'd never had it. And now she needed it.

'Kate, d'you not think I should leave you for a bit? You need to drink that soup, come to slowly and then we can talk. I've put off this evening's meeting, so I'm all yours. But I'd rather you were up and dressed, not lying here in bed.' He was moving towards the door, 'Can I make you some toast? You're probably starving. I've already had supper, but a bit of food inside you might not go amiss.'

'No,' she said, 'this is fine. A drop more soup would be lovely, but please come back.'

As he went out of the door, the longing in her was almost violent. She couldn't believe she had just discovered this. It was as though something had sparked off in her brain – someone had released the catch – and wham! Her reaction was as unexpected as it was sudden. She was going to have to ask for it – even if it meant begging him. She must be allowed to have it – just for once in her life. Compassion! Oh God! What a wonderful, healing thing – why had she never thought of it before? She needed compassion. To be held, kissed, comforted – and to know deep in her soul, that someone understood.

When he came back, she found she did not really want the soup. He put it down gently on the bedside table and made to go out. But she called him back. 'Michael!' She wanted him. So badly. She wanted again that look in his eyes. The way he'd looked at her when she was lying on the bed and he'd first entered the room. She'd give her right arm to get that look back again... and the promise of something more besides.

'Michael,' she said again, 'Please come and sit beside me. I need you.'

46

*T*here was a long pause. He looked at her again with that kindly light in his eyes, but there was worry too. In the end he came to her and sat on the edge of the bed. She held out her hand.

'Kate,' he said, taking it gently in both of his.

They looked at each other. There was none of the *frisson*, the electricity of that first time, when she was leaving his cottage. She remembered it so well. Catching her at the door. Eyes meeting. The rush of desire. So unexpected yet the more forceful because of that. Rising up from within, into her chest, pricking behind her eyes so that she knew they sparkled – almost overwhelming her for a moment. And then – just as suddenly – dying away as he'd let go, withdrawn. All that had been pure attraction.

This was different. In fact she couldn't believe the difference. He stroked her hand, tracing the veins from under her watch strap to where they angled, blue and a little proud of the skin up the back of her hand to disappear under her knuckle and just above, the white gold of her wedding band. There was such tenderness in these movements, in his eyes, the way he inclined his head; in that moment she recognised what she had missed. For many many years. And how much she needed it. And then, as if he remembered himself, he turned his head away, not daring to meet her own steadfast gaze. But this time, she was ready. She sensed his withdrawal; he in turn clearly sensed she was not going to allow it to happen again and there was an inevitability about what happened next.

With a rashness she had never known, careful, capable Kate threw herself into his arms and this time he took her. Held her. And for the second time that day, the tears welled up and she cried and cried. Cried for herself, cried for her parents – and even cried for Buster.

'I never really meant for him to die,' she sobbed, 'but I did hate him. And I did wish him gone – with all my heart. And I think I must have been living with that guilt ever since – although I blanked it all off in my mind. Instead, I transferred all those bad feelings to my parents. First my mother, then poor Pops...no wonder he got so cross when I kept questioning him. I probably even made him question himself. Yet I really believed it must have been them – partners in crime – planning the whole thing from beginning to end, so that Mama could return to him in Scotland.

'Oh Michael, I feel so ashamed. All the guilt I bore was my own! I was angry with my parents, because I felt so contaminated by what I thought *they'd* done. Every time something was said, it kept bubbling to the surface. Mama's confession was just the last straw. Yet, at the time of the accident – all those years ago – I must, subconsciously, have recognised how bad it was to wish someone dead. By pushing the guilt onto my parents, I was hoping to wipe the slate clean. After all, in the way of children, I probably thought at the time I was to blame – my fault that he'd drowned, my fault that Mama gave up trying to save him. My fault he died – because I hated him so.

'And even before the incident at sea. Wishing him dead … alone at night, in my bed, as I thought of them – together – in the room next door. When she should have been with my father… I just couldn't seem to stem the hatred…' her voice trailed off. Copious tears had dropped onto his shirt collar but he continued to hold her tight against him, so she would not have to meet his eye and read all the feelings that lay within.

She gulped then and he felt her hot breath against her neck, so he stroked her hair, very gently so she would not get distracted. She must be allowed to unburden herself whilst she still could '… And then Michael, after that – it was just a blank. But later, as I looked back, and tried to remember – I found I couldn't – so I must have pinned it on my mother. Only,' she paused and he could feel the effort as she tried to justify it all to herself, 'I was just a kid, Michael – I simply didn't know, didn't realise. Oh! what a mess this has been! It now seems to me I'm the guilty one. And have been all along. How could I have got it so wrong?'

'Kate,' he said again and for an answer merely tightened his arms around her back and with a tenderness she'd never known, caressed and loved her, his lips in her hair. 'My poor lovely Kate.'

'But I'm glad…' she sobbed, half-smiling through the tears, 'I'm glad he's dead and we came home to my father. And I know that's wrong, but how could I have changed it? And I'm glad about my mother too,' she sniffed, wiped away another tear and gazed over his shoulder through long wet lashes as though she could see it all again. 'Michael – she may have been very bad, but I'm so glad she wasn't a murderess, she really did try to save him … only, I still feel … she might have gone back to Pops, anyway. But probably not then. As for that day in the boat, she was also protecting me… she couldn't have done more than she did … could she?'

There was a long pause, and he unthreaded himself a little, held her square in front of him and looked deep into her eyes, unsmiling, serious. 'No, Kate, she couldn't. It's as it should be, Kate. Her child had to come first, and whatever you'd said or did not say in the boat that day would have made not a scrap of difference… you silly, silly Kate. Besides, her first instinct would have been to save herself too. Self preservation is very strong in these situations, and particularly if you're a mother. She was only human, Kate!'

He cupped his hand round the oval of her chin, and drew her gently towards him again. She felt his lips on her forehead, smoothing back a stray lock, touching her cheek, wiping away further tears with his fingers and all the while the other hand, rubbing her back. 'Kate, look at me,' his voice was young but commanding, 'You must realise – it wasn't your fault at all.' He kissed her again, this time on the nose, 'You've been torturing yourself all this time – and it wasn't your fault.'

'D'you really believe that?' her voice was tremulous and she subsided against his shoulder.

'Come on, Kate, you're a mum yourself. You must know that…' his firm fingers kneaded between her shoulder blades – as she'd done so many times for her two boys when they'd been injured or upset – it made her feel safe. '…And the coast guards would have known that, and the South African police. They'd have taken account of the weather, the conditions and where they found the body. And it wasn't like they wanted to lock you both up now, was it? You've always known your mother was completely in the clear after the accident.'

'Yes…but–'

'Yes, but nothing, Kate –' there was an edge to his voice just like that time before, when he had become exasperated with her and they'd almost had a row. 'You've been damn lucky today. Unblocking your memory like that was the best thing that could have happened… traumatic, yes – but it's kind of a miracle it happened that way.' He felt her tense and chose his words carefully, more gently. 'And now you know the truth, dearest Kate, you must just accept it and get on with your life. Like other people have to!'

'I guess I've been very selfish in my way.' She had stopped crying, but her eyes were downcast and he felt the shoulders slump forward, so that the arch of her spine collapsed under his grasp, and it would have been easier not to agree. He took a deep breath and carefully set her shoulders back.

'Yes, in a way,' he said. 'But luckily we're all safe and sound…and there've been no tragedies this time. Soon, having faced up to things, you'll feel much better. You must release yourself from the past and make up for lost time. Start to look forward again and …' he was turning her face upwards, towards him '…learn to be happy again!'

And in that moment as their eyes locked, they were kissing again but this time full on the lips.

And how long that kiss went on, she did not know. But it was so full of love, of comfort, so kind, it could have been eternity. And it filled her. It almost choked her but it was so healing she wanted it never to stop. And despite the intimacy, it felt so clean. Even when the saltiness of her tears had gone from her mouth and his tongue gently probed hers, it felt wholesome, almost chaste. It was all so different from anything she had ever known. Love, without lust – at least in those moments – she told herself later. Pure love and goodness and total understanding. She realised she was experiencing something she had never really known before.

And for that precious time, seconds, minutes, hours – she couldn't be sure – it was enough. Time had stood still. And then something changed. And the second hand was whirring again. Her breathing between the tears had been shallow. Now she felt a throbbing – deep down in the pit of her stomach – her breath coming in short, urgent rasps and she wanted more. And so, quite simply, she told him, 'Michael, please – please, I need you.'

And he sighed again and gradually released his grasp, as though awoken from a dream. She could feel the excitement within him, but he held her away and shook his head. 'Kate, I'm sorry. I shouldn't have done that. We can't…mustn't.'

'But Michael, we want each other, I need you! You can't stop now.'

'We must.' He looked at her, touched her hair gently, then let his hand fall to his lap and got up and paced round the small room.

'Kate, don't make this hard for us both. Of course I want you, I probably wanted you from the first day I saw you, although I didn't admit it to myself. But you're a married lady, Kate, I can't do it. I can't break all the rules I hold dear. I can't make love to another man's wife.' He came back to the bed and looked down at her, shaking his head, his hair tousled, his eyes bright, 'I can't do that, Kate. I'm sorry. I haven't made it easy – for either of us.'

'But Michael, you don't understand. I need you so much,' she took his hand and pressed it against her lips. 'I want to feel whole again. I want to feel a woman. I've been so numb all these months, years even – you don't know what I've been through.'

'Oh yes, I think I do, Kate,' he was still looking at her, but instead of taking her in his arms again, pushed her gently back against the pillows. 'I do know. And I wish it was as easy as you say, but it's not. I recognise you've been to hell and back. I know you think you need me. And you can have me – to talk, to help and advise, but I can't do that – any of it – if we start fucking! That would be the end of everything.'

'Michael!' she was shocked. 'I didn't want to fuck, I wanted you to make love to me. I feel so empty. You don't understand.'

He took her hand again. 'I do, Kate, but it's not right. It's as simple as that.'

She looked at him. Her heart was heavy. What she couldn't put into words was the need to be filled up – physically and utterly. Her mental side had taken over her life so completely, she needed to feel a woman again. Coming together in bed was the most natural thing in the world, it would fill up her body, her heart and her soul. It had been like that in the early days with James. The wonder and joy of real union. So different from the initial fumblings, the cavorting around with those earlier boyfriends. And invariably, that frenzied coupling – with the ultimate goal – on both parts – more selfish than giving. Now it all seemed so unimportant. What mattered more was the loving.

And she'd learned that in the early days with her husband. There'd been no hurry. It was such a relief. The excitement was in the build-up. The sheer delight of enfolding him. Flesh to flesh, heart to heart. Oneness. For her, that was the feeling that became the thrill; not the acrobatics that followed, nor even the climax which was so much easier – once she learned to let go. And when it didn't happen, it didn't really matter. What mattered was the knowledge. That she was containing him in only the way a woman can. That was what made the love act so special. The unification of all that was good from within, the innate melding of two bodies and two loving souls.

And now she wanted that feeling again, so badly. She was unsure she would ever find it again with James … things had changed … and she had felt empty and used. And right now there was a burning need in her. For the first time in years – a real desire. And if it could not be fulfilled now, she might never find it again. Love and tenderness was what she craved – and Michael had it in abundance. He had the power to make her feel whole. She could then face her life with a new sense of her own worth.

How could she begin to explain all this to him? She doubted he'd have a clue what she was talking about. Men never did about women's feelings – not when it came to sex. Neither would he understand how his taking charge this afternoon had made her realise just how vulnerable she'd always been. Or recently, how incomplete.

'Capable Kate,' he had called her when she first showed him how to sail the boat. Even this afternoon, he'd probably still seen her in that light – at least until the flash-back. But even then, he probably saw her weakness as temporary.

It was all a bit of a blur, but a few salient points were coming back. After her collapse, he'd taken complete charge of the boat. The voyage back had been bumpy but uneventful. Huddled in the stern under one of his fleeces, she'd shivered all the way back to shore. Leaving *La Bella* had been wobbly, but he'd steadied her with a kindly hand and she'd recovered enough to help him lug the vessel clear of the waves. After that, she remembered vaguely he'd gone to fetch the gardener. As the two men struggled to heave the vessel back on its planks, she'd sat in a heap on the sand. Had she cried? Maybe. Even rocked in that old childish way too. But nothing had been said.

Job done, he'd taken her by the hand – compassion again. Up the wooden steps they'd gone, then climbed the cliff path back to the cottage. She'd been cold and in shock, he said. He'd fiddled with the neatly laid fire in the grate and soon got it going with firelighters and driftwood. Made her sit on a stool in front of it while he fanned it with bellows. Made over-sweetened tea, fetched clothes and stuff and then hastened her off to bed with her drink and the hot-water bottle under her arm. He was so *kind*.

She remembered trying to argue she was fine, but he'd been very firm. After that, nothing. She had slept a long dreamless sleep and woken up to this!

He was moving towards the door now, but not before she'd spotted a new wariness back in his eyes. 'You'd better stay here tonight, Kate, but first let's reunite you with your clothes and we'll find you a toothbrush. D'you want to come and sit by the fire and drink a glass of red wine with me? Tomorrow's going to be a busy day – you've got your hotel to check out of and a plane to catch, I've got morning prayers and then visits all day. Whatever you want to say, we'd better do it now. But first, I'm going to insist you have something to eat, so hang on a minute and I'll go on and get your jeans; they should be dry by now, as well as everything else.'

He was back in a few minutes and tossed some clothes on to the bed. She noticed he kept a good distance between them. Then he was gone, stoking up the fire and busying himself in the kitchen. She wondered how they'd ever got to this stage where something so special, so reassuring, so intimate – had dissolved back into normal behaviour – almost as though it hadn't happened.

In the bathroom, she studied her reflection. Her eyes looked enormous in a paler than normal face, her hair was a mess, slightly curly where the spray had soaked it in front, turning up into ducks' tails at the back. Her tan seemed to have disappeared since this morning but she looked well enough, despite her ordeal. Her lips were cherry-red with kissing but her teeth probably needed a good brush. She tidied up, put on her own clothes – which seemed silly when it was going on for midnight – and found some scent in her bag to dab behind her ears and on her wrists. By the time he had laid down a tray of left-over stew for her and some cheese for them both on the coffee-table, she was feeling decidedly better.

A bottle of Portuguese burgundy had been warming in the hearth. He now opened this with some ceremony and poured out two goblets. 'To new beginnings, Kate!' he smiled.

'To new beginnings,' she said, trying not to sound flippant as she added, 'does that mean for you too?'

'I hope so,' he said. 'I'm still waiting to hear if I've got a parish to go back to when I return to England, and if that happens, the next step is to be ordained.'

'And then you'll become a fully fledged vicar?'

'That's right, although I prefer the word 'priest'...vicar sounds too much like those TV soaps, all garden parties and kissing babies, whereas I want to be taken seriously and do some good in the world.'

'Well, you've made a good start with me.'

'Oh, Kate, I haven't,' said Michael, feeling far enough away to look her straight in the eye. 'I liked you from the beginning rather too much...yes, you could say there was a chemistry there and it was probably foolish of me to give you my number.'

'But if you hadn't, where would I have been now?'

'Maybe in less of a muddle, than you are now. I'm sorry I tempted you like that. I didn't exactly plan it to happen.'

'Michael, it had to happen! You know that! The fact I wanted you, still want you so much is because you made me feel you really understood. I don't think you can begin to appreciate this, but I've never really had anyone recognise my need and really cuddle me before. Apart from Papa perhaps, but then he was taken away from me. But, seriously. Even as a tiny child, I was always expected to be sensible. You gave me comfort and warmth and you held me. No one's ever done that for me – not like that.'

'But then, it went beyond that,' he said, seriously. 'Kate, the truth is – I couldn't stop kissing you.' He laughed awkwardly, got up and fished in a back pocket for his cheroots. 'Do you mind if I do this whilst you eat?'

She shook her head and concentrated for a moment on the food. She was, in fact, starving and the stew was delicious. He'd thoughtfully added a baked potato and she was gulping it all down.

'The thing is, Kate, if you'd been single – it would all be quite different. I don't suppose you'd fancy being a priest's wife, but I would happily have married you. You're everything I admire in a woman, sensitive, beautiful, spirited and with a good mind. The fact you've been a bit screwed up lately only added to your charms...guys like a challenge.'

'I'm not so sure about that,' she said, 'James definitely wishes I was far less complicated.'

'He may say that,' said Michael pacing the room, 'but I very much doubt it.'

'The point is though, Kate, you may be just what I want, but you're not for me.'

'But I could be, if you let me.'

'What – an affair? No, Kate – I told you, I can't go there. Don't even want to. It may sound pure corn to you, but the love of God is more important every time than the love of man... and I mean that. I couldn't live with myself if I broke the rules. I'd be destroyed.'

'But if God is pure love, like you church people all think he is,' she said, 'surely He'd understand? You told me yourself He didn't expect us to measure up – and I thought anyway, belief was all about forgiveness. Isn't that what sets Christianity aside from the other religions – tolerance and forgiveness, and er – compassion? Jesus was all compassion – or whatever it is they say.'

'Yeah, but you don't go deliberately breaking the rules every day of your life because of that. It would make a mockery of everything. Forgiveness is about having done something and being really sorry. Not capitalising on it by going out of your way to do it again…and again!'

'Well, I still think He'd understand and anyway, I only wanted to do it once…I think!' She pushed her hair back and felt the flush creeping up her neck again. Her words sounded so banal. 'I mean – I wanted you so badly in that bedroom just now, I can't tell you how much it would have meant to me to be loved properly – the whole way. I've never strayed before. But just this once! It would have made me feel complete again. I could have walked out of here a new person!'

'Really? Oh, Kate, now you're tormenting yourself and me. You know it wouldn't have ended there. Once we'd gone there, we'd have wanted more. At least I know I would have. That's why I've never touched drugs – not even the so called harmless ones. If you don't know what you're missing, hopefully – you don't then miss.'

'But I would have been out of your hair tomorrow – conveniently away on my plane!' said Kate. 'It would naturally have come to an end…a really fulfilling end. And I could have gone home restored and you'd be left with a good memory, and it would have been oh so…' she gave a little shiver of anticipation and looked up at him, smiling, 'well – you know – *delicious*.'

'Like forbidden fruit! And there's you telling me how immoral your parents were and how *could* your mother have been tempted by Buster? Kate! Can't you see now? We all have our weaknesses, even you – and that's the very reason I'm so lucky to have my faith, because without that – I'd be succumbing and getting hurt and foundering in the dark. Because without some sort of moral guidance in today's modern society – where *are* the boundaries? Where *do* you stop? How can one cope with temptation without fucking other people's lives up?'

She remembered at the moment why she'd first been attracted to him. That moment in the plane when he'd mildly sworn – he was so honest in that way – especially for someone in his position. 'But we could have been grown up about it,' she said, taking a longer than usual sip of her wine. And as she said the words, she felt again the blush. Because again it sounded so very superficial – and not worthy of her – or him.

He stubbed out his cheroot and looked at her. In that moment, she saw again the tenderness – and for a fleeting moment – it reminded her of the look of Christ hanging on the cross in a painting by Raphael. And Christ was looking at the thief who hung beside him and despite his own suffering, there was real compassion. In bucketfuls. And she wondered at it. And then wondered again, how she had gone all through life and never really discovered it in another human being.

Or had she?

Perhaps it had been there all along, but in such small glimpses she hadn't noticed. Not everyone was as practised as Michael. Old Philismena back in those early days in Portugal, honest Archie in Scotland – simple people, rough diamonds even – but now she thought about it – full of compassion. Her friend Mima, who led such a busy life, but was never too busy to help her out with the kids – she too understood compassion. Perhaps even her father, well concealed under a mask of cynicism because like her, he too was complicated …hadn't there been moments? She had been so self-absorbed, so busy trying to find answers, she hadn't stopped to consider – or return it. Or be grateful. And what about James? Had she ever given him a chance really to show it? Had she ever showed him? To help him show her?

God – how selfish she had been! In so many ways she was her mother's daughter, only in a different way. As they sat by the fire and she looked into the dying embers, Kate realised that what Michael had given her was an insight into her own life without any word of preaching, condemnation or trying to convince. Just by his own behaviour, he had made her ask questions of herself. And with a sudden shock, she realised those questions were far more important and relevant to her future happiness than all the questions she had come here to the Algarve to solve.

And now that he'd shown her another kind of love – and Leah too in her way – Kate recognised something very precious indeed. She knew this quality was going to help her in her own future life. It was something to share and to spread outward. And if she could approach those about her with the same care and understanding, it would rebound on her a thousand-fold as well as making life immeasurably better for everyone else.

Thus, for the second time in their short acquaintance, Kate realised she was in the presence of a very good man who had taught her a precious quality. She also saw that people like Michael who were prepared to go out into the world and help people in this way should be cherished, not contaminated. How wrong she'd been to try to tempt him to a one-night stand. He was human too, and what for her might have been a celebration of all that had passed between them; for him, could well have opened up a running sore. He did not deserve that.

And in that unexpected moment, it came upon her.

Suddenly she knew that whatever lay ahead of her at home, she was glad that she hadn't seduced him. For both their sakes. Life was complicated enough, and here at least was someone who knew where he was going. And he deserved a clear blue passage, without her coming along to muddy the water. And so at that point she stood up, put her hands on his shoulders and kissed him on the cheek.

'I think I'll go to bed now,' she smiled. 'I'm OK now, thanks to you! In fact – I think – everything's pretty ok. I can't thank you enough.'

Scotland – The next day

James was waiting for her as her plane landed at Inverness. 'I took a couple of days off work,' he said slowly, 'and came home early. It's strange – the last few days you were away, I felt a load of worry and needed to get out of London. I've got a good young guy from Newcastle Uni in the office at the moment. He's in his fourth year, but they get released for a couple of months to work in a firm and this one's exceptionally bright. I had no appointments so

I've left him to go through some special audits that I was going to do myself. The point is – I was able to leave with a clear conscience.'

'Clear consciences are important,' she said, more to herself than him. Then with a brilliant smile, 'That must be the first time you've ever allowed yourself to do that. You ought to do it more – it's lovely to be met.'

'You always do it for me,' he said, 'and I realised it was a pretty poor sort of marriage if I let you come home all alone and upset by what you'd witnessed in the Algarve. I haven't spoken to you since you rang me in Brussels, and the texts didn't give away much. I've thought long and hard about why you went, and felt I hadn't done enough. Are you really OK? Your last text was a bit cryptic.'

They were on their way to the carpark and he stopped and suddenly whirled her around by the ticket machine, and looked deep into her face. There was no one else around. 'Tell me you're OK, Kate. I can't tell you how much I've been thinking about you.'

'Really?' she said, genuinely surprised. 'You sounded far too preoccupied last time we spoke, I thought it might be a relief not to be rung time and time again.'

'Not true,' he said. 'In fact the opposite. I'm sorry about that time in Brussels, I'd probably had too much red wine at that business dinner. I couldn't concentrate on anything you were saying and was dog-tired from the most horrendous board meeting earlier that day. But the next morning, I felt really bad and then when you didn't ring … and only the texts … I thought, maybe you didn't really want to talk to me anyway and I should allow you some freedom to do what you really wanted. I even thought you might be with someone. I'm probably not intuitive like you women, but I sort of sensed something. If you hadn't come back now, I was going to get on a plane and come and find you.'

'Were you?' she said impressed and thought about it. Another smile spread over her face and she squeezed his hand.

'Well, all is well – and you don't have to.' Surprising even herself in that cold empty carpark, she drew closer. Autumn's leaves and last night's litter were swirling round their feet but she didn't see them; instead she looked up into two wary brown eyes and began to smooth out the little worry lines on either side with her two thumbs – wondering why she'd never noticed them before. Now, she found her finger was tracing the line of his jaw and then back behind his ear to the base of his skull, where his dark hair curled into the nape of his strong neck. The smell of warm, clean skin washed over her. Cupping the back of his head with her hand, she pulled it gently down towards her. He was struck by the tenderness in her touch. So was she; it felt all so different.

Suddenly, it happened. Something that hadn't happened for a long time. Their eyes locked. And in that same moment, he felt her arch her back against his widespread hand and her lips opened under his. A huge wave of wonder surged into James Fraser's heart; it was as if this person he'd scarcely known for the past two years had become flesh and blood again. In this cold, gritty carpark, the cool, detached stranger had fled. The woman he held in his arms now was Kate – the old Kate – his wife – a warm, compliant creature who was quite literally melting against him. As he clung to her in his thin wax jacket and held her tight his heart sang. And a lump came into his throat as he said, 'Let's get you home, my love. The boys are still at Mima's – I wanted to have you all to myself tonight… and then we can talk. And I don't mind how long it takes. I'm ready to hear everything.'

It was Sunday. She had left James and the boys to clear up after lunch and now she was climbing the steep hill in a protesting Land Rover to Lochaig House and her father. She had rung him as usual to warn that she was coming, but it was rare that he left his fireside or his Sunday Telegraph to come out and greet her. Today however, he must be out in the garden. She knew as soon as the dogs came bounding down the drive to meet her and she had to drive carefully because whilst the two Dobermans sped ahead like eager black gazelles, the old spaniel had a habit of bumping against the wheels to get as close as he could. By the time she arrived on the pink gravel, her father was just coming up from the terrace below and into sight, a crook in one hand, a huge bunch of late roses in the other, all wrapped up in newspaper to avoid the prickles.

He stopped at the corner of the house and unsmilingly surveyed her attempt to park the right way round all in one go. 'You won't do it!' he called, 'not with that clumsy machine!'

She laughed then, and resorted to the usual three point turn, carefully avoiding a stone greyhound and a couple of urns. 'Pity I don't have a Mercedes sports, like some people used to!' she called out of the open window.

'Ah ... so you've found out about that, then?'

'Yes, and lots more.'

'Better come in then, hadn't you? By the way, these are for you!'

She took the roses, sniffed them with real pleasure and followed him in. The crook went clacking down the stone floor, flagged in huge outsize pieces like some ancient mausoleum. 'Do you ever wonder how old these are?' she said, on the way to the library.

'My father always said they came out of Dunfermline Abbey, where the old Scottish kings were crowned, but who knows.'

'There might be some truth in it,' she said, wondering how much he still cared about the things he used to yearn for when he lived so far away.

'Cup of tea?' her father was stoking up the fire, sending a shower of sparks towards the dogs who had taken their cue and already backed well away.

'No thanks, I just wanted to see you.'

'Well, I hope it's as happy a visit as the last one.'

For a moment she wasn't sure if he was being sarcastic or had genuinely forgotten. Where before she would have been perplexed and even irritated, now she felt a huge wave of regret for having dug up all those old memories, and flew to his side. 'Pops,' she said, putting an arm round the still square but gaunt shoulders, 'I'm really sorry about that. I really am. I've had a lot of time to think things through and I should never have asked the questions I did. Will you forgive me?'

He looked at her curiously, the green tiger eyes a little dim but still sharply focussed. 'Catkin, there's nothing to forgive. You are you and I am me. You needed to ask your silly questions and I chose not to answer them. And you know the reason why? Because I did not know all the answers myself. And even if I had, I would not have answered them anyway. Because there are certain things in this world which are better left unsaid – and that, I guess, is to do with privacy and integrity and letting life go on. And that's been my motto for many a long year, probably learned during the war – if you really want to know. Because when you've seen your best friends shot to pieces all around, you know that what you say and what you ask and what you think – makes no sense at all. Some things have to take their course – so why bother? Let life roll on and do the best you can to keep up – and that way, there'll be less disappointments and less heartache.'

'Yes, Pops…I can see that now. What amazing advice!' She paused wondering if what she wanted to say would come out right. Then she took the plunge.

'I did just want to say one thing. I think you always were the most wonderful, kind father anyone could hope for under the circumstances. And whilst I've been away in the Algarve, the one thing that was remembered by everyone in that whole crazy episode – was…' her voice faltered a little, but she regained control and said it out loud so he could not be mistaken – '…your love for me.'

'Well of course,' he said. 'That was never in question, surely, my Kate?' he bowed his head and stroked the old spaniel behind the ears.

'No,' she swallowed hard, 'It wasn't. But all the same, I was terribly…well…you must have guessed, horribly confused.'

'Kate,' he said quietly, 'don't you think I was? I mean, when it all happened. '

'Ye-es,' she said, 'I know that. But I suppose at the time – I thought you'd worked out the answers…I mean, long before Mama died… which is why I came to you, as I – er – did.'

'And now you realise,' he said, ' that I hadn't…and never will.'

'I wish you'd told me that.'

'Oh Kate,' he said, 'how could I have done that without giving your mother away? I don't know how much you know, but if Leah's still alive – no doubt quite a lot by now. So be it. But the difference is, I loved your mother, Kate – despite everything. Clearly Leah, poor woman, does not!'

Now it was Kate's turn to fondle the old spaniel's ears. They sat in companionable silence for a while. Instead of changing the conversation in his usual way, he was going on.

'And I suppose what I've learned from all that time, is this. Few people who say they have all the answers, really have. In my case, I finally had to accept it was out of my hands. I also learned to believe that somehow it would come right – or partly right, eventually. Otherwise I wouldn't have been able to go on. One has to believe in something.'

'And it did in a way, didn't it Pops?'

He nodded. 'I got you back and miracle of miracles, Lochaig has now inherited a bright new generation who hopefully will make a much better job of things than the last lot!'

'Oh Pops!' she said and went to hug him, surprising herself by rubbing his back as he leant over her – just as Michael had done, with her.

Gradually, he pulled himself upright again. 'Look!' he said, the old eyes bright. 'I think the time has come to give you something. Perhaps I should have given it to you before, but it didn't seem appropriate with your mother still alive. There'd have been too many questions, knowing you! Hang on there a moment.'

He left the room, the dogs making as swift an exodus as he – all, except the old spaniel who shuffled along in their wake. Feeling remarkably relaxed, she wondered what he was up to as she piled a few more logs on the fire. Strange how little impression they made on the wide grate. A whole tree trunk might be more appropriate.

He was gone some time, but there was an air of excitement in his demeanour when he returned. He almost had a spring in his step.

'Here!' he said shoving something small and hard, wrapped up in tissue paper, unceremoniously into her hand.

She looked at him quizzically as she unwrapped it. 'Careful!' he cried, as she almost dropped it. 'People shouldn't drop rings, it can get them into all sorts of trouble.'

'Pops,' she said in surprise, 'How lovely!'

She was looking at a plain gold band, inlaid with what looked like dark green cornelian, or was it jade? She stared at him, eyes wide. Had she seen something like this before, in another place, on another hand, at another time? She pushed the thought from her mind. That was a door she was not going to open.

'Why, what a lovely thing? Was it yours?'

'Well, I'd hardly be giving it to you if it wasn't!' he laughed, his short bark making the dogs sit up suddenly and look around.

'But I've never seen you wear it!'

'Because I never have! It lived in my stud-box for years, but it doesn't mean I forgot about it. When she gave it to me, I didn't care for it at all. But as the years rolled on and she began to correspond again – through her lawyer – I never knew where you were, you understand – I began to feel a glimmer of hope. Then, in those moments when despair threatened to engulf me – I went to my room and took it out. Instead of reaching for the whisky bottle, I would sit there, and silly as it sounds, rub it – like a genie's lamp – but at the same time saying a silent prayer. I do still pray, sometimes, Kate.'

He turned his back to her then, and kicked back one of the logs which had strayed. 'The thing was – she said it was 'for eternity' – so gradually, a bit against my will, I began to hope. I was scared in a way, but I teased myself with the thought – maybe, one day, she *will* come back. And if she does – one thing I can be certain of – she'll bring you too, for eternity.'

Kate was about to interrupt and then saw the look on his face, and held her tongue. 'And so you see…she did. My prayer was answered. In time, it all came to pass, and… Well!' He was dusting the sawdust off his hands and all businesslike again. 'Here we are today – so I guess, you'd better have the ring. In celebration of eternity, as it were.'

'Oh Pops,' she said. 'I knew it, I knew it! So she did love you. Even at that age, I knew she'd choose you in the end, and…if it hadn't been for the accident…she would have come anyway, wouldn't she?'

'I've never dared asked myself that question, Kate,' he said. 'But all I can say is – in the end the ring lived up to its name. Now, although she's gone and left me again, I do still have you, and Charlie and Maurie…who could ask for more, really?'

A huge wave of compassion swept over her and she went to him again. And this time they held each other for quite a time.

'Thank you Papa…I'll get it made smaller and wear it. And if I may just add one thing, I promise I *always* knew you loved me. I want you to be very sure of that.'

'That's nice,' he said. 'I'm glad. So you didn't have to go Portugal to find that out?'

'No Pops,' she said firmly. 'That was never in any doubt.'

And as though in silent agreement, they walked back down the long hall, over the flagstones with the dogs at their heel and stood at the door. Again, she remembered the great door of the great house, where a single light bulb from an old gas bracket had dimly welcomed her home all those years ago.

'And it's nice for me to know Mama cared enough to keep at least that one promise,' she said, not daring to meet his eye in case, suddenly, he might take offence.

And to her great surprise, he laughed. 'She'd have liked that remark, my Catkin. I think what none of us realised at the time was what a great sense of humour your mother had. Unfortunately, she never stopped to consider how it could damage other people. Despite all that, I wouldn't be surprised if she wasn't laughing at us right now. What a merry dance she led us, and particularly you – over the past ten days.'

And together, hand in hand, they looked down the valley, father and daughter. And as the mist rolled in from the hill, they fancied they heard the trill of her laughter echo back at them, a little ruefully, across the loch.

The End

Lightning Source UK Ltd.
Milton Keynes UK
10 August 2010
158186UK00001B/23/P

9 781907 212048